By the Same Author

Star Witness

A Willa Jansson Mystery

LIA MATERA

Simon & Schuster

SIMON & SCHUSTER
Rockefeller Center
1230 Avenue of the Americas
New York, NY 10020

Simon & Schuster and colophon are registered trademarks
of Simon & Schuster Inc.

Designed by Elina Nudelman

Manufactured in the United States of America

ISBN 0-684-83469-3

foreword

Much of *Star Witness* is set in Davenport, California, which is a real town. But there is no San Vittorio Road there, and as far as I know, no strange sightings have been reported. Santa Cruz, California, is real, too, though no description could quite do justice to this flaky, funky, gorgeous place. I've included various of its buildings and landmarks in my story, but no characters are modeled after actual residents. No locals were harmed in the writing of this book.

In particular, my descriptions of the District Attorney's Office and its lawyers, and the Sheriff's Department and its deputies, are fictitious. Anyone coming to Santa Cruz for fun might recognize the town from my book, but anyone getting arrested here will be on unfamiliar turf.

Speaking of unfamiliar turf, I did not invent the UFO theories discussed in *Star Witness*. I concocted the UFOlogists but not their positions or assertions. Whether one "believes in" UFOs or not, the sheer number of reported sightings and abductions makes alien contact our fastest-growing oral tradition. In and of itself, that's a fascinating comment on life on Earth.

For interested readers, I have included a bibliography and video list at the end of the book. More material is available in my Web site, http://www.scruz.net/~lmatera/liamatera.html. Many of us are natural skeptics, and skeptics often conclude in advance that UFO evidence is faked. But take a look before writing it all off. Skepticism should be at least as much trouble as gullibility.

To Anna Matera, Lillian Rehon, and Pete Rehon, Sr.,
with love and thanks

It's the cursor of God's reality processor. When you see the blinking light in the sky, it means there's about to be a text insertion or deletion.

TERENCE MCKENNA

prologue

The ambulance slammed to a stop, lights swirling and siren blaring. Up ahead, backlit by searchlights, two cars were stacked like blocks. The top one, a small sports car, had flattened the roof of the big American car beneath. Both windshields had burst into hundreds of beads of safety glass, littering the lonely stretch of coastal highway.

Paramedic John Bivens glanced at his partner and said, "Wow!" Then he jumped out of the unit, hurrying toward waiting firemen.

Between the ambulance and the lime green engine of Davenport Fire & Rescue, damp road and chrome reflected strobing red and blue lights. Broken glass glinted like strewn gems.

Amped on adrenaline, his steel-shanked boots crunching over glass, John realized he'd have hated to miss this call. He'd have been jealous of any medic who got it instead of him, though he hadn't thought so when the radio jolted him out of a sound sleep at two-thirty in the morning.

He approached the two cars as Fire gave him a quick report: "We can see the guy inside the bottom car breathing, so we know he's alive. We can't get a response out of him—hasn't opened his eyes or moved or said anything. We're thinking if we cut away the back door and part of his seat, we can maybe get him out that way."

The top car, a Fiat, was wedged into the old Buick, its front end torpedoed into the passenger compartment so that the grille rested on the Buick's dash. The Buick's roof was squashed beneath it, with the rear bumpers piggybacked. The Buick's lights were off and the Fiat's were a mere flicker.

"Highway Patrol called it in," Fire continued. "But he didn't see it happen, so we don't know how long ago. He's off looking for the owner of the Fiat."

John's partner, Barry, was standing beside him now. "The Fiat must have come off there." Barry pointed up an embankment only fifteen or twenty feet steep. This part of Highway 1 was bracketed with low cliffs.

Just south of Davenport, about ten miles north of Santa Cruz, the road was cut like a channel through a hillside of farmland sloping toward the Pacific. Tonight the waves crashed loudly and the fog smelled of sea salt and cold kelp.

A siren could be heard—sheriff, most likely, maybe Highway Patrol returning. John pulled out his flashlight. A firefighter was shining a light under the back bumper of the top car, probably assessing its stability.

John crouched, aiming his light through the slit formed by the crushed frame of the driver's window. A few beads of safety glass still clung to it. The driver's torso, bleeding profusely, was visible. The seat had collapsed on impact and the driver was pinned almost supine. That was good. He'd never have survived being crushed upright.

John shifted the light, trying to get a look at the driver's head. He told Barry, "Head's cracked open; I think I see brain matter. But he's foaming, definitely breathing; he's still alive. We'll have to get him to a trauma center. We're going to need a helicopter."

John walked around the cars while Barry got on the radio and ordered helicopter transport. He quickly realized Fire was right. To get to the driver, John would have to wait for the back door to be cut away.

A highway patrolman approached, saying, "There's almost no traffic. We can make a landing zone for the helicopter right up the road. If you think this guy's going to make it."

"Yeah, good, the closer the better. Tell the 'copter to watch out for those power lines. You've got the highway blocked off?"

"Yes," a fireman told him.

"Any chance this thing's going to catch fire?"

"We've got flame retardant under the lower car."

For the first time, John noticed a thick sprinkling of something that looked like Kitty Litter.

"There's not much we can do about the upper car," the fireman admitted, "except keep the hoses handy."

"I'm going to need you to get this back door off pronto," John said. Barry had oxygen and IV bags ready.

"Jaws-of-Life is on its way from Santa Cruz," the fireman explained. "Our hydraulic cutter can't handle this one. They should be here any minute."

And in fact, the siren was audible.

Within minutes, firemen were leaping from a red engine and attacking the car door as single-mindedly as leaf-cutter ants. John was right behind them. The minute the opening was big enough, he contorted and squirmed his way inside to check on the driver.

He was fighting claustrophobia, shouting at Barry to aim the flashlight a little lower, when he heard the helicopter overhead. John could see its red side lights and bright searchlight reflect off twisted chrome. Its whirling blades were deafening.

By the time the helicopter landed, he'd made sure the driver's airway was clear, and he'd started a trauma line. But he knew the guy wouldn't survive, not with such severe head injuries. He'd be lucky to make it to the helicopter alive. Too bad—he was fairly young, maybe sixty. Not a bad-looking old man either, plenty of hair and reasonably slim.

John squirmed out of the car. Despite the seacoast chill, he was drenched in sweat. He'd been worried the Fiat would shift and collapse the passenger compartment completely, crushing him along with his patient.

He stepped away to let Fire cut out the seat back. There were two fire trucks on scene now, one in front and one behind the ambulance. A Highway Patrol car and a sheriff's car were parked on the shoulder. The helicopter was just up the road, smack in the center of the highway on the white line. Six vehicles, their lights swirling and flashing, and twelve men—quite a congregation for a single-injury car accident.

The MediVac helicopter began spilling out trauma nurses, bent at the waist to avoid the rotor.

When the firemen motioned to him, John squirmed back into the car to keep the patient's head and spine stable while they yanked the seat back out from under him. The trauma nurses were at their elbows, peering in at the driver while John shouted over the noise, describing the patient's condition.

"What about the driver of the other car?" one of the nurses asked.

"GOA," a fireman explained—gone on arrival.

"Hit-and-run, huh? Stupid son of a bitch, I hope they catch him."

When they helped load the patient through the helicopter's back doors, John thought his eardrums would burst, the blades beat the air so loudly.

John and Barry stood with Fire, watching the helicopter lift off and turn inland toward the trauma center. When they could no longer see its red lights in the sky, Barry called County Comm and cleared. They could return to quarters and go back to sleep.

The sheriff and Highway Patrol were still walking around the cars, shining their lights inside. A tow truck had pulled up alongside the ambulance.

Barry remarked, "Hit-and-run. Boy, that guy's in a world of trouble."

"Not as much trouble as the guy he landed on." John looked up the slope. "Jeez, that Fiat came down hard. I wouldn't mind taking a look up there."

Barry was about to say something when his pager went off. He clicked the button to hear the radio squawk, "SC-2, respond to a medical emergency at the end of San Vittorio Road in Davenport."

While Barry got details, John jumped into the back of the unit and stripped off his bloody jumpsuit, replacing it with the clean one. He'd be driving this time: Barry's turn to be patient person. But he still might have patient contact. And besides, he didn't like being bloody any longer than he had to.

It was less than two minutes before he was behind the wheel, threading carefully past the stacked cars and the fire engines. San Vittorio was just up the highway, not even a half mile away, right before Davenport itself.

They barreled down the rutted country road, their lights glinting off the dark windows of run-down houses. There was no traffic, so they kept the siren off. No use waking everybody at three-thirty in the morning.

Barry commented, "There's sure been a lot of calls around Davenport lately."

Davenport was a minuscule village—a deli, a P.O., a B&B on the highway, and a few hillocks of houses rising up around a cement plant. For a town with just a couple of hundred residents, they'd had an inordinate number of dispatches this past week.

"Yeah, well, this last call takes the cake." Then John predicted, completely erroneously, "We're not likely to see anything any weirder for a while!"

Ironically, I was watching the movie *Inherit the Wind* when I got the phone call.

Inherit the Wind is a fictionalized account of the Scopes "monkey trial," where Clarence Darrow—perhaps the last lawyer in America to be admired and respected—defended a teacher charged with the crime of explaining evolution to his 1920s high school class. Darrow lost the case despite some heavy oratory. That's because there's no defense against orthodoxy; by definition, too many people believe in it.

Today, evolution is part of our orthodoxy. But I managed to find out the hard way what its modern equivalent is. I managed to find the one idea that, despite volumes of supporting evidence and testimony, even a modern-day Darrow couldn't comfortably advocate. And unfortunately, I'm no orator; natural selection bred that quality out of lawyers to make room for creative billing.

I'd been perfecting my double-billing skills for the last year, working for a firm specializing in high tech, especially multimedia law. The job sounded hip; that's why I took it (and also because I'd been unemployed for the previous half year). But to the low woman on the totem pole it meant a lot of copyright-infringement, unfair-competition, and breach-of-contract suits. It meant way too much time in conference rooms with techie lawyers.

These shouldn't be confused with stereotypical nerds of either the

geek or cyberpunk variety. Lawyers have huge, spun-glass egos, so having the best equipment (computer equipment, that is) isn't just a way
of mainlining more data, it's a way of putting their claw marks higher
up the tree. And with plenty of money to waste, lawyers can afford a
little bark under their nails.

After almost a year of hearing three lawyers, two paralegals, and four
secretaries lust after technology that was "almost there"—that is, almost
equal to their transcendental or business purposes—I was sick to death
of computers. Even my stereo seemed offensively digital. All I wanted
to do was get away, go someplace where suits weren't required and
hardware wasn't deified. I was longing for the tech-free simplicity of my
hippie youth; I was looking for one of those cabin-with-no-phone kinds
of vacations. Instead, I got the call from Fred Hershey.

I was comfortably cocooned in bed watching *Inherit the Wind* when
the phone rang. In the ordinary course of things, I'd have let my answering machine pick up. But in my hooray-I'm-free-for-three-weeks bliss,
I'd unplugged it.

So along about the sixth or seventh ring, I became groggily concerned.
What if my father was sick? What if my mother, the world's oldest
Yippie, had broken her vow to stop getting herself arrested?

I staggered out of bed, cursing my inconvenient Ludditism, and
picked up.

Fred Hershey said, "Willa Jansson, time for you to return the favor
you owe me."

I would later learn that Fred can be pathologically blunt, an odd trait
in a psychiatrist, and one that natural selection will, perhaps, eventually
eliminate from the breed. This night, it surprised me. I'd spent only a
few hours with Fred last year, just long enough for his brother, my old
boyfriend, to put me deeply into Fred's debt.

I said, "Who is this?" But I suppose I knew. Being generally cranky
and antisocial, there are few people to whom I owe phone calls, much
less favors.

"Fred Hershey. I need you to come down to Santa Cruz first thing
tomorrow morning."

"I'm leaving to go on vacation."

"Perfect. You'll enjoy the weather here."

Fred's brother, Edward, had driven me crazy years ago when we lived together. And he'd made himself a pain in the butt several times since. Now it seemed to be Fred's turn. I could only wish their mother hadn't spared the rod.

On the other hand, Fred and Edward had helped me hide out a friend. But for them, he'd be in prison now. I might be there, too.

"Willa, listen. A patient of mine is about to be arrested for vehicular manslaughter and felony hit-and-run. I need you to represent him."

"I'm a business lawyer," I protested. In the five years since graduating from law school, I'd also been a labor lawyer, a corporate lawyer, and a federal judge's clerk. Lest Fred think me versatile, I added, "And I'm on vacation."

"You're the only lawyer I know who's crazy enough to take this case."

"Thanks a—"

"And you're the only one who owes me a favor."

The evening chill penetrated my sweat clothes. I hugged myself. I remembered Fred in therapist mode, his voice as modulated and mellow as an FM deejay's. I'd also seen him under stress, swearing and barking out cross orders. But I hadn't spent enough time with him to recall the details of his face; I kept visualizing Edward's, which engendered a Pavlovian impulse to bicker.

"Why don't you get him a local lawyer, a criminal lawyer? That's what he needs, not a—"

"I'll explain when you get here. Can you make it by lunchtime?"

"Who did your patient hit?" I could just see myself representing some jerk who'd sped off after mowing down a nun.

"They say his car went over a cliff and landed on the highway."

"What do you mean, 'They say'? Did it or didn't it?"

"It landed on top of another car, yes. The driver was crushed."

"And your patient drove away?"

"No. He wasn't in the car."

"So who was driving?"

"No one."

"It went over by itself? He didn't set the hand brake?"

Fred didn't answer immediately. "It's a lot more complicated than that, I'm afraid. But I think you should hear it from Miller."

"Miller being the guy who wasn't in the car when it killed someone?" Shades of Stephen King's *Christine*.

"Yes."

"Where does he say he was? Does he have an alibi?"

"That's the part that gets a little sticky. That's why I need you."

Why oh why didn't I ignore the ringing phone? Why didn't I leave for vacation just a half day sooner?

There was no getting around it; I did owe Fred Hershey a favor, a great big one.

"Yeah, okay, I can be there by lunchtime."

I went back to watching *Inherit the Wind*, little realizing I was about to be transformed from a thirty-seven-year-old, slightly graying, too-short blonde with an uninspiring résumé. I was about to hobble a strange, modern mile in Clarence Darrow's shoes: Willa Jansson, heretic lawyer, counsel for the infidel.

2

Alan Miller seemed like an okay guy; I didn't really care much one way or the other. My agenda was to convince him and Fred Hershey that they didn't need me, they needed the local public defender. I'd even packed my suitcase, hoping to keep driving south, maybe to Big Sur, preferably to Mexico.

Miller was in a Catholic hospital. He looked pale, sitting in a cramped bed in a tiny room with a window slit and a big crucifix on the wall. Miller's face, pained, scared, strangely resigned, was a match for any plastic Jesus. Beside his bed, an IV dripped clear fluid into his vein. I noticed they'd shaved a patch of dark hair off his hand before taping in the needle. His other hand, presumably unshaven, was hidden beneath the sheets.

Miller was a big man, maybe thirty, with a square stubbled jaw, unkempt dark hair, and slightly dazed eyes. He winced occasionally, either uncomfortable in the too-narrow bed or battered beneath his flimsy gown and blankets.

"There's no way I'd have left the highway, no reason I'd have driven through a Brussels sprouts field." His Fiat sports car had landed atop a northbound Buick on a lonely part of Highway 1 ten miles from Santa Cruz. Miller's voice was deep, even in exasperation. "Why should I pull off the highway just so I could cut back toward it a quarter mile later? That's assuming I could even get my old Spider across a sprouts field, which I'd probably break the damn axle, the car's such a piece of shit." Tears glinted in his eyes, a clear green ringed by black lashes. "God, I'll miss that car!"

"So let me understand this. The cars were . . . stacked?"

"Yeah. I've seen pictures. The sheriff took some, mostly out of the weirdness of it, I think. The Fiat was right on top of the Buick, not perpendicular like you'd expect. You'd have to drive along the cliff edge of the field for a while to come off at that angle. Even so, I don't see how you could land pointing straight up the road."

I'd just experienced the glorious drive down from San Francisco, two hours of sun on crashing surf, winding cliff highway, and, close to Santa Cruz, cultivated land on a thin verge between the road and the drop-off to the sea. Apparently the hills on the inland side of the highway were Brussels sprouts farms. But they were hardly "cliffs," they were only ten or twenty feet above the road.

"The cars were within sight of Davenport, facing north toward it," he continued.

Davenport, from what I recalled, looked like a group of giant scrub-covered gumdrops with a few houses laced between them. A cement plant, a couple of restaurants—that seemed to be the extent of the tiny town fifteen minutes north of Santa Cruz.

"They're saying I turned off the highway, went up the hill, cut through the field—which probably would have blown my tires and wrecked my muffler—and went over." Miller gestured with his IV'd hand, wincing when the line tugged the needle. "Only they can't say why—because it didn't happen. I would never have done that. The road I live on is south of Davenport. Why would I be heading north at two-thirty in the morning?" He glanced at Fred Hershey. "And no way I'd run from an accident. Not with someone hurt; no way."

Fred was sitting in a corner looking like a psychiatrist, sympathetic and noncommittal and very prosperous. He was tan and fit, his tight curls lightly gelled. He wore a flaxen sport jacket with pushed-up sleeves, a vanilla cotton shirt, twiny slacks, and glove-leather boots.

Despite the same heavy brows and strong nose, he didn't look enough like Edward to be recognizable as his brother. But then, I'd never seen Edward so well groomed.

Miller said to him, "I don't know what I told you in hypnosis, but I can't think of any reason I'd do what they say I did." Miller sounded plaintive, maybe a little scared.

"You hypnotized him?"

"Yes." Fred didn't offer any details.

"And he told you where he was that night? Whether he did it or not?"

"He certainly doesn't believe he did it." Fred spoke slowly, tranquilly, turning on the verbal Prozac.

If a distinction was being made, I wasn't getting it. "Does he have an alibi?"

"I think it's best if you finish interviewing Alan before we discuss the hypnotherapy session." His tone was as bland as the voice programmed into my computer at work. *You have mail, Ms. Jansson*, I expected him to say. "He's already been interviewed by the police and the district attorney and myself about this, so I assume there's no confidentiality problem?"

"I have no idea—I'm a business lawyer."

"I want him to stay," Miller put in. "I want him here."

"I guess it's up to you." "I guess" is not a good thing to hear your lawyer say. But Fred was right; Miller was already on record. And presumably, at some point Fred would overcome his reluctance to tell me what Miller said under hypnosis. I assumed the delay was a psychiatrist thing: no quick (or cheap) insights. "But, Mr. Miller, let me get the accident scene straight. They found your car still on top of the other car? It didn't bounce off, drive off, roll off?"

"Right smack on top. With nobody inside when the police and paramedics got there. And the guy"—he gulped—"underneath, in the Buick, I guess his car had a lot of rust damage, it was an oldie. The roof wasn't strong. The Fiat just squashed the shit out of it. They told me the driver's head cracked open like an eggshell." His color changed from ashen to ghostly. "The nurses here are—I guess they knew him from a few years ago, when he had cancer. One of them yelled at me about it; said she heard pieces of his skull were sticking out through his forehead." He glanced at his IV as if the nurse had taken vengeance with the needle.

"And this was how close to your house?"

"About a half mile from where I turn off. I live on San Vittorio, a funky little country road. I've got but two neighbors."

"So what were you doing that night?"

"I was up in San Francisco, up at a symposium all day. Then, you know, a buffet at the hotel with some of the people there. Gabbed with them awhile. I left maybe at eleven or so." He looked like he was hiding something.

"What kind of a symposium?"

"Mycology. Mushrooms. That's my specialty. I do regional field guides, teach classes through the natural history museum, take people out mushroom hunting, that kind of thing."

"He's something of a local celebrity," Fred Hershey added.

"No." Miller smiled slightly. "But I've helped out a couple of times here at the hospital when the docs needed spores identified. You know, in cases of mushroom poisoning when they didn't know what they were dealing with."

"Okay, so you were at a mushroom symposium in San Francisco until eleven o'clock or so?"

"Uh-huh. I stopped in Half Moon Bay for a cup of coffee. There was a girl standing out by the café door, asked me for a ride down the coast. I told her I was only going to Davenport, but that was okay with her."

"So she rode with you? All the way to Davenport?"

"I let her out at the beach, the one across from the Cash Store—I guess that's what you'd call downtown, for Davenport. But that was at like one o'clock, one-fifteen."

"Oh." I tried not to sound disappointed. An alibi witness would be a godsend, even if it took a while to locate her. "Then what?"

He glanced at Fred Hershey. "I'm not . . . I don't know, I'm not totally clear. I remember I pulled over to drop this girl off, and I was worrying about it. She looked awful young to be hitchhiking, and I thought maybe I should offer to let her crash at my place. It can be cold down on the beach. But she didn't seem to want to talk about it, she was acting pretty tough. And after that, I just can't . . ."

I waited a moment, then prompted him. "After that?"

"I can't quite get clear on it, can't seem to get a handle on the time. I don't really remember anything else until I woke up in bed the next morning."

"The accident was at two-thirty?"

"That's when it got reported. A Highway Patrol car spotted it."

"And you believe you were home asleep by then?"

Fred stirred in his chair. "Actually, the Highway Patrol went to his house at around three o'clock. They got his address by checking his license plates."

I could guess where this was going. "But he wasn't there?"

"No."

Miller's brow furrowed. "I can't explain it. I don't remember. I just woke up at home."

"What time?"

"About ten-thirty."

"But they'd checked your house at three."

"It's worse than that. The Highway Patrol went back at around five, and then the sheriffs checked at eight."

"So, as far as anybody knows, you were gone all night. Did they find you in bed at ten-thirty?"

"No. In the shower."

"The deputies slammed him to the floor, handcuffed him, and were reading him his rights before they noticed the kind of shape he's in." Fred's lips pinched tight. "He ended up being transported here by ambulance."

I tried to telegraph a silent *Help* to Fred. What did he expect me to do for Miller? The man couldn't offer an alibi. Moreover, he was injured, just like he should be if he'd been in a car wreck. In fact, the more I heard, the more likely it seemed that he was guilty.

"Do you think he might have hit his head in the crash? Wandered off? Wouldn't a concussion account for the memory lapse?" I checked my watch. Mexico or bust.

"His injuries aren't consistent with a car accident." Fred was keeping something to himself.

"They aren't?"

"After an accident, you'd expect compression fractures of the neck and vertebrae, maybe broken knees and a crushed chest from hitting the steering wheel, head trauma, facial trauma, cuts from broken glass, that type of thing."

"And that's not the case here?" It seemed to me Miller moved like a man with plenty of aches.

"No."

"So what kind of injuries does he have?"

"We'll go into more detail about that later." Fred Hershey was either a control freak or he didn't want to discuss it in front of Miller.

Well, the hell with that. To Miller, I said, "What have the doctors here told you?"

"They haven't really wanted to say much. They're the ones who called Dr. Hershey." Miller looked scared. "I can tell you how I feel."

"Yes?"

"It's like my head's stuffed with cotton, sinuses killing me. My leg hurts. But mostly it's my kidney. Man. I've been passing blood."

"So the sheriffs found you at home at around ten-thirty yesterday morning, and either they were too rough or something was already wrong with you and you needed an ambulance. They brought you here, checked you in. The doctors examined you, and then called Dr. Hershey." It's a lawyer's habit to make clients agree to some version of the facts before retrospection begins to airbrush them.

Miller's eyes filled with tears. He nodded.

"And you assume the sheriff will be back to arrest you?"

Using the hand with the IV needle taped to it, he tugged down the sheet covering his other hand.

It was handcuffed to the bed rail.

"Oh." I glanced at Fred.

"They came last night and charged him with gross vehicular manslaughter and felony hit-and-run. They'll take him straight to jail, formally book him, as soon as the hospital's ready to release him."

"I wish they'd take this thing off!" Miller clattered the handcuff. "It means bedpans—I hate it. It drives me nuts."

"As far as you know, they haven't proved yet you were driving?" It sure didn't look good: it was Miller's car, and he admitted being in it an hour or two before the crash.

When Fred shook his head, I asked him, "Why exactly did they call you in?"

"He was in a great deal of emotional distress, especially about his memory loss. And I was the on-call psychiatrist. Alan and I talked for a while, and I suggested he might be a good candidate for hypnosis. I explained the procedure and the part it might play in a legal proceeding."

"Did the DA have anything to do with the decision?" If I remembered correctly, prosecutors could request that witnesses, but not suspects, be hypnotized.

"The district attorney signed off on it. His approval was required."

"And you went ahead with this?" I asked Miller. "Without consulting a lawyer? Without having one present?"

"I had to know," Miller protested. "I couldn't believe I'd done what they thought I did. I'm the one that pushed for hypnosis."

"The DA had Alan sign a document stating that he knew the session would be tape-recorded, and that if charges were filed, the recording could be used as evidence against him."

"But I was sure I didn't go driving through a field off a cliff, no way," Miller put in. "I was all for it. I never thought I'd end up like this." He raised the cuffed hand as high as it would go.

I was trying to understand Fred's part in this. "So your tape recording ended up getting him arrested?" He'd helped Miller incriminate himself, then hired him a business lawyer instead of a criminal lawyer. Did Fred have it in for the poor man?

But Fred didn't seem abashed. "It obviously didn't prevent his arrest. When I realized it would be a matter for the public defender, I called you."

I sighed. "Mr. Miller, Dr. Hershey and I have . . . worked together before. But I wasn't acting as an attorney then." I was acting as an accessory to an assortment of crimes. "And I've got to tell you, I'm not a criminal lawyer. I'm a multimedia lawyer—basically business and intellectual-property law. I really don't think I could be of much use to you. Especially compared to a public defender, who tries criminal matters day in and day out."

Fred raised an imperious hand. "I don't think a public defender is a good idea."

"They're usually highly accomplished—"

"A PD would plea-bargain," he insisted. "They are very good lawyers, I agree; but they just wouldn't know what to make of this. It'll take someone creative. And preferably not from around here."

"What does that mean?"

"Let's just say it will have to be a rather . . . eccentric defense."

" 'Eccentric' as in, get an out-of-town lawyer to come here and make a fool of herself, then vanish?"

With barely a smile, Fred nodded. "You'll understand after you hear the tape recording."

Miller sat forward. "You'll let me listen?"

"You haven't heard it?" I was surprised.

"Dealing with this kind of memory loss, without knowing the reason for it . . ." Fred seemed to be struggling not to overexplain. "I thought it would be best to wait and see whether Alan began recovering the memories on his own."

"I haven't." Miller looked as frustrated as he sounded.

Fred removed a small tape recorder from his briefcase. "Under the circumstances, and especially since the district attorney has a copy of this tape, I think you're entitled to hear it, Alan." Fred didn't look happy about it. "I would certainly have preferred to work with you first. I would have liked to have seen the memories begin to reemerge on their own." He set the recorder on his knee. "Rather than blindside you with them, as it were."

Miller sat forward, his eyes round, his lips slightly parted, staring at the tiny tape recorder as if it were Pandora's box. "Just play it," he begged. "I want to know what I said. I want to know where that time went." He flicked me a glance. "It's not like I haven't *tried* to remember. I've tried every way I can think of. I really have."

Handcuffed to a hospital bed, he probably had done his best, all right.

"Let's hear it," I agreed. Fred's hints had piqued my curiosity. What kind of case would send someone scrambling for an "eccentric" hired gun from out of town?

Probably the same question Clarence Darrow asked when he got the call from John T. Scopes.

3

"What *is* that? What is that thing? Oh, my *God!*" Miller's voice screamed out of the tape recorder.

The sound of it, hysterical and tinny, emanating unnaturally from a plastic box, made this seem like an old radio drama. *Carjackers from Mars.*

"Oh, my God, the light; it's paralyzed me. It's like being dipped in glass, invisible restraints all over me. I hate the light, I hate it, I could just burst out of my body, just blow up like an overcooked wiener or something. Oh, my God, it's *awful!*" Miller's voice quivered on the verge of a freak-out.

Watching Miller listen to himself, I'd have bet his shock was genuine. He sat very straight, his neck craned forward, his face so attentive the muscles were slack.

"I can see I'm moving, I can look out the car window and see I'm moving. Not my body; it's paralyzed. But the car's moving with me inside it!"

Miller's muscles jerked as he listened. His head started shaking slightly. He looked like a man about to say, *No way!*

"Something's wrong, something's wrong. Moving so fast, like getting sucked up, but I don't feel it; there's no wind to it, no rushing noise, no engine noise. It's all wrong. I must be going crazy. God, I've gone crazy. Just like Grandma. Oh, my God!" The voice on the tape was tight, wary. "What the hell is that? What is that thing?"

Fred Hershey's best FM voice intruded. "Remember, Alan, you're here now, not there. You're remembering this from a place of safety, recalling something that happened in the past and is behind you. Try to stay with the memory. What do you see?"

"Man, I don't know. Some kind of a *thing.* It's gray. It's skinny, it's got little legs and arms as flimsy as a spider's. There's four of these spidery guys. Big black eyes, tiny noses, little slits for mouths. Skinny chested. They're like gray insects standing up, like little grasshopper men."

"What are they doing, Alan?"

"They put their arms into the car like it's not solid. And then I'm going right through the car, right up through the roof, through it like it's just a cloud. They pull me right up through the roof. Oh, my God. I must be crazy!"

"You're okay, Alan; you're safe now. Try to stay with it."

"It's like they're floating me. We're in some kind of room. They're floating me into a chair. Except when I sit down the chair molds itself to me, straightens me out. It's more like a gurney now, but it's shaped to me and I'm . . ." The voice on the tape whimpered. "They took my clothes! Oh God, I'm claustrophobic, can't stand it, can't stand it, I'll go nuts if I can't move."

"You're safe now, Alan. You're only revisiting the past. Try to stay with it if you can."

"One of them is taller and bigger. It's like a big old praying mantis or something. I must be insane. I must be dreaming." He screeched. "It's touching me! It's touching my face. I'm so cold, its touch is so cold. It puts words into my head."

"Words?"

"It says I'm not scared. But I am. It says it won't hurt, but it does hurt."

"What hurts, Alan?"

"It's like a syringe with two needles. It's filled with something hot and gold colored. It burns like hell going in. The tall one says it doesn't hurt, but goddam it, it does, it really does hurt."

Miller's shoulders were hunched. He was shaking, staring down at the thumb of his cuffed hand.

I strained for a look. I could barely make out two small puncture wounds.

"He keeps saying it won't hurt, but it all hurts, it all does. Not as much as before he put the words in my head, but I know that underneath his words, it still hurts. It's like I don't feel it, but I know it hurts."

"You say, 'It all hurts.' What else hurts, Alan?"

Miller hung his head, listening to a long description of tissue taken from the back of his leg, an apparatus placed over his genitals to extract something, a huge instrument lowered over the table and used to bore beneath his rib cage into the general area of his kidney, something pushed up his nostril deep into his sinus cavity.

The tale was as harrowing as it was preposterous. And Miller's voice was as terrified as any I ever expected to hear.

Miller, in person, looked like he might leap up and run screaming down the hall, dragging the bed by his handcuff.

When the tape ended, we were all silent for a moment.

"Well . . . ," I said, "I guess I agree the public defender would want to plea-bargain this one."

"What does it mean?" Miller's voice was intense. "Am I crazy? I don't remember anything like that. I mean, how could I? It's crazy, right?" He looked at Fred as if begging him to concur.

Fred crossed his legs, scowling. "Perhaps I should explain the dynamics of hypnosis, Alan."

"I mean, I must have hit my head or something. It must have been some kind of nightmare." Miller rubbed the punctures on his thumb as if trying to erase them.

"Hypnosis is a way of getting into your perceptions, your own highly individualized and filtered view of reality. It doesn't give us the quote-unquote facts, or the truth, or any of those abstract concepts. It only gives us what *you* make of what *you* see. It gives us your memories, in short. And memories are more personal than most people realize. They're shaped by your worldview, your history, the unique way you process impressions. Does that make sense?"

Miller lay back as if deflated. "So if I'm crazy, my memories are going to be crazy."

"But you see, your other memories, the ones you've shared with me —what you did that day, where you come from, what you do for a living—those memories appear to be competent. It would be unusual for you to have only a few hours' worth of 'crazy' memories, as you call them."

"But Fred," I interjected, "say he did hit his head. Couldn't that put weird ideas into his brain?"

"There's no sign of trauma to the head." Fred sounded cranky. "On the contrary, if we're going to look at the physical indications, we have puncture wounds on his thumb, an apparent generalized allergic reaction to an unknown agent, kidney problems, genital swelling, pain in his calf, a sinus ache, and a tendency to nosebleed."

I was beginning to think Fred was the crazy one. "You're not saying this really could have happened?"

Fred sighed. Miller closed his eyes, breathing shallowly, quickly.

"Fred, are you saying you want me to go into court and argue that this man got abducted by gray aliens with spider legs who put words into his head?"

Fred scowled. "Would you be surprised to know people all over the world are telling similar stories?"

Miller's eyes were shut so tight his lids looked like prunes. Tears leaked down his face.

"I've been doing some research," Fred continued. "The founder of the

Cambridge Psychiatric Hospital compiled seventy-some case studies. There are hundreds of others in other collections. Reputable scholars believe there are literally hundreds of thousands of Americans with recovered memories of similar experiences. Some of them put the number at close to four million."

"Yeah, well, millions of people believed Richard Nixon had a 'secret plan' to end the war in Vietnam, but that didn't make it true! People believe all kinds of crap." I glanced at Miller, hoping I hadn't given offense.

But his eyes popped open. He watched Fred hopefully, as if wanting him to agree.

Encouraged to see it, I continued. "I thought the whole repressed-memory thing got discredited." I recalled some lawsuits about it—a woman who kept "remembering" her father slaughtering her childhood friends; women who, at the instigation of their therapists, began attributing their problems to sudden "memories" of sexual abuse.

"Discredited, no. Controversial, yes. Ordinarily, when a traumatic event occurs, the memories around it might become distorted, sometimes highly distorted—compressed, expanded, forgotten—but memories of the trauma itself tend to be unnaturally sharp and focused. That's why Vietnam veterans have such a hard time, for example; they can't forget the horror, not even one detail of it, though they may have blotted out the day-to-day occurrences."

"So Mr. Miller should have remembered very clearly . . . whatever happened. Which probably means it didn't really—"

"This has been used to discount so-called repressed memories of childhood sexual abuse. But there *have* been documented cases of recovered memories being independently verified. In fact, attacks on repressed memories seem to be more an assault on certain kinds of therapists than a bona fide scientific position."

Great. I could just see myself jumping into the whole repressed-memory quagmire.

"But Alan isn't experiencing the usual pattern of some memories being repressed and others remaining intact within the same period. He's lost an entire well-defined, recent block of time. Amnesia, basically. And that's one of the recognized areas where hypnosis can be very helpful. It can be a problem when it's used to enhance existing memories—people are prone to embellish and confabulate. But when you're trying to get to the memory itself instead of getting at the details . . . I'm sure that's why the district attorney went along with its use in this case."

"I'll bet he wasn't expecting this."

"Memories of alien abduction . . ." Fred glanced away. He seemed embarrassed even saying the words. "If the case studies can be believed, they're unique in that they almost always follow a period of amnesia, what they call 'missing time.' They may slowly leak back into conscious recollection. Or a person may experience difficulties that take him into therapy, where close work or hypnosis jars them free."

We continued watching Fred.

He added, "One theory is that they are forced into suppression."

"Forced? You mean, the bug-eyed creatures *tell* everyone to forget?"

Fred looked like it was hard for him to nod.

"No," I said. "No way. I'm sorry. But I am not going to go into court and say that." I'd spent years trying to prove I wasn't a flaky hippie like my parents; I wasn't going to undo it in a single close encounter of the legal kind.

Miller surprised me. "I agree with her. I won't go into court and say I got sucked into a—" He stopped, hyperventilating again. "I can't do it. I mean, I'll be honest. I'll say I don't remember what the hell . . . But not this. Nuh-uh."

Fred sat up straighter. "I'm not advocating anything, I hope you understand that. But I do want you to consider two points. One is that stories like yours are being told all over the world—and personally vetted by reputable therapists. And secondly,"—he spoke quickly, before we could scoff—"none of the doctors here is likely to testify that your injuries are consistent with a car accident. If you accept a plea bargain simply out of embarrassment at what you'd have to claim in your defense, you could be doing yourself a disservice."

That was cause for nonspacey optimism. "What about the injuries? Why didn't they keep the DA from filing charges?" Perhaps I could just stay the night, have a talk with the DA tomorrow, persuade him he couldn't prove Miller was in the car when it crashed.

"The sheriff didn't find anyone else's fingerprints on the steering wheel; that's number one." Fred leaned forward, ticking the numbers off on his fingers. "They have his statement that he was driving the car earlier. And the car didn't run itself off the cliff—so they believe. As far as the DA is concerned, the accident speaks for itself. The simplest explanation is that Alan walked away unhurt. That his condition now is the result of something that happened later."

I tilted my head, watching Fred. There was something else, something more. I couldn't believe he'd accept alien abduction so easily, otherwise. "How long have you believed in this stuff, Fred?"

"I don't 'believe in' it. I'm just telling you this isn't an isolated, unique recollection."

"You heard about this at some point, right?"

"I heard that John Mack, the Harvard psychiatrist, had written a book about it; that he believed the seventy-plus cases he described were legitimate recovered memories of alien abduction."

"Did you read the book? Were you persuaded?"

"No, I didn't read the book." He ran an exasperated hand over his curls. "I was rather appalled when Harvard spent a year deciding whether or not to censure him for his public stance, but I had no particular interest in the subject."

"And you'd never heard this kind of story before, yourself?"

Fred didn't answer.

"Did you?"

"Not until this week," he replied.

I was about to ask whether he meant Miller, but he raised a hand to shush me.

"The crucial thing is for Alan to make an informed decision. What if he doesn't offer an explanation of what happened that night? What are the possible penalties?" He turned to Miller. "Would it make a difference to you to know you could go to prison for five or ten years?"

Miller blanched.

Fred continued. "I don't know what the penalty is for manslaughter, Alan. But it's likely to be stiff. Stiff enough to be worth some public embarrassment."

"That's true," I agreed. Might as well jump in with something vaguely lawyerly. "But you don't want a business lawyer. If there's a good criminal lawyer here in—"

Fred leaped to his feet. I assumed he was going to get ballistic about the favor I owed him. But he was staring behind me at the hospital door.

I turned, alarmed by the shock on his face.

An older woman, perhaps sixty, perhaps a hard-drinking fifty, stood there glowering at Alan Miller. Her hair was dyed blond, arranged in a country-bar bouffant that needed tending. Her eyes were ringed with black liner streaked by tears. Her face was wrinkled and lean. She wore tight black jeans, boots, a black top that looked home sewn, and black plastic earrings. Her hand fumbled at the zipper of a big vinyl handbag.

She looked for all the world like a Texas divorcée with some serious hell to raise.

I glanced back at Fred. He'd reacted so strongly to the intrusion. Did he know her?

Fred was sidling close to the bed, putting himself between Miller and the visitor. He'd puffed himself up somehow, looking bigger and more authoritative.

Behind him, Miller seemed to cower. I could hear the handcuff rattle on the bed frame.

By virtue of their reaction, the woman earned my full attention. I turned back to her.

She was clearly agitated, her head twitching slightly, her eyes wet, her stare fixed. The corners of her mouth turned down, lipstick bleeding into her wrinkles.

She said, "You can't hide forever!" I was almost surprised she didn't have a Lone Star accent.

Miller was stuttering something about how sorry for her he was, but that it wasn't, he didn't . . .

Fred interrupted him. "This is highly inappropriate. Do the nurses know you're here?"

She barely glanced at him. To Miller, she shrieked an outraged "Sorry? *Sorry*'s all I get? 'I'm sorry?' " She stepped into the room, the door swinging shut behind her, bumping her forward another inch. The stink of cheap liquor entered with her. "You ever been married, you jerk-off son of a whore?"

Fred strode toward her, almost stumbling over my feet as he passed my chair. He wore the determined scowl of a nightclub bouncer.

He was already grabbing her as she added, "Well, 'sorry' don't cut it, asshole. Don't cut it. You never been married, much less a second time. What are the damn odds I die alone? How many men you think the good Lord made like Francis? Hunh, Mr. I'm-so-sorry, bastard?"

I finally realized she was the dead driver's widow.

Fred, grappling with her as he tried to reach around and open the door, looked like he was doing the Texas two-step with her. He was using the Voice again, telling her her grief was understandable, but that her actions were inappropriate and must cease immediately.

That sent her over the top. She spewed profanity, struggling to shove Fred aside. Fred, in the fray, didn't notice what she was doing with her hands.

She was reaching into her big purse.

I stood, almost toppling my cheap plastic chair. I've grown to accept the fact that I'm more paranoid than most people. But then, my parents have been arrested seventeen times, two of my former bosses have been killed, and Fred's own damn brother gave me herpes. I think people are crazy to expect anything but the worst.

I closed the short distance between me and the widow's ugly vinyl bag.

I knocked Fred's elbow aside. The widow made eye contact then, and I knew I was right.

Her eyes, a little jaundiced, a little red, were as mean and angry as a gargoyle's.

I threw myself against the handbag, trapping her hand inside it. We were in a tight huddle now: Fred in front of the widow, me to one side, the bag hard between us, and the door behind us.

The next moment, a blast sent me stumbling across the room. My ears felt like they'd been boxed.

The widow's gun had gone off in her purse. Through smoke that smelled like saltpeter and melted plastic, I could see a ragged hole in the bag.

Fred staggered back, mouth agape.

Miller was saying, "Holy shit," about an octave higher than his usual speaking voice.

Only the widow kept her head. She opened the door and slipped out.

Seconds later, two nurses ran in. They stopped short, looking at Fred with his hand over his forehead, and me, sinking back into my chair.

"What was that noise? What's that smell?" They turned to Miller and demanded, "Do you have firecrackers?"

I pointed to a corner of the room. The bullet had to be there somewhere, lodged in the wall or the floor. "A gun." I was out of breath.

Another nurse came up behind them. "Was that a shot? I'm going to get security up here."

Fred regained his composure. "Hurry!"

Miller slumped back against his pillows. One of the nurses bent over him.

"Come on out into the hall, both of you," the latest nurse commanded. "We'll talk out there."

Fred turned and murmured something to Miller as I walked out.

God damn, the widow had come here to shoot Miller, just coldbloodedly shoot him for (she thought) driving his car off a cliff onto her husband's. With so many other elements—fate, coincidence, rust damage (never mind alien abduction)—she'd chosen to blame Miller.

She could as easily have railed against kismet for putting her husband on that bit of highway at that moment, or for sending Miller's car over at that spot. She could have wished they'd owned a sturdier car or installed a luggage rack. She could have picked the incident apart, regret by regret. Instead, she'd kept it simple. Miller killed her husband; Miller must die. It was as direct, and as dumb, as the plot to a Hollywood movie.

I looked down the quiet corridor, beige and peach with subdued prints. The nurses' station had a few peeps of color—pictures of children, potted violets—but nothing incongruous. Nothing operatic, nothing crazy.

Nothing like a tape recording of a man recalling medical experiments aboard an alien spacecraft. Nothing like an infuriated Kmart shopper with a loaded gun.

I glanced at Miller's room number, 2120: you have just been admitted to the Twilight Zone. I memorized the number as if to localize the insanity, label it and keep it on the other side of a closed door.

I sniffed my sleeve, suddenly convinced my clothes must stink of gunpowder. My semidressy sweater did indeed reek.

Fred was standing beside me now, nagging me about something.

"Willa! Willa, talk to me."

"What?" My tone was cross. I pulled up my collar to see if it stank, too.

Fred gripped my shoulder, forcing me to make eye contact. "How are you doing?"

I wanted to bat his arm away. This was his damn fault. I'd be doing some leisurely packing right now, planning a restful trip, but for Fred.

"How are you?" he repeated. His brows were knit so tightly a couple of the hairs touched his lashes.

"How should I be? I'm freaked out."

He nodded, looking relieved. He let go of my shoulder. "Of course you are," he said complacently.

As a tubby security guard trotted toward us, Fred added, "You will represent him, won't you?"

I'd very likely saved Miller's life in there. Didn't that repay the favor I owed Fred? Or did it add Miller to my karmic load?

I hesitated.

"Good girl," Fred said, as if the matter were settled.

4

Fred Hershey sat me down in his office, which was decorated to look like someone's sunroom. Glass-topped tables matched white rattan love seats and chairs with green cushions. A wall of windows overlooked a gulch of young redwoods and hardy ferns. I'd been to Fred's office once before, in the process of sinking myself into his debt.

Now he sat opposite the love seat I occupied, staring out the window at his picturesque gully. He sat low on his spine, legs splayed, arms crossed. His suntan was the only cheerful thing about him.

"I want you to hear something," he said slowly. "I'm trying to think of some rationale—any rationale—to play it for you."

"What is it?"

"A session with a patient early last week."

I was surprised. Surely that would violate the doctor-patient privilege.

"It would have to be strictly on the QT, off the record. I'd have to have your assurance that you wouldn't mention it to anyone. That you wouldn't allude to the tape's contents or to the fact that you'd heard it."

If I couldn't use it in any way, why even bother? "You're making me feel like a lawyer, Fred." A rare and not completely pleasant thing. "How can I promise? What if it could help acquit Alan Miller? I have a duty to my client." My client; Christ—I'd caved. I'd made the business equivalent of a shotgun wedding.

"If you can get this information from a different source, fine; use it. But what you hear in this office you've got to swear you won't use or refer to in any way."

"There's no loophole in the patient-doctor privilege, Fred." I might as well go the lawyerly distance. "If you tell me, you've violated it and it ceases to exist."

"That's why you can't let anyone know I did this."

Did Fred assume, because of the way we'd met, because I'd been on the run from the police, that my ethics were shaky? Did he assume I was, in general, a sleazy rule-bender?

On the other hand, it must be important for him to rationalize doing it.

Sleaze on: "Tell me."

Fred reached behind him, finessing open a drawer. From it, he extracted an audiotape. He held it up. "It's another one," he said.

"Another tape of Miller?"

"No." He fumbled his tape recorder out of his briefcase and popped the new tape in.

His voice, crackling out of the small speaker, was almost sickly sweet. "Now we're going to talk about what happened to you yesterday morning, okay? But if we get upset, we'll go right back to that nice safe place you described; do you understand? The dog pillow in the kitchen is right there for you if things get hard. But remember, where we're going is all in the past. It's all done with, and you're safe now, okay?" He sounded like Mr. Rogers.

When the other voice piped up, I understood why. It was a young boy's, a grade-schooler's high-pitched "Okay."

"Now let's go back to where you and Joey were that morning. Let's go right back to when you left your mom's house. Can you do that?"

"Uh-huh. We go to the store and get cinnamon buns and Snapple."

"What store is that?"

"Davenport Cash Store." The squeaky voice seemed to relish the memory. "The buns are sticky there. And big."

"Then where did you go?"

"Beach," he replied. "I want to find agates. Joey says beaches don't make agates, but do so. And shells. I got mussels with the hinges still on." A silence. "I looked up and Joey's not there anymore. Where's Joey? It's so sunny I can't see." The boy's breathing quickened. "It's too sunny. I can't see Joey."

"What can you see?"

"It's too sunny. And the beach is getting little."

"Getting little?" Fred sounded confused, if still avuncular.

"I'm on top of the beach. It's little, like if I'm on a mountain, but I'm not."

"Is there . . . anybody with you?"

"A gray man with big sunglasses."

"What's he doing."

"He gots my arm. He gots a silver suit and he's little like me but he's a grown-up."

"How do you know he's a grown-up."

"I just know. When he talks to me, he talks like a grown-up."

"What does he say?"

"He doesn't say. He talks straight into my head. That it won't hurt."

"What won't hurt?"

"They gots a table like at the doctor's but invisible. And stuff to put on me." His voice sounded frightened now. "I want my clothes. I'm cold."

"Don't be scared. That time is all over with. You're just remembering something that's all done. And you're safe now. Do you understand that?"

"I go, 'I'm cold.' But the doctor with the sunglasses says no, I'm not. He says it won't hurt and I shouldn't be scared. Like you."

"Does it hurt?"

"Nope."

"Were you scared?"

"Nope. Not after he says I'm not."

"What is he doing, the doctor with the sunglasses?"

"He's taking sperms."

There was a brief silence on the tape. "What kind of sperms?" Fred asked.

"Sperms, you know, like eggs and sperms."

"How is the doctor taking the sperm?"

"With a box."

"Does he ask you to put your sperm in the box?"

"No. He puts a box like a glove on me and says I don't feel it on me, and then he takes it off and says I was good and gave good sperms. But the next thing hurted."

"What was the next thing?"

"The invisible table turns over and they have to put a cold snake inside me." The boy sounded matter-of-fact, not frightened. "It even hurted after the doctor said it didn't. He had to touch my eyebrows with funny gloves to make it stop hurting."

"He touched your eyebrows with funny gloves?"

"Like at the Halloween store."

"What did the gloves look like?"

"Gloves."

"What shape were they?"

"Hand shaped!" The boy seemed to find this a silly question.

"Like the gloves that took your sperm?"

"No. That was like a box with a glove. This was like a Halloween glove."

"And he touched your eyebrows with it?" Fred apparently decided to move beyond the gloves.

"He says it doesn't hurt, and then it really doesn't. He's a good doctor. Better than you!"

Fred clicked off the tape recorder. He scowled at it for a moment. "This boy, Mickey, and his brother Joey were missing from Davenport Beach for almost three hours. His mother had everyone she could round up out there looking for them. And then all of a sudden, there they were walking in the surf, arguing."

"Arguing?"

"Mickey claimed he bent over to pick up a shell, and that Joey wasn't there when he straightened up. Joey says the same thing about Mickey. They were fighting over who lost whom."

"Where does Joey say he was?"

"Joey's a year younger than Mickey, which is why I played Mickey's tape; it's a little clearer. They both say they were at the beach the whole time. Only, to them, it seemed like about twenty minutes. Whereas in reality, they were gone over four hours." His frown tightened like a spring. "Their mother—there's a restraining order against the father; he abused the boys."

"You mean that day? At the beach?"

"When they were younger." Fred seemed sincerely pained. "It was a terrible thing. Their memories of it are fragmentary, confused, as the memories of young children tend to be. But, of course, when the boys didn't come home on time, the mother panicked. Her immediate fear, her first assumption, was that their father had kidnapped them. And frankly"—he rubbed his eyes—"that was my assumption, too. I was sure these were screen memories."

"Screen memories?"

"A psychological mechanism to deal with memories that are just too painful or frightening. A father who's raped you, for instance: you erect a screen in front of your mental images. Something that accounts for the actual event while diminishing its horror. You quote-unquote 're-member' a gray alien instead of your father. And the physical sensation is no longer a rape, it's a medical procedure. Instead of your father insisting he's not hurting you, you take the fact that doctors often say that. You try to transform the memory into a visit to the doctor's office. But you know deep down you didn't see your doctor; and you know your mother knows it. So you have to work a little harder, construct a screen that can't be seen through so easily."

"So, in essence, the boy made this up."

"Not consciously. But on a level so deep, it isn't retrievable as a regular memory. Getting to it requires hypnosis." He straightened, stretching slightly. "On the surface, both boys were convinced they'd been at the beach only a short time."

"Are screen memories common?"

Despite better posture, he looked tired. "Common? No. But they happen. I've encountered them before, usually in children. Children have a greater tendency to blend memory and fantasy, just in general."

"So you thought this was a screen memory. And then you hypnotized Alan Miller."

Fred winced. "Yes."

"What do you think now?"

"I think there are an astonishing number of similarities in their stories. Not to mention a locational connection." He scowled. "What can I say beyond that?"

"That wouldn't sound ridiculous?"

He raised his hands as if to say, *Well?*

"I can't do it, Fred. I can't let Alan Miller testify that he was abducted by aliens. He'll get laughed out of court."

"Unless there are other people in Davenport who might also come forward . . . ?"

"They'd all be laughed out of court. And they should be! This is stupid! This is crap!" I felt my cheeks grow hot. I felt tears sting my eyes.

Fred handed me a box of Kleenex, saying, "You were almost shot. You're entitled."

I waved the tissues away. "Psychiatrists are supposed to think everyone's entitled."

Fred's snort made it clear their private assessment didn't always match the party line. "The real question is, *can* you defend Alan Miller without bringing his hypnosis session into it? Can you defend him based on his word that he wasn't driving the car at the time?"

"The jury would wonder what he *was* doing," I conceded. "And to tell you the truth, I do, too. I don't buy this space aliens stuff. What about a screen memory?"

"In a man Miller's age?" He shrugged. "The possibility is remote, at best. I say this because, number one, he shows no overt symptoms of a serious psychological disorder. And absent that, screen memories are rare in adults. Adults have learned so many other coping techniques."

I mulled this over.

"And it would defy the laws of probability," Fred added, "to find matching screen memories among unrelated individuals from entirely different age groups and backgrounds."

"You're saying it stretches your credulity?" I couldn't keep the sarcasm out of my voice. "But alien abduction doesn't?"

"Well, let me put it this way. Mickey and Joey's father certainly didn't abduct Alan Miller." He sighed. "And after hearing Miller's story, I wonder whether Mickey and Joey's father abducted *them*."

"You're not about to talk me into representing the father, too?"

Fred smiled. "Take on Miller and we'll call it square."

"Only if I can do it without bringing up spacemen. That's where I draw the line, swear to God."

Fred couldn't guess how out there my parents were. He didn't realize I'd spent my childhood elbowing past loonies in their Haight Street flat. He didn't know my landlord traced his lineage back to the Martian quarter of Atlantis.

I had worked long and hard to be the least weird person of my acquaintance. To end up as counsel for an alien abductee carjacking victim?

"I'll talk to Miller's neighbors—maybe we can find some alibi evidence. I'll go have a look at the field he supposedly drove through. Maybe we can get a mechanic to say his car couldn't have made it. There might be something we can argue—something terrestrial. But we can't go into court with *I was on a spaceship at the time.* That just doesn't cut it as an alibi."

"I'll drive you up there," Fred offered.

I took a hard look at him. Miller wasn't a longtime patient or even a personal acquaintance. Why was Fred putting himself out for the man? "It's the boys, isn't it? You want to know for sure what happened to them."

"If you can find an explanation for what happened to Miller—"

"You can go back to your screen memory theory."

"And not worry that their father is being unjustly reaccused." He rubbed the back of his neck as if it ached. "But it's also about Alan Miller. I believe him when he says he had no reason to drive across that field. I believe him when he says he wouldn't have left the scene of an accident."

"How can you believe that without believing the rest of it?"

"I don't know yet," he admitted. "I'm working on it."

5

Fred bought me lunch at the Davenport Cash Store, a restaurant and ethnic arts emporium whose brick walls and high ceilings lent it a bistro air despite the musty smell of African carvings and Persian rugs. Fred's patient, Mickey, had told the truth about one thing: the cinnamon buns there were sticky. And big.

Davenport was right on the coast highway, but two lanes of traffic didn't spoil the lonely, Hitchcockian charm of the town. Hillocks flowed with spring weeds overrunning tough perennial scrub. In seams between them, streets converged like veins in a leaf. Untended houses with wet yards rose toward an adobe church with an arch and bell, and a tiny building with a Western facade dangled a shingle reading Jail. Up the highway, a cement plant with tall digesters backlit the camel-hump hills.

After lunch, we got back on Highway 1 and headed south, pulling onto a gravel shoulder about a quarter mile down the road. Beside us, a rise blocked what I presumed was a view of the beach. I could hear waves crashing on nearby rocks. I could smell seaweed and wet sand, even from the highway.

Fred climbed out of his immaculate Lexus and came around to open the passenger door. "This is where the accident happened," he told me. "That's the hill, across the highway."

I wasn't sure what he expected me to notice. But I climbed out of the car for a better look. The hill was even shorter than I'd supposed. It rose, clifflike, to a height of perhaps twenty feet. The rise on our side was less than ten. The route had obviously been cut through a slope running down to the sea.

I stared at the highway, zipping with Sunday traffic now that the fog was burning off. Up the road, a dozen parked cars were jammed onto a dirt verge. A few surfers were stripping off wet suits.

Fred was saying, "You can still see beads of safety glass over there. Near the poppies."

The sun was catching side-of-the-road bits of windshield like sprinkled glitter.

"You haven't seen the pictures," Fred continued. "What a sight. Miller's car was about the same length as the Buick from the driver's window to the taillights. And it wasn't just sitting on top, it was wedged into the Buick's interior with its tail end sticking up." He shook his head. "I understand it was a complicated extrication."

"I see what Miller means about the angle," I mused. "You'd think any car coming off that hill would be pointing more toward the ocean."

Fred nodded, opening his door. "Let's go take a look up there."

A few minutes later, we turned left onto a rural road. We passed more shrubs overrun with tangled greenery as if everything was trying to grow everywhere at once. We turned onto a bumpy road that was paved in spots and graveled in others. It went sharply up a short hill to a Brussels sprouts field.

The sprouts had been harvested some time ago. Chopped stalks, about six inches high, were ringed with broad, wilted leaves. There were perhaps a hundred neat rows of them, too close together to drive between. But the dry stalks looked as tough and stiff as bamboo; it would be a hell of a bumpy ride over them.

Fred didn't try to get the Lexus across the field. He parked at the end of the road and hopped out of the car.

I joined him at the edge of the field.

"A lot of farmers let their land sit for a while between crops," Fred explained. "They're just starting to plow it under and replant with artichokes."

"I assume the sheriff and the DA have been here?"

"If they found Miller's tire tracks, they didn't mention it to me or to him. The ones we're looking at are obviously from a bigger vehicle, probably the farmer's truck."

"If they didn't find Fiat tracks, I'll put the sheriff—or whoever checked this area—on the stand. I wonder if they brought a forensic photographer up here."

Staring out across the field, I felt utterly inadequate. In the last year, I'd never once worried about tire imprints. I'd worried instead about securing patents for an Internet broadcast company's hardware and negotiating its "rent" on preexisting cable and telephone wires. My newfound expertise wasn't likely to be of much use to Alan Miller.

We started toward the "cliff," walking slowly, looking for tracks. We stepped over quite a few that were too wide to belong to a sports car. Fred was probably right about them belonging to a farm truck or a small tractor.

It didn't take long to get across; the cultivated area wasn't much bigger than a football field. Where the chopped stalks ended, the ground was bare and hard for perhaps four feet. It was too dry to show tracks, instead showing scuffs that could as easily have come from boots. Beyond that, tough, dusty-leafed plants competed with yellow-flowered sorrel and wild radish, holding the cliff edge together.

"This should be just about the spot." Fred prodded the shrubs with his chichi ankle boot. "You'd think the greenery would be crushed if he drove over it."

The plants appeared hearty and unbroken as far as I could see.

I looked beyond the brambles onto the road. Even with cars speeding by, I could tell where the accident happened. Traces of the Highway Patrol's orange spray paint still marked the scene. In addition, the pavement was noticeably smeared with oil and gasoline. A few twists of metal and piles of safety glass littered the shoulder. But there was a similar spot down the way; apparently the area had had its share of crashes.

Across the highway, beyond where the shorter hill bracketed it, the land tapered quickly down to the ocean. I could make out a long line of pelicans skimming the horizon. I inhaled ocean mist, car exhaust, and fertilizer. Eau de Highway 1.

I turned, hearing an engine. A big pickup truck was cutting a bumpy diagonal across the field. Dirt rose around it, making a corridor of murk behind it.

It stopped a few feet away. A cranky-looking man in jeans and a checkered shirt jumped out. He was short and swarthy, with a drooping black mustache and a sunburnt bald spot.

"This is private property, posted 'No Trespassing,' " he barked.

Fred pulled out his wallet, extending a business card. "We're here about that car crash Friday night—or rather, Saturday morning—the one down below on the highway."

The man came closer, snatching away and scowling at Fred's card. But if he wondered why a psychiatrist was investigating an auto accident, he didn't say so. "A doctor, huh?"

"That's right." Fred gestured toward me. "And this is my associate from San Francisco."

The man looked much friendlier now. "Jesus"—his tone was confidential—"I heard the Fiat landed right on top of the Buick. Now what are the odds of that?" He looked up and down the field. "I drive through here, but it's no place for a sports car. You'd have to be crazy or stoned to try something like that in the middle of the night."

"The sheriff was up here after the accident looking for tire prints?"

"Not till dinnertime. My house overlooks the access road, so I know when I've got company."

"He didn't come first thing Saturday morning? With photographers, evidence collectors?"

"No, I seen him drive up for a quick look about three-thirty in the morning—just shined his light around. Checking nobody was up here, I suppose. But they didn't really walk the field till dinnertime, like I said." The farmer grinned. "But hell, it's clear enough the fella drove across here. There's no other way to land on a car down below."

"How tough are these plants?" Fred wondered. "Over here on the edge? Because I don't see where they were run over."

The farmer glanced down at Fred's boot. "They're tough enough; they hold the hill together when it rains. But you should be able to notice—not that I've ever seen them run over. I took a look yesterday morning."

"Before the deputies came out?"

"My field, so of course I'm curious."

"Did you notice anything?"

"No." The farmer looked concerned. "It's posted 'No Trespassing,' " he repeated. "You couldn't mistake this for a road. He must have been stoned on something."

"You didn't know either of the drivers, did you?"

"I don't know anybody drives a Fiat. I believe in buying American."

We stood in silence for a minute.

"Can I show you something?" the farmer asked unexpectedly. "I'm wondering what to think about it."

"Please do," Fred said.

The farmer gestured toward his truck.

There was plenty of room for three in the cab, but that didn't make it comfortable. The leather seat was cracked and collapsing, and it stank of manure and dust. There were dirty skeins of spiderwebs where the windshield met the dash, making me imagine spiders on my ankles and neck. I was a car slob myself, but I drew the line at driving an eco-system.

It was a bumpy ride across the field and onto the road. The farmer turned inland, barreling over ruts and potholes. A few minutes later, we reached a meadow of tall grasses, mottled beige and green, with flecks of pink and yellow from wild radish.

"It's the damnedest thing," the farmer said. "Come and take a look. I don't know if I'm supposed to report this kind of thing or what."

We walked into the field. As beautiful as the knee- and thigh-high grasses were, I couldn't help but wonder about snakes, ticks, jumping spiders. In the city, greenery is corralled into parks, where it can't hurt anybody.

About five minutes later, we stepped into an area of flattened grass. It didn't look crushed or dead, just lying flat. The downed area extended at least twenty feet ahead.

"Some kind of camp?" Fred guessed. "For tents and the like?"

"That's what the other fellows thought," the farmer agreed. "But I sure didn't notice the traffic, if folks have been camping here."

"The other fellows?" I repeated. I watched Fred walk farther out, following a swirl pattern in the mashed-down grass.

"The paramedics." The farmer wiped his forehead fretfully. "The ones that took the call, that tried to save the fellow in the Buick. When they got off work in the morning, they came up to look at the sprouts field, same as you."

It seemed to interest everyone but the sheriff.

"And you brought them over here to see this?"

"Uh-huh. You know, one summer, they drove their ambulance right across my artichokes to get me when I was hurt out in the field. If they were more worried about their ambulance than about me, they sure as hell didn't show it."

"The same medics who came to see you on Saturday?"

"No, no. On Saturday, they were young fellas. Nice as can be. You could see they were still shook up about it. One of them had to crawl into the car and start an intravenous line. You know, while the firemen cut the driver out. But to hear him tell it, he knew the poor fellow wasn't going to make it. His head was cracked open with chunks of his brain hanging out—he died on his way to the hospital." The farmer's eyes glinted with empathy. "You could tell it had got to him. And just think how much those boys see every day."

"Is there any way to reach this field besides the road we took?"

"On foot, sure. You could come from over that way." He pointed past

Fred to a rising hill. "Off-road maybe a half mile from San Vittorio, where the barn is."

"San Vittorio Road?" I tried to sound nonchalant. But I remembered Alan Miller saying he lived there.

6

When we finally climbed back into his Lexus, the first words out of Fred's mouth were, "Crop circle."

I was a little tired and more than a little distracted by itches. "Crop circle?" To me, this signified some kind of farmers' union or grange.

"It's a crop circle," he repeated. "That thing in the farmer's field. It's like the ones in England."

"What in England?"

He didn't engage the engine. He shifted on the plush leather seat to look at me. I could see his furrowed brows through the gray lenses of his sunglasses. "I met someone a while back, someone who was researching them. There have been thousands of these things in England. Hundreds of them appear every summer. And they've appeared in more than a dozen other countries."

"So what causes them?"

"They think . . ." He glanced away.

"They think . . ." I prompted. I suppose I expected him to say sinkholes or fungus or whirlwinds. Even after our strange morning, his reply caught me by surprise.

"Spaceships. They think crop circles are their landing patterns."

"Oh, Fred—please." I rolled my head back against the buttery leather.

"I'm just telling you the popular view there," he protested. "I'd like to get a better look at it from uphill, see if it forms a pattern."

"Make it so," I agreed. "Warp three."

San Vittorio Road was longer than I'd imagined, a rutted, winding few miles bordered by tangled hills occasionally leveling to lush fields. There weren't many houses on the road, and they tended to come in clusters. Most were rural to the point of looking third-world, with scrubby, terraced gardens, cars on cinder blocks, and untethered goats. At Alan Miller's end of the road, only two houses were visible. One was freshly painted with bright trim and hollyhocks climbing the porch supports. Lace curtains dressed the windows.

The other had green paint showing through weathered patches of yellow, and a driveway piled with auto body parts overgrown with ivy. The porch was so swollen it looked mossy, and an old sofa beneath the eaves sprouted mushrooms from its arms and back.

I suspected this one was Miller's.

When we stopped to gawk, a white van, parked between the two houses, started up and pulled a U-turn. As it sped past, I caught a glimpse of the passenger, a thirty-something man with a graying buzz cut.

"Where's the barn the farmer talked about?" I could see the end of the road, but it looked like these two houses were the only structures here.

"I don't know." Fred drove the Lexus a few hundred yards forward into a turnaround. At that point, we spotted a dilapidated structure behind some trees.

A broad path curved up a steep grade. We climbed out of the car and continued on foot. When we rounded the first bend, a big, new house confronted us. What we'd taken for a footpath was apparently wide enough for a car; a Toyota sedan was parked near the front door.

"Wonder what happened here," Fred muttered.

The otherwise well tended house had a boarded-up front window, a dangling porch light, and a slashlike gouge in the door.

As I stared at it, the door opened.

A heavy, balding man with a long nose, wide mouth, and pale eyes seemed surprised to see us. He reached unconsciously toward his shirt-tail as if to tuck it in. "Hello?"

"We wondered if you'd mind . . ." Fred tilted his head, scrutinizing the man. "Dr. Joseph Huizen? The author of *Simple As Pi* and *Sweet As Pi?*"

"Yes." The man squinted as if a clearer view might help him identify Fred.

"We met at the last University Night." Fred stepped forward, extending his hand. "Dr. Fred Hershey. I guest-lecture the psychology graduate students now and then."

"Oh, yes?" But it was clear he didn't remember Fred.

"This is Willa Jansson," Fred continued, as if any friend of his must be a friend of Dr. Huizen's. "She's an attorney from San Francisco. She's representing your neighbor, Alan Miller."

"My neighbor?" He looked bewildered. "Is he buying land or something?"

Lest I seem like Mrs. Fred, I spoke for myself. "He was involved in a car accident; charges have been filed against him. The accident was close by here and there's a possibility that we might have a view of . . . something relevant from a hill behind your house."

Dr. Huizen shook his head as if I'd spoken Greek to him. "He had an accident on my property?"

Before I could reply, Fred blurted out, "Did you know you have a crop circle back there?"

I was surprised by his chattiness. The tendency is trained right out of lawyers. Surely psychiatrists were also in the habit of being close-mouthed?

"Really?" Dr. Huizen looked interested.

"It's an odd coincidence, isn't it?" Fred added. "Don't you remember? At University Night, the Oxford scholar who was researching crop circles?"

"Ah!" His face lit up. "The fellow who kept on about 'sacred geometry.' Not that I don't appreciate geometry"—he turned to me—"I teach mathematics at the university. But good heavens above, what's sacred about it?"

"That's right—the sacred geometry of crop circles; he was writing a book." Fred looked excited. "The geometry of the patterns within the circles or something. I only remember because he wouldn't let anyone change the subject."

"How long ago was this?" I wondered.

"Not even a month," Fred guessed.

"The fifteenth of last month," Dr. Huizen confirmed. His face was friendlier now, a sparkle in his pale blue eyes. "Would you like to come in? You can get oriented from my patio."

When we followed him into the high-ceilinged foyer, we saw other signs of damage: a pile of shattered porcelain, scarred parquet, a broken chair leg.

The professor must have noticed our eyes on the disarray. He sounded apologetic "Apparently I did this."

"You?" Fred's tone was neutral, a nice, nonjudgmental, psychiatrist's reaction.

"Mr. Hyde . . ." He motioned us all the way in. "Would you like a cold drink?" His gaze strayed to a photograph of a young woman, circa 1950. A now-dead wife? One who'd trained him to offer refreshments to guests?

Fred glanced a question at me. "Cold water would be nice, thank you," I answered.

"The same for me," Fred said.

We followed our host into a square, white-walled kitchen with plenty of windows. He poured us water from a cooler.

Just when I began to doubt we'd get the skinny, he explained, "It was night before last. My first diabetic emergency. I didn't know I had diabetes." He handed us the water, looking rather ashamed of his condition. "It was a miserable shock, I'll tell you."

He opened a sliding door to a small patio with the usual white tube furniture. We had a view of a slight decline, and then a steep incline, all tangled with vines and flowers.

"I suppose I've been trying to take refuge in the chemistry of it, to use my training to make it more real to myself. It seems my body depleted my blood sugar and then began leeching it from my brain. I've never tolerated alcohol well and I'm not one for mind expansion, as they call it. So I've never been seriously altered before." He smiled wanly. "It put me nose-to-nose with something unimaginable to me. And I didn't care for the experience, not a bit."

"It must have been very disorienting." Fred sounded sympathetic—and maybe a little surprised. It wasn't easy to visualize Joseph Huizen, with his white hair and soft build, busting up a foyer.

"At the time," he continued, "I felt unfettered—I remember the sensation so distinctly: I felt lightened, as if my body were a weighted vest I'd managed to shrug off. I remember feeling joy at being free of this inconvenient mass—a sign I should go on a diet, I suppose. And then I started trying to dance. I had a notion of dancing across a tetrahedron buried in my floor like a fly in an ice cube."

"A tetrahedron?" Fred seemed to take a professional interest, as if he were documenting yet another case of pesky tetrahedral delusional disorder.

"It makes a funny kind of metaphorical sense. I've been flirting with tetrahedral mathematics, specifically tetrahedra within spinning masses like planets. For my next book, *Pi in the Sky.*"

"Wonderful title."

"It may sum up my likelihood of ever truly grasping the subject." The professor sighed. "But I suppose, when my brain suddenly flew into chemical chaos, that I *would* see myself dancing on a tetrahedron." He looked down at his hand. The back showed a big bruise around a puffy vein. A bad IV stick? "It must have been at that point that I called nine-one-one. I really don't recall doing it, but they assure me I did. Apparently I babbled at some length about tetrahedra. If an ambulance hadn't already been in Davenport finishing other business . . . they say I'd be dead now. My brain, damaged from the lack of sugar, would have forced me into a coma; and they tell me I wouldn't have awakened."

"That's a difficult realization for anyone." Fred remained in psychiatrist mode.

"By the time the ambulance reached me, I was outside, communing telepathically—I thought—with a pattern of stars that had descended to eye level to discuss tetrahedra with me." He grinned sheepishly. "They made a few good points, too. I've been working on them."

"The unconscious can put together a lot of data for us," Fred agreed.

"Then I saw this dazzling, impossibly bright white light. And a strobing blue and red. I was utterly blinded by it."

Fred cast me a glance. I sat forward. Was this elderly math professor about to describe the descent of a spaceship?

"I became terrified. I recall backing toward the house, then stopping, immobilized. Two strange beings approached . . ." His voice became dreamy, subdued. "They were speaking gibberish, clad in some type of uniform."

"What else do you recall about them?" Fred asked.

"At the time, I seemed to know instinctively that they meant to harm me. But I wasn't able to back up any farther. I must have thrashed about on the porch a bit before making my way back into the foyer. I have cuts to show I broke lamps and a chair. But it seemed only seconds before these evil beings pinned me down and strapped me tight. I felt I would die of fright, truly—it was such a horrific shock. But I couldn't overcome their restraints. They carried me along a river of light into an enclosure. And then one of the beings sliced away the sleeve of my shirt and began torturing me with a needle."

Beside me, Fred had grown pale under his tan. He ran a finger under the wire frames of his aviator sunglasses, wiping away sweat.

Joseph Huizen glanced at him, a smile spreading across his face. "And then, the ordeal ended quite abruptly. The being with the needle injected me with glucose and . . . he suddenly became a paramedic. The blindingly bright vehicle turned out to be their ambulance."

I had to laugh. Poor Fred looked so relieved.

"Yes, quite an experience for someone who skipped all that sixties LSD business!" The professor grinned. "The medic said hello to me and started asking questions—who was I, where was I, that type of thing—obviously designed to see if I was back in reality. Then he explained the mechanics of diabetes, the warning signs, the seriousness—"

He looked so troubled, Fred patted his arm. "Quite an experience."

"It's odd, you know. We hadn't gone fifty yards down the road before the ambulance stopped. The paramedic who was tending me seemed mystified. The driver called to him to come up front for a minute. I remember he looked rather angry—you know, checking the IV, then me, looking like he meant to protest. But when he did go up front, it was a few minutes before I heard the driver say, 'We'd better go.' "

"That certainly is odd," Fred agreed. He glanced at me. "And I would think potentially actionable."

Dr. Huizen dismissed the suggestion with a good-natured wave.

"What night was this?" I wondered.

"Friday night."

"What time Friday night?"

"Perhaps three-thirty, four o'clock. Saturday morning, actually."

"And your ambulance stopped just up the road?" I wondered what to make of it.

"Yes. Whatever happened, the medic looked upset when he came back to me. Not that he didn't seem competent and concerned. But he was also flustered."

"My client's accident happened that morning. I wonder if the ambulance stopped near his house. Maybe the medics saw something going on there. Do you remember their names?"

"The one who tended me, his name badge said 'Barry.' I imagine the hospital's paperwork would tell you more." His gray brows were raised. "Well, I hope I've inadvertently helped you. I was beginning to feel guilty about being so long-winded."

"Not at all," Fred assured him. "I hope your condition is easily kept under control?"

"I suppose I'll get used to it," he said glumly. "They sent me home with the latest blood-testing kits and stacks of pamphlets apparently written for sixth-graders—you know the kind, illustrated with competent-looking women in shirtdresses smiling at their children."

"If you need to talk this out, let me know. I'd be happy to recommend someone, Dr. Huizen."

"Please call me Joseph." The professor appeared embarrassed. "I'm fine, really. Just old age—we all have to make some accommodations . . . Why don't you tell me what you're trying to get a look at, and I'll walk you to the best vantage point. They say I need more exercise."

Five minutes later, we started up a tangled hill with no path.

Close to the top, the greenery dried to a less dense incline of tough-leaved shrubs. They smelled spicy.

"The fog line," Joseph pointed out. "It sits in a trough between the hills, keeping the lower part wetter than the upper."

When we reached the top of the rise, I looked down a steep hill and over smaller mounds to a series of meadows. One of them showed the big circle. I was surprised to see how many smaller circles ringed it.

Apparently, Fred was, too. He let out an appreciative whistle. "That's quite a footprint."

"My Lord," Joseph agreed. "It reminds me of something—I wish I could put my finger on it."

"It looks like a six-planet solar system with one too-small planet and one multiple-mooned planet," I ventured.

"How was it made?"

"Your guess is as good as mine," Fred told him. "It's smashed into the grass in a kind of spiral pattern. The circles inside circles are grasses swirled in different directions."

"It looks like something," Joseph repeated tentatively. "A schematic I've seen recently."

"Do you have any idea who could have done it? Or why? Have you heard any commotion out behind your house?"

"No. But I haven't been home since Friday night."

I continued staring down at the pattern. The way it reflected sunlight, it gave the impression of hovering above the meadow. Maybe that's what suggested spacecraft to the British.

Fred started down the hill, presumably for a closer look.

By the time we joined him, he was pacing off the size of the inner circle.

Maybe it had to do with pitching tents. Maybe it was performance art. Maybe it was some kind of cult thing. Or maybe Alan Miller had made them. Maybe he'd done it in the wee hours of Saturday morning, crashing the car on his way home.

Beneath my feet, at least three kinds of wild grasses bent to the left in a broad swirl, coming together in the circle's center. I squatted, examining a few stalks. They weren't bruised or broken. The only signs of damage were in the joints, some of which seemed browner than they should be. Most of the stalks were bent at the lowest joint, as if sudden heat—or something—had wilted them from within. Some grass leaves showed a rumpling like stretched crepe paper on one side.

Fred returned, saying, "The big circle's about twenty-five yards across. Five of the smaller circles are about five yards. That one over there is only about three yards. And one of the five-yarders has a three-yarder up above it, with three even smaller circles around it."

"Does it mean anything to you?"

The look he gave me said, *Oh right*.

Joseph Huizen was squatting in the center of the big circle. The droop of his head told me there was more to his posture than simple interest in the wild grasses.

I hurried to him. "Are you okay?"

Without looking up, he asked, "Don't you feel it?"

I motioned for Fred to join us. To Joseph, I said, "Why don't you sit down. You must be tired."

As Fred trotted over, Joseph murmured, "There's some kind of a charge here. Don't you feel it?"

Fred looked worried. He dropped to his knees, easing Joseph out of his squat so that he sat in the spiraled grass. "What's your insulin dose and when did you last take it?"

"No, I'm not unwell." But sweat beaded his cheeks. "It's like a static charge. Can't you feel it?"

"No." Fred was checking Joseph's pulse.

Joseph insisted, "Look at the back of my neck."

The hairs there were standing up.

Fred seemed a little nonplussed. "Your pulse is strong."

"And that crackle," Joseph added. "Did you hear it?"

"No. Willa?"

"No."

"It zipped by, a minute ago."

I reminded myself that Joseph had just been in the hospital because of a blood sugar imbalance. And, as Fred had pointed out, he'd begun taking a new medicine.

But I was afraid the truth was simpler than that. Fred, by bringing up crop circles, had slipped Joseph the most potent drug of all: suggestion.

7

It was a relief to leave before Fred reiterated the theory that spaceships create crop circles. I tried to sit quietly in the car, suspecting Fred wouldn't enjoy my sarcasm any more than his brother, Edward, had in years past.

Fred backed out of the dead end turnaround, starting to say something. But he stopped midword, abruptly braking.

Up ahead, smoke tumbled across the road.

Fred cut the engine, fumbling for his dash-mounted cell phone. I got out of the car and started down the road. The smoke was coming from Alan Miller's house.

As I passed his tidy neighbor's, I noticed no sign of life there—no one peeping through the window or the door, no interior lights, no chatter from a television.

Even before I reached Miller's gate, smoke stung my eyes. It hung over his porch like a billowing gray curtain. I paused where the road met his yard. His windows were opaque with smoke. I doubted it was safe to get closer.

Even from here, I could see that the front door hung strangely, as if a hinge had snapped free of the wood frame. I wished Fred and I had checked it earlier. I wished I knew whether sheriff's deputies had damaged it bursting in to search for Miller. If it happened today, it meant arson.

I heard Fred shouting, "Back up! Get away from there." I turned, coughing, to find him running toward me, still holding his cell phone. "Into the field."

I joined him in a tiny pasture across from Miller's house.

"There's a fire station a stone's throw from the Cash Store," Fred panted. "They should be here any second."

"That white van. Remember the white van parked here when we first drove up?"

Fred nodded, eyes glued to Miller's house. He stuffed his cell phone into his slacks pocket.

"Did you notice the license number?"

He shook his head.

A moment later, an explosion of flames knocked the front door down, licking over the porch and curling over the eaves before retracting into the house.

Fred grabbed my shoulder, pulling me several yards farther into the field.

We could hear sirens now. Fred was saying, "It's smoke inhalation that kills people. All the toxic matter in houses now, the fumes are poisonous."

"Do you remember the men in the van well enough to describe their faces?" I only had a clear enough memory of one of them.

"Holy sh—look at this!" Fred crouched to pick something up. Still squatting, he held up a black bauble of an earring. I took it from him while he searched the ground more thoroughly.

I let the earring dangle from my fingers. I wasn't completely sure, but it looked like those clipped to the ears of the widow who'd tried to shoot Alan Miller this morning. I imagined her, sometime since, standing in this spot. Before we got here, waiting for Miller to return home? Or more recently, waiting for his house to catch fire?

I glanced at Fred, examining the ground between fluffy grasses and low weeds. Funny that he'd happened upon this earring. If it were anyone but Fred, I might suspect the widow had dropped it in the hospital room and that Fred had palmed it to "discover" later.

It was easy enough to suspect a man who'd dragged in an out-of-town business lawyer and then championed an alien-abduction defense.

But I tried to quiet my worries. Fred had saved my neck last year. He was Edward's brother, and I trusted Edward. And he had no reason—none I knew of—to do Alan Miller a disservice.

Fire engines were barreling down the road now. Fred rose, standing beside me.

Miller's house was wrapped in smoke so thick that interior flames glowed dimly, like a lightbulb through a scarf.

The fire trucks stopped in the middle of the road. Men leaped off, some working valves and yanking huge hoses, while others ventured closer to the house. One firefighter, in thick protective garb, ran next door and began pounding at the doors and windows. A moment later, he kicked open the door and disappeared inside.

Fred walked briskly toward the trucks.

I watched the firefighter emerge from the neighbor's house a moment later, speaking into a radio and gesturing for another man to join him.

Fred was giving a fireman his card, presumably explaining that he'd phoned in the call. The man nodded, gesturing him away from the scene.

Fred returned to where I stood, telling me they'd asked us to remain on hand until someone could question us. Considering their fire trucks blocked the road, we had no choice.

Fred hustled me toward his Lexus, several yards past Miller's neighbor's house. "Let's get well clear of the smoke. The air in my car should be good. You're all right?"

Assuring him I was okay, I let him hand me into the passenger side. He slid in behind the wheel, and for a while we just sat and watched.

One of the firefighters climbed onto Miller's roof and poked a hole into it. Another positioned a huge fan at the door. Within minutes, smoke from the porch and front of the house was being funneled up through the roof. Firefighters went inside.

I was still gripping the black plastic earring. I put it on Fred's dashboard. Against the backdrop of hardwood and glove leather, it stood out like a cheap hooker.

I considered all the phone calls I had to make. I had to talk to Miller's doctor, see how quickly we could get him released—I didn't want him to remain a sitting duck. I wanted to get him booked and out on bail as soon as possible. I wanted to examine the forensics reports, see how much evidence the DA had; look over what was left of Miller's Fiat; hire a detective to search for the hitchhiker he'd picked up; interview his neighbor.

It made me tired just thinking about it. In the leather womb of Fred's fine car, I wanted to curl up and sleep. This was supposed to be my vacation. I was supposed to be resting and relaxing.

But another siren made me sit up straight. An ambulance was bumping across the shoulder of the road, edging past the fire trucks.

It pulled close to Miller's neighbor's house. Two medics, both women, leaped out, one of them joining a firefighter on the porch and the other opening the ambulance's side doors. She grabbed three large black bags and followed the other medic into the house. A few moments later, a firefighter returned to the ambulance, pulling a gurney from the back.

Fred said, "I'd better see if they need a doctor in there." When he opened the car door, acrid smoke stung my nose.

I remained in the car a few more minutes, debating whether to follow him. I reluctantly decided that something at the neighbor's might bear on my case.

I got out of the car, gagging at the stench. But hardly any smoke rose through Miller's roof now. And several firefighters were gathered at the truck, retracting the hose. The fire, I assumed, was out. I just hoped Miller could salvage something from it.

When I started up the walk to the neighbor's, a firefighter trotted toward me, shouting at me to get back.

I pointed to the house, calling, "I'm with the doctor." I hurried before he could block my way.

I stepped into a tidy house with buffed wood floors. A firefighter and a medic were crouched on either side of a supine woman. The medic was pumping a bag attached to a tube taped to her lips. The firefighter had both hands positioned on her chest, exposed where her T-shirt had been cut away. He was doing chest compressions. Fred knelt at the woman's head, shining a tiny flashlight into her open eyes. The second medic adjusted some kind of monitor.

I staggered back a step. The woman was waxy white and her eyes didn't blink.

The firefighter noticed me, but he didn't say anything.

I could hear a slight pneumatic wheeze from the air bag. And I could hear a cracking sound with each compression of her chest.

Damn, the woman looked so young, younger than me. What could have happened to her?

I looked around her house. Every surface gleamed. Bowls of wild-flowers sat on colored straw mats. Bookcases were loaded with novels. The back window curtains were nailed into an artistic drape against the wall. Through it, a wildflower-dappled hillside showed no sign of anything to invade her privacy.

On a corner desk, a small computer was still on, its screen saver glowing with a stained-glass pattern. Amid the flowers and waxed wood, it created the impression of being in a small rural church.

But I didn't see any open windows. And the stink of smoke was lighter in here than outside. Could the woman possibly have succumbed to smoke inhalation?

Fred was murmuring to the paramedics. He took over pumping the bag while they went tête-à-tête over the monitor. Whatever it should have measured, it showed only a flat line.

I edged toward the door. Maybe if I didn't hear them pronounce her dead, the image of her lying there exposed to the view of strangers, her ribs cracking, her mouth stuffed, her eyes glassy, would fade from my memory more quickly.

As I turned to go outside, I glanced at a small table next to a coatrack. It was stacked with library books. Poor woman, I wondered if she'd had a chance to read them.

I touched the topmost cover, opening the book. The liner showed a due date thirteen days away. She'd checked out the books only yesterday.

I glanced at the title: *Abduction*, by John E. Mack. I tilted my head to see the spines of the other books: *Close Encounters of the Fourth Kind, The UFO Encyclopedia, Communion, Roswell Revisited.*

I stood there, hardly breathing. Why? Why had this woman gone just yesterday to check out a stack of UFO books?

I looked at Fred, wishing I could ask him, wishing he could give me some answer that would make my flesh stop crawling.

But Fred was shaking his head, watching the paramedics remove leads from small round pads on the woman's chest.

He approached me, saying, "She's been gone some time—probably a massive heart attack. They had to go through the motions. But it's time to get the coroner over here."

8

Miller was released from the hospital Sunday night and booked into the County Jail. He was arraigned Monday morning and out on bail by afternoon. Tuesday and Wednesday we selected his jury. And through it all, I waffled.

I never thought I could be so discouraged in a case where the District Attorney's Office had so little tangible evidence. In fact, the assistant district attorney had almost nothing: no Fiat tire prints in the field above Highway 1, no eyewitness to the accident, and absolutely no proof Alan Miller was inside his car when it landed atop poor Francis Everett Addenaur.

What the assistant DA did have was Miller's admission he was driving the Fiat earlier that night, his inability to provide a credible alibi, and—most persuasive of all—the notion that cars don't just fall out of the sky.

So even though the ADA's case was purely circumstantial, one of the circumstances was our basic understanding of how the universe works. I could cast doubt on every other aspect of the charge. But it was no use relying on reasonable doubt to suggest the car hadn't sailed off the cliff, tracks or no tracks. I either had to prove someone else was driving, prove Miller was elsewhere, or—God help me—prove that cars did indeed just drop out of the sky sometimes.

I'd get nowhere trying to prove someone else was driving. Where were his or her fingerprints on the door handle, on the steering wheel, on the hand brake? And where the hell was the person? Barring a stroke of magnificent good fortune—finding the hitchhiker and having her confess to carjacking, for example—I wouldn't get far with this argument.

Nor had Miller budged on his alibi. His memory was returning, but so far—to his distress—it continued to match the wild tale he'd told under hypnosis. And that was no more of an alibi than *My car fell from the heavens* was a defense.

With the trial just around the corner, I was forced to make the choice I'd dreaded since first hearing Fred's tape. I could ask the jurors to agree the state hadn't met its burden of proof, hadn't proved beyond doubt that Alan Miller was driving his own car at two-thirty, even though he admitted having driven it a little earlier and refused to say where he was at the time. And I could wave good-bye to Miller as they led him away to jail.

Or I could put on an affirmative defense, the only one available to me: that Alan Miller's car and person had been outside his control that morning.

The absence of tire tracks worked in our favor. So did the nature of Miller's injuries. So did Fred's audiotaped hypnosis session and his expert opinion. So, according to Fred, did many other experts' opinions. But how much good did expert opinions do John T. Scopes?

And though it might be the best defense, I just couldn't make myself believe it. I reminded myself lawyers don't have to believe, only defend. But most lawyers only risk losing their client's case. They don't end up tarred with the same brush.

I was in San Francisco when I finally made the decision. I'd returned to grab some clothes and do a little late-night computer research at my law firm.

I was still hedging when I stopped by my parents' flat for dinner. Maybe a dose of there-but-for-practicality would put me right.

As usual, my mother got up a dozen times during dinner to take phone calls, most of them about a caravan to deliver used computers to Cuba. Never mind that the Cubans had only two hours of electricity a day and precious few phone lines—my mother was sure socialism would flourish in cyberspace.

I poked at my stir-fry until my father, a slender, dimpled man, observed, "It's only been thirty years since the household went vegetarian —maybe you haven't given tofu a fair chance."

"What do you think of this alien-abduction stuff, Daddy?"

"Alien abduction? Coyotes at the border trucking in Mexicans?"

"No, space aliens, little gray men with bug eyes."

My mother reentered the room. Frowning as she was now, her skin looked as puckered as a deflated balloon. She wore her hair in the classic Women's International League for Peace and Freedom do—medium short, uncolored, and conscientiously unstyled. She was only a little overweight but she'd burned her bra thirty-five years ago, and it showed. The scary thing was, she'd looked a lot like me when she was my age.

She was seething as she crossed the dining room—if one could call it a dining room. Every sideboard and shelf was stacked with fliers, pamphlets, petitions, and diskettes. A sheet was tacked over the far wall for quick slide shows on the immorality of NAFTA.

Mother pushed away her half-eaten meal. "They're punishing him"— Castro, I presumed—"for being the last unrepentant socialist in the world."

"At least there's one left."

The doorbell rang, sending Mother through the door again. My father's chopsticks were poised partway to his lips as he waited to see which invading army would encamp here tonight. Would he spend the evening discussing Chinese labor camps, congressional e-mail box stuffing, or the politics of AIDS?

This time, Mother ushered in a group of aging cyberpunks, a recent coterie. My father, a true infoaddict, looked pleased. He'd recently fallen in love with the Internet. And my mother, grasping an opportunity for cheap mass mailing, was determined to work cyberspace like a street corner whore. The cutting edge had always managed to slash into our home life. It was a rare evening that every living room cushion wasn't a soapbox for someone with a monochromatic world vision. I'd grown up assuming we lived in a nation of ranters.

Tonight's cyberians were high on virtual avatars and erotic Web pages. They thought I was cool because my firm represented a group developing an Internet broadcast system. They didn't realize the damage done by recent movies glorifying techies, hackers, and nerds. Geeks in tight leather now talked kiss-kiss, do-lunch Hollywoodese. It was not a pretty sight.

Eventually, my father recalled the question I'd asked him over dinner, posing it to the group.

Moag, a thirtyish white guy with a bad Klingon haircut, immediately said, "I've been abducted."

I guessed they'd thrown him back.

"Not by the Grays, by the Pleiadeans." He crossed his plump legs into a half lotus. "They're not into the experiments. They're into communication and soul advancement."

My mother snorted. "Advancement doesn't come from other galaxies. It comes from a strong, united workforce—right here on earth!"

"There's more to life than the minimum wage," Moag pointed out. "Why should a guy dying of Ebola in Africa care how much some white asshole at the Ford plant makes? So imagine the rest of the universe giving a shit."

"And someone from the Pleiades is going to tell you what to care about?" Mother's cheeks were flushed.

Another netnerd spoke up, a ponytailed man with a bald spot and a squinty leer. "Have you seen the UFO Web sites? The video clips are great."

I turned to him. "What video clips?"

"Spacecraft mostly. A lot of sightings in Mexico, as usual. Another wave recently in Gulf Breeze, Florida."

"And the sightings were videotaped?"

"Tons of footage. In Mexico during the eclipse, home videos from people all over the city all showed the same ships."

"They weren't airplanes?"

"No way. Get on-line. Take a look."

"If there's video footage available, how come it's not broadcast?" But I already knew CNN and other stations had an aversion to news.

"In Mexico, it's on all the major channels. My wife watches their news all the time. Her English isn't very good."

A woman sitting beside Moag said, "There's a UFO conference here now."

"In town?"

"In the East Bay somewhere. I know the alien-propulsion-systems guy."

"The what?"

"He explains the antimatter reactor and space-bending mechanism used in the space ships."

My mother waved her arm impatiently. "This is just another way of turning our faces from the problems we have at home. Spaceships in Mexico! Let's talk about car manufacturers slinking down there. Let's talk about penniless, exploited Mexican truck drivers being manipulated into coming up here to undercut the Teamsters!"

My father chimed in, "I understand quantum physicists believe parallel universes might be intersecting this one. That might account for some of what people have been seeing." He glanced guiltily at my mother. She had forbidden him to mention his new hero, physics guru Brother Mike. To Mother, physics was just one more distraction from politics.

I still hoped to talk myself out of an alien abduction defense. So I egged Moag on: "You were saying the Pleiadeans differ from the Grays?"

"The Pleiadeans are called Nordics. They basically pass for good-looking Scandinavian types. And they don't get into the weird experiments, they don't do anything nonconsensual. They're not like the Grays. There's no way they'd sign that kind of treaty with us."

"You're saying we have a treaty with the Grays?"

He nodded emphatically. "Area Fifty-one in Nevada, the military's got a huge underground bunker there. Everybody's known about it for years, way before *Independence Day*. The government doesn't even bother denying it anymore. Instead, they land-grabbed the ridges overlooking it from the Indian reservations. But there's all kinds of videos of spaceships flying out of there, getting test-driven. Even Las Vegas news filmed one and showed it." He scratched a spot beneath his Worf goatee. "In return for the Grays giving us the technology, they get to abduct whoever they want—nobody high-ranking, just plebes—and the government doesn't try to stop them. And it keeps it out of the news as much as it can. Or makes it look ridiculous if it does get reported."

My mother jumped to her feet. "People actually put their energy into these beliefs?" Versus hers.

I wanted to reassure her: people believing in this government conspiracy might also be inclined to credit her conspiracies of choice.

"Area Fifty-one's for real," Moag insisted. "Just take a look at the videos."

"Well"—my father's tone was meant to soothe my mother—"but you're a computer videographer—you know how easy it is to fake video."

"There's been footage around for years—way before undetectable fakeability. One guy's Gulf Breeze pictures are in stereo film—that stuff's impossible to fake—plus people all over town took pictures of the same object. And look at the Mexico City eclipse films. How do over a dozen people in different parts of the city all fake the exact same thing from different perspectives? Same with the videos from Nevada and Florida. You've got footage from different people at different times in different cities of identical objects. They're here. They've decloaked."

I turned to the woman. "How can I find out where the UFO conference is?"

She looked at me pityingly. "Use a search engine." Search engines guided one through the Internet.

Presumably some UFO Web site would have posted a full schedule. It was getting so much more convenient to be flaky.

9

The trial would begin on Tuesday. I didn't have the luxury of waiving the speedy-trial date and cobbling together a brilliant defense—or even taking a crash course in oratory. I'd barely had time for my quick trip back to San Francisco. But I made time to stop by the UFO conference.

I was explaining to Alan Miller, "It changed my mind."

"About alien abduction?" Miller looked alarmed. In spite of his precarious legal position, he still seemed to hope someone would disprove his story.

"No—not about that. About your defense." A major distinction.

Though Miller looked better than he had at his bail hearing, he still looked fragile and pale despite a strapping frame and manly jaw. He still looked shell-shocked.

Today we sat in Edward Hershey's living room. Edward had locked the place up for three months while undertaking a macho-man sail through the Panama Canal. Fred decided his brother wouldn't mind a house-sitter for the few weeks remaining until his return.

I'd been to Edward's several times. The place hadn't improved over the years. The wood floors were little better than rough planks after being repeatedly soaked with salt water from fishing gear, rubber boots, and wet suits. The kitchen was stacked with accumulating mail and fly-fishing lures. The living room was a musty accumulation of old sofas and easy chairs with broken springs. The bedroom—well, I'd vowed never to set eyes on it, and I saw no reason to change my mind now.

Alan Miller, with his mushroom-sprouting porch sofa, was probably not offended by Edward's decor, however. Miller's major regret about the fire seemed to be that he'd lost most of his slides and photographs of mushrooms. His obsession was to teach enough classes to replace his camera.

And his worry was that he'd go to jail instead of getting the chance. So I definitely had the man's full attention.

"You changed your mind about my defense?" he repeated. "But not about the plea, right?"

I'd come this morning with news that Assistant District Attorney Patrick Toben, your typical suit with a smug smile, had offered a deal. He'd drop the felony hit-and-run charge if Miller changed his plea to guilty of vehicular manslaughter. It would shave some years off the sentence.

"No, not about the plea. I still think we should go for broke. That's what I'm here to talk about. Going for broke means more than trying to disprove their case. It means putting on one of our own."

He finger-combed a curtain of dark hair off his forehead. "I don't get the difference."

"We probably can't win unless we put you on the witness stand and have you tell your story."

His eyes widened as he pressed himself against the back of Edward's couch. Either he hated the idea, or a broken spring had lanced him. "But you said I'd get laughed out of court."

"I talked to some people yesterday who are willing to offer expert testimony." I could feel myself flush. "They're all credentialed to the hilt."

Miller was looking distinctly mistrustful. "Psychiatrists?"

"One of them's a psychiatrist. One of them's a science librarian. One's a detective. One's a retired air force colonel."

"What would they testify about? None of them's looked at the Brussels sprouts field or anything?"

I never thought I'd give such crazy advice: "We need them to testify that UFOs are real. That's their area of expertise. I found them at a UFO conference. I handpicked the most credible, least eccentric of the lot."

And what a lot it had been: a best-selling science fiction novelist weeping over the beauty he'd found in his (he claimed nonfiction) abductions; a "forensic" artist who specialized in drawing the sixteen races of aliens housed in secret government compounds; Roswell experts faulting a recent alien autopsy video because the alien had too many fingers; the founder of an abduction support group specializing in child abuse survivors; a muttering sharp-eyed man tracing the government's "conspiracy of silence" back to the Freemasons and (inescapably) the Trilateral Commission; a "freelance exohistorian" documenting gene manipulations by aliens throughout our evolution; members of an alien-human hybrid organization; crop circle investigators so moved by "agriglyphs" that they became enraged by mundane questions about how they were formed.

But the conference was also packed with intelligent-looking post-docs and computer wizards, as well as hippies and "experiencers" of every stripe. It was totally devoid of *Star Trek* uniforms and *Dr. Who* T-shirts, which surprised me. And many of the presentations were impossible to dismiss. The information was impressive, if only for its volume and consistency.

"The psychiatrist is prepared to present the statistics: thousands of reported abductions. At least, I'll coach him to say thousands—he puts the figure at five to seven million, but I don't want to blow our credibility. He'll say that nothing we know of—mass delusions or the power of suggestion or the Jungian unconscious—can account for it. He'll say it has to be a real phenomenon."

Miller kept gulping as if he might cry. I knew he was in a bind. If he didn't believe this, he was crazy. If he did believe it, he was the victim of something too horrible to accept.

"The detective has video footage and still shots of UFOs. He'll talk about interviewing four hundred people who've reported sightings. And he's got scientific analysis of crop circles—showing that some are hoaxes but most of them couldn't be man-made. We'll use him as more proof that something physical is definitely happening, something that can't be explained away."

As way-out as some of the people at the conference had been, the fact remained: there was a mountain of pictorial evidence that something weird was going on. I just wished I'd remained in hidebound ignorance of it; seeing, in this case, was bewildering.

"I don't know, Willa. I don't know. Just because you've got experts saying it doesn't mean people won't laugh at it."

"A lot of people believe in this stuff already. Who knows how many of your jurors are in that boat?"

I'd tried to choose young, open-minded folk without overly conventional accessories. I'd favored Birkenstocks over Naturalizers or even Nikes. I'd stayed away from vinyl handbags with matching pumps. I'd rejected double-knit slacks and Nancy Reagan hair. It was a far cry from hiring a jury consultant, but I hoped it would help.

"You said you had a scientist?" Miller tried to sound hopeful.

"He used to work for NASA's library. He ended up using old NASA photos to prove they're hiding a lot of their current space images from us—apparently they're censored by the National Security Agency. And the last guy, the colonel, he's got charts and diagrams of secret military installations he says are hangars for alien spacecraft. It sounds nuts, but it's pretty convincing when he runs through it." I gave Alan a moment to digest this. "That's the game: to make the jury think it might be possible, and to show them smart-looking men with credentials and documentation who believe it. Then we'll hammer on the fact that the assistant DA, with all his forensics people, can't prove you drove through the sprouts field."

Miller looked glum. He slumped, elbows on his knees, staring at Edward's filthy rag rug.

"I wish I knew what really happened," he told me for the hundredth time. "I wish I had something certified real, a piece of paper like my doctorate, something I could hang on to to tell myself I wasn't crazy."

I didn't know what to say. I wished a law degree were that potent.

I'd barely managed, in the last few days, to acknowledge the evidence behind claims I'd previously dismissed as bogus. After what I'd seen and heard, after meeting Alan Miller, I could no longer be blithely derisive. But making a case for something is a far cry from believing it.

And if I was having trouble in this tiny corner of the Twilight Zone, I could imagine Alan's struggle.

"I won't do it if you insist that I don't. But I think it's your best chance." I never thought I'd hear myself say so, but, "I'm willing if you are."

He threw his head back, letting it loll on Edward's none-too-clean afghan. I noticed the tapered end of a deep scratch disappearing into the neckline of his "Fungus Amongus" T-shirt.

"That scrape—it's not from the night of the accident?" One argument for Miller's not having been in an accident was that he should have been cut: his windshield had popped out and shattered. But as I understood the doctors' reports, Miller's injuries had been internal, including impaired kidney function and inflammation associated with "sharp instrument trauma"—through unmarked skin—into a calf muscle and a kidney. I didn't recall a notation about scratches.

Miller shot me a shamefaced look. "You won't— It's not a big deal, okay? I don't want you to mention it to anyone, all right?"

"What happened?"

"I ran into her again."

"The hitchhiker?" She was very much on my mind. I'd just spoken to the detective I'd hired to track her down; he'd picked up a lead at a homeless camp. There was a possibility she could help establish Miller's alibi. But even if her story incriminated him, I wanted to find her before Assistant DA Toben did. It had been a long time since I'd tried a criminal case, and I didn't want to be blindsided. I'd do an amateurish enough job, I was sure.

"Not the hitchhiker. Addenaur's widow."

"Why didn't you tell me? You ran into her—or she stalked you?" Didn't he understand she might have burnt his house down? We'd shown him the earring. We'd handed it over to the police. They'd remained tight lipped about the arson investigation, except to say kerosene had been used. But clearly they suspected her.

"I saw her in the courthouse the day of the jury stuff."

"You saw her during voir dire and you didn't say anything?" I felt like slapping him.

Bad enough he'd told the sheriff that she hadn't threatened him with a gun, that the whole thing looked to him like an accident. The only reason she wasn't currently under arrest was that no one could find her.

"Sorry." He glanced at me. "I was going to tell you, but . . ."

"But what? She tried to shoot you and she probably burned your house down. For all we know, she scared your next door neighbor to death."

"Poor lady."

I hoped he meant thirty-two-year-old Donna Nelson, who'd moved next door to him earlier that month. Tough luck to have a massive heart attack at that age.

"I don't believe she was going to shoot me," Alan persisted.

"I know it's hard to think about how the accident affected her, but—"

"No, no—I get it that she's devastated, I'm not in denial. I just think she was raving. I didn't feel from her that she'd go to that length. You'd feel it if someone was really going to kill you."

"No, you wouldn't." Unfortunately, I spoke from experience.

"Another thing . . . don't you think Dr. Hershey could have gotten her earring stuck on his jacket when he wrestled her? It doesn't seem very likely that he'd come across it by accident in a big old field. I mean, isn't that a little hard to believe?"

I was with him on that one. But as to the rest of it: "She was going to shoot you, all right. Even if you couldn't 'feel' it, I could. That's why I grabbed her handbag."

But he continued looking unconvinced. Why the hell did he feel so guilty about her husband's death if, as he believed, he wasn't even in the car?

"Tell me about the courthouse. What did she do to you?"

He pulled down the neck of the T-shirt. Even through his dark weave of chest hair, I could make out healing claw marks. "She kind of got my back a little bit, too. It's not bad, though."

"What did she say? What else did she do?"

"The same stuff—that she'd never find anyone like him again, that she'd die alone." He looked pained. "I don't suppose you've got an alcoholic in your family?"

"No." Just a couple of old radicals drunk on politics.

"I've had to deal with a few—basically, my mom and my aunts on her side. That's what's going on here, if you want my opinion. People get worked up when they drink, and she's been hitting it."

"How did you stop her?"

"A couple of deputies came out of the men's room."

I humphed. "What are the odds of that happening next time? We need to tell the sheriff about this."

I wondered if Toben could possibly use Miller's failure to report this against him. Could he infer Miller's guilt from it? Could he argue that Miller's consciousness of wrongdoing was behind his silence?

Questions like this just don't come up in patent searches.

10

I worried about the fact that Fred was picking up the tab for the expert witnesses. It might become an issue in the trial, where his audiotape and psychiatric testimony would figure prominently. I vowed not to mention Fred's name to any of the witnesses; I didn't want them blurting it out in response to a fee question from the assistant DA. I didn't want it to look like Svengali Fred had hypnotized the story into Miller's head, then hired experts to lend it credence.

I sent plane tickets to each of the four UFOlogists and arranged to put them up at a local hotel the day before I expected them to testify. I would meet with each the evening he arrived. It's customary to spend some time going over a witness's testimony. But I'd blocked out extra hours to get up to speed on a subject I'd never deigned think about. The UFOlogists had been amiable about staying on an extra day, perhaps two, if there was a delay in the proceeding. (It certainly helped that Santa Cruz had miles of beaches and lots of cute bars to spend Fred's money in.)

So I was expecting to turn my attention to UFO experts. I just wasn't expecting to turn it so soon, and to turn it toward the one UFOlogist I'd resolutely crossed off my list. The ironic thing was, I wouldn't have had to deal with Reginald Fulmer at all if I hadn't stupidly asked him a few questions at the UFO conference.

At the time, he'd seemed so scattered and unfocused I'd doubted he was listening to me. Unfortunately, he was.

He'd just presented an hour-and-a-half slide show of crop circles in

England. His comments on each slide had been effusive, extravagant, full of upper-class British stutters and pedantic drawls. As fascinating as the crop circle patterns had been—triangles within circles, orbit rings, spiderwebs, flower shapes, concentric swirls—this man, who'd spent every summer for the last eight years sleeping in grainfields to try to see a crop circle being formed, bombarded us with hyperbole until I was numb.

With his long flared nose, thin cheeks, down-turned lips, and flyaway bush of hair, he resembled a commedia dell'arte version of Mr. Ed. He alternated pacing manically or dropping into a chair to sit on his spine with his knuckles dragging on the floor. I'd seen fewer dramatic flourishes at Finocchio's.

Though I learned that over two thousand increasingly complex crop circles had been appearing as if by magic in British fields for decades, I didn't learn much else from the presentation—it was, ironically, mostly chaff. But because there were circles so close to Alan Miller's house, I toyed with the idea of inviting Reginald Fulmer down to testify.

I cornered him after his slide presentation, waiting while a gaggle of organic-food hippies rhapsodized with him. From one of them, I learned that hundreds more circles had appeared in a dozen other countries.

When I finally got Fulmer to myself, I still felt as if I were in a crowd. I couldn't cut through his posturing and gesticulating, had to weather a long word-spree about how he hoped he'd done well, but really, if people were going to want to cover the same ground every year—facts available in all the books, for goodness' sake—rather than looking, really *looking* at the pictograms themselves . . . after all, these glyphs must be allowed to speak for themselves, to speak directly through the visual cortex into that part of us that isn't tediously fussing over the same old dry statistics about when the circles are formed and in what direction the grain is swirled and whether it's suitable for harvest—really, why can't people separate out what's important, why can't they look at the damn circles and see them and experience them at the level at which they choose to communicate with us?

Since I'd stayed behind especially to ask him the questions he scorned as philistine, I kept it short.

"The crop circles that looked like a solar system—rings with circles around bigger central circles—do you know of any like them in this country?"

A plain, sensible-looking woman appeared behind him and began putting away his slides. He glanced at her as if she were an intrusive servant.

"Solar systems?" He rolled his eyes. "What a stupid assumption. They aren't solar systems, for pity's sake."

"I just meant that's what they looked like to me. Do you know the ones I mean?"

"Of course I know the ones you mean." His tone was sarcastic. "Americans always want to call them solar systems, God help us. It's all your *Star Trek* and *Star Wars*—you've no imagination left. What about the so-called solar systems?"

We were off to a brilliant start. "Have you seen anything similar to them in this country?"

"You don't get crop circles in this country." His tone made it clear we didn't deserve them. "Perhaps the odd one here and about, I don't know. It may be you people mow them down as a nuisance, just as you do your redwood forests." He began stuffing papers into a briefcase full of protractors and straightedges.

"Can I draw a crop circle for you, one I've seen? I'd like to know if you've encountered anything like it."

He raised his supercilious brows as if to say that wasn't bloody likely.

Nevertheless, when I drew the thing in the field behind Joseph Huizen's house, he spent several minutes scowling at it.

"Where is this?"

"In Santa Cruz county. A town called Davenport."

He squinted at me suspiciously. "You're quite sure it's a crop circle and not something else entirely?"

"You tell me—what are the hallmarks of a real crop circle?"

"The grain's not broken. It rather wilts at the growth nodes. And it's precisely swirled and woven, not pathetically, raggedly stomped down like the hoax circles by Doug and Dave, who fooled no one but the media with their amateurish grab at the limelight. Occasionally, there might be a sort of charge in the air—an indescribable physical effect— if the circle's quite fresh." This was more information than he'd provided in his entire slide presentation.

I wondered whether, with precise questioning, he might be useful on the witness stand, after all.

He answered my silent question by wadding up the paper I'd drawn on and throwing it at me. "Solar systems! Idiots raised on telly pabulum. Why, why, why must we always be looking for spacemen muttering *'Klatu barada'* and dum-dum-dum-dum?" He hummed the notes from the movie *Close Encounters.* "You find yourself in the presence of a communication from an ancient other, brilliantly editing itself, elaborating upon its previous utterances to produce the magnificent geometries I showed you today, and what do you Americans always think? *Oh, Mildred, turn off* Wheel of Fortune; *the spacemen have landed."* He gestured with both arms. "Have you any concept of how ancient a thing we're dealing with here? Think Merlin, not Mork! Do you suppose it's a coincidence that two thousand agriglyphs have appeared in the exact area where we have nine hundred stone circles, including Stonehenge?"

I backed away, saying, "Guess not."

The woman behind him dropped a slide tray. He turned to her with a vexed "For godsake! What now?"

I left quickly.

Luckily, I encountered a detective later in the conference who'd accumulated botanical data about crop circles, including microscope analysis of the affected grain. He could prove the grain had dramatically enlarged "cell pits," suggesting an unknown physical process involving intense microwave energy (like a spaceship landing?). By that time, my brain was awash in statistics—I'd been to several presentations by UFOlogists backing their claims with math (and math goes over my head at the point beyond which I can use it to balance my checkbook).

I had hoped never to set eyes on Reginald Fulmer again. I never dreamed my drawing—the one he'd crumpled and thrown at me— would bring him to Davenport.

I'd spoken to him on Saturday. That night, he contacted a colleague, the Oxford scholar who'd met Joseph Huizen and Fred Hershey during University Night. He, in turn, spoke to Joseph, who verified the circle's existence and provided the exact location.

As elaborately detailed as recent crop circles in England had been, the one in Davenport was at least as complex. This was especially remarkable because the wild grasses were a less dense, uniform palette than grain. So the following morning, Reginald Fulmer came to take a look.

And he didn't go away soon enough to keep his weirdness from tainting Alan Miller's trial.

On Monday morning, I picked up the local paper and saw a color photograph of the Davenport crop circle on the front page. Half a column inch later, Reginald Fulmer was effusing: "The earth is speaking to us directly, if we will only turn off the boob tube and take the trouble to look."

That seemingly innocuous statement must have touched a nerve: it was picked up by the wire services and reprinted in the *L.A. Times* on Tuesday. By Wednesday, it started pilgrimages: "Wicca" (witch) covens, New Agers, UFO "experiencers," the curious, the flaky, minor gurus and their coffee shop followers, and, of course, Reginald Fulmer himself, charging $40 a head for on-the-spot seminars that probably amounted to no more than "Look at the circle, and don't bother me with questions!"

The pilgrimages, in turn, brought puff-piece newscasters from ten counties—*look at the hippies, Ma*. If I'd been worried before about my defense being noticed and laughed at, now I felt doomed.

The local newspaper went on a full-out assault to prove that Santa Cruz was a levelheaded, business-friendly haven of rational consumers. One local columnist slammed the crop circle pilgrims as "superstitious, gullible throwbacks to an era of inquisitions and charlatans, willingly preyed upon by mental midgets pushing New Age snake oil."

And into the stage I'd inadvertently set myself, Alan Miller and I had to make our courtroom entrance.

11

On the first day of trial, I awakened early. There was still a deep-night chill in the air and the light was sallow. I was disoriented for a moment, missing the familiar smells of old apartment and heaped laundry, the pencil line of sunlight through gapped curtains.

Instead I smelled a fabric-softened duvet. I opened my eyes, surprised to find myself beneath a white eyelet comforter in a white room dotted with peaceful watercolors. My first thought was the Betty Ford Clinic —this level of tranquillity suggested upscale recovery. Then I sat up: Fred's guest room was a dream of expensive blandness, matching the rest of his waxed-hardwood-and-matte-white townhouse.

I climbed out of bed, perversely missing my messy, downscale flat. But I'd managed, even on so short a stay, to put my stamp on this place. My suitcase, on an upholstered bench beneath a window, appeared to have erupted with clothes and clutter.

I crossed to it, rummaging for underwear. I looked out the window into Fred's backyard, where severely pruned shrubs flowered meekly. Except for a few big pines, it was the most castrated garden I'd ever seen. Like Fred's condo, it showed little regard for profusion.

I heard a sliding glass door open below, and watched Fred step outside. In shorts and a T-shirt, he began trotting down his walkway. I figured I'd be out of the shower before he finished his morning run, so I didn't bother taking my business suit into the bathroom with me.

Later, drinking coffee in Fred's Swedish wood kitchen, I went over my notes obsessively, never calming down enough to really read them. I'd lost the last case I'd tried. I hadn't considered hara-kiri, but the experience had left me feeling unimpressive.

I was surprised, leaving for court, to find Fred standing beside my car. He stiffened when he saw me, taking a backward step.

"I'm off to the wars," I told him.

He didn't say anything. When I got closer, I noticed he wasn't sweating, didn't even have a runner's blush.

Frowning slightly, he cleared his throat. "That time already?"

"Yes." I was surprised to find my Honda door unlocked. I slid into the driver's seat, tossing my briefcase onto the seat beside me.

I glanced up at Fred, expecting some comment of encouragement. And some reason to believe he hadn't just been snooping in my car.

But Fred seemed wrapped in his own thoughts. He was still standing there when I turned the corner.

12

I sat at the defense table with Alan and watched the jurors. The judge, a beagle-faced man with half glasses, took his time shuffling through papers.

The jurors appeared expectant and alert. I hoped they weren't mulling this morning's news about multiple arrests of beach campers in Davenport, the first wave arriving to gawk at the crop circle. I hoped they weren't irritated about morning traffic through downtown streets inconveniently clogged with Grateful Deadheads, barefoot Rastafarians, and crystal-wearing blessing givers. As they fought for parking places around the courthouse, I hoped they hadn't been muttering about yet another influx of grooving, oh-wow transients.

I glanced over at Assistant DA Toben, a thin, buffed-out boomer with comb lines in his hair. He was leaning back in his chair, a corner of his mouth curled as if he was trying hard not to smile. With my expert witness list in front of him, he had every reason to look like the cat who'd swallowed the canary. We were going ahead with the *Outer Limits* defense; he didn't look too worried.

The courtroom itself was standard issue, with wood paneling and a big state seal between an American flag and a California flag. Below the judge, flanking him, a clerk and a court reporter sat looking patient and practical. Their lives were made up of delays.

The pews seemed a little on the full side for a vehicular manslaughter case. But Addenaur's widow hadn't shown up; that had been my main concern.

That is, until Alan Miller glanced at the audience and bent close to whisper, "Leonard Deally's here."

I turned to look. Leonard Deally was a columnist who in this morning's paper equated believing in crop circles to devolution into pre-*sapiens* ignorance. He wasn't likely to have much respect for our defense. But who'd tipped him off? Why had he come here?

"Which one?" I whispered. There were a few men in the audience with unstyled hair and sport coats, underdressed for lawyers and overdressed for passersby.

"With the three-piece."

I was surprised. I'd taken the portly young man for a stolid financial planner with a Rotary meeting later in the day. I'd met a lot of reporters, but never one who looked like a banker manqué.

The judge was looking over the rim of his half glasses as if our whispering demeaned him. Put a man behind a maple bench and he thinks he's Zeus.

There was a stirring in the courtroom, pure anticipation. The judge had already welcomed the ladies and gentlemen of the jury and thanked them for performing this valuable civic duty. So I knew what he was about to say: batter up.

I watched my opponent walk suavely toward the jury and smile like a genial MC. He greeted them, then launched straight into a rap about circumstantial evidence: "You've probably heard the term on television dramas and in the news. You might know already that it means evidence drawn from looking at the circumstances of the crime. It's not an eyewitness account or a confession, but that doesn't make it any less reliable. Circumstantial evidence asks you to reach logical conclusions from the facts of a case; that's all. We'll do our best to explain those facts to you. And the judge will give you careful instructions on how to reach your conclusions from them. All of us representing the People of the state of California will do our best to ensure that the ends of justice are served. And we know you'll do your best . . ." Blah blah blah.

If I was no Clarence Darrow, at least he wasn't William Jennings Bryan.

But the opening statement wasn't about engaging jurors' intellects, it was about winning their trust. Patrick Toben, detailing the accident scene, previewing the testimony of highway patrolmen, sheriff's deputies, and paramedics, wasn't merely presenting his data—he'd do that later. He was, instead, showing his compassion and his grit: on behalf of the People of California, he cared about a life cut short; and any caring juror would trust his perspective and take him at his word.

I watched him critically. The jurors looked interested, even when their thoughts might have begun straying toward lunch. But they weren't in his pocket, not yet. I'd have to be careful not to put them there.

So the lunch hour would have been a perfect time for some sort of Zen centering or method lawyer's affirmation to improve performance. Maybe I'd have even thought of one. But I didn't get the chance.

As I sat with Alan Miller in the basement cafeteria, he glanced at the front page of the local paper's "Living" section. It showed two color photographs. One was an aerial view of the crop circle, shaggier than the day Fred and I stood atop the hill. The other was an on-the-ground shot of happy pilgrims circling it, holding hands.

Alan grabbed my arm, pointing to one of them. "That's her! That's my hitchhiker!"

13

A breathless phone call to our detective resulted in a busy lunch hour with no time to rethink my opening statement. Before I knew what hit me, I was introducing myself to the jury, half my mind still on the hitchhiker.

To make matters worse, Alan caught my eye and rubbed the lapel of his borrowed sport coat. When I glanced at my own lapel, I saw fuzzy little blooms from a tree near the outdoor pay phone I'd used to avoid eavesdroppers. There was no inconspicuous way to brush it off, so, with a sigh, I did it conspicuously.

I was off to a Willa Jansson start, that's for sure.

"The assistant district attorney has explained circumstantial evidence to you and promised you detailed instructions on how to weigh it. What he hasn't promised you, and can't promise you, is enough circumstantial evidence for you to find Alan Miller guilty of vehicular manslaughter or hit-and-run."

God, I already had the flop sweats. I'd be looking for a demure way to wipe my cheeks in a few minutes.

"You'll learn that no one saw the accident that killed poor Mr. Addenaur. You'll learn there isn't a single tangible piece of evidence to prove that the accident happened the way the prosecution says it did. And you'll hear physicians testify that Alan Miller's injuries weren't consistent with his being in a car crash."

I went through these points more fully, hammering on evidence the prosecution should have found but didn't.

Then I took a deep breath. "The prosecution says its case depends on circumstantial evidence. But don't confuse circumstantial evidence with nonexistent evidence. A lack of evidence is not a circumstance, it's only a lack of evidence." Well duh, Willa.

I was getting nervous, conscious of Leonard Deally behind me in the pews. Toben must have tipped him off, told him to come here and listen to me talk about space aliens. No one but the assistant DA knew the guts of my defense, no one but Fred. No one else had a stake in seeing it ridiculed in the newspaper.

I looked at the jurors. They seemed like nice, white-collar people with polite faces. Before Leonard Deally made me doubt my strategy, I'd decided to prepare them for what they would later hear from me. I'd decided they needed all the time I could give them to get used to the idea.

But they weren't sequestered. And there was no way to insulate them from Deally's derisive ink.

When in doubt, hedge. "An implication here, an *It stands to reason* there, an *it must have happened that way*—these don't add up to circumstantial evidence. These are guesses made in a void, made precisely because there is no evidence. And multiple surmises don't equal a fact. Three times zero is still zero."

I could hear a stirring behind me and wondered if Toben was standing up to object, to make it look like I was mischaracterizing the evidence. The strategy had worked for O. J. Simpson's prosecutors; they'd won that round, though they'd lost the case.

I forged ahead. "Alan Miller isn't obligated to do anything but sit back in the courtroom and watch the prosecution try to add up the zeros: zero witnesses, zero tire tracks, zero accident injuries to Mr. Miller. Alan Miller isn't obligated by any rule or law or even stratagem to testify before you or to bring others here to testify on his behalf. But he will."

I launched into a syrupy biography of Miller: how he'd put himself through college after his parents died, how he'd helped shape a mycology graduate program out of the university's botany curriculum, how he'd come to be a respected mushroom expert, teaching classes through the museum and writing local field guides.

"The fact is," I concluded, "Alan Miller cares about this community and is an important part of it. He cares too much about his reputation to sit back and let the prosecution fail to prove him guilty. Alan Miller is going to do something he's under no obligation to do: he's going to prove his innocence."

During closing arguments, I'd remind the jurors a dozen times that the prosecution had the burden of proof and that they must find Miller not guilty whether he'd "proved his innocence" or not. But for now, it sounded good.

And for now, it would have to be enough. I didn't want to preload Leonard Deally's gun for him. Let him wait a few days until the first of our experts spoke the A-words: "alien abduction."

I managed a concluding smile. I hoped I looked more confident than I felt. They say jurors, like dogs, can smell fear.

Whatever impression I'd made on the jury, Alan Miller was ecstatic. His color was almost as high as his denial. He whispered to me, "That was great! Great! You were so good, maybe—" His eyes were bright and hopeful. "Maybe we could just stick with that. You know, not even bring up the other stuff."

The judge scowled at us for whispering. I shushed Alan until court was dismissed for the day. I was glad he'd liked my opening statement, but if he trusted jurors to acquit him based on little more than an absence of eyewitnesses, he was being naive.

We discussed it in my car on the way to the detective's office. By the time we arrived, Miller looked deflated.

The detective I'd hired, Carl Shaduff, had been recommended by Fred. It seemed that Edward, also a private eye, hired him whenever he needed backup.

Shaduff worked out of a studio in front of his house. The neighborhood, just a block over from Edward's, was a mix of shabby rental Victorians and yuppified bungalows. It was close enough to downtown that I could see the sprawling deck of a café crowded with students.

I'd expected to find Shaduff alone, I hoped with news of the girl pictured in the newspaper. I didn't expect to walk in and find her there with him, sitting at a rickety conference table finishing a take-out Mexican dinner.

Beside me, Alan choked back what he'd been saying. The girl glanced up, dropping her fork when she saw him.

She looked barely postpubescent, with freckled round cheeks, shoulder-length brown hair razored short above the ears, and full lips ravaged with cold sores. Her sweater, though stretched tight, appeared warm and new beneath a layer of dirt. At her feet, a big backpack was almost empty.

I glanced at Shaduff, a strapping buzz-cut blond obviously of Scandinavian descent. Despite his tidy gray suit, his red face suggested he'd just come in from ice fishing.

He said, "This is 'Mackenzie.' " He spoke the name as if he didn't believe it for a minute. "Just Mackenzie."

The girl flashed him an annoyed look.

Alan was stuttering, "I'm—look, I'm glad—glad you're—Are you okay?"

"Uh-huh." But her posture changed. She seemed to curl around an invisible weight on her chest.

"I found her at the crop circle," Shaduff explained. "There's a regular encampment out there."

I sat at the table opposite the girl. The room was spartan: the table, a desk, some computer equipment, filing cabinets. Right now, it smelled of burritos.

"My name is Willa Jansson. You've met my client, Alan Miller?"

She hugged herself, nodding.

"Would you tell me the circumstances of your meeting?" I didn't want to lead her. I wanted to know the worst, if that's what she had to offer the prosecution.

"Why?" Her tone wasn't the sullen default of many teenagers. She sounded worried.

I caught Shaduff's eye, wondering what he'd said to get her here. He rubbed his thumb over his fingertips, letting me know he'd had to pay her.

"There was a car accident involving Alan's car. It was at two-thirty the morning of the night you met. We're talking to everyone Alan saw that night. The time line is very important in our case."

"He told me," she glanced at Shaduff, "that I wouldn't have to testify in court."

"That's not what I said," Shaduff objected. "If your story doesn't have any bearing, the lawyers won't call you to testify; that's what I said."

"That's right," I assured her. "If your statement isn't relevant, you won't be asked to testify." But the prosecution would almost certainly find her testimony relevant, if only to prove Miller was driving his car earlier that night. "In the meantime, you're considered a material witness, and the district attorney is searching for you."

She looked alarmed, tears springing to her eyes. "Why?"

"We're trying to find out what happened between the time Alan left San Francisco that night and the time the accident happened. That's all. There's nothing for you to worry about. Let's just start with when and how you met Alan, okay?"

"I don't want to talk to the district attorney." She pushed away from the table.

She displayed more than the usual amount of anxiety about becoming a witness in a court case. She was probably a runaway.

"Why don't you tell us what happened that night? And I'll be honest about whether I think the DA will want you to testify, all right?"

"Will he arrest me?"

Alan stared at her with openmouthed intensity. Wondering if her question meant she was involved in the accident?

"You won't be arrested unless you participated in the crime. The DA just wants to know what time you accepted a ride from Alan and what happened after that. Look, I can answer your questions much more fully after you've answered mine."

"What's your name again?"

"Willa Jansson."

"And you're a lawyer?" She sounded as if that were a marvel, an attainment not remotely within her grasp.

"That's right. Can you tell me where and what time you first met Alan?"

She hesitated.

"You *have to* tell me." I gambled she was young enough to be in the habit of doing what adults commanded.

"Friday night." She leaned forward as if monitoring my face for early signs of hostility or danger. "Hitchhiking. In some little town."

Alan began, "It was—"

But I held up a hand for him to be quiet. The last thing I wanted was for him to feed her answers—answers she might change for Patrick Toben.

But she just sat there. I finally offered, "Half Moon Bay?"

"I guess so," she confirmed.

"You'd never been through there before? Where were you coming from?"

"Just . . . I was just traveling. I have some friends here." She flushed. She might have friends here now, but I doubted she'd had any when she arrived.

"So you saw Alan in Half Moon Bay. Then what happened?"

She looked at Alan again. For another answer?

"I asked him for a ride, and he said okay."

"Where did he take you?"

"I don't know. Here. I'm here, aren't I? I don't know the exact spot." She was sounding a little panicked.

"Well, why don't you tell me the circumstances when Alan stopped the car. Did you get out in a town, a beach, a residential area, a business district? You don't have to know the place-names, just describe the general area where you stopped."

Her breathing grew audibly ragged. "I don't know. It was weeks ago."

"Not even two weeks," I pointed out. "You remember meeting Alan and accepting a ride from him. I'm only asking you when and where you got out of the car."

"I don't know!" she repeated. "I can't testify if I don't know."

"That's not true." I had to make her understand that feigned ignorance wouldn't help her. "Even if you don't remember anything else, your testimony would prove Alan was driving earlier that night." I let it sink in. "It's only if you answer our questions fully, and both sides decide we don't need your information, that you won't have to testify. That's why you're better off searching your memory and cooperating with us."

Her mouth tightened to an I-won't-cry line.

"You're a runaway, aren't you? You're afraid the district attorney's office will send you back home."

She remained statue still.

"If you're having problems at home, you're much better off talking to someone in the DA's office about it. There are probably a lot of alternatives you haven't thought of. They can help you."

She shook her head.

Shaduff piped up. "This is not a good town to be on the streets at night, believe me. I can take you to a friend of mine at Child Protective—"

"No! I'm staying with friends. I'm not a runaway. I'm nineteen." She looked barely sixteen.

"Mr. Shaduff's just saying we'd like to help. I wish you'd trust me; I want to help." I waited until she looked a little calmer. "But for right now, you've got to make an effort to remember when and where you left Alan. He's been charged with two very serious crimes, and his freedom's on the line. It's really important that you be honest with us."

I glanced at Alan, leaning against a wall. He pressed a thumb and finger into his closed eyes as if trying not to cry. The stress of finding this girl but getting no information from her seemed too much for him.

The girl watched him, too. Her shoulders drooped. She looked nearly spent by her effort to appear decisively nineteen. But after a pause, she repeated, "I don't remember. It was weeks ago."

"How about the next morning? Did you wake up in Santa Cruz? In Davenport? On a sidewalk? In a bed? On the beach? This would be your first morning in the area. You'd remember your first morning, right?"

"On the beach, I guess; I don't really remember." She sat as still as a mouse facing a snake.

"Here in Santa Cruz?"

"Maybe. I don't know."

"What did you do that first morning? Did you walk on the beach? Talk to kids downtown?"

"It was too long ago! How'm I supposed to remember?" But she certainly remembered something: her lips curled downward and her brows furrowed. Whatever had happened, it had been a hard morning.

"Okay, then"—maybe if I started over, nice and friendly—"let's go back to Half Moon Bay. Were you having a bite to eat there?"

For the next hour, I did my best to act supportive, to win her trust. But I battled an accelerating desire to shake her.

Carl Shaduff sat behind his desk, rubbing his chin and looking tired. Alan slumped in a chair against the wall, apparently lost in thought. The girl kept her eyes on the remains of her burrito. Spellbinding I'm not.

In a last-ditch effort, I laid it on the line. "I'm going to tell you exactly what this case is about. I want you to know what Alan's up against here. Maybe then you'll understand why it's crucial that you make an effort."

I described the accident. I described the police search for Alan. I described his condition when they found him, his hospitalization, his amnesia, the difficult alibi he'd offered under hypnosis.

Only my description of Alan's hypnosis won me her full, startled eye contact.

"Do you understand what I'm telling you? Long after you really are nineteen and things are going fine for you, Alan Miller could still be in prison. Think how you'd feel then, knowing you held back information. Your memories of that night could make all the difference—if you'll just put your mind to it." My voice was rising in pitch. I was going to lose it soon, stand up, reach across the table, and try to slap an answer out of her.

She continued staring at her dinner as if it were a television screen. Her eyes flickered with thoughts and unspoken comments, as if some story unfolded in her paper plate.

Finally she repeated, rather huskily, "I don't remember."

"Would you be willing . . ." Toben might object. And it could turn out badly for Miller, I didn't know. "There's a psychiatrist named Fred Hershey. He's a very caring person, and you can trust him. What he could do, if you'll consent, is try to hypnotize you, try to nudge your memory."

She rose suddenly, knocking over her chair. "No! No way!"

Alan Miller freaked out, too, though less dramatically. "You don't think—Are you saying she was with me when they abducted—"

"No." I gestured for him to shut up. I didn't want to plant memories she didn't have. "No. I'm just suggesting we try to jog her memory."

The girl was backing toward the door. With a smooth inconspicuous motion, Shaduff slid out of his seat and stood between her and the exit.

She was so young—maybe she had comic book ideas about hypnosis. "Hypnotism is a very well respected, nonharmful procedure. Dr. Hershey would relax you and invite you to recall what happened that night, that's all. I've been hypnotized. It doesn't hurt, and the doctor doesn't intrude on other—"

"No! I won't do it! I don't have to!" She'd grown so red faced she looked like a toddler having a tantrum. "I don't remember anything. And you can't make me stay here saying so over and over."

"At least tell me this: What have you been doing since that night? Where are you living? How did you end up in that newspaper photo?"

"I haven't been doing anything. Just staying with friends. I have a right to do that, don't I?"

Only if you really are nineteen. "Have you spent much time in the crop circle?"

The change of subject seemed to calm her a little. She shrugged. "It's raggedy now. Some of the grass is standing back up. And all the people walking to it, a lot of the field's mashed." She sounded apologetic. "It still looks sacred, I guess."

"Do you know much about sacred geometry?" I wanted to ask if she'd been taken under the tiresome wing of Reginald Fulmer. But she didn't do well with direct questions.

"Yeah." She didn't sound sure.

"Maybe you could explain it to me sometime? We could go out there together."

She didn't exactly look like an ad for Little Sisters of America. "I might not go back."

"What does the pattern look like to you? A solar system?"

"No!" Her scorn made me positive she seen Fulmer. "The pattern is understood on a deeper level. That's where the geometry comes in." She backed up, looking defensive. "Why are you asking about the circle?"

"It's close to Alan's house." The remains of Alan's house, that is.

"Well, I've already told you everything I—" She turned to find Shaduff blocking her. "Hey! You can't keep me here."

"Better make the call now," Shaduff suggested.

"I'm sorry," I explained. "You're wanted for questioning because you might be a witness to a crime. That means I have to contact the assistant district attorney in charge of the case."

She turned back to me, looking flabbergasted. "You're going to call him? I thought you were on opposite sides."

"We are. But I have to let him know you're—"

"You were going to call him all along, weren't you? You knew you were going to call him, but first you tried to sneak answers out of me."

Well put. "I'm entitled, as Alan's lawyer, to question you before the DA does. What I can't do is question you, then sit back while you disappear. I can't cheat the DA out of his opportunity. I can stay close by when he questions you, if you like. Anytime you need me there, you can reach me through Mr. Shaduff or Dr. Hershey."

Her eyes were wide and wet with betrayal. "So what you said about me trusting you, you were only trying to get the answers you wanted. And just because you didn't, you're going to call the police on me!"

"No, you heard me say from the beginning that you'd have to talk to Assistant DA Toben." I tried to see it from her point of view: I was calling in the State to stomp around her fragile new life. "A man's freedom is at stake—of course the lawyers on both sides need to talk to you. We can't have a fair trial without all the witnesses."

Shaduff seemed to think I was being verbose. He motioned toward the phone.

I gave the girl a minute to respond. Instead she whirled around, trying to knock Shaduff aside.

I quickly made the phone call. We couldn't put ourselves in the position of restraining her. But there would be hell to pay if she got far.

Luckily, Toben was at his desk. "We have the hitchhiker at Carl Shaduff's office," I told him. "You'd better get someone over here. She's determined to leave."

He was no slouch; he dispatched deputies to cruise the area. They found Mackenzie less than twenty minutes later, not half a mile away.

After my hour with her, I suspected she'd be just as reticent with Patrick Toben as she'd been with me.

If only.

14

I've had many horrible days in court. My first year practicing law, I represented a kid who refused to register with the Selective Service even though we hadn't had a draft in over a decade. He insisted on scorning my advice and making a political statement; he practically clawed his way over me to get into jail. When I watched the bailiff take him away, possibly to four years in federal prison, I thought being a lawyer couldn't get much worse.

I've also been arrested twice and convicted once for protesting the war in Vietnam. I spent two horrible months in the San Bruno jail. I still get night sweats, dreaming I hear women's sobs echoing up and down the cell block. The judge who sentenced me became a personal enemy; it had been hell facing him again in court as a lawyer.

Plus, I'd been to most of my parents' civil-disobedience trials. And believe me, it's not easy watching the people you love most led away to prison. It's wrenching for an adult, but it's terrifying for a child—huddled alone in a sleeping bag at some acquaintance's house, fretting over what might be happening to them in prison, seething over being subordinated to their political ideals.

So I'm no stranger to things going wrong for me in court. But the first week of Alan Miller's trial, while the prosecution presented its case, things spun so far out of control that it was all I could do not to slink out the back door and jump a tramp steamer.

It wasn't just that the assistant DA did an excellent job. I expected he would. Patrick Toben presented the accident as a case of *Res ipsa loquitur*, "The thing speaks for itself": a car doesn't land atop another absent malfeasance by the driver. He made the most of the fact that Alan, when questioned by police and doctors, steadfastly failed to provide an alibi. He put up poster-board diagrams of the accident and the Fiat's trajectory off the cliff. He displayed a four-color map: green for Addenaur's route, purple for Alan's drive down from San Francisco, blue for the road to Alan's house, and red for the next turnoff, leading up to and across the field. Questioning a highway patrolman about the map, he suggested a scenario: Alan missed the turn onto San Vittorio Road, took his next left in order to backtrack, and ended up cutting through the field, crashing his car, and running away.

A serologist testified that it takes four to eight hours for blood alcohol levels to dip from legally drunk to zero. The DA was able to suggest that Alan left San Francisco later than he admitted and stopped to do some drinking; that he fled the accident to avoid drunk driving charges, staying gone long enough to sober up.

But I'd expected all that.

The hitchhiker was the problem. Mackenzie, as she continued to call herself, spent two nights in custody after leaving Carl Shaduff's office. A material witness is required to give information, and Toben refused to believe she couldn't remember anything. He also refused to believe she was nineteen. She was required, as a juvenile, to explain why she wasn't in school and wasn't living with a parent or guardian. She didn't. Hence, the nights in lockup.

What she told Toben Thursday morning, after a night of suicide threats, sent us reeling. She claimed she'd been abducted, along with Alan, by a UFO. She would give no descriptive details, nor discuss the time of night this happened, nor consent to hypnosis.

She would say only that gray aliens performed an experiment to make her pregnant.

And it turned out she was, indeed, pregnant. This was confirmed by a minute level of a hormone in her system. She had been impregnated anywhere from nine days to six weeks prior.

Needless to say, Toben didn't believe she'd been abducted and impregnated by aliens. It only gave him more fodder for scoffing at Alan's tale.

It also gave him a hell of a big stick.

I met with him Friday night to discuss Mackenzie's bombshell. He ushered me into a little conference room in the county building, a cement box attached by a glass-walled walkway to the courts.

As usual, he looked in fine fettle. He was a handsome man, I suppose, too conventionally tailored and muscled to be my type. But he didn't flirt, which set him above most jock lawyers.

"You'll be interested in the latest, Ms. Jansson." He motioned me into a chair, then dropped a stack of files onto the conference table. Behind him, windows glowed with the golden light of late afternoon. Only two hours south of San Francisco, the weather here seemed latitudes better.

"The latest being?"

"We've consulted experts, child psychologists, psychiatrists." He paused, as if waiting for me to debate Mackenzie's age. "Not Dr. Hershey, of course."

"Of course." Fred was on my witness list; I had dibs.

"I'm giving you their names and vitae. And I don't mind discussing what their testimony will be, if we decide to call them to the stand."

"Please do." I braced for bad news. If he was cocky enough to lay it out in advance of adding them to his witness list, he knew it would make me squirm. He wanted a ringside seat.

"Your client told the deputies he dropped Mackenzie off at around one o'clock in the morning. He claims a memory lapse after that." The corner of his mouth twitched; he was making an effort not to gloat. "Here's what our psychologists think: your client pulled the car off the road, but not to let Mackenzie out. To rape her."

"What the—!"

"Hear me out; we're not just whistling in the wind. We think this accounts for a number of things—including your client's memory lapse, if it's genuine."

"If Alan Miller was capable of raping a teenager to begin with, he wouldn't be traumatized enough to get amnesia about it." My God, were they serious? Or just maneuvering, trying to bargain?

"It would explain your client's swerving off onto the wrong road. He could have attacked her up there in the field. Or he could have been flustered afterward and missed his turn. And also . . . are you acquainted with the term 'screen memory'?"

"Yes. But it's not applicable here."

"Oh, come on. Miller says aliens touched his genitals. Mackenzie makes the same claim. We know there aren't little green men running around this planet touching peepees." He shook his head as if to say, *We're all rational lawyers here.* "Either they're both lying or they're both dealing with a traumatic experience."

"Or one of them's lying—she's lying. It's obvious she ran away from home because she missed her period, she was afraid she was pregnant. You should be looking for her family, maybe for a rapist father or brother. She's only talking about alien impregnation because I discussed my defense with her."

Toben tilted his well-groomed head. "Why would you do that?"

"To persuade her to answer my questions."

"By telling her your client was kidnapped by space lechers?"

"The point is, I brought it up. And she saw a way to get herself off the hook for becoming pregnant."

He simultaneously chuckled and sneered. A neat trick, and one he'd mastered. He continued to sit in easy hubris, not bothering to reply.

"Is there any more information you'd like to share with me?" I asked him. "Because I didn't come here to discuss my defense. Or your opinion of it."

"Just wanted to let you know about the two new experts." He grinned. It's customary to amend witness lists by mail or fax.

I stood. "You've got some papers for me?"

He handed me a file folder, and I left.

If I couldn't persuade the judge to disallow this testimony, Toben would finesse the time discrepancy. In the process, he'd offer a reason for Alan's careening onto the wrong road and off a cliff. And he'd explain why Alan might erase his own memories, masking them behind false images of sperm-extracting aliens.

Where Toben had previously scoffed at Alan's recovered memory, he would now welcome my introducing testimony about it. He would use that testimony to piggyback in his own psychiatrists. He was lying in wait, rubbing his hands in anticipation.

But my biggest problem wasn't the assistant district attorney. It wasn't even his new experts. It was that almost *any* story is easier to believe than alien abduction.

15

My meeting with the assistant DA was a wake-up call. I realized the trial wouldn't wrap up quickly. I began to doubt I'd make it back to work a week from Monday.

Because I'd taken the case pro bono and on my own time, I hadn't bothered letting my firm know. Now, barring unforeseen luck, I'd have no choice. As hard as it would be to tell a courtroom full of strangers that my client had been fondled by space aliens, it would be even harder to explain in proper legalese to a group of business lawyers.

But I didn't make the mistake of thinking things couldn't get worse —I try not to tempt fate.

That evening, Mackenzie showed up at Carl Shaduff's office. She threatened to kill herself if I didn't come immediately and talk to her.

Shaduff, thinking I was with Alan, called him at Edward's. Alan reached me at Fred's.

"I'm just around the corner from Shaduff's," Alan pointed out. "You want me to go over? I could wait with her till you come."

"No. Stay by the phone." He was still crashing at Edward's. "I'll call if I need you."

Fred, too, was champing at the bit. "I should come along. She's obviously having a lot of problems. You could use me."

"No—it's weird enough I'm camping at a witness's house." If it came out during Fred's cross-examination, the jurors might discount his testimony, thinking I'd pillow-talked him into it. "I don't want you to know any more details. Anything you blurt out on direct becomes fair game on cross."

He'd just come in from running, and he looked hot and damp and cross. He kept pacing his white-walled, white-carpeted living room. I couldn't tell if he was agitated or just cooling down. "Do you have any experience with troubled adolescents?"

"Only if you count my parents." I grabbed my jacket. "I'll be fine."

"It's her I'm worried about. You say she—"

"I'll call you if I need you."

I left Fred's townhouse and rushed to Shaduff's.

I found Mackenzie prowling his office like a caged cat. Her first words to me were, "You said you wanted to help me. You said I could trust you. You've got to hide me!"

Shaduff sat behind his desk. The look on his face said he'd raised no daughters and congratulated himself on the choice.

I ushered Mackenzie into a chair.

"Hide you? From who?"

She was definitely the worse for wear. Her eyelids were swollen from crying, her cold sores had turned into furious scabs, she looked puffy, pale, exhausted.

"That jerk Toben."

"Are you feeling all right?"

She bowed her head, her lower lip trembling. "He put me in jail. He had a doctor come and . . ." She'd had an obstetrics exam, courtesy of the county of Santa Cruz. "I hate him. He just wants to use his power against me. Lock me up, and what he had the doctor do. Now he's going to try to send me back home. Isn't he?"

Ten minutes with him exceeded my tolerance threshold, so I could empathize with her. "Well, he doesn't believe your alien abduction story."

"It's not a story!" She regarded me defiantly. "You believe Alan."

I didn't reply.

"They were this tall." She held her hand about three feet off the ground. "They had gray skin and black eyes with no white part. They put me on a steel table and put a needle-tube kind of thing in through my belly button. And a taller one told me telepathically that I was pregnant now and they'd be back later to take the baby." Her cheeks glowed with hot red patches.

Her story was no crazier than Alan's—not surprising, since it was modeled after his. The difference was that Alan refused to accept it, would have preferred to be thought delusional. And her story sounded like a convenient excuse, the synopsis of an *X-Files* episode or a cheesy television movie.

"It just . . . it sounds like the only lie you could think of." I tried to keep my tone nonthreatening. "Did you run away from home when you missed your period? Did you take a home pregnancy test? Because you do have choices, you know, even as a teenager."

She swallowed hard several times. "I told you how I got pregnant. It was the aliens. But now . . . they'll find out."

Did she mean the aliens? "Find out what?"

"My grandparents." She slumped in her chair. "They're from—well, they're foreign. My grandmother and grandfather came here after my mom was born. Their country's like some old-fashioned planet, at least they think so. It probably changed, but they don't know that. They visualize it being like it was when they left." Her lower lip trembled. "My mother wasn't married. So after she had me, they . . . they say they told her to leave the house because she disgraced them. But really?" She looked at me with big wet eyes. "They killed her."

"How do you know that?" I was relieved to hear a likelier story, however sordid.

"She never tried to call or come back."

"But you say she was banished, sent away in disgrace. You don't know how that might have affected her. I gather she was young?"

Mackenzie nodded. "But she'd have tried to phone her friends in town. They all think so. I talked to them. I looked them up in my mother's old yearbook. My grandparents forgot to burn it."

"They burned your mother's stuff?" Jeez, no wonder this girl was a mess.

"Uh-huh. If they ever find anything of hers in an old box or whatever, they tear it to shreds like crazy people. They swear and scream and rip it up like wolves killing something." She looked terrified just thinking about it. "I know they killed her. My mother would have called her friends"—her eyes said, *and me*—"if she was alive."

"So you thought your grandparents would kill you when they found out you were pregnant?" I was singing a silent hallelujah. As sorry as I felt for this girl, this was something I could put on the witness stand. And Patrick Toben could eat his damn expert witnesses.

A canny look crossed her face. "I told you: I got pregnant after I left. On the spaceship."

I supposed she was hedging her bets, keeping this story as insurance in case her grandparents found her. But I could hardly imagine them believing it. "Then why did you run away?"

"Because they killed my mother. And they . . ." She looked ashamed. "If they thought I was sneaking out with boys, if a guy phoned me or one of my friends made a comment about someone—you know, an innocent comment . . ."

"They'd beat you?"

She didn't say anything.

"Tell the assistant DA about this. I know he's—" I stopped myself from calling him a jerk. "Regardless of what you think of Mr. Toben, he can help you. His office can arrange a new home for you. They won't send you back to an abusive family." I hoped.

"No! It would kill them." Tears spilled down her cheeks.

"But if they beat you—"

"Sometimes. Most of the time they're crazy about me. They cook for me and make me things. They love me. It's just that, about boys . . ." She stopped to catch her breath. "They're different, you know? Like they were raised on another planet with upside-down ideas about things. They love me, but they're not like Americans, they're not calm, they're not from this century."

"But if they love you, wouldn't they rather know you were safe? Even if it meant you were with a foster family?"

"No, no, no. You don't get it." She leaned forward, as if proximity would help her explain. "The DA's going to find them and call them and they'll come here. And all he'll see is how nice they are and how much they love me. And then they'll take me home and we'll be alone and they'll kill me. Just like they killed my mother. They'll stop being relieved that I'm back, that I'm okay; and they'll just snap. They can't help themselves, they're not like Americans." She wiped her tears away. "You don't know what it's like to have a crazy family."

I wish. "Let me to talk to Mr. Toben about this. If he knows what to expect from them—"

"No! You've got to hide me from him. It's the only way! Otherwise, they'll kill me."

I watched her. Why come to me? Why not just take off? Hide on her own?

"Do you need money? Is that it? Help getting an abortion?"

She pulled herself straight, nodding.

"Look, I'm sorry, but I'm Alan's lawyer. That means I've got to put his welfare above everything else. If I hid you and the assistant district attorney found out—God, especially if I paid for an abortion—he'd assume it was an admission on Alan's part."

"Huh?"

As much as I hated to add to her burdens: "Mr. Toben is suggesting Alan raped you two weeks ago. Your pregnancy could be as recent as nine days."

"Alan?" She swayed with the shock of it.

"It's a way for the prosecution to offer a theory that guilt made Alan drive recklessly and have an accident. Mr. Toben will say you both concocted false memories to cover up what really happened, that it was too traumatic for you."

She shook her head, murmuring inaudibly.

"So if I help you, everyone will take it as proof. They'll say I hustled you away so you couldn't testify that Alan raped you. If I pay for an abortion, it'll look like an attempt to avoid a paternity test. Or like I was bribing—"

I didn't get a chance to finish my sentence. Carl Shaduff's front window exploded into shards of glass, spraying the floor and tabletop.

Shaduff dove across the room, pushing me off my chair.

I could tell by the smell it was a shot. A gunshot—Jesus. I scrabbled toward Mackenzie while Shaduff crawled back to his desk. He took something from a drawer.

Mackenzie had leaped to her feet, keening with panic. She kicked me in the face, as clumsy as a spooked colt.

Shaduff edged along a wall, loading a gun. Mackenzie lurched past him, pushing the front door wide.

Shaduff shouted, "Chee-rist!" and ran out after her. I could see him pause, aiming left, then right, like a cop in a shoot-'em-up movie.

I hid behind Shaduff's desk, my heart pounding, waiting for a gunman —Addenaur's widow?—to burst in and finish the job. I pulled the desk phone to the floor and dialed 911.

A few minutes later, Shaduff returned. He slammed the door, his face so red he looked skinned alive.

"Whoever it was, he's gone."

I remained on the floor. I touched the cheek Mackenzie had kicked, feeling for broken skin. I could hear night breezes stirring shards of glass near the window.

"What happened to Mackenzie?"

"Who knows?" He looked at me as if it were normal for a lawyer to cower behind his desk. "Are all your cases this interesting?"

"Only the ones here on Earth."

16

While I was leaking angst all over a hypercalm policeman, Patrick Toben showed up.

Shaduff, by then, had said his piece and was sweeping up broken glass. As the cop finished his report and handed me his business card, Shaduff produced, from somewhere in his house or yard, two rectangles of plywood. He began nailing them over the window, leaving me to Mr. Smug.

"So what was Mackenzie doing here?" Toben was as nonchalant as someone asking for a football score.

I wished I could be equally cool: *Nothing much, she just wanted me to hide her from you and pay for her abortion.* "She came to talk to me."

"About?"

I was obliged to give him notes and recordings of meetings with witnesses. Period. "We were interrupted." I gestured toward the window.

Shaduff was hoisting the second sheet of plywood, holding it in place with his shoulder while he positioned nails and swung the hammer.

Toben said, "We found her folks."

"Where?"

"We matched her with a missing-person report from up in Grants Pass, Oregon."

I sat, feeling suddenly exhausted. "Who are they? Who is she?"

"Her name's Maria Nanos. She's fifteen. She lives with her grandparents." He sat, too. He glanced at his wristwatch, looking tired. "I wish we'd run this down last night, while we still had her in custody. But we know where she's been staying. And she doesn't know about this. So hopefully we'll find her there."

"What's the story on the grandparents? Why'd she run away from them?"

"Everything I know, you know." He cocked his head as if to ask if I could say the same.

"They're not here in town, are they? The grandparents?"

"I couldn't tell you. I suppose if they hopped a direct flight the minute they heard. But I doubt it."

"They haven't checked in with your office?"

"No."

My attention strayed to Shaduff, hammering in the last of the nails.

Patrick Toben followed my gaze. "You're not suggesting the shooter was after Maria Nanos?"

"No, I'm not." Especially since Toben would be likely to suspect Alan Miller of the crime.

"Okay, then, I'm taking off. We're doing our best to find Betty Addenaur—soon, I hope. Keep safe tonight. Where are you staying?"

"I gave the officer the local address." Let him learn from the police report that it matched that of a witness. "But I'm heading back to San Francisco for the weekend."

"I wrap up Monday morning. Who's first up for you?" His expression was ingenuous.

"It's in my papers," I reminded him.

I'd bought into the lawyers' trick of withholding direct answers, of making my opponent jump through hoops for no reason except that I'd jumped through his. Reciprocal dickhood, the first thing lawyers learn in the field.

Toben was too seasoned to react to minor chain jerking. He gave a huge yawn, not bothering to cover his mouth.

17

I thought about the unself-conscious guyness of that yawn the next morning, as I stood atop Joseph Huizen's hillside, doing the same.

It was quarter to eight. I wanted to get to my apartment early, try to get in a full day of slovenly hermitry.

But first, I took a detour into Davenport to look for Mackenzie/Maria.

Longing for home, I'd tried to talk myself out of it: Maybe Maria Nanos was self-dramatizing, like most teenagers. Maybe she was lying about her grandparents beating her. And probably she was wrong about them killing her mother.

But I wanted to talk to her again before the police found her and reunited her with them. I couldn't hide her, and I wouldn't warn her— that would only result in her flight. But I could offer to go with her to the DA, to intercede with Child Protective Services.

I'd even toyed with the idea of asking Fred to follow me here, to stand by to do his therapist thing. But I'd gotten no reply when I knocked at his bedroom door; either he was out jogging or he was a very sound sleeper.

Stifling another yawn, I looked down at what had once been a distinct pattern of circles in circles. The field, though lush, wasn't as dense as a wheat field. Some grasses had withered and been replaced by wildflowers. Footpaths crisscrossed the now-ragged circles. The swirls within swirls had been mashed till they lost definition.

But even at seven-forty-five in the morning, there was a group inside the large central circle. They sat on blankets, watching a gesticulating figure.

I thought I recognized his extravagant arm-flinging and manic loping back and forth. It was almost certainly Reginald Fulmer.

I was even more startled to see checkpoint sawhorses and a table under a café umbrella where the field met the farmer's road. Between it and the circles was an encampment of at least a dozen tents.

As often as the farmer had emphasized to us that his fields were posted No Trespassing, he'd allowed all this. I wondered why.

I backtracked past Joseph Huizen's house to my car. If Maria Nanos was camping beside the farmer's road, I wanted to be parked nearby. If I persuaded her to come with me, I didn't want to risk leaving her to second-think the decision while I retrieved my Honda.

I went back along San Vittorio, stopping for a moment at Alan's house. Yellow plastic tape was liberally laced in front, warning passersby that it wasn't safe to go inside. But except for a boarded-up door, a plywood-covered hole in the roof, and some blistered paint, it didn't look a great deal worse from the outside.

I sped farther down the road toward the highway, past ratty yards crowded with old trucks and lounging dogs. I turned onto and almost immediately off the highway, going up a hill and beyond the Brussels sprouts field. I parked behind the sawhorses, in a row of dusty cars. But if someone was supposed to be manning the table beneath the umbrella, he didn't show himself. I cut straight over to the encampment.

About a third of the tents were zipped shut. I didn't see Maria in any of the others. Instead I found friendly neohippies spreading blankets and breaking bread. More than one advised me to have a nice day. None knew or would admit to knowing a girl calling herself Mackenzie or Maria.

"Are you here with permission?" I asked a plain-faced woman with long graying hair and a flowered jumper.

She'd run a clothesline from her tent to a ground stake. She was hanging purple thistles upside down from it, presumably to dry them.

"We pass the hat every morning," she told me, in a cheerful contralto.

"For what?"

"To pay the use fee." She looked with satisfaction at the row of large, thorny flowers.

"You're being charged money to stay here?"

She nodded. "A farmer comes and collects every morning. There's a separate fee for the seminar."

"Reginald Fulmer's seminar?"

"Uh-huh. He started about twenty minutes ago, if you want to do it today."

"How much is it?"

"Forty." She looked wistful. "We don't have that kind of money. But the ones who go try to keep the rest of us filled in."

"What does he say about the circles?"

"It's exciting: this is the first one he's encountered with a recognizable pattern." She glowed with satisfaction. "Right here in California! The ones in England, as fabulous as they are, only speak to the unconscious. 'Only'!" She laughed. "Communication on that level is probably the most powerful kind there is. But if our conscious mind can't grasp it, well . . . it's a little frustrating. Like a Zen koan."

In a neighboring tent, someone began hacking and coughing. Nearby, a man shouted to a frolicking dog.

"We traveled in Peru for a while," the woman continued. "We got so deep into Andean jungle we met a tribe that had never set eyes on the modern world. They wove their clothes out of wild cotton; true hunter-gatherers. We had our guides show them pictures, photos we'd taken, magazine pages, but they absolutely couldn't see anything in them. Not anything at all, just colors. They'd never seen printed images before. And our perceptions depend so much on what we're used to looking at." She grinned. "Maybe that's us with the crop circles. We don't know how to perceive them yet."

"Except for this one? This pattern's recognizable?"

"Mm-hm." She sniffed the air, apparently distracted by the scent of nearby coffee. "I wonder where that's coming from? We're not allowed to cook here—no campfires or stoves; the fire hazard is too high."

"So what is it?" I asked her. "What's the pattern?"

"One of the sugar molecules."

"Sugar." I took a backward step. "Not glucose?"

"That's right." She continued sniffing, head turned, like a dog.

"Glucose? You're sure?" The substance Joseph Huizen nearly died for lack of.

"You could ask Reggie," she pointed out. "I think that's what he said: the simplest form of sugar. I'm going to go track down that coffee!"

As much as I longed to follow her and get myself a cup, I traipsed through the field toward Reginald Fulmer and his small audience.

As I approached, Fulmer stopped talking. He took a few steps toward me, shouting crossly, "Two rules: no interruptions, and no trooping in late. If you can't be bothered to greet the dawn with us, then go piss away the rest of the day, I don't care. But don't distract the group with—"

He stopped, arms arrested midgesture. "The solar systems lady! From that ghastly conference."

"Yes. I'm sorry to interrupt, but I need to speak to you."

His half dozen students watched us. Tired looking and older, they might have been left over from a Pete Seeger concert.

"I'll be done in an hour."

"This won't wait." And then, to forestall protest, "It's a legal matter."

"Oh, not that bloody girl again!"

I gathered the police had already been here looking for her.

"Among other things," I admitted.

"Bother!" He scowled at his seminar. "Sit here for five minutes. Remember your techniques."

The techniques seemed to involve sitting cross legged with head bowed and eyes closed. He strode past them and over to me.

"Now, what do you want?" he demanded. "A legal matter, indeed."

I looked up at the man, who was at least a foot taller than I was. With his flaring nostrils and extraordinarily narrow face, he looked like a caricature from an illustrated Dickens or Swift.

"I'm a lawyer. I'm trying a case in which Maria Nanos, probably known to you as Mackenzie, is a material witness."

"Well, bully for you. As I've already told your policemen, I'm a scientist, I am not a baby-sitter."

"When was the last time you saw her?"

He waved his hand impatiently. "Oh, who bloody remembers?"

"Did you see her last night?"

"Certainly not. I'm not sleeping out here, you know. The first two nights, when it was fresh, yes. But there's no point anymore, is there? It's been fairly well squashed, hasn't it? Tomorrow's the limit, I'd say." He looked over his shoulder, shaking his head at the crop circle's disintegration.

"Where have you been staying?"

He snorted. "As if I have a choice of accommodations! The Davenport Bed and Breakfast, if one can call it that. They don't serve breakfast until after dawn—and a lot of damn use to me that is."

The bed-and-breakfast was directly over the Cash Store. In a town of a few hundred people, I could well believe they didn't get much call for predawn meals.

"Can you tell me anything about Mackenzie? Any observations at all?"

He bent closer, as if gawking at a madwoman. "Do you suppose she could be of the least interest to me? When I've got all this to worry about?" He nodded toward the circle.

"I hear you've identified it as a glucose molecule." I was afraid if I phrased it as a question he'd find a way to be nonresponsive.

"So much for your solar system." He flicked a finger as if I were a gnat. "Solar system! The minute I set eyes on it, I knew it couldn't be anything but a molecule. I should have guessed immediately which one. Sugar is the bloody basis for plant life, the basis for food preservation. It's also the greatest reward we can give our taste buds—our most primary sensual delight, the first thing children crave. Only think of what this tells us in terms of a communication uniquely tailored to us! Glucose is the basic unit of that which is most pleasing and precious and crucial to us." He nodded, flushing with excitement. "And here it is —right here. Within a stone's throw of me! And the timing of it: the one scholar likely to decipher the pictogram is in the neighborhood— not in his own backyard in southern England, where the circles usually form. To think I've worried about leaving on lecture tours. Well, this shows how silly I've been." He nodded solemnly. "They follow me, when they have to."

And I'd thought the assistant DA guilty of hubris.

"Yes, they follow me!" he repeated. "Can you fathom the urgency they must feel? Can you begin to understand how hard they worked to lay down a pattern of such complexity? To use this shabby mess of weeds as a medium?"

"To use me as a middlewoman?" It was all I could do not to smile.

He raised his brows, apparently not wanting to dignify me with the title.

Back to business: "You say you're leaving the area soon?"

"Oh, yes. I've had people out to photograph it. I've got what I need. I expect it'll cause the sort of stir we saw with the Mandelbrot Set."

I shook my head to indicate I didn't know it.

"Mandelbrot? As in the inventor of fractal geometry? As in chaos theory, the degree of irregularity remaining constant across different scales?" When I didn't say, *Oh, that Mandelbrot,* he rolled his eyes. "And I suppose you've a college degree? Well, take my word for it. If you feed Mandelbrot's extremely famous"—another roll of the eyes—"iteration into a computer, it gives one a pattern, a very distinctive shape. A perfect reproduction of which turned up in a field not so very far from where he happened to be at the time."

"Really? Like a message to him?"

He looked at me as if I were hopeless. "To a few more people than that!"

"Have you analyzed the plants here?" I mentioned a test one of my expert witnesses had recommended.

"Cell pits and growth nodes—what rubbish! These are *pictograms,* darling! One need only *look* at a picture."

"Would you be interested in lab results from the local university?" What I really wanted was his address. I might, in dire circumstances, need him to testify.

"Don't trouble yourself." His tone was snide. "We've all had our fill of Colin Andrews by now."

I'd watched one of Colin Andrews's videos at the UFO conference. An early crop circle researcher, Andrews focused on their physical features, including botanical changes. Unlike Fulmer, I'd appreciated his lack of pretense and bullshit.

"It's no trouble; I'll be happy to send them. Let me jot down your address."

With a twist of the lips and a sour sigh, he rattled off something that sounded more like directions than an address. "It's near Avebury. That's in England, so do put the extra stamp on."

He turned away, returning to his fidgeting groupies.

I wondered what he'd do if I shouted a few parting comments: That the crop circle had nothing to do with Reginald Fulmer. That just over the hill, a mathematician was writing a book about the spin of planets. That, on the night this pictogram appeared, Joseph Huizen would have died without an injection of glucose.

Glucose. Sugar might be the basis for plant life, a fine food preservative, and a child's first delight. But in addition, just two weeks ago, it kept alive the author of the forthcoming *Pi in the Sky*.

I walked back to my car in a daze. I didn't know what to think.

I made a call from a phone booth in Davenport. I asked Carl Shaduff to contact the paramedics who'd picked up Joseph Huizen the night of his diabetic emergency. They should be easy to find. They were on the prosecution's witness list because they'd tended Francis Addenaur earlier that morning. The ADA hadn't called them, relying instead on the testimony of cops and doctors. But he'd have their home phone numbers handy.

"I'm going to subpoena them, maybe put them on the stand toward the end of next week; I'm not sure. And one other thing . . ."

"Yes?"

"Find me some drawings of a glucose molecule?"

"Okay." His voice told me he envisioned a highly eccentric direct examination.

I drove home wondering why none of the news features about the crop circle had mentioned the resemblance to glucose. Was it because journalists had done their research and found none? More likely, Fulmer hadn't reached his conclusion until after they went home.

Maybe it didn't matter, one way or the other. Until I powwowed with my experts, I couldn't be sure it would pay to mention the circles.

I spent the weekend mainlining coffee and going over my notes, preparing questions for direct examination of my first witnesses. I jittered around the apartment telling myself I could budget in a break, take a short walk. But I knew how I'd feel if Alan Miller went to prison. My stomach would clench every time I thought about it; I'd second-guess every question I'd asked, every motion I made. I thanked God I wasn't (usually) a criminal lawyer—and I made myself keep working.

18

I was both relieved and disappointed on Monday: Patrick Toben didn't manage to wrap up his case before lunch.

I was still in the courtroom, stuffing my notes into my briefcase and looking forward to a bad lunch, when he approached me.

"I just got word," he said. "Maria Nanos's grandparents are in my office wanting to talk. You're welcome to join us."

Alan, leaning against the counsel table waiting for me, suddenly straightened. "They don't think I—? You didn't tell them I—?"

Toben clobbered him with a how-dare-you-speak glance. To me, he said, "If you want to come, come now."

"I'm right behind you," I assured him. To Alan, I said, "I'll join you in the cafeteria when I'm done."

I left him standing with his mouth open, poised as if to persuade us to take him along.

I followed Patrick Toben through the courthouse hall and into the adjoining county building. He walked past coworkers and clericals as if they were invisible. He led me into the usual conference room.

A short man in a well-fitting blue suit and cashmere vest stood behind a woman in dignified green wool. Her old-fashioned patent handbag, on the table, was as black as her dyed, sprayed hair. Her age showed in her choice of accessories, not in her skin.

Her husband strode toward us. His round face and sleekly combed hair made him look drawn onto a balloon.

His accent was so slight I couldn't identify it. "You have Maria?"

The DA extended his hand. "Mr. Nanos, hello. I'm the assistant district attorney trying *The People versus Alan Miller.* He withdrew his hand when Nanos didn't shake it. "Mr. Miller is the man who picked up your granddaughter hitchhiking in Half Moon Bay and brought her to this county."

Nanos bared a hint of teeth. His nostrils flared slightly. "You have Maria?" he repeated. "Friday you are telling us you know where is Maria. And so we pass a day on the bus and another one in the hotel. Today they say we will wait and talk to you. We are waiting since you phone us three days ago!" His voice was growing high pitched with exasperation. "You have Maria ready? She is ready to go home?"

But Toben was not to be rushed. "This is Mr. Miller's attorney."

"Hello," I said.

Mrs. Nanos flinched, rising partway out of her chair. The motion was slight, but her rush of feeling went further. I took a backward step.

"Where is Maria?" The grandmother braced her palms against the table edge. It seemed to be the only thing keeping her from flying at me. "What your Miller did with my granddaughter?"

"Please have a seat." Toben seemed to be performing some kind of hosting ritual. "Let's discuss why Maria left home and where she might be now."

"You can have no reason to keep my granddaughter!" The woman's voice was rising.

Her husband said, "We will take care. Where is Maria?"

"Please sit down." Toben's tone made it clear this conversation wasn't happening until they did.

Finally, Mr. Nanos sat beside his wife. He yanked her back into her seat.

Toben and I took the other side of the table.

"We don't know Maria's exact whereabouts, I'm sorry to say." His tone was brisk; for him, this was business as usual. "Ms. Jansson last saw her Friday night. Since then, we've been trying to locate her, for many reasons. One of them is that we'd like to call her as a witness. Do you know if she has any friends here in town?"

I watched the elderly couple. Toben's cool tone seemed to increase the heat of their seething.

He waited a moment before adding, "Maybe we should start with why she ran away. What can you tell us about that?"

"I tell you I will break her legs!" Nanos's words were barely audible, whispered like a prayer. His lips hardly moved. "Before she will hitch-hike with men, I will break her two legs."

Beside him, Mrs. Nanos nodded, tears streaming down her face.

"Mr. Nanos," Toben said patiently, "that's no kind of solution. It's also illegal. I know you're upset, but I hope you realize that we need to address the underlying problem here. All of us do. That's the reason I'm asking you, why did Maria run away?"

Nanos looked appalled that anyone would be in doubt of the reason. "This criminal, he has convinced Maria."

Toben's brows rose. "Our information is that she met Alan Miller just sixty miles north of here. So most of Maria's trip would have been in other company. She may have left with someone she knew or she may have hitched rides with strangers. Either way, the question remains, why did she leave in the first place?"

"Television!" Nanos spat the word out. "What a young girl she sees on the television . . . men and women going together like pigs." That drew a moan from Mrs. Nanos. "Even good children they are ruined."

"You think television influenced Maria to seek out more freedom?"

"Not just the television, even the teachers at Maria's school. Even the teachers in America they are like pigs, they are like animals."

"Was there a particular teacher? A male teacher? Someone she had a crush on?"

Mr. Nanos looked angry enough to pummel Toben just for hinting it.

"I'm asking for a reason, Mr. Nanos. Maria is pregnant."

It was obviously news to them.

Mr. Nanos dived across the tabletop, grabbing Toben's lapels and cursing him in a voice so high pitched it was difficult to resolve into speech.

Mrs. Nanos fell over backwards in her chair. I watched it happen, but I still don't understand how a person could arch her back and go over like that.

Christ, and I thought my family was strange.

I went around to Mrs. Nanos, assuming the DA didn't need my help handling a man twenty years his senior.

Mrs. Nanos made no move to rise. She lay partly splayed over the chair, the opaque tops of her panty hose showing and the weight of her torso forcing her neck into a painful-looking angle.

I thought for a second she'd had a heart attack and died. But then I saw her face contort with sobs so strong they sounded like a slow hiss. She seemed to have no energy left for rearranging her body.

When I tried to help her up, she was dead weight. I looked over at Patrick Toben, hoping he could help. But he had his hands full. He was no longer protecting himself from Mr. Nanos. He was trying to prevent the man from bashing himself repeatedly in the face.

Nanos was smashing his fists against his head. Toben was trying to get a forearm between Nanos and his fists. He was shouting for help.

Two men in suits ran in. They stopped for a minute, apparently shocked to find two well-dressed seniors causing such commotion.

The grandmother still seemed catatonically unable to do anything but cry. I suggested the men call for a medic, and one of them left. The other helped Toben force Mr. Nanos into a chair.

Nanos was screaming, "Kill me yesterday, God, kill me yesterday!"

A woman in a red suit entered the room, her elbows lifted as if bracing herself for an imminent tackle. Toben shouted, "Over there."

She went around to Mrs. Nanos. I backed out of the way, trying to imagine how this scene would have played had Maria been here. Would her grandfather have dived for her, trying to punch her, trying to break her legs?

One thing was sure: Maria had worried too much about her grandparents fooling the DA. She'd worried too much about being handed back over to them, at least right away.

I considered the places a kid without money might be. I'd slept under a few bridges in my hippie youth, flowing with a river of protesters to Washington, D.C. My main memories, besides endless political debate, were of being cold and hassled. But that was before Reagan emptied the mental hospitals, before the war on drugs incited dealers to buy guns.

The streets were an armed madhouse now. But I supposed anything beat getting your legs broken.

I stayed until paramedics arrived for Mrs. Nanos. Then I left the conference room.

But I'd lost my appetite for lunch. In the twenty minutes before court reconvened, I strolled to a park near the courthouse.

It was about seventy degrees out. The sky was streaked with clouds. Ducks squabbled in a jade green pond. I sat on a bench and watched them.

When the bailiff called court back in session, Toben seemed a little distracted, a little off. It took him the rest of the day to wind up his case in chief.

It was probably just as well I had the extra night to prepare. I played phone tag with the paramedics who'd picked up Joseph Huizen. Carl Shaduff said they'd been chatty about picking up and treating Joseph, but evasive about stopping the ambulance near Miller's house during transport. I prepared subpoenas in case I decided to put them on the stand.

I touched base with my four UFO experts, confirming their arrival on Wednesday.

I went through my questions for the next day's witnesses.

And I pretended to be surprised that it had grown too late to phone my boss at Curtis & Huston.

19

I put on a parade of witnesses Tuesday: investigators and forensic photographers to discuss the inconclusive evidence of the Brussels sprouts field; sheriff's deputies, paramedics, and doctors to establish that Alan Miller had been injured but that his injuries weren't typical of a car accident. I asked the deputies and doctors whether Alan remembered how he'd gotten hurt. Toben objected that this was hearsay, and I countered that it was offered to explain the witnesses' subsequent conduct. What it really did was set the stage for Fred Hershey's testimony and audiotape.

But something happened Tuesday night to make me worry about my most important witness.

I was preparing Fred's testimony, going over questions the assistant DA was likely ask on cross and suggesting ways he might couch his answers. My notes were strewn across a blond wood table in a kitchen that looked like the Swedish Modern nook of a home improvement store. Fred, ever the good host, had set out bagels and toppings and juices, any of which would have lain like lead in my nervous stomach.

"I'll start by running through your résumé at some length—your credentials are impressive, so I'll beat them to death. I especially want the jury to know you've testified in over a hundred trials, eighty of them for the DA. It'll give your testimony weight, make you seem unbiased." With luck, Fred would be a dream witness. He was old enough to have authority but young enough to exude vitality. His clothes looked expensive without being too New Yorkish. And he came across as confident, concerned, relaxed. "I'll ask how you came to interview Alan Miller; why you suggested hypnosis; whether the DA consented to it; the conditions and circumstances under which hypnosis is considered most reliable. I'll zip through these questions with you tonight, but I'm just laying a foundation for introducing the taped hypnosis session. After the jury hears the tape, that's when the thing gets tricky. I want you well prepared for anything Toben's likely to ask on cross."

Fred leaned back in his chair, sighing. His testimony could only invite ridicule. He'd be associated with the tale on the audiotape even though it wasn't his.

We were about half an hour into it when I excused myself to take a bathroom break. I returned to find that Fred had clicked off the kitchen light. The sliding door to Fred's backyard was partway open.

"Fred?" I crossed the dark room, glancing out into the yard. One of his walkway lights was flickering. Maybe he'd gone out to check it?

I pushed the door open farther so I could get through. But a quick glance told me he wasn't out there.

I stepped back inside, walking through the downstairs rooms. Then I went upstairs, calling for him. His bedroom door was open, but the spare, well-ordered room was empty.

He'd certainly made a speedy getaway. But where the hell had he gone?

I spent the next hour and a half going over my notes and fuming. How could Fred flake out on me? Why would he take off like this?

I'd left the sliding door open. The air was sweet with the smell of jasmine and cool enough to keep me alert. At about ten o'clock, I heard a sound outside. Footsteps?

I jumped to my feet. By the time I reached the door, I could see Fred standing in front of the walkway light, tapping it as if to get it to come back on.

"Fred! Where did you go?"

He looked up, startled. "I just came out to check on . . ."

I hated to sound like a shrewish wife, but he didn't seem to have any more to say. "To check on what? What have you been doing all this time?"

I couldn't see Fred's face. The bit of light from the flickering lamp didn't reach that high.

"What time is it?" Fred asked.

"Ten! And we've still got a lot of ground to cover."

"Ten?" He just stood there. "I'm sorry, I must have dozed off on the bench."

"What bench?" I stepped out into the garden. How could I have missed him?

Fred pointed to some rhododendrons pruned to look like boxes. I hadn't thought to check behind them.

"I called your name. You didn't hear me?"

"No, I'm sorry. I just sat down for a second. I don't usually nod off like that."

I turned to go back inside. I couldn't afford the doubts I was having. Fred Hershey was a key witness; my whole case depended on him. But he'd hired a lawyer who didn't usually try criminal cases. Then he'd sneaked out and stayed gone for much of the time allotted to coaching his testimony.

I didn't know what to think. Fred was the brother of someone I'd known since I was eighteen. And he'd helped me out last year, big time. Surely I could trust him?

When we resumed our seats at the table, I looked him over carefully. He seemed a little distracted, but ready to get back to business.

I just prayed he didn't have something up his sleeve, didn't have some agenda that would end up backfiring on Alan Miller.

20

Audio- and videotapes are always fun for the jury, like watching movies in class instead of listening to lectures. I could see the jurors perking up, especially after an hour of hearing about Fred's résumé and background.

But I hadn't prepared the jurors in my opening statement for what they were about to hear. As I produced the tape and handed it to the bailiff to feed through the court's audio system, I tried to keep the worry off my face.

I looked out into the pews. As usual, columnist Leonard Deally looked hot and cranky in his undertaker's three-piece. He was shaking his head, lips pursed, already writing in his notebook. He knew what was coming, I was sure of it.

A moment later, Alan Miller's voice screamed out of the speakers, "What *is* that? What is that thing?"

As the tape rolled on and the jurors realized what they were hearing, they sat very still, sneaking peeks at one another. One appeared to be stifling nervous laughter.

In the pews, someone did giggle.

The sound made Alan jerk as if he'd been struck. He stared at his hands, braced against the table, and struggled to keep his face blank. But his blush was painful to see.

Leonard Deally would later print that Alan "smirked like a man enjoying his big joke on the court."

After signaling for the tape to be turned off, I asked Fred, "Is this an accurate recording of your session with Alan Miller?"

"Yes, it is."

"What is your professional opinion, as an experienced psychiatrist, about Alan Miller's condition at the time you made this recording?"

"He appeared fully hypnotized."

"At the time you hypnotized Mr. Miller, what kind of story, if any, did you expect him to tell you?"

"Nothing like this." He looked surprised. "I had no set expectation, but I certainly didn't anticipate hearing about aliens or spacecraft."

"Did you have any interest in his mentioning spaceships or aliens?"

"None whatever."

"During this session, did you make any kind of hand gestures or signals, or do anything else that wouldn't be apparent to someone listening to the tape?"

"No, I didn't."

"What was your reaction when Mr. Miller brought the subject up?"

"I was very surprised." Fred nodded firmly. "Yes, I certainly was."

A few titters.

"Can you tell us, what is the role of a therapist during a hypnosis session?"

"It's a hypnotherapist's role to listen carefully and help the patient explore his recollections, not to point him in some particular direction by approving or disapproving of what he says."

"On the day you hypnotized Alan Miller, had you heard of other hypnosis sessions in which patients claimed to have been abducted into spaceships?"

I expected an objection on the grounds that this was irrelevant. Other therapists and patients might be flakes or red-hot UFOlogists, their sessions might further some obscure goal, their memories might be fantasies or screens.

I'd prepared a response to this. But Toben didn't object. Presumably he preferred to wait and hammer these points on cross-examination.

"I was slightly acquainted with the work of Dr. John E. Mack of Harvard University," Fred admitted.

Again, Toben might have objected. Mack wasn't on my witness list; he wouldn't be available for the assistant DA to cross-examine.

But my rebuttal—that these questions were intended only to shed light on what Fred knew at the time and could therefore "implant"—was again wasted. Patrick Toben sat there looking bemused and unruffled.

"Dr. Hershey, can you tell us what you knew about Dr. Mack's work before you hypnotized Alan Miller?"

The judge, hand straying to his gavel, watched Toben.

Fred answered, "I knew he'd collected some seventy-five accounts of people claiming, usually under hypnosis, to have been abducted by aliens. But I hadn't actually read his book at that time. I'd only followed the controversy around it."

"So when you hypnotized Alan Miller, you didn't know details of other alien abduction stories?" Recalling the boys Fred had hypnotized, I quickly amended this: "That is, you knew these accounts existed in Dr. Mack's book, but did you know any details of the accounts?"

"No, I didn't. I only knew that Dr. Mack had worked with these people and believed they were sincere. I knew their stories involved alien abduction, but I didn't know any particulars. I didn't know how they claimed to have been abducted or what happened to them after that."

"You said a moment ago that you'd followed the controversy around Dr. Mack's book. What did you mean?"

"I'd read in a number of professional journals that Harvard University put together a panel to decide whether to censure Dr. Mack for his involvement with UFO abductees."

"To your knowledge, does it violate some medical or psychiatric code of ethics to work with people who claim they've been abducted by UFOs?"

"No, it doesn't." Fred frowned. "But judging by Harvard's reaction, it's risky to believe their claims."

"So, speaking hypothetically, a psychiatrist who knew that Dr. Mack had risked censure by his university for believing claims of alien abduction . . . do you think that psychiatrist would purposely steer a client toward claiming he'd been abducted?"

"No. I doubt it very much." Fred's tone made it clear it was the last can of worms he'd want to open.

I was beginning to think Patrick Toben was on quaaludes. It's a rare hypothetical that isn't assailed for being confusing, improperly presented, or too different to be relevant.

"Immediately after your taped session with Mr. Miller, did you discuss with him what he'd said on the tape?"

Fred said, "No, I didn't."

"Why didn't you?"

"He seemed to have no recollection of the events he'd described. I didn't want to suggest them to his conscious mind. I wanted him to have the opportunity to recall them at his own pace, if possible."

"Would you say you were being particularly careful not to endorse or reinforce his memories of alien abduction?"

"Yes. Very careful."

Not even an objection that I was leading the witness. Man, if all DAs were this easy (or this confident?), business lawyers would try criminal cases as a lark.

"Dr. Hershey, can you tell us what a repressed memory is?"

"In certain instances, particularly involving psychological trauma, a person can choose, as it were, not to remember something that would cause him what he would consider unbearable stress or hardship."

"Have you encountered repressed memories in patients before?"

"Yes, I have."

I knew Toben would be prepared to dismiss repressed memories as controversial, at best. I was also afraid the jurors had heard of hotly contested cases of repressed memories of child abuse. I was afraid they'd watched women on *Oprah* or *Geraldo* recanting false memories that had ruined their families' lives.

"How, if at all, do repressed memories differ from what laypeople call 'amnesia'?"

We spent a long time distinguishing between forgetting everything within a certain block of time, as Miller had, and selectively repressing some memories within a larger time frame. I wanted the jurors to know this case was different from those they'd heard blasted on tabloid television. Miller might claim spacemen had abducted him for his sperm, but at least he wasn't slandering his daddy.

"As a psychiatrist and licensed hypnotherapist, are you trained to decide, based on your patients' demeanor, whether they themselves believe what they're saying?"

The judge himself almost objected to that one. Expert witnesses can offer conclusions, but they've got to be supported by facts. Arguably, a patient's demeanor wasn't a fact.

"We look at a number of factors to assess whether patients are sincere, yes."

I let Fred know with a quick "Thank you" that he'd answered my question. I didn't want him making any distinction between "sincere" and "truthful"; let Toben do that.

"Dr. Hershey," I continued, "were you present when the audiotape we played here in court was first played back to Mr. Miller?"

"Yes, I was."

"What, if anything, did you notice about Alan Miller's demeanor then?"

Fred glanced at the assistant DA, expecting to be silenced. When he wasn't, he said, "It was my strong impression that Mr. Miller would have preferred to be thought quote-unquote 'crazy' than to actually believe what he'd heard himself say on tape."

There were murmurs behind me in the pews. I almost turned around to check on Toben, to make sure he was still in the room.

Fred's "strong impression" could be considered a conclusion outside his area of expertise, a mere guess about a stranger's veracity. I'd never ever gotten away with this much in civil court.

What the hell did Toben have up his sleeve? Moses himself swearing there were no alien beings in the universe? A videotape of Fred and Alan in bed together?

I stood there stewing for a minute, trying to figure out prosecution's strategy.

Finally I said, "Thank you, Dr. Hershey. No further questions."

No doubt Patrick Toben would have plenty more. And unless there was Thorazine in the courthouse water supply, I was bound to object to some of them.

But so far so good, especially since I hadn't prepared Fred as well as I'd hoped to.

Over lunch, I fretted to him, "I can't figure out why the ADA didn't object to any of my questions. He's planning a sucker punch. Just try to stay cool, okay? Look professional, bring up your education and credentials whenever you can. Try to keep it on your turf: if he uses derogatory phrases, correct him with the proper psychological terms."

Fred nodded, looking a hell of a lot calmer than Alan or me.

A half hour into his cross-examination, he flicked a glance across the courtroom, meeting my eye. He was about to take my advice.

In response to a prosecution question about "false memories," he said, "The term I would use in this case is 'recovered memory.' The fact that a memory is not immediately retrievable doesn't say anything one way or another about whether it's true or false."

"I understand that, Dr. Hershey." Toben sounded ever so patient. "But I'm asking if you're aware of a phenomenon called 'false memory syndrome'?"

"I'm aware of the term. I wouldn't agree that it's a phenomenon. It's a hypothesis."

To give Fred his due, he looked cool, all right—maybe a little too cool. It's not good to have your experts appear overly detached and cerebral. Juries are, above all, just folks.

"Would you say it's a hypothesis for which there's considerable support in the psychiatric community?"

When Fred hedged further, Toben began asking if he'd read various tomes, papers, and journal articles on the subject. Fred said he had.

"Don't these authors conclude that a large percentage, more than a majority, of 'recovered' memories, as you call them, are false?"

"More than a majority of *non*recovered memories might be false," Fred pointed out. "Our memories are highly colored by our emotional, intellectual, and economic context. They are notorious for being out of line with verifiable history."

"What is usually meant in the literature by a 'false memory'?"

"Often it refers to something that never happened, but which a patient believes happened."

"By way of an example, are you familiar with . . ." He mentioned an experiment Fred knew nothing about. Then he asked about one Fred said he'd heard of.

"Isn't it true that in the course of this experiment, psychologists, during their therapy sessions with—"

"Objection, Your Honor. Counsel is testifying."

"Overruled."

"During therapy sessions," Toben continued, "psychologists repeatedly referred to a bogus childhood incident involving a patient being lost at a shopping mall, isn't that correct?"

"Yes, I believe so."

"Did the patients eventually begin to 'remember' the incident and elaborate upon it under hypnosis?"

"Those therapists drew on biographical data about the patient. I didn't know Mr. Miller at all when I hypnotized him."

"Are you aware of an experiment in which volunteers were asked to imagine, to simply make up, an alien abduction while under hypnosis?"

"Yes, I am."

Toben glanced at the jury, looking gratified. "Isn't it true that, while hypnotized, they were able to offer detailed and convincing abduction stories?"

"Well," Fred hedged, "but they were given permission to do so."

"Permission to lie under hypnosis?"

"Yes."

"Are you saying that without permission," Toben spoke the word sarcastically, "a person can't lie under hypnosis?"

I tried not to squirm. Toben wouldn't be asking unless the answer was no.

"I'm saying that experiments of the type you describe are fundamentally flawed because the subjects have the therapists' permission to lie. No conclusion can be drawn one way or the other."

"Let me understand this, Dr. Hershey. Are you testifying that people do not lie under hypnosis?"

"No. I'm testifying that the experiment you described doesn't answer that question."

"Do people lie under hypnosis?"

"Properly hypnotized, people faithfully describe their unconsciously edited and often inaccurate perceptions. That's all memories are."

Though I hoped the jury was persuaded, I found myself fearing that Fred protested too much. Was he worried that somehow, however subtly, he'd influenced Alan Miller? Was that why he'd skipped out on part of witness prep last night?

"So," Toben continued, "it is your testimony here today that no one willfully and knowingly lies under hypnosis?" This was lawyer code for *I have a truckload of experts ready to say they do.*

Fred seemed to know it. He sat straighter. "No therapist could make such a broad claim. I can only repeat that experiments designed to prove that point are inherently flawed because the subjects were *asked* to lie."

"Dr. Hershey, have you ever heard the term 'confabulation'?"

With a slight sigh, Fred said, "Yes, I have."

"What do you understand the term to mean?"

"It is the filling in of details not actually recalled. The replacement of fact with fantasy on an unconscious level."

"Does this occur under hypnosis?"

"It occurs in all states of consciousness."

"Is it considered a particular problem with hypnosis?"

"By some therapists, yes."

Without skipping a beat, Toben moved on to screen memories, asking Fred if he'd read certain articles about them.

I debated whether to object. All this harping on false memories and confabulation and screen memories would no doubt give the jurors additional reasons to dismiss Miller's story. But Fred was handling the questions well enough, and his familiarity with the literature might make him seem more, not less, credible.

And I worried that objecting too often would backfire, would make me look scared—especially after Toben's sanguine silence during direct.

Toben knew local juries. He knew the judge. I hoped I wouldn't regret it, but I decided to adopt his strategy: I wouldn't dignify my opponent's implied arguments with objections. I wouldn't let Toben make me look histrionic. When in Santa Cruz, lay back as the locals do.

I boiled redirect down to one question: "Dr. Hershey, given your extensive study and experience, do you feel that Alan Miller, under hypnosis, recovered genuine memories?"

Though I'd asked him this very question in last night's practice session, Fred seemed taken aback. He paused for a moment as if holding his breath. Then he blinked and straightened. He leaned a little closer to the witness microphone.

"Yes." He cleared a slight rasp from his throat. "I believe Mr. Miller recovered genuine memories."

21

I'd chosen my UFO experts based on how rational they seemed, how much scientific data they'd marshaled, and how good their résumés looked. It never occurred to me that there might be warring UFO camps. I didn't realize UFOlogists were no more monolithic than leftists. I'd spent decades watching communists denounce socialists, Yippies denounce liberals, the New and Old Left denounce each other, and just about everybody denounce the ACLU. So I was in no mood to hear UFOlogists accuse one another of spreading "disinformation."

My first mistake was putting them up at the same hotel, a local landmark advertising that every room had an ocean view. I thought having them at the same place would be convenient for meetings with them. I also thought it would give them a chance to walk on the beach. Instead, they apparently spent the afternoon in the hotel bar, bickering.

I'd asked them to meet me for dinner in the adjoining restaurant, a beige-and-mauve family-friendly place with piped-in elevator music. I was late because I'd stopped to see Carl Shaduff, and he'd put me on the phone with the medics who'd picked up Joseph Huizen.

Now, I spotted the four men at a bar table far from the ocean-view windows. The tabletop was cluttered with beers and chasers, soggy napkins and pretzel crumbs.

Three of them were speaking simultaneously. I lingered in the doorway, getting a hit of my witnesses.

The psychiatrist, Dr. Gene Karollas, a natural baritone, was the loudest: "Bart, Dan, this is a lose-lose. You're getting way off track. You're not discussing the same aspects—"

He was being squeaked down by Bart Bustamonte, a human Jabba the Hut, sweating in his tent of a shirt. "We've got so much verification it's ridiculous." He stabbed his finger at ex–NASA librarian Dan Fichman. "How can you possibly whine about sloppy science when we spent seventy-two hours running the data through a supercomputer?"

Dan Fichman, not a perfectly sprayed hair out of place, scoffed, "You could spend seventy-two *hundred* hours on computer analysis of your data and still reach a completely erroneous conclusion." Even with his collar open, he was as natty as a TV newsman.

"How? How can you argue with a perfectly clear ultrasound of an atomic reactor four hundred and fifty feet under a mesa?" Bustamonte's fleshy face was blotching red. "It's just like we've been saying, just like the Hickory Apaches out there have been saying, just like the nearest rancher neighbor has been saying. There's a multilevel military complex under that mesa, and it's hiding alien spacecraft. Hell, you can go sit on Apache land and watch ships fly out of there for your own damn self. The rest of us have done it. You've seen the videos we took."

"I'm talking about methodology, Bart." Fichman's words were precisely pronounced to full patronizing effect. "It's no use bothering to interpret data—however thoroughly—if you have a flaw in a major design parameter. It's going to be garbage in, garbage out. Look at what you piped through your buried transceivers to get that ultrasound: the woo-woo-woo Billy Meier *claims* he recorded from beamships visiting him over thirty years."

"Because of its sonic range. Other sounds would have worked. They chose Meier's because it has thirty-two bands, six of them subsonic, meaning—"

"Meaning zilch. Because we know now that Billy Meier is a fraud— leaking out pictures and videos from reclusion in Scandinavia, feeding us the latest quote-unquote wisdom from his Pleiadean buddies. Making himself the hermit guru of feel-good abductees." Fichman shook his head. "Korff's book proves Meier's lying, which means you used an invalid parameter—"

"Are you even listening to me?" Bustamonte shook like Mount St. Helens. "It's the range of sound that matters, not—"

Fichman made a sarcastic noise. "Then what was all that hooey about expecting Gray aliens to come screaming out of their underground labs and hangars because they'd think their Pleiadean enemies were after them?"

"Now that's disinformation! Who the hell told you that? And why the hell would you believe it?" Bustamonte looked close to pushing the table over.

A few other bar patrons, over near the windows, looked up in alarm. I fought the urge to turn around and leave. I'm rarely in the mood for bombast.

"Bart, Bart," Fichman continued, as if perfecting his pitying tone. "If we don't adhere to the standards of good science, if we aren't rigorous in our testing procedures, then our results are not scientific!" He took a calm sip of his drink.

Fichman's presentation at the UFO conference had certainly reflected his determination to appear scientific. He'd shown NASA slides of planets and moons, collected during his years as a science librarian. He'd overwritten them with geometric notations purporting to prove that certain features were too precisely and identically arranged on too many planets to be natural. His presentation had been methodical and intense, and he'd shown no sign of slowing even after three hours. Every discipline had its Trotskyites.

Dr. Karollas, a lean psychiatrist in regulation Izod, jumped back into the discussion. "I don't see any purpose to attaching negative tags to our disagreements. Words like 'disinformation' shoot us all in the foot. We've got enough to worry about on other fronts without sniping at one another, gentlemen, and you know it." He glanced at the fourth member of the group for support.

But Melvin Kraduck, a retired air force colonel with a white crew cut and mean gray eyes, remained deadpan. He sat back as if it would take an army of Grays and Gordon Liddy himself to get a word out of him.

So I was surprised when he boomed, "Science be damned, Fichman! Science is a different animal altogether every decade. Science is just a bad guess with money behind it."

Fichman shook his head. "Applications and theories change. But the scientific method got us to the stars. And it can get the stars to give up their secrets to us. Unless we abandon it in favor of—"

"Of what?" Bustamonte slapped his hand onto the table, making pretzel salt bounce. "You want the evidence to jump through hoops for you? Twist itself into math formulas? Well, I'll tell you something I've learned from twenty years as a private investigator, Dan. Evidence comes like it comes, not like you want it."

I'd eavesdropped too long already, observing this pack of UFOlogists in the wild. I forced myself to walk to their table. I'd grown up among ranters; it wouldn't do to become squeamish about vehemence now.

"Hello," I greeted them. "Thank you all for agreeing to meet me tonight."

Dan Fichman stood suavely, smiling like a product representative, a Scientific Method salesman. He was wearing quite possibly the only double-breasted jacket in all of scruffy Santa Cruz.

"Our pleasure," Fichman said. "We've just been having a collegial discussion."

Bart Bustamonte snorted.

Dr. Karollas and Colonel Kraduck murmured greetings.

"I'm sorry I'm late. I had to make a stop."

Dr. Karollas checked his wristwatch. The colonel had already risen. Bustamonte still scowled at Fichman.

Fichman took on the role of host, leaving money on the bar table, clapping Colonel Kraduck on the back, taking my elbow and leading the group into the dining area.

Once seated, the men looked at me. The colonel said, "So? What do you expect from us?" He pushed away the menu as if military men were always ready to order.

"I've told you generally what the case is about. Let me tell you where we are in the trial so far." I brought them up to date. "Now I want to offer expert testimony to convince the jury that Miller's alibi isn't crazy, that this stuff . . ." I couldn't quite make myself conclude, *really happens.*

Dr. Karollas said, "I've seen about a hundred and eighty patients personally. And I can tell you about hundreds of others."

"Your testimony will be the most directly relevant," I agreed. "It will let the jury know my client's not alone in this. The danger is . . . the DA could turn it around on us. If there are books full of these accounts, if they're featured in movies of the week, then they're available as alibis of last resort for the desperate and the delusional."

Karollas nodded. "Yes, I've heard that many times. My usual response is that even if you discount some percentage of the stories, you can't discount them all. No one who's met abductees can fail to be struck by how ordinary they are. Just regular, bewildered workaday folks, most of them. So even getting draconian and ignoring three quarters of the claims, what about the ones that remain? The most modest estimate puts that reduced number in the hundreds of thousands. Worldwide, it may be several million."

"Are the claims believable?"

"There are hundreds of multiple-abduction cases where groups of people are abducted together and all recover the same memories under hypnosis—the same craft and same type of examination, down to minute details. Plus, I've had two dozen people from different parts of the country, with no knowledge of one another, write down for me a series of symbols they've seen inside a craft. It's always the same unusual glyphs in the same odd pattern. And I have purposely never published this information! Add to that the fact that abductees repeatedly pass polygraph tests. And this is simply abduction cases. There have been millions more UFO sightings."

I couldn't hide my skepticism.

"There was a mass sighting by a million people in China in nineteen eighty-three," Bustamonte put in. "At least that many sightings in Mexico in the corridor between Mexico City and Oaxaca since the solar eclipse in ninety-one. Reports in this country are almost never picked up by the wire services, so it's hard to get numbers. But it's at least in the hundreds of thousands. Plus over four thousand trace cases."

"Trace cases?"

"Scars, scorched earth, radioactive ground, radiation burns on witnesses. You've heard of Cash and Landrum?"

"No."

Bustamonte raised his brows. "Famous court case. Betty Cash and Vicki Landrum got horrible radiation poisoning—nausea, hair loss, oozing sores, eventually cancer—from a huge spaceship that flew over their car on a highway in Texas. The craft was being escorted, or at least followed, by army Chinook helicopters, so the women ended up suing the government to recoup the cost of six weeks in the hospital. The court said their physical conditions alone didn't prove anything. So they had someone photograph that part of the highway—it was black from the heat where the ship flew over it. Within days, unmarked machinery dug up and replaced that whole piece of road."

"Did they win their case?"

"Against the government?" He snorted. "Of course not."

The waiter was at my elbow now, asking if we needed more time to decide.

The colonel said, "Steak medium and fries, black tea, and more water."

The rest of us needed quick consultations with the menu. The colonel sat back looking like a man disappointed in his troops.

To cover my inefficiency, I told him, "After Dr. Karollas testifies, I'll put you on the stand, colonel. I guess what I'm looking for is a list of credible people—astronauts, military men, scientists—who say they've seen UFOs."

The colonel nodded. "Plenty of astronauts: Ed White and James McDivitt saw them over Hawaii, James Lovell and Frank Borman spotted one from a *Gemini* capsule, Neil Armstrong admitted at a NASA symposium that he saw one while he was on the moon. Gordon Cooper and Donald Slayton reported them when they were fighter pilots. Cooper was on television awhile back talking about it: an armada of saucers higher than the fighters could fly. Other pilots saw the same ones, hundreds of them over the next day and a half. Air force finally had to say something, so they wrote them off as airborne seed pods." Kraduck shook his head. "Imagine telling your best pilots they're so stupid they can't tell seed pods from manufactured craft."

"We've got forty-two hundred confirmed sightings by military and commercial pilots," Bustamonte added.

"What do you mean, confirmed?"

"The pilots reported the sightings. There's paperwork on it." Bustamonte had cooled down. He looked more like Sydney Greenstreet now. "We couldn't begin to estimate the sightings pilots don't report. Military pilots and astronauts who report UFOs run the risk of getting grounded for two weeks while they have psychological tests and most of their orifices probed. They definitely get the message that it's best to shut up about it if you see something up there."

Colonel Kraduck took back the floor. "Presidents Reagan and Carter saw them. Scientists: Hermann Oberth and Robert Oechsler, fathers of modern rocketry; Wehrner von Braun, Robert Sarbacher. Military men: General George Marshall, Admiral Roscoe Hillencoetter, first director of the CIA—he even joined a UFO group after he retired."

"You should have the colonel talk about the CIA's role in all this." Bustamonte's glance suggested he'd have plenty to say. "When one of our groups hit the CIA with a Freedom of Information Act request, they said they didn't have a thing on UFOs. Not a thing—can you believe the chutzpah? Then after years of appeals, they cough up nine hundred pages—nine hundred!—of information on UFOs . . . with most of the text blacked out. And that's only a fraction! They admitted they were holding back dozens upon dozens of documents from other agencies—OSI, FBI, Department of State, DEA, NSA." Bustamonte dabbed his forehead with his paper napkin. "We tracked down hundreds of National Security Agency documents, but they convinced the judge not to let us see most of them—too sensitive. So don't let anyone tell you the government's not hiding what it knows about UFOs!"

"Government's right to worry about spies." The colonel buffed his scant crew cut. "The aliens have propulsion systems that blow away anything we've got. Whichever country figures it out first has a tremendous advantage; we can't be sharing what we learn from downed spacecraft. And you don't talk to your friends without your neighbors finding

out—that's where the FBI and NSA come in. If you want to keep a
secret, you've got to deny everything straight across the board, to your
own citizens same as to the Russians or Iraqis."

"There's more to it than that." Bustamonte waggled his hand. "The
government made a deal with the aliens, probably back in July of fifty-
two, after they showed up en masse in D.C." He looked at me. "You
didn't know about that little sky show? People always say to me, 'If
there really are aliens, why don't they just fly over the White House?'
Well, they did. I could show you photos from several sources—seven
glowing objects in formation over the Capitol dome. They showed up
on three different sets of radar. We had fighter planes ready to go after
them, but they kept disappearing from the radar screens, playing peeka-
boo with us. Thousands of people saw the formations two Saturdays in
a row. It made the front page of the *New York Times*, the *L.A. Times*, the
London Times, all the D.C. papers. And Eisenhower got the message, all
right: *We can fly rings around you and we can mess with your radar. Nyah
nyah nyah.*"

I looked around the table, expecting Fichman, at least, to deny it ever
happened. But the men all seemed to agree on the mass sightings.

"After that, from all appearances"—Bustamonte shrugged—"the government let the aliens abduct anyone they wanted. It protected them
with disinformation, and it made sure whoever reported UFOs got
ridiculed and ghettoized in tabloids—isolated behind the 'laughter curtain.' And for what? What did we get in return? The technological
equivalent of their Model T's."

Fichman shook his head. "You're behind the times, Bart. The news
leaks, the tabloid stories, the TV shows—ever ask yourself *why?* Why
would the government be feeding information to *X-Files*, *Sightings*, and
Unsolved Mysteries? Why the public celebration of Martian bacteria
inside that meteor? They're getting ready to make an announcement."

"Announcement, my butt. The information's out there because *we*
dug it up. Hell, you're the one who keeps complaining about the NSA
taking jurisdiction over NASA." He turned to me. *"Apollo, Gemini*, the
space shuttle, *Orbiter*, they used to video-feed live to universities, news-
rooms, amateur astronomers. Now everything goes through the NSA
and they decide what to release. Remember the moon landing? If it
happened today, you wouldn't see it. You might see some photos weeks
or months later—*if* the NSA was feeling generous."

Fichman smiled. "Ah, but NASA is an organization of scientists, and scientists just won't put up with restricted information, not for long. NASA's already drafted protocols for a formal announcement of alien visitation."

"You're waiting for the good scientists to save us? To storm the Pentagon in their white lab coats?" Bustamonte waved dismissively. "In your dreams, Fichman. They all work for the damn military, one way or another. If they aren't actually in uniform, they're on the payroll of some company with a big defense contract. Besides, that NASA protocol's been on the books for years. Along with Federal Regulation one-two-one-one, saying it's illegal to come in contact with an alien. Five thousand dollar fine and one year imprisonment."

I must have looked surprised.

"That's right." Bustamonte read my mind: "Convince the jury your client got abducted by aliens, and the FBI could march right into court and arrest him. Pretty serious stuff considering the Feds supposedly don't believe UFOs are anything more exotic than weather balloons and swamp gas!"

22

For four hours after dinner, I talked to the UFOlogists individually, ensconced in their respective rooms. The first thing each of them said to me was that one of the others was not what he seemed.

Bustamonte was adamant: "Colonel Kraduck's one of the biggest disinformation specialists the government has. Try to get hold of his military records—you won't be able to. Rumor has it he was an aide for one of the bigwigs in Project Blue Book, an air force commission put together back in the sixties to discredit and hush up UFO reports. Its members admitted later their orders were to release flaky reports to the press and bury valid ones. So this is not a man who decided to join UFO groups for fun after he retired. He's career military! Just because he wears civvies now doesn't mean he's out of uniform."

"You're afraid he'll give me false information?" I moved my feet farther from Bustamonte's strewn changes of clothes lying between the hotel chairs.

"Not if you limit your questions to which astronauts saw UFOs and that kind of thing—that stuff's too well documented for him to lie about." Bustamonte sat on the hotel bed because none of the chairs were wide enough. "But he'll put you on the map. Everything you say to him, everything he finds out you know, it'll get reported back to his superiors. And watch what kind of harassment you're in for when the shadow government learns about you! You'll get your house searched for sure. A few times out in the desert, they practically bounced their unmarked helicopters off our cars—all we could do not to crash. They've got deep pockets—some Pulitzer Prize–winning articles back in eighty-seven put the black budget at thirty-five billion, and you know it's higher by now. That's a hell of a slush fund. And they are mean sons of bitches! And Kraduck's their man."

Colonel Kraduck, on the other hand, pointed the finger at Dan Fichman.

"I hope you don't trust that phony bastard!" he barked to me from his hotel wing chair. "Anybody can scribble lines all over NASA photos and call it geometry. The man's a smooth talker, running a mathematics shell game, that's all. He gets the liberal arts majors out there all het up with his razzle-dazzle numbers and angles, and he's got half the UFO community convinced our ancestors came from Mars." He shook his head in gruff disgust.

"You think he's distracting UFOlogists from something more important?"

"Hell yes! What's his point?—just ask yourself. That a bunch of aliens traveled through the cosmos building pyramids and interbreeding with local humanoids? That we're part alien ourselves? Don't you see where that takes you? Don't you see the danger in a knuckleheaded story like that?"

"Well . . ."

"The rest of us are worrying about real aliens who kidnap and torture American citizens. Whereas Fichman's going around flim-flamming people into believing they're our long-lost cousins. The man's a menace. He'll have people walking up to the aliens with bouquets in their hands —Uncle Henry, welcome back—when they're here to steal our goddam genetic material!"

When I got to Dan Fichman's room, he warned me about Gene Karollas.

"Just a word in your ear," Fichman said suavely. He still wore his sport jacket and his hair remained wig perfect. "I know your defense is based on the alien abduction phenomenon. But I wouldn't question Gene Karollas too extensively. He doesn't have the stature of a John Mack or a Budd Hopkins, and there's a reason for that."

"There is?"

Fichman nodded portentously. "I'm not saying this is true of your client, but far too many so-called abduction cases are bogus. And Gene Karollas seems to specialize in them. Actually, I'm sorry to admit this to you, but I think this abduction stuff . . ." He shook his head.

"You don't think it's real?"

Fichman leaned toward me, his tone intimate. "Here's the mistake well-meaning investigators like Bustamonte make. They see the government engaged in an obvious cover-up, hiding hard evidence of flying saucers. Then they hear reports of aliens taking abductees, and they conclude the two things are related. But what we've really got is separate phenomena. One of them is flying disks, which the government certainly is studying for strategic military purposes. That's why they're hiding as much evidence as they can of alien artifacts here and on other planets. But the presence of extraterrestrial beings now and in the past does *not* mean they're kidnapping humans and playing with our genitals!"

Oh, great. I hoped he didn't say this under cross-examination. "So how do you explain the alien abduction reports?"

"Oh, *something* is happening. Up here." Fichman tapped his forehead. "Succubi, incubi, elves, demons . . . we humans have been visited and kidnapped by other kinds of beings without pause throughout our history. I think that whatever it's about, it involves a quantum-mechanical dimension of mind, shall we say? A psychophysical part of the human machinery—but nothing *extra*terrestrial."

"So you're saying these unwelcome visitors aren't aliens, they're . . . some kind of mental manifestation?"

"That's right—somehow part of us, emanating from us or coexisting with us. The infusion of aliens into our popular culture, starting with science fiction movies and pulp novels of the forties and fifties, causes us to interpret our timeless abductors as gray aliens with laser scalpels. But the experience, in its essence, is exactly the same as that of a thirteenth-century girl being raped by succubi. It's the Gene Karollases among us"—Fichman cocked a brow—"who encourage people to fill in memory lapses to match recent fictional portrayals of the future."

Needless to say, Gene Karollas's take on this was completely different.

"I could have had the kind of lucrative, satisfying practice my medical school classmates have now." Karollas stared out the hotel window as if lost in a happy fantasy of curing rich bipolar women. Two floors below, spotlit surf raced over packed sand. "But once I'd heard a few dozen of these abduction stories, I no longer had the luxury of disbelief. The trauma to the abductees is simply indescribable to anyone who hasn't met them. For people to imply they're after some kind of notoriety, well, comments like that could only come from the pettiest ignorance. That's our real enemy: the closed mind. And the easy put-down."

Just when I thought I was going to have a normal witness prep session, he added: "That's why fellows like Bart Bustamonte are so dangerous."

"But Bustamonte believes in—"

"He's simply over the top! How can we ever convince people of the truth when we've got overgrown kids sneaking around the desert piping spaceship music through underground speakers? He makes us all look foolish! Telling wild tales to a news media already laughing at our expense . . . Do you believe him? Do you believe there are subterranean hangars full of flying saucers? I hate to use the word, because it hurts us all to have it bandied about, but Bustamonte *is* passing along disinformation. He may not be aware of it, but he's the best friend the government could have in its cover-up of alien abduction!"

By the time I walked out to my car, I was sick to death of all of them. And despite being barraged with evidence—Bustamonte's photos of flying saucers, Karollas's case studies, Fichman's NASA photos of artifacts on other planets, Kraduck's government cover-up documents—I was too overloaded to believe any of it. Even the Business and Professions Code made more sense.

I'd also spent about as much time in company—especially paranoid, big-ego male company—as I could stand.

Unfortunately, I didn't even make it out of the parking lot before my solitude ceased. Our detective, Carl Shaduff, suddenly appeared in my headlights, waving for me to stop.

I slammed on my brakes, unlocking the door for him. He climbed into the passenger seat, looking rattled. "You okay?" he said.

"Yes. What are you doing here?" I could see his car parked on the street a half block down from the hotel.

"The question is, what the hell are *they* doing here?" He slumped so that he could squint out the windshield at something in the sky.

I felt my chest tighten with panic. Was Shaduff about to point out UFOs? Were we about to get abducted?

I followed Shaduff's gaze, but I didn't see anything. Only stars, nice and stationary. "What's who doing here?"

"Let your eyes get used to the dark a minute."

We were hardly in the dark. The hotel parking lot was bathed in the glow of searchlights trained on the tide line. I kept looking at the sky.

"I knew you were here talking to your witnesses," Shaduff said, still watching whatever he saw in the sky. "I came about the paramedics. One of them decided to 'fess up. I've been over to his house interviewing him." Shaduff's eyes moved slowly to the left as if following something.

" 'Fess up?" I finally made out shapes in the sky. "Are those helicopters? Why don't they have any lights on?"

"Not your usual helicopters. I'm not sure about this because it's so dark up there . . . but it looks like they're unmarked."

"Unmarked helicopters? Is that legal? Aren't they required to have identifying numbers like planes? And shouldn't they have their lights on?"

"I've heard about black helicopters." He followed them with his eyes, looking as excited as a teenager. "They're supposed to be almost silent, almost invisible in the night sky."

"If they're designed to be invisible, why are they flying so low?"

"The rumor is they show up when one of the alphabet agencies is working with the military. CIA, NSA, DEA—when these babies pop out of the clouds, somebody's running special ops."

I could barely see them, a few hundred feet out over the tide line, hovering like black dragonflies.

"Of course, our view's not the greatest. And the surf's going to cover some of their noise. They could just be police choppers looking for something on the beach. Or coast guard, I suppose."

"Or they could want the UFOlogists to spot them," I realized. "From the hotel windows."

Shaduff nodded. "They could be making a statement. To one or all of them. Maybe to you."

"Do you have a camera?" But I knew it was too dark to get a picture.

"No, but it wouldn't—"

The helicopters turned then, flying seaward until they were out of sight.

"Where did they come from?" I wondered.

"There's an airport up in Bonny Doon above Davenport, another one down in Watsonville. There's military bases all over central California; Travis Air Force is probably the closest. You could ask your experts."

I hesitated. The last thing I wanted to do was go back into the hotel and talk to them some more. I shifted in the Honda seat to face Shaduff. Fred Hershey would be paying plenty of overtime, it seemed.

"What did the paramedic say?" I asked him.

"He admits now that he and his partner stopped on San Vittorio after they picked up Joseph Huizen." Shaduff's eyes remained on the horizon, ready if the helicopters came back into sight. "The one I talked to, John Bivens, he was the driver. He says as soon as he turned out of Huizen's drive onto the road, he was almost blinded by a bright light. He slammed on the brakes about fifty yards short of Donna Nelson's house."

"Miller's neighbor." I was disappointed; I'd hoped to hear something involving Miller.

"Get this: the bright light was pointing straight into her window. Bivens couldn't see what the light was coming out of, but it was up in the sky at the height of a four- or five-story building. It was as bright as daylight and as big as a water-slide tube at an amusement park—his words."

"What would create a light beam like that?" I was getting scared. It was night and I was far from home.

"It might not have been as bright as he remembers." He nodded toward the shoreline. "Or maybe it was a helicopter. But Bivens says he's used to MediVac helicopters, that he'd have recognized a searchlight."

"Did the light do anything?"

"They couldn't stay long. Bivens says he slammed on the brakes and called his partner up front. But they couldn't hang around to watch."

"Donna Nelson went to the library the next day and checked out an armload of UFO books," I told Shaduff. "It's obvious what she thought it was."

"I could probably get her library records," Shaduff offered. "If you're thinking of trying to do something with this."

"The paramedic seems credible?"

"You never know. But it's hard to figure his reason for making it up. Imagine the shit he'll get at work. He stops an ambulance in the middle of transporting a patient. And you could certainly construe his statement as a UFO sighting. Even if his bosses don't care, he's bound to get a ration from his coworkers."

Shaduff was right. Paramedic John Bivens was likely to join my client behind what Bart Bustamonte had called the "laughter curtain."

I would soon learn what an uncomfortable place that could be.

23

I was jittery driving back to Fred Hershey's. I found myself watching the sky as much as the road. Try as I might, I could no longer dismiss space as an empty expanse with the occasional floating rock or distant gas ball. Now it seemed like some teeming ocean with strange life-forms breaching the surface.

I reminded myself that I didn't have to believe or debunk or even decide. I didn't have to get caught up in it; I only had to plead Miller's case.

And I didn't have to do that until tomorrow. Right now, I needed a respite. I needed some solitude and maybe some ice cream. I hoped I'd find Fred Hershey already in bed.

But when I rounded the corner onto Fred's street, I knew I wasn't going to get a break. There was a police car parked in front of his townhouse. Fred's front door was wide open. Every light in the place was on.

I pulled up behind the cop. Last night someone shot out Carl Shaduff's window. The bullet, lodged near the ceiling of the back wall, hadn't come close to hitting anyone. But it had scared the hell out of me. I tried to make myself stop for a second and get a grip.

Instead I ran up the walkway, trying to assure myself I wouldn't find Fred dead inside. There would be more police cars if anyone was hurt. There would be an ambulance, a fire truck, paramedics. There would be a commotion, a police line.

Nevertheless, I was so relieved to see Fred, looking frazzled in black sweat clothes, that I lowed like an ox.

"Willa." Standing beside a policeman, Fred waved his arm and snapped, "Can you believe this?"

The living room had been trashed: sofa cushions strewn, magazines scattered, paintings and pictures yanked off the walls. Through the kitchen door, I saw utensils on the floor.

"Every room in the house is like this," Fred complained. "This is Officer Groom."

"Hi." I didn't look at the cop; there was too much else to notice. "What's missing?"

"Nothing, I don't think. You'd better check the things in the guest room."

I ran upstairs. My clothes were tossed around the floor. So were a few of my papers. Most of them, luckily, were in my briefcase in my car.

I picked up my blue suit jacket, brushing white carpet fibers off it. I did a quick count: suits, blouses, shoes, everything was still here.

I rejoined Fred and Officer Groom. "My stuff's okay. Were they searching for something? Or just being malicious?"

Officer Groom stopped writing on his clipboard.

"I mean, nothing's taken apart. The couch cushions aren't unzipped. My bed's barely mussed. Did they mess with your computer, Fred?"

"Not that I know of."

"So . . ." The officer circled a number from a list on his paperwork. "You think this might be an act of mischief? Spite? Do you know who might have done it?"

"If it's spite . . ." Fred sighed.

"Fred testified in a trial today. The widow of"—I didn't want to go into the merits. "An aggrieved party, Betty Addenaur; she might have done it."

Fred added, "If you contact Sheriff's Deputy Brazel and Police Officer Rose, you'll find out she tried to take a shot at us, and that she's also under suspicion for another shooting incident."

I was surprised Fred knew the name of the officer who'd come to Carl Shaduff's Friday night.

Groom, a round-faced, freckled man who would probably always look too young, scribbled down the information. Fred spelled Addenaur's widow's name for him.

"Obviously you weren't here," I said. I was surprised by the note of suspicion in my voice. I recalled tapping on his door early Saturday and getting no answer, returning to the kitchen last night to find him gone. Last week, he'd claimed to be running, but I'd found him beside my car without a bead of sweat on him. What wasn't he telling me? Where was he really going?

"I went straight from the gym to dinner," Fred explained. "I'm thinking I must have left the kitchen window up—it's open now. Anyway, I came home about an hour ago and found this." He waved his arm. "I hope my insurance will pay for a cleaning service."

Straight from the gym to dinner, then home an hour ago. It was close to midnight now. Had he really eaten so late?

I glanced at the cop uncertainly. "Another witness in the case I'm trying . . . she expressed concern that her grandparents might be unstable, might be out to harm her. I have no reason to think this is related, but her name is Maria Nanos. She was with me when a shot was fired through a private investigator's window Friday night—Officer Rose can give you the police report." I gave him Patrick Toben's number, too. "He can give you details about the grandparents, if you want to check on them."

Fred was nodding. "I guess it's possible."

"Anybody else?"

Fred flushed. I knew he had three ex-wives and a brood of kids. I didn't know anything about his relationship with them.

I wondered whether to bring up the black helicopters. I kept hearing Bart Bustamonte's warning: now that "they" knew about me, I could expect a visit to my house.

"Let me call my client before you go. Let me just make sure he's okay."

I crossed to the phone and dialed Alan at Edward's house. I got Edward's answering machine.

"Alan, if you're listening, pick up," I urged. "Alan?" I waited. "Call me at Fred's if you check Edward's messages."

Very likely, Alan was asleep. But I hung up feeling troubled.

Fred wrapped things up with the policeman. I added my name and address to the information already on his clipboard. He scribbled the case number across two of his business cards, handing us each one. I was getting quite a collection of cops' cards. Maybe they'd be valuable someday.

When we were alone, Fred put his arm around me and gave me a brisk squeeze. "Tell me you're not anal retentive."

"Hardly." My apartment didn't look much better than this at the best of times.

"Then we'll leave it. Let's get some sleep and worry about the mess in the morning."

I'd be putting the UFOlogists on the stand in the morning; I had a worse mess to worry about.

24

I found Fred in a slightly tidied kitchen reading the newspaper and shaking his head. When I greeted him, the look on his face—startled, hesitant—told me there was bad news.

"Leonard Deally?" I guessed.

"Afraid so."

I took the editorial section from him. Deally's column was headlined *Twinkie Defense Meets Lost in Space*. "Dan White got away with murder because he ate too many Twinkies," it began. "Now Alan Miller, whose car crushed local contractor Francis Addenaur, is trying to get away with murder . . . by claiming he *is* a Twinkie. Or I should say that he was abducted by *alien* Twinkies."

"The laughter curtain," I murmured, skimming further.

"What?"

"That's what one of the UFOlogists calls it." I set the paper down on the table. "It's what I expected. There's no reason for Deally to be in court every day unless he plans to milk it."

Fred handed me the front page.

Another article, also under Deally's byline, discussed the trial. It quoted Fred's testimony and talked about the upsurge in reports of alien abduction since the topic had been popularized by novelists and screenwriters. It quoted Carl Sagan sneering at abduction reports and accusing therapists of implanting false memories. A sidebar listed bizarre defenses in other trials. Another interviewed Addenaur's friends and grandchildren, all of whom were outraged by the sleazy depths to which Miller's lawyer and therapist would sink to get him off.

"We're lucky they didn't find some preachers willing to call us satanic."

Fred smiled wanly.

"Look, Fred, I don't live here. I'm not even a criminal lawyer; I'll go back to multimedia law like none of this ever happened." Even if I did go back in dire need of a vacation. "What about you? Is this going to affect your practice?"

"I can't let that matter to me, can I?"

But I couldn't shake the feeling he was keeping something from me, some purpose beyond or even at odds with helping Miller.

He continued, "A good part of my work is for county agencies. If this tarnishes my credibility with them . . ." He sat back in his chair. "But I expected this. I'm okay with it. I just hope you are, too."

An hour later, in court, I was sincerely doubting it.

"The defense calls Dr. Gene Karollas." I tried to sound confident. But I worried that my UFOlogy experts would find ways to slander one another on the stand as they had in their hotel rooms.

Dr. Karollas was sworn in, looking at least as well tailored as Fred, in his silk turtleneck, a blue blazer, and gray slacks. No bargain basement experts for me.

I questioned him about his résumé, got the scoop on how and why he'd started working with abductees, how he checked patients' claims of "missing time," his reasons for and methods of conducting hypnosis, his experience with multiple abductees whose stories matched, and his documentation of abductees' physical effects, such as scars, bruises, and nosebleeds.

Just when I was beginning to congratulate myself on how sane and dignified the doctor seemed, he went and got strange on me.

"Dr. Karollas, is there any reliable estimate of how many of these cases have been reported?"

"The estimates range from several hundred thousand to several million worldwide." Unfortunately, he added, "I'm talking about alien abduction cases, mind you, not the cases attributed—wrongly, in my opinion—to abduction by so-called black budget elements of our own government."

I quickly asked a question about something else entirely. But I supposed Toben had noticed the perverse little toad hopping out of my witness's mouth.

During cross-examination, he could barely keep the smirk out of his voice. "A few moments ago, you mentioned cases of abduction not by aliens but by United States military personnel. Can you tell us how many *non*alien abduction cases have been reported, Dr. Karollas?"

"That's irrelevant," I objected. "These claims are not the same type made by the defendant."

"Your Honor," the assistant DA said patiently, "there's already been a great deal of testimony about unverifiable abduction claims. The People have the right to impeach based on how broad these claims are."

"Your Honor, the witness stated that his testimony does *not* take this type of claim into account. So any follow-up about them is irrelevant—on par with asking about abductions by the Symbionese Liberation Army."

The judge disagreed, overruling my objection.

Dr. Karollas looked upset. Maybe he realized he'd shot himself, as well as the rest of us, in the foot.

And boy, what an "us" I'd let myself get drafted into.

"I don't know of any estimate," Karollas answered the DA.

"Can you tell us how these stories differ from the ones you claim number in the hundreds of thousands?"

Dr. Karollas's lean face looked pinched. "Air force personnel are either alongside the aliens in the examination area or are working alone, using memory-wiping techniques such as those employed by the aliens."

I could hear a stirring in the pews, a pre-snicker, if there's such a thing. With a sharp look, the judge silenced it.

Toben paused as if to control his own smile. "So there are individuals who believe that air force personnel fly around in spaceships?"

"They don't necessarily believe or disbelieve anything."

"Well, in your experience, how do therapists interpret these stories?"

"Too often, as evidence of an alliance between our military and an alien race referred to as the Grays."

"Do you believe that, Dr. Karollas?"

"Objection. This is not the doctor's area of expertise."

"Overruled."

"No." Karollas was emphatic. "I do not believe, as some people do, that our government would ally itself with creatures capable of inflicting so many indignities and causing so much pain and trauma!"

Obviously he hadn't heard of Joseph Stalin or the Shah of Iran, of Pinochet or Duvalier or Somoza.

"You stated under direct examination that you began hearing accounts of alien abduction from your patients in nineteen eighty-two?"

"Yes."

"Are you aware of a book published in nineteen eighty-one by Budd Hopkins, titled *Missing Time*?"

"Yes."

"Doesn't this best-selling book describe case histories of individuals supposedly abducted by gray alien beings?"

"Yes."

"Are you aware of a nineteen eighty-seven best-selling book by Whitley Strieber titled *Communion*?"

"Yes."

"Isn't it a detailed account by a popular horror novelist of abductions by gray aliens?"

"Yes."

"Does it describe, among other things, intrusive physical exams and the taking without consent of a sperm sample?"

"Yes." Dr. Karollas was squirming with the desire to say more, to explain why he didn't think his patients' stories were mere paraphrasings.

But Assistant DA Toben kept his questions narrow: "Since nineteen eighty-seven, have any of your patients told you stories similar to the one in *Communion*?"

An irritated "Yes."

"Would you say, in fact, that the majority of your patients' stories track this one, give or take some details?"

Alan scribbled a note to me. It read, "I've never heard of *Communion*! Or that other book!"

Karollas replied, "A substantial number of my patients have experienced ordeals similar to Mr. Strieber's at the hands of the Grays."

"Are you aware that a movie was made of *Communion*?"

And on the ADA went, implying that Dr. Karollas's patients had been so enamored of Strieber's tale of alien torture that they'd claimed it for their own.

But then, who knew? This was a country that had reelected Nixon and Reagan; we obviously weren't above embracing painful debasement.

Toben continued his list of "Did you know's": that after the 1951 movie *The Day the World Stood Still*, UFO sightings "skyrocketed" to a then record fifteen hundred; that reports of gray aliens did the same after the publication of *Missing Time* and *Communion*; that reports of mysterious government agents in black did so after an *X-Files* episode? Did he know that after forty years of popular fiction, there were five times more believers in UFOs than there were fundamentalist Christians, twice as many as there were Catholics?

I repeatedly objected that the ADA was testifying, and I was repeatedly overruled.

I began to suspect that Toben's silence during my questioning of Fred Hershey owed less to strategy than to long acquaintance with this judge.

Toben then began raising problems with the use of hypnosis to recover "alleged memories of alien abduction." He'd covered much the same ground with Fred Hershey, but seemed delighted to do so again. He concluded with a series of questions about "sleep paralysis," about which Fred had claimed ignorance.

Unfortunately, Dr. Karollas was able to describe sleep paralysis as a condition where, for a few moments upon awakening, the sleeper was conscious but unable to move.

"Dr. Karollas, isn't another characteristic of sleep paralysis being prone to hallucinations?"

"I've never encountered a case of sleep paralysis with hallucinations. But I've seen mention of it in the literature."

"Isn't it true that most so-called alien abductions occur when a patient is wakened from sleep?"

"Most of them occur late at night, so, yes." Karollas glanced at the jury as if hoping they appreciated his point.

When I stood, a few minutes later, to do a little witness rehabilitation on redirect, I noticed Leonard Deally slipping out the courtroom doors. I guessed he wasn't interested in my rebuttal. He had all the negative stuff in his notes; he was ready to go write his column.

Ah, if only.

It turned out Deally left the courtroom to go phone his pal Timothy Elgin, the head of the news bureau for a local network affiliate. By the time I was halfway through questioning Bart Bustamonte, news cameras were being hoisted onto the shoulders of cameramen in the corridor outside.

I saw the broadcast later.

It began with a long shot of the chipmunk-cheeked newsman on the courthouse steps. His voice was both mellow and emphatic. "Just another day in court? Well, yes . . . if you live in Santa Cruz, California." He smiled, showing many white teeth. "Yes, Santa Cruz, where Jerry Garcia's Deadheads gathered in the thousands to mourn him . . . and never quite left. Where every year lesbian activists parade topless to show their, uh, *liberation*. Where just last week, hundreds of New Age pilgrims congregated to feel the vibes from so-called crop circles . . ."

They cut to film footage of kids in tie-dye dancing inside the main circle.

"Well . . ." Now the newscaster was shown in a wood-paneled portion of the courthouse corridor. "You wouldn't expect Santa Cruz to have the usual kinds of legal cases, would you? But just how far out *was* Courtroom Number Two today? Would you believe . . . in a far-distant solar system called Zeta Reticuli?"

They showed Bart Bustamonte outside the men's room, looking cranky after an afternoon of bad treatment by the assistant DA.

Bustamonte, sweating profusely, was trying to hold up UFO video stills and photographs he'd brought to court. But the cameraman was making no effort to zoom in on them. No doubt they'd rolled plenty of film of Bustamonte rattling off his data—thousands of sightings per year, types of craft sighted repeatedly in diverse locations, mass sightings, video-recorded sightings, radar-verified sightings, authentication of the film and photographs, trace-evidence cases showing irradiated ground and burnt grass—Bustamonte had plenty of statistical and pictorial backup.

But the only snippet the news chose to run was Bustamonte's comment that the aliens were widely reported to be small gray humanoids from Reticulum 4, the fourth planet of the Zeta Reticuli system, which had a binary sun that might account for the dark film over their eyes.

Having made Bustamonte look like a flake, Timothy Elgin then goaded Colonel Kraduck into a temper tantrum.

Kraduck, my final witness of the day, had been unshakable on the stand. There were over four thousand UFO sightings reported by American pilots, and by God, the colonel wasn't going to let the assistant DA get away with calling thousands of American boys liars.

But the colonel, confronted by a crew of derisive newspeople, became as testy as Ross Perot. The television segment cut straight from Bustamonte's pronouncement that aliens came from Reticulum 4 to Kraduck snapping, "Of course the air force knows about it! Don't be stupid! Contrary to popular belief, the U.S. military knows how to keep a secret!"

The camera returned to Elgin, alone in the corridor. "Well, it's nice to know that someone, in this era of news leaks, has faith in our government to keep a secret! Let's see if Dr. Eugene Karollas, a therapist specializing in alien abductions, agrees."

They segued to Dr. Karollas, who fielded their curveball with the pronouncement, "Hundreds of thousands of people have had contact experiences. So no, no, no, this is not a secret in any sense of the word."

A last shot showed Elgin again alone in the courthouse corridor, a glass wall behind him. Through it, a skinny Rastafarian with long dreadlocks could be seen approaching. "But what does any of this have to do with Courtroom Number Two? Let's ask attorney Willa Jansson. Her client, Alan Miller, is accused of killing Francis Addenaur when his car drove off a cliff and landed on top of Addenaur's."

I was suddenly ambushed by cameras as I left the courtroom. My face looked like a companion piece to Munch's *The Scream*, something titled *Oh, Shit*.

"Miss Jansson, your client says his car didn't go off a cliff, as the police have charged. He says it fell out of a spaceship?" Elgin sounded like he might burst out laughing.

I noticed Leonard Deally standing behind one of the camerapeople, looking satisfied.

Without a word, I went back inside the courtroom to warn Alan, a few seconds behind me, not to come out.

The news segment concluded with the assistant district attorney saying, "Well, I really can't comment." Then, piously, "But I will say that it's tragic Francis Addenaur lost his life."

"Do you believe the car that killed him fell out of a spaceship?"

Toben grinned sourly. "No, of course not."

"Well," Elgin wrapped up, "San Francisco had the Twinkie defense, and now Santa Cruz has the space cadet defense." He sighed telegenically. "As we love to say here in Surf City: 'Only in Santa Cruz' . . . and Zeta Reticulum Four. This is Timothy Elgin reporting."

25

I found Alan Miller in Edward's backyard, an overgrown weed patch and parking lot for a kayak, a surfboard, an inflated boat on a small trailer, and a filthy Jeep that had once served as my getaway car.

Some getaway: I'd escaped last year's police problems only to become obliged to Edward's brother this year. I'd traded last year's escape for this year's vacation.

I put my hand on Alan's shoulder. He was sitting on an upside-down kayak supported by cinder blocks. He was staring at Edward's eight-foot plank fence, his back to me.

"Alan?" He'd certainly heard me rustle through accumulated leaves and dry grass. But he hadn't even glanced over his shoulder.

"It's just so stupid," he said.

"The reporters today?"

"All of it. Everything we're saying. Everything the witnesses said."

Uh-oh, we were back to basics. "You can't help what you remember," I pointed out. "You're just trying to be honest."

"What about those studies the DA talked about? Maybe Dr. Hershey was, you know, suggesting alien abduction to me. Without being too obvious."

I was a little worried about that myself. But we were committed now. "You heard the tape. It didn't sound like it to me."

"Or maybe it was that sleep paralysis thing. Maybe I'm one of the people that gets hallucinations along with it."

"Have you ever experienced sleep paralysis before?"

"No." He looked up. His eyes were rimmed red. "But it makes more sense than getting snatched by aliens, doesn't it?"

"It's no use worrying about what makes sense. We have to go with the evidence we've got."

"Yeah, well you don't have to live in this town."

"If you're acquitted, you won't have to, either." It came out sounding harsh. "Look, I'm sorry all this got heaped on you. But I've got a few more things to add to the pile."

He sighed, staring back across the yard at the fence.

I walked to the other side of the kayak. I was still in my suit, so I didn't sit on the filthy plastic. But at least I could look Alan in the face, even if he was determined not to look at me.

"I just talked to Patrick Toben." I'd stopped by his office to discuss what happened to Fred's apartment. "Maria's grandparents are still refusing to go home. They seem to hold the DA's office—and us—responsible for losing her. Toben suggested we be cautious, keep an eye out for them and report any harassment." I hastened to add, "In a way, this is good. It's shut Toben up about screen memories for rape, at least for now. It seems obvious Maria's just trying to keep her grandfather from breaking her legs." But the charge, I was afraid, would surface again when Maria did.

Alan covered his face with both hands. His shoulders rounded.

"I didn't get a chance to talk to you about this today, but I think you should know. Someone broke into Fred's condo last night and tossed his stuff all around. They didn't take anything, but it was a mess." Still no response. "Please be careful, Alan. You're the flash point for all this."

Finally, Alan looked up.

"The other thing is, remember I mentioned going back to the crop circle Saturday morning? I told you about Reginald Fulmer. I've decided to put him on the stand."

I reached into my briefcase and pulled out one of the science-book

Xeroxes Carl Shaduff had provided. I handed it to Alan, saying, "Glucose."

He stared at it a minute or two, tilting his head from side to side.

Rendered as connected spheres, like most molecule diagrams, it didn't look much like a crop circle. But I'd done my share of head tilting, too.

"Imagine it as a two-dimensional line drawing. It can be sketched to look like the crop circle." I waited for him to agree. Finally, I continued, "I'll put Dr. Huizen on the stand and have him mention he's writing a book about the mathematics of spinning planets. He'll describe his diabetic emergency the night of your car crash. He'll testify that the medics gave him glucose, and that it saved his life. That if the ambulance hadn't been right in the neighborhood—they'd just put Addenaur into a helicopter—he'd have died."

Alan stared up at me, his face flushing. He swallowed a few times before saying, "Why? What will it prove? That there was a goddam silver lining?"

"There's more. On the way to the hospital, the ambulance slammed on its brakes in front of Donna Nelson's house. The medic who was driving admits now that he saw a bright light from the sky shining straight into her window."

Alan murmured, "No." He scowled. "The medic could be lying. Or he could be mixed up in this."

"Mixed up in what?"

"Maybe it's a drug thing. Maybe Fred's part of it—paramedics, a psychiatrist. Maybe they're drugging people to give them false memories. Maybe the medics made the crop circle."

He closed his eyes, looking exhausted.

I told myself Alan was weaving stories from the tatters of his denial. But Fred's level of involvement—including paying all expenses—troubled me, too. "As long as you know everything I know, I've done my bit. Right now, I've got to make a phone call. I'll come back out in a while and we'll talk some more."

If I couldn't persuade my own client his defense made sense, how would my boss, Cary Curtis, react?

As I walked inside to use Edward's phone, I decided the best tactic was to avoid details.

So, after some desultory "How have you been's" and what's-happening-at-work chat, I kept it general.

"Cary, an old friend of mine needed a favor. He asked me to defend one of his patients on a vehicular manslaughter charge. He contacted me the day my vacation started, and, well, I just assumed the case would be wrapped up by now."

Silence.

I continued. "It isn't. The trial was scheduled to last a week—it should have concluded Tuesday, yesterday at the latest. But now it looks like it could go maybe three or four more court days."

Cary cleared his throat. "It hasn't been easy without you around here. We've been going crazy with the extra work, to tell the truth. We've got the digital signatures . . ."

Several states were making it possible to "sign" Internet and e-mail documents using a private encryption key, with the receiver using a public unencryption program. This was supposed to make each "signature" as unique, theoretically, as handwriting. But disputes were already arising over types and ownership of encryption software.

"Plus we've got more domain name troubles."

Two of our corporate clients had been blindsided by clever young men registering Internet domain name addresses that matched corporate business names. When the corporations saw the wisdom of Internet advertising with online ordering, they found they couldn't use their own names in cyberspace—not unless they paid someone off or fought him in court.

"And we've got a shitload of copyright work, as usual."

The Internet was a copyright lawyer's dream come true. Art, literature, and music were swiped, reproduced, and sent all around the world every day.

"We need you back," he concluded.

"I want to be back, Cary, believe me. I never dreamed this case would drag on like this. But what can I do? I can't leave this guy twisting in the wind."

"If I may be blunt, shouldn't you have thought of that before? Before you went and took on a case? And as to that—you know, you *do* work for us. We do have a contract provision about other employment."

"I know. But this is completely outside our area of practice. And I'm doing it on my own time, pro bono. It's just a favor for a friend, Cary. I didn't think it would take so long, that's all."

"Jesus, the position you put me in here! What am I supposed to do? You don't leave me a hell of a lot of choice. If I say come back—as you are obligated to do—you leave your client in the middle of a case and he sues you for malpractice, and ends up going after this firm because we've got the friggin' pockets!"

Cary was taking this less well than I'd hoped. Though an excitable man, he almost never swore.

"I'm sorry, I really am. If I could make it go away today, I would. But like you said, I can't leave my client in the middle of trial. You can charge this time off against my next year's vacation. But what can I do?"

"What's this case about, anyway?"

"Vehicular manslaughter and felony hit-and-run. They can't prove my client was driving the car at the time, so I didn't want him to plea bargain."

"Where does he say he was when the accident happened?"

"It was two-thirty in the morning. He doesn't remember being awake then." True—as far as it went.

"So what is it, his word against what?"

"They didn't find anyone else's prints on the driver's side. And he wasn't home right after the accident."

"So what's the basis of your case—anything besides his denying it?"

"The way the prosecution claims the accident happened . . . well, they can't produce any evidence."

"Of what?"

"Look, it's no use arguing the merits. The problem is that both sides ended up bringing in expert witnesses. It's dragging out longer than I'd hoped." I prayed Cary wouldn't get stubborn about hearing the details.

"I guess I'm troubled that you would take a case without so much as running it past anybody here. I mean, really, your reputation is our reputation. We can be harmed by your representing certain kinds of clients. You must realize that?"

"Yes, I do. I really do." I'd been pacing Edward's ratty living room, cordless phone in hand. Now, I dropped into his dusty sofa, tired with the effort of remaining contrite. "Like I said, it's a small pro bono thing

on my own time. The client is a nice Ph.D. who honestly doesn't believe
he did anything illegal. I owed his therapist a favor. I thought I'd be
done by now. I'm really sorry, Cary."

During the ensuing pause, I prayed: If Cary let me leave it at that, all
might be well. If he asked for details, if he dug deeper into my defense,
who knew what would happen?

"I'll discuss it with the others. Call me tomorrow and I'll be speaking
for more than just myself. In the meantime, what's your number there?
What's the case name?"

I gave him Fred's number. "It's a Santa Cruz County case, *People
versus Alan Miller.*"

Little did I know Cary would go to his Palo Alto home that night and
see Timothy Elgin's news story. Elgin's network affiliate, it seemed,
reached as far north as Palo Alto and as far south as Big Sur. And who
knows, maybe as far up as Zeta Reticuli.

26

I don't know why I found the article in the newspaper more disturbing than the television
news story. Maybe because Elgin's story was as shallow as it was clichéd,
whereas Leonard Deally's acid burned deep.

A PREMEDITATED EXCUSE, Deally's headline read. "Maybe it's just
the system," he began,

> that encourages lying: All's fair in court and war, and every-
> one's entitled to the best defense—just ask Nicole Simpson's
> family. But what happens when a defendant is so flagrant in
> his lying—whoops, I mean defense—that the hypocrisy itself
> seems criminal? Case in point: Local mushroom expert Alan
> Miller says his car fell out of the sky when he was abducted by
> spacemen. Laughable, you say? The jury couldn't possibly buy
> it—you hope! Well, but this is California, where Dan White
> served three years per corpse and O. J. Simpson's out on the
> golf links right now.

Deally inserted a brief biography of Francis Addenaur, who was

> driving along minding his own business when he got squashed
> like an unimportant little bug, first by Miller's car and now by
> a legal system that lets slick city lawyers substitute trendy
> hokum for the truth.

As if that wasn't bad enough:

> There are larger issues at stake here. When a lawyer can pass
> off UFO buffs as expert—yes, *expert!*—witnesses, what does
> that do to science? Aren't we reintroducing medieval demons
> to run amok in a world that supposedly outgrew them with
> Galileo?

Deally missed the irony of Galileo's having been laughed at and imprisoned for taking an unorthodox stand.

> Isn't the court leading us right back into the middle ages, when
> the truth cowered in fear while superstition wore judicial
> robes and turned the thumbscrews?

Then Deally got personal.

> But here's the kicker: Alan Miller's dishonesty is premeditated,
> reaching all the way back to his college years, when he wrote
> his doctoral thesis on—can you guess?—outer space aliens.
> That's right. Our own UC Santa Cruz awarded Miller a Ph.D.
> for the preposterous theory that mushrooms are an alien life-
> form. And here you thought they were something you smoth-
> ered over T-bone steaks!

"What does this tell us," Deally concluded, "about what passes for science nowadays? And what does this case tell us about what passes for law?"

I reread the part about Alan Miller's Ph.D. thesis, then put down the paper.

I sat back in the kitchen chair. I was alone this morning. I assumed

Fred had gone early to his office, but for all I knew he was sleeping on his backyard bench again. I'd nearly been driven out myself by the stink of industrial cleaner from the janitorial service he'd hired to tidy his place.

I pulled the phone closer and dialed Alan at Edward's house.

I was leaving a message on the machine when he picked up.

"Hi. I'm here. I just don't like to answer if it's not for me."

"Alan, what was your Ph.D. thesis about?"

"My doctoral thesis?" He sounded surprised, obviously hadn't seen the morning paper. "The ability of spores to survive for long periods without any of the apparent prerequisites for life."

"Such as?"

"Oxygen, carbon dioxide, water, light, pretty much any kind of atmosphere or nutrient; you name it, spores can survive without it. They won't fruit, but they don't lose the potential."

"So basically they can survive in outer space?"

"Uh-huh. They've been collected in samples of what should be empty space above our atmosphere. So we know they drift up through the ozone layer. And they're able to germinate even after bombardment with solar and other kinds of radiation. Spores are probably the hardiest life-form on Earth."

"Do you think they could drift all the way to other planets?"

"Given enough time, I don't see why not."

"Do you think they could have come from other planets?"

"It's possible. There's a growing body of thought that solar systems and planets are like archipelagos. So particles and spores and what-have-you may be slowly washing up on each other's shores. They could also be hitching rides on asteroids or meteors. Why do you ask?" His tone was cheerful, what you'd expect from someone discussing pet theories. He didn't seem to connect them with aliens and abduction.

"So you did write a doctoral thesis saying spores may have reached Earth from some other planet?"

"Millions of years ago, but sure. Fungi are such a boon to plants— they sheath and protect rootlets and help them absorb nutrients, they were pivotal to evolution. Things didn't really start to rock-and-roll botanically until the fungi kicked in. But they're different from plants, that's for sure. On a cellular level, they're closer to beetles, did you know that? Their cell walls are made of chitin, like insect shells. They're heavy on protein, like bugs. They're like rooted animals—different from anything else in the world." His voice glowed with proprietary happiness.

"Leonard Deally's column makes it sound like your thesis says mushrooms are spacemen."

There was a long silence. "I love fungus," he said, as if Deally had attacked it, not him. "My thesis is about what spores can endure. What they can survive. It just looks at possibilities."

"We're going to have to put you on the witness stand to say that."

"I thought you didn't know yet if I should testify."

"Deally's forcing our hand. I don't think we can count on the jurors not to hear about this. And we don't want them thinking you've been obsessed with space aliens your whole life."

"Oh." His tone told me how depressed he was.

I hung up to take a call-through.

It was Cary Curtis. "Willa, what the hell are you doing down there?" he demanded.

"What do you mean, Cary?"

"I mean I saw you on the news last night. Luckily I know someone who got it on tape so I was able to show it to the others this morning. What the hell are you doing?"

"Trying a case."

"Shoveling shit! What kind of a case is that? Abducted by aliens—come *on!*"

"There's a lot more to it than you saw in that tabloid puff piece, Cary. The prosecution says Miller's car went over a cliff, but they didn't find his tire tracks in the dirt up there. They say Miller was driving, but he doesn't have any injuries you'd expect from a car accident. And when he was hypnotized to find out where he was, this is what he came up with."

"The hypnotist probably suggested the whole story. You hear about these quacks all the time."

"He's a respected psychiatrist—and a friend of mine."

"Well someone's sure as hell lying! Or crazy."

"I'm just arguing the facts, Cary. Just like any good lawyer would. I'm not doing anything weird."

"The hell you aren't! Alien abduction? Are you trying to make us all look ridiculous here? Look who our clients are—high-tech companies, for godsake. Do you think they want their law firm associated with this kind of antiscience?"

"Antiscience? There's plenty of evidence—photographs, videos, traces of—"

"Of what? Maybe some Martian bacteria from billions of years ago. But spacemen roaming the earth? Are you *nuts?*" Cary's voice was reacquiring its New York accent, something that happened only under stress.

"Science means looking at the evidence, right? Not dismissing it just because it's strange. *That's* antiscience. Four hundred years ago, astronomers called heliocentrism heresy; two hundred years ago, doctors attacked the idea of germs; a century ago, scientists swore machines could never fly. Science always thinks it knows everything—until it's proved wrong! Besides, the issue is simpler than that. The evidence supports Miller. If I don't argue the evidence, he loses. That's not the way it's supposed to work. That's not fair to him."

"You work for us, you know. How about what's fair to us?"

"All I'm taking away from you is a few days of my time."

"Let's talk about credibility, let's talk about accountability, let's talk about the prestige and goodwill this firm has accumulated over the last eight years!"

I groped for my coffee as if it were Valium. I waited for the pronouncement I hoped wasn't coming.

"The others agree: we want you to withdraw from the case. Today. For the sake of this firm's reputation. I'm afraid this isn't a request."

There it was.

I took a swallow of room-temperature coffee, trying to remain lukewarm myself. "Cary, if you let me give you a nontabloid account of this case, you'll feel differently about it. I'm only doing what any lawyer would do. I'm arguing the facts."

"You'll have to withdraw," Cary repeated. "Right now. Before your verdict gets national press and you're linked to us."

"I can't do that. You said yourself I'd be sued for malpractice."

"Yes, and you will indemnify us for any judgment against the firm. We're drawing up the papers now."

"What if I were to win the case?"

"Either way, the unwelcome attention—Good Lord, how could we reassure clients this firm didn't mean to rely on astrology or palmistry when we went to try their cases? No, either way, we refuse to be burdened by the publicity."

We were both silent.

He added, "You know, we're being generous even offering you this option. You didn't discuss this with us, clear it with us, even warn us we'd be linked to news reports like the one last night. You've put us in the terribly unfair position of scrambling to do damage control. We expected better treatment from you, Willa!" With that, he hung up.

I replaced the receiver slowly. I stood up and finished getting ready for another day in *Space People's Court*.

I walked into the courts building just in time to see my mother get up on her toes and lean close to Colonel Kraduck's face.

She was shouting, "I recognize you, all right!"

"Oh, no!" I couldn't have been more horrified to see my mother sucked into a beam of white light. At that moment, it might have been a relief.

She wheeled to face me. "Do you know who this man is?" She looked unusually tidy in unfaded jeans, a relatively new blue sweater, and clean white sneakers. Her dress protest clothes—worn, no doubt, to avoid embarrassing me.

"Colonel Kraduck," I said contritely, "I'm so sorry. She doesn't—"

"So you do know! You know this man is an officer in the air force?" This seemed to settle something, as far as my mother was concerned.

I walked up to her, flung an arm around her, and began marching her down the hall toward the ladies' room. Pushing the door open, I demanded, "What the hell are you trying to do to me? Why are you hassling Colonel Kraduck?"

"Don't you recognize him?" From the look on her face, I expected her to tell me he was Josef Mengele. "He used to work at Travis Air Force Base. He was there twice when we got arrested. You were with us one of the times."

"No, I don't recognize him. And even if he was there, so what?" I could see myself in the mirror above the bathroom sink. I looked like I was going to jump out of my skin. "The military police arrested you for trespassing, not because a particular colonel didn't like the look of you." I took a breath. "What are you doing here?"

"Moag called me. He saw you on the news." She looked disgusted.

"Of course, he thought it was marvelous. But I just had to come and talk to you—I didn't get a chance the other night."

"Talk about what? Make it fast!" I had to go assuage Colonel Kraduck. And I had a case to try in less than half an hour.

"The Republican plan to resurrect the Strategic Defense Initiative, Star Wars! They're going after more funding." She shook her head as if the topic were obvious. "Three different times, Ronald Reagan made remarks about what would happen if we learned about a threat from outer space. Three times! Because he knew Russia wouldn't be our excuse forever. And when George Bush—former head of the CIA!—couldn't shake enough money out of Congress, he started funneling Iran-Contra money into the Star Wars project. The government's been working on this weapons system for over ten years now, Willa, making up for shortfalls with secret operations and black budget money. And the whole time, they've been planting and exploiting paranoia about an alien invasion, about alien abduction. They've been doing it to justify SDI, so they can pressure Congress to—"

"I've heard this all before, Mother. You could have saved yourself a trip."

"But don't you see? When Democrats object, the Republicans will just point up to the sky. They'll have the people believing all this aliens nonsense by then. That was the whole point of *Independence Day*—Hollywood's playing right into their hands. And Congress will do anything it thinks their constituents want." She scowled, hot red spots appearing on her cheeks. "People will applaud an immoral waste of resources—resources diverted from desperately needed social programs—because they're afraid of little gray men invented just to scare us. And you're helping them do it!"

I knew from long experience that it was useless to argue with her. I cut to the chase: "What are you planning to do about it?"

"Some local members of WILPF"—Women's International League for Peace and Freedom—"are going to meet with me to discuss a teach-in."

"Fine. Have a teach-in." The Republicans would quake in their boots, no doubt. "Just leave my witnesses alone. And stay away from the courthouse!" I took a step toward her. "You hear me, Mother? My client's got a lot at stake. I'm not kidding."

I left her in the bathroom. I try to walk away early when I fight with her. If I stay too long, I say too much, and I just feel guilty later. I've learned the hard way: You can't change your mother, and you can't stop loving her. All you can do is watch your mouth.

When I got back out into the hall, Colonel Kraduck was nowhere to be found. I stepped into the courtroom for a quick discussion with the bailiff. I described my mother and told him to keep her out of court because she'd harassed a witness. I didn't trust her to put my wishes above her dogma.

Leonard Deally was already in the pews, fifteen minutes early. I turned and glared at him.

He met my gaze and cocked his pudgy face forward like a turtle's. His eyes told me he hated me and everything I represented. Or maybe just every*one* I represented.

At that moment I realized it might be personal, having nothing to do with antiscience and the flaws in our judicial system. It might be a lot more simple.

Maybe Leonard Deally had it in for Alan Miller. Maybe Deally knew Alan better than either of them let on—well enough to know the topic of Alan's Ph.D. thesis and well enough to hate him.

I checked the corridor again. Colonel Kraduck hadn't returned. I peeked into the ladies' room. My mother was gone, too. Before reentering the courtroom, I made a decision. Everyone was so damn sure stories like Miller's were ruses, lies, or antiscientific scams. They were sure enough to denounce me, harangue me, and even order me to withdraw from the case.

I went out to the pay phone and made a call.

When I got back, I ran into Dan Fichman on a padded bench in the corridor, awaiting his turn on the stand. I thanked him for coming and warned him that there might be a delay.

I entered the courtroom to find Alan sitting at the defense table, looking tired and listless. I murmured a greeting, then approached the assistant DA. I told Patrick Toben I wanted to add four more witnesses to my list. He knew their identities because I'd already subpoenaed them, just in case.

I then spent almost an hour in the judge's chambers persuading him the eleventh hour additions were relevant and necessary and not a waste of the court's time. In the meantime, Carl Shaduff alerted the witnesses that they would be expected at the courthouse this afternoon.

It was time to get serious, time to give Alan Miller everything I had.

I tried not to think about Cary Curtis's demand.
It looked like I'd get my vacation, after all.

27

Dan Fichman should have made a better first impression. I could see the jurors looking away, as if in embarrassment, when he began showing NASA photographs with circled anomalies. I didn't ask him to offer theories about the unexpected, unexplained objects and blips of light. Instead, I asked him to authenticate the photographs based on his experience cataloging them for NASA's library.

I asked him if similar features had shown up in recent NASA photographs, and he explained that only *some* new photographs were released to the public by the National Security Agency.

I asked him if he considered himself a scientist, and if he felt that science was well served by this change.

I watched the jury, hoping that Fichman's cheerleading for science would show them that not all scientists had rejected the possibility of UFOs and alien contact.

By the end of Fichman's direct examination, I could see the jury beginning to make a little timid eye contact with him. I'd saved him for last because his testimony was the least directly relevant. But I also thought he'd play best, looking as well groomed and practical as a TV anchorman.

And with luck, the jury would carry away the idea that there was some context, including NASA pictures, for the thousands of alien abduction stories.

Because we'd spent an hour in the judge's chambers, questioning Fichman took us up to lunch.

I was too wound up to eat. I spent the time preparing my afternoon witnesses—if harried conversations can be called preparation.

I noticed, when I started back into the courtroom, that news trucks were parking out front. Apparently, Elgin's feature had chummed the waters. There would be infotainment sharks aplenty by the close of the court day.

My first witness that afternoon was Joseph Huizen. I was disturbed to see him looking tired, with his suit hanging badly. Though he'd needed to lose weight, sudden illness had stripped the pounds off too quickly.

I asked him about his credentials and publications, especially his forthcoming mathematics-of-spinning-planets book, *Pi in the Sky*.

I asked if he was Alan Miller's neighbor. I asked where he was on the night Miller's car landed atop Francis Addenaur.

I asked about his medical problem that night, inviting him to describe his ambulance ride—especially the part where it stopped partway down the road.

Since he'd offered undisputed facts and no opinions, there wasn't much for Toben to cross-examine him about. He asked whether Joseph had seen or heard anything going on at Alan Miller's that night.

My next witness was John Bivens, the paramedic who'd driven the ambulance. His partner hadn't been reachable this morning. And for all I knew, he wouldn't have supported Bivens's testimony.

Bivens was a tall young man with short black hair, a friendly face, and a sport coat he didn't seem used to. He glanced nervously at the jurors. I felt a pang: he hadn't wanted to get dragged into this, and I could hardly blame him.

"Mr. Bivens, can you tell us what you and your partner did when you arrived at Joseph Huizen's home?"

"Well, first off, we had to restrain him."

"Why is that?"

"It happens in diabetic emergencies. The body uses up the blood sugar and then starts leaching it out of the brain. It makes the patient altered and combative." Bivens looked confident, discussing a medical matter he'd handled many times.

"What did you do after you restrained Dr. Huizen?"

"My partner started an IV—an intravenous line—on him."

"You didn't wait until you reached the hospital?"

"No ma'am," he said, making me feel old. "You don't want to let the body steal too much of the brain's sugar or the patient will go into a coma."

"What substance did you give Dr. Huizen intravenously?"

"Glucose."

I introduced into evidence my science-book Xerox. I asked the medic to verify that it represented a glucose molecule.

I could hear the jury stirring, probably wondering what possible relevance the drawing could have.

"What happened after you left Dr. Huizen's house?"

Bivens scowled. I could feel his unhappiness. "Down the road a few hundred feet . . . I know this is going to sound crazy, but . . ."

"Please go on."

"There was this incredibly bright light."

"Where was it?"

"Coming out of the sky." He stopped, looking like a deer caught in headlights as he recalled the moment. "I couldn't tell where it came from. It was like a tunnel of bright light leading to a fixed point maybe seventy-five, a hundred feet up."

"Where was the light aimed?"

"Into the window of a house."

"How many houses down the road from Dr. Huizen's?"

"The first house."

I'd made a point of asking Dr. Huizen where his house was in relation to Alan Miller's. With luck, the jury realized we were talking about Miller's next-door neighbor.

Apparently the audience got the point. The judge had to ask for silence in the courtroom.

"Did you stop to observe this light?"

He hung his head. "Yes."

"What did you observe about it?"

"It was bright, majorly bright. Aimed, like I said, into the window of this house."

"Did you observe anything else about it?"

"That's about it."

"Did anyone else observe the light?"

"I . . ." He flushed. "It was so bizarre. I called my partner, Barry, to the front to look."

"How long were the two of you parked there?"

"Maybe a minute."

"Was the light still there when you left?"

"Yes. But we had to go, obviously. We had a patient to transport."

On cross, Patrick Toben asked him if it was customary for medics to stop an ambulance during transport of a sick patient. He asked if it was a company policy for the driver of an ambulance to hold up transport to stare at "bizarre" sights. He asked if Bivens had ever done so before. Never? Or had he stopped at times, but not bothered to report it? Had he reported this stop to his employer? Did he think his employer would approve of him stopping an ambulance, even for a short time, with a sick patient in back? Bivens, tongue-tied, rattled, and shamefaced, answered no to every question.

My next witness was the farmer whose field hosted the crop circle and the stragglers who'd come to camp around it. He'd already testified for me once, stating he hadn't noticed Fiat-sized tire tracks in his Brussels sprouts field the morning after the accident.

Now I asked him to describe the location of his land in relation to Joseph Huizen's and Alan Miller's houses. I asked him if he'd seen anything unusual on his property the day after the accident.

I asked him to describe the crop circles. I offered into evidence a newspaper photograph of the circles, asking him to verify that this was the pattern in his meadow.

My next witness worked in the university's botany lab. He didn't have anything relevant to say—the tests had shown "inconclusive amounts" of cell-pit and growth-node damage. But I thought the jury would think the crop circles were phony if I didn't offer some kind of botanical analysis.

"You were asked to collect wild grasses from the circles and analyze them, is that correct?"

"Yes." He was a longhaired man with a balding crown and a cranky squint. I'd hated to put him on the stand because he was needlessly combative. I hoped to keep him to simple yesses and noes.

That worked until it was time to ask what he'd noticed about the grasses.

"Some cellular damage, and lateral splitting in some growth nodes. Easily caused by any number of stresses to the plants."

"Would ordinary farming techniques such as fertilization cause this type of stress?"

"Not the fertilizers I've seen."

"Frost?"

"No."

"Whirlwinds?"

"No."

"Microwave radiation?"

"What?"

"Microwave radiation."

He all but rolled his eyes. "Conceivably."

I had to leave it at that.

The assistant DA went over the lab results more thoroughly, having him point out several times that no test results struck him as unusual.

Then Toben asked him, "Did you see anything in your test results to rule out the so-called crop circles being made by ordinary human beings?"

"No, I didn't."

"Can you suggest a method by which they could have been made?"

"Objection. Calls for speculation."

"He's an expert on grasses, Your Honor," Toben pointed out.

"But not on how to make crop circles."

"It's within his expertise," the judge agreed. "Overruled."

"Lawn rollers should work," the witness guessed. "Even a board should flatten that stuff out."

"Is there anything in your laboratory results that's inconsistent with the circles having been made by, say, people with lawn rollers?"

"No."

"To your knowledge, are others in the botany department familiar, in general, with crop circles?"

"Oh, yes," the witness said dryly. "About a month and a half ago, we had a professor from Oxford over here who wouldn't talk about anything else."

By the time Toben was done, he'd created the impression that the English crop circles scholar, the same one Fred met during University Night, had inspired botany students to conduct a local circle-making experiment.

I cursed my decision to give the jury an expert it "expected."

All I could do on redirect was ask, with feigned assurance, "Do your tests rule out exposure to microwave energy?"

"Common sense does that."

"Please answer the question."

"No, they don't rule out microwave energy."

"Could microwave radiation cause the cell-pit damage and the crepey effect you observed on one side of the grass leaves?"

"It would have to be a pretty short exposure. Very long, and the grass would start to look cooked."

"No further questions."

I tried to look cheerful. Testimony about cell-pit damage was bound to be confusing to the jury. Maybe they'd interpret my confidence as a sign they'd missed something exculpatory.

The good news was that I had an ace up my sleeve: Toben didn't know why I'd shown the paramedic a glucose molecule drawing. He'd simply indulged me by not objecting.

The bad news was that there was only one witness I could call to make the connection between the molecule and the crop circle. My final witness that day was Reginald Fulmer.

Fulmer flounced into the courtroom like Scarlett O'Hara in high dudgeon. The phone call from Carl Shaduff had caught him at the checkout desk of the Davenport Bed and Breakfast. Only Shaduff's promise of getting him on a later flight—and paying him $500—had persuaded him to delay.

"Mr. Fulmer, can you tell us your educational and employment background?"

Fulmer crossed his legs and arms so that it appeared he had a couple of extra limbs. With his hawk nose, flyaway hair, and sour expression, he looked like a caricature in *Anglophobe* magazine.

"I took a first at Oxford in philosophy," he began pompously, "and I have, at times, been a public school teacher. What you would call private schools here," he added hastily, lest we suspect him of mingling with commoners.

"Do you consider yourself an expert on crop circles?"

"I am a well-known cereologist, yes."

"What have you done to gain expertise in this area?"

He shot me a look. "Merely camped out in the corn for eight consecutive summers, personally mapped and photographed roughly a hundred agriglyphs per season, and traveled all around the world lecturing and showing slides on the subject."

"Have there been very many crop circles appearing over the last eight years?"

"About twenty-four hundred in ten countries. I suppose you would call that 'many.'"

I could feel the jury begin to dislike him. I kept it short. "Have you seen the crop circle located in Davenport?"

"Seen it? Good Lord, I've been there all day every day for the last nine days!"

"That would be this one in the newspaper photograph?" I named the exhibit for the record.

"Yes, yes."

"Does the pattern of the circles suggest anything to you?"

"It's a sugar molecule."

I thought I heard the assistant DA's chair scrape; for once, he might be planning to object.

I quickly asked, "Glucose? Do you mean the form of sugar called—"

"I object, Your Honor. This is outside the witness's area of expertise. He's no more qualified to interpret a pattern than anyone else."

"Sustained."

Talk about an inconvenient time for the word to appear in the judge's vocabulary.

"But Your Honor," I pointed out, "Mr. Fulmer's opinion that it's glucose is based on eight years of experience mapping and photographing crop circles."

"His photography expertise is irrelevant to pattern interpretation," Toben repeated. "He's no more qualified to do that than—"

"I have already ruled!" The judge looked ready to throw his gavel at us. "Objection sustained."

But it didn't matter: I'd repeated the word I wanted burned into the jurors' brains: glucose.

Reluctantly, I said, "No further questions."

There was no way Fulmer would help me make crop circles seem "real" to the jury. He'd refuse to discuss botanical traits and ramble instead about pictograms, snapping out rude responses until the jury discounted everything he said.

Nor would he point out, as Bart Bustamonte would have, the relationship between increased sightings of lights in the sky and the appearance of circles.

It was my own damn fault. I should have asked Bustamonte about it during his testimony yesterday. But I'd still been waffling about introducing the crop circles. I hadn't wanted to overwhelm the jury.

Or maybe I just hadn't been ready to pull out all the stops. Nothing like getting fired to make a person get serious.

I looked at the jury, and wished I could repeat the word "glucose" one more time. I wished I could say *Joseph Huizen* and *Pi in the Sky*. But they must have gotten the point—they looked a little stunned.

I could hardly blame them. Eventually this case would end and we would all leave behind the crutch of duty—to a client, to the court, to the community. Then we'd have to make up our minds for real.

Maybe the jurors were ready to do that. I sure as hell wasn't.

28

Outside the courthouse, Reginald Fulmer encountered a trio of television cameras. He postured, preened, and declaimed in front of them so long that he missed his second flight. I waited beside my car like a patient chauffeur, ready to deliver the promised ride to the airport. But he was too damn busy strutting to heed my semaphoric signals.

When he finally tore himself away, I broke the news, with some satisfaction, that he'd never make the evening plane.

He demanded to be put up for the night. I reminded him he'd known the plane's departure time and had missed it through his own blabbing fault. I told him he was on his own. We proceeded to have a shouting match in the parking lot of the county building.

The last straw was him calling me a wren-tit. I have no idea what kind of bird that is; maybe it's adorable, maybe it looks like a short blond lawyer. I didn't care. I lost it. I called Fulmer a pretentious dick, a New Age drama queen, and an insult to rational discourse. And that was before we raised our voices.

About the time he was commenting on my lawyering skills ("I've heard better oratory from Harpo Marx—honk, honk!"), I noticed a white van cruising slowly, one row of parked cars away.

I struggled for a glimpse of the driver, convinced it was the same van I'd spotted on San Vittorio Road before Alan Miller's house burned. Fulmer, annoyingly, was in my way. Thinking only of catching sight of the van's driver, I put my hand on Fulmer's arm and gave him a bit of a push, the slightest jostle so I could see past him.

Fulmer responded with an oath, then punched me just below the collarbone. In addition to having the wind knocked out of me, I was as mad as a hornet (certainly madder than a wren-tit). And I remained determined to see more of the van, if it wasn't too late. I shoved Fulmer again, harder this time.

He started shrieking and slapping at me as if he were shooing away a mosquito. I slapped back. And then, abruptly, a wall of deputy sheriff stood between us.

The deputy, his car parked just a few feet away in the sheriff's section of the lot, began barking out instructions: "Hands up, don't move. I said, let me see your hands. I mean it, don't move! Move again, and you'll find yourself under arrest."

And so I might have been if Patrick Toben himself hadn't come out and vouched for me. As it was, Fulmer and I were warned at humiliating length that the matter would be dropped only if neither of us wished to press charges.

Fulmer assured the deputy I didn't deserve the title of criminal, not for shoving one about like a bloody fishwife and hurling paltry insults!

It was all I could do not to lunge at him again. (A fishwife was clearly a demotion from a wren-tit.) I was especially peeved to realize I hadn't gotten the van's license number.

When Fulmer stomped off to go God knew where, the assistant DA invited me into his conference room to discuss Maria Nanos. I went along, despite his annoying little smile.

As we climbed the charmless cement stairs, Toben commented, "I don't think I've ever duked it out with a witness, especially not my own."

"I didn't want to call him as a witness, believe me."

"Well, I probably shouldn't admit this, but I wasn't expecting that glucose thing."

I nodded. "It surprised me, too, when I found out."

"Coincidences are like that," he said blandly.

I trailed after him. As he held the door of the conference room open for me, he added, "We'll be calling the guys who made those circles as witnesses."

I turned. "What are you talking about?"

"We just picked them up making some more. Botany graduate students. You know how they are at that age."

"You're saying you found students making crop circles?"

"That's right."

"Making them today?"

"Uh-huh."

"And they claim they made the glucose molecule?"

"I haven't talked to them yet, so I'm not sure what they claim. But it stands to reason, doesn't it?"

"It stands to reason they heard about the crop circle—saw the picture in the paper, saw it on the news—and decided to try to copy it." I hoped. Oh God, did I ever hope. "Where's this circle you caught them making?"

"I'm not sure yet. We'll let you know."

He wouldn't "let me know," he'd tell me the exact location before I left the damn building. If there was one thing I'd learned from my mother, it was how to make a nuisance of myself.

A young man in a dark suit intercepted us at the conference room door. He asked Toben for a minute. Toben waved me inside before stepping away for a quick in-the-hall conference.

When he joined me at the table, he said, "Good news! They found Maria Nanos. They've got her in a car on her way here."

"Who's they?"

"Big Sur park rangers turned her over to some deputies. She should be here in a couple of hours."

"Are the grandparents still in town?"

"They were yesterday." He didn't look very happy about it. "And they sure didn't express plans to leave."

I remembered Monday's scene. "You're not turning Maria over to them, are you?"

"That's up to Child Protective Services."

"Her grandfather threatened to break her legs."

Toben ran a casual hand over his hair. "And if he meant it, that's one thing. If it was just shock, that's another." He smiled. "They'd just heard for the first time that their fifteen-year-old grandaughter was pregnant.

I think you'd get a pretty strong reaction to that from a lot of people."
When I started to protest, he added, "You're not going to tell me you
don't lose your temper sometimes?"

I felt myself blush. Goddam Fulmer.

"Where have the grandparents been staying?"

"Holiday Inn." The hotel was a stone's throw from the courthouse.
"Waiting. To some purpose, luckily."

"What are you going to do with Maria tonight?"

"We'll have to keep her in custody until she testifies."

Unfortunately, I'd been right. The rape/screen memory theory had
returned with Maria.

As if to confirm my fear, Toben said, "So this puts her back on
the witness list. She'll be our first rebuttal witness. Followed by our
psychiatrists—you've got their names already."

I sighed. The case would last another week for sure. But what the
hell, thanks to Cary Curtis, I had the time.

29

I'd planned to go home for the weekend. In fact, I'd planned to leave that evening. But
thank goodness I'd stowed a pair of jeans in my trunk. It would be hours
before I knew when and whether I could get away.

I went straight from Toben's office to Edward Hershey's. I wanted to
talk to Alan Miller about Maria Nanos's return. And because the DA
was going to put her in custody, I wanted to see her as soon as possible,
let her know she could call me anytime.

"She might admit the truth—who the father really is—once she's
confronted with her grandparents. Who knows?" I felt guilty offering
Alan this slight hope. But he needed it; he'd just heard himself ridiculed
on the evening news. "In the meantime, Carl Shaduff's coming by for
us. Some botany students made a crop circle up near the university. I
want to take pictures of it, see if there are enough similarities for Toben
to link it to the one behind Joseph's."

Alan looked alarmed, so I was glad to hear a knock.

But when I opened the door, I could tell by Shaduff's face he hadn't come about the crop circle.

He said, "Kraduck's been shot."

I took a backward step. "The colonel?" As if he'd tell me about some other Kraduck.

"In the hotel parking lot. I heard the news on a police scanner—private frequency, which I'm not supposed to have access to. I've been over there the last half hour."

"Is he—? He's not—?"

"He's fine. Bruised as hell and possibly a broken rib from the impact."

"Who shot him? Did they catch the guy?"

"He was shot from a car driving by the parking lot, he says. Didn't get the license number, all they have is a description." Shaduff stepped past me into the room. His red face made his hair look like polar bear fur. "He'd have two bullets in his chest except for the vest."

"Why was he wearing it?"

"Beats the hell out of me. I didn't get anywhere near him. I did get one of the city cops to talk to me a little bit. Was Kraduck wearing a vest in court?"

I recalled the colonel in a blazer and open-collared shirt. "I don't think so. He might have been wearing one today when I saw him; he had on a bulkier jacket."

"The better vests aren't too obvious. He was wearing a windbreaker over it tonight. Climbing into a rental car." Shaduff jerked his head toward the door. "We should go."

"To the hospital?"

"No, they won't let us near Kraduck, not for a while. I was thinking we should talk to Bustamonte and Fichman. Neither of them's checked out yet. They might know something."

I turned to grab my jacket, and found Alan flattened against a bookcase. His eyes were wide and he seemed to be holding his breath. "Do you want me to come?"

"We should minimize your contact with witnesses; it just complicates things." I didn't want to be answering subpoenas for nonexistent notes and tapes of Miller's meetings with them.

Alan exhaled, looking relieved.

I followed Shaduff out to his Road Ranger.

"I tried Fred Hershey's pager when it happened," Shaduff said. "Tried to get a message to you."

"But Fred didn't get back to you," I guessed. Fred had a way of being gone when one was looking for him.

Shaduff, scowling as he got his truck into gear, didn't reply.

Ten minutes later, we were in Bart Bustamonte's room, a hovel of heaped clothes and scattered notebook pages. Dan Fichman hadn't checked out, but he wasn't in the hotel.

Behind Bustamonte, a picture window framed gulls spinning over a silver gray sea.

He was saying, "I don't get it, I just don't get it. Kraduck's one of the government's biggest disinformation specialists. Why would they try to whack him?" He ran a beefy hand over his cheeks, wiping away sweat.

"You think the government had something to do with it?" The man was as paranoid as my mother.

"Who else gets off a couple of nice, clean shots, then gets away? It's got to be the military or one of the alphabet agencies."

"The shots," Shaduff pointed out, "weren't so nice and clean—torso shots from a moving car right there in the parking lot. Seems to me the military would have put a marksman somewhere farther away. And they'd have aimed for the head. If they even do shit like this, which, who knows?"

Bustamonte waved the suggestion aside. "They'd only do it that way if they wanted to leave a calling card! Kraduck's military—he'd know the current weapon of choice and the standard approach. It's no coincidence he had on a bulletproof vest."

"Whoever did it might have it in for UFOlogists in general." Shaduff seemed to be baiting him. "Not Kraduck in particular."

"Come on. A man's shot twice and it turns out he's wearing a vest? Kraduck saw it coming. Maybe a few nuts have it in for UFOlogists, I don't know. But I'll tell you this—the only times I wished I had a bulletproof vest, I was in the desert near Area Fifty-one being chased by black helicopters!"

"Maybe someone who watched the news about the trial," Shaduff continued. "Some religious nut, someone who thinks you guys are full of shit."

"Yeah, yeah, plenty of people think we're full of shit. But so what?" Bustamonte demanded. "Who isn't?"

"When did you last see Kraduck?" We could get existential some other time.

"About six o'clock he knocked on my door to say so long. He said he was on his way to Travis."

"Travis Air Force Base?" My mother had hassled him in the courthouse corridor just this morning, accusing him of having her arrested at Travis. "Why was he going there?"

"He didn't say; I didn't ask." Bustamonte shook his head cynically. "I assumed he was going to report in. I'm telling you, Kraduck's not retired."

"Did he mention needing to talk to me?" Why had he come to the courthouse this morning? What would he have done there if he hadn't been set upon by my mother? Watch the rest of the trial? Or relay a message, confide some problem?

"No, he didn't mention you. Except to say you put us up in a better hotel than Fulmer."

"Reginald Fulmer? What did he mean?"

"He said you put Fulmer at the Holiday Inn."

"Why did Kraduck think that?" Had he witnessed the scene in the parking lot? Spotted Fulmer flouncing toward the nearest hotel?

Bustamonte shrugged. "I didn't care, so I didn't quiz him. He's probably got operatives watching everything we do."

Shaduff looked puzzled. "Why did he say good-bye to you? You in particular?"

"Good question," Bustamonte agreed. "We're not pals, no. But Karollas is already gone. And I suppose Fichman wasn't in his room."

I knew from my interview with Kraduck that he didn't approve of Dan Fichman.

"He puts on a bulletproof vest," Bustamonte continued, "then he knocks at my door and tells me where he's going. Like he wants me to know, in case he doesn't make it back."

"I heard someone . . ." I didn't want to drag my mother into this. "Someone mentioned he'd been stationed at Travis."

"Well, I doubt he was on his way to a reunion party, not in that vest."

Shaduff stood at the picture window. Outside two gulls hovered, caught in an updraft. They were as motionless as the other night's unmarked helicopters.

"We're going to lose our daylight," Shaduff pointed out.

I stood. I needed to photograph the new crop circle before it got trampled. "There's something else you could do for us," I told Bustamonte. "If you don't have other plans?"

Bustamonte glanced at his papers. "You pay me, and my plans can wait."

We left immediately, Shaduff driving his Road Ranger as if it were a monster truck. He sped past the university entrance up a steep, winding mountain grade. He pulled up to a fire access gate hung with university No Parking signs.

As we climbed out, Bustamonte nodded up the road. "You know they're building parts for stealth bombers just ten or so miles from here?"

"No, I didn't know that."

We skirted the gate, starting down a path through an oak-studded meadow. I was surprised my mother hadn't mentioned a manufacturer of stealth bombers, one so close to home.

"Wait a minute . . ." Years ago, we'd reached a moutaintop Lockheed plant by taking a turn somewhere off Highway 1. A group of us protested their building first-strike nuclear weapons. We sat for hours in front of a chain-link fence while security guards milled around a distant, inaccessible guardhouse. I'd returned home covered with mosquito bites. "Is it a Lockheed plant? Building nuclear missiles?"

"Used to build missile triggers; now it's stealth bomber guts." Bustamonte nodded. "Scary looking place way up where this road dead-ends; all fenced off, warning signs everywhere, not even an intercom for visitors to try to talk their way in."

The path wound through mixed forest with madrones blossoming as if hung with white piñatas. Tiny irises dotted the duff.

Bustamonte added, "That's probably why you get UFOs up here. Most sightings are near air force bases, nuclear test sites, weapons research and development plants. Lockheed's probably your magnet."

I wondered if I should bring it up in court. Or would jurors resist the suggestion they were living near a UFO "magnet"? Especially one that presumably employed hundreds of locals.

"They seem to monitor us," Bustamonte continued cheerfully. "Regular sightings started over Nevada the year we began testing A-bombs there. The more bombs we dropped, the more of them we spotted. We've still got them in droves over the Nevada and New Mexico desert, where we fly fighters and test weapons." He stopped abruptly when the path reached another meadow. "There it is."

The new crop circle was only some twenty yards to our right. The trail, I'd been told, ended above a science building housing the botany labs.

As if reading my mind, Bustamonte commented, "They weren't out to fool anyone, putting it so near their own department."

I noticed he was wheezing with the exertion of the short hike, sweating profusely despite a cool evening breeze. But then, he carried more weight than Shaduff and I combined.

We waded through thigh-high grasses with fluffy beige and green heads. Out of the shade, the air buzzed with insects and the warm meadow smelled like hay.

Shaduff unslung his camera and snapped the cover off the lens.

Bustamonte stopped us a few feet from the circle, looking at it. "Classic pattern," he commented.

It was a smallish circle, perhaps fifteen feet across, with four smaller ones bracketing it like a cross.

"A quincunx," he continued. "A Celtic cross. They show up a lot, sometimes several times per season. The kids who made this obviously did their homework."

I scrutinized the main circle for the swirl pattern I'd seen behind Joseph Huizen's house.

Bustamonte followed my gaze. "Nice clockwise spiral. They definitely know their stuff."

"A crop circle expert visited the university last month. I'm told he talked about them nonstop."

Shaduff was starting to snap pictures. I'd hoped they would show a shabby, asymmetric mess, not a fine forgery like this.

"So it could pass for a real crop circle?"

"Oh, no," Bustamonte scoffed. "It doesn't look like a real circle. I'm just saying the hoaxers tried hard. They went to a lot of trouble and they did a good job. I'm impressed."

He walked to one of the smaller circles.

I followed. It, too, looked like Joseph Huizen's circles. The mix of grasses might be slightly different, but they were flattened in the same spiral pattern.

"What's wrong with this one?" I asked. "How can you tell it's a fake?" I motioned Carl Shaduff over to take a picture of whatever the problem might be.

I almost cursed when Bustamonte said, "You can feel it, for one thing." He noticed the look on my face. "No, really. A crop circle's got a whole different energy signature—measurable, if you have a dowsing rod. And if you've been inside enough of them, you get to recognize a certain je ne sais quoi."

"Yeah, well, je ne sais quoi doesn't exactly hold up in court."

Shaduff was squatting, looking at the swirled grass. "The grass looks a little different."

"Of course," Bustamonte agreed. "It's smashed, mashed, and torn." He plucked a stalk, holding it out to me.

The base was held together only by stringy plant fibers.

"If this were a real circle, you might have some splitting at the lowest growth nodes. You might have swelling or darkening of the nodes. But usually you find healthy-looking grain with very little rupture or splitting where it bends. You don't find trampled-looking, broken grass like this." Bustamonte nodded. "They probably attached a plank or a lawn roller to a central spool of string to get the spiral; you know, basically walked around the maypole. But they put too much pressure on the grass as they went around."

"The DA will use this circle to discredit the other one. Even if the students admit they didn't make that one, the DA will show all kinds of photos of this. He'll go on about how perfect and well swirled it is. And the jury will think, If someone faked this one, someone else faked the other one."

"Probably," Bustamonte agreed. "I've seen it happen: Multiple UFO sightings somewhere, and next thing you know, the air force is all over the sky flying everything you can think of. The next time there's a report, they say, See, it's just us. Same with the crop circles. This isn't the first time I've seen phony circles get made to divert attention from real ones."

It was hard not to have a knee-jerk reaction to his conspiracy talk; I'd been supersaturated by my mother. On the other hand, I was standing inside a hoaxed crop circle that could ruin my case. And one of my expert witnesses was in the hospital.

Shaduff began photographing individual mashed stalks. "So who's making the crop circles? Really?"

"Not who, what. Some of them are phony, no doubt about it—you can tell when you get down and look closely; it looks like this. But the genuine circles, the grain's not broken—the cell-pit and growth-node changes are similar to what you'd get if you microwaved the grain for thirty or forty seconds. The ground underneath isn't marked at all, no crumbling of fragile dirt clods. And the grain isn't just swirled, the stalks are interwoven. A lot of those circles are preceded by sightings of small balls of light, sometimes high in the sky, sometimes down low, just a few feet off the ground. And I don't mean a few sightings—we have dozens and dozens of witness statements."

Shaduff looked skeptical. "Little light balls? How little?"

"Six inches, a foot."

"And how do they make the circles?"

"Our best guess? Remember, no one's actually seen them getting made—at least, not that we can verify; you always get claims, some of them pretty ridiculous. But judging from the microwave-zapped look of the grain and zero disturbance to dirt underneath . . ." He stared at the quincunx. "We assume the patterns are painted into the crop from above. Quick swirling strokes of light or energy or radiation, like an expert's brush on a canvas."

Shaduff sighed, shaking his head slightly. He went back to photographing stalks.

"So you think Fulmer's right?" I perished the thought. "About them being pictograms?"

"Pictograms? How could I begin to guess? We could be dealing with something that doesn't visualize or process images the way we do. Would you hold up a bit of greenery chomped by a snail and call it a pictogram? What about the pattern of dots when an octopus moves its legs? Or the trail a beetle leaves in the dust? The whole concept of pictograms is meaningless if you don't know what you're dealing with. That's what makes Fulmer an idiot. He's so sure we're being given an *answer*. Well, I'm sorry, but we don't even know what the question is. *If* there's a question. We've only got what we've got. We've got what's in front of our eyes."

Shaduff rose from his squat, appraising him. "So you don't have a pet theory? Based on what you've seen?"

"What I've seen? Look, when white men first weighed anchor in the New World, the Indians saw the rowboats the sailors were using to get to shore, but they couldn't see the big European ships farther back in the water. They thought they saw some clouds, but they couldn't recognize ships. Because they'd never seen any craft bigger than a canoe before." Bustamonte waved an arm over the phony crop circle. "We're just as culture bound in our perceptions. You know, I was just having this conversation with that damn chihuahua Fichman. He's up in arms over funding cuts to SETI."

Knowing Fichman's unbridled faith in scientific projects, I wasn't surprised he supported NASA's Search for Extraterrestrial Intelligence.

"Here's SETI," Bustamonte continued, "with its big old antennae pointing out into space listening for radio signals from beyond. What are the odds that anything out there communicates like we do, and on wavelengths we can monitor? I mean, good heavens, isn't that like assuming they drink black tea with two lumps of sugar? It's so culture bound it's embarrassing."

"And so is trying to interpret the crop circles?" I followed up.

"Did you know you can buy crop circle Tarot cards now? The pictograms have been interpreted by channelers—Change, Renewal, Dissatisfaction." To Shaduff, he said, "You're a private investigator, just like me. You go where the evidence is, and you look at it and you record it, and you believe it because it's right in front of your nose. You don't scientific-method yourself out of seeing what you see, like that prissy Fichman. And you don't force it into a Tarot deck, either. If crop circles are symbols, they're not *our* symbols. If they were, we'd have agreed years ago what they meant."

"The Celtic cross is one of our symbols," I pointed out. "You say it shows up in the wheat fields pretty often."

"Yeah, yeah. But you know, the Celtic cross comes from the area where these circles appear. It could be the Celts took something they kept seeing in their fields and hung it on their buildings, who knows?"

"What about the glucose molecule?" I pressed. "Showing up behind Joseph Huizen's house the same night glucose saved his life?"

"I think it's a bunch of baloney. You say the formation looks a little like a glucose molecule—*if* you twist up and flatten a drawing of what we *think* the molecule looks like. You want to bet me fifty bucks I could find something it looks even more like, something meaningful to me?"

I must have looked a little miffed.

He added. "I know you're trying a case and you're going with what works. You're doing your best to convince people there's a real phenomenon going on here. But see"—he mopped his cheeks with his shirtsleeve—"I already know it's real. I don't have to buy every circle or every theory; I can keep an open mind."

"So just out of curiosity," Shaduff chimed in, "what do you think of Alan Miller?"

"Hiding something," Bustamonte said. "He's lying about something." An apologetic glance at me. "Judging by how he acts. I've met almost four hundred abductees. They're in denial, they're emotional, they're a lot of things. But they're not furtive, they don't have that weird extra thing Miller's got."

"They're not on trial for manslaughter," I pointed out.

"That's true. That could be it." Bustamonte shrugged. "But also, his story's so . . . generic. Usually, they have some weird little signature, some observation that's part of who the person is, not part of what happened. Miller's tape, it didn't have anything like that; it sounded like an abstract, it sounded phony to me." He lowered himself to the ground as if unable to support his bulk any longer. Beads of sweat glistened through his thinning hair. "But again, I've got the luxury of knowing these stories are true. I've interviewed a lot of folks, and I believe them, so I know it's not bullshit. I can point to an individual story and say, *That's a piece of crap.*"

"Whereas I have to believe Miller or I got fired for no reason." I spoke before thinking.

Shaduff whistled. "Your law firm fired you? Man, that's cold."

Bustamonte looked up at me. "Fuck 'em if they can't take the truth." He smiled. "Now there's a slogan for your new business card."

30

We barely made it back to Shaduff's Road Ranger before night fell. I was exhausted from a long day and itchy from standing in a bug-filled field.

But after picking up my car, I stopped at Edward's house. I told Alan the new crop circle was different from the one behind Joseph Huizen's. I hoped he'd be relieved to hear Bustamonte would testify to that effect.

Alan, it turned out, was less than effusive. Presumably he wanted to be acquitted, but he definitely didn't want any of this to be true.

I didn't like to add to his burdens, but I couldn't forget Bustamonte's suspicions. "Alan, is there something I should know?"

He squirmed on Edward's couch. "What do you mean?"

I voiced my most concrete suspicion: "There's history between you and Leonard Deally, isn't there?"

His face went blank. It looked like an expression he'd practiced. "No."

"You didn't know him in college?"

"No."

"But you met him somewhere—you pointed him out to me in court."

"I've seen his picture in the paper. Sometimes they run it next to his column."

"But you seemed afraid of him."

Alan jumped when the phone rang. We sat in silence while the machine screened the call.

It was Patrick Toben. I picked up.

"We've got a problem," Toben said. "We were doing okay with Maria Nanos till she saw her grandparents. Then she got hysterical—you ever watch a cat when a big dog comes in the room? She practically ran straight up a wall. Anyway, don't ask me how the kid managed it, but she got away from us."

"She got away? From you and the deputies?" I couldn't keep reproach out of my voice. Maria might never get her life straightened out now, might never have a second chance. "You let her run away?"

"We didn't want her handcuffed, not for the family meeting. And deputies in the room just add to the tension." He didn't even sound defensive. "She absolutely flipped. We weren't prepared for it. She was so hyper she made it past everybody—right out the building. We've got cars cruising the neighborhood now, looking for her."

"What are the grandparents doing?"

"I have to tell you, they're not calm. They're talking a lot of crazy talk. We had to get some Family Support people up here to deal with it."

"When you find Maria, you're not going to send her home with them, are you?"

"That's not up to this department."

"What about murder investigation? That's up to you. Maria thinks they killed her mother."

I was distracted by the doorbell.

"Why don't you go ask them—?" Watching Alan answer the door, I lost my train of thought.

When I saw who stood on the porch, I said, "Oh, never mind," and hung up.

Maria Nanos stepped inside, looking over her shoulder. She almost collided with Alan, who was stuttering out sentence fragments.

"Oh, good; it's you!" She slammed the door shut. "I wasn't sure what address . . . the phone book under 'Hershey.' I guessed Fred was short for Edward."

I was confused. Had I mentioned bunking with Fred?

She leaned against the closed door, looking none the better for her days of camping. Her hair was stringy, her sweater streaked with dirt, her jeans stiff. Her backpack was gone, probably still in a County Jail locker.

She spoke in a rush. "I have to leave here, they'll look here. You've got to help me—please!"

"Maria, I know this is hard, but you have to go back and face—"

"No!" She flattened against the door as if I'd struck her. "You've got to help me get away! I'll kill myself if they put me in jail again!" Her face twisted like a sobbing toddler's.

Within seconds, she snapped out of it, looking manically around the room. "Is there a back door? Could I have some money?"

Alan was reaching into his pockets. I stepped up behind him and grabbed his arm. I shuddered to think what the assistant DA would do with his giving her cash.

"You have to go back, Maria. I'm sorry, but you really do. I guarantee you won't end up with your grandparents again." Somehow I'd make good on the promise. "You can't keep running. You'll never be free of this, you'll never have a chance to get past it. And your baby—"

But she was already dashing into other rooms, looking for a door. She was muttering, "Oh my God, oh my God, they'll *be* here."

Alan looked at me as if I were a monster.

As Maria backtracked from the bedroom, she pushed me aside, knocking me into the bookcase. She ran into the kitchen. Alan followed.

It took me a second to regain my balance. I got to the kitchen as Maria flung open the back door. But I wasn't in time to stop her from erupting out into the yard. Alan, hand digging into his pocket, was right behind her.

I watched him follow her through the back gate.

By the time I got there, they were halfway down the alley. I could see that Alan wasn't chasing her, wasn't even passing her cash. He was running with her.

I started after them, my mind boggling at what this could do to my case, to Alan's life.

But worry didn't make me any fleeter of foot. When I emerged from the alley onto the street, I saw that they were already at the next corner.

Gasping for air after an unaccustomed sprint, I stood in the chilly night. Down the street, a coffee shop with a porch full of outdoor tables lit the pavement.

As Alan and Maria ran past it, he reached out his hand and she took it. They rounded the corner moving fast, holding hands.

Holding hands.

I stood there awhile trying to believe I was mistaken. Then I walked back to Edward's, hoping Alan had joined her out of sympathy and compassion, not self-interest or complicity.

But I was shaken by Bart Bustamonte's take on Alan. I was rattled by the sight of him running off with Maria. And I had trouble believing Maria had found us by misinterpreting the phone book.

I wondered what the police would make of it if they caught them together. I knew how Patrick Toben would argue it.

I went back through Edward's gate and yard, stopping for a glass of water in the kitchen. When I entered the living room, I saw someone there. I screamed.

"Willa! Don't do that! You scared me!" My mother, still in this morning's dress jeans, was sitting on Edward's couch.

"I scared *you?*" Even from here, I could smell cigarette smoke on her clothes. Since she didn't smoke, it meant she'd been to a meeting. "How did you find me, Mother?"

"I assumed you'd stay with Edward." Her tone was carefully neutral.

We'd had a few battles over her lingering fondness for my former boy-friend. "You didn't answer, so I came inside to wait."

"Edward's sailing through the Panama Canal. I'm staying with his brother, Fred."

"But this is Edward's house," she pointed out.

I dropped onto the couch beside her. The afghan stank of fish lures and mildew and visiting dogs. "It's Edward's house, but I'm not staying here. My client is. It's lucky you caught me."

"I wish you'd have let me come listen to your case today," she pouted. "I haven't heard you in court in ages."

"Next time." I shuddered involuntarily at the idea of Leonard Deally interviewing her.

"I didn't mean to embarrass you there at the courthouse, Baby. But when I saw *that* man . . ." Her expression again reflected an encounter with Dr. Mengele.

"Tell me about Colonel Kraduck. You say you remember him from Travis. What year was this?"

"Oh, about the time you got back from Boston. Right before you went to—" She stopped herself, knowing I hated any reference to the two long, painful months I'd spent in jail.

"What was Kraduck doing then? Do you remember his uniform? His rank?"

"A uniform's a uniform." Strands of flyaway yellow-white hair drooped over her forehead. With her bright blue eyes and old-handbag skin, without makeup or jewelry, she looked like the Minnesota-Lutheran-turned-union-activist-turned-radical-dinosaur that she was. "It was quite a few years ago."

"But you remember Kraduck's face? Are you sure?"

She nodded. "You know me and faces."

"He was shot tonight," I told her.

She jerked as if I'd slapped her. "He's dead?"

"He might have been. But he was wearing a bulletproof vest."

"Oh, good—then it has nothing to do with your case." She looked mostly relieved, maybe a little disappointed.

"Why do you say that?"

"Well, if he knew somebody was after him, then it has to do with his life, not yours. Right?"

"Maybe you have a point." I didn't tell her I'd been shot at twice since coming to town. "They didn't catch whoever did it. It was a drive-by."

She didn't comment.

"So you came down here to hassle me about SDI and alien abduction stories?"

"I came especially on a Friday so I could ride back with you." My mother wasn't one for polite denials. "I'm so glad I caught you."

"I was going to stay here this weekend. There've been a lot of developments." I had a sudden horrifying vision of my mother in Santa Cruz for the duration of my trial. "But . . ."

It was only two hours each way. For a mere four hours in transit, I could assure myself of a Mother-free courtroom. I could also pick up my mail and sleep in my own bed.

A pounding on the door interrupted my musing.

I opened it, expecting the police. I got a two-fer. Patrick Toben stood beside a cop.

"We had a lead Maria Nanos was in this neighborhood," he said. More likely, he'd attributed my suddenly hanging up on him to Maria appearing on the porch. "Is she here?"

"No." Without actually saying I'd put down the phone to greet my mother, I made a point of telling him she'd just arrived.

I'd have liked to be honest, to admit Maria had shown up here, then bolted. I wanted to help him; I wanted Maria to get counseling, find a foster family, go to college—things she'd never manage without intervention.

But I couldn't say more without getting my client into trouble we might never talk his way out of.

"Do you mind if we look around?" Toben asked.

"Go ahead. But you know this isn't my place. Don't touch any of the owner's stuff, okay?"

My mother jumped to her feet, clearly indignant over his request. I told her with a gesture to shut up.

Toben noticed. "We just want to look in the other rooms," he assured me. "We won't disturb anything."

The cop started in the kitchen. I could hear him open the back door and go out into the yard.

My mother was scowling, lips pursed as if to break into speech.

I didn't want a confrontation; I didn't want Toben asking point-blank if I'd seen Maria.

I babbled, "What did you do with the grandparents?"

"They're at the Holiday Inn again. Waiting."

The cop came back inside, leaving the kitchen and crossing to Edward's bedroom.

"That's Edward's private area!" my mother protested.

I flashed her a Medusa look. "I'm sure his underwear's all put away, Mother."

I moved close enough to elbow her, if need be.

"So where's Miller?" Toben wondered.

I was honest: "I don't know."

"He was here when I called."

"Why do you say that?" I'd answered the phone. Miller hadn't made any background noise, not that I recalled.

Were the police watching the house?

I felt myself scowl. If they were watching the front, they'd seen Maria enter. They'd seen her arrive, but not leave.

Was that why they'd come here? To catch her—and to catch us harboring her?

Toben and I had a staring contest. Finally he said, "I just had the impression Miller was here when I called."

The cop came out of Edward's bedroom. "Nobody," he confirmed.

"Well, what did you expect?" my mother fumed.

I squeezed her arm. I didn't want her prolonging the encounter. But I shot Toben a look telling him the accusation wasn't lost on me, either.

He chewed the inside of his cheek. "Okay, well . . . We'll call you when we get her back."

"If it's tonight, try me at my San Francisco number. I'm going back right now." Ten minutes with my mother had convinced me I couldn't risk her showing up in court next week.

Toben glanced at the cop, then asked, "You're returning to Santa Cruz when?"

"In the morning." I sighed for another lost weekend.

"I'll be in the office all weekend if you need me." Toben sighed, too.

31

My apartment was stuffy and stank of neglected perishables. My mail was mostly junk. And my bed wasn't as comfortable as I remembered.

I had a funny thought as I packed a fresh suitcase. Maybe I should move to Santa Cruz. Put a little distance between myself and my parents.

I'd spent a week in the Santa Cruz mountains last year. This year, in town, I was still liking what I saw. I could find a place near the beach. Maybe I needed a change.

Maybe not. First, I'd have to see if I got laughed out of town.

I stopped in Davenport on my way down the coast. I drove along San Vittorio Road. Yellow Caution Do Not Enter tape was still strung between fire department sawhorses in front of Alan Miller's house.

Alan had been escorted in by fire marshals and allowed to take some of his things from certain rooms. He'd been kept out of the living room, where the floor and walls were unstable.

As far as I knew, the arson investigation continued, but no one was saying anything beyond the fact that a space heater had sparked some kerosene. I'd have to try to get more details by Monday, before I wound up my case in chief.

I continued down the road. Donna Nelson's house looked vacant. The shades were pulled and the hollyhocks were wilted. The gate was wide open. A yellow dog moseyed through the yard.

The hill behind the houses was dotted with purple wildflowers that hadn't been in bloom last week. Overhead, big white clouds drifted through a pale blue sky. The field across the street rustled in the breeze. Even this far inland, I could smell the ocean.

It was a perfect Saturday. If I didn't get back on Highway 1 soon, I'd certainly get caught in beach traffic.

But first, I continued down the road, turning up Joseph Huizen's bumpy driveway. Yesterday, he'd left the courtroom before I'd had a chance to talk to him.

We'd had only minutes to prepare his testimony, so I'd decided not to tell him the crop circle resembled a glucose molecule. I hadn't wanted him to become self-conscious; I hadn't wanted him stumbling over a description of the IV, overemphasizing it or giving it short shrift.

But I wondered how he'd reacted to later testimony, what he'd thought of Fulmer's theory.

I knocked at his door, assuming he was too much a scientist to buy it. I imagined he'd agree with Bustamonte that it took an inordinate amount of twisting to make the molecule model two-dimensional. And that the model was just a conceptual guess, anyway.

Maybe I'd come here for a comforting dose of conventional science.

When Joseph opened the door, I stepped back in alarm. He wore pajamas and a robe, he needed a shave, there were circles under his eyes, and his thin white hair hung in limp, uncombed strands.

"Are you okay?" My manners didn't equal my concern.

"Oh, the pajamas; I'm sorry. I didn't make it to bed last night. Last night was *marvelous!*" He grinned like a boy on a bumper car. "Please, come in."

I stepped inside, hoping his mania hadn't led to more smashed lamps and broken furniture. I followed him into his airy kitchen, relieved to see things unharmed, if untidy.

He practically skipped to the table—not something I expected from a man his age or his size. Behind him, picture windows framed a flower-dotted hill. A hummingbird with invisibly quick wings stared in at us, then flew off as if jerked by a string. I felt as if I'd suddenly wandered into an outtake from *Mary Poppins*.

"I got it, I really got it. I can hardly believe it, but I've been checking it and checking it, and it still works." His pale blue eyes glittered. "I solved it. The tetrahedron inside the spinning mass, it—Oh, never mind the details. If there's one thing I've learned over the years, it's that it doesn't make sense to people one invites in for coffee." He pulled out a chair. "Is coffee all right? Is there anything you'd rather have?"

"Coffee's perfect."

I sat at a table an inch deep in scratch paper anchored with calculators, rulers, and protractors. The calculators had about forty extra buttons. The papers were penciled with equations and diagrams and measured angles. Some were marked in red pen. A few numbers were circled in blue. The floor around my chair was also littered with paper, most of it traversed with impatient cross-outs.

Joseph bent close to the tabletop, setting his cheek on the papers. He turned his face and kissed them several times. Then he went to the counter and began making coffee.

"I'm sorry to be so selfish. You probably have things you want to talk about." He cast me a look that said, *If so, get it in now.* "It's just that I've never had such a breakthrough, such a 'Eureka!' moment."

"I take it you discovered something last night?"

"Not just discovered something. Not the way academics 'discover' things today. This is *real*, not a mere embellishment on so-and-so's footnote in someone else's journal article. This is . . . well, I don't want to explode with hubris, but it may be the kind of thing that comes along only once in a generation. Unless I've gone completely foolish." He looked stricken by the notion. "But I've checked it over and over again. It seems to work, it really does."

"The mathematics of spinning bodies?"

"To drastically oversimplify it, yes."

"Is this . . . ?" I hated to bring up anything so flaky. "Is this what you were talking about—you know, outside with the imaginary lights—when the medics picked you up?"

"That's right! I was consulting a pattern of stars—I mean, as part of my hallucination. And they gave me a suggestion. What a suggestion!" He grinned. "It took glucose starvation for me to get this clue. And perhaps I should be embarrassed that it came to me in an altered state. But it works! I finally figured out what I was trying to say to myself that night. I finally got the numbers to click."

He finished pouring water through the coffee cone. I noticed his hand was trembling.

While the coffee brewed, he fumbled through his notes, trying to explain to me, in layman's terms, what he'd concluded. It was so far over my head it would have taken a spaceship to get me anywhere close to understanding it.

But I was grateful for the coffee. And he gave up blessedly soon on the explanation.

"Did you stay for the rest of the court session yesterday?" I asked him.

"Oh, yes! The glucose molecule crop circle! Only this"—he nodded at the notes he'd just gathered and stacked—"could have driven it from my mind."

"So you heard Reginald Fulmer's testimony?"

"My first thought was that it couldn't be possible. It gave me such a case of heebie-jeebies I could hardly drive home." He looked alarmed recalling it. "It seemed the most oppressive burden. Imagine the universe leaving graffiti in your yard."

"That's why I came to see you today. It gave me the heebie-jeebies, too," I confessed. "And I wanted to make sure you weren't angry."

"Angry?"

"That you didn't think I'd exploited you or played up a weird coincidence at your expense; something like that."

"Heavens, no. You have to do your job as a lawyer." He patted my hand. "When I got over the, well . . . *physical* reaction to the strangeness of it, I started to think, What if it's true, old man? What does it mean?"

He looked at me as if expecting an answer.

"I flipped it this way and that way and every which way," he continued. "But it continued to suggest an interest in me. An interest large enough, cosmic enough . . . Well, I'm afraid I'll get stricken down dead if I go on in this Olympian way. But thinking about it put me in the oddest mental state, almost a meditation. It was so shocking, it drove everything else from my head." He looked puzzled. "I've never gone in for Eastern religions, but this must be close to what they're talking about. Emptying your mind of all its noisy little thoughts to make room for something larger. That's what it was like. It was like a mantra. A marvel that I turned over and over like a jewel."

"But you were okay?" I needed to know, even in the face of his obvious bliss, that I hadn't harmed him.

"More than okay. That's when the insight struck, just like that, in an instant, a nanosecond. My life's toil didn't amount to a hill of beans by comparison. I just . . . *got* it. It suddenly made perfect sense. I saw how it worked and why it worked."

His smile was so young, so dashing. I felt I saw him, for the space of that quick grin, as the boy he'd been fifty years ago.

"You can work with mathematics for an entire career, write books, teach others, and have it be mere industry. You might as well work in a numbers mine, chipping and piling and equating. It's so easy to forget that mathematics is magic, that it's the poetry of the universe."

He sighed, taking a long swallow of coffee. "Actually," he confided, "I hate poetry. It always seems like too many words, spoken with more meaning than they really have. I've been dating a poet since my wife died. So I never get to say how I feel about it." He snickered. " 'Open mike,' in my opinion, is a synonym for 'purgatory.' "

I laughed. The universe had chosen a worthy recipient for it's glucose-shaped love note. Even if it had, possibly, spoken through botany students armed with twine and a lawn roller.

32

On my way down the coast, I slowed at the scene of Miller's accident. Naturally, there was no trace left. And naturally, the cars behind me honked.

They were even less glad to see traffic stalling up ahead of me.

In no mood for a traffic jam, I pulled onto the access road to the farmer's sprouts field. I might as well have another look up there. Maybe I'd see something I'd missed before, some clue we'd all ignored. Or maybe the universe had decided to leave me a cosmic Post-it, like Joseph's.

The field, I found, had been rototilled and replanted with rows of spiky-leafed plants. I had a vague idea they were artichokes. Apparently the time had come to segue from Brussels sprouts to something edible.

I parked near the No Trespassing sign and started picking my way through plants so jaggedly pointed they looked like they were being grown as weapons. About a third of the way across I stepped over ruts left between rows by the farmer's truck. The tire tracks, deep in irrigated dirt, were easily a foot across. Two of my Honda tires would have fit inside.

The prosecution was right about one thing: If this truck had driven over Fiat tracks, it would have obliterated them.

I continued toward the "cliff" and began walking between the cultivated area and the weedy verge dropping off to the highway. Now that the field was irrigated, the dirt was softer near the unwatered edge, still dry but less like hardpan. Three weeks ago, Toben and the deputies argued, this margin had been too hard to show tracks. When I reached the spot where the accident happened, I looked down.

Twenty feet below, northbound traffic clipped along. But the other lane wasn't moving at all. Perhaps a quarter mile up, two shirtless men pushed a Jeep toward a turnout.

I wondered, with a commuter's impatience, why it was taking them so long. As I turned, I almost fell over the wooden handle of a gardening tool sticking out of the weeds.

Annoyed, and a little concerned that a clumsier person (if one existed) might stumble off the cliff, I yanked it out of the greenery. It was a rusty metal rake, twice as long as I'd supposed.

I prodded the vegetation. Uneven growth made the edge appear level, made it look like three feet of flat, weed-covered ground ending abruptly. But beneath the plants, the ground dropped off at a forty-five degree angle before plunging straight down to the highway. Never having poked through the flora, I hadn't realized it.

I looked out across the field. If Miller's car really had sailed off the cliff here, sailed off at sufficient speed, his tires might not have made contact with the hidden slope. There was a chance, at just the right spot, that a car wouldn't crush plants between the ground and the wheels, after all.

No wonder the sheriff's deputy testified that a "disembanking" car wouldn't necessarily damage any greenery. But he hadn't made his reasoning clear; not to me, anyway. Not even under cross-examination, when he'd merely cited the "slope angle."

I could only hope the jury had missed the point, too. And that Patrick Toben didn't prepare a diagram to use in closing arguments.

I walked back to my car worrying: That the farmer really had overridden Miller's tracks sometime before the sheriff arrived to check the field. That Alan Miller did indeed sail off this field onto the highway. That he was lying about the alien abduction. Or that he was crazy, as he seemed to fear.

That he was guilty of manslaughter, after all.

I climbed into my car recalling how Miller had taken hold of Maria

Nanos's hand last night, how he'd run away with her. I hoped it was impulsive gallantry. I feared there was some preexisting attachment between them.

I was relieved to find Highway 1 traffic moving again. I slowed down out of curiosity when I passed the stalled Jeep. It was up on jacks with two tires off. Two flat tires: easy to see why it had taken so long to push it. I was impressed the men had rolled it so far on its rims.

But suddenly, it made me wonder. Having opened myself to one paranoia, I found another piggybacking in.

No one had witnessed Miller and Addenaur's accident. No one knew how long the cars had been stacked there before discovery.

What if Addenaur's car hadn't been crushed beneath the sprouts field at all? What if the accident happened a little farther south, where another field rose above the highway? What if the cars had been rolled to the spot where they were found?

I remembered noticing, when Fred and I looked down from the Brussels sprouts field, the stains of another accident on the highway.

I tried to calm down. Think of the cleanup it would have involved: sweeping and moving glass beads and twists of metal. All at night. And easily foiled by a single passing car.

No, it didn't make sense. Not unless someone didn't want the police looking in the right field for tire tracks.

I slowed my Honda. I guess I was afraid not to check. I was afraid an unjustified lack of confidence in my client would show, that the jurors would smell it on me, hear it in my voice.

I turned onto the next inland road. There, I found an easily accessed field that dropped straight off onto the highway. It was freshly tilled, stinking of fertilizer. Any tracks that might have been on it were gone now.

I told myself it didn't prove anything. What would Miller be doing here in the wee hours of a Saturday morning? As with the sprouts field farther north, there was no reason for him to take the side trip.

On the other hand, this would be an easier field mistakenly to veer into and across—if one were already heading west on this road.

Instead of returning to the highway, I followed the road inland to see where it went. I climbed through redwoods and oaks and pine-lined curves up into the coastal range. I'd spent a week in these mountains last year. Funny how much more beautiful the scenery was when the police weren't after you.

I turned onto another road, thinking I recognized it as the road to Lockheed. I'd been in the back of someone's VW when I'd gone there to protest with my parents, so my memories of the route were hazy. But it seemed worth a ten-minute detour to try to find Santa Cruz's UFO magnet.

I soon found myself at an end-of-the-road military-looking facility. But if it was Lockheed, it was totally unidentified.

A sign on a twelve-foot Cyclone fence read, "Absolutely No Trespassing or Loitering; Forbidden by Law." Slightly smaller signs read, "No Entry Without Permission; Closed to Public," and, "Trespassers Will Be Prosecuted Under Penal Code Sections 602," followed by a long list of subsections. Another sign read, "Photography Strictly Prohibited." Through the fence, I could see a guard station with one-way mirrored glass. Squinting, I could barely make out some of the writing on the sign beside it: "No Smoking, No Firearms, No Tape Recorders, No Cameras. All items to be deposited with guard until leaving facility." Beyond the guard station, a road wound through a compound of barrackslike structures. Behind them, a stand of trees blocked further view.

It had all the welcome signs I vaguely recalled decorating Lockheed's fence. But it should have been labeled "Lockheed Missile and Space Company." I remembered staring at the words, years ago, while mosquitoes rose out of roadside duff to bite every inch of me.

I wasn't sure if I'd found Lockheed or stumbled upon some other mountain stronghold. I made a mental note to ask Bustamonte.

I was turning my car around, backing onto the shoulder of the road, when I saw helicopters. There were two of them, big, dark ones, flying inland toward this facility. I couldn't guess whether these were the same type I'd seen at the hotel; it had been too dark that night, and these were too far away. I couldn't tell if either pair was "black." But they couldn't have scared me more if they'd been Black Riders from *The Lord of the Rings*.

The UFOlogists had spooked me with their shadow-government stories.

I was tucked beside the road, under cover of redwoods. For once, I was glad my Honda was a drab green. I cut the engine, hoping I wasn't visible from the air.

I watched the helicopters fly overhead, over the fence. I decided to wait a few minutes rather than risk being seen—and perhaps pursued —by them.

The next thing I knew, I was startled out of an uncomfortable doze by two large deer rustling along the shoulder of the road not two feet from my windshield. I looked at my car clock. It was past noon.

How could that be? How could I have lost almost two hours? I sat up, feeling achy and a little nauseated. My unintended nap had left me anything but refreshed.

I glanced at the guard station down the road, on the other side of the warning-laden Cyclone fence. It occurred to me—a little late in the game—that anyone inside could see me. If there was a guard in there and he had a radio, he might send someone out after me.

I took off down the mountain.

I careened around curves, remembering Bart Bustamonte's tale of black helicopters chasing him through the desert, bouncing off the roof of his car. I tried to take reassurance from it: Bustamonte was still around to tell the (maybe not so) paranoid tale. And he was a bona fide investigator, presumably a thorn in their side.

Except that I didn't know who "they" were. For all I knew, this compound belonged to a conservative committee of the State Bar, gunning for flaky lawyers.

I raced the rest of the way to Highway 1. Once there, I rolled down my window, drinking in the salty perfume of a sunny seacoast day.

I made myself stop wondering what kind of facility hides on a mountaintop without a single identifying plaque. I stopped thinking about the helicopters I'd watched fly into it. Because I couldn't afford to reflect on my sudden nap, not now. After the stories I'd heard lately, I was afraid I'd put a label like "missing time" on the experience.

No wonder Alan Miller couldn't believe he'd been abducted by a spaceship. I couldn't even come to grips with a couple of helicopters and a two-hour siesta.

33

I prayed, as I knocked at Edward's door, that I'd find Alan Miller there. When I didn't, I used one of the duplicate keys Fred made for us. I looked around. There was nothing in the living room to indicate whether Alan had returned.

Nor could I tell by the number of cups and dishes in the kitchen sink. I have an untidy woman's way of not noticing clutter, so it was hard to measure what I saw against last night's mess.

I was forced to break my long-standing vow and set eyes on Edward's bedroom. The room was surprisingly spartan, with old-fashioned wood furniture and a bed with no backboard.

The curtains were closed, but enough light filtered through the cheap weave for me to appreciate Edward's Navajo blankets and his dresser display of Northwest Indian carvings.

Right now, the cedar objects were pushed aside. The dresser top was covered with waxed paper, and several clusters of mushrooms were spread over it. I picked through them, amazed at how different they were from the ones in the supermarket. One group had frilly-looking caps with edges melting into black goo. A few were fluorescently bright red or yellow and seemed made of wax. Some weren't even shaped like mushrooms; they looked like little brains and corals and glops.

A tattered field guide lay beside them. I picked it up and began flipping through it. I saw pictures of fungi resembling fingers, clubs, nets, octopi; others you could dye with, write on, bake into cookies; some that attracted spore-transporting flies by stinking of carrion; carnivorous ones that invaded beetle bodies and consumed their flesh until only fungus filled the shiny insect shell (the photo showed a mushroom protruding from a beetle's back). I could understand Alan's thesis that fungi might be an alien life form. But then, I felt that way about Republicans, too.

I was about to replace the book on the dresser when my attention was caught by a section headed "Poisonous Mushrooms":

The most lethal of commonly occurring mushrooms in North America is the *Amanita phalloides*, or Death Cap, and it's springtime relative, the *Amanita ocreata*, or Destroying Angel. Its toxins typically do not cause illness for several hours or even two or three days, when they have caused enough liver and kidney damage that those organs no longer screen out everyday toxins. The body will, as it accumulates toxins, become susceptible to bruising, and there may be blood in the urine and delirium from poor liver function. Depending on the amount eaten, liver and/or kidney transplants may be the only hope for sustaining life.

I sat down on Edward's bed, book in hand, straining in the darkened room to read the rest of the section entitled "The Deadly Amanitas." Not only were they common, according to this author, but their survivors often remarked that the flavor was good. The picture showed big, standard-shaped mushrooms with nothing about them to disgust or deter.

Delirium and blood in the urine: it sounded like Miller's experiences before the sheriff's deputies came for him.

I slumped on Edward's bed, thinking. Alan had been at a mycology conference in San Francisco before the accident. Could a fellow fungus expert have poisoned him?

Or, given how long it took for the effects to be felt, maybe he'd been poisoned before he left Davenport. Maybe he was supposed to collapse at the conference, where other mycologists would be suspected of some kind of mistaken mushroom identification.

Maybe mushroom poisoning had made Alan Miller disoriented enough to take the wrong road, drive through a field, and land on top of Francis Addenaur.

I snickered, wondering if the jurors were having even half the doubts plaguing defense counsel.

I stood, about to return the book to the dresser. I checked the title page for author and publisher, thinking I'd buy a copy. It was published by an arty press in San Francisco, and I'd never heard of the author, K. L. Korlovatz. But the inscription made me catch my breath.

It was autographed, "To Leonard, Thanks for the great publicity."

Leonard Deally?

The possibility sent me on a brief detour through downtown, a bustling row of Italianate buildings, corner flower stands, and outdoor cafés. I picked up a triple espresso and a less soiled copy of the mushroom book. Maybe K. L. Korlovatz, if I tracked him through his publisher, could tell me how Leonard Deally and Alan Miller were connected.

Then I drove on to Fred's house.

Fred wasn't there. But for once he'd made himself easy to find. He'd left me a note asking me to phone his office. I stared at his tidy handwriting. Good news was easily jotted down. Only bad news needed telling.

Fred answered the phone with a clipped "Yes?"

"Hi." I couldn't quite bring myself to ask.

"Come to my office."

"Is it—? Have you talked to Alan?"

"Just come. We'll talk here."

"Is it about Alan?"

"Not directly. I'd rather talk here," he insisted.

"But—"

He hung up before I could finish objecting.

I found I was reluctant to meet him. It seemed to me that, once too often, Fred hadn't been where I'd expected him to be. I was beginning to worry that he had a secret agenda. Or worse, that he was following someone else's, perhaps reporting in to that person.

So before I rushed to oblige him, I made a few other phone calls. My first was to the hospital. Colonel Kraduck had been discharged. I tried the hotel, but he hadn't reregistered—perhaps being shot in its parking lot had soured him on the place.

Then I phoned the assistant DA. True to his word, Toben was in his office on this sunny Saturday.

"It's Willa Jansson. I'm back from San Francisco. Did you find Maria Nanos?"

All morning, I'd been in a fever to know. But I'd wanted to appear calm, no more concerned than I should be, not like someone whose client had run off with a witness. My unscheduled nap had made it easy to wait until afternoon.

"No. We've got deputies and city police looking. But it's hard on the weekend. We get anywhere from fifteen to fifty thousand tourists on a nice day like this. Unless she shows up at a beer brawl or a boardwalk knifing, everybody's pretty busy."

"What about her grandparents? Did you ask about their daughter, Maria's mother?"

"Yes." A pause. "I asked them."

"What did they say?"

"They were very . . . excitable on the subject. But their basic point was that she was a prostitute. That she left Maria with them and took off to live that life."

"They called her a prostitute? That's probably just their old-fashioned ideas. They're so—"

"Maybe." He sounded a little peeved. "We have the mother's name; we're checking for arrests. But you know, it could be Maria's romanticizing things—girls come up with the most amazing *Perils of Pauline* stuff at her age. And if her mother really was a prostitute, you can see how the grandparents would want to keep the brakes on Maria."

I had a sudden suspicion: "Do you have teenage daughters?"

"Two of them."

No wonder our conversation was going nowhere. In part, he was talking about his overdramatic daughters and I was talking about my crazy parents.

"Call me if you find her." I gave him Fred's number.

On the way to Fred's office, I drove past beaches with high waves chasing flocks of shore birds. I dangled my arm out the window to feel the sun on my skin: the ten-minute vacation.

As I walked across Fred's tiny parking area, my worries begin to synergize. I tapped at his outer office door, feeling like just another patient with a panic disorder.

Fred, in a polo shirt, linen pants, and boating shoes without socks, looked like a man who should be lounging with a pink drink in his hand. But his face was anything but relaxed. His brows were pinched and he looked pale. His shoulders were hunched.

He said, "Those boys I told you about, Joey and Mickey?" He motioned me into the inner office and shut the door. "I played you Mickey's—"

"I remember." I hadn't heard so many alien abduction tapes that I was likely to forget one.

I settled into the rattan couch near the picture window. I was getting a bad case of spring fever; I couldn't keep my glance from straying to the view of redwoods in a sunlight-dappled gully. I could have been in Big Sur now.

Fred dropped into his usual chair. "The FBI arrested the father yesterday." He cringed slightly.

That got my attention. "Have you discussed Mickey's tape with them?"

"You don't understand." Fred ran both hands down the back of his head. "The father confessed. They found . . . he had pictures."

We stared at each other a minute.

"So what Mickey said under hypnosis, the aliens and all that . . . they *were* screen memories? His missing time was . . ." Horrible, poor kid, but not otherworldly.

Fred nodded. "Apparently some of it was straight out of an *X-Files* video they saw the night before. But that doesn't say anything one way or the other about Alan Miller's memories."

"Unless he saw the same *X-Files* episode. Which seems a lot more likely than a cruise ship from Zeta Reticuli docking in Davenport three weeks ago." Maybe it was just as well: I was sick of the strain of trying to believe something so unconventional. And maybe I needed reminding that usually, if not always, a nap is just a nap.

"You couldn't have offered testimony from those children anyway," Fred pointed out.

"It doesn't make any difference to my case," I agreed. "But it makes a difference to me, Fred. Me personally. I'm having a crisis of confidence." I shook my head wearily. "Worse yet, a crisis of flakiness."

34

Alan Miller was sitting on Edward's couch. He was scowling, elbows on splayed knees, his fingers laced, his head down. He looked like a kid getting yelled at by his mother. Or, more accurately, by his lawyer.

"Now I can't put you on the witness stand," I complained. "They'll ask you the last time you saw Maria Nanos, and you'll convict yourself right there."

"But all I did was get far enough away with her to give her some money." He looked up, his green eyes beseeching me to understand. "You saw how scared she was. And you said yourself the DA doesn't act like he believes her about her grandparents. I just wanted to help her."

"Money's not going to help her. Living on the street's not going to help her. She's not even sixteen, she's pregnant; she needs to get all this settled and get on with her life." I was confounded that he didn't see it that way. "Are you telling me everything?"

He sat up. "What do you mean?"

"I mean, you didn't just run after her, you took her hand."

"She was going so slow. I was speeding her up till we got past all those people outside the coffee place."

I continued pacing. Alan claimed he'd returned within half an hour to find me gone. This morning, he'd taken a brief hike, accumulating the mushrooms I'd found on the dresser. Then he'd showered and gone downtown.

He'd seemed surprised I hadn't realized he'd been back. "What about all the extra dishes in the sink? And the mushrooming gear?" He'd pointed to rubber boots, a filthy basket, and a trowel in a corner near the door.

I repeated, "Whatever your reasons, this is a real mess. I think the police spotted Maria coming here; I think that's why they searched the house. I could be disbarred for lying to the assistant DA." Technically, I hadn't lied, but it had been a matter of semantics. And semantics weren't much of a defense. "Now there's no way we can put you on the stand."

His relief showed.

"I realize you don't want to testify, but remember my opening statement? We promised to put your butt up there." With a sigh, I sat beside him. "Your story's most convincing coming from you. You don't seem like a weirdo; that's important to jurors."

He didn't respond.

"Do you know a mycologist named K. L. Korlovatz?"

"Why do you ask?"

"I bought his book today. Was he at your mycology conference? The one in San Francisco?"

"Uh-huh. There were mycologists there from all over the world." Alan watched me blandly. "It's a pretty good field guide; it's small enough to tote around. It's not as good as David Arora's." His tone told me no field guide was.

"What's K. L. Korlovatz like?"

He shrugged. "Loves mushrooms. Takes good pictures." He stood. "Give me five minutes. Nature calls."

I watched him head toward the bathroom.

He hadn't corrected me when I called K. L. Korlovatz a "he." But according to the publisher, Kathleen Korlovatz was definitely a "she."

Alan came out a few minutes later, prattling about Maria. "Whatever the DA says about it, it's his fault. She wouldn't have run away if he didn't threaten to keep her in jail. And if he didn't act like he was going to send her back to her grandparents." He sat beside me again. "I mean, I get your point about how she should straighten her life out. But it's not like I told her to run away; she was already out of here. I just caught up to her and gave her money so she'd have a place to sleep."

"She was going to be a witness against you. Now you've given her money so she can run away and not testify. Don't you see how that looks? This isn't about her, it's about you. It's about blowing a chance for acquittal." Maybe I'd gone too far; he looked stricken. "Not your only one. But damn, I wish I could put you on the witness stand."

He didn't say anything. It was a chance he'd blown willingly. Because he didn't want to testify? Because some other part of his testimony would be perjured?

"Where did you part company with Maria? Where do you think she was going?"

"Maybe Davenport. She said she lived in a tent village there for a while."

"It's not up anymore." Before I left Joseph's, I'd walked up the hill for a quick look. The circles were ragged now, blending back into the meadow. And the tents were gone, every one of them. "Where did you leave her?"

He hesitated. "The Boardwalk area."

I stood, not at all confident he was telling the truth. I was getting angry. If he couldn't see the foolishness of giving money to a pregnant runaway at a time when it could land him in prison; if he couldn't see the wisdom of telling his lawyer everything . . .

"Is the city library open on Saturdays?" I asked him.

He nodded. "It's the one-story building with all the glass walls, a couple of blocks this side of downtown."

I grabbed my handbag and set out.

I got to the library about twenty minutes before closing. In addition to the usual complement of parents with kids, large-print seniors, and high-schoolers laboring miserably over reports, the library seemed to be a dumping ground for street people, their arms flung across tabletops as they slept. Their smell mingled with book dust and Xerox exhaust and the faint breeze of blossoming trees outside. The large room was cool and quiet, reminding me of afternoons I'd escaped the madhouse at my parents' to hide in the library with a yellowed *Scaramouche.*

With the help of a reference librarian, I found the microfilm room.

I typed the name "Korlovatz" into a computer and found a half dozen references, all from the year the mushroom field guide came out. I began looking them up.

Sure enough, one was Leonard Deally's column. It effused about the poetic writing, wittily presented information, and fabulous photographs in a field guide no one should be without. I popped a quarter into the microfilm reader to make a copy.

A later review in the paper's arts supplement agreed that it was a fine field guide, although not on par with that of "mushroom king" David Arora, or as "antic" as the work of "mushroom bishop" Terence McKenna. (Making Alan Miller a mere mushroom pawn?)

In later newspapers, there were brief mentions that the author was signing books at local bookstores.

But the last of the articles, dated six months after the others, announced the engagement of Kathleen Korlovatz. The photograph showed a dark-haired, heavy-chinned woman in logger's flannel holding up a huge mushroom. Seated beside her was Leonard Deally.

At least, that's what the caption read. Leonard Deally, in presumably happier times, hadn't looked much like the priggishly overdressed and balding man he was today. Seated beside his fiancée, a slimmer Deally wore a T-shirt reading "Santa Cruz Fungus Fair."

The headline was *Columnist to Wed Mushroom Queen*. At least the paper didn't mix its metaphors.

I hastily fed in another quarter before the librarian shooed me out.

I sat on a bench in front of the library, smelling the dusty blossoms of nearby trees and watching their pollen catch the sun like drizzle. In the distance, in front of some sidewalk café, a jazz quartet played " 'Round Midnight," heavy on the vibraphone.

I'd found no follow-up article, no Deally-weds-Korlovatz. Something had gone wrong. And Deally no longer had possession of the field guide inscribed to him by his wife-to-be.

Somehow Alan Miller had ended up with it.

Alan and Kathleen, two pieces in the mushroom chess set; they had plenty in common. Perhaps they'd become romantic. And now, Leonard Deally was getting his revenge.

Or maybe Deally and Alan had been friends once. Maybe Deally had given Alan the book, not wanting to be reminded of a broken engagement.

Hell, for all I knew the book was Edward's.

With the sun in my face, I almost didn't care. I lay on the bench like the hippie I'd once been, and I basked, just basked. I wondered if anyone ever got any work done in this town.

35

On Sunday, I met with Bart Bustamonte to go over his testimony about the hoaxed crop circle.

We were in the hotel cocktail lounge. On the other side of huge windows, kids played volleyball in the sand. Beyond them, the waves crashed in and out, leaving twenty feet of foamy surf. Cliffs mantled in ice plant curved away to a tiny lighthouse.

"You'll be my last witness," I told Bustamonte. The assistant DA planned to question the botany students; I might as well jump the gun. Better to call Bustamonte now than to make him wait around to be a rejoinder witness. "After I put you on the stand, I'm done."

"You're not putting your guy on?" He looked surprised.

"No. He doesn't want to testify."

Bustamonte tapped a copy of the Sunday paper he'd brought to the table. Today, Leonard Deally cited the campus crop circle as proof Miller was a liar and a fraud. "He's embarrassed?"

I shrugged, leaving it at that.

"Yeah, I know the feeling. I once had the Great Debunker himself, Carl Sagan, may he rest in peace, attack me in a national magazine. And you should hear what he said about Fichman." He grinned. "Sagan went, okay, there are a bunch of pyramids on Mars, and they're in an area a lot like Gizeh in Egypt. But, said Mr. Science Sagan, what's the chance of pharaohs on Mars? This is how deep a thinker Sagan was. Like if you don't have pharaohs, you can't have pyramids." Bustamonte leaned forward. "Here's another example. These two retirees, Doug and Dave, they call the English press corps one day and say, *You know all these crop circles over the last fifteen years? We made them, just to fool everyone.* They offer piddling proof, they don't even *try* to explain the circles in other countries. Colin Andrews confronts them with questions about specific circles, and they say, *Oh, heh heh, no, we didn't mean those circles.* That was in ninety-one; there have been hundreds every summer since. So did Carl Sagan say, *Prove it, Doug and Dave!* Or, *Why didn't you send a registered-mail drawing of a pattern to the press the day before a circle appeared?* No, Sagan's last book has a chapter about how easily fooled we were by this crop circle crap, when it was Doug and Dave all along." He grinned. "Hell, I could phone the papers today and say I've been abducting all these thousands of folks. Scientists like Sagan would go, *See, told you it was nothing to worry about.*"

"Well, you've been dealing with this stuff for years; you've developed a sense of humor about it. Alan Miller doesn't even believe it himself. He's really having a hard time."

It wasn't just Alan Miller. I couldn't stop thinking about the vegetation on the verge above the highway. Or the next field south, all traces plowed away. "Me, too. I shouldn't say this, I guess, but I have big-time doubts. I can't prove Miller didn't go off that cliff. And I keep thinking of other equally terrestrial ways the accident could have happened."

"The rowboats," Bustamonte said. "Remember the explorers' rowboats? The Indians weren't able to see the big ships, only the rowboats, because they looked like canoes. That's you. You're looking at something so strange to you that you're having trouble recognizing it. Instead you're seeing what you're used to: a client lying, an accident happening the way accidents usually do, somebody hiding evidence, whatever—things you've seen before. Canoes."

"Maybe."

"You know I'm not a hundred percent on your client. But we should all try to look past our canoes. The more habits of perception you break, the better your chances of seeing that big, important, unfamiliar thing out there."

Bustamonte glanced out the window, where kids were falling over backward to make sand angels.

"There have been a lot of circles on sand, did you know that? And in snow. I've photographed several myself. There were no tracks leading to them. No way Doug and Dave could have made them. Although one guy suggested pogo sticks."

I made a note to ask him a question about this in court.

"Ice, too. Lots of ice circles in Siberia and Greenland. The pattern is melted in."

A beach ball hit the window, and Bustamonte jumped. "I'll be glad to leave here. Too crowded, too hot." He wiped sweat from his cheeks. "Coastal Washington's just right for me—nice and cool."

I guess he didn't mind a little rain. "You must get a lot of mushrooms up there." I'd been reading Kathleen Korlovatz's book; I had mushrooms on my mind.

Bustamonte made a *ffftp* sound, indicating that they certainly did.

"Are you a mushroom hunter?"

He shook his head. "No, but I have friends up there who are into it. Their mushroom god lives in this area somewhere."

I leaned forward. "Kathleen Korlovatz?"

"No, somebody Arora. How do you know Kathleen?" He frowned, lips pursing.

"I'm reading her mushroom book. Do you know her?"

"Unfortunately. We all do. She was at the UFO conference, you know."

"She was? Why?" And why didn't I remember a name like Korlovatz being on the program?

"She calls herself Ninti, after the Sumerian extraterrestrial who gave birth to the first test-tube baby, Adam. Ninti!" He snorted. "The rest of us call her Ninny."

"Adam? Of Adam and Eve?"

He nodded. "You get a lot of nuts at these things. Part of the package," he sighed.

"And Kathleen Korlovatz is one of them?"

"A big one of them."

"What does she believe?"

"That ETs called the Annunaki came to earth four hundred and fifty thousand years ago. They mined gold so they could suspend particles as a radiation shield around their own planet. But a hundred thousand years later, their workers revolted—formed Earth's first labor union. Management decided to go for indigenous labor, but the only thing running around back then was *Homo erectus*, barely smarter than an ape. So they did some genetic engineering. They took an egg from a *Homo erectus* female and fertilized it in vitro with Annunaki sperm. Then Ninti, their chief medical officer, destined to live in legend as a fertility goddess, had the egg implanted into her womb. Ten months later, she gave birth to the first of a slave race they called Adamu. They gave Ninti the nickname Mammi, the root of the universal 'mama.' This is from six-thousand-year-old cuneiform tablets. The story, the names, even an illustration of the lab setup were supposedly handed down to the Sumerians through the generations."

"Kathleen Korlovatz believes a Sumerian creation myth? That humans were genetically engineered to be a slave race?"

" 'With sweat on your brow shall you eat your bread,' just like it says in Genesis. Actually, the Sumerian word for 'life' was the same as their word for 'rib,' as in Adam's rib. And the text says the Annunaki lived in E.Din." He shrugged. "You get your same basic spacemen in Mayan and Hopi stories. I'm not saying it's all crap; myths can be based on history. And the Sumerians did know a thing or two. They left tablets with depictions of our solar system. The planets are shown revolving around the sun—about four thousand years before Galileo got the idea. And they're the right sizes in relation to each other. Plus—here's the kicker —Pluto, Neptune, and Uranus are on the tablet. We didn't discover those planets till this century. Here's an ancient culture with no telescopes, supposedly. How did they know?"

I waited for an answer.

He continued, "When anthropologists and archaeologists vouch for this stuff, you think, Well, maybe." He shook his head. "But then you get Kathleen-Ninti and her airy-fairy overlay about 'positive' ETs and 'negative' ETs, channeling the mushroom, spore vibrations . . . it just about makes you want to turn your back on the whole thing and become an accountant."

"Channeling mushrooms?" Kathleen Korlovatz reborn as a Sumerian goddess; I was still trying to master my shock.

"According to her, when the Annunaki waved good-bye to Earth, they left behind mushrooms to guide the Adamu. Psilocybin's found in cow dung, and that encouraged the Adamu to follow cattle around, eventually domesticating them and using them for farming. Plus, the mushroom-alien talked to them through it, helped them evolve." He scrutinized me. "You're about my age. You know what it reminds me of?"

"What?"

"The sixties, all the psychedelic talk back then."

"Korlovatz's mushroom book seems so normal."

"She was still normal when she wrote it. Now she's part Annunaki—maybe they have more attractive last names." He snickered. "You should hear her story. First she becomes persuaded mushrooms are ETs. Then she decides to let the mushroom-ETs speak through her. She starts scarfing psilocybin—magic mushrooms—and pretty soon she's channeling Ninti, diva from another planet!"

"Alan Miller did his Ph.D. thesis on spores drifting here from other planets."

"There you go," he said. *Spore Trek.*"

"I wonder if that's when she met Alan." I glanced at Bustamonte's newspaper. "I wonder if Alan consulted her about his theory, explained it to her."

And got her started on a line of research that ended up taking her away from a mere earthling like Leonard Deally.

"If he did," Bustamonte said, "it would explain why he's so embarrassed. If I helped create Ninti Korlovatz, I'd go join the Foreign Legion."

36

Bustamonte asked to see the fenced facility I'd stumbled upon yesterday. "If Lockheed took its shingle off the door, it could mean something."

I wasn't thrilled about going back; I dreaded encountering the un-marked helicopters again. But Bustamonte pooh-poohed my fears.

"If they wanted to get you, they'd wait till after the trial—less notice-able. Next month sometime, a thug in an alley . . ." Seeing my face, he burst out laughing. "Kidding, just kidding. Come on, show me this place."

I was glad to leave the hotel, to be out of its air-conditioned, sound-muffled, beach-behind-glass environment. It was around seventy-five degrees with an ocean breeze; no one thinner than Bustamonte would have considered it too hot.

But anyone would have agreed it was too crowded. The beach and wharf area looked like a giant hand had picked up a dozen high schools, some in Mexico, and emptied them within sight of the hotel.

After helping Bustamonte into my Honda—not an easy fit, though he was too polite to complain—we drove up Highway 1. Even in Sun-day traffic, it was less than twenty minutes to Davenport.

The winding road up the mountain took longer. And despite the forest shade, it grew hotter. Bustamonte turned his face to the open window like a dog panting for air. I wondered how he'd survived his jaunts to air force bases in Nevada and New Mexico. It said something about the strength of his convictions and his curiosity.

"Wait, wait, wait," he said. "What the hell is that?"

I slowed. We were winding through a fringe of thick forest, with small oaks and knobcone pines beside the road and redwoods rising high behind them. I couldn't see anything but trees and scrub. A red-tailed hawk circled overhead.

"Stop. Back up." He was trying to twist and look over his shoulder.

I shifted into reverse, breaking into a sweat as we rolled backward on the hairpin turn. This was my first car, and I'd owned it only a few years. I bought it when I worked for an L.A. firm, using it to create a slow lane for one.

"Right here!"

I stopped, not bothering to park on the shoulder. We'd seen no traffic since leaving the larger road.

"Here?" I still couldn't see anything but forest.

"Well, I'll be damned!" Bustamonte flung open the passenger door. "I didn't know anybody was still doing this!"

I got out, too. I reached his side of the car as he hoisted himself to his feet, bracing one hand on the seat and the other on the door frame.

"Doing what? What are we looking at?"

"You don't see it?" His face lit up. "Right over there." He nodded ahead into the woods.

I saw splotches of shadow, trees, bushes, birds, light through fluttering leaves . . . ordinary sights, except that one of the shadows—

"Oh, wow!" A pattern of shadow and light suddenly resolved itself into a huge cistern. But it wasn't camouflaged in any way I'd ever seen before. It wasn't splotched beige, green, and black like camouflage fatigues. It was a wild abstract of curves and angles and slashes. "It looks like Sister Corinna on acid. Or Peter Max with a boring palette. I can't believe I didn't see it."

"It's called dazzle camouflage. They were big on it during and after World War One. They'd take a huge ship and they'd paint it in the most way-out patterns you could dream of. Looked like you'd be able to see it a hundred miles away. But you know"—he started walking toward the cistern—"German subs couldn't spot them from the water, and planes couldn't map their velocity. The crazy patterns masked the shape, just like the angles on this thing made it look like shadows and trees and shafts of light. I think the basic principle is that if it's too weird and unexpected, your brain turns it into something familiar, part of the background."

We picked our way over vines—I hoped not poison oak—to get closer. The water tank was twice my height, as long as a limo.

"For fire department use?" I guessed. "It must get dry up here."

"They probably have a mostly volunteer fire department. Why the hell would they want to camouflage a water tank?"

"Maybe they have a problem with siphoning."

"Water's a very damn heavy thing to steal. No." He shook his head. "You might be right about it being for fire protection. But it's privately owned. It belongs to the thing at the end of the road, Lockheed or whatever it is."

I was getting the creeps. "What do you mean, whatever it is?"

"Well, they've got a good supply of extra water. It's possible they've got unmarked helicopters to chase folks away." I'd told Bustamonte about seeing helicopters here yesterday. "And they know their camouflage."

But if he expected something dramatic at the front gate, he must have been disappointed. (I, on the other hand, was relieved.) We encountered no vehicles of any kind, and no people, military or otherwise, armed or not. We simply drove up to the fence labeled "Absolutely No Trespassing or Loitering; Forbidden by Law." We stared at the guard station. We read the warnings and statute numbers.

"This isn't Lockheed," Bustamonte said. "It's on the wrong road, it doesn't have Lockheed written on it. It's just mimicking Lockheed. It's camouflaged, every bit as much as the water tank."

Then we walked into the woods far enough to be convinced the fence didn't just end.

Returning to the entrance, Bustamonte continued to look excited. "The whole setup—the warnings, the guardhouse, those whatever-the-hell barracks things . . . it's supposed to look like Lockheed, only more military. It's like a Potemkin village. You know, like the facades General Potemkin built to fool Catherine the Great into thinking she was riding through villages." He rubbed his neck as if his collar were burning him. "It's a Potemkin Lockheed. It's supposed to look scary, a place with armed guards ready to radio for troops to take you away!"

The place had certainly spooked me yesterday. I'd driven away in a lather of fear that black helicopters, that the shadow government—of this planet or some other—would come and get me . . . for nothing more than driving (and napping) on a public road.

Back at the front gate, Bustamonte stared through the chain-link. "It's just like a movie set, isn't it? Twelve-foot fence with barbed wire on the top, guardhouse, barracks. The road going off into the woods so you wonder what kind of big creepy building they've got tucked away in there—does it look like the Borg ship?" He made a voilà gesture. "The whole thing says, *Stay out*."

"Of what?"

"Couldn't begin to guess," he admitted.

As we drove back down the mountain, Bustamonte seemed lost in thought.

Suddenly he exclaimed, "This is where your client came! The Potemkin Lockheed, it's where Miller came after he dropped off that teenager. Betcha anything!"

I swerved slightly. "You don't have any reason to believe that."

"Think about it: He was missing all night; that's mystery number one. This unmarked thing is sitting at the end of a lonely road not so far from his house; that's mystery number two. You've got helicopters hovering as subtly as pterodactyls outside the hotel rooms of your expert witnesses, and then you see the same helicopters here." He tapped his head. "It doesn't take a genius. Somebody at Potemkin Lockheed hired the helicopters to excite and titillate your UFO experts. Ergo, this is not about UFOs at all—they're just dazzle camouflage. And if this isn't about UFOs, then your client is lying. That puts him in cahoots with whoever hired the helicopters. And since they parked here, probably he did, too."

My luck: I take my witness for a drive and he becomes convinced of my client's guilt.

37

The next morning, Bustamonte proved to be an ideal witness. He was smart, sure, and quick to contradict unspoken assumptions in the assistant DA's questions. By the time he was dismissed, I wasn't as worried about Toben's botany students. I hoped we'd neutralized their testimony.

I announced that I had no further witnesses and I took my seat beside Alan Miller. The hound-faced judge asked Patrick Toben to begin his rebuttal case.

I caught Bustamonte's eye as he lumbered out of the courtroom. He looked boyishly eager. My detective, Carl Shaduff, waited for him in the hall. They were going back up to the facility Bustamonte persisted in calling Potemkin Lockheed.

Shaduff had looked up title to the land. It was owned by a corporation whose name suggested nothing in particular and whose business was unspecified. To Bustamonte, this meant intrigue.

I hoped their visit would lay Bustamonte's suspicions to rest. But if there was evidence Miller had hidden out up there, I wanted it now. I wanted no last-minute surprises.

The assistant DA didn't begin his rebuttal with the crop circle forgers. He was probably giving the jury time to forget Bustamonte's testimony.

He started with two doctors willing, for a fee, to interpret Miller's medical chart in a way that proved he'd been in an auto accident.

On cross, I asked each of them how they explained the lack of compression injuries to the spine. Both cited the cushion effect of landing on a car roof. I asked how they accounted for the absence of lacerations. They replied, tautologically, that Miller hadn't been cut. I asked them how blood might have appeared in Miller's urine. They answered, stress.

I took them phrase by phrase through the findings and testimony of examining physicians. I asked if, in general, the observations of attending doctors would be more reliable than later conclusions based only on reading a patient's chart. They said, not necessarily.

I couldn't resist asking, "How do you account for the double puncture wound in Mr. Miller's thumb?"

One of them said, "Bee stings, perhaps."

The other said, "Any heavy-duty staple could leave such a mark."

I had no idea if they'd done us damage.

I sat with Alan during the lunch break. The judge, hoping to wind up quickly, had lengthened the court day and shortened the lunch hour. So we'd taken our places in a cafeteria line crowded with county-building workers.

A group of laughing women clicked by in their high heels. At metal tables, well-groomed men puzzled over sports scores. Secretaries with good haircuts nibbled salads. A hundred people talked at once, gossip ringing through the big basement room. It was crowded enough to offer privacy.

We had a small table to ourselves. I couldn't resist asking Alan, "Have you ever been up to a fenced facility at the top of the mountain? It's unmarked except for No Trespassing signs."

"Lockheed? On Empire Grade?"

"No." I verbally retraced my route. "It's closer to Davenport."

Alan unwrapped his cafeteria sandwich as if it were a complicated and delicate task. Finally, he said, "I've seen it."

"Have you been there lately?"

He bit into the sandwich, shaking his head.

I stared down at my square of white bread fringed with wilted romaine. It would have been hard enough to summon an appetite for it. Right now, I couldn't have eaten anything.

Right now, I was struggling with an occupational hazard. I believed my client was lying.

I just wondered how much he was lying about. All of it?

I was startled to hear him saying, "Willa? Willa?"

I turned to him. "Yes?"

"What is it?"

A practical lawyer would have said, *Nothing.* The trial was almost over; what was the point?

I said, "You didn't tell me about Kathleen Korlovatz, for starters."

"What about her?" His tone was guarded, his sandwich arrested a few inches from his lips.

"Didn't you talk to her about your doctoral thesis?"

He put the sandwich down. "I guess you spoke with her?"

I didn't reply.

"She was at the university as a guest lecturer. She mentioned she'd done some research in spore mutation. And since my thesis was on the effects of cosmic radiation . . . She was really helpful." He sighed. "And then . . ."

"She got more involved in the theory than you expected?"

"She got into mushrooms being alien, yeah." He slumped, straining the seams of his borrowed suit. "I'm interested in the idea theoretically, but, man, she really took off on it."

"Beyond the point where you shared her beliefs?"

"See, I'm in love with fungus; my object was to show one more remarkable thing about it. This culture's so misinformed about mushrooms—afraid to let their kids near them, afraid the least bit of contact will poison them." He ran his hand over his dark hair. "That's what all these years of teaching classes at the museum have been about. Showing people how diverse they are—how much you can do with them. How much fun they are. But at least a dozen times a season, some freaked-out mom comes into the museum with something from her backyard, going, 'Oh my God, Johnny touched this; what should I do?' Like just touching a mushroom's going to—Anyway, you see what I'm saying?"

"I'm not sure." I suspected he was changing the subject.

"People who make a lot of noise about the psychedelic mushrooms just make my job harder. They just make little Johnny's mom more paranoid. They keep mushrooms bad rapped."

"And Kathleen Korlovatz focuses on psychedelic mushrooms?"

He nodded.

"I thought she did something with Sumerian mythology."

"Maybe. I mean, I know she's supposed to be channeling or something. She uses a different name now, Nitsy or something. But it's her thing about *Stropharia cubensis*—a kind of psilocybin—having an alien voice, that you can talk to an alien if you eat magic mushrooms—that's the stuff I hate."

"Why didn't you tell me any of this when I asked you about her?"

"Because I hate it! I hate what happened." He pushed his sandwich away. "She was a good scientist. She was a good thesis advisor. Now she's on mushroom trips talking to alien spore men!"

"You blame yourself?"

He looked surprised. "Blame myself? Why would I?"

"For suggesting to her that spores came from outer space."

He shook his head. "It was a book about *Stropharia cubensis* that did that—an interesting book; a lot of good research by an ethnomycologist. It's just that Kathleen went overboard with it. Changed her name and started coming to conferences in robes and stuff. Got very weird about the mushroom, made it her whole life."

"Is it addictive?"

"Psilocybin? No. But it makes you feel like you're communing with something—not an alien spore creature, but something spiritual. I think what hooked her was the mind expansion or the spiritualism or whatever you want to call it. It's the New Age stuff that's addictive, not the mushroom."

"But you weren't the one that got her into it?"

He shook his head.

"Leonard Dealy thinks you were."

"He does?"

"Doesn't he?"

"I don't know. I've never talked to him."

"Even when he was engaged to Kathleen?"

"I knew they were dating—she gave me a book because she didn't like her inscription to him. But I didn't really socialize with her. The time I spent with her, we were in the labs or in her office up on campus."

I looked at the handsome, green-eyed man filling out Edward's borrowed suit better than Edward ever had.

"You seem to feel so guilty about Leonard Dealy's columns, almost like you have his cruelty coming." I rubbed the spot between my brows, hoping to stave off a headache. "I thought you must feel responsible for Kathleen breaking up with him. I thought her mushroom-goddess stuff must have come from you."

His brows rose. "I feel guilty because Francis Addenaur's dead. And his widow's gone crazy. And it was my car that killed him."

"You don't believe your own alibi, do you?"

He winced. "No. I don't."

38

The botany graduate students were on and off the witness stand in an hour. They admitted getting the idea to make crop circles from last month's visiting expert. They described how easy it had been to make the campus crop circle: how few implements they'd needed, how quickly they'd finished. But they didn't claim to have made the circles near Joseph Huizen's house. And I'd already rebutted (prebutted?) their testimony with Bustamonte's.

The assistant DA then called the administrator of the Bonny Doon airport, which was, apparently, not far from Potemkin Lockheed.

He testified that a helicopter could easily hover above a house like Donna Nelson's and shine a searchlight into a window. And that, in fact, there had been many complaints about helicopter fly-overs in the mountains these last months.

I felt a pang for the medic who'd been forced to admit stopping to gawk. Deally's vitriolic editorial claimed he'd hallucinated a spaceship. Now everyone would laugh that he'd misidentified a helicopter.

On cross, I asked the witness what kind of helicopters the majority of complaints involved.

He admitted that virtually all were attributable to the federal Campaign Against Marijuana Planting program that searched for hidden pot fields.

I asked if he'd ever heard of CAMP helicopters hovering over houses at night, aiming their high beams into windows.

He said no.

But the witness left me more shaken than I'd left him.

I imagined a black helicopter would be invisible in the unlighted countryside at night. It would be inaudible over an ambulance siren. Its light would appear to be shining down from nowhere, from space, from an unseen alien craft.

But why would it be shooting a light into Miller's neighbor's house? Mistaken address?

Had it come to pick Miller up? Had it flown him away before the sheriff could find him?

Patrick Toben's final rebuttal witness was one of the deputies who'd examined the crime scene. He went back over details of the accident, deriding the "supernatural" explanations our witnesses attached to it.

He made a point of explaining why the Sheriff's Department hadn't investigated the Brussels sprouts field until 5:43 P.M. "We took a quick look right after the accident in case there was anybody hurt up there. Or anything, you know, important. But we didn't bother checking for tracks then because it was absolutely positively clear the car couldn't have come from any other location. It had to come off the cliff directly above the highway where it landed, no question." He stated that Fiat tire prints were of a size to be wholly obscured by truck tracks. "And at least four sets of truck tire tracks postdated the accident due to the landowner driving back and forth across his field to look down at the site."

And, to my chagrin, he explained why field-edge vegetation needn't have been crushed.

On cross, I hammered him hard for waiting fifteen hours to examine the field for tracks. I suggested that, because of it, his evidence and conclusions were mere guesses. I asked if he had any proof beyond his own supposition that truck tires had obscured preexisting tracks. We went round and round about what "proof" meant.

I asked him if he had any proof beyond his own supposition that Miller was driving the Fiat. We went around about how much information it takes to "know" something.

The deputy held his own.

When I was done, the prosecution rested.

I had one rejoinder witness.

Joseph Huizen, glowing with the thrill of equations that still worked out, took the stand.

If Patrick Toben objected to my line of questions, I could only call it a day. Joseph's testimony had nothing to do with the Miller case, not strictly speaking. But Toben was looking cocky after a good witness.

I gave it a shot. I asked Joseph if Reginald Fulmer's testimony about the crop circle had surprised him. I asked him what he'd done since learning Fulmer's theory that the circle pictogram represented a glucose molecule. Joseph could barely contain his excitement over his mathematical breakthrough. I let him ramble on about it.

At first, Toben didn't object. I caught a glimpse of him out of the corner of my eye; he didn't look concerned.

But as Joseph continued, I could hear Toben's chair scrape, almost feel him realizing it was too late.

Joseph said, "I am now convinced that something not of this world spoke to me the night the crop circle appeared. I am convinced that viewing the crop circle, believing it must relate to my need for glucose that night . . . I'm certain these things triggered my insight. I feel deeply that this breakthrough was a gift to me. That it was a communication from another place, perhaps another world."

He looked so much younger and stronger and happier today. The jurors must see that *something* had happened to him. I just hoped they wouldn't believe, as I did, that the something had been Joseph's doing, that the communication had come from an inner galaxy.

I said, "No further questions, Your Honor."

Toben had Joseph reiterate that he'd been in a state of organic hallucination when he'd received his so-called communication. He asked Joseph whether any two-dimensional rendition of a molecule could really be said to represent it, except by previous agreement between scientists. He asked if glucose was ever represented as swirled circles within circles in the scientific world.

Joseph admitted that it wasn't.

When Toben concluded, I said, "The defense rests."

Toben rose. "As you know, Your Honor, we have been unable to locate one of our witnesses, Maria Nanos. We have no further witnesses at this time. But we would ask that court be adjourned for the day so that we might continue in our attempts to locate her."

The judge called us over to sidebar. He asked Toben, "How likely are you to find this witness tonight?"

"I don't know, Your Honor. We have deputies and city police searching."

"Searching specific locations?"

"No." The assistant DA looked chagrined.

As much as I hated to launch into my closing statement, it was to Miller's advantage to wind this up before Maria was found.

"Your Honor, basically Mr. Toben is hoping the witness will walk right out in front of a police car. He has no reason to believe she's even in this state any longer."

"Well?" The judge regarded Toben over the tops of his reading lenses.

"We were able to locate her previously," Toben pointed out.

"And they lost her previously. Last time they found her in Big Sur. So it's likely she's left the county again." I tried to look impatient. "I would like to get on with the trial. I don't think the People have any reasonable expectation of producing this witness tomorrow."

"I agree." The judge checked his Rolex. "Let's get this trial over with. You've got three hours to finish up your closing statements. Let's try to keep them short and free this courtroom up, Counsel."

Toben watched me through narrowed eyes. Considering Alan Miller gave Maria Nanos her running-away money, I could hardly blame him for being suspicious.

Within moments, I stood before my comfortable-shoes-and-no-hairspray jurors.

"Ladies and gentlemen of the jury," I said, "during my opening statement and during the assistant district attorney's, we spent quite a while discussing the meaning of the term 'circumstantial evidence.' We explained to you that it referred to what may be deduced from the circumstances surrounding the crime.

"The assistant district attorney is going to tell you in his closing statement that he's presented you with enough circumstantial evidence to convict Alan Miller. Circumstantial evidence . . . from a crime scene that has no tire prints where they should be, no broken vegetation where you would expect to find it, no witnesses, and . . . nothing else at all—nothing!—to prove my client was driving his car at the time. The assistant district attorney calls this 'circumstantial evidence' that Alan Miller committed vehicular manslaughter.

"Well, you don't have to accept that.

"You've heard from a psychiatrist who has testified for the prosecution in dozens of previous cases. He testified here that Alan Miller has absolutely no memory, conscious or unconscious, of having been inside his car when the accident happened.

"If Alan Miller wasn't in his car, it really doesn't matter where he was. If he wasn't in the car, you cannot convict him of this crime. It's that cut-and-dried.

"But the defense has, at great embarrassment to Mr. Miller, tried to explain the terrible thing that happened to him that night.

"You don't have to have an opinion or take a position about any of the information we've presented to you. We presented it because we felt you had a right to know where he was. But for the purposes of this inquiry, you do not have to believe anything except that the prosecution did *not* prove Alan Miller was in his car at the moment the accident occurred.

"That's the only question before you. Not whether or not we are alone in the universe. You've heard that many thousands of people have grown to believe we are not. You've learned that many of them are credentialed and credible people. You've seen photographs and video clips of some of the objects they've sighted.

"But these were shown to you so that you would not dismiss as lies or delusions the statements made by Alan Miller under hypnosis. They provide a context for a horribly traumatic experience that is, unfortunately, not an uncommon one.

"But you are not being asked to decide what you think about it or where you stand on this issue."

And, God, did the jurors look relieved to hear me say so.

"You are only being asked to decide whether the prosecution has proved—*proved* beyond a reasonable doubt—that Mr. Miller was driving his car at approximately two-thirty that morning.

"The prosecution has *supposed* it, and they have reconstructed where the hard evidence *should have been* if the accident had happened the way they claim it did. But they *did not* find that evidence. They did not prove anything except that Alan Miller's car landed on top of Francis Addenaur's. That's because, from the actual evidence in this case, no one could prove any more than that.

"So don't be distracted by the bigger debate about our place in the universe. We promised to provide you with an explanation of where Mr. Miller was that night, regardless of the derision that would be heaped on him because of it."

The DA could certainly have objected to that one. The jurors had avoided reading about the trial, had ignored Leonard Deally's scathing articles—in theory.

"But all of this is, in a sense, irrelevant. The prosecution has not proved Alan Miller was driving his car. It has not proved his injuries that night were consistent with a car accident. It has not even bothered, as we have, to present you with a scenario of where Mr. Miller was after the accident.

"How can there be no reasonable doubt that Mr. Miller was driving his car? Where are his tire tracks? What are the odds of them being obliterated in this convenient way? Where are his accident injuries—the lacerations, the compression injuries, the bruises? You saw photographs of the cars. Do you believe Mr. Miller could have jumped out of that car without a nick? Do you believe he could have jumped out of that car and run so far neither the Highway Patrol nor the Sheriff's Department could find any trace of him for seven hours? And if so, why have they offered no evidence about where Mr. Miller supposedly hid himself?

"They haven't proved a thing, ladies and gentlemen. They don't have a single piece of evidence. They don't have a single explanation that isn't an outright guess. And it would be wrong to convict a man based on guesses.

"So you have to acquit Alan Miller. Because all explanations and theories aside, no one has proved to you that he was inside his car when the accident happened."

I looked at them, wishing some dramatic ending would occur to me.

It didn't. I said, "Thank you."

I returned to the table to sit beside Alan. He stared straight ahead, the corners of his lips turned down, tears gleaming in his eyes.

The assistant DA stood up and gave a stock speech about how important a part of our system the jurors were and how much the People depended upon and appreciated them.

Then he scoffed, "No circumstantial evidence in this case? Is that what the defense is asking you to believe? Why, they might as well be asking you to believe in . . . flying saucers!"

I gave him points for that one.

Unfortunately, he didn't lose speed. He ran through every bit of evidence they'd presented, contrasting it with what we were asking the jury to believe instead.

"They tell you that in a field where a farmer routinely drives a big truck, you couldn't reasonably conclude that the farmer might have driven over a single set of tire tracks. They ask you instead to believe that the defendant's car was dropped out of the sky by a flying saucer.

"They quibble about the exact nature of injuries to the defendant. They tell you the injuries aren't consistent with a car accident, though we've presented abundant medical testimony that they are. They ask you instead to believe the injuries were caused by spacemen doing sexual experiments."

And so on. By the time he finished his list, it was all I could do not to slink from the courtroom in shame.

I certainly had asked the jury to swallow a mountain of weirdness.

As the assistant DA walked back to his table, I noticed several jurors glancing into the pews.

I was afraid to turn my head. I was afraid I'd catch sight of Leonard Deally, bristling with indignation.

We sat through twenty minutes of the judge instructing the jury, his tone ponderous and pompous.

At four-forty, the jury was dismissed to begin its deliberations. The judge was obviously not one to sanction an early dinner.

He instructed the assistant DA and me to remain available from nine to six each day of deliberations, ready to return within an hour of being summoned.

But Toben had another trial coming up and asked for four hours' notice on certain days. I said I needed to return to San Francisco, and asked for a full day's notice. Behind us, spectators murmured. Some could be heard shuffling their way to the aisle. The noise level rose as the courtroom doors opened to let them out.

Toben and I wrangled with the judge for quite a while, trying to reach an accommodation. The judge, as cranky as an importuned parent, was determined to work out a varying schedule, depending on the day. I ended up agreeing to be in court by five-fifteen any day I was notified by eleven. I could return to San Francisco.

Then the bailiff cried, "All rise," and we watched the judge whoosh off to his robing room.

I gave Alan's arm a squeeze. His muscles were knotted so tight it felt like he was flexing. I tried to think of something uplifting to say, but I had so little practice.

With a sigh, I began stuffing my briefcase. Behind me, lingering spectators chatted, others hurried down the aisle. The open doors brought in waves of excited talk and laughter.

I tried again to console Alan. "It went okay. It'll be over soon."

He was sitting as still as a wax statue, staring at the empty jury box. I took my time putting away my notes; no use rushing into the hallway throng. At the prosecution table, Toben smiled at something a woman with a file folder was saying to him.

As we stood to leave, I noticed the bailiff returning to the courtroom, which seemed a little odd. He approached me, blinking like he had dust in his eyes.

He said, "Jury's reached a verdict."

"What?"

"The judge wants to reconvene now to hear it read." He didn't sound convinced it would be worth reading. "You're available now, right?"

"Yes."

I couldn't look at Alan. Instead, I watched the bailiff approach Toben, lean close, and speak to him.

Patrick Toben flashed me a wild look. We were probably mirror images of dread.

Behind me in the courtroom, I could hear rushing footsteps, voices in the hall. I heard spectators hurriedly returning to their seats.

Five minutes later, the bailiff announced that court was back in session. I watched the judge billow in and sit at the bench. It took him a few minutes to quiet everyone down and order that the jury be brought in. My heart was beating so fast it seemed to have forgotten how to pump blood to my brain.

In a daze, I watched the jury file in and take their seats. They didn't look at us.

Beside me, Alan visibly trembled. I wanted to apologize to him. My defense was so stupid, so crazy, that the jury rejected it within half an hour, out of hand, with hardly any deliberation at all.

The judge asked the foreman if the jury had reached a verdict on both charges.

The foreman said, "Yes, Your Honor, we have."

I noticed that her clothes didn't match; I'd chosen her for that reason, among others. I'd hoped it meant she was no slave to the common view. Maybe she was just clueless.

I wasn't sure which would work most to my advantage.

The judge asked defendant and counsel to rise. We did.

The bailiff collected the verdict and handed it to the judge. The judge looked it over it and handed it back.

Finally, the foreman read it aloud.

"On the charge of vehicular manslaughter, we, the jury, find the defendant, Alan Miller, not guilty."

I grabbed Alan's arm. There was a roar of disapproval in the pews behind us. The judge rapped his gavel.

Startled, the foreman took a moment to continue. "On the charge of felony hit-and-run, we, the jury, find the defendant, Alan Miller, not guilty."

Leonard Deally shouted, "No!"

The judge rapped his gavel again, threatening to cite anyone else who spoke.

Alan Miller dropped into his chair, covering his face with his hands. He began shaking with sobs. I squeezed his shoulder. I found myself wondering if he wept with relief or guilt.

The judge told us to be seated. He polled the jurors, then thanked them at some length. He commented that they had witnessed one of the more unusual cases to be tried in his courtroom. Several of them laughed. A few nodded.

When he dismissed the jurors, I watched them file out. I still couldn't believe it. I was afraid one of them would turn around at the jury room door and shout, *No! What was I thinking?*

For a moment, the judge peered sourly over the tops of his reading glasses. Then he said, "The defendant, Alan Miller, having been acquitted of all charges against him, is hereby remanded to his own custody. And court is hereby adjourned."

The bailiff cried, "All rise," and again the judge departed.

I began congratulating Alan—or, more accurately, consoling him as he wept away the stress of the trial.

The assistant DA came and offered me a manly handshake, quipping, *"Klatu barada nikto."* When I looked bewildered, he explained, "It's what the spaceman says in *The Day the Earth Stood Still.*" He tried to smile, but couldn't quite manage it. He lowered his voice. "You know what's really too bad? I think you believe your client. And I think you're going to go home and realize it couldn't possibly have happened the way he said it did. It couldn't possibly have happened any way except how the People presented it."

Spectators buzzed around us, saying something or other, trying to interpose themselves between me and Toben. I did my best to block their view of Alan until he could pull himself together. I lost sight of Patrick Toben.

Joseph Huizen stood on the other side of me. He began diverting people from our table, saying, "Not now, please; not now."

Alan finally got a grip, apologizing for the outburst.

I tried to soothe him, but I could barely keep still. It was finally sinking in: damn, I'd won. Against all rational prediction, I'd won this weird case. I wanted to jump on the table and dance, high-five everyone, phone Curtis & Huston and invite them to choke on it.

I noticed Joseph turning hastily. I thought perhaps he was leaving. I wheeled around, starting to thank him for his testimony and his support.

But he wasn't moving. He was standing very straight, elbows slightly bent as if about to engage in battle. His posture was so militant, so protective, it startled me into silence.

Leonard Deally faced Joseph as if in a showdown. The two stood frozen—Deally leaning forward to spray us with verbal acid, and Joseph apparently determined to shield us from it.

I caught my breath. Joseph was a sixtyish man, overweight and diabetic, standing before a priggish younger man with a bone to pick. That's all; nothing grander.

But they seemed to eclipse the battle between the People and Alan Miller. They were the true faces of this strange coin: Joseph had been given something, and Deally had had something taken from him.

In tomorrow's papers, Deally would write the story the way it was likely to be remembered: as an embarrassment to the legal system and an insult to science. But Joseph's work might eventually nudge the boundaries of orthodoxy. Watching Joseph hold his ground—and ours, too—I almost enjoyed a moment of optimism.

Good thing I'd built up my resistance.

The bailiff moseyed over then, expressing his preference for getting the courtroom cleared out so he could go home to dinner.

Deally flashed Alan a look, then turned and strode away.

The bailiff commenced shooing out other bystanders. On his way back past us, he patted Joseph on the arm and smiled.

"I saw the jurors looking at you in the pews during closing," he told Joseph. "You won this case for them!"

To me, he said, "But of course they'll say the deputy lost it by not looking in the field before the tracks got covered." He seemed to take satisfaction from the thought. "Come on, Judge says to let you out through chambers."

I gave Joseph a hasty hug, and turned back to Alan. He stared at the spot where Deally had been standing, stared as if the gorgon reporter had turned him to stone.

Or maybe he felt too guilty to leave the defendant's table.

I gave him a shove, forcing him to follow the bailiff. Guilty or not, he was a free man.

39

We left through the judge's chambers, where the judge indiscreetly agreed that the sheriff lost the case by letting the tire tracks get obliterated. Obviously our UFO evidence hadn't made a believer out of him.

But he complimented my closing statement. "The prosecution just didn't put your client in the car. They didn't have any of it—tracks, injuries, witnesses. And you didn't let them get away with it." He shook his head. "It's good you didn't close with that outer space stuff, though . . . that was a big waste of the court's time."

I smiled politely. Better to waste the court's time than Miller's life.

To avoid the press, we took a circuitous route out the back of the building. On our way, Alan grew progressively cheerier. He seemed to be realizing, at last, that he didn't have to worry about prison, that, except for a burnt house and a ruined reputation, he'd averted disaster.

Almost.

Ten paces into the back lot where I was parked, we saw Betty Addenaur. At first, I didn't recognize her. She looked frailer than I recalled, her shiny black blouse hanging loose, its flounced collar gaping over gaunt bones and wrinkled skin. Dark roots showed through her badly ratted hair.

She just stood there, ten feet from us, arms dangling. Behind her in a nearby lot, sheriff's deputies parked their cruisers, perhaps preparing for a change of shift.

She said, "Ain't this always the way." One of her hands fluttered at her side like a drunk bird. "You kill my poor Francis and get away with it. And I have to hide so's they don't arrest me."

I took a step toward her. "Come in with us now. There's a good chance they'll drop the charges. We'll try to persuade them. The district attorney understands your grief."

I considered telling her Alan had already tried to cover for her. And I wasn't above changing my story and lying for her. Because I didn't want her to be right: I didn't want this to always be the way.

She made an angry chopping motion. "Just stop that, stop it! You'd like me to be arrested. But I got it covered this time." She squinted. "You don't want me out free. 'Cause I remind you of the real truth without any of the crap. I scare you, don't I?"

She would have, if she'd been armed. But she didn't have a handbag. She didn't even have a jacket.

"Francis used to say lawyers could get away with anything, but I never ever dreamed you'd get away with this. No, I really didn't think you would." She had the earnest voice of a drunk person who thinks she's fooling everyone. "I lost one good husband already. I used to promise myself I wouldn't lose another one and end up crying every night like my mama." Tears began to slide down her cheeks, taking her mascara with them. "I had the surgeries and I watched my figure. I watched what I said, and I did my very best with Francis. And ain't this always the way?"

Behind her, only a few parking spaces away, I noticed a white van. The one parked near Miller's house before the fire?

I extended my arm like a barrier in front of Alan. I took a backward step, trying to push him back with me. If the white van belonged to Betty Addenaur, we might be in trouble. I'd seen two men inside it before the fire.

It was dawning on me that Betty might not be alone today. Her handbag and jacket might be in the van. With her accomplices.

I murmured to Alan, "Get back inside!"

Instead, he gushed, "Oh God, I'm so sorry, really." He slapped my arm away impatiently. "I'll do anything I—"

"Alan! She's not alone!" I could see movement in the van now. Someone was in there.

"Not alone? How could I be *more* alone?" She came flying at me, her hands knotted into fists.

Alan jumped in front of me, taking her pummeling.

"Alone, alone!" She kept sobbing the word. "Alone."

I could see bleeding gashes on Alan's neck. She was clawing him and he was letting her.

I got behind her, pulling her by the shoulders, trying to yank her away from Alan, detach her claws from his flesh.

She was so small boned it felt like I was grabbing a bird. She stank of cigarettes, booze, and body odor. I pivoted, hoping to keep my eyes on the van. But for a critical second, I had a face full of bleached, ratted hair.

Alan was still pleading with her. "Come in with us. We'll do everything we—"

"Watch out!" I screamed.

A passenger had leaped from the van, a man with a sandy crew cut. I recognized him from the day of Miller's fire.

He was Betty's minion, I was sure.

At the hospital, I'd stopped Betty Addenaur from taking "justice" into her own hands. But she'd gotten no satisfaction through the courts. She had only managed, with the help of the men in the van, to burn Alan's belongings. That couldn't compensate for the loss of a beloved husband.

So she'd come here to finish what she'd started. Her friends—employees?—would either use or hand her a gun. And she would kill Alan Miller just as (she thought) he'd killed Francis Addenaur.

I let go of Betty and began pushing Alan back. I waited for the sound of a gunshot, my dread half convincing me I'd already heard it.

I pushed Alan with all my might to force him back, to get us both inside the building. I despaired of making it, but it wouldn't be for lack of trying.

I pressed the crown of my head and both hands against Alan's chest and I gave it everything I had. Despite his resistance, we almost reached the door.

That's when I heard the shots. There were two of them, rapid-fire. They sounded like caps or small firecrackers. But a breeze blew acrid smoke our way; there was no mistaking the smell.

I would have kept pushing till Alan went right through the side of the building, my adrenaline was so high. Fear had turned me into superchicken.

But Alan started pushing back hard, scooting me forward. I couldn't figure it out. Why would he run toward people who were shooting at him? It didn't make sense. And it pissed me off.

Finally, Alan grabbed my shoulders and flung me away like a doll. I ended up on my butt in the parking lot, making freaked-out hooting noises and scrambling to get on all fours so I could scurry to safety. My only consolation was that, so far, only my dignity had been wounded.

I'd finally won a case, and I was about to get murdered for it.

Goddam Betty Addenaur! I was shaking with rage as I struggled to my feet. I was ready to tear the head off the first person who didn't shoot me first.

But the men were kneeling in the parking lot, their backs to me, obscuring Betty Addenaur from my view.

I wasn't sure whether to run inside the building and hide or try to help Alan. From the rear, he seemed all right. The other men appeared busy at something, weren't noticeably threatening him.

Unsure and unsteady, I shuffled a little closer. That's when I saw the blood. There was blood all over the pavement.

I wanted to run away. Whatever the situation—and I was hard pressed to guess, at this point—I wanted to ignore it. I wanted to celebrate my victory and then go home. Back to my own little cocoon to deal with my own problems, which were not seeming so bad anymore, not by comparison.

But I moved closer.

Alan was holding Betty Addenaur's shoulders, and the two men, far from threatening him, seemed to be begging him.

"Please, you've got to lay her down. Let us look at her," the man with the crew cut urged. "Lay her down gently." He was hunched close to her, his hands cupped as if prepared to hold her head.

But Alan seemed determined to keep Betty upright, to lean her against him. He was muttering, "You're going to be okay, you're going to be okay."

I could see that her black blouse was wet and sticking to her scrawny chest. At least one of the two shots had hit her.

The other man, obscured from my view by Alan, was saying something. I thought I heard my name, but I was too aghast to understand or respond.

Alan was crooning, "Nobody's going to charge you with anything. And you won't be alone; you can live with me, if you like." His voice was so low it sounded like he was in a barrel. "You're going to be all right."

The other man was definitely calling my name. He was saying, "Ms. Jansson! Call nine-one-one! Hurry!"

I watched Betty Addenaur's eyes roll back in her head. A bloody froth spilled from her mouth down her front, all over the sleeve of Edward's jacket.

The man with the crew cut pried her out of Alan's grip, laying her down.

Suddenly, behind us, there were repeated high-pitched screams; they almost sounded like a car alarm.

I turned. A group of county workers had come out the back door.

The man who knew my name yelled, "Call an ambulance. Call nine-one-one right away!"

The flock disappeared inside.

The other man lamented, "I wish we had an ambu bag out here!" He squeezed between Alan and the now-supine Betty.

"I always meant to stick one in the van. Just in case."

Alan had been knocked out of his kneeling position. He sat on the pavement in Edward's ruined suit, crying as if he'd known Betty Addenaur his whole life.

I stared beyond him, over the shoulder of the crew-cut man. I could see Betty's mascara-streaked face. Her eyes and mouth were wide open. She didn't move at all.

And I could see the man who knew my name. It was John Bivens, the paramedic who'd testified for us. He was ripping open Betty's blouse. The man with the crew cut pulled off his sweatshirt. He held it against a wound above her shriveled breast.

There was some kind of leather strap and bag on her chest. A holster? The men exchanged pessimistic looks.

I backed away, pressing my knuckles to my lips. I could see a gun lying in a pool of blood close by.

Betty Addenaur had had a gun, after all. But she hadn't turned it on us, she'd used it on herself.

Alan was whispering something about the charges being dropped even if he had to serve her sentence himself; that she wouldn't always feel so alone, if she'd just hang on a little longer.

But it was easy to see she was already gone.

Paramedic John Bivens and his partner, Barry Burns, did what they could until an ambulance pulled up. By then, sheriff's deputies had sprinted out of the county building.

The deputies greeted the medics by name and they pushed away a photographer who'd happened to come around to the back of the building. They pulled me and Alan out of the way. And after Betty was placed in the ambulance, they herded the rest of us inside to take our statements.

John Bivens walked beside me into a basement foyer. "I know this is a hard sight for a layperson. Are you doing okay?"

I felt boggled, blown away, numb. "Yes." The deputies unlocked a massive door and motioned us into a corridor. "Why were you here?"

"My partner and I just came to tell you we were glad for you. I wanted to wish you luck the other day, after I testified, but you were talking to someone in the parking lot. We just wanted to say that we know a lot of people are laughing at you and hassling you. You and Mr. Miller." He seemed embarrassed just mentioning it. "But we saw that light the night we picked up Dr. Huizen, so we know it's for real. And we just wanted you to know not everybody thinks you're . . . you know."

"That was your van in the parking lot the other day?"

He nodded. "That's how I knew which car was yours today. So I could wait for you."

"And on San Vittorio Road a couple of weeks ago?"

"You saw us?" He blinked as if his eye itched, then trapped his hands beneath his armpits. He obviously knew better than to rub his eyes with bloody hands.

His partner was up ahead in the hallway, talking to the deputies, saying, "She just reached into her blouse and pulled it out. We couldn't believe it! She was probably aiming for her heart—got it, too. We get a lot of suicides where a partner's died or run off and the survivor shoots herself in the heart. We had two last Valentine's Day."

Alan shuffled beside them as if he were a zombie.

John Bivens sounded embarrassed. "We sat out in front of Donna Nelson's house three or four times. I guess to see if anything like that was going to happen again, or if there was something different about the house—I don't know. We were just so tripped, we didn't know what else to do."

"I'm sorry everyone had to find out. Where you work, I mean. You must have taken a lot of teasing. I hope your boss wasn't too hard on you?"

Bivens stopped walking. He lowered his voice. "Actually, the insurance company, our employer's malpractice insurance, it freaked out. Especially after what the newspaper said about us having hallucinations.

Insurance was afraid the company would get sued if it let us run any more calls. Because we'd been delusional while on the job; that's how they put it."

"What are you saying?" I looked at the fit young man. He seemed so straightforward and practical, and I'd just seen how good he was in a pinch. How could an insurer conclude he'd been delusional?

"Well, to be fair to my bosses, the insurance company threatened to raise the rates big time if they didn't get rid of me and Barry. They said any call we went on from now on, the company could get sued for sending medics with a public history of hallucinations on the job." He shrugged. "Maybe it was the kick in the butt I needed to move on."

"I used to be a labor lawyer," I said. "I'll do anything I can to get you reinstated, both of you. No charge. Okay?"

His brows rose. Despite his brave front, he looked grateful. "If you really think . . ."

"Give me your phone number. We'll get right on this."

"God, that'd be great! Especially for Barry—he's got a mortgage and kids."

He glanced up the hall, at Alan trotting beside the sheriff. Farther ahead, a deputy inserted a key into an elevator lock. I'd be glad to leave the harsh fluorescence of the basement.

"If you're sure you're okay . . . ?" Bivens waited for my nod. "I'm just going to go talk to Miller for a minute. The way he's draggin'; just make sure he's not going into shock or anything."

He strode forward, catching up to Alan at the elevator door. "How you doin'?" I heard him ask.

Of all the people to be fired as a medic . . . Betty Addenaur's words rang in my ears: *Ain't it always the way?*

40

Fred Hershey came to the courthouse to find me after his last appointment of the day. He'd heard the closing statements, then he went out for a few minutes to answer a beeper call. In that short time, he missed the verdict. And when he got back to the courtroom, Alan and I were already gone.

While Betty Addenaur shot herself in front of us, Fred was having dinner downtown with Joseph Huizen. When he dropped Joseph in the parking lot to pick up his car, he noticed the crime scene tape. News reporters and photographers were swarming by then, as they would be for days. Worry made Fred hop out of his car and ask what was going on. It didn't take him long to track us to the Sheriff's Department.

We'd given our statements by then, and were sitting in a drab waiting room while the deputies did some last-minute paper shuffling.

A few of them knew Fred; they let him in to sit with us.

He spent most of that time talking to Alan Miller. I could tell by his soothing tone that he was worried about Alan, about his reaction to both the verdict and the shooting.

By the time Fred turned back to me, his manner was deeply clinical. But I couldn't afford to start expressing my feelings; right now, I'd drown in them.

I cut him off quickly. "Did Bustamonte and Shaduff get back?"

For a therapist, Fred sure could look avoidant. "Let's get you guys home and give you some dinner," he suggested.

"What's up? What did they say?" My God, they hadn't found evidence of Miller's guilt inside the mountain facility? They hadn't found evidence he'd fled behind its fence after the accident?

I could still see Betty Addenaur's slack, dead face. If Miller was guilty and I'd won him an acquittal, I'd helped pull the trigger.

"Or isn't this the place to discuss it?"

The main workroom of the Sheriff's Department, visible through the open door, was bustling; Friday night was apparently prime time.

Fred followed both my glance and my train of thought. "It's not that." His voice was quiet; he shifted a little closer. "They left a message at about two." He scowled, his thick brows shading his eyes in the overlighted room. "Shaduff was calling from his cell phone. He said they found something." He averted his gaze.

"What? Just tell me." I'd had too trying a day to mess around with the amenities, to wait for the right moment.

"I don't know." He gave me one of those really-look-at-you looks.

"Before Shaduff hung up, as an aside, he said he hoped they hadn't been found, as well."

"What were his exact words?"

"I believe they were, 'We've definitely got something,' or maybe it was 'some activity.' Then he said, 'I hope it doesn't have us, too.' That was at two o'clock. I checked my machine again before and after dinner. Half an hour ago."

"Could you check it now?" It sounded like Shaduff was warning us they might get—what?—detained, attacked? It sounded like they might need help.

Fred stopped to soothe Alan again first. I tried not to be a jerk about rushing him. But Bustamonte and Shaduff had left for the Potemkin Lockheed at around noon. By two o'clock, they'd found something. It was now past six-thirty. They should have returned. They should have phoned back.

In the few minutes Fred was gone, we were brought statements to sign. We were given deputies' business cards (for my collection).

The party was escorted through the main room and out into the hall. I jotted down John's and Barry's phone numbers and promised to call them in the morning. I'd get started hassling their employer and their union rep. I'd get them reinstated if I had to wage a one-woman guerrilla war.

They left.

While waiting for Fred to return, I yanked a red garbage bag out of Alan's hand and threw it in a trash can. The deputies had asked him to remove his bloody jacket and place it inside. They were fussy about their furniture.

We owed Edward a suit.

The deputies also had Alan scrub his hands with Hexol, which was a good thing, since he kept rubbing his eyes.

Finally Fred walked toward us. He was shaking his head. "No message."

"Take me up there?" I didn't trust myself to drive; I felt dazed and foolish. I wasn't unaccustomed to the feeling, but I get tired of being flipped off and passed on the right. "Will you? I'll show you the way."

"Do you think we should spend a little time making sure Alan's . . . ?" There was no tactful way to finish the sentence, I guess.

"I'm okay," Alan said. "I'm just . . . I mean, God, poor lady."

I had to agree with Fred that Alan didn't look okay. But I didn't want to go up the mountain alone, not with only an hour of daylight left. I looked at Alan. "You want to come?"

"He's not up to it," Fred murmured.

Alan surprised me by saying, "You're going up Pine Flat and Bonny Doon Road, up to that area?"

Had I mentioned where we were going? "Uh-huh." I'd asked him about the place over lunch, but had I mentioned sending Shaduff and Bustamonte there?

"I should go with you." Alan waved away the objection he could see Fred about to make. "I know the mountain. You can get into a lot of trouble up there. You better take me."

Fred was asking, "What kind of trouble?"

But I didn't want to waste time arguing. I started for the exit.

We stopped just long enough for Fred to pop the trunk of his Lexus and pull out his gym bag. He wasn't about to let Alan climb in with a spattered shirt and pants with bloody knees. He tossed Alan some sweat clothes. Using the car as a screen, Alan changed right there.

On our way out of the parking lot, we pulled behind an exiting news van.

I made a mental note not to watch the news tonight. The chances were slim to nil that we'd be congratulated for going out on a limb with the only defense that fit the facts. And juries were rarely praised for reaching difficult, unpopular verdicts.

The judge was right. The jury's quick verdict could only reflect reasonable doubt that Miller was in his car when it landed on Addenaur. The sheriff had failed to collect the necessary evidence and the prosecution had failed to prove it by other means.

It had probably been wise to introduce Miller's alibi, however strange —to offer no explanation would have damned him in the jurors' eyes. But no jury could have endorsed alien abduction so quickly and decisively. The verdict had certainly been rendered on the narrowest possible grounds.

That wouldn't matter to the press. The jurors would be excoriated and ridiculed for accepting the "spaceman defense." Reporters wouldn't bother being analytical when they could be sensational.

Betty Addenaur's suicide in front of the defendant and his lawyer,

that would be the lead: a miscarriage of justice with tragic consequences. There would be only one side to the news coverage, the easy
side. The monster of orthodoxy liked its food predigested.

We cruised past Shaduff's office, making sure he hadn't returned.

Then I told Fred how to get where we were going. Alan, in the back,
suggested a quicker route.

I could see Alan's reflection in the rearview mirror mounted outside
the door. He stared through the window, cloud shadows racing across
his face. Only when we got near Davenport did he sit up a little. When
we turned and started up the mountain, he leaned close to the car
window as if inhaling the scenery.

He'd expected a guilty verdict. I could see it in his reverence.

I relaxed into my seat. Thank God Miller wasn't in jail tonight. At
least I didn't have to live with that, didn't have to relive my own jail
time.

The evening sun bathed fields in golden light. We sped around curves
lined with horsetails in the shade and wild irises in the sun, past redwood thickets and Maxfield Parrish meadows, past tangles of wild roses
and fields with grazing horses, past dark gullies and feathery meadows
buzzing with mosquitoes and sprinkled with purple vetch. Here and
there, odd rock formations rose like badly drawn castles.

Alan told Fred where to turn.

Ten minutes later, we spotted the dazzle-camouflaged water tank.
Carl Shaduff's Range Rover was parked a little farther up the road,
under an overhang of live oaks. The fenced facility wasn't in view; it
was another quarter mile or so up the mountain. This was a less conspic-
uous place to park, but I doubted Bustamonte had appreciated the hike.

There was barely room for Fred to pull over.

I walked around the Range Rover, peering into the windows. I didn't
see anything revealing inside. Two jackets lay across the backseat. Foil
wrappers from two film rolls littered the passenger seat.

I looked up to find Alan walking toward the water tank, frowning as
if he were seeing through it. He went behind it.

I hurried to catch up.

Alan was walking as fast as the wooded, viney terrain allowed.

"Alan!"

He didn't turn.

I didn't want to lose him, too, add him to the list that already included Shaduff and Bustamonte. And Maria Nanos.

"Alan," I called again.

He turned, looking bigger than usual in Fred's too-small gray sweats. Even in the shade of mixed forest, I could see his face was contorted.

"Maria," he said. "I wanted to tell you. She's not . . ."

"Not what?"

Fred was charging forward, in full doctor mode, ready to tone-of-voice us some more.

"What about Maria?"

"In Half Moon Bay, at the Denny's—"

"Alan?" Fred was looking seriously kindly. "Maybe this isn't the best time for you to be—"

I grabbed Fred's arm to shush him. "In Half Moon Bay?"

Alan knotted his fists, crossing them over his chest self-protectively. A response to having a psychiatrist freaking out about him?

"What about Maria?" I prompted.

"She's not the hitchhiker."

"What do you mean, she's not . . ." There was only one thing he could mean. "She's not the girl you picked up in Half Moon Bay?"

"No."

"But you said she was! You saw her picture in the paper, a picture of her at the crop circle, and you said she was your hitchhiker." I was too surprised to do anything but state the obvious.

"I recognized the picture, that's true," he admitted. "And we were looking for the hitchhiker, so I thought that's who was in the picture."

"But she said she was the hitchhiker." And besides, "When she came to Shaduff's office the night the police picked her up, you guys recognized each other."

"I recognized her from someplace else. But she wasn't the hitchhiker."

"Then who is she? How could you get confused about something like that?"

I glanced at Fred, half expecting him to offer a theory. But his lips were pressed into a resolute line, as if he resisted feeding Alan psychiatric terms and jargon.

"I dropped off the hitchhiker, another girl; I have no idea who. Brown haired and young like Maria. I dropped her off just like I said. I guess

her face wasn't that clear in my head; I was mostly looking at the road."
He put a hand over his brow as if checking to see if he was overheating.
"When I saw the picture in the paper and recognized the face, I assumed
it was her. Right then, I didn't remember anything besides what I told
Fred."

I repeated, "But Maria said she was your hitchhiker. Why would she
do that?"

"When she came to Carl Shaduff's and I saw her in person, I remembered. When she walked in, it came to me. I dropped off the hitchhiker
—the real one—then I took the turn into Davenport to go home. And
Maria, she flagged down my car. She pounded on my window. She
begged me to help her."

"Under hypnosis, you didn't say anything about this." Fred sounded
too calm.

"I didn't remember it."

"That's the function of hypnosis, to bring out what you don't remember."

No wonder Alan doubted the contents of the tape. He knew at least
part of it was a lie. He knew something had happened in addition; he
knew it as soon as he saw and recognized Maria.

If he was telling the truth now.

"You must have been very determined to keep this encounter buried,"
Fred continued. "Do you know why? Do you recall what else happened?"

"Like I said, she pounded on my car window. She kept saying a
helicopter was chasing her. She said she was trying to camp up on the
mountain, but a helicopter chased her away." He started rubbing his
chest. "I know there are helicopters up here. Lockheed's building stealth
bombers, and CAMP's looking for pot fields, and there's fire and medical
helicopters, and military ones from Monterey and Travis. But I'd never
seen a helicopter at night. And I couldn't imagine one chasing her—I
thought she might be on drugs or something. I was going to take her
home, let her sleep on my couch. She looked so scared; she was so
young."

"And what happened?"

"I have no idea. As far as I know, we went to my house and I went to
bed." He buried his fists in his armpits. "Except, obviously we didn't.

Maybe the helicopter took us somewhere; maybe I mixed up a helicopter with a—That's why I ran after her the other day, when she came and asked for money. That's why I chased her; I couldn't stand not knowing. I couldn't stand wondering and wondering what happened, why this didn't come out when I was hypnotized. If maybe it was a helicopter that took us . . . I went after her to ask her, just ask where we went, what we did there."

"You didn't believe her story that she was abducted by aliens with you."

"I wasn't abducted by aliens!" He scowled at us. "My hypnosis was wrong—it left out the part about Maria, didn't it? Why should I trust any of the rest of it? It was all wrong!" He took a few gasping breaths. "I was a liar and a jerk for not saying so during the trial. And now Betty Addenaur's dead."

"Alan, don't you see?" Fred's tone was gentle. "You're looking for ways to deny what you heard yourself say on the tape. Especially now that you're safe, now that the trial's over. And after what you witnessed in the parking lot."

Man, was I confused. Did Fred think Alan was delusional about Maria *not* being the hitchhiker?

I tried to steer us back to the tangible. "Last Friday, what did Maria say when you caught up with her?"

Fred flashed me a look: Don't interfere with the Doctor-King.

"She looked at me like I was crazy. She might have even called me crazy."

"Alan," Fred began.

"Please, Fred! I need to hear this." I'd just watched Betty Addenaur shoot herself; I needed facts, not psychology.

"I asked Maria where we went after I picked her up in Davenport. She said, God, maybe I really did believe in flying saucers; maybe I really was mental. And she wiggled free of me. I ended up running after her, not running with her." He still looked shaken by her accusation. "I lost her in the crowd at The Boardwalk." He drooped, looking discouraged.

"Why didn't you tell me this before? I'm your lawyer—you're supposed to talk to me."

"She told everyone she was the hitchhiker. I couldn't contradict her.

Especially after someone shot through the window. I mean, what if they were shooting at her? What if she had some good reason for saying that?" His expression begged forgiveness. "I didn't want to lie to you. Fred, I'm sorry—you spent all that money on expert witnesses and I didn't want to lie to you. Willa, you spent all this time." He closed his eyes tight. "I didn't want to lie about being abducted."

Fred and I exchanged glances. He was right about Alan; I understood that now.

There was no possible reason for Maria to claim to be Miller's hitch-hiker if she wasn't. It only embroiled her in a court case, landed her in custody, and set the police looking for her. If she'd denied it, she'd have been just one more runaway, eventually falling through the cracks.

So Alan had lied, all right—to himself. He'd lied about Maria not being the hitchhiker. He'd intertwined memories of meeting her with prosecution testimony about helicopters. He'd rearranged his actual recollections so he could use them to negate the ones he'd repressed.

The trial was over now, and he was left to face the petrifying story he'd committed to tape under hypnosis. Alan Miller didn't need a law-yer anymore, he needed a psychiatrist.

Fred put his arm around him. "This acquittal was very much to be desired, Alan. For you to lose your freedom would have been a tragedy; you have every right to be happy with this result. As for me paying the expert witnesses, that was my choice. And you had no control over Mrs. Addenaur. Her reactions and actions were her responsibility, not yours."

I smelled the cool pine of the forest and looked around at the dappled golden light on the duff. Throughout the trial, I had nursed every suspi-cion of Alan Miller, refusing to believe he told the whole truth.

I still didn't know what the truth was. Patrick Toben might be right. It might have happened exactly as he'd presented it: Alan Miller had gotten to Davenport later than he admitted. He'd been sleepy or drunk, and he'd taken a wrong turn, bouncing across a field and over a cliff, his Fiat tracks later obscured by the farmer's truck. He'd wandered from the accident, roaming the night away in a state of delusion and distress. And as he lay beside some road or in some field, he'd had nightmares based on an *X-Files* episode or a television movie.

I hadn't proved otherwise. I hadn't demonstrated it in court, though I'd won the case. And I certainly hadn't convinced myself.

But right now, watching Miller try so hard to fool himself about Maria, try so hard to discount the experiences he'd relived under hypnosis, I was sure of one thing: However much he wanted to doubt it, however hard he worked to deny it, Alan Miller absolutely believed the story he'd recited into Fred's tape recorder.

I'd preferred, at times, to hope he was lying. I didn't think so anymore.

It didn't necessarily mean it had happened that way. But I was finally persuaded he thought so. On the deepest possible level, despite all his protestations to the contrary, Alan Miller believed his horror story.

Maybe someday, safe in bed, I'd try to decide what I thought that meant. What thousands of stories just like it meant.

"We've got to find Bustamonte and Shaduff," I urged. "We don't have much light."

Alan turned away from Fred.

Fred said, "Alan, please. Try to forgive yourself for doing nothing more than allowing yourself to be hypnotized. And for being unable to censor yourself under hypnosis."

Alan, his voice husky, said, "The fenced-off area's up ahead. We can reach it faster through here than up the road."

"Let's go," I beseeched Fred. "While we have the light."

Fred's lips were parted as if he had plenty more to say. But when Alan started walking, he followed.

It would have been easy for us to stroll abreast, but I suppose none of us felt like chatting.

We were soon on uneven terrain, pine and oak forest with occasional stands of redwoods and open patches of duff. Within minutes, we reached a spot where a twelve-foot Cyclone fence, topped with barbed wire, turned a corner.

"The Potemkin Lockheed?" I asked.

"The—? Oh, yeah, I guess it does look like Lockheed," Alan agreed. "From where you stop your car and look in through the gate, it's a hike to get to this spot." Alan pointed back behind us. "But from the water tank, if you know where you're going, it's pretty close. Farther on, the fence turns a corner and stops at a gorge. For all intents and purposes, the mountain ends at this facility."

"Have you ever tried to get in?"

"Some parts of the mountain, I don't worry too much about fences.

It's just folks wanting privacy or keeping their horses corralled. But up here, you've got Lockheed building missiles and bombers, pot farmers guarding their crops, local militia on makeshift shooting ranges. This far off the beaten path, you've got to take fences seriously. There's plenty of unfenced mountain—it's no use asking to be shot at or have dogs sicced on you."

"Do you have any idea what this place is?"

"No. I always assumed the government owned it; all those signs out front."

"Bustamonte thinks the military/Lockheed-looking stuff is just for show."

"Why does he think that? It sure looks real."

"I guess he thinks it looks *too* real." But Bustamonte was predisposed to look for the circle beneath the square.

Fred said, "If I could make a suggestion . . . let's go back to the car the other way, the long way, keeping to the fence. It's getting dark fast. We've got just enough light to try and spot Shaduff and Bustamonte through the chain-links."

As much as I didn't relish the hike, I had to agree.

We walked in silence, listening to the rustle of duff, the creak of tree limbs, the scramble of small animals. Through the wire mesh, I saw nothing but trees, vines, pecking jays. I saw no buildings, no vehicles, no helicopters, no goons. And no detectives.

It was fully dark by the time we reached the front entrance. But floodlights blazed above the gate, around the guard station, and along the road that curved behind the trees.

The front gate was unchained and open wide enough for a truck to roll through. A uniformed man stood just outside the station. A rifle was slung across his back. He spoke into a radio.

Tonight the place looked like Lockheed on steroids.

Two men trotted toward us. "Please identify yourselves and state your purpose," one of them barked.

He wore a security guard's uniform, not a military one.

I hurried forward. "My name is Willa Jansson. I'm looking for two men, Carl Shaduff and Bart Bustamonte."

No use being coy. If they had Bustamonte and Shaduff, I wanted to know right now.

One of the guards held up a hand, keeping us from coming closer.

The other put his radio to his lips and walked away, speaking quietly into it.

Headlights in the parking lot popped on. A doorless Jeep sped toward the gate. Two more security guards jumped out.

One of them, craggy and overweight, approached. "You're looking for a Carl Shaduff and a Bart Bustamonte?" As if there were several.

"Yes. Are they here?"

He said nothing until he was close enough for me to smell the onions he'd had for dinner. He loomed for a moment. Was he going to try to detain us? We hadn't breached the fence.

"What's your business with these men?" He watched us suspiciously.

"They phoned and said they were at the water tank down the road. That's the last we heard from them."

"What was their purpose in coming here?"

"I don't know. I just know they're late and we're looking for them."

"Why?"

"We're going dancing. Do you know where they are or not?"

"A Carl Shaduff and a Bart Bustamonte were placed under citizen's arrest for trespassing at fourteen-forty this afternoon. They were later transported by Sheriff's Department personnel to the County Jail in Santa Cruz. You might try looking for them there."

"They were booked for trespassing? They weren't given citations and released?"

"No ma'am," the guard said. "The statute numbers are clearly posted on the fence; trespassing at this location is a criminal offense. Photography is strictly prohibited. Refusal to turn over photographic equipment and/or failure to leave when requested to do so will result in arrest and prosecution."

Jesus, the guy talked like a penal code.

I wanted to sit down in the duff, just sit there until some semblance of energy and stamina returned to my weary limbs and overtaxed brain.

While we'd hightailed it to their rescue, Bustamonte and Shaduff were being shuffled around the County Jail, right across the street from the courthouse.

They'd probably posted bail by now—probably not much more than a simple citation would have cost, just more of a hassle. More of a message.

"Did you come here in a vehicle?" the Stepford guard demanded.

"It's down the road."

He motioned to someone behind him, saying, "Escort these people to their vehicle."

We could have refused the escort. But a ride was a ride.

We barreled down the hill in the windy, doorless Jeep. The console had a radio with lots of buttons.

"So is this a military base?" I asked the driver.

He didn't say anything.

"Part of Lockheed?" Still nothing. "A dude ranch? A detox center?"

Fred put his hand on my arm to shut me up.

When we got out, I tried again. I asked the driver, "Is that place part of Lockheed?"

He replied, "It's private property."

Gee, no kidding.

But the tight security told me one thing. Bart Bustamonte was wrong about Alan Miller having hidden out there.

The guard waited for us to get into Fred's Lexus. Then he drove behind us all the way to the main road.

It was a step down from a helicopter escort, but just as effective.

41

I hoped Fred continued to feel good about the verdict after assessing the publicity's effect on his practice—and writing all the necessary checks.

Right now, he seemed a trifle annoyed with Bustamonte for reminding him to include the cost of bail.

We were sitting around Shaduff's office, behind his new, shuttered windows. Alan had excused himself, leaving to go back to Edward's. He'd declined Fred's repeated offers of company, saying he wanted to be alone. I knew the feeling.

"I would have left you guys another message," Shaduff complained, "but those dickheads kept us waiting for the sheriff almost two hours, just sitting in the parking lot on the ground. Wouldn't let me near my cell phone."

"Searching us, taking the film out of our cameras—can you imagine?" Bustamonte looked scorched. He'd have sunburn blisters on his rain-coast Washington forehead tomorrow. But he didn't seem disappointed in the outcome of the trip. "There's definitely something up there!"

"No shit, Sherlock." Carl Shaduff looked like he'd had enough of Bustamonte and then some. "I kinda got the hint from the half dozen burly guys ripping film out of our cameras and getting us arrested!" To me, he said, "It's obviously some kind of government-contract facility. It's no eccentric recluse with a tall fence, not with that kind of security. It's a branch office of Lockheed or some other military subcontractor. Probably quite a few of them in odd nooks around the state." Another fed-up glance at Bustamonte. "Nothing sinister about that."

"Uh-uh," Bustamonte disagreed. "They've got serious shit up there—maybe even alien spacecraft. Did you see how many guards came at us from every which way when we jumped that fence? They've got cameras in the woods. They knew where we were parked. They are hiding something big up there," he repeated. "They're as well guarded, if not better, than Lockheed. And they're more remote, better hidden, and nobody knows about them, not even our people." He nodded with satisfaction. "That will soon change! I'll be making some phone calls and getting people down here ASAP."

Shaduff looked beleaguered. Fred looked alarmed.

"You'll be staying in Santa Cruz?"

"On my own dime, of course. You know, it's not really well known that Lockheed operates here, at the end of a mountain road, miles from any convenience." He raised his brows. "And now here's this other place, practically its twin, but unmarked!"

"Granted—they're doing some kind of top-secret research work; you can tell by the set up. But that's not a crime. They don't want protesters and mobs of job applicants up there, so what?" Shaduff demanded.

"So they've been brilliant about keeping a low profile, keeping tucked away, keeping the spotlight on other locations. That tells you something right there. It tells you they're doing something important."

"Every research and development place thinks it's doing something important," Shaduff pointed out.

"This is exactly where you get UFO sightings. Over air force bases, nuclear test sights, NASA research facilities, Lockheed Space and Missile—and spooky places with no name on the gate."

He looked at us, then grinned. "You think I don't know it sounds crazy? You think I have no perspective how this strikes people who haven't put ten years into researching it? But do me a favor before you write me off as a nut."

Fred obliged him by asking, "What?" He handed Bustamonte a check for his days of testimony and, presumably, his bail.

"Just keep your ears open. See if you don't start hearing more and more astronauts admitting what they saw in outer space, NASA workers breaking their silence about what they know, military pilots speaking up. See if you don't hear more and more nice people like Alan Miller telling weird stories." He looked over Fred's check, then he tucked it into his pocket. "There's going to be plenty of discussion here in Santa Cruz about these issues!" he predicted. He smiled at me. "I'm so glad you invited me down."

I'd helped make Santa Cruz a flakier place. I guessed the downtown merchants would be coming around soon to measure me for a statue.

42

By morning, the police confirmed that the bullets from the gun that killed Betty Addenaur matched the ones fired through Carl Shaduff's window and into Colonel Kraduck's vest.

Her grief had made her eclectic as well as crazy. She'd tried to shoot Miller (or perhaps herself) at the hospital. Then she'd tried, with partial success, to burn down his house. Then she'd tried to shoot him (or perhaps me) through a window after following us to Shaduff's office.

Later, her fury over Fred's testimony led her to sneak in through his window and throw things around his condo. I don't know why she chose more drastic measures for Colonel Kraduck. Maybe, like later commentators, she found him to be my most impressively "American" and unassailably "sane" expert; maybe his credibility had infuriated her.

She probably tracked him by following me or Carl Shaduff to the hotel. She saw Kraduck alone in the parking lot and fired at him from a borrowed car. The bullet casings (and half a jug of kerosene from setting Miller's fire) were found right on the passenger seat.

The colonel, ironically, owed his life to my mother. Two nights before encountering Mother in the courthouse corridor, he'd seen the helicopters hovering outside his hotel window.

Then, an unstable-looking woman (his description) accosted him in the courthouse and began besieging him about his years at Travis Air Force Base. He decided the two events, taken together, could be interpreted as a threat. He was being told to shut up, and he didn't like it.

So he put on his bulletproof vest, and he let Bustamonte know he was on his way to Travis. He was prepared to have a shouting match with former colleagues who seemed to think they could make him stop speaking the truth.

My mother saved the life of someone who, years ago, had had her arrested. There was a kind of beauty in it, not quite on par with Joseph Huizen's crop circle resembling a glucose molecule.

I phoned her with the news.

She mulled it over for a minute. "Maybe he'll place a higher value on pacifists now."

"Or on bulletproof vests."

"You know who we're having for dinner, Willa? Speaking of all this UFO business? He knows you, he says."

"Who?"

"Reggie Fulmer."

"What? Why? Why are you having that ass over to dinner?"

I could tell by the brief silence that she didn't agree with my assessment of him.

"When WILPF held that meeting down there, remember? To organize a teach-in about how this UFO nonsense is being used by the Republicans as an excuse to raise the defense budget—"

"Mother, I don't want to get into all that. Just tell me why Fulmer's coming to dinner."

"This *is* why. I *am* telling you. He's going to be one of our featured speakers."

"Fulmer thinks the UFO threat is being used to beef up military spending?" Maybe she was kidding. Maybe she'd developed a sense of humor in her old age. "A guy who believes crop circles are subliminal messages from Merlin?"

"He doesn't say he believes that! Just that they're a pictographic phenomenon." She continued hastily, "But what he absolutely doesn't believe is that they have anything to do with UFOs!"

"And that's enough to get him on your debunkers faculty?"

"Well, we were going to invite some scientists. But they believe two men made all the crop circles in England just because the men said so —we want someone more analytical than that. Reggie says scientists are too easily taken in by publicity hounds."

She was always good for a straight line.

I hung up. Reginald Fulmer at my parents' dinner table. I looked out the window of Fred's condo. The sky was blue with feathery trails of cirrus clouds. A breeze played through the open window, carrying the scent of mowed lawn and jasmine.

I tried to think of a reason not to keep seventy-five miles between me and my wonderful but highly exasperating kin.

My second call was to Cary Curtis. If I still had a job waiting, that would be reason enough. But it proved to be a quick conversation.

Cary wasn't impressed that I'd won Miller's case. "What do you expect from a Santa Cruz jury?"

He asked me when I'd be cleaning out my office.

I phoned John Bivens, the paramedic who'd been fired for telling the truth under oath on the witness stand.

"I still want your case," I told him. "You might be my first clients"— albeit pro bono—"in a new practice. I'm thinking about moving down here."

"You'll like it," he assured me. "Except during tourist season. And weekends when the students are in rut."

I packed my bag and went downstairs to thank Fred for his hospitality. If I'd been shanghaied, at least it had been to a tree-lined beach town. And the favor I'd repaid had been a huge one.

I found Fred at his kitchen table, slumped over a cup of coffee. I'd never seen him look so tired. But then, I'd never seen him unshaven, either. I'd never seen his hair uncombed, much less ungelled.

The sight stopped me short. I dropped my suitcase in the doorway and walked slowly toward him.

"Fred? Are you okay?"

I prayed he wasn't going to tell me the thing I most dreaded hearing —that Alan Miller was indeed guilty, that Fred had, during hypnosis, implanted the memories of his wild alibi.

Fred's behavior had certainly been odd: getting the DA's permission to hypnotize Miller, calling in a business lawyer to represent him, breaking the doctor-patient privilege to play Mickey's tape for me, disappearing for two hours in the middle of our witness prep. Now that I'd done all he'd hoped—or, judging from his downcast face, more than he'd hoped—would he confess to me that my client was guilty, after all? In helping to free Miller, had I also helped delude him?

"Fred!" I repeated. "What's up?"

He looked at me, his eyes red rimmed. "I wish I knew. It happened again, just now. I came downstairs to make some coffee. I was going to go back up and change into my running clothes, take a run. Coffee'd be ready when I got back. Then I'd set out some breakfast, have a shower."

I noticed for the first time that Fred was in plain cotton pajamas resembling hospital scrubs.

I walked to the table, squatting beside him. "So what happened?" Close up, he looked ill. I was getting spooked.

"Nothing. Nothing at all happened, except that it's almost two hours later. Two hours later and here I still am in the kitchen. I don't have my running clothes on. I haven't been back upstairs. I haven't been anywhere or done anything, not that I'm aware of. And yet"—his eyes widened—"all that time passed."

He'd lost two hours this morning. As he'd lost them the night I was preparing his testimony? The morning he'd set out to go running but, when I saw him later beside my car, hadn't broken a sweat?

"What are you saying, Fred?" I knew what he was saying. That he'd experienced "missing time."

"You asked me the real reason I brought you down here, Willa." He sounded bone weary. "This is it. What Alan Miller described, I'm afraid . . ."

"That it's been happening to you, too?" I didn't know how to respond. "Have you been hypnotized?"

He shook his head. "I didn't want to taint my testimony for Miller. In case the DA asked if I'd ever experienced anything like it myself, I didn't want to have to answer yes. I didn't want to undercut my credibility."

"You've been getting up too early, that's all." All I could make myself believe. "You've been under stress and you've been driving yourself too hard. The most likely explanation is that you've been dozing off, catching up on your sleep. You're exhausted—your body's just forcing you to slow down."

"Maybe," Fred agreed.

"Weird ideas are contagious, Fred. I've seen it with my parents a hundred times. Some conspiracy theory starts out seeming too far-fetched, even for them. But the more they hear about it, the more normal and plausible it begins to sound. And next thing I know, they've bought in. It makes perfect sense to them and they revise their version of reality to accommodate it. That's what this UFO stuff is doing to you. If you'd never heard all this from Miller, from the UFOlogists, you'd be fine with the idea of nodding off now and then."

I wondered if he'd risk going to a hypnotist. If I were him, I wouldn't tempt fate. I wouldn't jeopardize a relatively comfortable worldview.

He leaned forward and embraced me. In a brisker tone, he said, "Thank you, Willa."

I knew he wasn't endorsing my advice. He was thanking me for taking Miller's case. I understood now the secret worry that had fueled his request.

I hugged him back. Whatever else might need to be resolved, we'd done it. We'd won.

43

I wanted to say good-bye to Alan Miller. I wanted to make sure he was okay. I knew today's paper would be especially brutal.

I knocked at the door of Edward's little house. Edward would be home from Panama in a week or so. But Alan's place would be fit to rehabilitate before then.

We'd added the final piece to the arson investigator's report: Betty Addenaur had kerosened the area around Alan's heater, then clicked on the *high* button and left. It had probably taken hours to ignite. The damage had mostly been confined to the front corner of the house. Alan's landlord had already contracted out the repairs. Alan agreed to do the finishing work himself so he could return sooner.

I knocked again. It was ten-thirty on a gorgeous Tuesday morning. Maybe Alan was out mushroom hunting, enjoying the freedom he'd almost lost. I was turning to leave when I thought I heard a sound inside.

I hesitated. Maybe Alan heard the knock but wasn't answering. The man was entitled to his solitude. He'd been through enough to make anyone become a hermit for a while. And he'd certainly seen enough of me lately.

I knocked again. Again, I thought I heard a stirring.

I tried the door, finding it unlocked. I pushed it open slowly, hating to invade his privacy, afraid I might catch him in a depressive's dishabille.

I found him semiconscious on the floor. His face was battered and bleeding. One of Edward's wooden chairs had been shattered against a wall. A leg of it, splintered and with nails protruding, lay covered in blood beside Alan.

"Alan!" I bent over him. The blood on his face was still sticky.

Alan opened his eyes. One was swollen half shut from a scratch across the lid, perhaps from a sliver of the chair leg. Blood soaked his T-shirt. His sweatpants were ripped and bloody at the thigh.

"Alan?" My voice was squeaky with worry. "What happened? Oh my God."

I flung my arm back as if the phone would rush to meet my hand. I scooted backward to grab it. I dialed 911.

"We need an ambulance," I told the operator.

"No. Wait." Alan's voice was woozy. "How long—Oh, shit." He sat up, holding his head.

I gave 911 Edward's address.

"No, no, let me talk." He reached for the phone.

"I don't know what happened," I told the emergency operator. "He's been beaten."

"Let me talk!"

I handed him the phone.

"I'm okay; don't send an ambulance. But you've got to get the police after an old couple with a teenage girl." He was curled over his knees, he could barely keep upright. "They're going to kill her."

"Oh, Jesus," I said to him. "Maria?"

"Maria Nanos is her name. Tell the police her name. They know about her already. Her grandparents went crazy. They're going to kill her. Tell them." He repeated Edward's address. "I think they're on foot, maybe still in the neighborhood."

He hung up, getting to his feet and staggering into the bathroom. I followed.

He splashed water on his face. "She came here for money again. For help. This morning. They were right behind her." He winced. "They must have been watching the house. Followed us here from court or something." He gripped the sink with both hands. Blood dripped onto the wet porcelain. "They smashed things. They screamed I was her boyfriend and they'd kill me."

He grabbed my arm, pulling me toward the back door. "Come on," he said.

"You're in no shape—Lie down." He looked a little better without the dried blood, but his nose appeared broken, his cheek and eye were hugely swollen.

"I'm okay—just had to clear my head." He continued pulling me toward the kitchen. "They're going to kill her, come on."

"Come where?"

"They dragged her out the back. It wasn't that long ago. They can't have gotten far, not if they're on foot." He bent forward so that momentum carried his shuffling body along.

In the kitchen, he made an effort to straighten. He grabbed his torso, crying out. But he stayed upright. He picked up speed, going out the back door.

There were drag marks and scuffed areas all across the dirt. Alan stopped and braced himself on Edward's kayak so he wouldn't fall. I passed him on my way out the gate.

I looked up and down the tranquil alley. "Maria!" I screamed. "Mariiii-iia!" I put as much noise as I could into it, but there was no response.

I ran left toward the coffee shop and tried again, still getting no response.

Not knowing what else to do, I doubled back to the other end. I noticed trash cans tipped over in the next alleyway, their contents spilled.

I dashed across the street. I raced past the downed cans. I could hear Alan's footsteps, in ragged groupings, behind me.

When I got to the end of the second alley, I called out again.

This time, I thought I heard something in reply. A faint, high-pitched cry.

Up ahead, the alley became little more than a gravel path flanked by huge tangles of wild roses and ivy-covered sheds behind crumbling Victorians.

"Maria?"

I heard a thin whistle, the kind of scream you force out of your lungs during a paralytic nightmare.

Alan caught up to me, running past me like he'd pitched himself down a hill, his gait uneven and staggering.

We could see them now. They were in a bower of ivy and weeds, an overgrown portion of a half-collapsed garbage enclave.

Maria was on the ground, arms raised to protect her head. Her grandparents were stooped over her in their elegant suits, attacking her with the ferocity of tigers.

Alan reached them a few seconds before me. He grabbed a garbage pail lid as the grandfather was about to smash it back down onto Maria. I could hear Alan grunt as the grandfather turned to attack him.

The grandmother was using her fists and feet, kicking Maria's legs over and over and screaming something in another language. I ran up behind her and tried to pull her away, to pull her farther down the alley.

It was like taking hold of a huge wild dog. She was strong and crazy, clubbing my head with her fists, shouting shrill epithets I didn't understand.

"Run, Maria," I called to her.

But she just sat there trembling, forearms crossed over her head.

As Alan and I struggled with her grandparents, she curled into a fetal position and began sobbing. I thought I heard her calling for her mother.

A police siren screamed in my ear. Pivoting and staggering with Maria's grandmother, I hadn't noticed the car racing down the alley toward us.

It took the cop, me, and Alan to get Maria's grandparents into the back of the police car.

Alan turned his attention to Maria. The cop phoned for an ambulance. And I watched the old couple in the backseat of the police car collapse into convulsive sobs.

When the ambulance came for Maria, the paramedics insisted on taking Alan, too. One of the medics, despite his haste, was good enough to tell me he didn't see anything drastic or permanent in their injuries. But they would definitely need stitches and painkillers and X rays.

As the ambulance pulled out of the alley, the grandparents extended their arms toward it as if to hold on to their wounded child. I saw the stricken looks on their faces, the anguish, the sorrow; they loved Maria. She'd told me they did, but until now, I hadn't believed her.

I'd been scared many times these last few weeks, but this moment was the worst. No alien being could be as frightening as someone truly crazy who truly loves you. Mickey and Joey proved it to Fred, and Maria had just proven it to me.

The policeman took notes while I described what I'd seen. Then he gave me his card, yet another one for the stack. I gave him my phone number and promised to make myself available to the district attorney, if necessary. He drove away.

I walked the few blocks back to Edward's, trying to smell the flowers and catalog the profusion of plants poking through back fences.

I tried not to think about things that could reach out of the sky and pluck people away. I tried even harder not to think about things that could reach out of people's own homes to do much worse.

I walked back into Edward's yard, closing the gate behind me. I went into the kitchen and locked the back door.

The living room was a mess. The wall was damaged where the chair had splintered, and there was blood on the floor.

I swept the mess away and mopped the hardwood with peroxide.

I was sitting on the couch wondering what to do next, whether to stop at the hospital, go back to Fred's, or just drive on home.

I looked up to find Edward Hershey himself standing in his doorway, obviously very surprised to see me there. His hair was long and wild, the tips of his windblown curls bleached golden. He sported a medium-length beard, and his face was tanned a deep clay. He looked like someone who'd just sailed through the Panama Canal.

He dropped his duffel bag, mouth gaping.

"Willa!" He looked alarmed. "What are you doing in my house? What are you doing in Santa Cruz?"

"The short answer?" I smiled. "I moved here."

bibliography

Andrews, Colin, and Pat Delgado. *Circular Evidence*. Phanes Press, 1989.

Blum, Howard. *Out There*. Simon & Schuster, 1990.

Bova, Ben, and Byron Preiss, eds. *First Contact*. Plume, 1990.

Brookesmith, Peter. *UFO: The Complete Sightings*. Barnes & Noble, 1995.

Bryan, C. D. B. *Close Encounters of the Fourth Kind*. Knopf, 1995.

Cousineau, Phil. *UFOs: A Manual for the Millennium*. HarperCollins West, 1995.

Drake, Frank, and Dava Sobel. *Is Anyone Out There?* Delta, 1994.

Fiore, Edith. *Encounters*. Ballantine Books, 1989.

Good, Timothy. *Alien Contact*. William Morrow, 1991.

Grossinger, Richard, ed. *Planetary Mysteries*. North Atlantic Books, 1986.

Hancock, Graham. *Fingerprints of the Gods*. Crown, 1995.

Hopkins, Budd. *Missing Time*. Richard Merck, 1981.

Horn, Arthur. *Humanity's Extraterrestrial Origins*. A. & L. Horn, 1994.

Jacobs, David M. *Secret Life*. Fireside, 1992.

Korff, Kal K. *Spaceships of the Pleiades*. Prometheus Books, 1995.

Lindemann, Michael, ed. *UFOs and the Alien Presence*. The 2020 Group, 1991.

Mack, John E. *Abduction*. Ballantine Books, 1994.

McKenna, Terence. *Food of the Gods*. Bantam Books, 1992.

Mouton Howe, Linda. *Glimpses of Other Realities*. Vol. 1. LMH Productions, 1993.

Randles, Jenny. *UFOs and How to See Them*. Sterling Publishing, 1992.

Sagan, Carl. *The Demon-Haunted World*. Random House, 1995.

Sitchin, Jecharia. *Genesis Revisited*. Avon, 1990.

Strieber, Whitley. *Breakthrough*. HarperCollins, 1995.

———. *Communion*, Century Hutchison, 1987.

Terr, Lenore. *Unchained Memories*, Basic Books, 1994.

Thompson, Keith. *Angels and Aliens*. Fawcett, 1991.

Thompson, Richard L. *Alien Identities*. 2nd ed. Govardhan Hill Publishing, 1995.

Vallee, Jacques. *Revelations: Alien Contact and Deception*. Ballantine Books, 1991.

———. *Passport to Magonia*. Contemporary Books, 1993.

Videos

Above Top Secret

Alien Archaeology (with David Childress)

The Alien Autopsy

Aliens Among Us (with Bill Hamilton)

Are We Alone? (with Jecharia Sitchin)

Arthur Horn; Need to Know (with Arthur Horn)

Beamship Trilogy (with Billy Meier)

Bob Lazar; Excerpts from the Government Bible

Countdown to Alien Nation (with Michael Lindemann)

Crop Circle Update (with Colin Andrews)

Cropcircle Communiqué

Dulce Update (with Sean Morton)

Farewell Good Brothers

Flying Saucers Are Real, Vol. I (with Stanton Friedman)

Flying Saucers: The Government Coverup (with John Lear)

From Legend to Reality

Geometric Metaphors of Life (The Meru Foundation with Stan Tennan)

The Grand Deception: UFOs, Area 51 & the U.S. Government (with Norio Hayakawa)

Hidden Memories: Are You a UFO Abductee? (with Budd Hopkins)

Hoagland's Mars I: The NASA-Cydonia Briefings (with Richard Hoagland)

Hoagland's Mars II: The UN Briefing (with Richard Hoagland)

Hoagland's Mars III: The Moon/Mars Connection (with Richard Hoagland)

John Mack; Human Encounters with Aliens (Thinking Allowed Productions)

Lost Was the Key (with Leah Haley)

Masters of the Stars (with Britt and Lee Elders)

Messengers of Destiny (with Britt and Lee Elders)

The Mystery of the Crop Circles (with Michael Hesemann)

One on One: Alien Abductions

One on One: Phenomenon of the Crop Circles

The Pleiadian Connection (with J. Randolph Winters)

Roswell Revisited

The Secret of the UFOs (with Marc Davenport)

A Strange Harvest (with Linda Moulton Howe)
UFO Cover-up: Down in Roswell (with Paul Davids)
UFO Diaries, vols. 1–6
UFO Secret: The Roswell Crash
UFO Sightings (with Michael Lindemann)
UFOs: A Need to Know
UFOs & the Alien Presence (with Michael Lindemann)
UFOs and the New World Order (with Michael Lindemann)
UFOs & Underground Bases (with Bill Hamilton)
UFOs: Secrets of the Black World (with Michael Hesemann)
UFO's . . . The Hidden Truth
UFOs: The Secret Evidence (with Michael Hesemann)
Undeniable Evidence (with Colin Andrews)
Visitors from Space: Films of the Nations

These videos are available from Lightworks Audio & Video, 1-800-795-TAPE, and UFO Central, 1-800-350-4639.

THE HUMAN BRAIN

ITS CAPACITIES AND FUNCTIONS

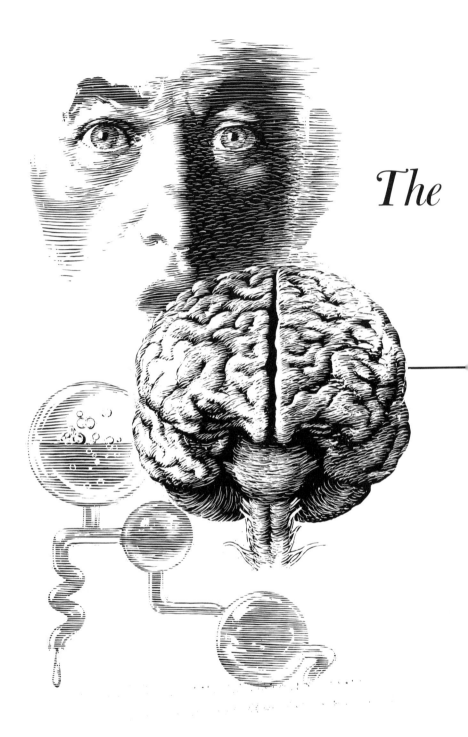

The

HUMAN BRAIN
ITS CAPACITIES
AND FUNCTIONS

BY ISAAC ASIMOV

ILLUSTRATED BY

ANTHONY RAVIELLI

HOUGHTON MIFFLIN COMPANY BOSTON

Sixth Printing   R

COPYRIGHT © 1963 BY ISAAC ASIMOV
ALL RIGHTS RESERVED INCLUDING THE RIGHT
TO REPRODUCE THIS BOOK OR PARTS THEREOF
IN ANY FORM. LIBRARY OF CONGRESS
CATALOG CARD NUMBER: 63-14549
PRINTED IN THE U.S.A.

To Gloria and William Saltzberg,
who guarded the manuscript

ACKNOWLEDGMENTS

To Professors John D. Ifft and Herbert H. Wotiz for their reading of the manuscript and their many helpful suggestions, I would like to express my appreciation and gratitude.

I.A.

CONTENTS

INTRODUCTION

In 1704, a Scottish sailor named Alexander Selkirk was a member of the crew of a ship sailing the South Seas. He quarreled with the captain of the ship and asked to be marooned on an island named Más a Tierra, which is one of the Juan Fernández Islands in the South Pacific, about 400 miles west of central Chile.

He remained on the island from October 1704 to February 1709, a period of almost four and one-half years, before being taken off by a ship that passed by. He survived the period well and went back to sea, attaining the position of first mate by the time of his death. The story of his years of isolation was written up in an English periodical in 1713, and it proved to be a fascinating story.

The tale intrigued the English author Daniel Defoe, among others, who proceeded to write a fictional treatment of such a marooning, and improved it in some ways. His sailor was marooned in the Caribbean (perhaps on the island of Tobago) and he lived there for twenty-eight (!) years.

The name of the sailor and of the novel was Robinson Crusoe, and it has remained a classic for two and a half centuries and will undoubtedly continue to remain so for an indefinite time in the future. Part of the interest in the book arises out of Defoe's masterly way of handling details and of making the account sound real. But most of the interest, I think, arises out of being able to witness one man alone against the universe.

Crusoe is an ordinary human being, with fears and anxieties and weaknesses, who nevertheless by hard labor, great ingenuity, and much patience builds a reasonable and even a comfortable life for himself in the wilderness. In doing so, he conquers one of man's greatest fears, solitude. (In cultures where direct physical torture is frowned upon, hardened criminals are placed "in solitary" as the ultimate punishment.)

If Robinson Crusoe fascinates us, surely it is the fascination of horror. Which of us would be willing to take his place in isolation, regardless of what physical comforts we might be able to take with us? What it amounts to is that a society consisting of a single human being is conceivable (for one generation at least) but in the highest degree undesirable. In fact, to make a society viable, it is a case, up to a certain point at least, of "the more the merrier." Nor is it entirely a matter of company, or even of sexual satisfaction, that makes it well for a society to consist of a good number of individuals. It is the rare human being who could himself fulfill every variety of need involved in the efficient conduct of a society. One person may have the muscular development required to chop down trees and another the ingenuity to direct the construction of a house and a third the patience and delicacy required in good cooking.

Even if one presupposes a quite primitive society, a number of specializations would be in order, including, for instance, someone who understood some rule-of-thumb medicine, someone who could manage animals, someone with a green thumb who could keep a garden under control, and so on. And yet if such a many-person society has its obvious advantages over Robinson Crusoe alone, it also has some disadvantages. One person may be lonely, but at least he is single-minded. Two people may quarrel, in fact probably will; and large numbers of people left to themselves will certainly be reduced to factionalism, and energy that should be expended against the environment will be wasted in an internal struggle. In other words, in the list of specialties we must not forget the most important of all, the tribal chieftain.

He may do no work himself, but in organizing the work of the others, he makes the society practical. He directs the order of business, decides what must be done and when, and, for that matter, what must cease to be done. He settles quarrels and, if necessary, enforces the peace. As societies grow more complex, the task of the organizer grows more difficult, at a more rapid pace than does the task of any other specialist. In place of a chieftain, one finds a hierarchy of command, a ruling class, an executive department, a horde of bureaucrats.

All this has a bearing on the biological level.

There are organisms that consist of a single cell, and these may be compared to human societies of a single individual (except that a single cell can reproduce itself and persist into the indefinite future, whereas a single human being can survive for only one lifetime). Such single-cell organisms live and flourish today in competition with multicellular organisms and may even in the long run survive when the more complicated creatures have met their final doom. Analogously, there are hermits living in caves even today in a world in which cities like New York and Tokyo exist. We can leave to philosophers the question as to which situation is truly superior, but most of us take it for granted it is better to be a man than an amoeba, and better to live in New York than in a cave.

The advance from unicellularity to multicellularity must have begun when cells divided and then remained clinging together. This does indeed happen now. The one-celled plants called algae often divide and cling together; and the seaweeds are huge colonies of such cells. The mere act of clinging together, as in seaweeds, involves no true multicellularity, however. Each cell in the group works independently and is associated with its neighbor only by being pushed against it.

True multicellularity requires the establishment of a "cellular society" with needs that overbalance those of the individual cell. In multicellular organisms, the individual cells specialize in order to concentrate on the performance of some particular function even to the point where other quite vital functions are allowed to fade or even to lapse completely. The cell, then, loses the ability to live independently, and survives as part of the organism only because its inabilities are made up for by other cells in the organism that specialize in different fashion. One might almost regard the individual cell of a multicellular organism as the parasite of the organism as a whole.

(It is not too farfetched to make the analogy that the human citizens of a large modern city have become so specialized themselves as to be helpless if thrown on their own resources. A man who could live comfortably and well in a large city, performing his own specialized function, and depending on the vast network of services offered by the metropolis — and controlled by other equally but differently specialized citizens — would, if isolated on Robinson Crusoe's island, quickly be reduced to animal misery. He would not survive long.)

But if cells by the trillions are specialized, and if their various functions are organized for the overall good of the organism, there must, in analogy to what I have said about human societies, be cells that specialize as "organizers." The job is a perfectly immense one; far more terrifyingly complex on the cellular level of even a fairly simple creature than any conceivable job of analogous sort could be in the most complex human society.

In *The Human Body*[*] I discussed in some detail the structure and operation of the various organs of the body. The operation is obviously complexly interrelated. The various portions of the alimentary canal performed their separate roles in smooth order. The heart beats as a well-integrated combination of parts. The bloodstream connects the various portions of the body, performing a hundred tasks without falling over its own capillaries. The lungs and kidneys form complicated but efficient meeting grounds of the body and the outer environment.

Organization is clearly there, but throughout *The Human Body*

[*] *The Human Body* was published in 1963, and the book you are reading now may be considered a companion piece.

I glossed over the fact. In this book, however, I shall gloss over it no longer. In fact, this book is devoted entirely and single-mindedly to the organization that makes multicellular life possible and, in particular, to the organization that makes the human body a dynamic living thing and not merely a collection of cells. The brain is not the only organ involved in such organization, but it is by far the most important. For that reason I call the book *The Human Brain*, although I shall deal with more than the brain. The whole is generally greater than the sum of its parts, despite Euclid, and if in *The Human Body* I considered the parts, in *The Human Brain* I shall try to consider the whole.

THE HUMAN BRAIN

ITS CAPACITIES AND FUNCTIONS

1

OUR HORMONES

ORGANIZATION

Even primitive man felt the need for finding some unifying and organizing principle about his body. *Something* moved the arms and legs, which of themselves were clearly blind tools and nothing more. A natural first tendency would be to look for something whose presence was essential to life. An arm or leg could be removed without necessarily ending life; or even diminishing its essence, however it might hobble a man physically. The breath was another matter. A man just dead possessed the limbs and all the parts of a living man but no longer had breath. What is more, to stop the breath forcibly for five minutes brought on death though no other damage might be done. And, to top matters off, the breath was invisible and intangible, and had the mystery one would expect of so ethereal a substance as life. It is not strange, then, that the word for "breath" in various languages came to mean the essence of life, or what we might call the "soul." The Hebrew words *nephesh* and *ruakh*, the Greek *pneuma*, the Latin *spiritus* and *anima* all refer to both breath and the essence of life.

Another moving part of the body which is essential to life is the blood; a peculiarly living liquid as breath is a peculiarly living gas. Loss of blood brings on loss of life, and a dead man does not bleed. The Bible, in its prescription of sacrificial rites, clearly indicates the primitive Israelite notion (undoubtedly shared with neighboring peoples) that blood is the essence of life. Thus, meat must not be eaten until its blood content has been removed, since blood represents life, and it is forbidden to eat living matter. Genesis 9:4 puts it quite clearly: "But flesh with the life thereof, which is the blood thereof, shall ye not eat."

It is but a step to pass from the blood to the heart. The heart does not beat in a dead man, and that is enough to equate the heart with life. This concept still lingers today in our common feeling that all emotion centers in the heart. We are "broken-hearted," "stouthearted," "heavyhearted," and "lighthearted."

Breath, blood, and heart are all moving objects that become motionless with death. It may be an advance in sophistication to look beyond such obvious matters. Even in the earliest days of civilization, the liver was looked upon as an extremely important organ (which it is, though not for the reasons then thought). Diviners sought for omens and clues to the future in the shape and characteristics of the liver of sacrificed animals.

Perhaps because of its importance in divining, or because of its sheer size — it is the largest organ of the viscera — or because it is blood-filled, or for some combination of these reasons, it began to be thought by many to be the seat of life. It is probably no coincidence that "liver" differs from "live" by one letter. In earlier centuries, the liver was accepted as the organ in charge of emotion; and the best-known survival of that in our language today is the expression "lily-livered" applied to a coward. The spleen, another blood-choked organ, leaves a similar mark. "Spleen" still serves as a synonym for a variety of emotions; most commonly anger or spite.

It may seem odd to us today that, by and large, the brain was ignored as the seat of life; or as the organizing organ of the body. After all, it alone of all internal organs is disproportionately large in man as compared with other animals. However, the brain is not a moving organ like the heart; it is not blood-filled like the liver or spleen. Above all, it is out of the way and hidden behind a close concealment of bone. When animals, sacrificed for religious or divining purposes, were eviscerated, the various abdominal organs were clearly seen. The brain was not.

Aristotle, the most renowned of the ancient thinkers, believed that the brain was designed to cool the heated blood that passed through it. The organ was thus reduced to an air-conditioning device. The modern idea of the brain as the seat of thought and, through the nerves, the receiver of sensation and the initiator of motion was not definitely established until the 18th century.

By the end of the 19th century, the nervous system had come into its own, and actually into more than its own. It was recognized as the organizational network of the body. This was the easier to grasp since by then mankind had grown used to the complicated circuits of electrical machinery. The nerves of the body seemed much like the wires of an electrical circuit. Cutting the nerve leading from the eye meant blindness for that eye; cutting the nerves leading to the biceps meant paralysis for that muscle. This was quite analogous to the manner in which breaking a wire blanked out a portion of an electrical mechanism. It seemed natural, then, to suppose that *only* the nerve network controlled the body. For instance, when food leaves the stomach and enters the small intestine the pancreas is suddenly galvanized into activity and pours its digestive secretion into the duodenum. The food entering the intestine is bathed in the digestive juice and digestion proceeds.

Here is an example of excellent organization. If the pancreas secreted its juices continuously that would represent a great waste, for most of the time the juices would be expended to no purpose. On the other hand, if the pancreas secreted its juices intermittently (as it does), the secretions would have to synchronize perfectly with the food entering the intestine, or else not only would the secretions be wasted but food would remain imperfectly digested.

By 19th-century ways of thinking, the passage of food from the stomach into the small intestine activated a nerve which then carried a message to the brain (or spinal cord). This, in response, sent a message down to the pancreas by way of another nerve, and as a result of this second message the pancreas secreted its juices. It was not until the beginning of the 20th century that, rather unexpectedly, the body was found to possess organization outside the nervous system.

SECRETIN

In 1902 two English physiologists, William Maddock Bayliss and Ernest Henry Starling, were studying the manner in which the nervous system controlled the behavior of the intestines and of the processes of digestion. They made the logical move of cutting all the nerves leading to the pancreas of their experimental animals. It seemed quite likely that the pancreas would fail to secrete digestive juices at all, once the nerves were cut, whether food passed into the small intestine or not.

That was *not* what happened, to the surprise of Bayliss and Starling. Instead, the denervated pancreas behaved promptly on cue. As soon as food touched the intestinal lining, the pancreas began pouring forth its juice. The two physiologists knew that the stomach contents were acid because of the presence of considerable hydrochloric acid in the stomach's digestive secretions. They therefore introduced a small quantity of hydrochloric acid into the small intestine, without food, and the denervated pancreas produced juice. The pancreas, then, required neither nerve messages nor food, but only acid; and the acid needed to make no direct contact with the pancreas itself but only with the intestinal lining.

The next step was to obtain a section of intestine from a newly killed animal and soak it in hydrochloric acid. A small quantity of the acid extract was placed within the bloodstream of a living animal by means of a hypodermic needle. The animal's pancreas reacted at once and secreted juice, although the animal was fasting. The conclusion was clear. The intestinal lining reacted to the trigger action of acidity by producing a chemical

that was poured into the bloodstream. The bloodstream carried the chemical throughout the body to every organ, including the pancreas. When the chemical reached the pancreas it somehow stimulated that organ into secreting its juice.

Bayliss and Starling named the substance produced by the intestinal lining *secretin* (see-kree'tin; "separate" L),* since it stimulated a secretion. This was the first clear example of a case in which efficient organization was found to be produced by means of chemical messages carried by the bloodstream rather than electrical messages of the nerves. Substances such as secretin are in fact sometimes referred to rather informally as "chemical messengers."

The more formal name was proposed in 1905, during the course of a lecture by Bayliss. He suggested the name *hormone* ("to arouse" G). The hormone secreted by one organ, you see, was something that aroused another organ to activity. The name was adopted, and ever since it has been quite clear that the organization of the body is built on two levels: the electrical system of brain, spinal cord, nerves, and sense organs; and the chemical system of the various hormones and hormone-elaborating organs.

Although the electrical organization of the body was recognized before the chemical organization was, in this book I shall reverse the order of time and consider the chemical organization first, since this is the less specialized and the older of the two. Plants and one-celled animals, after all, without a trace of anything we would recognize as a nervous system nevertheless react to chemical stimuli.

---

* In this book I shall follow the practice initiated in *The Human Body* of giving the pronunciation of possibly unfamiliar words. I shall also include the meaning of the key word from which it is derived with the initial — L, indicating the derivation to be from the Latin and G indicating it to be from the Greek. In this case, the derivation from "separate" refers to the fact that a cell forms a particular substance and separates that substance, so to speak, from itself, discharging it into the bloodstream, into the intestines, or upon the outer surface of the body. A secretion is thought of as being designed to serve a useful purpose, as, for instance, is true of the pancreatic juice. Where the separated material is merely being disposed of, it is an *excretion* ("separate outside" L); thus urine is an excretion.

In line with this mode of progression, let us begin by looking at secretin more closely; from its behavior and properties we shall be able to reach conclusions that will apply to other and far more glamorous hormones. For example, a question may arise as to what terminates hormone action. The gastric contents arrive in the small intestine. The acidity of those contents stimulates the production of secretin. The secretin enters the bloodstream and stimulates the production of pancreatic secretion. So far, so good; but there comes a time when the pancreas has produced all the juices it need produce. What now stops it?

For one thing, the pancreatic secretion is somewhat alkaline (an alkaline solution is one with properties the reverse of those of an acid solution; one will neutralize the other, and produce a mixture neither acid nor alkaline). As the pancreatic secretion mixes with the food, the acid qualities the latter inherited from the stomach diminish. As the acidity decreases, the spark that stimulates the formation of secretin dies down.

In other words, the action of secretin brings about a series of events that causes the formation of secretin to come to a halt. The formation of secretin is thus a self-limiting process. It is like the action of a thermostat which controls the oil furnace in the basement. When the house is cold, the thermostat turns on the furnace and that very action causes the temperature to rise to the point where the thermostat turns off the furnace. This is called "feedback," a general term for a process by which the results brought about by some control are fed back into the information at the disposal of the control, which then regulates itself according to the nature of the result it produces. In electrical circuits we speak of input and output; but in biological systems we speak of *stimulus* and *response*. In this case, the successful response is sufficient in itself to reduce the stimulus.

This sort of feedback is surely not enough. Even though secretin is no longer formed, what of the secretin that has already been formed and which, one might expect, remains in the bloodstream and continues to prod the pancreas? This, however, is taken care of. The body contains enzymes* specifically designed to catalyze the destruction of hormones. An enzyme has been located in blood which has the capacity of hastening the breakup of the secretin molecule, rendering the hormone inactive. Enzymes are very often named for the substance upon which they act, with the addition of the suffix "ase," so this enzyme to which I have referred is *secretinase* (see-kree'tih-nays).

There is consequently a race between the production of secretin by the intestinal linings and the destruction of secretin by secretinase. While the intestinal linings are working at full speed, the concentration of secretin in the blood is built up to stimulating level. When the intestinal linings cease working, not only is no further secretin formed but any secretin already present in the blood is quickly done away with. And in this fashion, the pancreas is turned on and off with a sure and automatic touch that works perfectly without your ever being aware of it.

AMINO ACIDS

Another legitimate question could be: What is secretin? Is its nature known or is it merely a name given to an unknown substance? The answer is that its nature is known but not in full detail.

Secretin is a protein, and proteins are made up of large molecules, each of which consists of hundreds, sometimes thousands, sometimes even millions of atoms. Compare this with a water molecule (H_2O), which contains 3 atoms, 2 hydrogens and 1 oxygen; or with a molecule of sulfuric acid (H_2SO_4), which contains 7 atoms, 2 hydrogens, 1 sulfur, and 4 oxygens.

It is understandable, therefore, that the chemist, desiring to know the exact structure of a protein molecule, finds himself faced with an all but insuperable task. Fortunately, matters are eased

---

* Enzymes are proteins that behave as catalysts — they hasten particular reactions when present in small quantities. That is all we need to know for our present purposes. If you are interested in the nature and the method of operation of enzymes, I refer you to my book *Life and Energy* (1962).

somewhat by the fact that the atoms within the protein molecule are arranged in subgroupings called *amino acids* (the first
word is pronounced either "a-mee′noh" or "a′mih-noh"; you may
take your pick — I prefer the first).

By gentle treatment with acids or with alkali or with certain
enzymes, it is possible to break up the protein molecule into its
subgroup amino acids instead of its separate atoms. The amino
acids are themselves rather small molecules made up of only 10
to 30 atoms and they are comparatively simple to study.

It has been found, for example, that all the amino acids isolated
from protein molecules belong to a single family of compounds,
which can be written as the following formula:

$$NH_2-\underset{\underset{H}{|}}{\overset{\overset{R}{|}}{C}}-COOH$$

The C at the center of the formula represents a carbon atom
(C for carbon, of course). Attached to its right, in the formula
as shown, is the four-atom combination COOH, which represents
a carbon atom, two oxygen atoms, and a hydrogen atom. Such a
combination gives acid properties to a molecule and it is called a
carboxylic acid group (carbon plus oxygen plus acid). Attached
to the left is a three-atom combination, NH_2, which represents
a nitrogen atom and two hydrogen atoms. This is the *amine group,*
because it is chemically related to the substance known as "am-
monia." Since the formula contains both an amine group and an
acid group this type of compound is called an amino acid.

In addition, attached to the central carbon is an H, which
simply represents a hydrogen atom, and an R, which represents
a *side-chain.* It is this R, or side-chain, that is different in each
amino acid. Sometimes the side-chain is very simple in structure;
it may even be nothing more than a hydrogen atom in the very
simplest case. In some amino acids the side-chain can be quite

complicated and may be made up of as many as 18 atoms. For our own purposes, we don't have to know the details of the structure of the side-chains for each amino acid. It is enough to know that each structure is distinctive.

Amino acids combine to form a protein by having the amino group of one amino acid connected to the carboxylic acid group of its neighbor. This is repeated from amino acid to amino acid so that a long "backbone" is formed. From each amino acid unit in the chain a side-chain sticks out, and it is the unique pattern of side-chains that makes each type of protein molecule different from all others.

There are more than two dozen amino acids to be found in various protein molecules, but of these only 21 can be considered as being really common. To give ourselves a vocabulary we can use, I shall name these:

1. *Glycine* ("sweet" G, because of its sweet taste),

2. *Alanine* (a name selected for euphony alone, apparently),

3. *Valine* (from a compound called valeric acid, to which it is chemically related),

4. *Leucine* ("white" G, because it was first isolated as white crystals),

5. *Isoleucine* (an isomer of leucine; isomers are pairs of substances with molecules containing the same number of the same type of atoms, but differing in the arrangement of the atoms within the molecules),

6. *Proline* (a shortened version of "pyrrolidine," which is the name given to the particular atom arrangement in proline's side-chain),

7. *Phenylalanine* (a molecule of alanine to which an atom combination called the phenyl group is added),

8. *Tyrosine* ("cheese" G, from which it was first isolated),

9. *Tryptophan* ("trypsin-appearing" G, because it appeared, when first discovered, in the fragments of a protein molecule that had been broken up by the action of an enzyme named trypsin),

10. *Serine* ("silk" L, from which it was first isolated),

11. *Threonine* (because its chemical structure is related to that of a sugar called threose),

12. *Asparagine* (first found in asparagus),

13. *Aspartic acid* (because it resembles asparagine; although aspartic acid possesses an acid group, COOH, in the side-chain and asparagine possesses a similar group, $CONH_2$, with no acid properties),

14. *Glutamine* (first found in wheat gluten),

15. *Glutamic acid* (which differs from glutamine as aspartic acid differs from asparagine),

16. *Lysine* ("a breaking up" G, because it was first isolated from protein molecules that had been broken up into their sub-groupings),

17. *Histidine* ("tissue" G, because it was first isolated from tissue protein),

18. *Arginine* ("silver" L, because it was first isolated in combination with silver atoms),

19. *Methionine* (because the side-chain contains an atom grouping called the "methyl group," which is in turn attached to a sulfur atom, called *theion* in Greek),

20. *Cystine* (sis′teen; "bladder" G, because it was first isolated in a bladderstone),

21. *Cysteine* (sis′tih-een; because it is chemically related to cystine).

I shall have to use these names fairly frequently. To save space, let me give you the commonly used abbreviations for each of them, a system first proposed and used in the 1930's by a German-American biochemist named Erwin Brand. Since most of the abbreviations consist of the first three letters of the name, they are not difficult to memorize:

glycine	gly	asparagine	asp·NH_2
alanine	ala	aspartic acid	asp
valine	val	glutamine	glu·NH_2
leucine	leu	glutamic acid	glu

isoleucine	ileu	lysine	lys
proline	pro	histidine	his
phenylalanine	phe	arginine	arg
tyrosine	tyr	methionine	met
tryptophan	try	cystine	cy-S-
serine	ser	cysteine	cy-SH
threonine	thr		

Of the abbreviations that are more than the first three letters of the names, ileu, asp·NH$_2$, and glu·NH$_2$ should be clear. The abbreviations for cystine and cysteine are more cryptic and deserve some explanation, for they will be important later on.

Cystine is a double amino acid, so to speak. Imagine *two* central carbon atoms, each with a carboxylic acid group and an amine group attached. The side-chain attached to one of these central carbon atoms runs into and coalesces with the side-chain attached to the other. Where the side-chains meet are two sulfur atoms. We might therefore symbolize cystine as cy-S-S-cy, the two S's being the sulfur atoms that hold the two amino acid portions together.

Each amino acid portion of cystine can make up part of a separate chain of amino acids. You can get the picture if you imagine a pair of Siamese twins, each one holding hands with individuals in a different chain. The two chains are now held together and prevented from separating by the band of tissue that holds the Siamese twins together.

Similarly, the two amino acid chains, each holding half a cystine molecule, are held together by the S-S combination of the cystine. Since chemists are often interested in the makeup of a single amino acid chain, they can concentrate on the half of the cystine molecule that is present there. It is the "half-cystine" they usually deal with in considering protein structure and it is this that is symbolized by cy-S-.

One way of breaking the S-S combination and separating the two amino acid chains is to add two hydrogen atoms. One hydrogen atom attaches to each of the sulfur atoms and the combination is broken. From -S-S-, you go to -S-H plus H-S-. In this way, one cystine molecule becomes two cysteine molecules (there's the relationship that has resulted in two such similar names, hard to distinguish in speaking except by exaggeratedly and tiresomely pronouncing the middle syllable in cysteine). To show this, cysteine is symbolized cy-SH.

STRUCTURE AND ACTION

Now if I return to secretin and describe it as a protein molecule, we know something of its structure at once. What's more, it is a small protein molecule, with a molecular weight of 5000. (By this is meant that a molecule of secretin weighs 5000 times as much as a hydrogen atom, which is the lightest of all atoms.)

A molecular weight of 5000 is high if we are discussing most types of molecules. Thus, the molecular weight of water is 18, of sulfuric acid 98, of table sugar 342. However, considering that the molecular weight of even average-sized proteins is from 40,000 to 60,000, that a molecular weight of 250,000 is not rare and that proteins are known with molecular weights of several millions, you can see that a protein with a molecular weight of merely 5000 is really small.

This is true of protein hormones generally. The hormone molecule must be transferred from within the cell, where it is manufactured, to the bloodstream. It must in the process get through, or *diffuse* through, the cell membrane and the thin walls of tiny blood vessels. It is rather surprising that molecules as large as those with a molecular weight of 5000 can do so; but to expect still larger molecules to do so would certainly be expecting too much. In fact the molecules of most protein hormones are so small, for proteins, that the very name is sometimes denied them.

When the amino acid chain of a protein molecule is broken up into smaller chains of amino acids by the action of the enzymes in the digestive juices, the chain fragments are called *peptides* ("digest" G). It has become customary to express the size of such small chains by using a Greek number prefix to indicate the number of amino acids in it: a *dipeptide* ("two-peptide" G) is a combination of two amino acids, a *tripeptide* ("three-peptide" G) of three, a *tetrapeptide* ("four-peptide" G) of four, and so on.

Where the number is more than a dozen or so but less than a hundred, the chain is a *polypeptide* ("many-peptide" G). Secretin and other hormones of similar nature are built up of amino acid chains containing more than a dozen and less than a hundred amino acids and are therefore sometimes called *polypeptide hormones* rather than protein hormones.

Having said that secretin is a polypeptide hormone, the next step, logically, would be to decide which amino acids are to be found in its molecule and how many of each. This, unfortunately, is not an easy thing to determine. Secretin is not manufactured in large quantities, and in isolating it from duodenal tissue a variety of other protein molecules are also obtained. The presence of such impurities naturally complicates analysis.

In 1939, however, secretin was produced in crystalline form (and only quite pure proteins can be crystallized). These crystals were analyzed and it was reported that within each secretin molecule there existed 3 lysines, 2 arginines, 2 prolines, 1 histidine, 1 glutamic acid, 1 aspartic acid. and 1 methionine. This is a total of 11 amino acids in a molecule which, from the data available, seems to contain 36 amino acids altogether. Using the Brand abbreviations, the formula for secretin, as now known, would be:

$$lys_3arg_2pro_2his_1glu_1asp_1met_1X_{25}$$

X standing for those amino acids still unknown.

Even if with further progress all the amino acids in the secretin molecule were determined, that would not give us all we need to determine the exact structure of the secretin molecule. There would still remain the necessity of discovering the exact order of the various amino acids within the chain. If you knew that a certain four-digit number was made up of two 6's, a 4, and a 2, you would still be uncertain as to the exact number being referred to. It might be 6642, 2646, 4662 or any of several other possibilities.

There are fixed methods for calculating the number of possible patterns that can be built up of different sets of units and the results are startling. Suppose that the 36 amino acids of the secretin molecule consisted of two of each of 18 different amino acids. The total number of possible arrangements would be somewhat in excess of 1,400,000,000,000,000,000,000,000,000,000,000,000. This may sound incredible but it is quite true. This, mind you, is for a small protein molecule. The situation for even an average-sized one is far, far more complicated, and this helps account for the difficulties biochemists have in attempting to work out protein structure.

It also speaks amazingly well for the fact that biochemists, since World War II, have actually developed ingenious techniques that have made it possible for them to work out the exact order of the amino acids (out of trillions upon uncounted trillions of possible orders) in particular protein molecules.

Emphasizing the complexity of structure of a protein molecule, as I have just done, gives rise to the natural wonder that cells can elaborate such complex molecules correctly, choosing one particular arrangement of amino acids out of all the possible ones. This, as a matter of fact, is perhaps the key chemical process in living tissue, and in the last ten years much has been discovered about its details. Unfortunately, this book is not the place to consider this vital point, but if you are interested, you will find it in some detail in my book *The Genetic Code.*

Even if we grant that the cell can elaborate the *correct* protein molecule, can it do it so quickly from a cold start that the spur of the acid stimulation of the stomach contents suffices to produce an instant flood of secretin into the bloodstream? This would perhaps be too much to expect, and, as a matter of fact, the start is not a cold one.

The secretin-forming cells of the intestinal lining prepare a molecule called *prosecretin* ("ahead of secretin") at their leisure.

This they store and therefore always have a ready supply of it. The prosecretin molecule requires, apparently, one small chemical change to become actual secretin. The stimulus of acid is not, therefore, expected to bring about a complete formation of a polypeptide molecule, but only one small chemical reaction. It is logical to suppose that prosecretin is a comparatively large molecule, too large to get through the cell membrane and therefore safely immured within the cell. The influx of acid from the stomach suffices to break the prosecretin molecule into smaller fragments, and these fragments — secretin — diffuse out into the bloodstream. The prosecretin might be thought of as resembling a perforated block of stamps. It is only when the stamps are torn off at the perforations and used singly that they bring about the delivery of ordinary letters; but the blocks can be bought and kept in reserve for use when and as needed.

Another question that may well arise is this: How do hormones (and secretin in particular, since I am discussing that hormone) act to bring about a response? Oddly enough, despite more than a half century of study, and despite amazing advances made by biochemists in every direction, the answer to that question remains a complete mystery. It is a mystery not only with respect to secretin but with respect to all other hormones. The mechanism of action of not a single hormone is indisputably established. At first, when secretin and similar hormones were discovered and found to be small protein molecules that were effective in very small concentration,* they were assumed to act as enzymes. Enzymes are also proteins that are effective in very small concentration. Enzymes have the ability to hasten specific reactions to a great degree and it seemed very likely that hormones might do the same.

When secretin reached the pancreas, it might hasten a key reaction that, in the absence of secretin, would proceed very slowly. This key reaction might set in motion a whole series of reactions

---

* As little as 0.005 milligrams of secretin (that is, less than one five-millionth of an ounce) is sufficient to elicit a response from a dog's pancreas.

ending with the formation and secretion of quantities of pancreatic juice. A small stimulus could in this way easily produce a large response. It would be like the small action of pulling a lever in a firebox, which would send a signal to a distant firehouse, arouse the firemen, who would swarm upon their fire engines, and send them screaming down the road. A large response for pulling a lever. Unfortunately, this theory does not hold up. Ordinary enzymes will perform their hastening activity in the test tube as well as in the body and, in fact, enzymes are routinely studied through their ability to act under controlled test-tube conditions.

In the case of hormones, however, this cannot be done. Few hormones have ever displayed the ability of hastening a specific chemical reaction in the test tube. In addition, a number of hormones turned out to be nonprotein in structure and, as far as we know, all enzymes are proteins. It seems, then, that the only conclusion to be drawn is that hormones are not catalysts. A subsidiary theory is that hormones, although not themselves enzymes, collaborate with enzymes — some enzyme, that is, which is designed to hasten a certain reaction and will not do so unless a particular hormone is present. Or perhaps there is a whole enzyme system that sets up a chain of reactions intended to counteract some effect. The hormone by its presence prevents one of the enzymes in the reaction chain from being active. It *inhibits* ("to hold in" L) the enzyme. This stops the entire counteraction, and the effect, which is ordinarily prevented, is permitted to take place. Thus, the pancreas might always be producing secretions but for some key reaction that prevents it. By blocking that key reaction, secretin may allow the pancreatic juice to be formed. This seems like a backward way of doing things, but such a procedure is not unknown in man-made mechanisms. A burglar alarm may be so designed that an electric current, constantly in being, prevents it from ringing. Break the electric current, by forcing a door or a window, and the alarm, no longer held back, begins to ring.

Unfortunately, here too the cooperation between a particular hormone and a particular enzyme is very difficult to demonstrate. Even where some cooperation, either to accelerate or to inhibit the action of an enzyme, is reported for some hormone, the evidence remains in dispute.

Still another theory is that the hormone affects the cell membrane in such a way as to alter the pattern of materials that can enter the cell from the bloodstream. To put this in human terms, one might suppose that the workers constructing a large skyscraper one day were presented with loads of aluminum siding. They would on that day undoubtedly work on the face of the building as far as they could. If, instead, large loads of wiring arrived but no aluminum siding, work would have to switch to the electrical components of the building.

In similar fashion, the hormone action might determine cellular action by permitting one substance to enter the cell and prohibiting another from doing so. It may be that only when secretin acts upon the cell membranes of the pancreas is the pancreas supplied with some key material needed to manufacture its digestive juice.

But this theory, too, is unproved. The whole question of the mechanism of hormone action remains open, very open.

MORE POLYPEPTIDE HORMONES

I have been concentrating on secretin, so far, to a much greater extent than is strictly necessary for its own sake, because secretin is a minor hormone, as hormones go. Nevertheless, it has the historical interest of being the first hormone to be recognized as such and, in addition, much of what I have said in this chapter applies to other hormones as well.

But it is important to stress the fact that there *are* other hormones. There are even other hormones that deal with pancreatic secretion. If secretin is purified and added to the bloodstream, the pancreatic juice that is produced is copious enough and alkaline enough, but it is low in enzyme content, and it is the enzymes that do the actual work of digestion. A preparation of secretin that is less intensively purified brings about the formation of pancreatic juice adequately rich in enzymes.

Evidently a second hormone, present in the impure preparation but discarded in the pure, stimulates enzyme production. Extracts containing this second hormone have been prepared and have been found to produce the appropriate enzyme-enriching response. This hormone is *pancreozymin* (pan'kree-oh-zy'min; which is a shortened form of "pancreatic enzymes").

Secretin seems to have a stimulating effect on the liver too, causing it to produce a more copious flow of its own secretion, which is called *bile*. The bile produced in response to secretin is low in material (ordinarily present) called *bile salt* and *bile pigment*. The gallbladder, a small sac attached to the liver, contains a concentrated supply of liver secretion, with ample content of bile salt and bile pigment. This supply is not called upon by secretin, but still another hormone produced by the intestinal lining will stimulate the contraction of the muscular wall of the gallbladder and will cause its concentrated content to be squirted into the intestine. This hormone is *cholecystokinin* (kol'eh-sis-toh-ky'nin; "to move the gallbladder" G).

The secretion of cholecystokinin is stimulated by the presence of fat in the stomach contents as they enter the intestine. This makes sense, since bile is particularly useful in emulsifying fat and making it easier to digest. A fatty meal will stimulate the production of unusually high quantities of cholecystokinin, which will stimulate the gallbladder strongly, which will squirt a greater-than-usual supply of bile salt (the emulsifying ingredient) into the intestine, which will emulsify the fat that started the whole procedure and bring about its digestion.

I have mentioned that one of the effects of secretin is to neutralize the acidity of the stomach contents by stimulating the production of the alkaline pancreatic juice. This is necessary because the enzymes in pancreatic juice will only work in a slightly alkaline medium and if the food emerging from the stomach were to remain acid, digestion would slow to a crawl. Part of this desirable alkalizing effect would be negated if the stomach were to continue to produce its own acid secretions at a great rate after the food had left it. However necessary those secretions might be while the stomach was full of food, they could only be harmful if produced in an empty stomach and allowed to trickle into the intestine. It is not surprising, then, that yet another function of the versatile secretin has been reported to be the inhibition of stomach secretions.

This is more efficiently done, however, by a second hormone designed just for the purpose. Several of the different substances in food serve to stimulate the intestines to produce a substance called *enterogastrone* (en′ter-oh-gas′trohn; "intestine-stomach" G, that is, produced by the intestine and with its effect on the stomach). Enterogastrone, unlike most hormones, inhibits a function rather than stimulates one. It has been suggested that substances which are like hormones in every respect except that they inhibit instead of arousing be called *chalones* (kal′ohnz; "to slacken" G). Nevertheless, the name has not become popular, and the word "hormone" is used indiscriminately, whether the result is arousal (as "hormone" implies) or the opposite.

But if food in the upper intestine releases a hormone inhibiting stomach secretion of digestive juices, then food in the stomach itself ought to bring about the release of a hormone stimulating that secretion. After all, when the stomach is full, those juices are wanted. Such a hormone has indeed been detected. It is produced by the cells of the stomach lining and it is named *gastrin* ("stomach" G).

Other hormones that affect the flow of a particular digestive secretion one way or another have been reported as being produced by the stomach or small intestine. None of them have been as well studied as secretin, but all are believed to be polypeptide in nature. The only real dispute here is over the structure of gastrin. There are some who believe that the gastrin molecule is made up of a single modified amino acid. All these hormones collaborate to keep the digestive secretions of the stomach and intestines working with smooth organization, and they are all lumped together as the *gastrointestinal hormones.*

If polypeptide hormones bring about the production of digestive juices, the compliment is, in a way, returned. There are digestive juices that produce polypeptide hormones in the blood. This was discovered in 1937, when a group of German physiologists found that blood serum and an extract of the salivary gland mixed were capable of bringing about the contraction of an isolated segment of the wall of the large intestine. Neither the serum nor the salivary extract could accomplish this feat singly. What happens, apparently, is that an enzyme extracted from the saliva has the ability to break small fragments off one of the large protein molecules in the blood (like tearing individual stamps off a large block of them). The small fragments are polypeptide hormones capable of stimulating the contraction of smooth muscle under some conditions and its relaxation under other conditions.

The enzyme was named *kallikrein* (kal-ik'ree-in) and it, or very similar enzymes, have been located in a number of other tissues. The hormone produced by kallikrein was named *kallidin* (kal'ih-din). It exists in at least two separate and very similar varieties, called *kallidin I* and *kallidin II.* The actual function of kallidin in the body is as yet uncertain. It lowers blood pressure, for one thing, by stretching the small blood vessels and making them roomier. This causes the vessels to become a bit leakier, a condition that in turn may allow fluid to collect in damaged areas, forming blisters, while also allowing white blood corpuscles to get out of the blood vessels more easily and collect at these sites.

A substance similar to kallidin is produced in blood by the action of certain snake venoms. The net effect on tissues is similar in various ways to that produced by a compound called histamine but is somewhat slower in establishing itself (30 seconds against

5 seconds). The kallidin-like substance produced by the venom was therefore named *bradykinin* (brad′ih-ky′nin; "slow-moving" G). Eventually, bradykinin, kallidin, and all similar hormones were grouped under the name *kinins*. There are kinins, ready made, in the venom of the wasp. These are injected into the bloodstream when the wasp stings and are probably responsible, at least in part, for the pain and the swelling that comes with the accumulation of fluid as the small blood vessels grow leaky.

The molecules of the kinins are simpler than are those of the gastrointestinal hormones. Being made up of no more than 9 or 10 amino acids, they are scarcely even respectable polypeptides. The comparative simplicity of their structure has made it possible for biochemists to work out the exact order of the amino acids. Bradykinin, for instance, turned out to be identical with kallidin I and to have a molecule made up of 9 amino acids. These, in order, and using the Brand abbreviations, are:

arg·pro·pro·gly·phe·ser·pro·phe·arg

Kalladin II has a tenth amino acid, lysine (lys), which occurs at the extreme left of the bradykinin chain.

And yet, knowing the exact structure, however satisfying that may be in principle to biochemists, doesn't help in one very important respect. Even with the structure in hand, they can't tell exactly how the kinins bring about the effects they do.

2

OUR PANCREAS

DUCTLESS GLANDS

The word "gland" comes from the Latin word for acorn, and originally it was applied to small scraps of tissue in the body which seemed acornlike in shape or size. Eventually the vicissitudes of terminology led to the word being applied to any organ that had the prime function of producing a fluid secretion.

The most noticeable glands are large organs such as the liver and pancreas. Each of these produces quantities of fluid which are discharged into the upper reaches of the small intestine through special ducts. Other smaller glands also discharge their secretions into various sections of the alimentary canal. The six salivary glands discharge saliva into the mouth by way of ducts. There are myriads of tiny glands in the lining of the stomach and the small intestine, producing gastric juice in the first case and intestinal juice in the second. Each tiny gland is equipped with a tiny duct.

In addition, there are glands in the skin, sweat glands and sebaceous glands, that discharge fluid to the surface of the skin by way of tiny ducts. (The milk-producing mammary glands are modified sweat glands, and milk reaches the skin surface by way of ducts.)

But there arose the realization that there were organs producing secretions that were not discharged through ducts either to the skin or to the alimentary canal. Instead, their secretions were discharged directly into the bloodstream, not by means of a duct but by diffusion through cell membranes. A controversy arose as to whether organs producing such secretions ought to be considered glands; as to whether it was the secretion or the duct that was crucial to the definition. The final decision was in favor of the secretion, and so two types of glands are now recognized: ordinary glands and *ductless glands.* (The simple term "gland" can be used for both.)

The nature of the secretion is differentiated by name as well. Secretions that left the gland (or were separated from it, in a manner of speaking) and were led to the skin or alimentary canal are *exocrine secretions* (ek'soh-krin; "separate outside" G). Secretions that left the gland but remained in the bloodstream so as to circulate within the body, are *endocrine secretions* (en'doh-krin; "separate within" G). The former term is rarely used but the latter is common to the point where the phrase *endocrine glands* is almost more frequently used than "ductless glands." The systematic study of the ductless glands and their secretions is, for this reason, called *endocrinology.*

The gastrointestinal hormones, discussed in Chapter 1, are produced by cells of the intestinal lining which are not marked off in any very noticeable way, making it difficult to define actual glands in that case. It is better to say, simply, that the intestinal lining has glandular functions. This is an exception. In the case of virtually all other hormones definite glands are involved. Often these glands constitute separate organs. Sometimes they are groups of cells marked off, more or less clearly, within organs dedicated principally to other functions. An interesting example of the latter is that of a group of endocrine glands inextricably intermingled with an exocrine gland, and a very prominent one, too. I refer to the pancreas.

Since the 17th century at least, the pancreas has been known to discharge a secretion into the intestines, and in the early 19th century, the digestive function of that secretion was studied.

The pancreas has a prominent duct and produces a secretion that contains so many different digestive enzymes that it is actually the most important single digestive juice in the body. There seemed no particular reason to think that the pancreas had any secretory function other than this one.

However, the cellular makeup of the pancreas showed curious irregularities. A German anatomist, Paul Langerhans, reported in 1869 that amid the ordinary cells of the pancreas were numerous tiny clumps of cells that seemed marked off from the surrounding tissue. The number of these cell clumps is tremendous, varying from perhaps as few as a quarter million in some human beings to as many as two and a half million in others. Still, the individual clump is so small that all of them put together make up only 1 or 2 per cent of the volume and mass of the pancreas. Since the human pancreas weighs about 85 grams (3 ounces) the total mass of these clumps of cells in man would be in the neighborhood of one gram. The clumps have received the romantic-sounding name of *islets of Langerhans* in honor of their discoverer.

The islets, whatever their function, can have nothing to do with the ordinary secretion of the pancreas. This is shown by the fact that when the pancreatic duct is tied off in an animal, the ordinary cells of the pancreas wither and atrophy (as muscles do when because of paralysis they are not put to use). The cells of the islets, nevertheless, remain vigorous. Their function is not interfered with by the tying off of the duct so that if they have glandular function, it is ductless in nature.

Furthermore, if the pancreas is removed from the body of an experimental animal, one would fully expect that digestion would be interfered with; but there seemed no reason at first to suspect that anything else would happen. It was certainly not expected that the removal would be fatal; and if predigested food were fed the animal, it seemed reasonable to suppose the animal would not even be seriously discommoded.

Nevertheless, when two German physiologists removed the

pancreas of a dog, in 1889, they found that a serious and eventually fatal disease was produced that seemed to have nothing to do with digestion at all but which, instead, strongly resembled a human disease known as *diabetes mellitus* (dy'uh-bee'teez meh-ly'tus). Grafting the pancreas under the skin kept the dog alive, although in the new position its duct was clearly useless. Whatever the pancreas did to prevent diabetes mellitus, then, had nothing to do with the ordinary pancreatic juice which in normal life was discharged through that duct.

When, a little over a decade later, Bayliss and Starling worked out the concept of a hormone, it seemed very likely that the islets of Langerhans were ductless glands producing a hormone and that lack of this hormone brought on diabetes mellitus.

Diabetes mellitus is a disease that has been recognized among human beings since ancient times. It is one of a small group of diseases characterized by the production of abnormally high quantities of urine, so that water seemed simply to pass through the body in a hurry. This gave rise to the name "diabetes," from a Greek word meaning "to pass through." The most serious variety of the disease is characterized by an abnormally sweet urine. (This was first attested to by the fact that flies swarmed about the urine of such a diabetic, but eventually some curious ancient physician must have confirmed the fact by means of the taste buds.) The word "mellitus" is from the Greek word for honey. Diabetes mellitus may therefore, in popular terminology, be called "sugar diabetes" and often is referred to simply as "diabetes" without any modifier.

Diabetes mellitus is a common disease since between 1 and 2 per cent of the population in Western countries develop it at some time during their life. There are well over a million diabetics in the United States alone. Its incidence increases in middle age, is more common among overweight people than in those of normal weight, and is one of the few diseases that is more common among women than among men. It tends to run in families, so that relatives of diabetics are more apt to develop the disease than are

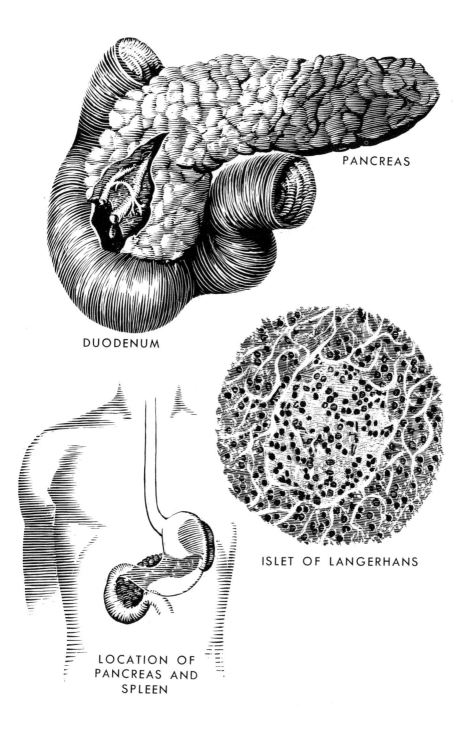

PANCREAS

DUODENUM

ISLET OF LANGERHANS

LOCATION OF
PANCREAS AND
SPLEEN

people with no history of diabetes in their family. The symptoms include excessive hunger and thirst and yet, even by eating and drinking more than normally, the untreated diabetic cannot keep up with the inefficiency of his body in handling foodstuffs. Urination is excessive and there is a gradual loss of weight and strength. Eventually, the diabetic goes into a coma and dies.

The disease is incurable in the sense that a diabetic can never be treated in such a way as to become a nondiabetic and require no further treatment. However, he can submit to a lifelong treatment that will enable him to live out a reasonably normal existence (thanks to the developments of this century), and this is by no means to be scorned.

INSULIN

For a generation, attempts were made to isolate the hormone of the islets of Langerhans.

Success finally came to a thirty-year-old Canadian physician, Frederick Grant Banting, who in the summer of 1921 spent time at the University of Toronto in an effort to solve the problem. He was assisted by a twenty-two-year-old physician, Charles Herbert Best. Banting and Best took the crucial step of tying off the pancreatic duct in a living animal and waiting seven weeks before killing the animal and trying to extract the hormone from its pancreas.

Previous attempts had failed because the hormone is a protein and the enzymes within the ordinary cells of the pancreas, some of which are particularly designed for protein digestion, broke up the hormone even while efforts were being made to mash up the pancreas. By tying off the duct, Banting and Best caused the pancreas to atrophy and its ordinary cells to lose their function. The hormone could now be isolated from the still-vigorous islets and no protein-destroying enzymes were present to break up the hormone. Once methods for producing the hormone were worked out, patients with diabetes mellitus could be treated successfully. For his feat, Banting received the Nobel Prize in Medicine and Physiology in 1923.

Banting suggested the name of "isletin" for the hormone, since it was produced in the islets of Langerhans. However, before the hormone had actually been isolated, the name *insulin* ("island" L) had been advanced, and it was the Latinized form of the name that was adopted. Insulin is one of a group of hormones that acts to coordinate the thousands of different chemical reactions that are constantly proceeding within living tissue. All these thousands of reactions are intermeshed in an exceedingly complicated fashion, and any substantial change in the rate at which any one of these reactions proceeds will affect other reactions that make use of substances produced by the first reaction. The reactions that are thus secondarily affected will in turn affect still other reactions, and so on.*

This interconnectedness, this mutual dependence, is such, that a drastic slowdown of a few key reactions, or even in only one, may be fatal, and sometimes quickly so. There are some poisons that in tiny quantities act quickly and put a sudden end to life by virtue of their ability to stop key reactions. It is rather like an intricate display of canned goods, or an elaborate house of blocks, in which the removal of one can or one block can lead to a quick and complete shattering of order.

But if the general pattern of metabolism is so intricate as to be vulnerable to the intrusion of a bit of alien poison, it might also be vulnerable to the general wear-and-tear of normal events. In our analogy, even if no one came up to a display and deliberately removed a can from the bottom row, there would still be the chance that the vibration of traffic outside, the thud of footsteps within the store, the accidental touch of a toe, might push a can out of place. Presumably, store employees passing such a display would notice if a can were dangerously off-center and push it back into position. It would be even more convenient if the dis-

* It is to this vast complex of chemical reactions within living tissue that we refer when we speak of *metabolism* ("to throw into a different position" G).

play were somehow so organized that a can out of position would automatically trip a circuit that would set up a magnetic field to pull it back into place.

Our metabolism, better organized than the displays in a store, has just such self-regulating features. Let's take an example. After a meal, the carbohydrate content of the food is broken down to simple sugars, mostly one called *glucose* ("sweet" G). This diffuses across the intestinal wall and into the bloodstream.

If the bloodstream accepted the glucose in full flood and if matters ended there, the blood would quickly grow thick and syrupy with the glucose it carried, and the heart, no matter how strongly it might work, would have to give up. But this does not happen. A short vein called the *portal vein* carries the glucose-laden blood to the liver, and in that organ the sugar is filtered out of the blood and stored within the liver cells as an insoluble, starch-like material called *glycogen* (gly′koh-jen; "sugar producer" G).

The blood emerging from the liver immediately after a meal will usually have a glucose content of no more than 130 milli-grams per cent* as a result of the storage work of the liver. This quickly drops further to somewhere between 60 and 90 milli-grams per cent. This range is called the "fasting blood glucose."

Glucose is the immediate fuel of the cells. Each cell absorbs all the glucose it needs from the blood, then breaks it down, through a complicated series of reactions, to carbon dioxide and water, liberating energy in the process. With each cell drawing upon the glucose, the total glucose supply in the blood might be expected to last only a matter of minutes. The glucose is not used up, however, because the liver is perfectly capable of breaking down its stored glycogen to glucose and delivering that into the bloodstream at a rate just calculated to replace the amount being abstracted by cells.

And so the liver is involved in maintaining the glucose level in the blood in two different ways, one opposed to the other, and

* A milligram (mg.) per cent is one milligram per hundred milliliters of blood.

both involving a number of intricately related reactions. When the glucose supply is temporarily greater than needed, as after a meal, glucose is stored in the liver as glycogen. When the glucose supply is temporarily smaller than needed, as during fasting intervals, glycogen is broken down to glucose. The net result is that the level of glucose in the blood is (in health) maintained within narrow limits; with a concentration never so high as to make the blood dangerously viscous; nor ever so low as to starve the cells.

But what keeps the balance? Meals can be large or small, frequent or infrequent. Fasting intervals may be long. Work or exercise may be greater at one period than at another so that the body's demands for energy will fluctuate. In view of all these unpredictable variations, what keeps the liver maintaining the balance with smooth efficiency?

In part, at least, the answer is insulin.

The presence of insulin in the bloodstream acts somehow to lower the blood glucose level. If for any reason, then, the glucose level should rise unexpectedly above the normal range, that high level in the blood passing through the pancreas stimulates the secretion of a correspondingly high quantity of insulin and the blood glucose level is pushed down to the normal range again. As the blood glucose level drops the stimulus that produces the insulin flow falls off, and so does the insulin. When the blood glucose level reaches the proper point, it falls no lower. Naturally, there is an enzyme in the blood designed to destroy insulin. This *insulinase* sees to it that no insulin remains to push the blood glucose level too low.

Again the condition is one of feedback. The condition to be corrected stimulates, of itself, the correcting phenomenon. And the response, as it corrects the condition, removes the very stimulus that calls it forth.

In the diabetic the capacity of the islets of Langerhans to respond to the stimulus of high glucose concentration fails. (Why this should be is not known, but the tendency for such failure is inherited.) As a result, the rise in glucose concentration after a meal is counteracted with increasing sluggishness as the extent of islets' failure increases. In fact, clinicians can detect the onset of diabetes at an early stage by deliberately flooding the blood with glucose. This is done by having the suspected person drink a quantity of glucose solution after a period of fasting. Samples of blood are then withdrawn before the meal and periodically afterward, and the glucose content is measured. If, in such a *glucose-tolerance test,* the rise in glucose concentration is steeper than is usually the case and if the return to normal is slower, then the patient is probably in the early stages of diabetes.

If the disease is not detected and is allowed to progress, the islets of Langerhans continue to fail to an increasing extent. The insulin supply goes lower and the glucose concentration becomes permanently high and, then, higher. When the concentration reaches a level of 200 mg. per cent or so (rather more than twice normal) the *glucose threshold* is passed and some glucose is lost through the kidneys. This is a waste of good food, but it is the best thing to be done under the unfortunate circumstances. If the glucose were allowed to continue to pile up, the blood would become dangerously, even fatally, viscous.

Ordinarily, the urine contains only traces of glucose, perhaps as little as 1 mg. per cent. In untreated diabetics, the concentration rises a thousandfold and is easily detected. By the time sugar is detected in the urine, however, the disease has progressed uncomfortably far.

The islets of Langerhans, having once failed, cannot have their function restored by any treatment known to man. The patient can, nevertheless, be supplied with insulin from an outside source. The insulin taken from the pancreas of a slaughtered steer is as effective in reducing the blood glucose concentration as is the insulin supplied by the patient's own pancreas. One or two milligrams of insulin per day will do the job.

The difficulty is that, whereas the patient's own pancreas in its days of health and vigor supplied insulin in the precise quantity needed and in a continuous but varying flow, insulin from the outside must be supplied in set quantities that can be made to match the need only approximately. The adjustment of the body's metabolism must therefore proceed by jerks, with the glucose concentration being driven too low at the first flood of insulin and being allowed to drift too high before the next installment. It is as though you placed the thermostat of your furnace under manual control, pushing it up and down by hand and trying to attain a continuously equable temperature.

It is for this reason that a diabetic, even under insulin treatment, must watch his diet carefully, so that he places as little strain as possible upon the blood glucose level. (You could control the thermostat manually with somewhat greater success if there were no sudden cold snaps to catch you by surprise.) The use of externally produced insulin has the disadvantage also of requiring hypodermic injection. Insulin cannot be taken by mouth, for it is a protein that is promptly digested in the stomach and broken into inactive fragments.

A possible way out lies in an opposite-tack approach. The insulin-destroying enzyme insulinase can be put out of action by certain drugs. Such drugs, which can be taken by mouth, would therefore allow a diabetic's limited supply of insulin to last longer and could, at least in some cases, replace the hypodermic needle.

INSULIN STRUCTURE

It is easy to observe that insulin lowers the blood glucose level. This level, however, is the result of a complex interplay of many chemical reactions. How does insulin affect those reactions in order to bring about a lowering of the level? Does it affect just one reaction? More than one? All of them?

In the search for answers to these questions, suspicion fell most strongly on a reaction catalyzed by an enzyme called *hexokinase* (hek'soh-ky'nays). This was chiefly the result of work by the husband-and-wife team of Czech-American biochemists, Carl Ferdinand Cori and Gerty Theresa Cori, who had worked out much of the detail of the various reactions involved in glucose breakdown and had, for that reason, shared in the Nobel Prize in Medicine and Physiology for 1947. The Coris maintained that the hexokinase reaction was under continual inhibition under ordinary circumstances and that the action of insulin was to counteract this inhibition and to allow the reaction to proceed. They were able to demonstrate how the effect on that one reaction would account for the lowering of blood glucose concentration.

However, this seems to have been too simple an explanation. The metabolism of the diabetic is disordered in various ways. Although it is possible to account for a variety of disorders through the effect of the upsetting of a single reaction (so interconnected is the metabolic web), to account for all the disorders in diabetes mellitus out of the one hexokinase reaction required a great deal of complicated reasoning that grew the less convincing as it grew more complicated. The most recent experiments seem to indicate instead that insulin exerts its effect on the cell membranes. The rate at which cells absorb glucose depends partly on the difference in concentration of glucose within and without the cell; and also on the nature of the cell membrane through which the glucose must pass.

To make an analogy: if men are entering a building from the street, the rate at which they will enter will depend partly on the number of men trying to get in. It will also depend on the width of the door or on the number of open doors. After a certain point of crowding is reached, only a certain number of men can enter the building each second, no matter how many men are in the street pushing to get in. An attendant, however, who quickly opens two more doors at once triples the rate of entry.

Apparently insulin molecules attach themselves to the membranes of muscle cells and of other types of cells as well and act to increase the permeability of those membranes to glucose. (In

effect, opening additional doors.) So, when glucose floods the
bloodstream after a meal, insulin is produced. This opens the
"membrane doors" and the glucose concentration in blood is rapidly reduced, since it vanishes within the cells, where it is either
utilized or stored. In the diabetic, glucose knocks at the various
cell membranes, but in the absence of insulin it knocks to a certain extent in vain. It cannot enter with sufficient speed and it
therefore accumulates in the blood. Obviously, anything else
that will facilitate entry of glucose into the cells will, at least par-
tially, fill the role of insulin. Exercise is one thing that will, and
regular exercise is usually prescribed for the diabetic.

We must inevitably ask: What is it that insulin does to the cell
membrane to increase the facility with which glucose enters?
It is partly in the hope of answering this question (and partly
out of sheer curiosity) that biochemists attempted to determine
the exact structure of the insulin molecule.

The molecule of insulin is a polypeptide, as are those of the
gastrointestinal hormones, but it is more complicated. While
the secretin molecule is made up of 36 amino acid units, the insulin molecule is made up of about 50. Since the problem of
secretin's exact structure has not been solved, one might reasonably suppose that insulin's exact structure would also be still
unknown; but the drive for a solution to the problem in the case
of insulin, which is involved in mankind's most serious "metabolic disease," is far greater than the drive to solve the problem
of the structure of the gastrointestinal hormones, which have
little clinical importance. In addition, far greater quantities of
pure insulin are available for analysis.

By the late 1940's it had been discovered that insulin had a
molecular weight of a trifle under 6000. (Its molecules have a
tendency to double up and to join in even larger groups so that
molecular weights of 12,000 and even 36,000 had been reported
at first.) The molecule was then found to consist of two chains
of amino acids held together by cystine molecules after the fashion explained on page 12. When the chains were pulled apart,

one (chain A) turned out to consist of 21 amino acids, while the other (chain B) consisted of 30.

The individual amino acids in each chain were easily determined by breaking down the chains separately and then analyzing for the different amino acids.* But, as I explained in the previous chapter, knowing the individual amino acids is only the beginning. One must also know the exact order in which they are arranged. The 21 amino acids of chain A can be arranged in any of about 2,800,000,000,000,000 ways. The 30 amino acids of chain B offer more leeway, obviously, and can be arranged in any of about 510,000,000,000,000,000,000,000,000 different ways.

The problem of determining the exact arrangements in the actual molecule of insulin obtained from the ox pancreas, out of all the possibilities that could exist, was tackled by a group headed by the British biochemist Frederick Sanger. The method used was to break down the amino acid chains only partway by the use of acid or of various enzymes. The breakdown products were not individual amino acids but small chains containing two, three, or four amino acids. These small chains were isolated and studied and the exact order of the amino acids determined. (Two amino acids can only be placed in two different orders, A-B and B-A. Three amino acids can be placed in six different orders: A-B-C, A-C-B, B-C-A, B-A-C, C-A-B, and C-B-A. Even four amino acids can only be placed in 24 different orders. The possible arrangements in the case of the small fragments can be checked and the correct one chosen without insuperable difficulty. At the most, a couple of dozen possibilities are involved and not a couple of quintillion.)

Once all the small chains are worked out, it becomes possible to fit them together. Suppose that chain A has only one molecule of a particular amino acid that we shall call q, and suppose that two short chains of three amino acids each have been located,

* The method of doing this involves a procedure called *paper chromatography* that was first developed in 1944 and has succeeded in revolutionizing biochemistry. If you are interested in this, you will find the procedure described in some detail in the chapter "Victory on Paper" in my book *Only a Trillion* (1957).

one being *r-s-q* and the other *q-p-o*. Since only one *q* is present, there must be a five amino acid sequence in the original molecule that goes *r-s-q-p-o*. You will then get either *r-s-q* or *q-p-o*, depending on which side of the *q* the chain breaks.

It took eight years for Sanger and his group to work out the complete jigsaw puzzle. By 1955 they had put the fragments together and determined the structure of the intact molecule. It was the first time the structure of any naturally occurring protein molecule had ever been determined in full, and for this Sanger was awarded the Nobel Prize in Chemistry for 1958.

The formula of the molecule of ox insulin, in Brand abbreviations, is as follows:

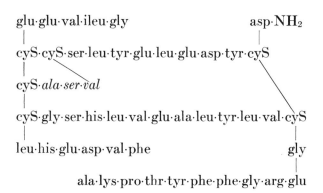

OX INSULIN

Unfortunately, nothing in the structure of the molecule gives biochemists any clue as to why insulin affects the cell membrane as it does.

It might be possible to tackle the matter by comparing the structures of insulin produced by different species. Swine insulin is just as effective for the diabetic as ox insulin is. If the two insulins differ in molecular structure, then only that which they possess in common need perhaps be considered necessary to their functioning, and attention could be focused to a finer point. When swine insulin was analyzed, it was found to differ from ox insulin only in the three amino acids italicized in the formula given above, the three that are pinched off in a corner, so to speak, between the two cystine groups.

Whereas in ox insulin the three amino acids are ala-ser-val, in swine insulin they are thr-ser-ileu. These same three amino acids and *only* these three also vary in the insulin molecules of other species. In sheep it is ala-gly-cal, in horses it is thr-gly-ileu, and in whales it is thr-ser-ileu. Of these three the one at the left can be either alanine or threonine, the one in the middle can be either serine or glycine, and the one at the right can be either valine or isoleucine.

While many other species remain to be tested, it does not seem likely that startling differences will be found. Furthermore, any change imposed on the insulin molecule by chemical reaction from without, unless the change is a rather trifling one that does not seriously affect the complexity of the molecule, produces loss of activity. Whatever it is that insulin does to the cell membrane, all, or virtually all, of the molecule is involved, and that is about as much as can be said. At least so far.

GLUCAGON

Where a hormone exerts its push in a single direction, as insulin does in the direction of lowered glucose concentration in the blood, it would be reasonable to suspect that another hormone might exist which exerts an opposing effect. This would not result in a cancellation of effect, but rather in an equilibrium that can be shifted this way and that more delicately and accurately through the use of two opposing effects than through either alone. You can see this best perhaps when you consider that a tottering ladder is most easily steadied by being held with both hands, the two pressing gently in opposing directions.

There does exist such an "opposition hormone" for insulin, one also produced in the islets of Langerhans. This second hormone is far less well known than insulin because there is no clinical disorder that is clearly associated with it; nothing, that is, corresponding to diabetes mellitus.

The islets of Langerhans contain two varieties of cells, named *alpha cells* and *beta cells*. (Scientists very often, perhaps too often, follow the line of least resistance in distinguishing a series of similar objects by use of the first few letters of the Greek alphabet.) The alpha cells are the larger of the two types and are situated at the outer regions of the islets, making up about 25 per cent of their total volume. At the centers of each islet are the smaller beta cells. It is the beta cells that produce the insulin, and the alpha cells produce the hormone with the opposing effect.

This second hormone was discovered when, soon after Banting's discovery of a method of insulin preparation, some samples were found to induce an initial rise in blood glucose concentration before imposing the more usual lowering. Something that exerted an effect opposed to that of insulin was therefore searched for and located. The new hormone was found to bring about an acceleration of the breakdown of the glycogen stored in the liver. The glycogen was broken down to glucose, which poured into the bloodstream. In this fashion the blood glucose level was raised.

When the presence of a hormone is only suspected by the effects it brings about, it is named after those effects in many cases; this new hormone was therefore named *hyperglycemic-glycogenolytic factor* (hy'per-gly-see'mik gly'koh-jen'oh-lih'tik; "high-glucose, glycogen-dissolving" G) in order to mark the manner in which it raised the blood glucose level and lowered the quantity of glycogen in the liver. Since biochemists don't really like long names any more than do the rest of us, this was quickly abbreviated to *HGF*. In recent years an acceptable name, shorter than the first, has become popular — *glucagon* (gloo'kuh-gon).

By 1953 glucagon had been prepared in pure crystalline form and was easily shown to be a polypeptide with a molecule made up of a single chain containing 29 amino acids. At first thought it might have seemed that perhaps glucagon was a fragmented insulin molecule, but a closer look disproved that. By 1958 the order of the amino acids had been worked out, by use of the methods introduced by Sanger. Here it is:

$$his·ser·glu·NH_2·gly·thr·phe·thr·ser·asp·tyr·ser·-$$
$$lys·tyr·leu·asp·ser·arg·arg·ala·glu·NH_2·asp·phe·-$$
$$val·glu·NH_2·try·leu·met·asp·NH_2·thr$$

GLUCAGON

There is, as you see, no similarity in this chain to either of the chains in insulin. As a matter of fact, some of the amino acids present in glucagon (methionine, say) are not present in insulin at all, while others (as, for example, isoleucine) which are present in insulin are not present in glucagon. There is no question but that insulin and glucagon are two completely different hormones.

EPINEPHRINE

Insulin and glucagon are by no means the only hormones that affect the metabolism of carbohydrates in a manner that shows up in the level of glucose concentration in the blood. Another hormone with such an effect is produced by two small yellowish organs, roughly pyramidlike in shape, about one or two inches in length in the adult and weighing about 10 grams (⅓ ounce) each. They lie in contact with the upper portion of either kidney and are the first organs I have had occasion to mention that are completely endocrinological in functioning.

Because of their location, the organs are called the *adrenal glands* (ad-ree'nul; "near the kidneys" L), or *suprarenal glands* (syoo'pruh-ree'nul; "above the kidneys" L); see illustration, page 75.

The adrenal glands are made up of two sections, an outer and an inner, and these are different in cellular makeup, in function, and in origin. In the more primitive fish, the material corresponding to the two sections of the adrenal glands exists separately. What is in us the outer portion is an elongated structure in these fish, about as long as the kidneys. Our inner portion forms two lines of small collections of cells, running nearly twice the length of the kidney. In amphibians, reptiles, and birds, the glandular material is more compact and the two sets of cells become intermingled. Among the mammals compactness reaches the extreme, and one set of cells entirely encloses the other.

The outer portion of the adrenal glands, which makes up about nine tenths of the mass of the organs is the *adrenal cortex* (kawr'-teks; "bark" L, because it encloses the inner portion as the bark encloses a tree). The inner portion is the *adrenal medulla* (meh-dul'uh; "marrow" L, because it is within the outer portion as marrow is within a bone). The hormone to be discussed now is formed in the medulla.

As long ago as 1895 it was known that extracts of the adrenal glands had a powerful action in raising the blood pressure. In 1901 a pure substance was obtained from the glands by the Japanese biochemist Jokichi Takamine and this markedly raised the blood pressure even in very tiny quantities. The name by which this compound is best known is *Adrenalin* (ad-ren'uh-lin), which, however, is only one of many trade names for the material. The proper chemical name for the compound is *epinephrine* (ep'ih-nef'rin; "on the kidney" G).

The year after Takamine's feat, Bayliss and Starling demonstrated the possibility of chemical coordination in the absence of nerve action. Once that was clearly understood, it was recognized that epinephrine was a hormone. It was the first hormone to be isolated in pure form, and the first hormone to have its structure determined. This is less remarkable than it might otherwise appear: of all known hormones, epinephrine has the simplest structure.

Where secretin, insulin, and glucagon are all made up of chains of several-dozen amino acids, epinephrine is, in its essentials, a modified version of a single amino acid, tyrosine. This is most clearly shown by comparing the chemical formulas. Even if you are not familiar with such formulas and don't understand the details of what is represented, the resemblance between the two substances will still be clear:

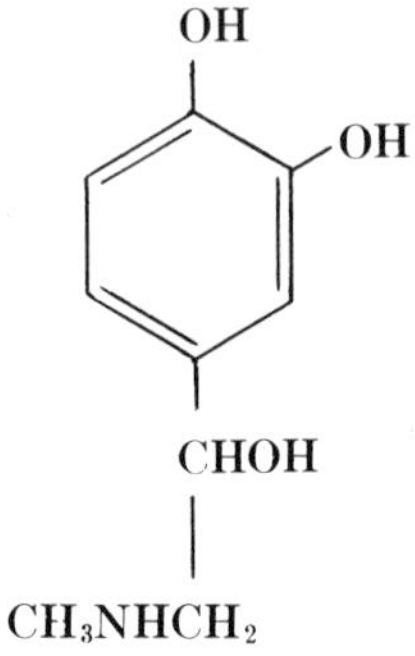

OH

OH

CHOH

CH₃NHCH₂

EPINEPHRINE

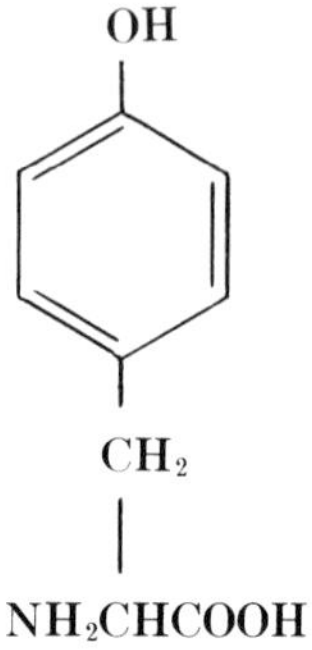

OH

CH₂

NH₂CHCOOH

TYROSINE

Chemists have had little difficulty in showing that the adrenal medulla manufactures its epinephrine out of tyrosine.

As far as its effect on carbohydrate metabolism is concerned, epinephrine resembles glucagon in hastening the breakdown of glycogen to glucose so that the blood level of glucose rises. The difference is this: glucagon works under normal conditions; epinephrine works in emergencies. To state it differently, glucagon maintains a more or less steady effect designed to help keep the glucose level constant (in cooperation with the opposite action of insulin) under the ordinary fluctuations of glucose supply and glucose consumption. Epinephrine, in contrast, is called into play under conditions of anger or fear, when a massive supply of glucose is quickly needed to supply the energy requirements of a body about to engage in either fight or flight.

Then, too, where glucagon mobilizes only the glycogen supplies of the liver (supplies that are for the general use of the body), epinephrine brings about the breakdown of the glycogen in muscle as well. The muscle glycogen is for use by the muscles only, and by stimulating its breakdown epinephrine makes possible the drawing on private energy supply by the muscles (which will be primarily concerned in the fight-or-flight situation).

Epinephrine has other effects on the body beside the mobilization of its glucose reserves. For one thing, there is the effect on blood pressure, by which its existence was first recognized, and its ability to speed the heartbeat and the breathing rate. These last effects are brought about via the interplay of epinephrine and the nervous system, something I shall discuss in more detail in Chapter 9. I might pause to mention, though, that the two levels of organization, the chemical (hormones) and the electrical (nerves) are by no means independent, but are interrelated.

The situation, incidentally, whereby a single modified amino acid functions as a hormone (and is classified as one) is represented by more than one case. There is *histamine*, for another example, a compound very similar in structure to the amino acid histidine, as the following formulas show:

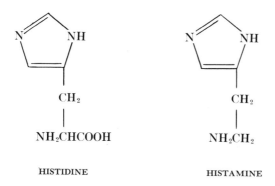

HISTIDINE   HISTAMINE

In small concentrations histamine stimulates the secretion of hydrochloric acid by the glands in the stomach lining. There are biochemists who suspect that gastrin (one of the gastrointestinal hormones pointed out in the previous chapter, see p. 20) is really histamine. This is by no means certain yet.

As in the case of epinephrine, histamine affects blood pressure and other facets of the body mechanism. (The kinins, described on page 22, have some effect similar to histamine.) Histamine is believed responsible for some of the unpleasant accompaniments of allergies (runny nose, swelling of the mucous membrane of nose and throat, constriction of the bronchioles, and the like). Apparently the foreign protein, or other substance, which sparks the allergic reaction does so by stimulating the production of histamine. Drugs that counteract the effect of histamine (antihistamines) relieve these symptoms.

3

OUR THYROID

There is still another hormone that is a modified amino acid, one a bit more complicated in structure than either epinephrine or histamine is. To discuss it properly, I shall begin by introducing a new organ. The prominent cartilage in the neck, commonly called the "Adam's apple," is more correctly termed the *thyroid cartilage*. The word "thyroid" is from a Greek term meaning "shieldlike," in reference to the large oblong shields carried by Homeric and pre-Homeric warriors which had a notch on top for the chin to rest upon. You can feel the notch on top of the thyroid cartilage if you put your finger to your neck.

Now at the bottom of the thyroid cartilage is a soft mass of yellowish-red glandular tissue about two inches high, a bit more than two inches wide, and weighing an ounce or a little less. It exists in two lobes, one on either side of the windpipe, with a narrow connecting band running in front of the windpipe just at the bottom boundary of the thyroid cartilage. Seen from the front, the gland resembles a letter H. The gland, for some centuries, has borrowed its name from the cartilage it hugs and is therefore known as the *thyroid gland* even though there is nothing shieldlike about it.

Before the end of the 19th century, the function of the thyroid gland was not known. It is somewhat more prominent in women

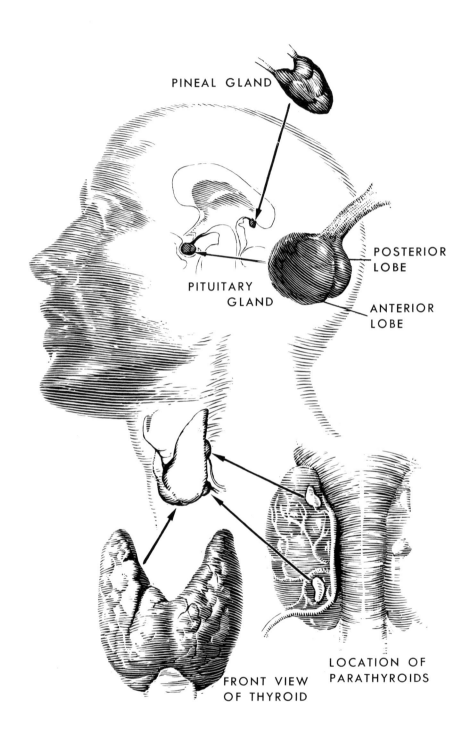

PINEAL GLAND

POSTERIOR LOBE

PITUITARY GLAND

ANTERIOR LOBE

FRONT VIEW OF THYROID

LOCATION OF PARATHYROIDS

than in men, and for that reason the opinion was variously maintained that the thyroid was nothing more than padding designed to fill out the neck (of women especially) and make it plumply attractive. There were regions of Europe where the thyroid (again, particularly in women) was enlarged beyond the normal size, and this, which meant a somewhat swollen neck, was accepted as an enhancement of beauty rather than otherwise. An enlarged thyroid gland is referred to as a *goiter* ("throat" L).

The cosmetic value of a goiter was rather deflated when it came to be recognized about 1800 or so that the condition could be associated with a variety of undesirable symptoms. Confusingly enough, goitrous individuals were apt to have either of two opposing sets of symptoms. Some were dull, listless, and apathetic, with soft, puffy tissues, cool, dry skin, and slow heartbeat. In contrast, some were nervous, tense, unstable, with flushed, moist skin and fast heartbeat. And finally, as you might guess, there were people with goiters who showed neither set of symptoms and were reasonably normal.

That this connection of the goiter and at least one set of symptoms was no coincidence was clearly demonstrated in 1883, when several Swiss surgeons completely removed goitrous thyroids from 46 patients. (Switzerland is one of the regions where goiter was common.) The thyroids had enlarged to the point where they were interfering with surrounding tissue, and there seemed no logical argument against removal. Unfortunately, in those patients the symptoms of the dull, listless variety appeared and intensified. To remove the entire thyroid appeared *not* to be safe.

Then in 1896 a German chemist, E. Baumann, located iodine in the thyroid gland. Not much was present, to be sure, for the best modern analyses show that the human thyroid at most contains 8 milligrams (or about 1/2000 ounce) of iodine. About four times the amount is distributed throughout the rest of the body. The rest of the body, however, is so much more massive than the thyroid that the iodine content there is spread thin indeed. The iodine concentration in that one organ, the thyroid gland, is more than 60,000 times as high as is the concentration anywhere else in the body.

Certainly this sounds significant now, but it didn't seem so in 1896. Iodine had never been located in any chemical component of the human body, and it seemed reasonable to suppose that it was an accidental contaminant. The fact that it was present in such small quantities made this seem all the more probable, for it was not yet understood in 1896 that such things as "essential trace elements" existed; elements that formed parts of hormones or enzymes and were therefore necessary to proper functioning of the body and even to life itself, without having to be present in more than tiny quantities.

It was a decade later, in 1905, that David Marine, an American physician just out of medical school, took Baumann's discovery seriously. Coming to the American Midwest from the East, he wondered if the relative frequency of goiter in the Midwest had anything to do with the relative poverty of the soil in iodine.* Perhaps the iodine was not merely an accidental contaminant, but formed an integral part of the thyroid; and perhaps in the absence of iodine the thyroid suffered a disorder that evidenced itself as a goiter.

Marine experimented upon animals with diets low in iodine; they developed goiter, showing the dull, listless set of symptoms. He added small quantities of iodine to the diet and cured the condition. By 1916 he felt confident enough to experiment on girls and was able to show that traces of iodine in the food cut down the incidence of goiter in humans. It then took another ten years to argue people into allowing small quantities of iodine compounds to be added to city water reservoirs and to table salt. The furious opposition to such procedures was something like

---

* Iodine is actually a rare element; the sea is richer in iodine than the land is. Seaweed is a major source of iodine because plant cells actively concentrate the iodine of the sea. The iodine in soil is often there only because storms spray the coastline with droplets of ocean water that evaporate, leaving the tiny bits of salt content to be blown far inland. The salts contain iodine, and as a matter of course land near the sea would, all things being equal, be richer in iodine than areas far inland.

the similar opposition to fluoridation today. Nevertheless, iodination won out; iodized salt is now a commonplace; and goiter, in the United States at least, is a rarity.

The symptoms that accompany goiter depend on whether the goiter forms in response to an iodine deficiency or not. The thyroid gland consists of millions of tiny hormone-producing follicles, each filled with a colloidal (that is, jellylike) substance called, simply enough, *colloid* ("gluelike" G). The colloid contains the iodine and so does the hormone it produces.

If the iodine supply in the diet is adequate, and if for any reason the thyroid increases in size, the number of active follicles may be multiplied as much as ten or twenty times and the hormone is produced in greater-than-normal quantities. The nervous, tense set of symptoms are produced, and this is *hyperthyroidism.* If, on the contrary, there is a deficiency of iodine, the thyroid may enlarge in an effort to compensate. The effort inevitably must be unsuccessful. No matter how many follicles form and how much colloid is produced, the thyroid hormone cannot be manufactured without iodine. In that case, despite the goiter, the hormone is produced in less-than-normal quantities and the dull, listless set of symptoms results. This is *hypothyroidism.* *

The two forms of goiter can be distinguished by name. The form of goiter associated with hypothyroidism is simply *iodine-deficiency goiter,* a self-explanatory name. The form of goiter associated with hyperthyroidism is *exophthalmic goiter* (ek'sof-thal'mik; "eyes out" G) because the most prominent symptoms are bulging eyeballs. The latter form is also called *Graves' disease,* because it was well described by an Irish physician, Robert James Graves, in 1835. In hypothyroidism, the puffy flabbiness of the tissues seems to be brought about by an infiltration of mucuslike

* "Hyper" is from a Greek word meaning "over" and "above," and "hypo" is from the Greek for "under" or "below." The former prefix is commonly used to indicate any condition involving overactivity of an organ or the production or occurrence of some substance in greater-than-normal quantities. The latter prefix is used to indicate the opposite. It is a pity that opposites should sound so alike and offer such chance of confusions, but it is too late to correct the Greek language now.

materials, and the condition is therefore called *myxedema* (mik'suh-dee'muh; "mucus-swelling" G).

The symptoms in either direction, that of hyperthyroidism or hypothyroidism, can be of varying intensity. A reasonable measure of the intensity was first developed in 1895 by a German physician, Adolf Magnus-Levy, and that was partly a result of accident. At the time, physiologists had developed methods for measuring the uptake of oxygen by human beings and deducing the rate at which the metabolic processes of the body were operating. Naturally, this rate increased with exercise and decreased during rest. By arranging to have a fasting person lie down in a comfortably warm room and under completely relaxed conditions it was possible to obtain a minimum waking value for the rate of metabolism. This was the *basal metabolic rate*, usually abbreviated *BMR*, and it represented the "idling speed" of the human body.

Magnus-Levy was briskly and eagerly applying BMR measurements to the various patients in the hospital at which he worked in order to see whether the BMR varied in particular fashion with particular diseases. Obviously if it did, BMR determinations could become a valuable diagnostic tool and could help in following the course of a disease. Unfortunately, most diseases did not affect the BMR. There was one important exception. Hyperthyroid individuals showed a markedly high BMR and hypothyroid individuals a markedly low one. The more serious the condition the higher (or lower) the BMR was.

In this way the overall function of the thyroid hormone was established. It controlled the basal metabolic rate, the idling speed. A hyperthyroid individual had, to use an automotive metaphor, a racing engine; a hypothyroid individual had a sluggish one. This lent sense to the two sets of symptoms. With the chemical reactions within a body perpetually hastening, a person would be expected to be keyed-up, tense, nervous, overactive. And with those same reactions slowed down, he would be dull, listless, apathetic.

THYROXINE

The search for the actual thyroid hormone started as soon as the importance of iodine in the thyroid gland was recognized. In 1899 an iodine-containing protein was isolated from the gland. This had the properties associated with a group of proteins called "globulins" and was therefore named *thyroglobulin* (thy'roh-glob'-yoo-lin). It could relieve hypothyroid symptoms as well as mashed-up thyroid could, and do it in smaller quantities; so it might be considered at least a form of the thyroid hormone.

However, thyroglobulin is a large protein molecule, possessing a molecular weight, we now know, of up to 700,000. It is far too large to get out of the cell that formed it and into the bloodstream in intact form. For this reason it quickly seemed clear that thyroglobulin was at best merely the stored form of the hormone, and that what passed into the bloodstream were small fragments of the thyroglobulin molecule.

Iodine assumed increasing significance as biochemists labored in this direction. The thyroid gland, rich in iodine though it might be compared with the rest of the body, is still only about 0.03 per cent iodine. Preparations of thyroglobulin itself were 30 times or so as rich in iodine as was the intact thyroid gland and contained up to almost 1 per cent iodine. Furthermore, when the thyroglobulin molecule was broken down, the most active fragments had iodine contents as high as 14 per cent. Iodine was clearly the key. It was even possible to add iodine to quite ordinary proteins, such as casein (the chief protein of milk), and to produce an artificial *iodinated protein* containing some degree of thyroid hormone activity.

Finally, in 1915 the American chemist Edward Calvin Kendall isolated a small molecule that had all the properties of the thyroid hormone in concentrated form and yet seemed to be a single amino acid. Since it was found in the thyroid and since it controlled the rate of oxygen utilization in the body, the molecule was named *thyroxine* (thy-rok'sin).

An additional decade was required to determine the exact molecular structure of this amino acid. It turned out to be related to tyrosine, differing in its possession of a sort of doubled side-chain. You can see this clearly in the formulas below:

TYROSINE   THYROXINE

The most unusual point about the structure of the thyroxine molecule is the fact that it contains four iodine atoms, symbolized in the formula above by I. (If the four iodine atoms were removed, what would be left of the molecule would be named *thyronine*.)

The four iodine atoms are quite heavy, much heavier than all 31 carbon, hydrogen, nitrogen, and oxygen atoms making up the rest of the molecule.* For that reason, iodine makes up about 63 per cent of the weight of the thyroxine molecule.

Apparently the thyroid gland traps the small traces of iodine

* Of all the atoms that are essential to life, iodine is by far the heaviest. The four most common atoms in the body are all quite light. Thus, if the weight of the hydrogen atom is considered 1, then carbon has an atomic weight of 12, nitrogen of 14, and oxygen of 16. Compare this with iodine, which has an atomic weight of 127.

present in food, adds them to the tyrosine molecule, doubles the side-chain, and adds more iodine to form thyroxine. (This can be done artificially, to a certain extent, by adding iodine to casein, as I mentioned above.) The thyroxine molecules are then united with other, more common amino acids and stored as the large thyroglobulin molecule. At need, the thyroxine content of the thyroglobulin is stripped off and sent out into the bloodstream.

For some thirty-five years after the discovery of thyroxine, it was considered *the* thyroid hormone. In 1951 the British biochemist Rosalind Pitt-Rivers and her co-workers isolated a very similar compound, one in which one of the iodine atoms was absent from the molecule, leaving only three in place. The new compound, with its three iodine atoms, is *tri-iodothyronine*, and is rather more active than thyroxine. For this reason I shall refer hereafter to "thyroid hormone" rather than to any one particular compound.

Now where thyroid hormone is severely deficient, the BMR may drop to half its normal value; where it is quite excessive, the BMR may rise to twice or even two and a half times its normal value. The thyroid control can therefore push the rate of metabolism through a fivefold range.

Yet what is it that thyroxine, tri-iodothyronine, and possible related compounds do to bring about such changes? What particular reaction or reactions do they stimulate in order to lift the entire level of metabolism? And how does iodine play a role? This is perhaps the most fascinating aspect of the problem, because no compound without iodine has any thyroid hormone activity whatever. Furthermore, there is no iodine in any compound present in our body except for the various forms of thyroid hormone.

By now you should not be surprised at learning that there is no answer as yet to these questions. The answer, when it comes, will have to explain more than a simple raising or lowering of the BMR, since that is by no means the only effect of the thyroid hormone. It plays a role in growth, in mental development, and in sexual development.

It sometimes happens that children are born with little or no thyroid tissue. Such children live but one can scarcely say more than that. If the condition is not corrected by the administration of hormone, the deficient creatures never grow to be larger than the normal seven- or eight-year-old. They do not mature sexually and are usually severely retarded mentally. They are often deaf-mutes. (These symptoms can be duplicated in animals if the thyroid is removed while they are young; actually it was in this fashion that the symptoms just described were first associated with the thyroid gland.)

Such virtually thyroidless unfortunates are called *cretins* (kree′tinz). The word is from a southern French dialect and means "Christians." The use of this word is not intended as a slur on religion but is, rather, an expression of pity, as we might say "poor soul." It could also be a hangover from an earlier day, reflecting the widespread belief among many primitive peoples that any form of mental aberration is a sign that the sufferer is touched by a god. (And do we not sometimes say of a madman that he is "touched in the head"?)

This inability of a thyroidless child to develop into an adult is also evidenced among the lower vertebrates; most startlingly among the amphibians. In amphibians the change from the young to the adult forms involves such dramatic overhauls of body structure as the replacement of a tail by legs, and of gills by lungs. Such changes cannot be carried through partway without killing the creature. The change is either completed or it is not begun.

If thyroid tissue is removed from a tadpole, the change is never begun. The creature may grow, yet it remains a tadpole; but if thyroid extract is added to the water in which the tadpole is swimming, it makes the change and becomes a frog. In fact, if thyroid extract is added to the water in which small tadpoles are swimming (tadpoles too small to produce their own hormone and change to frogs in the course of nature) the change nevertheless takes place. Tiny frogs are produced, much smaller than those produced under normal conditions.

There are creatures called axolotls, which are amphibians that remain tadpoles, so to speak, throughout life. They remain water creatures with gills and tail, but differ from ordinary tadpoles in that they can develop sexual maturity and reproduce themselves. They evidently are naturally hypothyroid, but through evolutionary processes have managed to survive and adjust to their lot. Now if the axolotl is supplied thyroid extract, it undergoes the change that in nature it does not. Legs replace the tail, lungs replace gills, and it climbs out upon land, a creature forever cut off from the rest of its species.

The sensitivity of amphibians to thyroid hormone is such that tadpoles have been used to test the potency of samples of thyroid extracts.

THYROID-STIMULATING HORMONE

One would expect the thyroid hormone to be produced in amounts matching the needs of the body. Where the rate of metabolism is high, as during exercise or physical labor, the hormone is consumed at a greater-than-normal rate and the thyroid gland must produce a correspondingly greater amount. The reverse is true when the body's needs are low, as when it is resting or asleep.

In the case of insulin, the blood glucose level can act as a feedback control. No such opportunity seems to be offered the thyroid gland. At least no blood component is, as far as we know, clearly affected by the quantity of thyroid hormone produced, and so there is no shifting level of concentration of some component to act as a thyroid control.

The concentration of thyroid hormone in the blood must itself vary. If body metabolism rises, so that the hormone is more quickly consumed, its blood level must show a tendency to drop. If body metabolism is low, the blood level of the hormone must show a tendency to rise. It might seem, then, that the thyroid could respond to the level of its own hormone in the blood passing through itself. This is clearly dangerous. Since the thyroid produces the hormone, the blood concentration in its own vicinity would always be higher than in the remainder of the body, and it would receive a blurred and distorted picture of what is going on. (It would be something like an executive judging the worth of his ideas by the opinions of his yes-men.)

The solution is to put a second gland to work; a gland in a different region of the body. The second gland turns out to be, in this case, a small organ at the base of the brain. This is the *pituitary gland* (pih-tyoo'ih-tehr'ee; "phlegm" L). The name arises from the fact that, since the gland is located at the base of the brain just above the nasal passages, some of the ancients thought its function was to supply the nose with its mucous secretions. The idea held force till about 1600.

This, of course, is not so; the only secretions produced by the pituitary are discharged directly into the bloodstream. Nevertheless, the name persists, although there is the alternative of *hypophysis cerebri* (hy-pof'ih-sis cehr'uh-bree; "undergrowth of the brain" G), or simply *hypophysis*. This term, which came into use about half a century ago, is at least accurately descriptive.

In man the pituitary gland is a small egg-shaped structure about half an inch long, or about the size of the final joint of the little finger; see illustration, page 46. It weighs less than a gram, or only about 1/40 of an ounce, but don't let that fool you. In some respects it is the most important gland in the body. The location alone would seem to indicate that — just about at the midpoint of the head, as though carefully hidden in the safest and most inaccessible part. The gland is connected by a thin stalk to the base of the brain, and rests in a small depression in the bone that rims the base.

The pituitary is divided into two parts, which (as in the case of the adrenal glands) have no connection with each other functionally. They do not even originate in the same way. The rear portion, or *posterior lobe*, originates in the embryo as an outgrowth of the base of the brain, and it is the posterior lobe that remains attached to the brain by the thin stalk. The forward portion, or *anterior lobe,* originates in the embryo as a pinched-off portion of the mouth. The anterior lobe loses all connection with the mouth and eventually finds itself hugging the posterior lobe. The two are lumped together as a single gland only by this accident of meeting midway and ending in the same place. (In some animals, there is an *intermediate lobe* as well, but in man this is virtually absent.) Both lobes produce polypeptide hormones. The anterior lobe produces six hormones that have been definitely isolated as pure, or nearly pure, substances, and these may be spoken of, generally, as the *anterior pituitary hormones.* (The existence of several other hormones is suspected.)

Of the six anterior pituitary hormones, one has the function of stimulating the secretion of the thyroid gland. This is easily shown, since removal of the pituitary in experimental animals causes atrophy of the thyroid gland, among other unpleasant effects. This also takes place in cases of *hypopituitarism,* where the secretions of the pituitary gland fall below the minimum required for health. The symptoms of this disease (which are quite distressing since they tend to show up in young women and to induce premature aging, among other things) were described by a German physician named Morris Simmonds, so the condition is often called *Simmonds' disease.*

On the positive side, the administration of preparations of pituitary extracts to animals can cause the thyroid gland to increase in weight and become more active. It is reasonable, therefore, to suppose that at least one of the anterior pituitary hormones is concerned with thyroid function. The hormone has been isolated and has been labeled the *thyroid-stimulating hormone,* a name usually abbreviated as *TSH.* It may also be called the *thyrotrophic hormone* (thy′roh-troh′fic; "thyroid-nourishing" G).*

---

* There is a tendency to use the suffix "tropic" in place of "trophic" in the case of TSH and certain other hormones. The suffix "tropic" is from a Greek word meaning "to turn" and makes. no sense in this connection. Unfortunately, the difference lies in but one letter and few biochemists seem to be terribly concerned over the proper meaning of a Greek suffix, so "thyrotropic" is a fairly common term and may become even more common.

With two hormones at work, a mutual feedback can take place. A lowering of the thyroid hormone concentration in the blood stimulates a rise in TSH production; and a rise in thyroid hormone concentration inhibits TSH production. Conversely, a rise in TSH concentration in the blood stimulates a rise in thyroid hormone production; and a fall in TSH concentration inhibits thyroid hormone production.

Now suppose that, as a result of racing metabolism, inroads are made on the thyroid hormone supply, causing the blood level to drop. As the blood passes through the anterior pituitary, the lower-than-normal level of thyroid hormone stimulates the secretion of additional TSH, and the blood level of TSH rises. When the blood passes through the thyroid carrying its extra load of TSH, the secretion of thyroid hormone is stimulated and the demands of the high metabolic rate are met.

If the thyroid hormone should now be greater than the body's requirements, its blood level will rise. This rising thyroid hormone level will cut off TSH production, which will in turn cut off thyroid hormone production. By the action of the two glands in smooth cooperation, the thyroid hormone level will be maintained at an appropriate blood level despite continual shifts in the body's requirements for the hormone.

The working of the "thyroid-pituitary axis" can, understandably, be imperfect. The mere fact that a second gland is called into action means there is another link in the chain, another link that may go wrong. It is likely, for instance, that hyperthyroidism arises not from anything wrong with the thyroid itself but from a flaw in the anterior pituitary. The secretion of TSH can, as a result, be abnormally high and the thyroid kept needlessly, and even harmfully, overactive. (The anterior pituitary serves as regulating gland, after this fashion, for several other glands in the body. It is this that makes it seem to be the "master gland" of the body.)

TSH is not one of the anterior pituitary hormones that have been prepared in completely pure form, and so information about its chemical structure is as yet a bit fuzzy. Its molecular weight, as it is formed, may be about 10,000; this would mean that its polypeptide chain could contain nearly a hundred amino acids. However, there seem to be signs that the chain can be broken up into smaller portions without loss of activity. This ability to confine the area of activity to a relatively small region of the whole molecule is true of some other hormones as well (though it does not seem to be true of insulin).

PARATHYROID HORMONE

Behind the thyroid gland are four flattened scraps of pinkish or reddish tissue, each about a third of an inch long. Two are on either side of the windpipe, one of each pair being near the top of the thyroid, and one near the bottom. These are the *parathyroid glands* ("alongside the thyroid" G); see illustration, page 46.

The parathyroids were first detected (in the rhinoceros, of all animals) in the middle 19th century, and little attention was paid them for some decades. If physicians or anatomists thought of them at all, it was to consider them as parts of the thyroid. There were cases when, in removing part or all of the thyroid, these scraps of tissue were casually removed as well. This proved to have unexpectedly drastic consequences. The removal of the thyroid might result in severe myxedema, but the patient at least remains alive. In contrast, with the removal of the parathyroids, death follows fairly quickly and is preceded by severe muscular spasms. Experiments on animals, which proved more sensitive to loss of the parathyroids than men were, showed that muscles tightened convulsively, a situation called *tetany* (tet′uh-nee; "stretch" G). This resembled the situation brought on by abnormally low concentration of calcium ion[*] in the blood and it was found that

---

[*] Some atoms or groups of atoms have a tendency to lose one or more of the tiny electrons that form component parts of themselves. Or they may gain one or more electrons from outside. Since electrons carry a negative electric charge, atoms that lose them possess a positive charge, and those that gain them possess a negative one. Atoms charged either way can be made to move through a fluid in response to an electric field, and are therefore called *ions* (eye′onz; "wander" G).

calcium ion levels in the blood were indeed abnormally low in animals that had been deprived of the parathyroids. As tetany progressed and worsened, the animal died, either out of sheer exhaustion or because the muscles that closed its larynx did so in a tight death grip so that, in effect, the animal throttled itself and died of asphyxiation. By the 1920's, surgeons grew definitely cautious about slicing away at the thyroid and supremely careful about touching the parathyroids.

As is now understood, the parathyroid hormone is to the calcium level in the blood as glucagon is to the glucose level. Just as glucagon mobilizes the glycogen reservoir in the liver, bringing about its breakdown to glucose, which pours into the blood, so the parathyroid hormone mobilizes the calcium stores in bone, bringing about its breakdown to calcium ions in solution, which pours into the blood.

The blood contains from 9 to 11 mg. per cent of calcium ion,* so the total quantity of calcium ion in the blood of an average human being is something like 250 milligrams (less than 1/100 ounce), whereas there is something like 3 kilograms (or about 6½ pounds) of calcium ion in the skeleton of the body. This means there is 12,000 times as much calcium in the skeleton as in the blood, so bone is a really effective reservoir. A small amount of calcium withdrawn from bone — not enough to affect perceptibly the strength and toughness of the skeleton — would suffice to keep the blood content steady for a long time.

The properties of an ion are quite different from those of an uncharged atom. Thus, calcium atoms make up an active metal that would be quite poisonous to living tissue, but calcium ions are much blander and are necessary components of living tissue. Nor are calcium ions metallic; instead they make up parts of substances classified by chemists as "salts." The difference between ordinary atoms and ions is expressed in symbols. The calcium atom is symbolized as Ca. The calcium ion, which has lost two electrons and carries a double positive charge, is Ca^{++}.

* Calcium ion is essential to blood coagulation, and to the proper working of nerve and muscle. To do its work properly, calcium ion must remain within a narrow range of concentration. If it rises too high or drops too low, the entire ion balance of the blood is upset; neither nerves nor muscles can do their work; and the body, through a failure in organization, dies. It is the proper functioning of the parathyroid gland which keeps this from happening.

Under the influence of the parathyroid hormone, those cells whose function it is to dissolve bone are stimulated. Bone is eroded at a greater-than-normal rate and the calcium ion thus liberated pours into the bloodstream. As this happens, phosphate ion also enters the bloodstream, for calcium ion and phosphate ion are knit together in bone and one cannot be liberated without the other. The phosphate ion does not remain in the blood but is excreted through the urine. It is possible that parathyroid hormone has as another function the stimulation of the excretion of phosphate ion in the urine.

It is the calcium ion level in the blood that controls the rate of secretion of parathyroid hormone (just as the blood glucose level controls that of insulin). If the diet is consistently low in calcium, so that there is a chronic danger of subnormal levels in the blood, the parathyroids are kept active and bone continues to be eroded away. If the diet is adequate in calcium, the raised level in blood acts to inhibit the activity of the parathyroid and the bone erosion subsides. It was reported in 1963 that the parathyroid produces a second hormone, *calcitonin*, acting in opposition to the parathyroid hormone, as insulin acts in opposition to glucagon. Calcitonin acts to reduce the calcium ion level of the blood. In addition, other processes (in which vitamin D is somehow involved — but that is another story) act to bring about buildup of bone, and any bone previously lost is replaced. Any excess calcium beyond what is needed is excreted through the urine.

It is possible for the parathyroids to remain overactive even when the blood level is adequately high. This can take place when a parathyroid tumor greatly increases the number of hormone-producing cells and the condition is *hyperparathyroidism*. In such a case, bone erosion continues unchecked, while the body survives by continually dumping excess calcium ion into the urine. Eventually bones may be weakened by calcium loss to the point where they will break under ordinary stresses, and such apparently reasonless breakage may be the first noticeable symptom of the disease.

The parathyroid hormone was isolated in pure form in 1960. It is a small protein molecule with a molecular weight of 9500 and a structure consisting of a chain of 83 amino acids. The molecule can be broken into smaller units, and a chain of 33 amino acids is found to exert the full effect of the parathyroid hormone. Why the other 50, then? The best guess seems to be that the additional 50 are needed to increase the stability of the molecule as a whole. (To use an analogy, only the blade of a knife cuts, and yet the wooden handle, though contributing nothing to the actual cutting, makes the knife easier to hold and therefore more useful generally.)

The exact order in which amino acids occur in the parathyroid hormone has not yet been worked out.

POSTERIOR PITUITARY HORMONES

Now that we have examples of how hormones like insulin and glucagon can maintain the level of concentration of an organic substance such as glucose, and of how hormones like those of the parathyroid gland can maintain the level of concentration of an inorganic substance such as calcium ion, it would round out matters to produce a hormone that controls the level of concentration of the water in which both inorganic and organic substances are dissolved. Water enters and leaves the body in a variety of ways. We take in water with the food we eat and with the fluids (particularly water itself) we drink. We lose water through perspiration, through the expired breath, through the feces, and, most of all, through the urine. Water loss can be increased or decreased with circumstances. The most common way in which we are subjected to unusually great water loss is through perspiration caused by unusual heat or by strenuous physical activity. We make up for that by drinking more water than usual at such times.

This is the "coarse control." There is a "fine control" too, which enables the body to adjust continuously (within limits) to minor changes and fluctuations in the rate of water loss, so we are not as slavishly tied to the water tap as we would otherwise be. In the fine control, the kidneys are involved. The blood, in passing through the kidneys, is filtered. Wastes pass out of the blood vessels and into the renal tubules. The phrase "pass out" is actually too weak a term. The wastes are flushed out by the lavish use of water; more water than we could ordinarily afford to lose. However, as the blood filtrate passes down the tubules, water is reabsorbed. What eventually enters the ureter and travels down to the bladder is a urine in which the waste materials are dissolved in comparatively little water. If the body is short of water, reabsorption takes place to the maximum of which the body is capable, and the urine is concentrated, scanty, and dark in color. (Desert mammals can conserve water to the point where the urine is so scanty as to be almost nonexistent; we do not have that talent.) If, on the contrary, we drink considerable water or other fluids, so that the body finds itself with more than it needs, the reabsorption of water in the tubules is repressed by the necessary amount and the urine is dilute, copious, and very light in color.

In the early 1940's, it was discovered that this ability of the body to control reabsorption of water in the tubules in order to help keep the body's water contents at a desirable level was mediated by a hormone. Extracts from the posterior lobe of the pituitary gland seemed to have a powerful effect on the manner in which water was reabsorbed. These extracts, usually called *pituitrin*, encouraged the reabsorption of water and therefore diminished the volume of urine. Now any factor which increases urine volume is said to be *diuretic* (dy'yoo-ret'ik; "to urinate" G). The posterior pituitary extract had an opposite effect and was therefore felt to contain an *antidiuretic hormone*, usually referred to by the abbreviation *ADH*.

In addition, as it turned out, pituitrin possesses two more important abilities. It tends to increase blood pressure through a contraction of blood vessels. This is referred to as vasopressor (vas'oh-pres'or; "vessel-compressing" L) activity. It also induces contractions of the muscles of the pregnant uterus at the time it becomes necessary to force the fully developed fetus out into the world. This is called the oxytocic (ok′see-toh′sik; "quick birth" G) effect. And, as a matter of fact, the preparation can be used to encourage a quick birth by forcing a uterus into action at some convenient moment.

The American biochemist Vincent du Vigneaud and his associates obtained two pure substances from the posterior pituitary extracts, of which one possessed the blood-pressure-raising effect and was named *vasopressin* and the other possessed the uterus-stimulating effect and was named *oxytocin*. There was no need to search for a third hormone with the antidiuretic effect: vasopressin possessed it in full. By the mid-1950's, therefore, the phrase "antidiuretic hormone" vanished from the medical vocabulary. ADH was vasopressin and the latter term was sufficient.

Du Vigneaud found oxytocin and vasopressin to be unusually small peptides, with molecular weights just above 1000. Analysis of these peptides by the methods worked out by Sanger was not difficult. Du Vigneaud found both to possess molecules made up of no more than 8 amino acids. He worked out the order in which they appeared:

$$\overset{\displaystyle \diagup\text{cyS}\!-\!\text{Scy}\diagdown}{\text{tyr}\cdot\text{ileu}\cdot\text{gluNH}_2\cdot\text{aspNH}_2\cdot\text{pro}\cdot\text{leu}\cdot\text{glyNH}_2}$$

OXYTOCIN

$$\overset{\displaystyle \diagup\text{cyS}\!-\!\text{Scy}\diagdown}{\text{tyr}\cdot\text{phe}\cdot\text{gluNH}_2\cdot\text{aspNH}_2\cdot\text{pro}\cdot\text{arg}\cdot\text{glyNH}_2}$$

VASOPRESSIN

As you see, the two molecules are very much alike, with only two amino acids of the eight different. That is enough, nevertheless, to make their properties completely different and shows what a minor alteration in the nature of the side-chains can do. (On the other hand, vasopressin obtained from hog pituitaries

contains a lysine in place of the arginine in the above formula —
which is for vasopressin taken from cattle — and that change
makes no significant difference.)

Du Vigneaud, having determined the structure of these two
hormones, went a step further. He built up an amino acid chain,
placing the amino acids in the order analysis had told him was
correct. In 1955 he prepared synthetic molecules that showed
all the oxytocic, vasopressor and antidiuretic functions of the
natural molecules. Thereby he was the first to synthesize a natural active protein (albeit a very small one), and for that feat
was, that very year, awarded the Nobel Prize in Chemistry.

It happens occasionally that vasopressin may fail to be produced in adequate quantities in a particular individual. When
this happens, water is not properly reabsorbed in the kidney tubules and urination becomes abnormally copious. In bad cases,
where water is not reabsorbed at all, the daily volume of urine
may reach twenty or thirty quarts, and water must then be drunk
in equally voluminous quantities. Such a disease, with water
"passing through" so readily, rightly deserves to be considered
a form of diabetes.

Since the ordinary wastes present in urine are not increased
in this condition but are merely spread thin through the large
quantity of water produced, the urine becomes very little removed from tap water. It lacks the odor and amber color of
ordinary urine. In particular, when compared with the sugar-
filled urine of the sufferer of diabetes mellitus, it lacks a taste.
The condition is therefore *diabetes insipidus* (in-sip'ih-dus;
"tasteless" L).

4

OUR ADRENAL CORTEX

So far, all the hormones I have discussed are based on the amino acid. Some, such as thyroxine, epinephrine, and histamine have molecules that are modifications of single amino acids; tyrosine in the first two cases, histidine in the last. Other hormones are chains of amino acids, made up of as few as eight members or as many as a hundred. There are, however, certain hormones that are completely unrelated in structure to the amino acid, and their story begins with that usually painful and certainly unromantic phenomenon we know as gallstones.

In 1814 a white substance with a fatty consistency was obtained from gallstones and was named *cholesterin* (koh-les′ter-in; "solid bile" G). The name was reasonable enough since gallstones precipitated out of the bile and could therefore be looked upon as a kind of solidified bile. Investigations into the molecular structure of the substance met with frustrating lack of success for over a century, but one fact that eventually turned up after some decades was that the molecule possessed one oxygen-hydrogen combination (-OH) as part of its structure. This is a group occurring, characteristically, in alcohols, and, toward the end of the 19th century, it became conventional to give the alcohols names ending with the suffix "ol." For this reason, cholesterin came to be called *cholesterol,* and the family of compounds of which it was a member came to be called the *sterols.*

As time went on, it was discovered that many compounds clearly related to cholesterol did not possess the -OH group and were therefore not entitled to names with the "ol" suffix. In the 1930's a more general term was proposed to include the entire class of compounds, both with and without the -OH group. The name proposed was *steroid* ("sterol-like" G).

And by then the molecular structure of cholesterol was finally worked out. The molecule is made up, it turned out, of 27 carbon atoms, 46 hydrogen atoms, and just 1 oxygen atom. Seventeen of the carbon atoms are arranged in a four-ring combination, which can be schematically presented as follows:

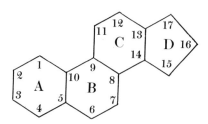

STEROID NUCLEUS IN CHOLESTEROL

The carbon atoms are arranged, you see, in three hexagons and one pentagon, joined together as shown. At every angle of these rings you can imagine a carbon atom as existing. The lines connecting the angles are the "bonds" connecting the carbon atoms. The rings are lettered from A to D and the angles (or carbon atoms) are numbered from 1 to 17, according to the conventional system shown above, which is accepted by all chemists. This particular four-ring combination of carbon atoms is called the *steroid nucleus*.

Each carbon atom has at its disposal four bonds by which connections may be made with other atoms. The carbon atom at position 2, for example, is making use of two of its bonds already, one for attachment to carbon-1 and another for attachment to carbon-3. This means that two bonds still remain and each of these can be attached to a hydrogen atom.* (A hydrogen atom

---

* It is conventional in such schematic formulas as I am using in this chapter to

has only one bond at its disposal.) As for the carbon at position 10, that is making use of three of its bonds, one leading to carbon-1, one to carbon-5, and one to carbon-9. It has only one bond left over.

Sometimes a carbon atom is held to the neighboring carbon atom by two bonds; this is referred to as a *double bond*. Suppose such a double bond exists between positions 5 and 6. In that case, carbon-5 is connected by two bonds to carbon-6, by a third bond to carbon-10 and by a fourth bond to carbon-4. All its bonds are used up.

Now let's return to cholesterol. Of its 27 carbon atoms, 17 are accounted for by the steroid nucleus. There remain 10. Of these, 1 is attached to the lone remaining bond of carbon-10 and 1 to the lone remaining bond of carbon-13. The final 8 form a chain (with a detailed structure that need not concern us) attached to carbon-17, with finally, a double bond between carbons 5 and 6.

What of the lone oxygen atom? This is attached to carbon-3. The oxygen atom has the capacity to form two bonds. One of these is taken up by the carbon-3 attachment, but the other is joined to a hydrogen atom, forming the -OH combination that is characteristic of alcohols. This gives us all the information we need to present a schematic formula for the cholesterol molecule:

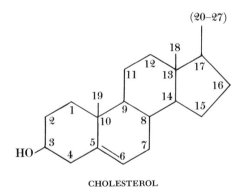

CHOLESTEROL

leave out the hydrogen atoms that are connected to carbon atoms, for simplicity's sake. Therefore wherever there are bonds left unaccounted for in a formula, as is true of those two extra bonds of carbon-2, you may safely assume that hydrogen atoms are attached.

I have gone into detail on the cholesterol molecule for two reasons: first, it is an important molecule in itself and, second, it is the parent substance of other molecules at least as important. The importance of cholesterol is attested by the mere fact that there is so much of it in the body. The average 70-kilogram (154-pound) man contains some 230 grams, or just about half a pound, of the substance. A good deal of it is to be found in the nervous system (which is reason enough to stress the compound in this book). About 3 per cent of the weight of the brain is cholesterol. Considering that 80 per cent of the brain is water, you can see that cholesterol makes up some 15 per cent, nearly a sixth, of the dry weight of the brain.

It is present elsewhere, too. The bile secreted by the liver contains 2½ to 3 per cent of dissolved matter, and of this about 1/20 is cholesterol. The bile in the gallbladder is stored in concentrated form, and the cholesterol content there is correspondingly enriched. The cholesterol in the bile may not really seem like a large quantity (about 1/10 of a per cent all told) but it is enough to cause trouble at times. The quantity of cholesterol in the bile within the gallbladder is just about all that the liquid can hold, since cholesterol is not particularly soluble in body fluids. It is not uncommon to have crystals of cholesterol precipitate out of the bile. On occasion such crystals conglomerate to form sizable gallstones that may block the cystic duct through which bile ordinarily passes into the small intestine. It is this blockage that produces the severe abdominal pains with which sufferers from gallstones are all too familiar.

Of the dissolved material in blood, about 0.65 per cent is cholesterol. This, too, is sufficient to make trouble on occasion. There is a tendency for cholesterol to precipitate out of blood and onto the inner lining of arteries, narrowing the bore, and roughening the smoothness. This condition, *atherosclerosis*, is currently the prime killer of mankind in the United States. (Mankind, literally, since men are affected more often than women.)

Cholesterol, although only very slightly soluble in water, is freely soluble in fat and is therefore to be found in the fatty portions of foods. Animal fats are far richer in cholesterol than plant fats are. In addition, there is some evidence to the effect that the body can handle cholesterol more efficiently if the diet contains a sizable quantity of fat molecules marked by several double bonds between carbon atoms. These are called *polyunsaturated fats* and are of considerably more common occurrence in plant fats than in animal fats. For this reason, the last few years have seen a swing in American dietary habits away from animal fat and toward plant fat.

Nevertheless, increasing consciousness of the dangers of atherosclerosis must not cause us to think of cholesterol as merely a danger to life. It is, in fact, vital to life. It is a universal component of living tissue and no cell is entirely without it. It is rather frustrating, as a consequence, to be forced to confess that biochemists have only the haziest notion of what it actually does in living tissue.

OTHER STEROIDS

There are other steroids in the body, which may be formed out of cholesterol or which are, perhaps, formed simultaneously with cholesterol by similar chemical processes. The bile, for instance, contains steroids called *bile acids* in concentrations seven or eight times that of cholesterol itself. (The bile acids create no troubles, though, because unlike cholesterol they are fairly soluble and do not come out of solution to form stones.)

The molecules of the bile acids differ from that of cholesterol chiefly in that the eight-carbon chain attached to carbon-17 (in cholesterol) is chopped off at the fifth carbon. That fifth carbon forms part of a carboxyl group (-COOH), and it is the acid property of this carboxyl group that gives the bile acids their name.

There are several varieties of bile acids. One has a single hydroxyl group attached to carbon-3, as in the case of cholesterol. Another has a second hydroxyl group attached to carbon-12, and still another has a third hydroxyl group attached to carbon-7. Each of these bile acids can be combined at the carboxyl group to a molecule of the amino acid, glycine, or to a sulfur-containing compound called "taurine." These combinations make up the group of compounds called bile salts. The bile salts have an interesting property. Most of the molecule is soluble in fat, whereas the carboxyl group and its attached compound is soluble in water. The bile-salt molecule therefore tends to crowd into any interface that may exist between fat and water, with the fat-soluble portion sticking into the fat and the water-soluble portion sticking into the water.

Ordinarily the interface represents a greater concentration of energy than does the body of either liquid, so the amount of interface is kept to a minimum. If oil and water are both poured into a beaker, the interface is a flat plane between the two. If the mixture is shaken violently bubbles of oil are formed in water, and bubbles of water are formed in oil. The energy of shaking is converted into the energy of the additional interface formed; but when the shaking ceases, the bubbles break and the interface settles back into the minimum area of the flat plane.

The presence of bile salts in the interface, however, lowers its energy content. This means that the interface can be easily extended so that the churning of the food within the small intestine easily breaks up fatty material into bubbles and then smaller bubbles. (The smaller the bubbles, the larger the area of interface for a given weight of fat.) Furthermore, the bubbles that are formed have little tendency to break up again, as bile salt crowds into every new interface formed. The microscopic fat globules eventually formed are much easier to break up through the digestive action of enzymes than large masses of fat would be, because enzymes are not soluble in fat and can only exert their effects on the edges of the bubbles.

A rather drastic change of sterol structure often occurs when one is exposed to ultraviolet light. The bond between carbon-9 and carbon-10 breaks and ring B opens up. The resulting structure is no longer, strictly speaking, a steroid, since the steroid nucleus is no longer intact. However, the molecule remains so clearly related to the steroids that it is usually discussed as though it were part of the group.

Many of these "broken steroid" molecules possess vitamin D activity; that is, they somehow encourage the normal deposition of bone. That deposition cannot take place in the absence of vitamin D. The broken steroid developed from cholesterol itself does not have vitamin D properties. Nevertheless, cholesterol is almost invariably accompanied everywhere in the body by small quantities of a very similar sterol that differs from cholesterol itself only in that it has a second double bond located between carbon-7 and carbon-8. This second compound, when broken by ultraviolet light *does* have vitamin D properties. There is cholesterol and its double-bonded partner in the fat layers in the skin. The ultraviolet of sunlight can reach it, forming the vitamin when it does so. For this reason vitamin D is called the "sunshine vitamin," and not because it, or any vitamin — or any material substance whatever for that matter — is in sunshine itself.

If vitamin D were formed by the body, particularly if it were secreted by some organ of the body, it would certainly be very tempting to consider it a hormone. It might even be considered a hormone that like the recently discovered calcitonin (see p. 61) opposed the action of the parathyroid hormone (depositing bone, whereas parathyroid hormone erodes it) as glucagon opposes the action of insulin. Since the body does not form vitamin D directly but must have it formed by the action of sunlight or, failing that, by absorbing such trace quantities as may be present in the food, it is called a vitamin.

A number of classes of steroids not formed in the human body are nevertheless found in the living tissue of other species. Almost invariably these have profound effects when administered to human beings even in small quantities. There are such steroids in the seeds and leaves of the purple foxglove. The drooping purple flowers look like thimbles, and the Latin name of the genus is *Digitalis* (dih-jih-tal'is; "of the finger" L, which is what thimbles certainly are). The steroids in digitalis are something like the bile acids in structure except that the carboxyl group on the side-chain combines with another portion of the chain to form a fifth ring that is not part of the four-ring steroid nucleus. This five-ring steroid combines with certain sugarlike molecules to form *glycosides* (gly'koh-sidez; "sweet" G, in reference to the sugar). Such compounds are used in the treatment of specific heart disorders and are therefore called the *cardiac glycosides* (kahr'dee-ak; "heart" G).

The cardiac glycosides are helpful and even life-saving in the proper doses, but in improper doses can, of course, kill. Steroids similar to those in the cardiac glycosides are found in the secretions of the salivary glands of toads, and these are called *toad poisons*. Another group of steroids, found in certain plants are called *saponins* (sap'oh-ninz; "soap" L, because they form a soapy solution). They are poisonous, too.

But why do steroids have such profound physiological effects in small quantities? For one thing, many of them, like the bile salts, tend to crowd into interfaces. Many physiological effects are dependent on the behavior of substances at interfaces. By changing the nature of those interfaces, steroids succeed in changing the behavior of substances generally and of the physiological effects dependent on that behavior.

For living tissue the most important interface of all is that between the cell and the outside world. The boundary of a cell is its *membrane*, which is an extremely thin structure. It is so thin that only in the 1950's, with the aid of the best electron microscopes available, could it really be studied. It appears to consist of a double layer of phosphorus-containing fatlike molecules (*phospholipid*), coated on each side with a single thickness of protein molecule. It is through this thin membrane that substances enter and leave the cell. Entry or exit may be by way of tiny pores existing in the membrane, or that are formed, but such entry or exit, whatever the mechanism, cannot be a purely passive thing. Some atoms and molecules can pass through more easily and rapidly than can other atoms and molecules of similar size. The fact that the cell membrane is made up of both phospholipid and protein may be significant here. The phospholipid is largely fat-soluble and the protein is largely water-soluble. It may be that the manner in which a particular substance can (or cannot) get through the cell membrane depends on the manner of its relative solubility in fat and in water.

In Chapter 1, I mentioned the theory that hormones achieved their effects by altering the manner in which the cell membranes allowed the entry and exit of particular substances. One can imagine a peptide molecule layering itself over the cell membrane and substituting for the original pattern of side-chains a new pattern that might, for instance, encourage the entry of glucose at greater-than-normal rates, thus lowering the glucose-concentration in blood. (This, as you may remember, is the effect of insulin.)

Now it would seem reasonable that, if a protein molecule could accomplish this by altering the pattern of the protein portion of the membrane, a fat-soluble molecule such as a steroid might also do so by altering the pattern of the phospholipid portion of the membrane. It may be in this fashion that vitamin D encourages the growth of bones, by altering the membrane of bone cells to permit the entry of calcium ions at a greater-than-normal rate. It may also explain the workings of other steroids that not only have hormone functions, as vitamin D does, but are elaborated by special glands and therefore carry the name of hormones, too.

In fact, all hormones fall into two, and only two, chemical groups. They are either (1) protein or amino acid in nature, and presumably affect the water-soluble portion of the cell membrane, or (2) steroid in nature, presumably affecting the fat-soluble portion.

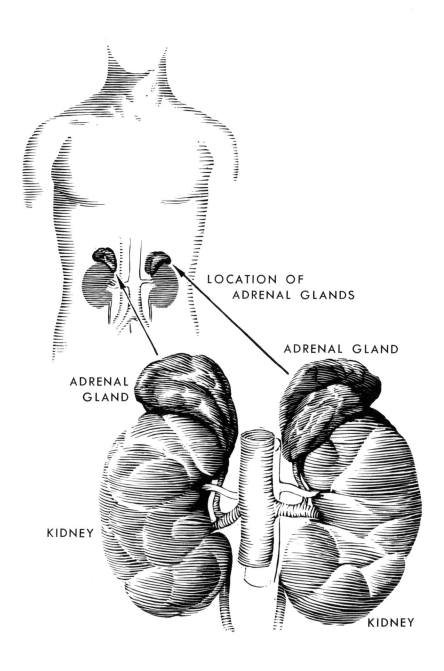

LOCATION OF
ADRENAL GLANDS

ADRENAL GLAND

ADRENAL
GLAND

KIDNEY

KIDNEY

CORTICOIDS

One of the glands that produces steroid hormones is the adrenal cortex. (I referred to it in passing on page 41 when I talked about epinephrine, which is formed by the adrenal medulla.)

The importance of the adrenal cortex was first made clear in 1855, when an English physician named Thomas Addison described in detail the clinical symptoms that accompanied deterioration of this organ (a deterioration sometimes brought on by the ravages of tuberculosis). The most prominent symptom was a discoloration of the skin, a kind of mottled-bronze or grayish effect produced by the overproduction of the skin pigment melanin. Anemia, muscle weakness, and gastrointestinal symptoms were also found. Modern methods of analysis have added to these marked abnormalities in water distribution and in the concentrations of glucose and of various inorganic ions ("minerals") in the blood. Thus, sodium ion concentration in the blood falls because too much is excreted in the urine and potassium ion concentration rises because too much escapes into the blood from the cells, where it is usually firmly retained. The disease grows progressively worse and death generally follows two to three years after its onset, if untreated. Because Addison was the first to describe the symptoms of the disease arising from adrenal cortical insufficiency with such care, it has been called *Addison's disease* ever since.

If there was any doubt that the adrenal cortex is essential to life, this was banished as a result of animal experimentation. Animals in which the adrenal cortex was removed rapidly developed all the symptoms of Addison's disease in exaggerated form and died within two weeks.

By 1929 methods were developed that enabled biochemists to prepare extracts of the adrenal cortex which served to lengthen the life of adrenalectomized animals (those from which the adrenal glands had been removed). By that time biochemists had sufficient experience with hormones to be quite certain that the extract, called *cortin,* had to contain at least one hormone. A number of different groups of researchers set about the task of locating it.

Throughout the 1930's two groups particularly, an American group headed by Edward Kendall (the discoverer of thyroxine) and a Swiss group headed by the Polish-born Tadeus Reichstein, followed hot on the trail. The success that stemmed from their researches led to both Kendall and Reichstein sharing in the Nobel Prize in Medicine and Physiology for 1950.

By 1940 more than two dozen different crystalline compounds had been prepared from the adrenal cortex. This was no mean task, for out of a ton of adrenals, obtained from hecatombs of slaughtered cattle, about half an ounce of a particular compound might be obtained. At first there was no notion of what the structure of these compounds might be. Kendall called them simply "compound A," "compound B," and so on, whereas Reichstein referred to them as substances rather than compounds. With investigation, however, it developed that these compounds were one and all steroid in character. They were therefore lumped under the heading of *adrenocortical steroids,* or, by telescoping the phrase, as *corticoids.*

The steroid nature of the various cortical substances solved one problem at once. The adrenal cortex is rich in cholesterol, richer than any other organ but the brain. Earlier this had been puzzling, but now it seemed clear that cholesterol was the store upon which the cortex drew in its manufacture of the various corticoids.

All the important corticoids have the same carbon skeleton, one differing from that of cholesterol chiefly in that the carbon chain attached to carbon-17 is reduced to 2 carbon atoms only, in place of cholesterol's 8. Therefore the corticoids have 21 carbon atoms altogether instead of cholesterol's 27.

The formula of one steroid produced by the adrenal cortex is presented schematically on page 78, with each of the 21 carbon atoms marked off by number.

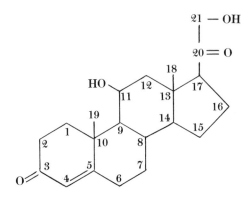

CORTICOSTERONE

Notice that it has four oxygen atoms instead of just one, as is the case of cholesterol. Two of the oxygens form part of the -OH alcohol group. The other two, however, are bound to a carbon atom by both bonds. This C=O group was first found to exist in a simple organic compound called "acetone." For this reason compounds possessing such groups are often given names with a "one" suffix. Since all the important corticoids possess a C=O group attached to carbon-3 (in place of the -OH group of cholesterol), all have this suffix. The particular compound shown above (which Kendall called "compound B" and Reichstein called "substance H" in the days before its structure was determined) is now called *corticosterone* (kawr'tih-kos'ter-ohn).

One effect of this hormone is to promote the storage of glycogen in the liver. This is similar to the action of insulin and opposed to the action of glucagon, so that it represents another item in the complex hormonal balance controlling the glucose level in the blood.

There are other corticoids with effects similar to corticosterone, and of these the best-known is one which Kendall called "compound E" and Reichstein "substance Fa." It differs from corticosterone in possessing a fifth oxygen atom, attached to carbon-17 in the form of an -OH group. In addition, the oxygen atom attached to carbon-11 is not an -OH group, as in corticosterone, but is a C=O group. To a chemist these differences are perfectly well described in the official name of the compound which is 17-*hydroxy*-11-*dehydrocorticosterone*. When this compound gained clinical importance, however, for a reason I shall shortly describe, a shorter name was absolutely necessary, and, by leaving out most of the letters, the word *cortisone* was arrived at.

In a couple of corticoids there is no oxygen attached to carbon-11. One of them, which Reichstein isolated from cattle, has a molecule with exactly the corticosterone structure, except for that missing oxygen. It is called, reasonably enough, *deoxycorticosterone*, a name usually abbreviated to *DOC*. DOC is not particularly concerned with glycogen storage, but instead with the maintenance of the proper balance of water and of mineral ions. It promotes increased reabsorption of salt in the kidney tubules, keeps potassium ions from leaving the cells to an undue extent, and maintains the proper volume of water outside the cells.

The corticoids have been divided into two groups: those which, like corticosterone and cortisone, possess an oxygen attached to carbon-11 are the *glycocorticoids* and are concerned with glycogen storage; those which, like DOC, do not possess an oxygen attached to carbon-11 are the *mineralocorticoids* and are concerned with the mineral balance.

The mineralocorticoids seem to be more immediately vital to life than are the glycocorticoids, for adrenalectomized rats are kept alive longer by the administration of DOC than by use of corticosterone.

In 1953, more than a decade after the discovery of four important glycocorticoids and two important mineralocorticoids, there came the rather surprising isolation of another mineralocorticoid. This was produced by the cortex in far smaller quantities than those previously discovered — which accounts for its late detection. However, it was also terrifically potent. Weight for weight, its efficiency in promoting the survival of an adrenalectomized rat was twenty-five times as great as was that of DOC.

This new mineralocorticoid had an unusual structure, too. In all other steroids, without exception, carbon-18 is attached to three hydrogen atoms, forming a *methyl group* (CH_3). In this new steroid, it was discovered, the carbon-18 is attached to a hydrogen and an oxygen. The resulting atom combination, -CHO, is called an *aldehyde group*, for reasons we need not go into. In consequence the new mineralocorticoid was named *aldosterone* (al-dos′ter-ohn).

Aldosterone is also unusual, for a mineralocorticoid, in possessing an oxygen at carbon-11. This, it would seem, should make it a glycocorticoid; but the aldehyde group making up carbon-18 has the ability to combine with the -OH group on carbon-11, a combination that neutralizes it, in effect. That, perhaps, is the particular importance of the unusual aldehyde group at carbon-18.

It might seem odd to put an oxygen at carbon-11 and then design the molecule in such a way as to neutralize it. Why not leave the oxygen off carbon-11 in the first place? Why this should be we cannot yet tell, but this point of putting the oxygen on, then neutralizing it, results in a mineralocorticoid that is much more powerful than any of those in which the oxygen is absent in the first place.

The various corticoids, singly and together, could be used in cases of adrenal cortical failure much as insulin is used in diabetes. This, nonetheless, would not suffice to make them nearly as important as insulin, for cortical troubles are by no means as common as diabetes.

However, after the isolation of the corticoids, their effects on various diseases of metabolism were inevitably studied. Hormones sometimes have such a wide variety of effects that one can never tell when one of them might not indirectly bring about at least a relief of symptoms, if not an actual cure. Nothing very startling was noted until 1948, when cortisone first became available in reasonable quantity. The American physician Philip Showalter Hench, working in Kendall's group, tried it on patients with rheumatoid arthritis. Surprisingly, it produced great relief.

This was something to crow about. Arthritis is a crippling disease and an extremely painful one. It can strike anyone, and there is no true cure. Anything that can relieve the pain and make it more possible to use the joints is to be hailed in glory even if it is not a cure. Hench shared the 1950 Nobel Prize in Medicine and Physiology with Kendall and Reichstein, in consequence.

Cortisone is also used to promote healing of skin lesions, in the treatment of gout, and as an anti-inflammatory drug. Despite all this, it has not attained the status of insulin as a savior of man. Cortisone, like the other corticoids, has a particularly complex effect on the body, and there is always the danger of undesirable side effects. Physicians must use it with caution; the more conservative ones prefer not to use it at all, if that use can be avoided.

Because the steroid molecule is a relatively simple one compared with molecules of even the smaller proteins, it has been possible to experiment a good deal with synthetic steroids, produced in the laboratory and not found in nature. To cite one case, a steroid that differs from the natural corticoids in possessing a fluorine atom attached to carbon-9 is an unusually active glycocorticoid, ten times as active as the natural ones. Unfortunately, its activity in bringing about undesirable side effects is also enhanced.

ACTH

The production of corticoids is not controlled by direct feedback as insulin is by the blood glucose level it controls, or parathyroid hormone by the blood calcium level it controls. Instead, as in the case of the thyroid hormone, a second gland must be called into the balance, and again it is the anterior pituitary.

In 1930 it was noticed that in animals from which the pituitary was removed, the adrenal cortex shriveled. Yet it has been found that when extracts from the anterior pituitary are injected into an animal the cholesterol concentration in the adrenal cortex drops precipitously, presumably because cholesterol is being used up in the manufacture of corticoids.

The connection is also made clear by the relationship of the pituitary to stress; that is, to sudden adverse changes in the environment of the body. Exposure to severe cold or to mechanical injury, to hemorrhage or to bacterial infection are all examples of stress. The body must shift balance radically to meet such changes and survive, and the burden of directing such changes seems to fall upon the corticoids. At least under stress the cholesterol content of the adrenal cortex falls, signifying that corticoids are being manufactured rapidly to meet the situation.

In an animal from which the anterior pituitary has been removed there is no such reaction to stress. Even if the adrenal cortex is still in working condition, nothing happens. Apparently, then, something among the anterior pituitary hormones stimulates the cortex.

The hormone that does so is named, very reasonably, the *adrenocorticotrophic hormone* (ad-ree'noh-kawr'tih-koh-troh'fic; "adrenal-nourishing" G) and is abbreviated, equally reasonably, as *ACTH*. In the late 1940's, when cortisone was found to be effective in combatting the painful symptoms of rheumatoid arthritis, ACTH was found to be likewise effective; not so much in itself as because it stimulated the adrenal cortex to form larger quantities of cortisone and other such hormones for itself. ACTH, like cortisone itself, made newspaper headlines and was on everybody's lips as a "wonder drug," particularly since in abbreviated form its name was so easy to rattle off.

Research into its molecular structure was carried on ardently, therefore, and by the early 1950's its molecular weight had been determined as 20,000. This is fairly large for a polypeptide hormone, and it was quickly found that if the isolated protein were subject to breakdown by acid or by enzyme it was possible to isolate molecular fragments which possessed full activity. These fragments are called *corticotropins*. One of them was found to contain 39 amino acids in the following sequence:

ser·tyr·ser·met·glu·his·phe·arg·try·gly·lys·pro·val·gly·lys·-
lys·arg·arg·pro·val·lys·val·tyr·pro·asp·gly·ala·glu·asp·-
gluNH$_2$·leu·ala·glu·ala·phe·pro·leu·glu·phe

CORTICOTROPIN

This corticotropin, obtained from the adrenals of swine, is still larger than it need be. A fragment consisting of the first 24 amino acids only is still fully active. In 1963 a 17-amino acid fragment was reported which had only 1/10 the corticoid-stimulating effect of natural ACTH but which still possessed certain other properties in full. Yet, if the serine group at the extreme left is removed, the loss of that one amino acid wipes out all activity.

The relationship between ACTH and the corticoids is analogous to that between TSH and the thyroid hormones. A fall in the corticoid levels of the blood below that required by the body stimulates the production of ACTH, which in turn raises corticoid production. Too high a corticoid level inhibits ACTH production, which in turn allows the corticoid level to drop.

Stress stimulates ACTH production, which in turn stimulates the production of corticoids. Stress does not affect the adrenal cortex directly. The stimulation of ACTH production by stress is mediated, it would seem, at least partly through the action of epinephrine (see pp. 40 ff.), which is secreted in response to some stressful situations. (This is another example of the complex way in which hormones mesh their labors.)

Where the pituitary (perhaps because of a tumorous overgrowth) produces a consistently too great quantity of ACTH, there is chronic overproduction of the corticoids and the condition that results has some symptoms similar to those of diabetes mellitus. The stimulation of glycocorticoid production produces a high blood-glucose level. The too great supply of glucose in the blood tends to be stored as fat, so sufferers from this disease tend to grow grotesquely obese. The first to describe the disease in detail was the American brain surgeon Harvey Cushing, and it has been called *Cushing's disease* ever since.

Similar symptoms can be produced where the tissue of the adrenal cortex is multiplied by a tumor of its own and begins to overproduce corticoids even without any encouragement from the pituitary. For reasons I shall explain on page 106, such adrenal tumors may bring on sexual precocity in children, or a marked increase in masculine characteristics in women, the latter condition being known as *virilism* ("man" L).

ACTH has the ability of influencing the skin pigmentation of animals, and even man is affected. As corticoid production falls with destruction of the adrenal cortex in Addison's disease, ACTH rises to considerable (but useless) heights. The pigmentation effect then produces the skin-darkening described on page 76.

Among the lower animals, particularly the amphibians, it was known that a special hormone existed which had its effect on pigment-producing cells and made it possible for such animals to darken many shades in a matter of minutes. The hormone is produced by the portion of the posterior lobe nearest the anterior lobe. Since this region is sometimes called the intermediate lobe, the hormone is named *intermedin*. For some years it was assumed that nothing like intermedin existed in mammals, but in 1955 biochemists at the University of Oregon were able to isolate from the mammalian pituitary a hormone that stimulated the activity of the *melanocytes* (mel'uh-noh-sites), which are the cells that produce the skin pigment melanin. The hormone was named *melanocyte-stimulating hormone,* in perfectly straightforward fashion, a name usually abbreviated as *MSH*. The molecule of the hormone, as obtained from swine pituitary, was found to consist of 18 amino acids in the following order:

asp·glu·gly·pro·tyr·lys·met·glu·his·phe·arg·try·gly·ser·-
pro·pro·lys·asp

MSH

If you compare the molecule of MSH with that of ACTH given on page 83, you will see that there is a seven-amino-acid sequence that the two hold in common: met·glu·his·phe·arg·try·gly.

The possession of this sequence in common may account for a certain overlapping of properties, as evidenced by the pigment-stimulating effect of ACTH. The production of MSH by the pituitary is, like the production of ACTH, stimulated by low corticoid levels. In Addison's disease both pituitary hormones are produced in higher than normal quantities and the MSH contributes even more to the skin-darkening than does the ACTH.

While we are on the subject of pigmentation, we can mention another small glandular organ that has several points of glamor and mystery about it. It is a conical reddish-gray body attached, like the pituitary, to the base of the brain. Because it vaguely resembles a pinecone in shape it is called the *pineal gland* (pin'ee-ul). It is smaller than the pituitary and is located on the other side of that portion of the brain which, extending downward, merges with the spinal cord. The pituitary lies to the front of this extension and the pineal to the rear; see illustration, page 46.

The pineal entered one period of glory in the early 17th century, when the influential French mathematician and philosopher René Descartes, under the impression that the pineal gland was found only in humans and never in the lower animals, maintained that this small scrap of tissue was the seat of the human soul. It was not long before this notion was put to rest, because the pineal occurs in all vertebrates, and is far more prominent in some than it is in man.

Much more exciting to the modern zoologist is the fact that the pineal was not always hidden deep in the skull as it is in human beings and in most modern-day vertebrates. There was a time, apparently, when the pineal was raised on a stalk and reached the top of the skull, there performing the function of a third eye, of all things. A primitive reptile on some small islands in the New Zealand area exists even today with such a "pineal eye" almost functional.

But turning to man, what is the function of the pineal? It seems glandular in structure, and when the hormones were being iso-

5

OUR GONADS
AND GROWTH

PLANT HORMONES

The hormones I have thus far discussed (with the exception of the gastrointestinal hormones) have as their function the holding of the body's mechanism in one place, or, at the most, of allowing it to vary over a very restricted range. Insulin, glucagon, epinephrine, and the glycocorticoids all combine their efforts to keep glucose concentration in the blood within a narrow range of values designed to best meet the needs of the body. The parathyroid hormone calcitonin and vitamin D do the same for the calcium ion concentration in the blood. The mineralocorticoids do the same for mineral ions generally. Thyroid hormone does the same for the overall rate of metabolism. Vasopressin does the same for the body's water content.

And yet the human body is not entirely an equilibrium structure, shifting this way and that merely to keep its balance and remain in the same place. For at least part of our life we go through a long period of imbalance, in which the general trend is not cyclic but progressive; not back and forth, but onward and upward.

In short, a child must grow; and in that simple phrase there is a wealth of complexity of fact.

The growth of a single cell, although complex enough chemically, has its rather simple physical aspects. As more and more food is turned into cellular components of one sort or another, the volume of the cell increases, and the membrane swells outward. Eventually the difficulty of absorbing sufficient oxygen through the slowly expanding area of the membrane to maintain the rapidly expanding bulk of the cell interior sparks cell division.

In multicellular animals, however, there is an added dimension to growth. The individual cells making up the body do indeed grow and divide, but there must also be coordination involved. No group of cells must be allowed to outgrow the limits set down for it, and all growth must be neatly balanced between one set of cells and another, so that at all times each group of cells can perform its functions efficiently, without undue interference from the rest.

In the human being, for example, some cells, such as those of the nervous system, do not multiply at all after birth. Other cells grow and multiply only in response to some out-of-the-ordinary need, as when bone cells will spring into action to heal a broken clavicle or when liver cells will suddenly resume rapid multiplication to replace a portion of a liver cut away by the surgeon's knife. (This is called *regeneration*.) Then, too, there are cells that continue to grow and multiply unceasingly throughout life, however extended that life might be. The best examples are the cells of the skin, which continue throughout life to reproduce and multiply in order to form the dead but protective epidermis — forever sloughed away and forever renewed.

This process of coordinated growth requires the most delicate and subtle adjustment of chemical mechanisms. One measure of the subtlety of these mechanisms is the fact that biochemists have not yet discovered the essential chemical steps initiating growth and keeping it under control. If this is ruled out as too subjective a measure, another form of evidence of the delicate complexity of the process is the unfortunate ease with which it can go out of order, allowing one batch of cells or another to involve itself suddenly in uncontrolled growth.

Uncontrolled growth is not necessarily rapid or wild; the danger lies in the mere fact of its being uncontrolled — in that the mechanisms ordinarily calling it to a halt are no longer in action. The cells growing in uncontrolled fashion do so indefinitely, burdening the body with their unnecessary weight, drowning out neighboring tissues, and gradually preventing them from carrying out their normal functions, in consequence outgrowing their own blood supply and sickening. The wild cells may break off sometimes and be carried by the bloodstream to another part of the body where they may take root and carry on their anarchic activity.

Any abnormal growth, anywhere in the body, is referred to as a *tumor* ("swelling" L). Sometimes the abnormal growth is restricted, forming warts or wens which may be unsightly and inconvenient but are not generally dangerous to life. Such tumors are *benign tumors* (bih-nine′; "good" L). Where the abnormal growth is not restricted but continues indefinitely, and in particular where it invades normal tissues, it is said to be *malignant* ("evil" L). Galen, a physician of Roman times, described a malignant tumor of the breast which distended nearby veins until the whole figure looked like a crab with its legs jutting out in all directions. Since that time, malignant tumors have been referred to as *cancers* ("crab" L).

Cancer has become far more common in our times than ever in the past, for three reasons. First, methods of diagnosis have improved, so that when a person dies of cancer, we know it and don't put the death down to some other reason. Second, the incidence of many other disorders, particularly infectious diseases, has been lowered drastically in the past century. Therefore, a number of people who in times past would have died of diphtheria, typhoid fever, cholera, or the like now live long enough to fall prey to cancer. Third, there are environmental conditions newly inflicted upon us by our advancing technology which are known to induce cancer, or are suspected of doing so. Among these are the radiations of X-rays and radioactive substances, various synthetic

chemicals, atmospheric pollution through coal smoke and automobile exhaust, and even inhaled tobacco smoke.

However, let us return to normal growth —

In view of the fact that hormones so delicately control the chemical processes within the body, it would be very strange if one or
more did not control this all-important phenomenon of growth.
It is another aspect of the universal nature of growth that it is here,
more than anywhere else, where we are conscious of hormones
even in the plant kingdom.

Growth in plants is far less bound within limits than is growth in
animals. The limbs of an animal grow in fixed numbers and in
fixed shape and size. The limbs of a tree, in contrast, grow in comparatively wide variety, neither fixed in numbers nor shape nor
size. And yet, even among plants controls are necessary.

Substances capable of accelerating plant growth when present
in solution in very small concentration were first isolated in pure
form in 1935. They were named *auxins* ("to increase" G). The
best-known of these auxins is a compound called *indolyl-3-acetic
acid,* commonly abbreviated *IAA.* It is another of the hormones
that are actually modified amino acids in structure. In this case,
the amino acid involved (and from which the plant cells manufacture IAA) is tryptophan:

TRYPTOPHAN   IAA

Auxins are formed in the growing tips of plants and move downward. They bring about an elongation of cells rather than actual cell division. Many of the movements of plants are governed by the distribution of these auxins. For instance, they are present in higher concentration on the side of the stem away from the sun. This side of the stem will elongate and the stem will therefore bend in the direction of the sun. In the same way, auxins will concentrate on the lower side of a stem held horizontally, curving the tip upward.

Plant hormones, like hormones generally, can cause disorders when present in excess. One of the most powerful of the auxins was discovered through studies of a plant disease. Japanese farmers cultivating rice plants had often observed that certain shoots would for no clear reason suddenly extend themselves high in the air, becoming weakened and useless. The Japanese referred to this as *bakanae*, which in English means (rather charmingly) "foolish seedling." In 1926 a Japanese plant pathologist noticed that such lengthened shoots were fungus-infested. A dozen years of work finally resulted in the isolation in 1938 of growth-stimulating compounds from the fungus. The particular fungus at fault belongs to the genus *Gibberella*, so the compound was named *gibberellin* (jib'ur-el'in).

The structure of the gibberellins (for there are a number of closely related varieties), worked out in 1956, is quite complicated, the molecule being made up of five rings of atoms. Gibberellins have been isolated from certain types of beans; this shows that they occur naturally in at least some plants and may therefore qualify as auxins. They (and plant hormones generally) can be used to hasten the process of germination, of flowering and fruiting. In short, they can race plants through life — to our advantage, of course.

Auxinlike compounds can also race plants through life to death — again to our advantage. There is a synthetic molecule, called *2,4-dichlorophenoxyacetic acid*, usually abbreviated as 2,4-*D*, that has auxinlike properties. Sprayed upon plants, it encourages a too rapid and too disorganized growth, killing them through what practically amounts to an induced cancer. Plants with broad leaves absorb more of such a spray than those with narrow leaves, and the former are therefore killed by a concentration of 2,4-D that leaves the latter unaffected. It often happens that the plants man wishes to cultivate, such as the various grasses and grains, are narrow-leaved, whereas the intruding and unwanted plants ("weeds"), which compete for sun and water with our pets, are broad-leaved. For this reason, 2,4-D has gained fame in recent years as an effective weed killer.

There are also plant hormones that accelerate actual cell division in otherwise mature and nondividing cells. This is useful whenever new tissue growth is necessary to cover externally caused damage. Compounds bringing about such repair-growth are called, dramatically, *wound hormones*. One example of these, a compound with a molecule composed of a chain of 12 carbon atoms, with a carboxyl group (-COOH) at each end and a double bond between carbon-2 and carbon-3, is called *traumatic acid* (troh-mat'ik; "wound" G).

GROWTH HORMONE

As for animals — and of course for the human being in particular — it is difficult to pin a complex phenomenon such as growth down to a single hormone. The misfunctioning of any hormone insofar as it upsets the body's chemical mechanisms is going to interfere with growth to some extent. The most extreme example I have mentioned is that of the thyroid hormone, the absence of which in children produces the dwarfish cretin.

Naturally, then, one would expect the pituitary, which works in conjunction with several glands (the thyroid and adrenal cortex have already been pointed out) to have an effect on growth. As a matter of fact, it was noted as long ago as 1912 that an animal from which the pituitary had been removed ceased growing. What is more, this pituitary effect is not entirely due to the atrophy of other glands brought about by the loss of certain hormones of the anterior lobe. In the 1920's and 1930's, pituitary extracts were prepared which, when injected into growing rats and dogs, caused growth to continue past normal and produced giant animals. Furthermore, these extracts could be purified to the point where such components as ACTH and TSH were definitely missing and where, indeed, no other glands were affected. The pituitary was doing it all on its own.

Apparently the anterior pituitary produces a hormone that does not act upon other glands (the only pituitary hormone not to do so) but upon the body's tissues directly, accelerating growth. The name for this substance in plain English is *growth hormone*. It may also be called, with a more scholarly tang, *somatotrophic hormone* (soh′muh-toh-troh′fik; "body-nourishing" G), which is in turn abbreviated, usually, *STH*.

The structure of the growth hormone is less well known than that of some of the other pituitary hormones. The hormone obtained from cattle is rather large for a protein hormone and has a molecular weight of 45,000. The molecule seems to be made up of some 370 amino acids arranged in two chains. Ordinarily, protein hormones obtained from different species of vertebrates may differ in minor ways and yet remain functional across the species lines. Thus insulin from cattle is slightly different from that of swine and yet both will substitute for human insulin with equal efficiency. Growth hormone obtained from cattle or swine, however, is without effect on man. Man is affected only (as far as is known) by growth hormone obtained from man himself and from monkeys. The molecules of such primate growth hormones have molecular weights of only 25,000 or so. It seems probable that the molecules of any growth hormone so far obtained could be broken down substantially without loss of biological activity.

Growth hormone has several overall effects on metabolism (though, of course, the exact details of its chemical effects are unknown). One of these is to accelerate the conversion of amino acids to protein, a natural accompaniment of any process that is to bring about growth. In addition, an oversupply of growth hormone administered to experimental animals increases glucose concentration in the blood and diminishes insulin. This may be because the wildly growing animal places so many demands on the energy mechanisms of the body that the insulin-producing cells wear out and die, leaving a more or less permanent diabetes behind.

Growth hormone encourages the enlargement of bones in all dimensions. Usually the secretion of growth hormone is high during childhood and youth, when the body (and skeleton in particular) is growing, and tapers off in late adolescence, when growth itself tapers off in consequence. If the secretion of growth hormone by the pituitary is less than normal during youth the bones cease growth prematurely, and the result is a midget. Such midgets (sometimes reaching heights of only 3 feet or even less), produced by underproduction of growth hormone, retain their proper proportions and, although retaining a childlike cast of features, are not deformed, grotesque, or mentally retarded. In some cases they even attain sexual maturity and become miniature but fully adult human beings. The most famous midget of this sort was Charles Sherwood Stratton, who was made famous by P. T. Barnum as "Tom Thumb." He was about 3 feet tall, but perfectly proportioned. He died in 1883 at the age of 45.

An oversupply of growth hormone during youth, or a supply that does not taper off appropriately with age, results in overgrowth and giantism. A recent example, which made the newspapers regularly, was that of Robert Wadlow, born in Alton, Illinois, in 1918. He grew with remarkable speed. There are pictures of him as a boy showing him head and shoulders taller than his normally sized father but with boyish features and proportions. He finally attained a height of 8 feet 9½ inches before dying at the age of 22.

It sometimes happens that the pituitary of an adult, who has achieved his full measurements and has ceased growing long since, begins to produce an oversupply of growth hormone. The bones have ossified and can no longer grow in proper proportions. Despite this, the ends of some of the bones at the body extremities still possess the capacity for growth, and these respond. The hands and feet enlarge, therefore, as do the bones of the face, particularly of the lower jaw. The result of this condition, which is called *acromegaly* (ak′roh-meg′uh-lee; "large extremities" G), is a rather grotesque distortion of features.

METAMORPHOSIS

Growth is not merely a process in which each organ lengthens and widens and thickens in proportion. In the course of the life of most creatures there come periods where qualitative changes take place as well as quantitative ones. Where such sudden qualitative changes are very marked, amounting to a radical alteration in the overall shape and structure of the creature, the process is referred to as a *metamorphosis* ("transform" G). It would be natural to expect a metamorphosis to take place under the control of one or more hormones. Among the vertebrates the most common example of metamorphosis is that by which a tadpole turns into a frog; and, as a matter of fact, I pointed out in Chapter 3 that this is mediated by thyroid hormone.

Metamorphosis also takes place among a number of invertebrate groups, notably among the insects, where the caterpillar-butterfly conversion is at least as spectacular and well known as the tadpole-frog conversion. In insects in the larval stage (as in caterpillars), growth takes place, so to speak, in jumps. The external skeleton prevents the smooth enlargement that is so characteristic of the growth of the soft-surfaced vertebrates. Instead, every once in a while the horny outer coat of the insect splits and then a new and larger coat is formed, one large enough to allow a spurt of growth. This business of exchanging an old shell for a new and larger one is commonly called *molting* ("change" L). A less common word for the process is *ecdysis* (ek′dih-sis; "get out" G).

Insect molting is controlled by a hormone produced by a gland located in the forward portion of the thorax and therefore called the *prothoracic gland*. This gland apparently produces a hormone named *ecdysone* (ek'dih-sohn), which is stored in a small organ near the heart. The action of a group of cells in the brain causes the organ to release some of the stored ecdysone periodically and this stimulates a molt. Ecdysone therefore is sometimes called *molting hormone*.

After a number of such molts, the young of many insect species enter a quiescent stage during which metamorphosis takes place. As a result of radical changes, an adult, sexually mature insect is formed. The caterpillar, encircling itself with a cocoon and becoming a butterfly, is, as I said before, the most familiar case.

But after which particular molt in the larval stage does the metamorphosis take place? One might think that this would be determined by a hormone that is secreted at the proper time, neutralizing ecdysone, ending the molts, and initiating metamorphosis. Instead, it is the reverse that takes place. A hormone is continuously secreted by a pair of glands in the head. This *prevents* metamorphosis and keeps the larva molting and growing. Once the formation of this hormone decreases and its concentration falls below a certain point, the next molt is then followed by metamorphosis.

Since this metamorphosis-preventing hormone keeps the insect in the larval form, it is called the *larval hormone*, or even the *juvenile hormone*. (There is something fascinating about the term "juvenile hormone" that brings to mind vague glimmers of thought concerning the fountain of youth; needless to say, these insect hormones are without effect on the human being.) So far, chemists have not worked out the structure of any of the insect hormones.

Human beings do not undergo metamorphosis in the sense that tadpoles and caterpillars do, and yet there are marked changes that do appear in adolescence as a boy becomes a man and a girl becomes a woman. They may not be as drastic as the change from water-breathing to air-breathing, or from crawling to flying, but it is not altogether unspectacular when the smooth cheeks of a boy begin to sprout a beard and when the flat chest of a girl begins to bulge with paired breasts.

These changes, associated with sexual maturity but not directly involved in the processes of reproduction, are referred to as the development of the *secondary sexual characteristics*. Such development represents a very mild human metamorphosis. It is to be expected that it is under the control of a hormone or hormones.

Occasionally in the past there were speculations as to the effect on adolescence, and the changes that took place at this time, of the *thymus gland* (from a Greek word of uncertain derivation). The thymus gland lies in the upper chest, in front of the lungs and above the heart, extending upward into the neck. In children, it is soft and pink, with many lobes, and is fairly large. When the age of 12 is attained it may reach a weight of 40 grams (or about 1½ ounces). With puberty, however, as the signs of adulthood begin to appear, the thymus begins to shrink. In the adult it is represented by no more than a small patch of fat and fiber.

One is tempted to think that the thymus might produce some secretion which, like the juvenile hormone of insects, keeps a child from maturing. It would then be the disappearance of the hormone (as the gland shrivels) that would bring about the onset of puberty. However, even the most intense investigation has brought to light no such hormone. The removal of the thymus in experimental animals does not bring on sudden maturity, and the injection of thymus extracts in young animals does not delay maturity. Consequently, that theory has been abandoned.

A second possibility arises from the fact that the thymus is composed of lymphoid tissue, very like that of the spleen, the tonsils, and the lymph nodes. It has seemed possible, therefore, that the thymus shared the functions of such lymphoid tissue and, one way or another, combatted bacterial infection. It might produce antibodies (protein molecules specifically designed to neutralize bacteria, bacterial toxins, or viruses), and if so, that is very important, for these antibodies are of prime importance in the body's mechanisms of immunity to disease.

This theory received strong support in 1962. Jacques F. A. P. Miller at the Chester Beatty Research Institute in London has shown that not only does the thymus produce antibodies but it is the first organ to do so. With time, the cells of the thymus migrate to other sites such as the lymph nodes. The thymus degenerates at puberty, then, not because its function is gone but because it has, in a sense, spread itself through the body.

In support of this notion is the fact that mice from which the thymus was removed very soon after birth died after several months, the various tissues engaged in immunological mechanisms being undeveloped. Where the thymus was removed only after the animals were three weeks old, there were no bad effects. By that time enough of the thymus had migrated to ensure the capacity of the animal to protect itself against germ invasion. Evidently this spreading out of the thymus is accelerated by the same hormones that bring about puberty, which is why the thymus shrinks rapidly after the age of 12 or 13.

Removal of the thymus in very young mice also makes it possible for the creature to accept skin grafts from other animals. These would ordinarily be rejected through the development of antibodies against the "foreign protein" of the skin graft. If thymus glands from other animals are inserted into such mice, they regain the antibody-manufacturing (and graft-resisting) ability. If the thymus inserts are from another strain of mice, skin grafts from that other strain will still be accepted. There is a distant hope here that someday techniques involving thymus grafts may make it easier to graft tissues and organs on human patients.

ANDROGENS

The organs directly connected with the appearance of secondary sexual characteristics are those which produce the cells essential to reproduction — the sperm-producing organs (testicles) in the male and the egg-producing organs (ovaries) in the female. These are grouped under the name of *gonads* (gon′adz; "that which generates" G). A more common name for them is *sex glands*. The connection between the gonads and the changes associated with puberty would seem a logical one, and might be accepted even without evidence. However, logic-minus-evidence has proved insidiously deceiving many times in the history of science. Fortunately there is ample evidence on the side of logic in this connection, evidence dating from prehistoric times.

Sometime before the dawn of history, the early herdsmen discovered, perhaps through accident at first, that a male animal from which the testicles were removed in youth (*castration*) developed quite differently from one that retained its testicles. The castrated animal was not fertile and, indeed, showed no interest in sexual activity. Furthermore, it tended to put on fat, so its meat was both tenderer and tastier than that of the uncastrated male. Additionally, it developed a placid, stolid disposition, which made the animal much easier to handle and easier to put to work than the uncastrated male would be. Through castration the savage bull becomes the slow-moving ox, the fierce stallion becomes the patient gelding, and the stringy rooster becomes the fat capon.

It would be naïve, alas, to expect that such a procedure should not be applied by man to his fellowman. A castrated man is a *eunuch* (yoo′nook; "to guard the bed" G), so called because his chief function was to serve as guard in the harem of rich men who needed wardens incapable of taking undue advantage of their ordinarily enviable position.

Where castration is performed in childhood, before the development of the male secondary sexual characteristics, those characteristics do not develop. The eunuch does not grow a beard and remains generally unhairy, although he retains the hair of his head and virtually never grows bald. (Baldness in males is in part a secondary sexual characteristic and bears a relationship to the male sex hormone concentration in the blood — although it is possible, and even very common, to be amply virile without being bald.)

The eunuch also retains the small larynx of the child, so his voice remains high and womanish. In Christian times, when polygamy and harems were frowned upon, eunuchs were still valued for their soprano voices, and such singers (called castratos) were renowned in the early days of opera. They were also used in choirs. It was not until 1878 that Pope Leo XIII abolished the inhuman custom of manufacturing eunuchs for use in the papal choir.

The eunuch puts on fat in feminine distribution, lacks a sexual drive, and develops (perhaps through association with women in the harem) the personality traits we ordinarily associate with women. His intelligence is not affected, however. The sly and intriguing court eunuch is a staple of historical fiction, and at least one eunuch, the Byzantine general Narses, was an able administrator and general, capable in his seventies of defeating the Goths and Franks in Italy.

With the close of the 19th century and the beginning of the 20th, chemists began to work with extracts of the testicles and found that changes occurring after castration (in experimental animals) could be prevented by injection of such extracts. Capons, in this way, could be made to grow the lordly comb of the intact rooster.

As knowledge of hormones developed, it became quite clear that the testicles, in addition to producing sperm cells, produced hormones capable of initiating the formation of secondary sexual characteristics. These were called *androgens* (an'droh-jenz; "male-producing" G) and may also be called the *testicular hormones* or the *male sex hormones*.

In the early 1930's, compounds with androgenic properties were isolated and proved to be steroids. This was accomplished chiefly through the labors of the German chemist Adolf Butenandt, who, as a result, shared the Nobel Prize in Chemistry for

1939 with the Yugoslav-born Swiss chemist Leopold Ruzicka, another worker in the field. (Butenandt was forbidden by the Nazi government to accept the Nobel Prize and was unable to do so until 1949, after a war which he survived and the Nazi government did not.) Two well-known androgens are *androsterone* (an-dros′tur-ohn) and *testosterone* (tes-tos′tur-ohn). The formulas are given below:

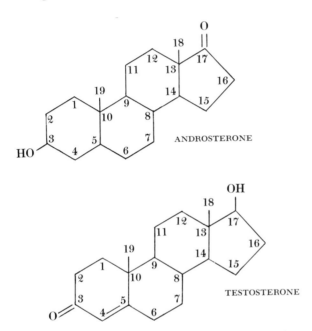

The androgens differ from the other steroids I have discussed in this book chiefly in lacking altogether the carbon-chain attachment at carbon-17. (You may remember that cholesterol has an eight-carbon chain attached at that site, bile acids a five-carbon chain, and corticoids a two-carbon chain.)

The androgens have an effect similar to growth hormone in that they somehow encourage the formation of protein from amino acids. However, growth hormone does this generally throughout the body, whereas the androgens do so, for the most

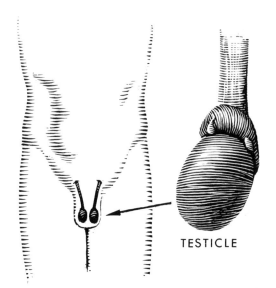

TESTICLE

PLACENTA

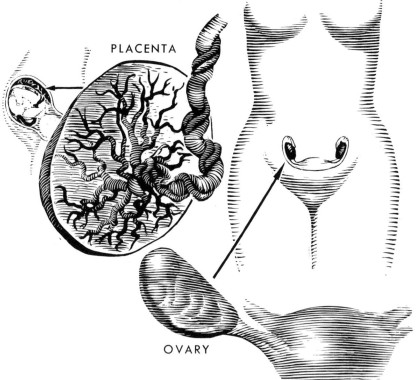

OVARY

part, locally and selectively, so those organs associated with reproduction or with the secondary sexual characteristics are chiefly involved. A general effect is not altogether absent. Until puberty boys and girls are not very different in size and weight, but after puberty, with androgens pouring into the blood, the male grows larger and more muscular than the female.

Testosterone is about ten times as active as androsterone; that is, it will produce equivalent effects in one-tenth the dose. An androgen more potent than testosterone does not occur naturally, but has been prepared in the laboratory. It is *methyltestosterone*, which differs from testosterone in that a one-carbon methyl group ($-CH_3$) is attached to carbon-17 in addition to the hydroxyl group already present.

It is also possible to prepare synthetic androgens that retain the general protein-forming property and not the specialized masculinizing one. An example is 19-*nortestosterone*, which differs from ordinary testosterone in that carbon-19 is missing.

ESTROGENS

At about the same time that the hormones produced by the testicles were being studied, those produced by the ovaries in females were isolated. Since ovaries are located well within the pelvic region and are not conveniently exposed as the testicles are, early man had far less experience with ovariectomy (removal of the ovaries) than with castration. Nowadays, however, ovariectomies conducted on young experimental animals result in the suppression of female secondary sexual characteristics and there is no doubt that there are *female sex hormones* (or *ovarian hormones*) analogous to the male androgens.

Extracts containing these hormones caused female rats to become eager to accept the sexual attentions of the male of the species. Ordinarily this took place only at periodic intervals when the female rat was "in heat," or, to use the more classical term, in *estrus* ("frenzy" G). The female sex hormones were therefore named *estrogens* (es'troh-jenz; "estrus-producing" G) and most of the individual hormones contain the letter-combination "estr" in their names. (The androgens and estrogens together may be referred to simply as *sex hormones.*)

The estrogens differ from the androgens chiefly in that ring A (the one at the lower left of the steroid nucleus) possesses three double bonds. This makes it a "benzene ring," in chemical language. Carbon-10, as you will see in the formula below, has all four of its bonds in use. Two lead to carbon-5, one to carbon-1, and one to carbon-9. No bond is available for the usual attachment of carbon-19 at that point and so that carbon is missing. (The compound, 19-nortestosterone, defined above, also has carbon-19 missing but it is not an estrogen. It lacks the necessary three double bonds in ring A.)

One of the best-known of the estrogens is *estrone* (es'trohn), which possesses the following formula:

ESTRONE

Two others are *estradiol* (es'truh-dy'ole), in which both oxygen atoms form part of -OH groups, and *estriol* (es'tree-ole), in which a third -OH group is attached to carbon-16.

As in the case of the androgens, the most powerful estrogens are synthetic. Thus, there is 17-*ethynylestradiol,* in which a two-carbon chain is attached to carbon-17 in addition to the hydroxyl group. This two-carbon chain possesses a triple bond and is called an *ethynyl group* (eth'in-il), which accounts for the name of the compound. Taken orally, 17-ethynylestradiol will produce the effects of the natural estrogens in one-tenth the dose.

Another synthetic estrogen is *stilbestrol* (stil-bes′trole), so called because it is related to an organic chemical called "stilbene"). It is not quite as powerful as 17-ethynylestradiol, but it is three to five times as powerful as the natural hormones. Stilbestrol is unusual in that it is not a steroid. This is useful, too, since its molecule is far easier to synthesize than the molecule of a steroid would be. Hence stilbestrol is cheaper and more easily available than either the natural or synthetic steroid estrogens.

The estrogens and androgens are quite similar in chemical structure. The molecule of estrone, for instance, differs from that of androsterone only in the presence of three double bonds and in the absence of carbon-19. Such a similarity in structure might seem by "common-sense" reasoning to imply a similarity in function. Nevertheless, it frequently happens in biochemical reactions that a particular compound will inhibit (that is, slow down or even stop) the working of a very similar compound by competing with it for union with a particular enzyme. The enzyme cannot, in effect, distinguish between the proper compound and the very similar inhibitor. The extent to which the enzyme will work and therefore possibly the entire course of metabolism will depend on slight changes in the relative concentrations of the two similar compounds. This is called *competitive inhibition.*

The two groups of sex hormones, so similar in structure, may very likely compete for the same spot on the cell membranes. The course of metabolism would then shift drastically in one direction or the other, depending on which group of hormones is predominant and wins the competition.

The effects of estrogens and androgens are opposed, and adding one is much like subtracting the other. To illustrate: the injection of estrogens will caponize a rooster just as castration (removal of androgens) will. And, predictably, the injection of androgens will have much the same effect on a female animal as an ovariectomy would. This is useful in the treatment of certain diseases involving the tissues most affected by these hormones. Estrogens have in this way been used to treat cancer of the prostate. Androgens stimulate the growth of the prostate and estrogens inhibit that growth even, sometimes, when the growth is cancerous.

The androgens and estrogens are so closely related chemically that it is perhaps unreasonable to expect that an organ capable of producing one should not be also capable of producing the other. Indeed, both testicles and ovaries produce hormones of each variety. A male is male not because he produces only androgens but only because he produces mostly androgens. The same, in reverse, is true of the female. Masculinity can be accentuated not merely by increasing the quantity of androgens produced but by getting rid, with increased efficiency, of any estrogens that are produced. Thus, a rich source of estrogen is the urine of the stallion.

One gland besides the gonads produces steroid hormones. That gland, the adrenal cortex, also produces sex hormones, and especially androgens. It is for this reason that a tumor of the cortex, leading to the overproduction of its steroids, does have a strongly masculinizing effect on women.

The business of being a female is in many ways more complicated than that of being a male. Once a male has attained sexual maturity, he continues on an even keel, producing sperm cells in regular fashion. The adult female, in contrast, undergoes a complicated sexual cycle in which an egg cell is produced every four weeks or so. The changes involved in this process are brought about by the action of a particular hormone. It seems reasonable that the very structure that produces the egg cell also produces the hormone.

The egg cell is produced by a follicle in the ovary, which, after it has reached pinhead size and ruptured (thus allowing the egg cell to escape into the Fallopian tubes, which lead to the uterus), turns reddish yellow. It becomes the *corpus luteum* ("orange-yellow body" L), and it is this which produces the hormone.

The first action of the hormone of the corpus luteum is to stimulate the growth of the inner lining of the uterus, preparing it for the reception of the fertilized egg. Since it thus paves the way for pregnancy, the hormone was first named *progestin* (prohjes'tin; "before pregnancy" L). When the hormone was shown to be a steroid, its name was altered to *progesterone.*

Progesterone resembles the corticoids more than it does the estrogens. Like the corticoids it has a 2-carbon chain attached to carbon-17, and it lacks the benzene ring of the estrogens. The chief difference between progesterone and the corticoids is that the latter have a hydroxyl group on carbon-21, whereas progesterone does not. As a matter of fact, except for that missing hydroxyl group, progesterone has precisely the formula of deoxycorticosterone (DOC); see page 79. But the one missing oxygen atom makes all the difference as far as function is concerned.

If the egg cell is not fertilized, the corpus luteum withers away and progesterone ceases to be formed. The lining of the uterus, with its blood supply, is sloughed off, and the menstrual period is the result. Some two weeks later there is another ovulation and the uterus is prepared for another egg cell and another try. If the egg cell is fertilized, then it embeds itself in the lining of the uterus, which is maintained by the continuing existence of the corpus luteum and the hormone it produces. Progesterone not only maintains the lining but also stimulates the formation of the placenta, the organ through which the developing embryo is fed. The role of progesterone in this respect has been made clear through work with experimental animals. If the ovaries of a rabbit are removed shortly after it has become pregnant, the embryo is not retained and there is an abortion. If extracts from the corpus luteum are injected into such ovariectomized animals, however, pregnancy can be made to continue normally to its natural conclusion.

Yet once the placenta (see p. 102) is formed, it too produces progesterone, supplementing that of the corpus luteum, which continues to flourish and to increase in size until the later months of pregnancy. In late pregnancy, with the placenta well established and its progesterone supply ample, the removal of the ovaries will no longer affect pregnancy.

Obviously, during the period of pregnancy, the ordinary cycle of egg cell production must be interrupted. It is part of the effect of progesterone to put a stop to the steady production of eggs at the rate of one every four weeks, at least for the duration of the pregnancy.

This has suggested a method for the development of oral contraceptives. Compounds having the effect of progesterone but capable of easy synthesis in the laboratory might render a woman infertile. If it could be shown that there were no undesirable side effects and if the conscientious objections of various religious groups could be overcome, this could become the most practical method for controlling the present-day overrapid expansion of population. Actually, such progesterone analogs have been manufactured and have passed many tests successfully.

GONADOTROPHINS

As with the corticoids and with thyroxine, there is an interplay between the various sex hormones and the pituitary. This can easily be shown to be so, because if the pituitary is removed from an experimental animal the sex glands atrophy and pregnancy will not take place, or will end in abortion if already under way. Then, too, lactation, if under way, will cease.

There turned out, not surprisingly, to be several different hormones produced by the anterior pituitary gland which affected sexual development. Each had its specialized function, but they are lumped together (along with substances of similar effect produced by other organs) as *gonadotrophins* (gon'uh-doh-troh'finz; "gonad-nourishing" G). One of these gonadotrophins has as a noticeable effect the stimulation of the growth of the follicles of the ovary, preparing them for the production of egg cells. It is therefore called the *follicle-stimulating hormone,* usually abbreviated *FSH.* Don't suppose, though, that this hormone has a function only in the female. In the male it stimulates the epithelium of the portions of the testicles that produce sperm cells.

A second hormone takes over where FSH leaves off. In the female it stimulates the final ripening of the follicles, their rupture to release the egg, and the conversion of the ruptured follicle into the corpus luteum. It is therefore called *luteinizing hormone,* usually abbreviated as *LH.* In the male this hormone stimulates those cells which form testosterone. Such cells (as well as analogous cells in the ovary, also stimulated by the hormone) are called "interstitial cells." For that reason a second name for the luteinizing hormone is *interstitial cell-stimulating hormone,* or *ICSH.*

This second name, although longer, would seem more reasonable. Otherwise there would be confusion with the third of the pituitary gonadotrophins, which carries on the work of the second, acting to maintain the corpus luteum, once formed, and to stimulate the production of progesterone. This third hormone is therefore the *luteotrophic hormone.* It has functions for the period following the completion of pregnancy, since it cooperates with the estrogens in stimulating the growth of the breast and the production of milk. This function was discovered before the effect of the hormone on the corpus luteum was worked out. Older names for it are *lactogenic hormone* (lak′toh-jen′ik; "milk-producing," a word of mixed Greek and Latin origin) and *prolactin* ("prior to milk" L).

Prolactin stimulated other post-pregnancy activities. Young female rats injected with the hormone would busy themselves with nest-building even though they had not given birth. On the other hand, mice whose pituitaries had been removed shortly before giving birth to young exhibited little interest in the baby mice. The newspapers at once termed prolactin the "mother-love hormone."

The interplay between the estrogens (or androgens) and the various pituitary gonadotrophins is exceedingly complex; the network of effect and countereffect has not yet been entirely worked out. In general, the gonadotrophin production is stimulated by a low concentration of sex hormones in the blood and inhibited by a high one.

A more direct influence, on prolactin at least, is the stimulating effect of suckling. This increases prolactin production and, therefore, milk secretion. Undoubtedly the occasional news reports of increased milk production by dairy cattle when soft music is played in the stalls is due to the stimulation of prolactin secretion by any environmental factor that brings on a sensation of well-being and freedom from insecurity.

Because of this interrelationship between the pituitary and the gonads, the failure of the pituitary to hold up its end is as surely asexualizing as castration or ovariectomy would be. Such pituitary failure in young produces dwarfism, a tendency to gross obesity, and arrested sexual development. The symptoms were described in 1901 by an Austrian neurologist named Alfred Fröhlich, and the condition has been called *Fröhlich's syndrome* ever since. (Syndrome, from Greek words meaning "to run with," is a term applied to a collection of symptoms of widely different character which occur together in a particular disorder — which run with each other, so to speak.)

Of the three gonadotrophins of the pituitary, lactogenic hormone is the only one to have been isolated in reasonably pure form. All are proteins, of course, (the pituitary gland produces only proteins) with molecular weights running from 20,000 to 100,000. Such preparations of FSH and ICSH as have been studied seem to contain sugars as part of the molecule, but whether these sugars are essential to the action is not yet certain.

The placenta produces a gonadotrophin of its own that is not quite like those of the pituitary. It is called *human chorionic gonadotrophin,* usually abbreviated *HCG.* ("Chorion" [kaw′ree-on] is the name, from the Greek, for the membranes surrounding the embryo.) As early as two to four weeks after the beginning of pregnancy, HCG is already produced in large enough quantities to give rise to the problem of its removal. At least some of it is excreted in the urine. The urinary content of HCG rises to a peak during the second month of pregnancy.

HCG can produce changes in experimental animals that would ordinarily be expected of the pituitary gonadotrophins. If the injection of extracts of a woman's urine into mice, frogs, or rabbits produces such effects, it is a clear sign that HCG is present and that the woman is therefore in the early stages of pregnancy. This forms the basis for the various now routine pregnancy tests that can give a reasonably certain decision weeks before the doctor could otherwise tell by less subtle examinations.

6

OUR NERVES

Throughout the first five chapters of this book I have described the manner in which the complex activities of the body are coordinated by means of the production and destruction of certain complex molecules, sometimes working in coordination and sometimes in balanced opposition, and achieving their effects (probably, though not certainly) by their addition to and alteration of the cell membrane. This form of coordination, present from the very beginning of life, is useful and practical but it is slow. Hormone action must wait on the chemical construction of molecules, on the piling together of atom upon atom. The product must then be secreted into the bloodstream and carried by that fluid to every point in the body, even though it may only be useful at one particular point. Then, its mission done, the hormone must be pulled apart and inactivated (usually in the liver) and its remnants must be filtered out of the body by the kidneys.

There is, however, an entirely different form of coordination that represents an advance in subtlety, efficiency, and speed. It is not complex molecules, but single atoms and particles far smaller than atoms. These atoms and other particles are not carried by the bloodstream; they move along special channels at velocities considerably greater than those at which the viscous blood can be forced through small vessels. These channels, furthermore, lead from (or to) specific organs so that this form of coordination, electric in nature, will stimulate a certain organ and do so exclusively, without the fuzzy broadcasting of side effects that often accompany hormone action.

The difference in the seeming intensity of life between plants and animals is due mainly to the fact that animals have this electrical form of coordination in addition to the chemical, whereas plants have only the chemical. But let's start at the beginning —

When the animal body is dissected, thin white cords are to be found here and there. They look like strings. The word *nerve* now applied to them is from the Latin *nervus*, which is traced back to the Sanskrit *snavara*, meaning a string or cord. Indeed, the term was originally applied to any stringlike object in the body; to tendons, for one. It was the tendons, the stringlike connections between muscles and bones, that were the original "nerves."

The Greeks of Alexandria in Julius Caesar's time recognized that the tendons themselves were tough connective fibers, whereas other strings were comparatively fragile and fatty rather than connective. The latter were connected to muscle at one end as the tendons were, but not connected to bones at the other. Galen, the Roman physician who lived A.D. 200, finally completed the semantic switch by applying the term "nerve" only to the nontendons, and this is what we still do today.

Nevertheless, traces of the pre-Galenic situation persist in the language. We say, when we make a supreme effort, that we are "straining every nerve," whereas we obviously mean that we are straining every tendon because of the fierce contraction of our muscles. Again, the unabridged dictionary gives "sinewy" as its first definition of "nervous." To speak of a hand as nervous, which today would imply weakness and trembling, would have meant precisely the opposite in older times — that it was strong and capable of firm action.

Throughout ancient and medieval times the nerves were felt to be hollow, as the blood vessels were, and (again like the blood vessels) to function as carriers of a fluid. Rather complicated theories were developed by Galen and others that involved three different fluids carried by the veins, the arteries, and the nerves respectively. The fluid of the nerves, usually referred to as "animal spirits," was considered the most subtle and rarefied of the three.

Such theories of nerve action, lacking a firm observational basis on which to anchor, went drifting off into obscurity and mysticism, and the structure so reared had to be torn down entirely and thrown away. And yet, as it turned out, the ancients had not entirely missed the target. A kind of fluid actually does travel along the nerves; a fluid far more ethereal than the visible fluid that fills the blood vessels, or even than the lighter and invisible fluid that fills the lungs and penetrates into the arteries. The effects of this fluid had been observed for centuries before the time even of Galen. As long ago as 600 B.C., the Greek philosopher Thales had noted that amber if rubbed gained the ability to attract light objects. Scholars turned to the phenomenon (now called "electricity" from the Greek word for amber) occasionally over the centuries, unable to understand it yet interested.

In the 18th century, methods were discovered for concentrating electricity in what was called a Leyden jar. (It was particularly studied at the University of Leyden in the Netherlands.) When a Leyden jar was fully charged, it could be made to discharge if a metal-pointed object were brought near the knob on top. The electricity jumped from the knob to the metal point and produced a visible spark like a tiny lightning bolt. Accompanying it was a sharp crackle like a minute bit of thunder. People began to think of electricity as a subtle fluid that could be poured into a Leyden jar and be made to burst forth again.

The American scientist Benjamin Franklin first popularized the notion of electricity as a single fluid that could produce electric charges of two different types, depending on whether an excess of the fluid were present (positive charge) or a deficiency (negative charge). More than that, Franklin, in 1752, was able to show that the spark and crackle of the discharging Leyden jar did not merely resemble thunder and lightning but were identical with those natural phenomena in nature. By flying a kite in a thunderstorm, he drew electricity out of the clouds and charged a Leyden jar with it.

The discovery excited the world of science, and experiments involving electricity became all the rage. The Italian anatomist Luigi Galvani was one of those drawn into the electrical orbit in the 1780's. He found, as others had, that an electric shock from a Leyden jar could cause a muscle dissected out of a dead frog to contract spasmodically, but he went further and (partly by accident) found more. He found that a frog muscle would contract if a metal instrument were touching it at a time when an electric spark was given off by a Leyden jar not in direct contact with the muscle. Then he discovered that the muscle would contract if it made simultaneous contact with two different metals even where no Leyden jar was in the vicinity.

Galvani thought the muscle itself was the source of a fluid similar to the electricity with which scientists were experimenting. He called this new fluid he thought he had discovered "animal electricity." Galvani was quickly shown to be wrong in his theory even if he was tremendously right in his observation. Galvani's compatriot Alessandro Volta was able to show, in 1800, that the electricity did not originate in the muscle but in the two metals. He combined metals in appropriate fashion — but in the complete absence of animal tissue of any sort — and obtained a flow of electricity. He had constructed the first electric battery and obtained the first electric current.

The electric current was in turn set to stimulating tissues, and it was quickly discovered that although muscles did contract under direct stimulation they were contracted more efficiently if the nerve leading to the muscle were stimulated. The concept grew firmer, throughout the 19th century, that nerves conducted stimulations and that the conduction was in the form of an electric current.

The source of the electricity in the lightning, in Volta's battery, and in the nerves was not truly understood until the inner structure of the atom began to be revealed about 1900. As the 20th century wore on it was discovered that the atom was composed of much smaller, *subatomic particles,* most of which carried an electric charge. In particular, the outer regions of various atoms consisted of circling *electrons,* tiny particles each of which carried a charge of the type that Franklin had arbitrarily described as negative. At the center of the atom, there was an *atomic nucleus* which carried a positive charge that balanced the negative charges of the circling electrons. If the atom were considered by itself, the two types of electric charges would balance and the atom as a whole would be neutral.

However, atoms interact with each other, and there is a tendency for some to gain electrons at the expense of others. In either case, whether electrons are gained or lost, the electrical neutrality is upset and the atom gains an overall charge and becomes an ion (see footnote, pp. 59–60). The electrons flowing from one set of atoms to another is like Franklin's fluid, except that Franklin had the flow in the wrong direction. (Nevertheless, we needn't worry about that.)

The atoms of the metals sodium and potassium have a strong tendency to lose a single electron each. What results are *sodium ion* and *potassium ion,* each carrying a single positive charge. On the other hand, the atom of the element chlorine has a strong tendency to pick up a single electron and become a negatively charged *chloride ion.**

The body is rich in sodium, potassium, and chlorine but the atoms of these elements invariably occur within the body in the form of ions.** It also contains many other ions. Calcium and

---

* It is "chloride ion" and not "chlorine ion" for reasons buried deep in the history of chemistry; it would be tedious to try to root them out. This is not a misprint.

** As a matter of fact, they occur in inanimate nature only in the form of ions. The neutral atoms of sodium and potassium make up active metals that can be isolated in the laboratory after expending considerable effort. And unless special precautions are taken, they will revert back to ionic form at once. Similarly, the neutral atoms of chlorine combine in pairs to form the poisonous chlorine gas that does not exist on earth except where it is manufactured through the manipulations of chemists.

magnesium each occur as doubly charged ions. Iron occurs in the form of ions carrying either two or three positive charges each. Sulfur and phosphorus combine with oxygen and hydrogen atoms to form groups that carry an overall negative charge. The groups of atoms making up the amino acid side-chains in protein molecules have in some cases a strong tendency to pick up an electron and in others to give one off (and in other cases neither), with the result that a protein molecule may have hundreds of positive and negative electric charges scattered over its surface.

Positively charged particles repel other positively charged particles and negatively charged particles repel other negatively charged particles. Positively and negatively charged particles, on the contrary, attract each other. These attractions and repulsions result in charges tending to exist in an even mixture. In any volume of reasonable size (say, large enough to be seen under the microscope) there is electrical neutrality therefore, as positives and negatives get as close as possible, each neutralizing the effect of the other. It takes considerable energy to maintain even a small separation of charge, and when this is done there is a tendency for the charges to mix once again. This can be done catastrophically in the form of a lightning bolt, or on a much smaller scale in the form of a Leyden jar discharge. In a chemical battery there is a small separation of charge that is continually set up in the metals; the electric current is the perpetual attempt of the electrons to flow from one metal to the other in an effort to restore neutrality.

If there is any form of electrical flow in the nerves, there must be a separation of charge first, and the answer to such a separation lies in the cell membranes.

THE CELL MEMBRANE

The cell is surrounded by a *semipermeable membrane*. It is semipermeable because some substances can penetrate it freely, whereas others cannot. The first generalization we can make is that small molecules, such as those of water and of oxygen, can pass through it freely; large molecules, such as those of starch and proteins, cannot. The simplest explanation of the method by which the membrane works would then seem to be that it contains submicroscopic holes so small that only small molecules can pass through.

Suppose this were so and that a particular small molecule bombarded the cell membrane from without. By sheer chance, a certain molecule would every once in a while strike one of the submicroscopic holes sufficiently dead-center to move right through into the cell interior. Such a molecule would be entering the cell by *diffusion* ("pour out" L). The rate at which molecules would enter the cell by diffusion would depend on the number of molecules hitting the tiny holes per unit of time. That would in turn depend on the total number of molecules striking the membrane altogether. And that would depend on the concentration of those molecules outside the cell. The greater the concentration, the larger the number of molecules striking the membrane and the larger would be the group finding their way through the holes. To sum up, the rate of diffusion into the cell depends on the concentration outside the cell.

If the particular molecule we are discussing existed also inside the cell, it would be bombarding the inner surface of the membrane as well. And occasionally a molecule inside would strike a hole and pass through out of the cell. Here also, the rate of diffusion out of the cell would depend on the concentration inside the cell.

If the concentration were higher outside the cell than inside, the rate of diffusion inward would be greater than that outward. The net movement of molecules would be toward the inside. The greater the concentration difference (or *concentration gradient*, as it is called), the faster this net movement. If the concentration were higher inside the cell than outside, the net movement of molecules would be outward. In either case, the net movement of molecules is from the region of higher concentration to that of lower concentration, in the direction of the slope of the concentration gradient, like an automobile coasting downhill. As the molecules move, the side with the low concentration builds up and that with the high concentration settles down. The concentration gradient becomes more gentle, the net movement slows, until at last, when the concentrations are equal on both sides of the membrane, no concentration gradient is left and there is no net movement at all.* It is like a coasting automobile reaching level ground and coming to a halt.

All this is to be expected of simple passive diffusion and, in fact, is found to be true of many types of molecules. In some cases, the cell acts as though it cannot wait upon the process of diffusion but must hurry it up. A substance such as glucose will enter the cell at a rate considerably faster than can be accounted for by diffusion alone (like an automobile moving downhill with its motor working and in gear). Such a situation is called *active transport* and consequently takes energy (the equivalent of the automobile's working motor). The exact mechanism by which this is accomplished is not yet known.

But let us apply this to ions. The cell membrane is freely permeable both to sodium ion and to potassium ion, which consist of single atoms and are not very much different in size from the water molecule. It might be expected, then, that if there were any difference in concentration of sodium ions and potassium ions inside and outside a cell the process of diffusion would equalize matters, and that, in the end, the concentration of these ions would be the same within and without. This, as a matter of fact, is true of dead cells. But not of living cells!

In living tissue, sodium ion is to be found almost entirely outside the cells in the *extracellular fluid*. The concentration of sodium ion is ten times as high outside the cell as it is inside. Potassium ion, in contrast, is found almost entirely within the cells in the *intracellular fluid*. The concentration of potassium ion

---

* With concentrations equal on both sides of the membrane, molecules are still moving, some going into the cell and some leaving. However, they go and leave at equal rates, so there is no net shift. Such a balance in the face of rapid movement in both directions is called a *dynamic equilibrium*.

is thirty times as high inside the cell as outside. What is more, under ordinary circumstances there seems no tendency to equalize this imbalance.

Such an unequal distribution of ions in the face of a concentration gradient can only be maintained through a continual expenditure of energy on the part of the cell. It is as though you were pulling apart one of those spring devices that gymnasiums use to develop the arm muscles. The natural state of the spring is one of contraction; but you can expand it through an expenditure of energy, and to keep it expanded requires a continuous expenditure of energy. If for any reason you were unable to maintain the energy expenditure, through weariness perhaps, or as a result of having some funny fellow poke you in the short ribs without warning, the spring contracts suddenly. When the cell dies and no longer expends energy, the ion concentrations on either side of the membrane equalize quickly.

The cell maintains the unequal distribution of ions by extruding the sodium ion — by kicking it out of the cell, in effect — as quickly as it drifts into the cell by diffusion; or, possibly, by turning it back before it even penetrates the membrane all the way. The sodium ion is thus forced to move against the concentration gradient like an automobile moving uphill. (Such an automobile cannot be conceived of as coasting; it *must* be expending energy; and so, likewise, must the cell.) To move sodium ion against a concentration gradient in this fashion is, to use still another simile, like pumping water uphill; the mechanism by which this sodium movement is accomplished is called the *sodium pump.* As yet no one knows precisely how the sodium pump works.

As the positively charged sodium ions are forced out of the cell, the interior of the cell builds up a negative charge, and the outside of the cell builds up a positive one. The positively charged potassium ions outside the cell are strongly repelled by the excess of positive charge in their neighborhood and are attracted by the negatively charged interior of the cell. They are thus both pushed and pulled into the cell. There is no "potassium pump" to undo this movement and the potassium ions remain inside the cell once there. Nor do they diffuse outward minus pump activity (as they would ordinarily, in order to equalize concentrations on both sides of the membrane), because the distribution of electric charge holds them in place. The inflowing potassium ions do not entirely neutralize the negative charge of the cell's interior. Instead, when all is done, a small negative charge still remains within the cell and a small positive charge remains outside.

The energy expended by the cell in running the sodium pump does three things. First, it maintains the sodium ion concentration unequal on the two sides of the membrane against a natural tendency toward equalization. Second, it maintains the potassium ion concentration unequal as well. Third, it maintains a separation of electric charge against the natural tendency of opposite charges to attract each other.

POLARIZATION AND DEPOLARIZATION

When there is a separation of charge, so that positive charge is concentrated in one place and negative charge in another, physicists speak of a *polarization of charge*. They do so because the situation resembles the manner in which opposite types of magnetic force are concentrated in the two ends, or poles,* of a bar magnet. Since, in the case we are discussing, there is a concentration of positive charge on one side of a membrane and a concentration of negative charge on the other, we can speak of a *polarized membrane*.

But whenever there is a separation of charge, an *electric potential* is set up. This measures the force tending to drive the separated charge together and wipe out the polarization. The electric potential is therefore also termed the *electromotive force* (the force tending to "move the electric charge"), which is usually abbreviated *EMF*.

---

* The magnetic poles derive their name, originally, from the fact that when allowed freedom of movement they pointed in the general directions of the earth's geographic poles.

The electric potential is spoken of as "potential" because it does not necessarily involve a motion of electricity, since the separation of charge can be maintained against the force driving the charges together if the proper energy is expended for the purpose (and in the cell, it is). The force is therefore only potential — one that will move the charge if the energy supply flags. Electric potential is measured in units named *volts*, after Volta, the man who built the first battery.

Physicists have been able to measure the electric potential that exists between the two sides of the living cell membrane. It comes to about 0.07 volts. Another way of putting it is to say it is equal to about 70 millivolts, a millivolt being equal to one thousandth of a volt. This is not much of a potential if it is compared with the 120 volts (or 120,000 millivolts) that exist in our household power lines, or with the many thousands of volts that can be built up for transmission of electric power over long distances. Notwithstanding, it is quite an amazing potential to be built up by a tiny cell with the materials it has at its disposal.

Anything that interrupts the activity of the sodium pump will bring about an abrupt equalization of the concentrations of the sodium ions and potassium ions on either side of the membrane. This will in turn automatically bring about an equalization of charge. The membrane will then be *depolarized*. Of course, this is what happens when the cell membrane is damaged or if the cell itself is killed. There are, nevertheless, three types of stimuli that will bring about depolarization without injuring the cell (if the stimuli are sufficiently gentle). These are mechanical, chemical, and electrical.

Pressure is an example of mechanical stimulation. Pressure upon a point in the membrane will stretch that portion of the membrane and (for reasons as yet unknown) bring about a depolarization. High temperature will expand the membrane and cold temperature contract it, and the mechanical change brought about in this fashion may also result in a depolarization.

A variety of chemicals will effect the same result, and so will a small electric current. (The last is the most obvious case. After all, why should not the electrical phenomena of a polarized membrane be upset by the imposition of an electric potential from without?)

When depolarization takes place at one point in a membrane, it acts as a stimulation for depolarization elsewhere. The sodium ion that floods into the cell at the point where the sodium pump has ceased to operate forces potassium ion out. The sodium ions, however, which are the smaller and nimbler of the two types, enter just a trifle more quickly than the potassium ions can leave. The result is that the depolarization overshoots the mark, and for a moment the interior of the cell takes on a small positive charge, thanks to the surplus of positively charged sodium ions that have entered, and a small negative charge is left outside the cell. The membrane is not merely depolarized, it is actually very slightly polarized in the opposite direction.

This opposed polarization may act as an electrical stimulus itself, one that stops the sodium pump in the regions immediately adjacent to the point of original stimulus. Those adjacent areas depolarize and then polarize slightly in the opposite direction, so as to stimulate depolarization in areas beyond. In this way a wave of depolarization travels along the entire membrane. At the initial point of stimulus the opposed polarization cannot be maintained for long. The potassium ions continue moving out of the cell and eventually catch up with the faster sodium ions; the small positive charge within the cell consequently is wiped out. This somehow reactivates the sodium pump at that point in the membrane, and sodium ions are pushed out once more and potassium ions drawn in. That portion of the membrane is *repolarized*. Since this happens at every point where the membrane is depolarized, there is a wave of repolarization following behind the wave of depolarization.

Between the moment of depolarization and the moment of complete repolarization the membrane will not respond to the usual stimuli. This is the *refractory period;* it lasts only a very short portion of a second. The wave of depolarization that follows a stimulus at any point on a membrane makes certain the cell's response to that stimulus as a unit. Exactly how the tiny electrical changes involved in a depolarization bring about a particular response is not known, but the fact of response is clear, and so is the fact that the response is unified. If a muscle is stimulated at one point by a gentle electric shock, it contracts, because this is the natural muscular response to a stimulus. But it is not just the stimulated point that contracts. It is an entire muscle fiber. The wave of depolarization travels through a muscle fiber at a rate of anywhere from 0.5 to 3 meters per second, depending on the size of the fiber, and this is fast enough to make it seem to contract as a unit.

These polarization-depolarization-repolarization phenomena are common to all cells, but are far more pronounced in some than in others. Cells have developed that take special advantage of the phenomena. These specializations can take place in one of two directions. First, and rather uncommonly, organs can be developed in which the electric potential is built up to high values. On stimulus the resultant depolarization is not translated into muscular contraction or any of the other common responses but makes itself evident, instead, as a flow of electricity. This does not represent a waste: if the stimulus arises from the activity of an enemy, the electrical response can hurt or kill that enemy.

There are seven families of fish (some in the bony fish group, some among the sharks) that have specialized in this fashion. The most spectacular example is the fish popularly called the "electric eel," which has the very significant formal name of *Electrophorus electricus*. The electric eel occurs in the fresh waters of northern South America: the Orinoco River, the Amazon River and its tributaries. It is not related to the common eels, but receives its name because of its elongated eel-like body, which reaches lengths of some 6 to 9 feet. This elongation is almost entirely due to tail — some four fifths of the creature is tail. All the ordinary organs are crowded into the forward 12 to 18 inches of the body.

More than half of the long tail is filled with a series of modified muscles that make up the "electric organ." The individual muscles produce no more potential than any ordinary muscle would, but there are thousands upon thousands of them arranged in such a fashion that all the potentials are added. A fully rested electric eel can develop a potential of up to 600 or 700 volts, and it can discharge as often as 300 times per second when first stimulated. Eventually this fades off to perhaps 50 discharges per second, but that rate can be maintained for a long time. The electric shock so produced is large enough to kill quickly any smaller animal it might use for food and hurt badly any large animal that might have the misguided intention of eating the eels.

The electric organ is an excellent weapon in itself. Perhaps more creatures would have specialized in this fashion if the organ were not so space-consuming. Imagine how few animals would have developed powerful fangs and claws if, in order to do so, more than half of the mass of the body would have had to be devoted to them.

The second type of specialization involving the electrical phenomena of cell membranes lies not in the direction of intensifying the potential but in that of hastening the speed of transmission of depolarization. Cells with thin elongated processes are developed, and these processes are, after all, virtually all membrane. They have as their chief function the very rapid transmission of the effects of a stimulus at one part of the body to another part. It is such cells that make up the nerve — which brings us back to the subject of concern at the beginning of this chapter.

THE NEURON

The nerves that are easily visible to the unaided eye are not single cells. Rather, they are bundles of *nerve fibers*, sometimes a good many of them, each of which is itself a portion of a cell. The fibers are all traveling in the same direction and are bound

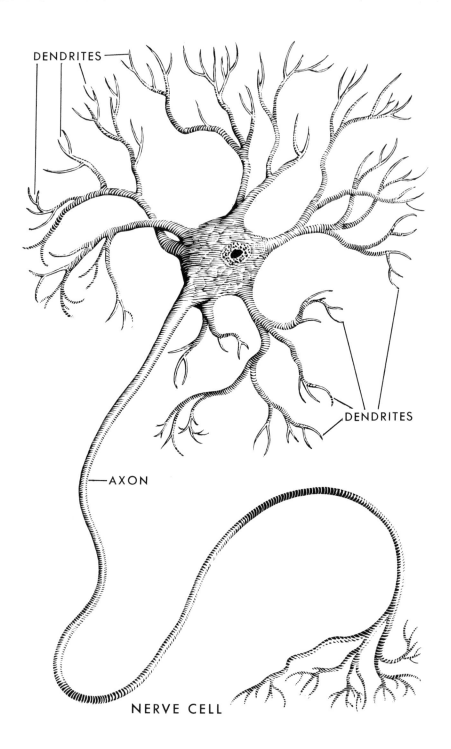

DENDRITES

DENDRITES

AXON

NERVE CELL

together for the sake of convenience, though the individual fibers of the bundle may have widely differing functions. The principle is the same as that in which a number of conducting wires, insulated from each other and each fulfilling its own function, are bound together for convenience's sake into an electric cable.

The nerve fiber itself is part of a *nerve cell*, which is also known as a *neuron* (nyoo'ron). This is the Greek equivalent of the Latin-derived "nerve" and was applied by the Greeks of the Hippocratic age to the nerves themselves and to tendons. Now the word is applied exclusively to the individual nerve cell. The main portion of the neuron, the *cell body*, is not too different from other cells. It contains a nucleus and cytoplasm. Where it is most distinct from cells of other types is that out of the cell body, long, threadlike projections emerge. Over most of the cell there are numerous projections that branch out into still finer extensions. These branching threads resemble the branchings of a tree and are called *dendrites* ("tree" G).

At one point of the cell, however, there is a particularly long extension that usually does not branch throughout most of its sometimes enormous length. This is the *axon* (so named for reasons to be given later). It is the axon that is the nerve fiber in the typical nerve, and such a fiber, although microscopically thin, is sometimes several feet long, which is unusual, considering that it is part of a single cell.

Depolarization setting in at some point of these cell projections are rapidly propagated onward. The wave of depolarization traveling along these nerve-cell processes is referred to as the *nerve impulse*. The impulse can travel in either direction along the processes; and if the fiber is stimulated in the middle the impulse will travel out in both directions from this point. However, in the living system it happens that the nerve impulse in the dendrites virtually always travels toward the cell body, whereas in the axon it travels away from the cell body.

The speed of the nerve impulse was first measured in 1852 by the German scientist Hermann von Helmholtz. He did this by stimulating a nerve at different points and noting the time it took for the muscle, to which it was attached, to respond. If an additional length of nerve was involved there was a small delay and that represented the time it took for the nerve impulse to cross that additional length. Interestingly enough, this demonstration took place just six years after the famous German physiologist Johannes Müller, in a fit of conservatism such as occasionally afflicts scientists in their later years, had stated categorically that no man would ever succeed in measuring the speed of the nerve impulse.

The impulse does not move at the same rate in all nerves. For one thing, the rate at which a nerve impulse travels along an axon varies roughly with the width of the axon. The wider the axon, the more rapid the rate of propagation. In very fine nerve fibers the impulse moves quite slowly, at a rate of two meters per second or less; no faster, in other words, than the motion of the wave of depolarization in muscle. Obviously, where an organism must react quickly to some stimulus, faster and faster rates of nerve-impulse propagations are desirable. One way of arranging this is to make use of thicker and thicker fibers. In the human body, where the smallest fibers are 0.5 microns in diameter (a micron being 1/1000 of a millimeter), the largest are 20 microns in diameter. The largest are thus 40 times as wide as the smallest and possess 1600 times the cross-sectional area.

One might think that since the vertebrates had a better-developed nervous system than do any other group of creatures, they would naturally have the fastest-moving nerve impulses and therefore the thickest nerve fibers. This is not so. The lowly cockroach has some axons thicker than any in man. The extreme, as far as sheer size is concerned, is reached in the largest and most advanced mollusks, the squids. The large squids probably represent the most advanced and highly organized of all the invertebrates. Combining that with their physical size, we find it not surprising that they require the fastest nerve-impulse rates and the thickest axons. Those leading to the squid's muscles are commonly referred to as "giant axons" and are up to a millimeter in diameter. These are 50 times the diameter of the thickest mammalian axons and possess 2500 times the cross-sectional area. The giant axons of the squid have proved a godsend to neurologists, who were able to perform experiments on them easily (such as measuring directly the electrical potential across the axon membrane) that could be performed only with great difficulty upon the tenuous fibers present in vertebrates.

And yet why should invertebrates outpace vertebrates in axon thickness when the vertebrates have the more highly developed nervous system? The answer is that vertebrates do not depend on thickness alone. They have developed another and more subtle method for increasing the rate of propagation of the nerve impulse.

In vertebrates, the nerve fiber is surrounded during its process of formation in very early life with "satellite cells." Some of these are referred to as Schwann's cells (shvahnz) after the German zoologist Theodor Schwann, who was one of the founders of the cell theory of life. The Schwann's cells fold themselves about the axon, wrapping in a tighter and tighter spiral, coating the fiber with a fatty layer called the *myelin sheath* (my'uh-lin; "marrow" G, the reason for the name being uncertain). The Schwann's cells finally form a thin membrane called the *neurilemma* (nyoo'rih-lem'uh; "nerve-skin" G), which still contains the nuclei of the original Schwann's cells. (It was Schwann who first described the neurilemma in 1839, so that it is sometimes called the "sheath of Schwann." As a result a rather unmusical and unpleasant memorial to the zoologist lies in the fact that a tumor of the neurilemma is sometimes called a "schwannoma.")

A particular Schwann's cell wraps itself about only a limited section of the axon. As a result, an axon has a myelin sheath that exists in sections. In the intervals between the original Schwann's cells are narrow regions where the myelin sheath does not exist, so that the axon rather resembles a string of sausages. These constricted unmyelinated regions are called *nodes of Ranvier* (rahn-vee-ay), after the French histologist Louis Antoine

Ranvier, who described them in 1878. The axon is like a thin line running down the axis of the interrupted cylinder formed by the myelin sheath. The word "axon" comes from "axis," in fact, with the "on" suffix substituted because of the presence of that suffix in the word "neuron."

The functions of the myelin sheath are not entirely clear to us. The simplest suggestion is that they insulate the nerve fiber, allowing a smaller loss of electric potential to the surroundings. Such a loss increases as a nerve fiber grows thinner, so that the presence of insulation allows a fiber to remain thin without undue loss of efficiency. Evidence in favor of this rests in the fact that the myelin sheath is composed largely of fatty material, which is indeed a good electrical insulator. (It is this fatty material that gives nerves their white appearance. The cell body of the nerve is grayish.)

If the myelin sheath served only as an insulator and nothing else, very simple fat molecules would do for the purpose. Instead, the chemical composition of the sheath is most complex. About two out of every five molecules within it are cholesterol. Two more are phosphatides (a type of phosphorus-containing fat molecule), and a fifth is a cerebroside (a complex sugar-containing fatlike molecule). Small quantities of other unusual substances are present, too. The existence of sheath properties other than mere insulation would therefore seem very likely.

It has also been suggested that the myelin sheath serves somehow to maintain the integrity of the axon. The axon stretches so far from the cell body that it seems quite reasonable to assume it can no longer maintain active communication throughout its length with the cell nucleus — and the nucleus is vital to cellular activity and integrity. Perhaps the sheath cells, which retain their nuclei, act as nursemaids, in a manner of speaking, for successive sections of the axon. Even nerves without myelin sheaths have axons that are surrounded by layers of small Schwann's cells with, of course, nuclei.

Finally, the sheath must somehow accelerate the speed of

propagation of the nerve impulse. A fiber with a sheath conducts the impulse much more rapidly than a fiber of the same diameter without a sheath. That is why vertebrates have been able to retain thin fibers and yet vastly increase the speed of impulse.

In the mammalian myelinated nerve, the impulse travels at a velocity of about 100 meters per second, or, if you prefer, 225 miles an hour. This is quite fast enough. The greatest stretch of mammalian tissue that has ever existed in a single organism is the hundred feet separating the nose end of a blue whale from its tail end; the nerve impulse along a myelinated axon could negotiate that distance in 3/10 of a second. The distance from head to toe in a man six feet tall could be covered in 1/50 of a second. The superiority of the nerve impulse, in terms of speed, over hormone coordination is, as you see, tremendous.

The process of myelination is not quite complete at birth, and various functions do not develop until the corresponding nerves are myelinated. Thus, the baby does not see at first; this must await the myelinization of the optic nerve, which, to be sure, is not long delayed. Also, the nerves connecting to the muscles of the legs are not fully myelinated until the baby is more than a year old, and the complex interplay of muscles involved in walking are delayed that long.

Occasionally an adult will suffer from a "demyelinating disease" in which sections of myelin sheathing degenerates, with consequent loss of function of the nerve fiber. The best known of these diseases is *multiple sclerosis* ("hard" G). This receives its name because demyelination occurs in many patches, spread out over the body, the soft myelin being replaced by a scar of harder fibrous tissue. Such demyelination may come about through the effect on the myelin of a protein in the patient's blood. The protein seems to be an "antibody," one of the class of substances that usually react only with foreign proteins, and often produce symptoms with which we are familiar as "allergies." In essence, the sufferer from multiple sclerosis may be allergic to himself and multiple sclerosis may be an example of an auto-allergic disease.

Since those nerves that receive sensations are most likely to be attacked, double vision, loss of the ability to feel, and other abnormal sensations are common symptoms. Multiple sclerosis most often attacks people in the 20-to-40 age group. It may be progressive — that is, more and more nerves may become involved, so that death eventually follows. The progress of the disease can be slow, however, death sometimes not following for ten or more years after its onset.

ACETYLCHOLINE

Any neuron does not exist in isolation. It usually makes contact with another neuron. This happens through an intermingling of the axon of one neuron (the axon branches at its extreme tip) with at least some of the dendrites of another. At no point do the processes of one cell actually join the processes of another. Instead there is a microscopic, but definite, gap between the ends of the processes of two neighboring neurons. The gap is called a *synapse* (sih-naps'; "union" G, although a union in the true sense is exactly what it is not).

This raises a problem. The nerve impulse does indeed travel from one neuron to the next, but how does it travel across the synaptic gap? One thought is that it "sparks" across, just as an electric current leaps across an ordinarily insulating gap of air from one conducting medium to another when the electric potential is high enough. However, the electric potentials involved in nerve impulses (with the exception of certain reported instances in the crayfish) are not high enough to force currents across the insulating gap. Some other solution must be sought, and if electricity will not help we must turn to chemistry.

A very early effect of a stimulus on a nerve is that of bringing about a reaction between acetic acid and choline, two compounds commonly present in cells. The substance formed is *acetylcholine* (as'ih-til-koh'leen). It is this acetylcholine which alters the working of the sodium pump so that depolarization takes place and the nerve impulse is initiated.

It is easy to visualize the acetylcholine as coating the membrane and altering its properties. This is the picture some people draw of hormone action in general, and for this reason acetylcholine is sometimes considered an example of a *neurohormone* — that is, a hormone acting on the nerves. The resemblance, however, is not perfect. Acetylcholine is not secreted into and transported by the bloodstream, as is true in the case of all hormones I described in the first part of this book. Instead, acetylcholine is secreted at the nerve-cell membrane and acts upon the spot. This difference has caused some people to prefer to speak of acetylcholine as a *neurohumor*, "humor" being an old-fashioned medical term for a biological fluid (from a Latin word for "moisture").

The acetylcholine formed by the nerve cannot be allowed to remain in being for long, because there would be no repolarization while it is present. Fortunately, nerves contain an enzyme called *cholinesterase* (koh'lin-es'tur-ays) which brings about the breakup of acetylcholine to acetic acid and choline once more. Following that breakup the cell membrane is altered again and repolarization can take place. Both formation and breakup of acetylcholine is brought about with exceeding rapidity, and the chemical changes keep up quite handily with the measured rates of depolarization and repolarization taking place along the course of a nerve fiber.

The evidence for the acetylcholine/cholinesterase accompaniment to the nerve impulse is largely indirect, but it is convincing. All nerve cells contain the enzymes that form acetylcholine and break it down. This means that the substance is found in all multicellular animals except the very simplest: the sponges and jellyfish. In particular, cholinesterase is found in rich concentration in the electric organs of the electric eel, and the electric potential generated by the eel is at all times proportional to the concentration of enzyme present. Furthermore, any substance that blocks the action of cholinesterase puts a stop to the nerve impulse.

And so the picture arises of a nerve impulse that is a coordinated chemical and electrical effect, the two traveling together down the length of an axon. This is a more useful view than that of the nerve impulse as electrical in nature only, for when we arrive at the synapse and find that the electrical effect cannot cross we are no longer helpless: the chemical effect can cross easily. The acetylcholine liberated at the axon endings of one nerve will affect the dendrites, or even the cell body itself, across the synapse and initiate a new nerve impulse there. The electrical effect and chemical effect will then travel down the second neuron together until the chemical effect takes over alone at the next synapse, and so on. (The impulse moves from axon to dendrites and not in the other direction. It is this which forces nerve messages to travel along a one-way route despite the ability of nerve processes to carry the impulse either way.)

The axon of a neuron may make a junction not only with another neuron but also with some organ to which it carries its impulse, usually a muscle. The tip of the axon makes intimate contact with the *sarcolemma* (sahr'koh-lem'uh; "skin of the flesh" G), which is the membrane enclosing the muscle fiber. There, in the intimate neighborhood of the muscle, it divides into numerous branches, each ending in a separate muscle fiber. Again there is no direct fusion between the axon and the muscle fibers. Instead, a distinct — if microscopic — gap exists. This synapse-like connection between nerve and muscle is called the *neuromuscular junction* (or *myoneural junction*).

At the neuromuscular junction, the chemical and electrical aspects of the nerve impulse arrive. Once more the electrical effect stops, but the chemical effect bridges the gap. The secretion of acetylcholine alters the properties of the muscle cell membrane, brings about the influx of sodium ion, and, in short, initiates a wave of depolarization just like that which takes place in a nerve cell. The muscle fibers, fed this wave by the nerve endings, respond by contracting. All the muscle fibers to which the various branches of a single nerve are connected contract as a unit, and such a group of fibers is referred to, consequently, as a *motor unit*.

Any substance that will inhibit the action of cholinesterase and put an end to the cycle of acetylcholine buildup and breakdown thus will not only put an end to the nerve impulse but will also put an end to the stimulation and contraction of muscles. This will mean paralysis of the voluntary muscles of the limbs and chest and of the heart muscle as well. Death will consequently follow such inhibition quickly, in from two to ten minutes.

During the 1940's German chemists, in the course of research with insecticides, developed a number of substances that turned out to be powerful cholinesterase inhibitors. These are deadly indeed. As liquids they penetrate the skin without damage or sensation, and, once they reach the bloodstream, kill quickly. They are much more subtle and deadly than were the comparatively crude poison gases of World War I. Germany did not make use of them in World War II, but under the name "nerve gases" mention is sometimes made of their possible use in World War III (assuming anything is left to be done after the first nuclear stroke and counterstroke).

Nature need not in this case take a back seat to human ingenuity. There are certain alkaloids that are excellent cholinesterase inhibitors and, therefore, excellent killers. There is *curare* (kyoo-rah′ree), which was used as an arrow poison by South American Indians. (When news of it penetrated the outside world, this gave rise to legends of "mysterious untraceable South American toxins" that filled a generation of mystery thrillers.) Another example of natural cholinesterase inhibitors is the toxins of certain toadstools, including one that is very appropriately entitled "the angel of death."

Even nerve gases have their good side, nevertheless. It sometimes happens that a person possesses neuromuscular junctions across which the nerve impulse travels with difficulty. This condition is *myasthenia gravis* (my-as-thee′nee-uh gra′vis; "serious muscle weakness" G) and is marked by a progressive weakening of muscles, particularly of the face. Here the most likely fault is that the acetylcholine formation at the neuromuscular junction is insufficient, or perhaps that it is formed in normal amounts but is too quickly broken down by cholinesterase. The therapeutic use of a cholinesterase-inhibitor conserves the acetylcholine and can, at least temporarily, improve muscle action.

Although muscle tissue can be stimulated directly and made to contract — by means of an electric current, for illustration — muscle is, under normal conditions, stimulated only by impulses arriving along the nerve fibers. For that reason, any damage to the fibers, either through mechanical injury or as a result of a disease such as poliomyelitis, can result in paralysis. An axon which has degenerated through injury or disease can sometimes be regenerated, provided its neurilemma has remained intact. Where the neurilemma has been destroyed or where the axon is one lacking a neurilemma (as many are) regeneration is impossible. Further, if the cell body of any nerve is destroyed, it cannot be replaced. (Nevertheless, all is not necessarily lost. In 1963 human nerves were transplanted successfully from one person to another for the first time. There is a reasonable possibility that the time will come when "nerve banks" will exist and when paralysis through loss of nerve function can be successfully treated.)

A particular nerve fiber shows no gradations in its impulse. That is, one does not find that a weak stimulus sets up a weak impulse, while a stronger stimulus sets up a stronger impulse. The neuron is constructed to react completely or not at all. An impulse too weak to initiate the nerve impulse does nothing effective; it is "subthreshold." To be sure, some minor changes in the membrane potential may be noted and there may be the equivalent of a momentary flow of current, but that dies out quickly. (If, however, a second subthreshold stimulus follows before that momentary flow dies out, the two together may be strong enough to initiate the impulse.)

It would seem that a small current of electricity won't last long in the nerve — its resistance is too high. On the other hand, a stimulus just strong enough to initiate the impulse ("threshold stimulus") results in an electrical and chemical effect which is regenerated all along the nerve fiber and does not fade out. (How the regeneration takes place is uncertain, though there is a strong suspicion that the nodes of Ranvier are involved.) The threshold stimulus produces the fiber's maximum response. A stronger stimulus can produce no stronger impulse. This is the "all-or-none law" and may be simply stated: a nerve fiber either propagates an impulse of maximum strength or propagates no impulse at all.

The all-or-none law extends to the organ stimulated by the nerve. A muscle fiber receiving a stimulus from a nerve fiber responds with a contraction of constant amount. This seems to go against common knowledge. If a nerve fiber always conducts the same impulse, if it conducts any at all, and if a muscle fiber always contracts with the same force, if it contracts at all, then how is it we can contract our biceps to any desired degree from the barest twitch to a full and forceful contraction?

The answer is that we cannot consider nerve and muscle isolated either in space or time. An organ is not necessarily fed by a single nerve fiber, but may be fed by dozens of them. Each nerve fiber has its own threshold level, depending on its diameter, for one thing. The larger fibers tend to have a lower threshold for stimulation. A weak stimulus, then, may be enough to set off some of the fibers and not the others. (A stimulus so weak that it suffices to set off only one nerve fiber is the *minimal stimulus*.) A muscle would merely twitch if a single motor unit would contract under the minimal stimulus. As the stimulus rises, more and more nerve fibers would fire; more and more motor units would contract. Eventually, when the stimulus was strong enough to set off all the nerve fibers (*maximal stimulus*), the muscle would contract completely. A stimulus stronger than this will do no more.

There is also the matter of time. If a nerve fiber carries an impulse, the motor unit to which it is connected contracts and then relaxes. The relaxation takes time. If a second impulse follows before relaxation is complete, the muscle contracts again, but from a headstart, so that it contracts further the second time. A third impulse adds a further total contraction, and so on. The faster one impulse follows another the greater the contraction of the muscle. The number of impulses per second that can be delivered by a nerve fiber is very high and depends upon the length of the refractory period. Small fibers have refractory periods of as long as 1/250 of a second, which, even so, means that as many as 250 impulses per second can be delivered. Ten times as many can be delivered by the large myelinated nerve fibers.

In actual fact, a muscle is usually stimulated by some portion of the nerve fibers that feed into it, each fiber firing a certain number of times a second. The result of these two variable effects is that, without violating the all-or-none law, a muscle can be made to contract in extremely fine gradations of intensity.

7

OUR NERVOUS SYSTEM

CEPHALIZATION

For nerve cells to perform their function of organizing and coordinating the activity of the many organs that make up a multicellular creature, they must themselves be organized into a nervous system. It is the quality and complexity of this nervous system that more than anything else dictates the quality and complexity of the organism. Man considers himself to be at the peak of the evolutionary ladder, and although self-judgment is always suspect there is at least one good objective argument in favor of this. The nervous system of man is more complex, for his size, than is that of any other creature in existence (with the possible exception of some cetaceans). Since our nervous system is the clearest mark of our superiority as a species, I think it is important to see how it came to develop to its present state.

The simplest creatures that possess specialized nerve cells are the *coelenterates* (sih-len'tur-ayts), which include such organisms as the freshwater hydra and the jellyfish. Here already there is a nervous system of sorts. The neurons are scattered more or less regularly over the surface of the body, each being connected by synapses to those nearest to it. In this fashion, a stimulus applied to any part of the creature is conducted to all parts. Such a nervous system in a sense is merely an elaboration on a larger scale of what already existed in unicellular creatures. Among them, the cell membrane is itself excitable and conducts the equivalent of a nerve impulse to all parts of itself. The nerve network of the coelenterate does the same thing, acting as a supermembrane of a supercell. The results of such an arrangement, however, represent no great advance. Any stimulus anywhere on the coelenterate body alerts the entire organism indiscriminately and results in a response of the whole, which proceeds to contract, sway, or undulate. Fine control is not to be expected. Furthermore, since there are so many synapses to be passed (each a bottleneck), conduction of the nerve impulse is in general slow.

The next more complicated group of animals are the flatworms, which, although still simple, show certain developments that foreshadow the structure of all other, more complicated, animals. They are the first to have the equivalent of muscle tissue and to make effective use of muscles; the efficiency of the neuron network hence must be improved. Such improvements do indeed take place in at least some flatworms. The nerve cells in these creatures are concentrated in a pair of *nerve cords* running the length of the body. At periodic intervals along the length of the cords, there emerge nerves that receive stimuli from or deliver impulses to various specific body regions. The nerve cords represent the first beginnings of what is called the *central nervous system,* and the nerves make up the *peripheral nervous system.* This division of the nervous system into two chief portions holds true for all animals more advanced than the flatworm, up to and including man.

In any creature with a central nervous system, a stimulus will no longer induce a response from the whole body generally. Instead, a stimulus at some given part of the body sets off a nerve impulse that is not distributed to all other neurons but is carried directly to the nerve cord. It passes quickly along the nerve cord to a particular nerve, which will activate a specific organ, or organs, and bring about a response appropriate to the original stimulus.

The coelenterate system would correspond to a telephone network in which all subscribers are on a single party line, so that any call from one to another rouses every one of the subscribers, who are then free to listen and probably do. The flatworm system resembles a telephone network in which an operator connects the caller directly with the desired party. We can see at once that the operator-run telephone network is more efficient than the one-big-party line.

Early in the evolutionary process, however, the nerve cords became more than simple cords. The nerve cord had to specialize, even in the flatworms, and this specialization arose, in all probability because of the shape of the flatworm. The flatworm is the simplest living multicellular animal to have *bilateral symmetry*, and its primeval ancestors must have been the first to develop this. (By bilateral symmetry, we mean that if a plane is imagined drawn through the body it can be drawn in such a way as to divide the creature into a right and left half, each of which is the mirror-image of the other.) All animals more complicated than the flatworms are bilaterally symmetrical; ourselves most definitely included. One seeming exception is the starfish and their relatives, for these possess *radial symmetry*. (In radial symmetry, similar organs or structures project outward from a center, like so many radiuses in a circle.) The seeming exception is only a seeming one, for the radial symmetry of the starfish is a secondary development in the adult. The young forms (larvae) exhibit bilateral symmetry; the radial symmetry develops later as a kind of regression to an older day.

Animals simpler than the flatworms, such as the coelenterates, sponges, and single-celled creatures, generally have either radial symmetry or no marked symmetry at all. The same is true of plants: the daisy's petals are a perfect example of radial symmetry and the branches of a tree extend unsymmetrically in all directions from the trunk. This grand division of living creatures into those with bilateral symmetry and those without is of vital importance. An animal with no marked symmetry or with radial symmetry need have no preferred direction of movement. There is no reason why one particular leg of a starfish should take the lead in movement over any other.

A creature with bilateral symmetry is usually longest in the direction of the plane of symmetry and tends to progress along that plane. Other directions of movement are possible, but one direction is preferred. If a bilaterally symmetric creature, by reason of its very shape and structure, adopts one preferred direction of movement, then one end of its body is generally breaking new ground as it moves. It is constantly entering a new portion of the environment. It is that end of the body which is the head.

Obviously, it is important that the organism have ways of testing the environment in order that appropriate responses be made, responses of a nature to protect its existence. It must be able to check the chemical nature of the environment, avoiding poison and approaching food. It must detect temperature changes, vibrations, certain types of radiation, and the like. Organs designed to receive such sensations are most reasonably located in the head, since that is the ground-breaking portion of the body. It meets the new section of the environment first. The mouth also is most reasonably located in the head, since the head is the first portion of the body to reach the food. The end opposite the head (that is, the tail) is comparatively featureless.

In consequence, the two ends of the bilaterally symmetric creature are in general different, and living creatures of this type have distinct heads and tails. The differentiation of a head region marked by sense organs and a mouth is referred to as *cephalization* ("head" G). The process of cephalization has its internal effects on the nervous system. If a bilaterally symmetric creature were equal-ended, the nerve cords would, understandably enough, be expected to be equal-ended as well. But with a distinct head region containing specialized sense organs, it would be reasonable to suppose that the nerve cords in that head region would be rather more complex than elsewhere. The nerve endings in the specialized sense organs would be more numerous than elsewhere in the body, and the receiving cell bodies (most logically placed at the head end of the cord, since this is the portion nearest the sense organs) would likewise have to be more numerous.

Even in flatworms there is an enlargement and enrichment of the nerve cord at the head end, therefore. Such an enlargement might be called the first and most primitive *brain.* Not surprisingly, the brain grows more complex as the organism itself grows more complex. It reaches the pinnacle of its development in the Phylum** *Chordata*, the one to which we ourselves belong.

The special position of Chordata with respect to the nervous system is shown in the very nature of the nerve cord. The double nerve cord of the flatworms persists in most phyla. It remains a solid tube in structure and is ventrally located; that is, it runs along the abdominal surface of the body. Only in Chordata is this general scheme radically altered. In place of a solid double nerve cord, there is a single cord in the form of a hollow cylinder. Instead of being ventrally located, it is dorsally located — it lies along the back surface of the body. This single, hollow, dorsal nerve cord is possessed by all chordates (members of the Phylum Chordata), and by chordates only; and, if we judge by results, it is much preferable to the older form that had been first elaborated by the distant ancestors of the flatworms.

THE CHORDATES

The Phylum Chordata is divided into four subphyla, of which three are represented today by primitive creatures that are not very successful in the scheme of life. In these three, the nerve cord receives no special protection any more than it does in the phyla other than Chordata.

---

* The word "brain" is from the Anglo-Saxon but it may be related to a Greek word referring to the top of the head. A less common synonym for brain is *encephalon* (en-sef'uh-lon; "in the head" G). This name is most familiar to the general public in connection with a disease characterized by the inflammation of brain tissue, since this disease is known as *encephalitis*.

** The animal kingdom is divided into *phyla* (fy'luh; "tribe" G, singular, *phylum*), each representing a group with one general type of body plan. A discussion of the various phyla and of the development of Chordata is to be found in Chapter 1 of *The Human Body*.

In the fourth and most advanced subphylum of Chordata, on the contrary, the nerve cord receives special protection in the form of enclosure by a series of hard structures of either cartilage or bone. These structures are the vertebrae, and for this reason the subphylum is called *Vertebrata* (vur'tih-bray'tuh) and its members commonly referred to as the vertebrates.

And it is only among the vertebrate subphylum that the brain becomes prominent. Of the other three subphyla, the most advanced (or, at least, the one that most resembles the vertebrates) is the one that contains a small fishlike creature called the amphioxus. The similarity to fish (resting chiefly on the fact that it has a cigar-shaped body) vanishes upon closer inspection. For one thing, the amphioxus turns out to have not much of a head. One end of it has a fringed suckerlike mouth and the other a finny fringe, and that is about all the difference. The two ends come to roughly similar points. In fact, the very name amphioxus is from Greek words meaning "both-pointed," with reference to the two ends. This lack of advanced cephalization is reflected internally; the nerve cord runs forward into the head region with scarcely any sign of specialization. The amphioxus is virtually a brainless creature.

Among the vertebrates, however, the situation changes. Even in the most primitive living class of vertebrates (a class containing such creatures as the lamprey, an organism that has not yet developed the jaws and limbs characteristic of all the other and more complex vertebrate classes) the forward end of the nerve cord has already swelled into a clear brain. Nor is it a simple swelling. It is, rather, a series of three — a kind of triple brain — the swellings being named (from the front end backward) the *forebrain, midbrain,* and *hindbrain.* These three basic divisions remain in all higher vertebrates, although they have been much modified and have been overlaid with added structures.

When the vertebrates first developed, some half-billion years ago, the early primitive specimens developed armor covering their head and foreparts generally. Such armor has the disadvantage of adding deadweight to the creature and cutting down speed and maneuverability; among vertebrates generally, the development of armor has never been a pathway to success.* And yet the brain had to be protected. A compromise was struck whereby the armor was drawn in beneath the skin and confined to the brain alone. In this way the skull was developed.

The vertebrates rely not on the passive defense of a shell but on speed, maneuverability, and the weapons of attack. The central nervous system — the brain and nerve cord — was excepted; for in all vertebrates it is carefully enclosed in cartilage or bone, a shelled organ within an unshelled organism. Certainly this seems a rather clear indication of the special importance of the brain and nerve cord in vertebrates.

The three sections of the brain show further specializations, even in primitive vertebrates. From the lower portion of the most forward portion of the forebrain are a pair of outgrowths which received the nerves from the nostrils and are therefore concerned with the sense of smell. These outgrowths are the *olfactory lobes* ("smell" L); see illustration, page 196. Behind the olfactory lobes are a pair of swellings on the upper portion of the forebrain, and these make up the *cerebrum* (sehr′uh-brum; "brain" L). The portion of the forebrain that lies behind the cerebrum is the *thalamus* (thal′uh-mus).** The midbrain bears swellings that are particularly concerned with the sense of sight and are therefore termed the *optic lobes* ("sight" G).

The hindbrain develops a swelling in the upper portion of the region adjoining the midbrain. This swelling is the *cerebellum* (sehr′uh-bel′um; "little brain" L). The region behind the cerebellum narrows smoothly to the point where it joins the long section of unspecialized nerve cord behind the head. This final region is the *medulla oblongata* (meh-dul′uh ob′long-gay′tuh;

---

* Examples of modern armored vertebrates are the turtles, armadillos, and pangolins, all relatively unsuccessful.

** This word is from the Greek and refers to a type of room. The name arose among the Romans who felt this section of the brain was hollow and therefore resembled a room.

"rather long marrow" L). It is "marrow" in the sense that it is a soft organ set within hard bone, and, unlike other portions of the human brain, is elongated rather than bulgy.

This is the essence of the brain throughout all the classes of Vertebrata. There are shifts in emphasis, though, depending on whether smell or sight is the more important sense. In fish and amphibians smell is the chief sense, so the olfactory lobes are well developed. In birds, smell is comparatively unimportant and sight is the chief sense. In the bird brain, therefore, the olfactory lobes are small and unimpressive, whereas the optic lobes are large and well developed.

The development of the brain into something more than a sight-and-smell machine involved the cerebrum primarily. The outer coating of the cerebrum, containing numerous cell bodies that lend the surface a grayish appearance, is the *cerebral cortex* ("cortex" being the Latin word for outer rind, or bark), or the *pallium* ("cloak" L). It can also be termed, more colloquially, the "gray matter." This, in fish or amphibians, is chiefly concerned with sorting out the smell sensations and directing responses that would increase the creature's chance to obtain food or escape an enemy.

In the reptiles the cerebrum usually is distinctly larger and more specialized than in fish or amphibians. One explanation for this may well be that the dry-land habitat of the reptile is much more hostile to life than the ocean and fresh water in which the older classes of Vertebrata developed. On land, the medium of air is so much less viscous than that of water that faster movement is possible, which in itself requires more rapid coordination of muscular action. In addition, the full force of gravity, unneutralized by buoyancy, presents greater dangers and again places a premium on efficient muscle action.

Therefore, although the reptilian cerebrum is still mainly concerned with the analysis of smell and taste sensations, it is larger, and in the part of the cerebral cortex nearest the front end there is the development of something new. This new portion of the cortex is the *neopallium* (nee'oh-pal'ee-um; "new cloak" L). It consists of tracts of nerve cell bodies involved with the receipt of sensations other than smell. In the neopallium a greater variety of information is received and more complicated coordinations can be set up. The reptile can now move surefootedly, despite the upsetting pull of gravity. The neopallium was developed further in that group of reptiles which, about 100 million years ago or so, underwent some remarkable changes — changing scales into hair, developing warm-bloodedness, and, in general, becoming mammals, the most complex and successful class of Vertebrata.

In primitive mammals the cerebrum is even larger than in reptiles, although remaining just as specialized for reception of smell sensations. At least the pallium remains so. However, there is a large expansion in the size of the neopallium, which spreads out to cover the top half of the cerebral cortex.

The larger the neopallium, which is the center of a great variety of coordinations among stimuli and responses, the more complex the potentialities of behavior. A simple brain may have room for only one response to a particular stimulus; a more complex brain will have room to set up neuron combinations that can distinguish different gradations of a stimulus and take into account the different circumstances surrounding the stimulus, so that a variety of responses, each appropriate to the particular case, becomes possible. It is the presence of an increased variety of response that we accept as a sign of what we call "intelligence." It is the enlarged neopallium, then, which makes mammals in general more intelligent than any other group of vertebrates and, indeed, more intelligent than any group of invertebrates.

During the course of mammalian evolution, there was a general tendency toward an increase in body size. This usually implies an increase in the size of the brain and, as a result, in the cerebrum and neopallium. With increase in size, it is at least possible, therefore, that an increase in intelligence would follow. This is not necessarily so, since, normally, the larger the animal the more complex is the coordination required, even when there is no advance in intelligence. Sensations arrive from larger portions of the environment and are therefore more complicated. The larger, heavier, and more numerous muscles require more careful handling. If an animal increases in size without increasing its brain in proportion, and even more than in proportion, it is likely to become more stupid rather than more intelligent.

An extreme example of this was in the giant reptiles of the Mesozoic Era. Some grew larger than any land mammal ever has, but very little of that increase went into the brain. In fact, one of the most startling things about the monsters is the pin-head brain they carried atop their mountains of flesh. There seems no doubt but that they must have been abysmally stupid creatures. In the worst cases, the creatures lacked enough brain to take care of the minimal requirements of muscular coordination. The stegosaur, to name one, which weighed some ten tons or more (larger than any elephant), had a brain no larger than that of a kitten. It was forced to develop a large collection of nerve cells near the base of the spinal cord which could coordinate the muscles of the rear half of the body, leaving only the front half to the puny brain. This "spinal brain" was actually larger than the brain in the skull. The phenomenon of large size associated with decreased intelligence exists in mammals, too, though in not nearly as marked a fashion. The large cow is a rather stupid mammal, not nearly so bright as the comparatively small dog.

Some mammals, as they increased in size, enlarged the area of the neopallium *more* than in proportion, so they increased in intelligence as well. To enlarge the neopallium at that rate, however, meant that it would outgrow the skull. With the larger and more recently developed mammals, therefore, the cerebral cortex, which by then had become all neopallium, must wrinkle. In place of the smooth cerebral surface found in all other creatures, even among the smaller and more primitive mammals, the cerebral surface of the larger and higher mammals rather resembles a large walnut. The surface has folded into *convolutions* ("roll together" L). The gray matter, following the ins and outs of the wrinkles, increased in area.

In terms of sheer bulk, brain growth reaches an extreme in the very largest mammals, the elephants and whales. These have the largest brains that have ever existed. What is more, the cerebral surface is quite convoluted; the brains of some of the whale family are the most convoluted known. It is not surprising that both elephants and whales are unusually intelligent animals. Yet they are not the most intelligent. Much of their large brain — too much — is the slave of the coordination requirements of their muscles. Less is left for the mysterious functions of reason and abstract thought.

To look for a record intelligence, then, we must find a group of animals that had developed large brains without neutralizing this by developing excessively huge bodies. What we want, in other words, is a large value for the brain/body mass ratio.

THE PRIMATES

For such an increase in brain-body mass ratio, we must turn to that Order of mammals called *Primates* (pry-may′teez), usually referred to, in Anglicized pronunciation, as the primates (pry′mits). The term is from the Latin word for "first," a piece of human self-praise, since included in the Order is man himself.

About 70 million years ago, the primates first developed out of the Order *Insectivora* (in-sek-tiv′oh-ruh; "insect-eating" L). The living examples of the insectivores are small and rather unremarkable creatures such as the shrews, moles, and hedgehogs, and the earliest primates could not have been much different from these. As a matter of fact, the most primitive living primates are small animals, native to Southeast Asia, called *tree-shrews*. They are indeed much like shrews in their habits, but are larger (the shrews themselves are the smallest mammals). They are large enough to remind people of diminutive squirrels, so they are sometimes called "squirrel-shrews" and are placed in the Family *Tupaiidae* (tyoo-pay'ih-dee; from a Malay word for "squirrel"). Their brains are somewhat more advanced than those of ordinary insectivores and they possess various anatomical characteristics which to a zoologist spell "early primate" rather than "late insectivore."

An important difference between the tree-shrew and the shrew lies in just that word "tree." The primates began as arboreal (tree-living) creatures, and all but some of the larger specimens still are. The arboreal environment is the land environment exacerbated still further, to almost prohibitive difficulty. The hard land is at least steady and firm, but the branches of trees do not offer a continuous surface and sway under weight or in the wind. The dangers of gravity are multiplied, too. In case of a misstep, an organism does not merely fall the height of its legs; it falls from the much greater height of the branch.

There are a number of ways in which mammals can adapt to the difficult arboreal life. Reliance can be placed on smallness, nimbleness, and lightness. For a squirrel, the thin branches are negotiable and the danger of a fall is minimized. (The smaller a creature, the less likely it is to be hurt by a fall.) With the development of a gliding surface of skin, as in the "flying" squirrel, the fall is actually converted into a means of locomotion. An alternative is to trade nimbleness for caution, to move very slowly and test each step as it is taken. This is a solution adopted by the sloths, which have attained considerable size at the cost of virtually converting themselves into mammalian turtles.

The early primates took the path of the squirrel. These include not only the tree-shrews but also the *lemurs* (lee'merz; "ghost" L, because of their quiet and almost ghostly movements through the night — they being nocturnal creatures). Together, the tree-shrews and the lemurs are placed in the Suborder *Prosimii* (prohsim'ee-eye; "pre-monkeys" L).

The whole Suborder is still marked by its insectivorous beginnings. The members have pronounced muzzles, with eyes on either side of the head; the cerebral cortex is still smooth and is still mainly concerned with smell. Notwithstanding, a crucial change was taking place. Slowly, more and more, the early primates tackled the difficulties of arboreal life head on. They did not follow a course of evasions. They did not merely patter along the branch but developed a grasping paw — that is, a hand — with which to seize the branch firmly.

Nor did they escape the dangers of gravity by developing a gliding membrane.* Rather, they relied on an improvement of the coordination of eye and muscle. In judging the exact position of a swaying branch, no sense is as convenient as that of sight, and even among the tree-shrews a larger proportion of the brain is devoted to sight and a lesser amount to smell than is true of the insectivores. This tendency continues among the lemurs.

The most specialized of the lemurs is the *tarsier* (tahr′see-ur; so called because the bones of its tarsus, or ankle, are much elongated). Here the importance of sight as opposed to sound makes itself evident in a new way. The eyes are located in front rather than on either side of its face. Both can be brought to bear simultaneously on the same object and this makes stereoscopic, or three-dimensional, vision possible. Only under such conditions can the distance of a swaying branch be estimated with real efficiency. (The tarsier's eyes are so large for its tiny face that its silent, staring appearance at night has given it the name "spectral tarsier.") With the development of grasping hands capable of holding food and bringing it to the mouth, the importance of the muzzle declines; the tarsier in reality lacks one, and is flat-faced like a man. The decline of the muzzle, together with the ascendancy of the eye, allows the sense of smell to become less important.

* There is an animal called a flying lemur, which has developed such a membrane, but it is an insectivore and not a primate.

The suborder including all the remaining primates is *Anthropoidea* (an'throh-poi'dee-uh; "manlike" G), and within this grouping are the monkeys, apes, and man himself. Among all of these, the traits in the tarsier are accentuated. All are primarily eye-and-hand-centered, with stereoscopic vision and with the sense of smell receding into the background.

Of all the senses, sight delivers information to the brain at the highest rate of speed and in the most complex fashion. The use of a hand with the numerous delicate motions required to grasp, finger, and pluck requires complex muscle coordination beyond that necessary in almost any other situation. For an eye-and-hand animal to be really efficient there must be a sharp rise in brain mass. If such a rise had not come about the primates would have remained a small, inconspicuous, and unsuccessful group with eyes and hands incapable of developing their full potentiality. But there *was* a sharp rise in brain mass. No other animal the size of a monkey has anywhere near the mass of brain a monkey possesses. (For their body size, the smaller monkeys have larger brains than we do.) Nor has any other animal its size a brain as convoluted as that of a monkey.

The higher primates are divided into two large groups, the *Platyrrhina* (plat'ih-ry'nuh; "flat-nosed" G) and *Catarrhina* (kat'uh-ry'nuh; "down-nosed" G). In the former, the noses are flat, almost flush against the face, with the nostrils well separated and opening straight forward. In the latter, the nose is a prominent jutting feature of the face, and within it the two nostrils are brought close together, with the openings facing downward, as in our own case.

The platyrrhines are to be found exclusively on the American continents and are therefore usually referred to as "New World monkeys." They frequently possess a prehensile tail; one able to curl about a branch and bear the weight of the body even without the supporting help of any of the legs. These prehensile-tailed monkeys are a great favorite at the zoos because of their breathtaking agility. Their four limbs are long and are all equipped for grasping.* The tail acts as a fifth limb. Often the tail and all the limbs are long and light, with a small body at the center. One common group of platyrrhines is commonly known as "spider monkeys" because of their slight, leggy build.

This is all very well as far as adaptation to arboreal life is concerned, but long arms that can stretch from branch to branch reduce the importance of the eye. A tail that can act almost literally as a crutch does the same. The adaptation to arboreal life is wonderful, but in effect some of the pressure is off the brain. The platyrrhines are the least intelligent of the higher primates.

The catarrhines are confined to the Eastern Hemisphere and are therefore ordinarily termed the "Old World monkeys." No catarrhine has a prehensile tail, which means one crutch less. The catarrhines are stockier in build and lack some of the advantageous agility of the platyrrhines. They are forced to make up for it by greater intelligence. The catarrhines are divided into three families. Of these the first is *Cercopithecidae* (sir′koh-pih-thee′sih-dee; "tailed-monkey" G). This family, as the name implies, possesses tails, though not prehensile ones. The most formidable of the family are the various baboons, which are stocky enough to have abandoned the trees for the ground but have not abandoned the tree-developed eye-and-hand organization, or the intelligence that developed along with it. In addition to their intelligence, they travel in packs and have redeveloped muzzles that are well equipped with teeth.

And yet even the baboons with their short tails must take a backseat in intelligence with respect to the remaining two families of the catarrhines. In the remaining two families there are no tails at all, and the hind legs become increasingly specialized for support rather than for grasping. It is as though intelligence

---

* Indeed, an old-fashioned name for monkeys is *Quadrumana* (kwod-roo′muh-nuh; "four handed" L), and this came to be applied to all higher primates except man. The term has fallen into disuse because this grand division between man on the one hand and all other higher primates on the other is zoologically unsound, however soothing it may be to our pride.

is forced to increase as the number of grasping appendages sinks from five to four, and then from four to two.

The second catarrhine family is *Pongidae* (pon'jih-dee), which includes the animals known as "apes." The name of the family is from a Congolese word for ape. The apes are the largest of the primates and therefore possess the largest brains in absolute terms. This, too, is a factor in making them the most intelligent of all the "lower animals."

There are four types of creatures among the apes. These are, in order of increasing size, the gibbon, the chimpanzee, the orangutan, and the gorilla. The gibbons (of which there are several species) are, on the average, less than three feet high and weigh between 20 and 30 pounds. Furthermore, they have gone nearly the way of the spider monkey. Although without tails, their forearms have lengthened almost grotesquely and they can make their way through the trees, hand-over-hand, with an uncanny accuracy that makes them a fascination in zoos. Between a small size and an overdependence on long limbs, it is not surprising that the gibbon is the least intelligent of the apes.

The remaining three pongids, approaching or even exceeding man in size, are lumped together as the "great apes." The weight of the brain of an orangutan has been measured at about 340 grams (12 ounces), that of a chimpanzee at 380 grams (13½ ounces), and that of a gorilla at 540 grams (19 ounces, or just under 1¼ pounds). Of these, the most intelligent appears to be the chimpanzee, since the greater mass of the gorilla's brain seems to be neutralized to an extent by the much greater mass of its body.

The similarities between the apes (particularly the chimpanzee) and man are unmistakable and sufficiently apparent to cause the Pongidae to be referred to frequently as the *anthropoid apes* ("manlike" G). And yet there are distinctions of considerable importance between apes and man, enough difference so that, quite fairly and without too much self-love on our own part, man may be put into a third catarrhine family all by himself, *Hominidae* (hoh-min'ih-dee; "man" L). Some millions of years ago the creatures ancestral to man branched off from the line of evolution leading to the modern apes. It was from this branch of the family that the first hominids developed. The hominids stood upright, finally and definitely. The hind legs became fully specialized for standing only and it is solely as a kind of stunt that a modern man, for instance, can pick up anything with his small, hardly maneuverable toes. The hominids became definitely two-handed, and the arms did not, as in the gibbon's case, unduly specialize themselves for a single function. The one specialization, that of the opposable thumb, rather served to accentuate the Jack-of-all-trades ability.

The loss of equipment again placed the accent on the brain. The hominids advanced in size, to be sure, outstripping the gibbon, and equaling or even slightly surpassing the chimpanzee. The hominids never attained the weight of the orangutan or the gorilla, and yet the hominid brain developed almost grotesquely; the expanding cranium came to overshadow the shrinking face.

The skull of the oldest creature we can definitely consider a hominid was discovered in Tanganyika in 1959. It has been given the name *Zinjanthropus* (zin-jan'throh-pus; "East Africa man"), from the native term for East Africa, the region in which it was discovered. The Zinjanthropus skull is much more primitive than any living human skull but also it is much more advanced than any living ape skull. Associated with the fossil, in the strata in which it was found, were tools. Therefore Zinjanthropus was a tool-making creature and deserves the name "hominid" in the cultural as well as the zoological sense. In 1961 the age of the strata in which Zinjanthropus was found was determined by measuring the radioactive decay of the potassium within it. The fossil, it would seem, is 1,750,000 years old. This is quite startling, because until the moment of the time measurement it had been felt that tool-making hominids had been inhabiting the planet only for half a million years or so. However, the finding is somewhat controversial, and perhaps the last word has not been said.

Zinjanthropus is an example of a small-brained hominid and there are other varieties, too, such as those popularly known as Java man and Peking man from the sites at which the first skeletal remains were discovered. The reference "small-brained" is only relative. Brought to life, such hominids would indeed look pinheaded to us, but their brains approached the 1000-gram (2¼ pounds) mark and were nearly twice the size of that of any living ape.

Nevertheless, as the hominid group continued to evolve, the accent continued to be on the brain. What we might call the "large-brained hominid" developed, and it was these only which survived to inherit the earth. Today (and since well before the dawn of history) only one species of hominid remains. This is *Homo sapiens* (hoh'moh say'pee-enz; "man, the wise" L), to whom we can refer as "modern man."

The specimens of modern man existing today are not actually the largest-brained hominids. An early variety of modern man, called the Cro-Magnons (kroh-man'yon; from the region in France where their skeletal remains were first discovered), seems to have the record in this respect. Even Neanderthal man (nay-ahn'der-tahl; so called from the region in Germany where their skeletal remains were first discovered), who seems distinctly more primitive than modern man in skull formation and in jaws, had a brain that was slightly larger than our own. However, between the Neanderthals and ourselves there seemed to be an improvement not so much in size of the brain as in internal organization. In other words, those portions of the brain believed to be most important for abstract thought seem better developed and larger in modern man than in Neanderthal man.

(Nevertheless, there are some who fear that the human brain may have reached its peak and may be on the point of begin-

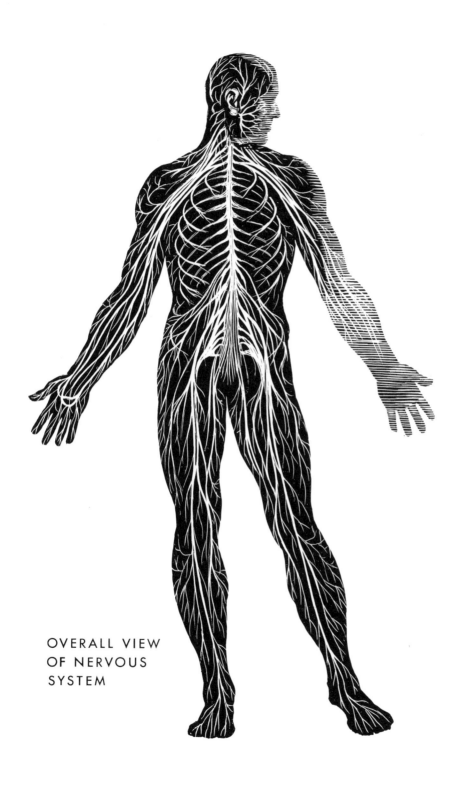

OVERALL VIEW
OF NERVOUS
SYSTEM

ning a downhill slide. They point out that individual intelligence is no longer of key importance, since all members of a society, intelligent or not, benefit from the accomplishments of the intelligent few, while those few are forced to pay the penalty of nonconformity by leading a less comfortable life. Evolutionary pressures would therefore now favor declining intelligence. This, however, may be an overly pessimistic view. I hope so, certainly.)

In modern man the brain at birth is about 350 grams (12 ounces) in weight and is already as large as that of a full-grown orangutan. In maturity, the average weight of a man's brain is 1450 grams (3¼ pounds). The average weight of a woman's brain is about 10 per cent less on the average, but her body is smaller too and there is no reason for thinking that either sex is inherently the more intelligent. Among normal human beings, in fact, there can be marked differences in weight of brain without any clear correlation in intelligence. The Russian novelist Ivan Turgenev had a brain that was just over the 2000-gram mark in weight, but Anatole France, also a skilled writer, had one that was just under the 1200-gram mark.

This represents the extremes. Any brain that weighs as little as 1000 grams is apparently below the minimum weight consistent with normal intelligence and is sure to be that of a mental defective. On the other hand, there have been mental defectives with brains of normal or more than normal size. Weight of brain alone, although a guide to intelligence, is by no means the entire answer.

If we consider the average weight of a man as 150 pounds and the average weight of his brain as 3¼ pounds, then the brain-body ratio is about 1:50. Each pound of brain is in charge (so to speak) of 50 pounds of body. This is a most unusual situation. Compare it with the apes, for example — man's nearest competitors. A pound of chimpanzee brain is in charge of 150 pounds of chimpanzee body (differently expressed, the brain/body ratio is 1:150), whereas in the gorilla the ratio may be as low as 1:500. To be sure, some of the smaller monkeys and also some of the hummingbirds have a larger brain/body ratio. In some monkeys the ratio is as great as 1:17½. If such a monkey were as large as a man and its brain increased in proportion, that brain would weigh 8½ pounds. The brain of such a monkey is in actual fact very small; so small that it simply lacks the necessary mass of cortical material to represent much intelligence despite the small amount of body it must coordinate.

Two types of creatures have brains considerably larger in terms of absolute mass than the brain of man. The largest elephants can have brains as massive as 6000 grams (about 13 pounds) and the largest whales can have brains that reach a mark of 9000 grams (or nearly 19 pounds). The size of the bodies such brains have to coordinate is far, far larger still. The biggest elephant brain may be 4 times the size of the human brain, but the weight of its body is perhaps 100 times that of the human body. Where each pound of our own brain must handle 50 pounds of our body, each pound of such an elephant's brain must handle nearly half a ton of its body. The largest whales are even worse off: each pound of their brain must handle some five tons of body.

Man strikes a happy medium, then. Any creature with a brain much larger than man's has a body so huge that intelligence comparable to ours is impossible. Contrarily, any creature with a brain/body ratio much larger than ours has a brain so small in absolute size that intelligence comparable to ours is impossible.

In intelligence, we stand alone! Or almost. There is one possible exception to all this. In considering the intelligence of whales, it is perhaps not fair to deal with the largest specimens. One might as well try to gauge the intelligence of primates by considering the largest member, the gorilla, and ignoring a smaller primate, man. What of the dolphins and porpoises, which are pygmy relatives of the gigantic whales? Some of these are no larger than man and yet have brains that are larger than man's (with weights up to 1700 grams, or 3¾ pounds), and more extensively convoluted.

It is not safe to say from this alone that the dolphin is more intelligent than man, because there is the question of the internal organization of the brain. The dolphin's brain (like that of Neanderthal man) may be oriented more in the direction of what we might consider "lower functions."

The only safe way to tell is to attempt to gauge the intelligence of the dolphin by actual experiment. Some investigators, notably John C. Lilly, seem convinced that dolphin intelligence is indeed comparable to our own, that dolphins and porpoises have a speech pattern as complicated as ours, and that a form of interspecies communication possibly may yet be established. If so, it would surely be one of the most exciting developments in human history. So far, the matter remains controversial, and we must wait and see.

8

OUR CEREBRUM

THE CEREBROSPINAL FLUID

Now that I have discussed the nerve cells (the mode of action of which is identical, as far as we can tell, in all animals) and have briefly taken up the manner in which their organization into a nervous system has grown more intricate through the course of evolution, reaching a climax in ourselves, it is time to take up the human nervous system in particular. The central nervous system (the brain plus the spinal cord) is clearly the best protected part of the body. The vertebrae of the spinal column are essentially a series of bony rings cemented together by cartilage, and through the center of those protecting rings runs the spinal cord. At the upper end of the neck, the spinal cord passes through a large opening in the base of the skull and becomes the brain. The brain is surrounded snugly by the strong, dense bone of the skull.

The protection of the bone alone is rather a harsh one, however. One would not like to entrust the soft tissue of the brain to the immediate embrace of bone. Such an immediate embrace fortunately does not exist, since the brain and spinal cord are surrounded by a series of membranes called the *meninges* (mehnin'jeez; "membranes" G). The outermost of these is the *dura mater* (dyoo'ruh may'ter; "hard mother"* L), and indeed it is

---

* The use of the word "mother" dates back to a theory of the medieval Arabs, who felt that out of these membranes all the other body membranes were formed.

hard. It is a tough fibrous structure that lines the inner surface of the vertebral rings of bone and the inner surface of the skull, smoothing and somewhat cushioning the bare bony outlines. Sheets of dura mater extend into some of the major dividing lines within the central nervous system. One portion extends downward into the deep fissure separating the cerebrum into a right and left half; another extends into the fissure dividing the cerebrum and the cerebellum. On the whole, though, the dura mater is a bone lining.

The innermost of the meninges is the *pia mater* (py′uh may′ter; "tender mother" L). This is a soft and tender membrane that closely lines the brain and the spinal cord, insinuating itself into all the unevennesses and fissures. It is the direct covering of the central nervous system. Between the dura mater and the pia mater is the *arachnoid membrane* (a-rak′noid; "cobweblike" G, so called because of the delicate thinness of its structure). Inflammation of the membranes, usually through bacterial or viral infection, is *meningitis*. Bacterially caused meningitis, in particular, was a very dangerous disease before the modern age of antibiotics. Even the membranes, taken by themselves, are not sufficient protection for the brain: between the arachnoid membrane and the pia mater (the *subarachnoid space*) is the final touch, the *cerebrospinal fluid*. One way in which the cerebrospinal fluid protects the brain is by helping to counter the effects of gravity. The brain is a soft tissue; as a matter of fact, its outermost portions are 85 per cent water, making this the most watery of all the solid tissues of the body. It is even more watery than whole blood. Hence it is not to be expected that the brain can be very hard or rigid — it isn't. It is so soft that if it were to rest unsupported on a hard surface the pull of gravity alone would be sufficient to distort it. The cerebrospinal fluid supplies a buoyancy that almost entirely neutralizes gravitational pull within the skull. In a manner of speaking, the brain floats in fluid.

The fluid also counters the effect of inertia. The bony framework of the skull protects the brain against the direct impact of a blow (even a light tap would suffice to damage the unprotected tissue of the brain). This protection in itself would scarcely be of much use if the sudden movement of the head, in response to a blow, smashed the brain against the hard internal surface of the skull, or even against the fibrous dura mater. It is of little moment whether it is the enemy club that delivers the blow or your own bone. For that matter, even the mere sudden lifting or turning of the head would be enough to press the brain with dangerous force against the skull in the direction opposite the movement. The cerebrospinal fluid acts as a cushion in all these cases, damping the relative motions of brain and skull. The protection isn't unlimited, of course. A strong enough blow or a strong enough acceleration can be too much for the delicate brain structure, even if the disturbance is not sufficient to produce visible damage. Even if the brain is not directly bruised, sudden twisting of the skull (as is produced in boxing through a hard blow to the side of the chin) may stretch and damage nerves and veins as the brain, through inertia, lags behind the turning head. Unconsciousness can result and even death. This is spoken of as *concussion* ("shake violently" L).

The cerebrospinal fluid is also to be found in the hollows within the brain and spinal cord, and this brings us to another point. Despite all the specialization and elaboration of the human brain, the central nervous system still retains the general plan of structure of a hollow tube, a plan that was originally laid down in the first primitive chordates. Within the spinal cord this hollowness is almost vestigial, taking the form of a tiny *central canal*, which may vanish in adults. This central canal, like the spinal cord itself, broadens out within the skull. As the spinal cord merges with the brain, the central canal becomes a series of specialized hollows called *ventricles.** There are four of these,

---

* "Ventricle," from a Latin word meaning "little belly," can be used for any hollow within an organ. The most familiar ventricles to the average man are those within the heart.

numbered from the top of the brain downward. Thus, the central canal opens up at the base of the brain into the lowermost of these, the *fourth ventricle*. This connects through a narrow aperture with the *third ventricle*, which is rather long and thin.

Above the third ventricle there is a connection, through another narrow aperture, with the two foremost ventricles, which lie within the cerebrum, one on either side of the fissure that divides the cerebrum into a right and left portion. Because of the fact that they lie on either side of the midline they are referred to as the *lateral ventricles*. The lateral ventricles are far larger than the third and fourth and have a rather complicated shape. They run the length of the cerebrum in a kind of outward curve, beginning near each other at the forehead end, and separating increasingly as the back of the skull is approached. A projection of each lateral ventricle extends downward and still outward into the lower portion of the cerebrum.

These hollows — the central canal and the various ventricles — are filled with cerebrospinal fluid. The cerebrospinal fluid is very similar in composition to the blood plasma (the liquid part of the blood), and in reality is little more than filtered blood. In the membranes surrounding the ventricles there are intricate networks of fine blood vessels called *chorioid plexuses* (koh′ree-oid plek′sus-ez; "membrane networks" L). These blood vessels leak, and are the source of the cerebrospinal fluid. The cells and subcellular objects within the blood, such as the white cells, the red corpuscles, and the platelets, do not pass through, of course; the leak isn't that bad. Nor do most of the protein molecules. Virtually all else in the blood does leak out, nevertheless, and pass into the ventricles.

The cerebrospinal fluid circulates through the various ventricles, and in the fourth ventricle escapes through tiny openings into the subarachnoid space outside the pia mater. Where the subarachnoid space is greater than usual, the fluid collects in *cisternae* (sis′tur-nee; "reservoirs" L). The largest of these is to be found at the base of the brain, just above the nape of the neck; it is the *cisterna magna* ("large reservoir" L). The total volume

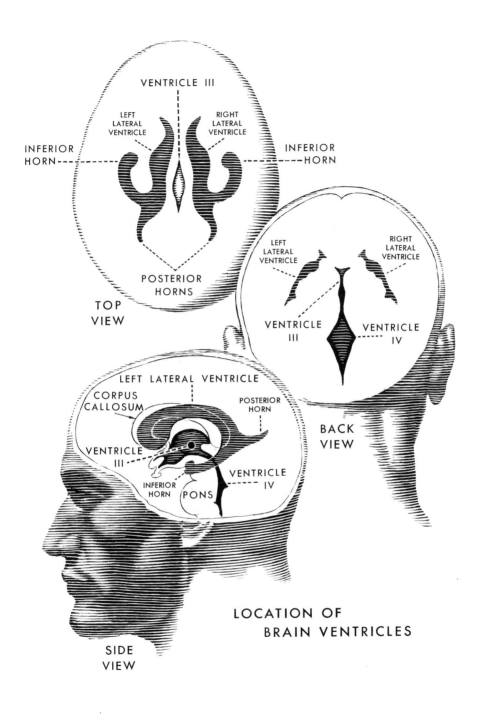

VENTRICLE III

LEFT
LATERAL
VENTRICLE

RIGHT
LATERAL
VENTRICLE

INFERIOR
HORN

INFERIOR
HORN

POSTERIOR
HORNS

TOP
VIEW

LEFT
LATERAL
VENTRICLE

RIGHT
LATERAL
VENTRICLE

VENTRICLE
III

VENTRICLE
IV

BACK
VIEW

LEFT LATERAL VENTRICLE

CORPUS
CALLOSUM

POSTERIOR
HORN

VENTRICLE
III

VENTRICLE
IV

INFERIOR
HORN

PONS

SIDE
VIEW

LOCATION OF
BRAIN VENTRICLES

of cerebrospinal fluid amounts to only a few drops in the new-born child but increases to 100 or 150 milliliters (about 4½ fluid ounces) in the adult.

Since cerebrospinal fluid is continually seeping into the ventri-cles, it must be allowed to escape somewhere. In the arachnoid membrane are small areas called *arachnoid villi* (vil'eye; "tufts of hair" L, so named because they have the appearance of tiny tufts). These are richly supplied with blood vessels, and into these the cerebrospinal fluid is absorbed. There is a resultant active circulation of the fluid from the chorioid plexuses, where it leaks out of the blood, through the ventricles, out into the sub-arachnoid space, and through the arachnoid villi, where it is ab-sorbed back into the blood.

It is possible for the circulation of the cerebrospinal fluid to be interfered with. There may be blockage at some point, perhaps through the growth of a brain tumor, which closes off one of the narrow connections between the ventricles. In that case, fluid will continue to be formed and will collect in the pinched-off ventricles, the pressure rising to the point where the brain tissue may be damaged. Inflammation of the brain membranes (men-ingitis) can also interfere with the reabsorption of the fluid and lead to the same results. At such times, the condition is *hydro-cephalus* (hy'droh-sef'ah-lus; "water-brain" G), or as it is com-monly referred to, in direct translation, "water on the brain." This condition is most dramatic when it takes place in early in-fancy, before the bones of the skull have joined firmly together. They give with the increased internal pressure so that the skull becomes grotesquely enlarged.

Cerebrospinal fluid can be removed most easily by means of a *lumbar puncture;* that is, by the introduction of a needle between the fourth and fifth lumbar vertebrae in the small of the back. The spinal cord itself does not extend that far down the column, therefore the needle may be inserted without fear of damaging spinal tissue. The collection of nerves with which the canal is filled in that region make easy way for the needle. Fluid may be obtained, with greater difficulty, from the cisterna magna, or even from the ventricles themselves if conditions are grave enough to warrant drilling a hole through the skull. From the fluid pressure and from its chemical makeup it is possible to draw useful conclusions as to the existence or nonexistence of a brain tumor or abscess, of meningitis or other infection, and so on.

The cerebrospinal fluid offers more than mechanical protection: it is also part of a rather complex system of chemical protection for the brain. The brain, you see, has a composition quite different in some respects from that of the rest of the body. It contains a high percentage of fatty material, including a number of unique components. Perhaps for this reason brain tissue cannot draw upon the material in the blood as freely as other tissues can. It is far more selective, almost as though it had a finicky taste of its own. As a result, when chemicals are injected into the bloodstream it is often true that these chemicals may be quickly found in all the cells of the body except for those of the nervous system. There is a *blood-cerebrospinal barrier* that seems to prevent many substances from entering the fluid. There is also a direct *blood-brain barrier* that prevents them from passing from the blood directly into the brain tissue.

The blood-brain barrier may be the result of an extra layer of small cells surrounding the blood capillaries that feed the brain. These cells make up part of the *neuroglia* (nyoo-rog′lee-uh; "nerve-glue" G) that surrounds and supports the nerve cells themselves. These neuroglial cells, or simply *glia cells,* outnumber the nerve cells by 10 to 1. There are some 10 billion nerve cells in the cerebrum but 100 billion glia, and these latter make up about half the mass of the brain. A coating of these about the capillaries would serve to deaden the process of diffusion between blood and brain and so erect a selective barrier. (It has usually been assumed that these glia cells serve only a supporting and subsidiary function in the brain. Some recent research, however, would make it appear they are more intimately concerned with some brain functions such as memory.)

The brain is highly demanding in another fashion. It uses up a great deal of oxygen in the course of its labors; in fact, in the resting body, ¼ of the oxygen being consumed by the tissues is used up in the brain, although that organ makes up only 1/50 of the mass of the body. The consumption of oxygen involves the oxidation of the simple sugar (glucose) brought to the brain by the bloodstream. The brain is sensitive to any shortage of either oxygen or glucose and will be damaged by that shortage sooner than any other tissue. (It is the brain that fails first in death by asphyxiation; and it is the brain that fails in the baby if its first breath is unduly delayed.) The flow of blood through the brain is therefore carefully controlled by the body and is less subject to fluctuation than is the blood flow through any other organ. What is more, although it is easy to cause the blood vessels in the brain to dilate by use of drugs, it is impossible to make them constrict and thus cut down the blood supply.

The existence of a tumor can destroy the blood-brain barrier in the region of the tumor. This has its fortunate aspect. A drug labeled with a radioactive iodine atom and injected into the bloodstream will pass into the brain only at the site of the tumor and collect there. This makes it possible to locate the tumor by detecting the radioactive region.

THE CEREBRAL CORTEX

Since we stand upright, our nervous system, like all the rest of us, is tipped on end. Where in other vertebrates the spinal cord runs horizontally, with the brain at the forward end, in ourselves the cord runs vertically, with the vastly enlarged brain on top. During the course of the development of the nervous system, new — and what we might call "higher" — functions (involving the more complex types of coordination and the ability to reason and indulge in abstract thought) were added to the forward end of the cord through the process of cephalization. Since in the human being the forward end is on top, it follows that when we speak of

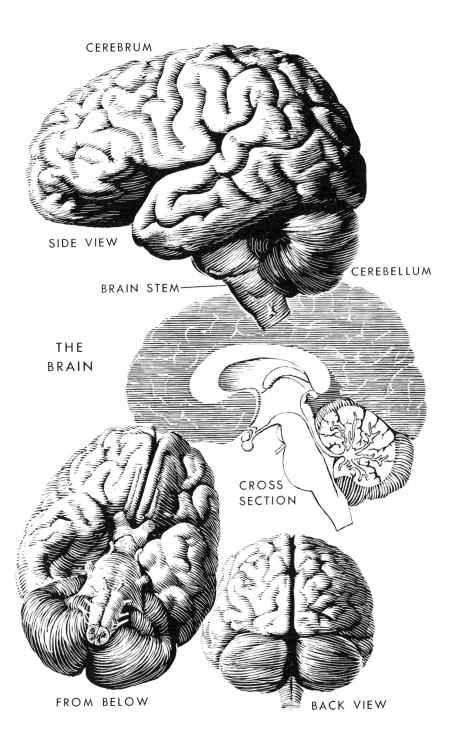

CEREBRUM

SIDE VIEW

CEREBELLUM

BRAIN STEM

THE
BRAIN

CROSS
SECTION

FROM BELOW

BACK VIEW

higher and lower levels of the central nervous system we mean this both literally and in some ways figuratively.

Furthermore, in the human being the higher levels have come to predominate not only in terms of our own estimate of importance but in that of actual mass. The central nervous system in the average man weighs about 1480 grams, or just over 3 pounds. Of this, the spinal cord — the lowest and most primitive level — weighing about an ounce, makes up only 2 per cent of the total. And of the brain, the cerebrum — which stands at the highest level and is the most recently developed — makes up 5/6 of the total mass.

In describing the central nervous system in detail, then, let us begin with the cerebrum, which is almost divided, longitudinally, into right and left halves, each of which is called a *cerebral hemisphere*. The outermost layer of the cerebrum consists of cell bodies which, grayish in color, make up most of the *gray matter* of the brain. This outermost layer of gray matter is the cerebral cortex (where "cortex" has the same meaning it has in the case of the adrenal cortex mentioned on page 41). Below the cortex are the nerve fibers leading from the cell bodies to other parts of the brain and to the spinal cord. There are also fibers leading from one part of the cortex to another. The fatty myelin sheath of these fibers lend the interior of the cerebrum a whitish appearance, and this is the *white matter* of the brain.

The cortex is intricately wrinkled into convolutions, as I mentioned in the previous chapter. The lines that mark off the convolutions are called *sulci* (sul′sy; "furrows" L), the singular form being *sulcus* (sul′kus). Particularly deep sulci are termed *fissures*. The ridges of cerebral tissue between the sulci, which look like softly rolled matter that has been flattened out slightly by the pressure of the skull, are called *gyri* (jy′ry; "rolls" L), the singular form being *gyrus* (jy′rus). The convoluted form of the cerebrum triples the surface area of the gray matter of the brain. There is twice as much gray matter, that is, lining the various sulci and fissures as there is on the flattish surface of the gyri.

The sulci and gyri are fairly standardized from brain to brain, and the more prominent ones are named and mapped. Two particularly prominent sulci are the *central sulcus* and *lateral sulcus*, which occur, of course, in each of the cerebral hemispheres. (The cerebral hemispheres are mirror images as far as the details of structure are concerned.) The central sulcus begins at the top of the cerebrum, just about in the center, and runs curvingly downward and forward. It is sometimes called the *fissure of Rolando*, after an 18th-century Italian anatomist, Luigi Rolando, who was the first to describe it carefully. The lateral sulcus starts at the bottom of the hemisphere about one third of the way back from the forward end and runs diagonally upward on a line parallel to the base of the cerebrum. It comes to an end after having traversed a little over half the way to the rear of the cerebrum. It is the most prominent of all the sulci, and is sometimes called the *fissure of Sylvius*, after the professional pseudonym of a 17th-century French anatomist who first described it. (See the illustration on page 172.)

These two fissures are used as convenient reference points by which to mark off each cerebral hemisphere into regions called *lobes*. The portion of the cerebral hemisphere lying to the front of the central sulcus and before the point at which the lateral sulcus begins is the *frontal lobe*. Behind the central sulcus and above the lateral sulcus is the *parietal lobe* (puh-ry'ih-tal). Below the lateral sulcus is the *temporal lobe*. In the rear of the brain, behind the point where the lateral sulcus comes to an end, is the *occipital lobe* (ok-sip'ih-tal). The name of each lobe is that of the bone of the skull which is approximately adjacent to it.

It seems natural to think that different parts of the cortex might control different parts of the body, and that through careful investigation the body might be mapped out on the cortex. One of the early speculators in this direction was an 18th-19th century Viennese physician named Franz Joseph Gall. He believed the brain was specialized even to the extent that different sections controlled different talents or temperamental attri-

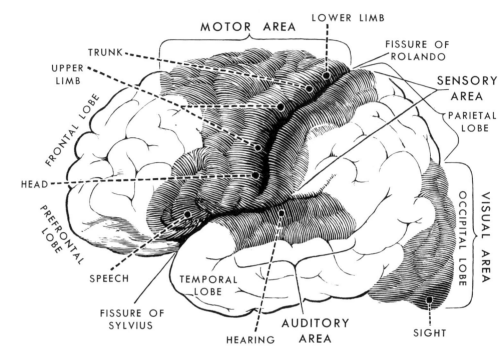

TRUNK
UPPER LIMB
MOTOR AREA
LOWER LIMB
FISSURE OF ROLANDO
SENSORY AREA
PARIETAL LOBE
FRONTAL LOBE
HEAD
PREFRONTAL LOBE
SPEECH
FISSURE OF SYLVIUS
TEMPORAL LOBE
HEARING
AUDITORY AREA
OCCIPITAL LOBE
VISUAL AREA
SIGHT

LOCATION OF IMPORTANT AREAS OF CEREBRUM

butes. Hence, if a portion of the brain seemed more than normally well developed, the talent or attribute should be correspondingly noticeable. His students and followers went further than he did. They conceived the notion that a well-developed portion of the brain would be marked by a corresponding bump on the skull, the bump being required in order to leave room for the overdevelopment of gray matter in that region. It followed that by taking careful note of the fine detail of the shape of the skull, so went the theory, one could tell a great deal about the owner of that skull. So began the foolish pseudoscience *phrenology* ("study of the mind" G).

But if Gall, and especially his followers, went off on a wrong turning, there was nevertheless something in their notion. In 1861 a French surgeon named Pierre Paul Broca, by assiduous postmortem study of brains, was able to show that patients with an inability to speak or to understand speech — a disorder called *aphasia* ("no speech" G) — possessed physical damage to a particular area of the brain. The area involved was found to be the third left frontal gyrus, which is often called *Broca's convolution* as a result.

Following that, in 1870, two Germans, Gustav Fritsch and Eduard Hitzig, began a line of research in which they stimulated different portions of the cerebral cortex of a dog in order to take note of what muscular activity, if any, resulted. (It was also possible to destroy a patch of the cortex and to take note of what paralysis might or might not result.) In consequence, the skeletal muscles of the body were to a certain extent mapped out on the cortex.

It was discovered by such lines of investigation that a band of the cortex lying in the frontal lobe just before the central sulcus was particularly involved in the stimulation of the various skeletal muscles into movement. This band is therefore called the *motor area*. It seems to bear a generally inverted relationship to the body: the uppermost portions of the motor area, toward the top of the cerebrum, stimulate the lowermost portions of the leg; as one progresses downward in the motor area, the muscles higher in the leg are stimulated, then the muscles of the torso, then those of the arm and hand, and finally of the neck and head.

The cerebral cortex in the motor area, as elsewhere, is composed of a number of layers of cells which are carefully distinguished by anatomists. One of these layers contains, in each hemisphere, some 30,000 unusually large cells. These are called *pyramidal cells* (from their shape), or *Betz cells* (after the Russian anatomist Vladimir Betz, who first described them in 1874). The fibers from these cells stimulate muscular contractions, each pyramidal cell controlling a particular portion of a particular muscle. Fibers from the smaller cells in the layers above the pyramidal cell layer do not by themselves stimulate muscle contraction, but instead seem to sensitize the muscle fibers so that they will more easily and readily respond to pyramidal stimulation.

The fibers from the motor area form into a bundle called the *pyramidal tract,* or *pyramidal system.* This leads downward through the various portions of the brain below the cerebrum and into the spinal cord. Because the tract connects the cortex and the spinal cord it is also called the *corticospinal tract.* The two portions of the tract, one from each cerebral hemisphere, happen to cross each other in the lower regions of the brain and in the uppermost portion of the spinal cord. The result is that stimulation of the motor area of the left cerebral hemisphere results in an effect in the right side of the body, and vice versa.

The existence of the pyramidal system is an indication of the way in which the nervous system is bound into a functional unit. That is, there may be separate anatomical parts, the cerebrum, the cerebellum, and others (which I shall discuss in some detail) but it is not to be supposed that each has a distinct and separate function. Rather, the pyramidal system in its control of motion draws on all parts of the central nervous system, from cortex to spinal column. There are also nerve fibers involved in the control of motion which do not stem from the pyramidal cells, and these, the *extra-pyramidal system,* likewise connect with all parts of the central nervous system. While the nervous system may be sliced up anatomically in a horizontal fashion, it is much better to slice it in a vertical fashion, functionally.

At each step of the descent from the motor area of the cortex, down through the lower regions of the pyramidal and extra-pyramidal systems to the muscle fibers themselves, there is a multiplication of effect. The fiber from a single pyramidal cell will exert an effect on a number of cells in the spinal cord. Each of these spinal cells will control a number of neurons in the peripheral nervous system (the portion outside the brain and spinal cord) and each neuron will control a number of muscle fibers. All in all, a single pyramidal cell may end up in indirect charge of possibly 150,000 muscle fibers. This helps in the coordination of muscular activity.

By controlling the amount of this "divergence," the body can be subjected to varying degrees of "fine control" as required. In this way the motion of the torso can be controlled adequately by relatively few pyramidal cells, since the necessary variety of motion is quite limited. Divergence is great here, and one pyramidal cell controls many thousands of fibers. A special situation exists with the fingers, which must be capable of delicately controlled motions of many varieties. Here there is considerably less divergence, and pyramidal cells are in control of definitely fewer muscle fibers.

But the cortex is not involved in merely controlling responses. To make the responses useful ones, it must also receive sensations. In the parietal lobe, therefore, just behind the central sulcus, is a band which is called the *sensory area* (see illustration, p. 172, for location of this and areas described below).

Despite this name, it does not receive *all* sensations. The sensations arising from the nerve endings in the skin and in the interior of the body are led through bundles of fibers up the spinal cord and into the brain. Some are sidetracked by the spinal cord itself, others by the lower portions of the brain. Most, however, finally reach the cortex. Those reaching the sensory area are primarily the sensations of touch and temperature, together with impulses from the muscles which give rise to knowledge concerning body position and equilibrium. These are the generalized body senses not requiring any specialized sensory organs.* The sensory area is therefore sometimes referred to in more limited fashion as the *somesthetic area* (soh'mes-thet'ik; "body sensation" G). Even this is overgenerous, since one important somesthetic sense, that of pain, is not represented here; it is received in lower portions of the brain. The fact that the sensations are received at various horizontal levels of the nervous system shows that here, too, there is a longitudinal unification of function. There is a *reticular activating system* which coordinates the various levels in their task of receiving sensations.

---

* I shall discuss these senses and the others, too, in some detail in Chapters 10, 11, and 12.

As in the case of the motor area, the regions of the sensory area in the cerebral cortex are divided into sections that seem to bear an inverse relation to the body. Sensations from the foot are at the top of the area, followed successively as we go downward with sensations from the leg, hip, trunk, neck, arm, hand, fingers. Below the area that receives finger sensations are the areas receiving sensations from the head. Lowest of all are the sensations from the tongue; here one specialized sense is involved, because it is in the lowest portion of the sensory area that taste is received. (The other chemical sense, that of smell, is received in a region at the floor of the frontal lobe — the remnant in man of the extensive olfactory lobes in most other vertebrates.)

The sections of the sensory area devoted to the lips, tongue, and hand are (as one might expect) larger in proportion to the actual size of those organs than are the sections devoted to other parts of the body. In fact, distorted little men are sometimes drawn along diagrams of sections of the brain in an attempt to match up graphically the cortex and the body. Both in the motor area and the sensory area, the result is a tiny torso to which a small leg with a large foot is attached in the direction leading to the top of the cranium, and a large arm with a still larger hand is attached in the other direction. Beneath is a large head that seems all mouth and tongue.

This is reasonable enough. As far as movements are concerned, the manipulations of the mouth and tongue that make speech possible and the manipulation of the hand that makes tool-wielding possible are what have been the main factors in making man. As for the senses, one must expect that the flexible manipulation of a hand could not be fully efficient if we did not know, at every moment and in great detail, what it was feeling. The senses related to the mouth are less distinctively human, but while food remains important (and it does, even to intellectual *Homo sapiens*) sensations from the mouth area will require great attention.

Each of the two important specialized senses, sight and hearing, has a separate lobe reserved to itself. That portion of the temporal lobe just beneath the sensory area is reserved for the reception of sound and is therefore the *auditory area* ("hear" L), or the *acoustic area* ("hear" G). The occipital lobe carries the *visual area*, which receives and interprets the sensation of sight. This is located at the extreme rear of each cerebral hemisphere.

ELECTROENCEPHALOGRAPHY

There are some 10 billion nerve cells in the cerebral cortex, as I have said, and all are capable of undergoing the chemical and electrical changes that accompany the nerve impulse. (If they didn't, they would be dead.) A specific cell would conduct an impulse only when stimulated, and it is only then, at perhaps rare intervals, when it would be undergoing variations in electrical potential. However, at any given moment a sizable fraction of the 10 billion cells would be firing, so the brain as a whole is constantly active.

Under ordinary conditions, sensations are constantly being funneled into the cerebrum and motor impulses are constantly being sprayed outward. Even if many sensations were cut off, if you were surrounded by complete darkness and silence, if there were nothing to smell or taste, if you were floating weightless in space and could feel nothing, there would still be sensations arising from your own muscles and joints to tell you the relative position of your limbs and torso. And even if you were lying in complete relaxation, moving no muscle consciously, your heart must still pump, the muscles of your chest still keep you breathing, and so on.

It is not surprising that at all times, awake or asleep, the brain of any living creature, and not of man only, must be the source of varying electric potentials. These were first detected in 1875 by an English physiologist, Richard Caton. He applied electrodes directly to the living brain of a dog on which he had operated for the purpose and could just barely detect the tiny currents.

During the half century after his time, the techniques of detecting and amplifying tiny changes in electric potential improved vastly. By the 1920's it was possible to detect the currents even through the thickness of skin and bone covering the brain.

In 1924 an Austrian psychiatrist named Hans Berger placed electrodes against the human scalp and found that by using a very delicate galvanometer he could just detect electric potentials. He waited until 1929 before publishing his work. Since then, the use of more sophisticated technology has made the measurements of these currents a routine affair. The process is called *electroencephalography* (ee-lek'troh-en-sef'uh-log'ruh-fee; "electric brain-writing" G). The instrument used is an *electroencephalograph*, and the recording of the fluctuating potentials is an *electroencephalogram*. The abbreviation *EEG* is commonly used to represent all three words.

The electric potential of the brain waves (as these fluctuations in potential are commonly referred to) are in the millivolt (a thousandth of a volt) and microvolt (a millionth of a volt) ranges. At the very beginning of the history of EEG, Berger noticed that the potentials fluctuated in rhythmic fashion, though the rhythm was not a simple one, but made up of several types of contributory waves.

Berger gave the most pronounced rhythm the name of *alpha wave*. In the alpha wave the potential varies by about 20 microvolts in a cycle of roughly 10 times a second. The alpha wave is clearest and most obvious when the subject is resting with his eyes closed. At first Berger's suggestion that the brain as a whole gives rise to this rhythm seemed acceptable. Since his time increasingly refined investigation has altered things. More and more electrodes have been applied to the skull in various places (the positions kept symmetrical about the midplane of of the skull) and now as many as twenty-four places may be tapped and the potential differences across a number of these can be recorded simultaneously. In this way it has been discovered that the alpha wave is strongest in the occipital region of the skull, or, to say it differently, in the area where the visual center is located.

When the eyes are opened, but are viewing featureless illumination, the alpha wave persists. If, however, the ordinary variegated environment is in view, the alpha wave vanishes, or is drowned by other, more prominent rhythms. After a while, if nothing visually new is presented, the alpha wave reappears. It is possible that the alpha wave represents the state of readiness in which the visual area holds itself when it is being only minimally stimulated. (It would be almost like a person shifting from foot to foot or drumming his fingers on the table as he waits for some word that will rouse him to activity.) Since sight is our chief sense and provides us with more information than any other sense does, and is therefore the chief single factor in keeping the brain busy, it is not surprising that the alpha wave dominates the resting EEG. When the eyes actually begin reporting information and the nerve cells of the cortex go to work on it, the "waiting" rhythm vanishes. If the visual pattern remains unchanged so that the brain eventually exhausts its meaning, the "waiting" rhythm returns. The brain cannot "wait" indefinitely, however. If human beings are kept for long periods without sensory stimulation, they undergo difficulties in trying to think or concentrate and may even begin to suffer from hallucinations (as though the brain in default of real information begins to make up its own). Experiments reported in 1963 indicated that men kept in environments lacking sensory stimulation for two weeks showed progressively smaller alpha waves appearing in the EEG.

In addition to alpha waves, there are also *beta waves*, representing a faster cycle, from 14 to 50 per second, and a smaller fluctuation in potential. Then, too, there are slow, large *delta waves* and rather uncommon *theta waves*.

The EEG presents physiologists with reams of fascinating data, most of which they are as yet helpless to interpret. For instance, there are differences with age. Brain waves can be detected in the fetus, though they are then of very low voltage and very slow.

They change progressively but do not become fully adult in characteristics till the age of 17. There are also changes in brain waves characteristic of the various stages of falling asleep and waking up, including changes when, presumably, the subject is dreaming. (Delta waves accompanied by rapid movements of the eyes are prominent during these dream intervals.) In contrast to all this variegation, the EEG of the various animals tested are quite similar in general characteristics among themselves and when compared with those of man. The brain, of whatever species, seems to have but one basic fashion of operation.

As far as analyzing the EEG is concerned, we might make an analogy with a situation whereby all the people on earth are listened to from a point out in space. It might be possible to detect human noise as a large buzz with periodic tiny irregularities (representing the passage of rush-hour traffic, evening hilarity, nighttime sleep, and so on) progressing around the world. To try to get information from the EEG as to the fine details of behavior within the cortex would be something like trying to analyze the overall buzz of the world's people in order to make out particular conversations.

Specially designed computers are now being called into battle. If a particular small environmental change is applied to a subject, it is to be presumed that there will be some response in the brain that will reflect itself in a small alteration in the EEG pattern at the moment when the change is introduced. The brain will be engaged in many other activities, however, and the small alteration in EEG will not be noticeable against the many complicated wave formations. Notwithstanding, if the process is repeated over and over again, a computer can be programed to average out the EEG pattern and compare the situation at the moment of environmental change against that average. In the long run there would be, it is presumed, a consistent difference.

Yet there are times when the EEG has diagnostic value in medicine even without the refined work of the latest computers. Naturally, this is so only when the EEG is radically abnormal and therefore when the brain is suffering from some serious malfunction. (Thus, the hypothetical listener to the overall buzz of the world's people might be able to detect a war, and even locate its center of action, by the unusual sound of artillery rising above the ordinary melange of sound.)

One case in which EEG is useful is in the detection of brain tumors. The tissue making up the tumor itself is not functional and delivers no brain waves. The areas of the cortex immediately adjacent to the tumor deliver distorted brain waves. If enough EEG records are taken over enough areas of the brain and if these are subjected to careful enough analysis, it is possible sometimes not only to detect the existence of a tumor but even to locate its position on the cortex. However, it will not detect a tumor in any part of the brain but the cerebral cortex.

The EEG is also useful in connection with *epilepsy* ("seizure" G), so called for reasons explained below. Epilepsy is a condition in which brain cells fire off at unpredictable moments and without the normal stimulus. This may be due to damage to the brain during prenatal life or during infancy. Often it has no known cause. The most dramatic form of such a disease is one where the motor area is affected. With the motor nerves stimulating muscles randomly, the epileptic may cry out as the muscles of the chest and throat contract, fall as the muscular coordination controlling balance is disrupted, and writhe convulsively. The fit doesn't last long, usually only a few minutes, but the patient can do serious damage to himself in that interval. Such fits, at unpredictable intervals, are referred to as *grand mal* (grahn mal; "great sickness," French). A more direct English name is "falling sickness."

In another version of epilepsy, it is the sensory area that is primarily affected. Here the epileptic may suffer momentary hallucinations and have brief lapses of unconsciousness. This is *petit mal* (puh-tee mal; "small sickness" French). Both areas may be mildly affected, so that a patient may have illusions followed by disorganized movements. These are *psychomotor attacks*.

Epilepsy is not very uncommon, since about 1 in 200 suffer from it, though not necessarily in its extreme form. It has a fascinating history. Attacks of grand mal are frightening and impressive, particularly in primitive societies (and some not so primitive) that do not understand what is taking place. During the attack, the epileptic's muscles are clearly not under his own control and it is easy to conclude that his body has been momentarily seized by some supernatural being. (Hence, the fit is considered a "seizure" and thus the name "epilepsy" arises.) Some famous people, including Julius Caesar and Dostoyevsky, have been epileptics.

The supernatural being may be conceived of as an evil demon, and the existence of epileptic seizures are partly to blame for the belief, even down to modern times, in demonic possession. The epileptic may be felt to have gained supernatural insights into the future as a result of his intimate relationship with the supernatural. A Delphic prophetess was always more impressive if she experienced (or counterfeited) an epileptic fit before delivering her prophecy. Modern mediums, during spiritualistic séances, are careful to writhe convulsively. To the Greeks epilepsy was "the sacred disease." Hippocrates, the "father of medicine" (or possibly some disciple), was the first to maintain that epilepsy was a disease like other diseases, caused by some organic failing, and potentially curable without recourse to magic.

The EEG is characteristic for each variety of epilepsy. Grand mal shows a pattern of high-voltage fast waves; petit mal, fast waves with every other one a sharp spike; psychomotor attacks, slow waves interspersed by spikes. The brain-wave pattern can be used to detect subclinical attacks that are too minor to be noticed otherwise. It can also be used to follow the reaction of patients to treatment by noticing the frequency and extent of these abnormal patterns.

Other uses of EEG are in the process of being developed. Thus, the brain, because of its critical need for oxygen and glucose, is the first organ to lose function in a dying patient. With modern techniques of resuscitation, it is not impossible that patients may be revived while the heart is still beating but after the higher centers of the brain are irretrievably gone. Life under those conditions is scarcely to be called life, and it has been suggested that loss of EEG rhythms be considered as marking death even though the heart is still struggling to beat.

EEG may be useful in diagnosing and even in learning to understand various psychotic states, which is something I shall come back to in Chapter 14.

THE BASAL GANGLIA

The portion of the cerebrum below the cortex is, as mentioned earlier in the chapter, largely white matter, made up of myelin-sheathed nerve fibers. Just above the various ventricles making up the hollow within the brain, for example, is a tough bridge of white matter, the *corpus callosum* (kawr'pus ka-loh'sum; "hard body" L), which binds the two cerebral hemispheres together (see illustration, p. 165). Nerve fibers cross the corpus callosum and keep the cerebrum acting as a unit, but in some ways the hemispheres are, at least potentially, independent.

The situation is somewhat analogous to that of our eyes. We have two eyes which ordinarily act as a unit. Nevertheless, if we cover one eye we can see well enough with the remaining eye; a one-eyed man is not blind in any sense of the word. Similarly, the removal of one of the cerebral hemispheres does not make an experimental animal brainless. The remaining hemisphere learns to carry on. Ordinarily each hemisphere is largely responsible for a particular side of the body. If both hemispheres are left in place and the corpus callosum is cut, coordination is lost and the two body halves come under more or less independent control. A literal case of "twin brains" is set up. Monkeys can be so treated (with further operation upon the optic nerve in order to make sure that each eye is connected to only one hemisphere), and when this is done each eye can be separately trained to do particular tasks. A monkey can be trained to select a cross over a circle as marking, let us say, the presence of food. If only the left eye is kept uncovered during the training period, only the left eye will be useful in this respect. If the right eye is uncovered and the left eye covered, the monkey will have no right-eye memory of his training. He will have to hunt for his food by trial and error. If the two eyes are trained to contradictory tasks and if both are then uncovered, the monkey alternates activities, as the hemispheres politely take their turns.

Naturally, in any such two-in-charge situation, there is always the danger of conflict and confusion. To avoid that, one cerebral hemisphere (almost always the left one in human beings) is dominant. Broca's convolution, see page 173, which controls speech, is in the left cerebral hemisphere, not the right. Again, the left cerebral hemisphere controls the motor activity of the right-hand side of the body, which may account for the fact that most people are right-handed (though even left-handed people usually have a dominant left cerebral hemisphere). Ambidextrous people, who may have cerebral hemispheres without clear-cut dominance, sometimes have speech difficulties in early life.

The subcortical portions of the cerebrum are not all white matter. There are collections of gray matter, too, below the cortex. These are called the *basal ganglia.* The piece of gray matter that lies highest in the cerebral interior is the *caudate nucleus* ("tailed" L, because of its shape). The gray matter of the caudate nucleus bends upon itself, and its other end is the *amygdaloid nucleus* ("almond-shaped," again because of its shape). To one side of the caudate nucleus is the *lentiform nucleus* ("lens-shaped") and between the two is the white matter of the internal capsule. The nuclei are not uniformly gray but contain white matter with fibers of gray matter running through it and giving

---

* The word *ganglion* (gang'lee-on) is Greek for "knot" and was originally used by Hippocrates and his school for knotlike tumors beneath the skin. Galen, the Roman physician who flourished about A.D. 200, began to use the word for collections of nerve cells which stood out like knots against the ordinarily string-like nerves, and it is still so used.

the region a striated appearance. The region including the two nuclei is therefore called the *corpus striatum*.

Within the curve of the caudate-nucleus, corpus-striatum, and lentiform-nucleus complex lies a mass of gray matter that represents the thalamus. (The reason for the name is given on page 145.) The thalamus is usually not included among the basal ganglia, though it is right there physically.

The basal ganglia are difficult to study, obscured as they are by the cerebral cortex. Yet there are indications of importance both in the passive and active sense. The white matter of the corpus striatum is a bottleneck. All motor nerve fibers descending from the cortex and all sensory fibers ascending up toward it must pass through it. Consequently, any damage to that region can have the most widespread effects. Such damage can, for instance, lead to loss of sensation and capacity for motion in a whole side of the body; the side opposite to that of the cerebral hemisphere within which the damage took place. Such one-sided loss is called *hemiplegia* (hem-ee-plee′jee-uh; "half stroke" G).*

It has been suggested that one of the functions of the basal ganglia is to exert a control over the motor area of the cortex (by way of the extra-pyramidal system of which it forms a part) and to prevent the motor area from kicking off too readily. When this function of the basal ganglia is interfered with, sections of the motor area may indeed fire off too readily, and then there are rapid involuntary muscle contractions. The muscles usually affected in this way are those controlling the head and the hands and fingers. As a result, the head and hand shake continuously and gently. This shaking is most marked when the patient is at rest and smooths out when a purposeful motion is superimposed; in other words, when the motor area goes into real action instead of leaking slightly.

---

* The loss of the capacity for motion is referred to as *paralysis* from a Greek word meaning "to loosen." The muscles fall loose, so to speak. Conditions that bring on sudden paralysis, as the rupture of a blood vessel in the brain, is referred to as a "stroke" both in plain English and in the Greek, because the person is felled as though struck by a blunt instrument.

Other muscles become abnormally immobile in such cases, although there is no true paralysis. The facial expression becomes comparatively unchanging and masklike; walking becomes stiff, and the arms remain motionless instead of swinging naturally with the stride. This combination of too little movement in arms and face and too much movement in head and hands receives the self-contradictory name of *paralysis agitans* (aj′ih-tans; "to move" L). The self-contradictoriness is maintained in the English name of "shaking palsy." (The word "palsy" is a shortened and distorted form, descended through medieval French, of "paralysis.") Paralysis agitans was first clinically described in 1817 by an English physician named James Parkinson; it is also commonly known as *Parkinson's disease*.

Relief from some of the symptoms has been achieved by deliberately damaging the basal ganglia, which seems to be a case of "a hair of the dog." One technique is to locate the abnormal region by noting at which point a touch of a thin probe wipes out, or at least decreases, the tremor and rigidity, and then cooling the area to $-50°$ C. with liquid nitrogen. This can be repeated if the symptoms recur. Apparently, nonfunctioning ganglia are preferable to misfunctioning ones.

Sometimes damage to the basal ganglia may result in more spasmodic and extensive involuntary muscular movements; almost as though a person were dancing in a clumsy and jerky manner. Such movements are referred to as *chorea* (koh-ree′ah; "dance" G). This may strike children as an aftermath of rheumatic fever, where the infection has managed to involve the brain. An English physician named Thomas Sydenham first described this form of the disease in 1686, so that it is usually called *Sydenham's chorea*.

During the Middle Ages there were instances of "dancing manias" that swept over large areas. These probably were not true chorea epidemics, but had roots in abnormal psychology. It is possible, however, that specific cases of mania may have been set off by a true case of chorea. Someone else might have fallen into line in hysterical imitation, others followed, and a mania was under way. It was felt at one time that to be cured of the dancing mania one ought to make a pilgrimage to the shrine of St. Vitus. It is for this reason that Sydenham's chorea has the common name of "St. Vitus's dance."

There is also *hereditary chorea,* often referred to as *Huntington's chorea,* from the American physician George Sumner Huntington, who described it in 1872. It is much more serious than the St. Vitus's dance, from which, after all, one recovers. Huntington's chorea does not appear until adult life (between 30 and 50). Mental disorders accompany it; it grows steadily worse, and is eventually fatal. It is an inherited condition, as one of its names implies. Two brothers afflicted with the disease migrated to the United States from England, and all modern American patients are supposed to be descended from them.

The thalamus acts as a reception center for the somesthetic sensations — touch, pain, heat, cold, and the muscle senses. It is indeed an important portion of the reticular activating system which accepts and sifts incoming sensory data. The more violent of these, such as pain, extreme heat or cold, rough touch, are filtered out. The milder sensations from the muscles, the gentle touches, the moderate temperatures are passed on to the sensory area of the cortex. It is as though mild sensations can be trusted to the cerebral cortex, where they can be considered judiciously and where reaction can come after a more or less prolonged interval of consideration. The rough sensations, however, which must be dealt with quickly and for which there is no time for consideration, are handled more or less automatically in the thalamus.

There is a tendency, therefore, to differentiate between the cortex as the cold center of reason and the thalamus as the hot focus of emotion. And, as a matter of fact, the thalamus controls the movement of facial muscles under conditions of emotional stress, so that even when cortical control of those same muscles is destroyed and the expression is masklike in calm states, the face can still twist and distort in response to strong emotion. In addition, animals in which the cortex is removed fall easily into all the movements associated with extreme rage. Despite the foregoing, this sharp distinction between cortex and thalamus would seem to be an oversimplification. Emotions do not arise from any one small part of the brain, it would appear. Rather, many parts, including the frontal and temporal lobes of the cortex, are involved — in a complex interplay. Removing the temporal lobes of animals may reduce their emotional displays to a minimum even though the thalamus is not affected.

In recent years, attention has been focused on certain portions of the cerebrum — old portions, evolutionarily speaking, related to ancient olfactory regions — which are particularly associated with emotion and with emotion-provoking stimuli such as hunger and sex. This region seems to coordinate sensory data with bodily needs, with the requirements of the viscera, in other words. It is therefore referred to as the *visceral brain*. The convolutions associated with the visceral brain were named the *limbic lobe* ("border" L) by Broca because they surrounded and bordered on the corpus callosum. For this reason, the visceral brain is sometimes called the *limbic system*.

THE HYPOTHALAMUS

Underneath the third ventricle and, consequently, underneath the thalamus, is the *hypothalamus* ("beneath the thalamus" G), which has a variety of devices for controlling the body. Among the most recently discovered is a region within it which on stimulation gives rise to a strongly pleasurable sensation. An electrode affixed to the "pleasure center" of a rat, so arranged that it can be stimulated by the animal itself, will be stimulated for hours or days at a time, to the exclusion of food, sex, and sleep. Evidently all the desirable things in life are desirable only insofar as they stimulate the pleasure center. To stimulate it directly makes all else unnecessary. (The possibilities that arise in connection with a kind of addiction to end all addictions are distressing to contemplate.)

Because of the several ways in which the hypothalamus sets up automatic controls of bodily functions, one can look upon it as having functions not very different from those of sets of hormones acting in cooperating antagonism (such as insulin and glucagon, for instance). There is, in reality, a physical connection between the hypothalamus and the world of hormones as well as a vague functional one. It is to the hypothalamus that the pituitary gland is attached, and the posterior lobe of the pituitary actually arises from the hypothalamus in the course of its development.

It is not surprising, then, that the hypothalamus is involved in the control of water metabolism in the body. I have already described how the posterior pituitary controls the water concentration in the body by regulating reabsorption of water in the kidney tubules. Well, it would seem that one can go a step beyond the posterior pituitary to the hypothalamus. Changes in the water concentration in the blood stimulates a particular hypothalamic center first, and it is the hypothalamus that then sets off the posterior pituitary. If the stalk connecting the hypothalamus to the posterior pituitary is cut, diabetes insipidus results, even though the gland itself remains unharmed.

The hypothalamus also contains a group of cells that acts as a very efficient thermostat. We are conscious of temperature changes, of course, and will attempt to rectify extremes by adding or subtracting clothing and by the use of furnaces and air-conditioners. The hypothalamus reacts analogously, but much more delicately and with built-in devices.

Within the hypothalamus appropriate cells are affected by the temperature of the bloodstream, and small variations from the norm bring quick responses. The body's furnace is represented by a constant gentle vibration of the muscles of from 7 to 13 times a second. (This was detected and reported in 1962.) The heat liberated by such muscular action replaces that lost to a cold environment. The rate of these vibrations increases as the temperature drops and, if it grows cold enough, the amplitude becomes marked enough to be noticeable and we shiver. The body's air-conditioner is represented by perspiration, since the evaporation of water absorbs heat, and the heat absorbed is withdrawn from the body. The hypothalamus, by controlling the rate of muscle vibration and of perspiration, keeps the body's internal temperature within a Fahrenheit degree of normal (98.6° F. is usually given as the normal) despite the alteration (within reason) of outside temperatures.

There are conditions where the setting of the hypothalamus thermostat can be raised. Most frequently, this is the result of the liberations of foreign proteins, or *toxins* ("poison" G), in the body by invading germs. Even small quantities of these toxins may result in raising the temperature of the body by several degrees to produce a *fever*. In reaching the higher-than-normal temperatures of fever, all of the body's devices for raising temperature are called into play. Perspiration is cut down, and the body feels dry and the muscles are set to shivering. This is customarily the reaction to cold; the patient, whose teeth may be chattering, complains of "chills"; hence the common expression "chills and fever." When the invasion of bacteria is brought under control so that body temperature can drop to normal, the body's cooling reactions become evident. In particular, the rate of perspiration is greatly increased. This sudden onset of perspiration is the crisis, and its appearance is, in many infectious diseases, a good sign that the patient will recover.

The raising of temperature hastens the destruction of protein molecules to a much greater extent than it hastens other types of reactions. Since there are numerous proteins in the body that are essential to life, a body temperature of 108° F., only 10 Fahrenheit degrees above normal, is sufficient to place a man in serious danger of death. (Such a raised temperature also endangers the functioning of the proteins of the alien bacteria; the ideal situation is to find a temperature high enough to kill the bacteria without being high enough to affect the human cells too adversely.)

The body is much less sensitive to temperatures lower than

normal, that is, to *hypothermia* ("below-heat" G). Human beings, trapped in snowdrifts, have been snatched from slow freezing and brought back to complete recovery from temperatures as low as 60° F. The lowering of temperature decreases the rate at which chemical reactions take place in the body (lowers the "metabolic rate"), and at 60° F. the metabolic rate is only 15 per cent normal.

As a matter of fact, many normally warm-blooded animals, such as bears and dormice, react to the cold season by dropping the thermostat of the hypothalamus precipitously. Everything slows down. The heartbeat falls to a feeble few per minute and breathing is shallow. The fat supply is then sufficient to last all winter. Man lacks this ability to hibernate, and if his temperature is forced below 60° F. death follows, apparently because the coordination of the heart muscle is destroyed. Nevertheless, there are times when hypothermia is useful; especially when operations on the heart itself are in progress. Through the sufficient lowering of rate of metabolism (but not too much for safety), heart action is slowed and the heart can be tampered with for longer intervals without harm.

The human body temperature can be lowered by brute force — by packing the anesthetized body in ice water, or in a blanket cooled by refrigerant circling within. Less drastic measures are required if the hypothalamus is tackled. This can be done by withdrawing the blood from an artery, sending it through refrigerated tubes, and restoring it to the body. If the blood is taken from the carotid artery in the neck and restored there, the brain is most directly cooled. The hypothalamus is frozen out of action, and after that the body temperature can be lowered more easily. Furthermore, the brain can be brought to an especially low temperature, lower than that of the rest of the body. This decreases the metabolic rate within the brain especially and drastically cuts down its need for oxygen. It is the brain's needs that limit the time for any operation which shuts off the blood flow for a while. Under these conditions, a heart operation has lasted for as long as 14 minutes without harm to the body.

A section of the central region of the hypothalamus controls the appetite of the body just as the thermostat area controls the heat. By analogy, this appetite-controlling region can be called the *appestat*. Its existence was discovered when animals began to eat voraciously and became grotesquely obese after the appropriate area of the hypothalamus was destroyed. It appears that as the thermostat tests the blood passing through for temperature so the appestat tests it for glucose content. When, after a period of fasting, the glucose content drops below a certain key level, the appetite is turned on, one might say, and the person will eventually eat if food is available. With the glucose level restored, the appetite is turned off. In this way the average human being, eating when hungry and not eating when not hungry, can maintain a reasonable weight with reasonable constancy — and without thinking about it too much.

There are people (all too many) who maintain their weight at levels considerably higher than is optimum for health. The simplest explanation is that such people are "gluttons"; and the most romantic explanation is that there is some psychiatric reason making it necessary for them to overeat. Between the two is the ordinary physiological suggestion that the appestat is for some reason set too high, so that they become hungry sooner and stay hungry longer. A recent suggestion is that there are two appetite-controlling centers: one to turn it on (a "feeding center") and one to turn it off (a "satiety center"), and that it is the latter which is often malfunctioning in the somewhat overweight person. It is not, perhaps, that he is actively hungry as that he is constantly ready to nibble; whereas the normal person would find such eating unnecessary and even distasteful.

Finally, the hypothalamus contains an area that has to do with the wake-sleep cycle. The human being has a twenty-four-hour cycle that must have originated in response to the alternation of light and dark as the earth rotates. (Modern air travel, which puts the human cycle out of phase with the earthly cycle, can disrupt a man's regular habits of eating, sleeping, and excreting.) During the periods of sleep, a man goes through a kind of very mild hibernation. His metabolic rate drops 10 to 15 per cent below the lowest wakeful values, his heartbeat slows, his blood pressure drops, and his muscle tone slackens.

The amount of sleep required varies from person to person but decreases generally with age. For a period after birth the baby sleeps whenever it is not eating. Children, in general, sleep from ten to twelve hours a day, and adults from six to nine hours.

The purpose of sleep, one would almost naturally assume, is to make up the wear and tear of the working day; but there are many organs that work constantly day and night, without much in the way of wear and tear. When wakefulness is enforced, no bodily functions go seriously awry except those of the brain. Apparently, extended wakefulness affects the coordination of various parts of the nervous system, and there is the onset of hallucinations and other symptoms of mental disturbance. This is quite enough, however. Lack of sleep will kill more quickly than lack of food.

The onset of sleep may be mediated by a section of the hypothalamus, since damage to parts of it induces a sleeplike state in animals. The exact mechanism by which the hypothalamus performs its function is uncertain. One theory is that it sends signals to the cortex, which sends signals back in response, in mutually stimulating fashion. With continuing wakefulness, the coordination of the two fails, the oscillations begin to fail, and one becomes sleepy. When the coordination is restored, arousal takes place, even if violent stimuli (a loud noise, a persistent shake of the shoulder) does not intervene.

The reticular activating system, which filters out sensory data, is also involved in the arousal mechanism, since by refusing to pass stimuli along, it encourages sleep, and by passing them it helps bring about waking, and, what's more, maintains consciousness during the waking interval. It is therefore referred to as an "activating system." The reason for the "reticular" portion of the name will be made clear later.

The working of the reticular activating system and the mutual stimulation of hypothalamus and cortex may be insufficient to maintain wakefulness in the absence of a normal amount of varying stimuli entering the cortex. Drabness or dullness of the surroundings may send one to sleep, and deliberate concentration on a repetitive stimulus (a swinging, glittering object, say) may induce the trance well known to all of us who have watched hypnotic demonstrations. And, of course, we commonly put babies to sleep by slow, rhythmic rocking. On the other hand, if the cortex is unusually stimulated, the failure of the hypothalamic signals may be insufficient to induce sleep. The unusual stimulation may be from without (a gay party, perhaps) or from within, when the cortex is absorbed in matters arising out of anxiety, worry, or anger. In the latter case especially, sleep may not come even when all the external factors (darkness, quiet, a soft bed) usually associated with it are present. Such *insomnia* ("no sleep" L) can be exasperating indeed.

There are diseases that inflame the brain tissue (encephalitis) and can produce continuous sleep. One variety, *encephalitis lethargica* (le-thahr'jih-kuh; "forgetfulness" G), commonly called *sleeping sickness,* can produce long periods of *coma* ("put to sleep" G). In extreme cases a patient can remain in such a coma for years, provided he is properly cared for and all his needs are met by attendants.

In Africa there is an endemic disease caused by a kind of protozoon called a *trypanosome* (trip'uh-noh-sohm'; "augur-body" G, from its shape). The disease, properly called *trypanosomiasis* (trip'uh-noh-soh-my'uh-sis), is commonly called "African sleeping sickness." It is spread from person to person by the bite of the tsetse fly, which carries the protozoon and is famous for that reason. Trypanosomiasis induces a coma that usually deepens into death. Large areas of Africa are deadly to men and cattle, as a result.

9

OUR BRAIN STEM
AND SPINAL CORD

All the structure of the brain from the cerebral cortex down to the hypothalamus is developed from the forebrain of the original fishy ancestor of the vertebrates. All this may therefore be referred to as the *prosencephalon* (pros'en-sef'uh-lon; "forebrain" G). This may be divided into two parts. The cerebral hemispheres themselves are the *telencephalon* ("end-brain" G), because this is the end of the central nervous system if you work from the bottom up, whereas the basal ganglia, thalamus, and hypothalamus are the *diencephalon* ("between-brain" G).

Although the forebrain has grown to be so overwhelmingly prominent a feature of the human nervous system, it does not follow that the brain is all forebrain. Below that there remain the midbrain and the hindbrain. The midbrain in the human being is comparatively small and lies about the narrow passage connecting the third and fourth ventricle. It appears as a pair of stout columns that extend vertically downward from the thalamic regions. Below it is the *pons* ("bridge" L), so named because it is a bridge connecting the midbrain with the chief portion of the hindbrain; and below that is the medulla oblongata (defined on p. 145).

The midbrain, pons, and medulla taken together form a stalk-like affair leading downward and slightly backward from the

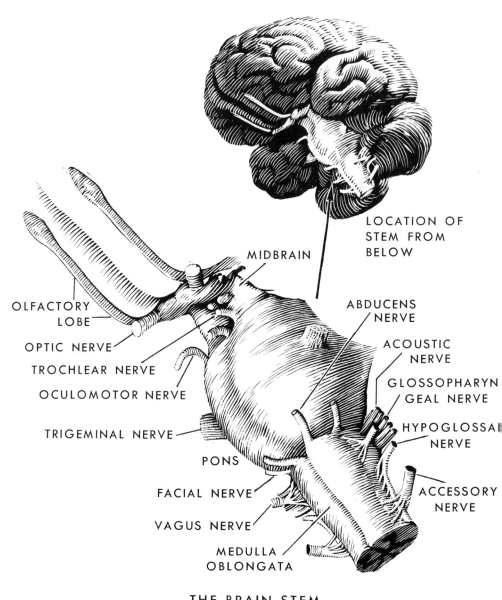

LOCATION OF STEM FROM BELOW

MIDBRAIN

OLFACTORY LOBE

OPTIC NERVE

TROCHLEAR NERVE

OCULOMOTOR NERVE

TRIGEMINAL NERVE

PONS

FACIAL NERVE

VAGUS NERVE

MEDULLA OBLONGATA

ABDUCENS NERVE

ACOUSTIC NERVE

GLOSSOPHARYN GEAL NERVE

HYPOGLOSSAL NERVE

ACCESSORY NERVE

THE BRAIN STEM

cerebrum. The cerebrum seems to rest on these lower portions as though it were a piece of fruit balanced upon its stem. The lower structure is commonly referred to as the *brain stem* for that reason. The brain stem narrows as it proceeds downward, until it passes out through an opening in the cranium, the *foramen magnum* (foh-ray'men mag'num; "great opening" L), at the base of the skull and enters the neural canal of the spinal column. There the brain stem merges with the spinal cord.

Attached to the brain stem, behind and above, and lying immediately below the rear overhang of the cerebrum is the cerebellum (see p. 145). This originated in the primitive vertebrates as a portion of the hindbrain. Like the cerebrum, the cerebellum is divided into two portions by a longitudinal fissure, these portions being the *cerebellar hemispheres.* There is a connecting structure between the hemispheres which, seen on edge from behind, seems thin, segmented, and elongated and is consequently called the *vermis* (vur'mis; "worm" L). Like the cerebrum, the cerebellum contains white matter within and the gray matter of the cell bodies occupies the surface, which is the *cerebellar cortex.* The cerebellar cortex is more tightly wrinkled than the cerebral cortex, and its fissures lie in parallel lines.

Each cerebellar hemisphere is connected to the brain stem by three *peduncles* (peh-dung'kulz; "little feet" L) made up of nerve fibers. The uppermost connects it with the midbrain, the next with the pons, and the lowermost with the medulla oblongata. There are also connections by way of the peduncles with the cerebrum above and the spinal cord below.

The brain stem has much to do with the more automatic types of muscle activity. For example, in standing we are actively using muscles to keep our back and legs stiff against the pull of gravity. We are not ordinarily aware of this activity, but if we have been standing a long time a feeling of weariness makes itself unpleasantly evident, and if we lose consciousness while standing we at once relax the muscles that counteract gravity, and crumple to the ground.

If we were forced to keep our muscles in completely conscious play in order to stand without falling, standing would become an activity that would occupy our minds greatly and prevent us from doing much of anything else. This is not so, fortunately. The muscular effort of standing is taken care of without much of a conscious effort. As a result, we can allow our minds to be completely occupied with other matters and, if circumstances so dictate, stand easily while lost in a brown study. No one falls simply because his mind is distracted. This automatic control of the standing muscles is centered in the brain stem, particularly in a portion of it characterized by a mixture of gray and white matter so interspersed as to give it a netlike appearance. This is the *reticular area* ("little net" L). It is here, too, that the sensory filter is located, which we have been referring to as the reticular activating system (see p. 193).

Assuredly we do not wish to stand all the time. In order to sit down, the standing muscles must relax. This is done in response to impulses from the basal ganglia above the brain stem. These impulses allow the body to fall down, one might say, in a controlled fashion and to assume the sitting position. If an animal's brain is cut between the cerebrum and the brain stem, these relaxing impulses from the basal ganglia can no longer reach the muscles. As a result the animal becomes rigid all over and remains so. Its war against gravity becomes permanent and uncompromising.

Standing is not a static matter, though it may seem so. The human body is in a relatively unstable position while standing, because it has a high center of gravity and is balanced on two supports placed close together. (Most other vertebrates are quadrupeds, with a relatively lower center of gravity, and balance on four supports, generously spaced, at the vertexes of a rectangle.) Consequently, if a man tries to stand absolutely rigid without moving a muscle under any circumstances, he can be easily toppled by a brisk push against the shoulder. In an actual situation of that sort, the man would automatically shift his muscular effort to counteract the force, spread his legs wider apart, and push back. If in the end he fell, it would only be after a struggle.

The forces tending to upset equilibrium are constant. If no kindly friend is testing you by a push, you still may be altering the position of your center of gravity by the natural motions of the body — by reaching, lifting, stooping. You may be withstanding the erratic pressure of the wind. In short, you are constantly tending to fall in one direction or another, and the muscles of your trunk and legs must constantly adjust their tensions in order to counteract and neutralize these falling tendencies.

Here there is an intimate connection, again, between the brain stem and the basal ganglia. The overall position of the body with respect to the pull of gravity is revealed by structures in the inner ear which I shall discuss later in the book. Nerve messages from the inner ear are received by the brain stem and the basal ganglia. In addition, sensations from muscles and joints continually arrive at the reticular activating system in the brain stem. In cooperation, basal ganglia and brain stem act so that appropriate muscles are stiffened or relaxed, so that equilibrium is constantly maintained.

Far from being troublesome, this constant necessity of altering muscular tension to produce equilibrium is useful. If we were to imagine a human being in perfect balance, we would see that the muscles would be forced to maintain a constant and unchanging tension and would grow weary more rapidly. By constant adjustment of equilibrium, different muscles bear the brunt at different times and each has a certain chance to rest. Actually, when we are forced to stand a long time we exaggerate these varying tensions on the muscles by altering the position of the center of gravity. We do this by shifting restlessly from foot to foot, or by shifting weight in other parts of the body.

Walking consists of throwing ourselves off balance by leaning forward and then catching ourselves before we fall by moving a foot ahead into a new position. It is a difficult feat for a child to learn, and during his early attempts it takes up all his concentration. If his mind wanders, he plops down.

However, walking involves rhythmic motion; the same muscles tense and relax in a fixed pattern that is repeated over and over again. With time, the control of these rhythmic muscular movements can be shifted to the brain stem, which can then keep the arms and legs swinging along without any need for much conscious effort on our part. We can even walk with reasonable efficiency while engaged in an absorbing conversation or with our head buried in a book.

This perpetual loss and regaining of equilibrium during standing and walking involves constant feedback. Thus, if the body is out of equilibrium and if the basal ganglia begin a change in the tension of particular muscles in order to restore equilibrium, sensory impulses must be received at each instant to indicate the departure from equilibrium at that moment, in order for the tension of the muscles to be constantly adjusted (feedback). This means the body must look ahead.

The reason for this may perhaps be more easily understood if we consider a mechanical analogy. If you are turning a corner while driving an automobile, you must begin to turn your wheel before you reach the corner, turning it more and more as you proceed, until you have reached maximum turn midway around the corner. Otherwise, if you reach the corner while your wheels are still perfectly straight, you will have to turn too sharply. Again, you must begin to straighten your wheel long before you complete the turn. You must begin to straighten it, in fact, as soon as you have reached midway around the corner, and adjust the straightening process in such a way that the wheels are perfectly straight, at last, just as you complete the turn. Otherwise, if your wheels are still turned when you are finally heading in the right direction, you will find yourself turning into the curb and forced to right yourself by a quick curve in the opposite direction.

So, you see, a proper turn requires you to look ahead, to be aware of not only your position at the moment but of your future position a few moments later. This is not easy for a beginner.

When first learning to drive a car, a man is forced to take corners very slowly in order to avoid turning erratically first this way and that. As experience grows, he begins to handle the wheel without conscious thought and to make smooth and perfect turns every time — well, nearly every time.

A situation exactly analogous to this takes place in the controlling centers of the nervous system when equilibrium must be maintained or when a specific motion of any sort is necessary. Suppose that you move your arm forward to pick up a pencil. Your hand moves forward rapidly but must begin to slow up before it quite reaches the pencil. The fingers must begin to close before the pencil is touched. If the hand looks as though it might go to one side, its position is adjusted correspondingly; if it looks as though it will overshoot the mark, it must be slowed further; or hastened, if it will fall short. All this continuous correction of motion is unconscious, and we might feel ready to swear that it does not take place. Nevertheless, it is why we look at the pencil we are to pick up, or the jaw we are to punch, or the shoe-lace we are to tie. It is the continual message sent to the brain by the eye which enables us to adjust the controls constantly. If you reach for a pencil without looking, even if you know where it is, you are very apt to have to grope a bit.

To be sure, looking is not always required. If you are told to touch your nose with your finger, you can do it quite accurately even in the dark. You are normally aware of the position of various parts of your body at all times through the somesthetic senses. Likewise, you might be able to type or knit without looking, but your fingers are making very short-range motions where, through long practice, there is scarcely room to go astray.

It is a chief role of the cerebellum, evidently, to take care of this adjustment of motion by feedback. It looks ahead, and predicts the position of the arm a few instants ahead, organizing motion accordingly. When the system fails, the results can be dramatic. A hand reaching for a pencil will overshoot the mark, come back, overshoot the mark in the reverse direction, go forward, and continue to do this over and over. There are wild oscillations that may resemble those of a novice driver trying to round a corner at too great a speed. In mechanical devices such oscillations are referred to as "hunting." Damage to the cerebellum induces such hunting, and anything that requires the coordination of several muscles becomes difficult or even impossible. An attempt to run leads to an instant fall. Motions become pathetically jerky, and even the attempt to touch the finger to the nose can result in a ludicrous miss of the target. This condition is called *ataxia* (a-tak'see-uh; "disordered" G). *Cerebral palsy* refers to any disturbance in muscle use resulting from brain damage taking place during fetal development or during the birth process. About 4 per cent of such cases show ataxia.

The brain stem also controls specific functions and motions of the digestive tract. For instance, the rate of salivary secretion is controlled by certain cells in the upper medulla and the lower pons. The sight and smell of food, or even the thought of food, will trigger those cells to stimulate salivary secretion so that the mouth "waters." On the contrary, fear or tension may inhibit their action so that the mouth grows dry. The process of swallowing brings about a number of automatic movements in the throat, and a subsequent wave of constriction in the esophagus that pushes the food ahead of it into the stomach. These, too, are under the control of cells in the brain stem.

Then, too, a region in the brain stem controls the respiratory rate. This is to a certain extent under voluntary control and hence amenable to impulses from the cerebrum. We can force ourselves to breathe quickly or slowly; we can even hold our breath. All these voluntary interferences with rate of respiration quickly grow difficult and wearisome and the automatic control of the brain stem takes over.

Below the brain stem, beyond the foramen magnum, is the lowermost portion of the central nervous system, the *spinal cord*. This is what is left of the undifferentiated nerve cord of the original chordates. The spinal cord is roughly elliptical in cross sec-

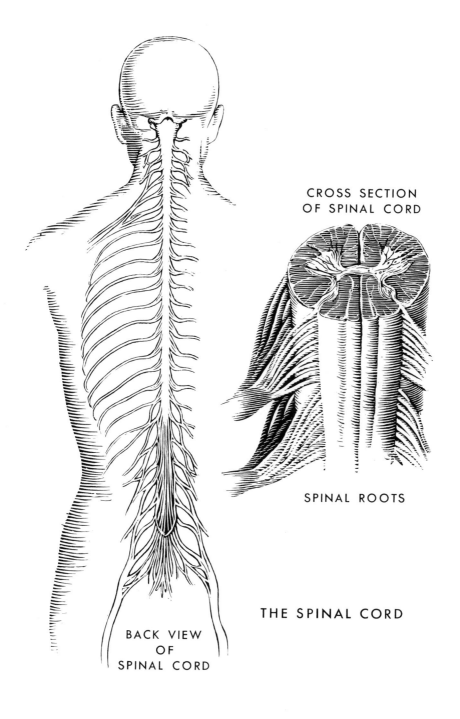

CROSS SECTION
OF SPINAL CORD

SPINAL ROOTS

THE SPINAL CORD

BACK VIEW
OF
SPINAL CORD

tion, being wider from right to left than from front to back. There is a furrow running down the back of the cord and a somewhat wider but shallower depression running down in front. Together these almost, but not quite, divide the cord into a right and left half that are mirror images. Running down the axis of the cord is the small central canal (which sometimes vanishes in adults), all that is left of the hollow in the original chordate nerve cord.

The inner portion of the cord is filled with a mass of nerve cell bodies, so the spinal cord has its gray matter as the brain has. Only, whereas the gray matter of the brain is on the outside cortex, that of the spinal cord lies within. When the spinal cord is viewed in cross section, the gray matter forms a more or less vertical line in both right and left halves. The two lines are connected by gray matter reaching across the central canal region. As a result, the gray matter in cross section looks like a rather straggly *H*. As shown in the illustration (p. 203), the lower bars of the letter H are those which extend dorsally — toward the back. They are relatively long and reach almost to the surface of the spinal cord. These are the *posterior horns,* or *dorsal horns.* The upper bars of the H, extending ventrally — toward the abdomen — are shorter and stubbier. These are the *anterior horns,* or *ventral horns.* Surrounding the H-shaped gray matter and filling out the elliptical cross section are the massed nerve fibers, which, because of their myelin sheathing, make up the white matter. In the spinal cord the white matter is on the surface, and not, as in the brain, in the interior.

The spinal cord does not run the full length of the spinal column in man. It ends at about the first or second lumbar vertebra, just in the small of the back. The spinal cord, therefore, is only about 18 inches long. It is about ½ inch wide and in the adult weighs about 1 ounce.

THE CRANIAL NERVES

Outside the brain and spinal cord, which make up the central nervous system, is the peripheral nervous system (see p. 140).

This consists of the various nerves that connect particular parts of the central nervous system with particular organs. The nerves in turn consist of bundles of hundreds, sometimes thousands, of individual nerve fibers. Some nerve fibers conduct impulses from the different organs to the central nervous system and are therefore *afferent fibers* (af'ur-ent; "carry toward" L). Because the impulses carried toward the brain and spinal cord are interpreted by the central nervous system as sensations of various sorts, the afferent fibers have the alternate name of *sensory fibers*. There are also nerve fibers that conduct impulses from the central nervous system to the various organs. These are *efferent fibers* (ef'ur-ent; "carry outward" L). They induce responses in the organs to which they are connected, and since the most noticeable of the responses are the motions induced in muscles, the efferent fibers are also called *motor fibers*.

There are a few *sensory nerves,* containing only sensory fibers, and *motor nerves,* containing only motor fibers. Most are, nonetheless, *mixed nerves* and contain both sensory and motor fibers. Nerves contain not only nerve fibers but sometimes, in addition, collections of the cell bodies to which these fibers are attached. These cell body collections are ganglia, a word I discussed on page 184.

In man 43 pairs of nerves, all told, lead into the central nervous system. Of these, 12 pairs are connected to the brain; they are the *cranial nerves* (see illustration, p. 196). The remaining 31 pairs join the spinal cord. The cranial nerves can simply be numbered one to twelve in Roman numerals (as they often are) according to the point of junction with the brain, beginning at the cerebrum and ending at the bottom of the medulla oblongata. Each has its own proper name, too, and these are as follows:

I. *Olfactory Nerve.* Each consists of a number of closely associated nerves (about twenty) that originate in the mucous membrane of the upper part of the nose. They extend upward, passing through small holes in the bones that make up the base of the cranium and ending in the olfactory lobes, which are small projections of the cerebrum, lying immediately above the floor of the cranium. As the name implies, these nerves are involved in the sense of smell.

The olfactory nerve is the only nerve to connect to the cerebrum; it reminds us that the cerebrum was originally primarily a smell organ until the mammals made something more of it. The remaining eleven cranial nerves are all attached to various portions of the brain stem.

II. *Optic Nerve.* This has to do with sight, as the name implies, and originates in the retina of the eye. The optic nerves from the two eyes extend backward and join at the midbrain. In this joined structure some of the fibers from each eye cross over to the opposite side, some remain on the original side. The fibers thus form an X shape; and the structure is the *optic chiasma* (ky-az'muh), because the Greek letter "chi" looks like our X (see illustration, p. 274). The optic nerve is not a true nerve, but is actually an extension of the brain structure.

III. *Oculomotor Nerve* (ok'yoo-loh-moh'tor; "eye movement" L). It extends from the midbrain to all but two of the muscles involved in the movement of the eyeball. Obviously, it controls eye movements.

IV. *Trochlear Nerve* (trok'lee-er). It is the smallest of the cranial nerves and extends from the midbrain to a muscle that helps to move the eyeball — one of the muscles not innervated by the oculomotor nerve. The word "trochlear" is from a Greek expression for a sheaf of pulleys. The muscle innervated passes through a ring of connective tissue so that it resembles a small pulley, whence the name.

V. *Trigeminal Nerve* (try-jem'ih-nul; "triplet" L). It is the largest of the cranial nerves. Whereas the olfactory and optic nerves are sensory and the oculomotor and trochlear nerves are motor; the trigeminal nerve is a mixed nerve, containing both sensory and motor fibers, each attached to the pons by a separate structure. The sensory fibers are in three groups (hence the name of the nerve as a whole) and are connected to different regions of the face. The *ophthalmic nerve* (of-thal'mik; "eye" G) supplies the skin of the forward half of the scalp, of the forehead, upper eyelid, and nose. The *maxillary nerve* (mak'sih-lehr'ee; "jaw" L) supplies the skin of the lower eyelid, part of the cheek, and the upper lip. The *mandibular nerve* (man-dib'yoo-ler; "chew" L) supplies the skin of the lower jaw and the regions of the cheeks behind those supplied by the maxillary nerve. The ophthalmic and maxillary nerves are sensory nerves, but the mandibular nerve is mixed. Its motor fibers control the movement of those muscles involved in chewing.

A *neuralgia* ("nerve pain" G) associated with the trigeminal nerve can be very painful. When it is spasmodic, it is associated with a twitching of the facial muscles. Such a twitch is usually known as a *tic* (a word arising from the same root that "twitch" does, perhaps). The painful muscular spasms associated with trigeminal neuralgia are sometimes referred to as *tic douloureux* (tik doo-loo-ruh'; "painful twitch" French).

VI. *Abducens Nerve* (ab-dyoo'senz; "lead away" L). It arises from the pons a little before its junction with the medulla and leads to the external rectus muscle of the eyeball. This muscle pulls the eyeball in such a way that the pupil moves away from the midline of the body, and it is from this that the name of the nerve arises. It is a motor nerve. (It may seem rather surprising that three of the twelve cranial nerves are concerned with motions of the eyeball, the abducens and trochlear nerves supplying one muscle each, the oculomotor nerve supplying the rest. In view of the importance of vision, it is perhaps not so surprising at that.)

VII. *Facial Nerve*. It arises from the pons just above its junction with the medulla. Like the trigeminal nerve, the facial nerve is a mixed nerve. Its sensory fibers arise from the forward two thirds of the tongue and it is through these that the sensation of taste reaches the brain. They also innervate the salivary glands and the tear-producing glands of the eye. The motor fibers lead to the various muscles of the face, which by their interplay give rise to the facial expressions that are so familiar to all of us.

VIII. *Stato-acoustic Nerve*. This sensory nerve is attached at the junction of the pons and the medulla. It innervates the inner ear and is concerned with the sense of hearing. For that reason it is frequently called the *acoustic nerve* ("hear" G), or *auditory nerve* ("hear" L). Since it also receives the sensations enabling the body to judge and control the equilibrium position while standing, the prefix "stato" ("stand" G) is added.

IX. *Glossopharyngeal Nerve* (glos'oh-fa-rin'jee-ul; "tongue-throat" G). This mixed nerve arises in the medulla, near its junction with the pons, and innervates the mucous membrane of the rear of the tongue and of the throat. These are sensory fibers. A motor fiber runs to a muscle in the throat.

X. *Vagus Nerve* (vay'gus; "wandering" L). Here is another mixed nerve. It receives this name because its course carries it over a far larger part of the body than is true of the remaining cranial nerves. The vagus nerve arises in the medulla as a series of rootlets that pass through the base of the cranium and join into a single nerve. Some of the motor fibers supply muscles in the larynx and the throat, and some reach downward to the muscles of the bronchi, to the heart muscle, and to the muscles of most of the digestive tract. It also innervates the pancreas and helps control that organ's rate of secretion of digestive juice (though the main job of regulating pancreatic secretion, as I explained in Chapter 1, rests with secretin).

XI. *Accessory Nerve*. This motor nerve supplies muscles of the throat and some of those in the arms and shoulder. A few of its fibers join the vagus nerve. It also receives some of its fibers from a spinal root. The name of the nerve arises from this fact, since spinal fibers are accessories to the nerve, as it is itself an accessory to the vagus nerve.

And, finally, there is —

XII. *Hypoglossal Nerve* (hy'poh-glos'ul; "below the tongue" G). This, another motor nerve, arises from the medulla and supplies the muscles controlling the movement of the tongue.

THE SPINAL NERVES

The spinal nerves differ from the cranial nerves in several respects. First, they are more regularly placed. The cranial nerves are attached to the brain at irregular intervals, many of them crowded into the region where the pons and the medulla oblongata meet. The spinal nerves, on the contrary, emerge from the cord at regular intervals in a manner that makes sense if we consider chordate history. The chordates are one of three segmented phyla — segmentation involving a division of the body structure into similar sections, as a train is divided into separate coaches. (The other two segmented phyla are the arthropods, which include insects, spiders, centipedes, and crustaceans, and the annelids, which include the earthworm.)

Chordates have specialized to the point where segmentation is not clearly marked. The clearest evidence of segmentation in the adult human is the repeated vertebrae of the spinal cord (one to each segment) and the repeating line of ribs attached to twelve of them. The nervous system also shows the existence of segmentation, and does so most clearly in the repeated and regular emergence of pairs of spinal nerves from between vertebrae all down the spinal column.

Whereas the cranial nerves are sometimes motor, sometimes sensory, and sometimes mixed, as has been shown, the spinal nerves are all mixed. At each segment of the cord a pair of nerves emerge; one from the left half and one from the right half of the H of gray matter. Each nerve, moreover, is connected both to the ventral horn and the dorsal horn of its side of the H. Each nerve thus has a *ventral root* (or *anterior root*) and a *dorsal root* (or *posterior root*). From the ventral root emerge motor fibers and from the dorsal root sensory fibers. These two sets of fibers join a short distance from the cord to form a single mixed nerve. The cell bodies to which the motor fibers are attached are found within the gray matter of the spinal cord itself. In contradistinction to this, the sensory fibers have their cell bodies lying just outside the spinal cord proper. These cell bodies are referred to as *ganglia of the posterior root.*

Each pair of spinal nerves, formed of the fusion of anterior and posterior roots, makes its way out between adjacent vertebrae. The first pair makes its way out between the skull and the first vertebra, the second pair between the first and second vertebrae, the third pair between the second and the third vertebrae, and so on. The first seven vertebrae are the cervical vertebrae of the neck region.* Consequently, the first eight pairs of spinal nerves, from the first which passes above the first vertebra, to the eighth, which passes below the seventh, are the *cervical nerves.*

Beneath the cervical vertebrae are twelve thoracic vertebrae of the chest region, and under each of these passes a pair of spinal nerves, so that there are twelve pairs of *thoracic nerves.* And since there are five lumbar vertebrae in the region of the small of the back, there are five pairs of *lumbar nerves.* Beneath the lumbar vertebrae is the sacrum. In the adult it seems to be a single bone, but in the embryo it consists of five separate vertebrae. These fuse into a solid piece during the course of our independent life in order to supply a strong base for our two-legged posture. However, the organization of the spinal nerves antedates the time when man rose to his hind legs, so there are still five pairs of *sacral nerves.* Finally, at the bottom of the spine are four buttonlike remnants of vertebrae that once formed part of a tail (when the animals ancestral to man had tails). These are the coccygeal vertebrae, and there is one final pair of *coccygeal nerves.*

To summarize: 8 cervical nerves, 12 thoracic nerves, 5 lumbar nerves, 5 sacral nerves, and 1 coccygeal nerve make up a total of 31 pairs of spinal nerves.

If the spinal column and the spinal cord it contained were of the same length, then one would expect the segments of the cord to run even with the vertebrae, and each successive nerve would just run straight out, horizontally. This is not so,

---

* For a detailed discussion of the various vertebrae, see *The Human Body.*

the spinal column is some ten inches longer than the cord, and the segments of the cord, therefore, are considerably smaller than the individual vertebrae.

As one progresses down the cord, then, the individual nerves must run vertically downward in order to emerge from underneath the proper vertebrae. The farther one progresses, the longer is the necessary vertical extension. Below the end of the cord there is a conglomeration of ten (to begin with) pairs of nerve running down the neural canal and being drained off, one could say, pair by pair at each vertebra. The lowermost portion of the neural canal thus seems filled with a mass of coarse parallel threads that seem to resemble the tail of a horse. And, indeed, the nerve mass is called *cauda equina* (kaw'duh ee-kwy'nuh; "tail of a horse" L). When anesthesia of the lower sections of the body is desired, the injection of anesthetic is made between the lumbar vertebrae, and never higher. At higher levels the cord can be injured. In the lumbar regions, the needle moves between adjacent nerves and does no mechanical damage. The technique is called *caudal anesthesia* (kaw'dul; "tail" L) because of the region of the body punctured.

After the spinal nerves leave the column they divide into two branches, or *rami* (ray'my; "branches" L), the singular form of the word being *ramus*. The *dorsal ramus* of each nerve supplies the muscle and skin of the back; the *ventral ramus* supplies the remainder of the body.

In general, the original chordate body plan had each pair of spinal nerves innervate the organs of its segment. Even in the human body the first four cervical nerves connect to the skin and muscles of the neck, whereas the next four connect to the skin and muscles of the arm and shoulder. In the same way, nerves from the lowermost segments of the cord supply the hips and legs. It is down here that the longest and largest nerve of the human body is to be found, passing out of the pelvis and down the back of the thigh and leg. It is the *sciatic nerve* (sy-at'ik; a word arising from a distortion of the Latin word *ischiadicus* meaning "pertaining to pains in the hipbone"). In-flammation of the sciatic nerve can be very painful. It is one form of neuralgia that has earned a special name for itself — *sciatica.*

The human body cannot be separated into clear segments, each handled by a special spinal nerve, however, because there are complications. For one thing, the segments are somewhat dis-torted as a result of evolutionary changes since the days of the first simple chordates. To illustrate: the diaphragm is a flat muscle separating the chest from the abdomen and lying in an area where one would expect it to be innervated by thoracic nerves; but in the embryo it develops, at least in part, in the neck region and is therefore innervated (as one might expect) by cervical nerves; when in the course of development the diaphragm moves downward to its position in the fully formed infant, it carries its cervical nerve supply with it.

Also, many muscles and other organs are formed in regions where nerves from two adjoining segments can be connected to them. This overlapping is quite usual, and there are few muscles that don't have a nerve supply reaching it from two different spinal nerves. This allows a margin of safety, by the way, since severing one nerve may then weaken muscles but is not likely to bring about complete paralysis of any region.

Lastly, the nerves themselves do not maintain a neat isolation after leaving the spinal column. Several adjacent nerves tend to meet in a complicated interlacing pattern called a *plexus* (see p. 164). They don't lose their identity there, apparently, but the intermixing is sufficiently tortuous to make it impractical to trace the course of the individual nerves. To give examples, the first four cervical nerves form the *cervical plexus* and the remaining four, plus the first thoracic nerve, form the *brachial plexus* (bray′kee-ul; "arm" L). The latter is so named because it is at the level of the upper arm. The other thoracic nerves remain individual, but the lumbar nerves join to form the *lumbar plexus*, and the sacral nerves form the *sacral plexus*.

In general, then, when the spinal cord is severed, through disease or through injury, that part of the body lying below the severed segment is disconnected, so to speak. It loses sensation and is paralyzed. If the cord is severed above the fourth nerve death follows, because the chest is paralyzed, and with it the action of the lungs. It is this which makes a "broken neck" fatal, and hanging a feasible form of quick execution. It is the severed cord, rather than a possible broken vertebra, that is fatal.

The various spinal nerves are not independent but are coordinated among themselves and with the brain. The white matter of the spinal cord is made up of bundles of nerve fibers that run up and down the cord. Those that conduct impulses downward from the brain are the *descending tracts* and those that conduct them upward to the brain are the *ascending tracts*.

I have already mentioned, on page 174, the pyramidal system, which is one of the descending tracts. It arises in the motor area of the cortex, passes down through the basal ganglia and the brain stem, then down the spinal cord on either side, right and left, forming synaptic connections with the various spinal nerves. In this way the muscles of the limbs and trunk, which are innervated by spinal nerves, are subject to voluntary movement and are under cortical control. Other descending tracts such as the extra-pyramidal system pass through the various levels of the nervous system. The muscles of the trunk and limbs, connected in this fashion to the brain stem via the spinal nerves, can be controlled by the cerebellum, for instance, so that equilibrium is maintained.

The ascending tracts collect the various sensations picked up by the spinal cord and carry them upward, through the reticular activating system. It is by use of this information that the various portions of the brain can evolve the appropriate responses.

THE AUTONOMIC NERVOUS SYSTEM

Nerve fibers can be divided into two classes, depending on whether the organs they deal with are under the control of the will or not. The organs we most commonly think of as being under the control of the will are the skeletal muscles. It is by the contraction of these that we move the hinged bones of the skeleton and move certain nonskeletal portions of the body as well. The movements of the limbs, the flexings of the torso, the motion of the lower jaw, and the various movements of the tongue and face are all under voluntary control.

The skeletal muscles sheathe the body and flesh out the limbs so that we can move virtually all parts of the body surface at will. To the casual eye, it seems that we can move the body itself, without need for qualification. For this reason nerve fibers leading to and from skeletal muscles are called *somatic fibers* (soh-mat'ik; "body" G).

Within the body, hidden from the casual eye, are organs not under voluntary control in the full sense of the word. You can force your lungs to pump air more slowly or more quickly, but it is an effort to do so, and as soon as you relax (or fall unconscious, if you are too persistent in your interference) breathing proceeds at an automatically regulated pace. And too, you cannot force your heart to beat more slowly or more quickly (although, if you are highly imaginative you can make it pound by indirect action, as by talking yourself into a state of terror). Other organs change without your being especially aware of it. The pupils of your eyes dilate or contract, the various blood vessels of the body may expand their bore or narrow it, various glands may secrete more fluid or less, and the like.

The internal organs not subject to the will can — most of them — be grouped under the heading *viscera* (vis'ur-uh). This term may arise from the same Latin root that gives us "viscous," implying that the organs are soft and sticky. Nerve fibers supplying the viscera are called *visceral fibers*. One would expect that nerve fibers which control organs in response to the conscious will would not follow the same paths as would those which control organs without regard to the will. The latter, in a manner of speaking, have to short-circuit our consciousness, and to do so something new must be involved.

Thus, sensory fibers, whether somatic or visceral, lead from the various organs directly to the central nervous system. Motor fibers that are somatic, and therefore govern voluntary responses, likewise lead directly from the central nervous system to the organs they innervate. Motor fibers that are visceral, and therefore govern involuntary responses, do not lead directly to the organs they innervate. That is the "something new" I referred to above. Instead, they make their trips in two stages. The first set of fibers leads from the central nervous system to ganglia (which are, you may remember, collections of nerve cell bodies) that lie outside the central nervous system. This first set of fibers are the *preganglionic fibers*. At the ganglia the fibers form synaptic junctions with the dendrites of as many as twenty different cell bodies. The axons of these cell bodies form a second set of fibers, the *postganglionic fibers*. It is these postganglionic fibers that lead to the visceral organs, usually by way of one spinal nerve or another, since the spinal nerves are "cables" including all varieties of nerve fibers.

These two sets of visceral fibers, the preganglionic and the postganglionic, taken together with the ganglia themselves, make up that portion of the nervous system which is autonomous — or, not under the control of the will. It is for this reason called the *autonomic nervous system*. The chief ganglia involved in the autonomic nervous system form two lines running down either side of the spinal column. They are outside the bony vertebrae, and not inside as is the gray matter of the spinal cord and the ganglia of the posterior root.

These two lines of ganglia outside the column resemble a pair of long beaded cords, the beads consisting of a succession of 22 or 23 swellings produced by massed nerve cell bodies. At the lower end, the two cords join and finish in a single central stretch. These lines of ganglia are sometimes called the *sympathetic trunks.** Not all ganglia of the autonomic nervous system are located in the sympathetic trunks. Some are not; and it is possible for a preganglionic fiber to go right through the sympathetic trunks, making no synaptic junction there at all, joining instead with ganglia located in front of the vertebrae. These ganglia are called *prevertebral ganglia*, or *collateral ganglia*.

The *splanchnic nerves* (splank′nik; "viscera" G), which originate from some of the thoracic nerves, have their preganglionic fibers ending in a mass of ganglia (a "plexus") lying just behind the stomach. This is the *celiac plexus* (see′lee-ak; "belly" G), and it represents the largest mass of nerve cells that is not within the central nervous system. In fact it is sometimes called the "abdominal brain." A more common name for it, and one known to everyone interested in boxing, is the *solar plexus*. The word "solar" refers to the sun, of course, possibly because nerves radiate outward, like the sun's rays. Another theory is that a sharp blow to the solar plexus (to the pit of the stomach just under the diaphragm) can stun a person in agonizing fashion, so that for him darkness falls and the sun seems to set, at least temporarily.

In some cases, the ganglia separating the preganglionic fibers from the postganglionic fibers are actually located within the organ the nerve is servicing. In that case, the preganglionic fiber runs almost the full length of the total track, whereas the postganglionic fiber is at most just a few millimeters long.

Those fibers of the autonomic nervous system that originate from the first thoracic nerve down to the second or third lumbar nerve (in general, the central stretches of the spinal cord) make

---

* The word "sympathetic" was in the past used to describe the autonomic nervous system, because of ancient theories of the control of organs through sympathy. "Sympathy" comes from Greek words meaning "with suffering." One's own actions may be dictated not through outside force but through an inner impulse of sorrow over another's suffering. In the same way, an organ might act not through being forced to do so by the will but through a kind of sympathy with the needs of the body. Nowadays, as I shall shortly explain, the term sympathetic is applied only to part of the autonomic nervous system.

up the *sympathetic division*. Because of the origin of the fibers involved, it is also called the *thoracicolumbar division*. The fibers starting from the region above and below the sympathetic division form another division. Some fibers start from the cranial nerves above the spinal cord. Others originate from the sacral nerves at the bottom of the spinal cord. These make up the *parasympathetic division* ("beyond the sympathetic"), or the *craniosacral division*.

The difference between the two divisions is more than a mere matter of origin. For instance, the divisions differ in structure. The preganglionic fibers of the sympathetic division end at the sympathetic trunks or at the prevertebral ganglia, so these fibers are quite short. The postganglionic fibers, which must travel the remaining way to the organs they are concerned with, are relatively long. The parasympathetic nerve fibers, on the contrary, travel to ganglia within the organ they are aiming at; as a result, the preganglionic fibers are quite long and the postganglionic fibers very short.

Also, the functions of the two divisions are in opposition to each other. The sympathetic division has the wider distribution to all parts of the viscera, but many of the visceral organs are innervated by fibers of both divisions. When this happens, what one does the other undoes. Thus, the sympathetic nerve fibers act to accelerate the heartbeat, dilate the pupil of the eye and the bronchi of the lungs, and inhibit the activity of the smooth muscles of the alimentary canal. The parasympathetic nerve fibers, on the other hand, act to slow the heartbeat, contract the pupil of the eye and the bronchi of the lungs and stimulate the activity of the alimentary canal muscles. The sympathetic nerve fibers act to constrict the blood vessels in some places (as in the skin and viscera) and to dilate them in others (as in the heart and skeletal muscles). Oppositely, the parasympathetic fibers, where present, dilate the first set of blood vessels and constrict the second.

The two divisions of the autonomic nervous system show an

interesting chemical difference, too. The nerve endings of all fibers outside the autonomic nervous system secrete acetylcholine when an impulse passes down them (see p. 134). This is true also of all the preganglionic nerve endings in the autonomic nervous system, but there is a deviation from this norm in connection with the postganglionic nerve endings. The postganglionic nerve endings of the parasympathetic division secrete acetylcholine, but the postganglionic nerve endings of the sympathetic division do not. They secrete a substance which, in the days before its molecular structure was known, was called *sympathin*. Eventually sympathin was found to be a molecule named *norepinephrine* (also called *noradrenalin*), which is very similar in structure to epinephrine (or adrenalin), discussed toward the end of Chapter 2 (see pp. 40–43). As a result, those nerve fibers which secrete acetylcholine are referred to as *cholinergic nerves* and those which secrete norepinephrine are *adrenergic nerves*.

The secretion of norepinephrine seems to make sense, since the effect of the sympathetic division is to put the body on an emergency basis in just the same way that the hormone epinephrine does. The sympathetic division speeds up the heart and dilates the blood vessels to the muscles and the heart so that muscle can expend energy at a greater rate. It dilates the bronchi so that more oxygen can be sucked into the lungs. It cuts down on the action of the muscles of the alimentary canal and on the blood vessels feeding the digestive apparatus and the skin because digestion can wait and the blood is needed elsewhere. It also suspends kidney action, hastens the release of glucose by the liver, and even stimulates mental activity. It does the things epinephrine does, as one might expect of a chemical compound that is virtually the twin of epinephrine.

As a matter of fact, we can see once again that the chemical and electrical controls of the body are not entirely independent, for the adrenal medulla itself is stimulated by sympathetic fibers and releases epinephrine in response, so its effect is added to that of the norepinephrine, which helps to conduct impulses along the sympathetic nerve fibers. The sympathetic system also stimulates the secretion of ACTH by the pituitary gland, which in turn stimulates the secretion of corticoids by the adrenal cortex, and these (see p. 83) are needed in greater-than-normal concentration in periods of stress. The parasympathetic division, in contrast, acts to bring the body back from its emergency posture when the need is passed.

The sympathetic system, and the adrenal medulla, too, are not necessary for life, except insofar as failure to react properly to an emergency may be fatal. The adrenal medulla can be removed and sympathetic nerves can be cut without fatal results. Indeed, if the organism can be guaranteed a placid and nonstressful life, it is not even seriously inconvenienced.

10

OUR SENSES

TOUCH

Now that I have described the structure of the nervous system, let us consider how it works. To begin with, it is easy to see that in order for the nervous system to control the body usefully it must be constantly apprised of the details of the surrounding environment. It is useless to duck the head suddenly unless there is some collision to be avoided by the action. It is, on the other hand, dangerous not to duck the head if a collision is to be avoided.

To be aware of the environment, one must sense or perceive it.* The body senses the environment by the interaction of specialized nerve endings with some aspect or another of the environment. This interaction is interpreted by the central nervous system in a way that is different for each type of nerve ending. Each form of interaction and interpretation may be distinguished as a separate kind of *sense perception*.

In common speech, five different senses are usually recognized: *sight, hearing, taste, smell,* and *touch*. Of these, the first four reach us through special organs which are alone involved in a particular sense. Sight reaches us through the eye, hearing through the ear, taste through the tongue, and smell through the

* The word "sense" is from a Latin word meaning "to feel" or "to perceive," whereas "perceive" itself is from Latin words meaning "to take in through"; that is, to receive an impression of the outside world through some portion of the body.

nose. These are therefore grouped under the heading of *special senses* — senses, in other words, that involve a special organ.

Touch involves no special organ. The nerve endings that give rise to the sensation of touch are scattered everywhere on the surface of the body. Touch is an example of a *general sense.*

We are apparently less aware of senses when specific organs are not involved, and so we speak of touch as though that were the only sense present in the skin generally. We say that something is "hot to the touch," yet heat and touch arise from different nerve endings. Cold stimulates still another type of nerve ending, and pressure and pain each have their own nerve endings also. All of these — touch, pressure, heat, cold, and pain — are examples of *cutaneous senses* ("skin" L), and are so designated because they are located in the skin. They also represent *exteroceptive sensations* ("received from outside" L). The "outside" of course exists within us as well — within the digestive tract, which opens to the outside world at the mouth and anus. Sensations received there are sometimes considered to be additional examples of exteroceptive sensations, but are frequently differentiated as *interoceptive sensations* ("received from inside" L), or *visceral sensations.*

Lastly, there are sensations arising from organs within the body proper — from muscles, tendons, ligaments, joints, and the like. These are the *proprioceptive sensations* ("received from one's self" L). It is the proprioceptive sensations with which we are least familiar but take most for granted. These arise in specific nerve endings in various organs. In the muscles, to illustrate, there are such nerve endings attached to specialized muscle fibers. The stretching or contraction of these fibers sets up impulses in the nerve endings, which travel to the spinal cord and through ascending tracts to the brain stem. The greater the degree of stretching or contraction, the greater the number of impulses per unit time. Other nerve endings respond to the degree of pressure on the soles of the feet or on the muscles of the buttocks. Still others respond to the stretching of ligaments, the angular positions of bones hinged at an individual joint, and so on.

The lower portions of the brain utilize these sensations from all over the body in order to coordinate and organize muscular movements to maintain equilibrium, shift from uncomfortable positions, and adjust similarly. However, although the routine work is done at the lower levels and we are not consciously aware of what is going on in our busy body while we sit, stand, walk, or run, certain sensations do eventually reach the cerebrum, and through them we remain consciously aware at all times of the relative positions of the parts of our body. We are quite aware, without looking, of the exact position of an elbow or a big toe and can point to it with our eyes closed if asked to do so. If one of our limbs is bent into a new position by someone else, we know what the new position is without looking. To do all this, we interpret the nerve impulses arising from the miscellaneous stretchings and bendings of muscles, ligaments, and tendons.

The various proprioceptive sensations are sometimes lumped together as the *position sense* for this reason. It is also sometimes called the *kinesthetic sense* (kin'es-thet'ik; "movement-feeling" G). How far this sense is dependent on gravitational force in the long run is uncertain. This question has become an important one to biologists, now that astronauts are put into orbit for extended periods and are in "free fall," unaware of the usual effects of gravity.

As for the exteroceptive sensations — touch, pressure, heat, cold, and pain — each originates from a definite type of nerve ending. For all but pain, the nerve endings that receive these sensations are elaborated into specialized structures named in each case for the man who first described them in detail.

Thus, the touch-receptors (and a "receptor" is, of course, any nerve ending capable of receiving a particular sensation) often end in *Meissner's corpuscle*, described by the German anatomist Georg Meissner in 1853. The cold-receptors end in *Krause's end bulb*, named for the German anatomist Wilhelm Krause, who described them in 1860. The heat-receptors end in *Ruffini's end organ*, after the Italian anatomist Angelo Ruffini, who described them in 1898. The pressure-receptors end in a *Pacinian corpuscle*, described in 1830 by the Italian anatomist Filippo Pacini. Each of these specialized nerve-ending structures is easily distinguishable from the rest. (The pain-receptors are, however, nerves with bare endings, lacking any specialized end structure.)

Each type of specialized nerve ending is adapted to react to one kind of sensation: a light touch in the neighborhood of a touch-receptor will cause that nerve ending to initiate an impulse; it will have no effect on the other receptors. In the same way contact with a warm object will fire off a heat-receptor but not the others. The nerve impulse itself is identical in every case (actually, it is identical, as far as we can tell, for all nerves), but the interpretation in the central nervous system varies according to the nerve. A nerve impulse from a heat-receptor is interpreted as warmth whatever the nature of the stimulus. Each of the other receptors similarly gives rise to its own characteristic interpretation whatever the stimulus.

(This is true of the special senses as well. The most familiar case is that of the optic nerve, which is ordinarily stimulated by light. A sudden pressure will also stimulate it, and the stimulus will be interpreted not as pressure but as light. This is why a punch in the eye causes us to "see stars." Similarly, the stimulation of the tongue by a weak electric current will result in the sensation of taste.)

The various cutaneous receptors do not exist everywhere in the skin, and where one is another is not. The skin can actually be mapped out for its senses. If we use a thin hair we can touch various points on the skin and find that in some places a touch will be felt and in others it will not. With a little more effort, we can also map the skin for heat-receptors and cold-receptors. The gaps between them are not very large, however, and in the ordinary business of life we are not apt to come in contact with a stimulus that will not affect some of the appropriate receptors. Altogether, the skin possesses some 200,000 nerve endings for temperature, half a million for touch or pressure, and three million for pain.

As is to be expected, the touch-receptors are found most thickly strewn on the tongue and fingertips, which are the parts of the body most likely to be used in exploration. The tongue and fingertips are hairless, but elsewhere on the body the touch-receptors are associated with hairs. Hairs themselves are dead structures and have no sensations; yet the lightest touch upon a hair is felt, as we all know. The apparent paradox is explained when we realize that when the hair is touched it bends and exerts a leverlike pressure on the skin near its root. The touch-receptors near the root are stimulated by this.

This is a useful arrangement, because it enables the environment to be sensed without actual contact. At night, inanimate objects (which cannot be seen, heard, or smelled) can make themselves impinge upon our consciousness, just short of actual contact, by touching the hairs on our body. (There is also the possibility of echolocation, something I discuss on pages 262 ff.)

Some nocturnal animals carry sensations-through-hair to an extreme. The most familiar examples belong to the cat family, including the domestic cat itself. Its "whiskers" are properly called *vibrissae* (vy-bris'ee; "vibrate" L, because the ends are so easily moved). These are long hairs that will be touched by objects at comparatively great distances from the body. They are stiff so that the touch is transmitted to the skin with minimal loss. They are located in the mouth region where the touch-receptors are thickly strewn. In this way, dead structures, unfeeling themselves, become extraordinarily delicate sense organs.

If a touch becomes stronger, it eventually activates the Pacinian corpuscle of a pressure-receptor. Unlike the other cutaneous senses, the pressure-receptors are located in the subcutaneous tissues. There is a greater thickness between themselves and the outside world, and the sensation activating them must be correspondingly stronger to penetrate the deadening pad of skin.

On the other hand, if a touch is continued without change, the touch-receptor becomes less sensitive to it and ends by being unresponsive. You are conscious of a touch when it is first experienced, but if the touch is maintained without change, you become unaware of it. This is reasonable, since otherwise we would be constantly aware of the touch of our clothing and of a myriad other continuing sensations of no import which would be crowding our brain with useless information. The temperature-receptors behave similarly in this regard. The water of a hot bath may seem unpleasantly hot when we first step in but becomes merely relaxingly warm when we are "used to it." In the same way, the cold lake water becomes mild and bearable once we have undergone the shock of plunging in. The reticular activating system, by blocking sensations that no longer carry useful or novel information, keeps our cerebrum open for important business.

In order for the sensation of touch to be continuous, it must be applied in a continually changing fashion, so that new receptors are constantly being stimulated. In this way a touch becomes a tickle or a caress. The thalamus can to a certain extent localize the place at which a sensation is received, but for fine discrimination the cerebral cortex must be called in. It is in the sensory area that this distinction is made, so that if a mosquito lands on any part of the body, a slap can be accurately directed at once even without looking. The fineness with which a distinction can be made concerning the localization of a sensation varies from place to place. As is to be expected, the mouth parts and fingertips, which are the most important areas for feeling generally, can be interpreted most delicately. Two touches on the tip of the tongue which are 1.1 millimeters (about 1/25 inch) apart can be felt as two touches. At the fingertip the two touches must be separated by 2.3 millimeters (about 1/10 inch) before being felt separately. The lips and nose tip are somewhat less sensitive in this respect. The nose requires a separation of 6.6 millimeters (about ¼ inch) before it can detect a double touch. Compare this, though, with the middle of the back, where two touches must be separated by 67 millimeters (nearly 3 inches) before being felt as two touches rather than one.

In interpreting sensation, the central nervous system does not merely differentiate one type of sense from another and one location from another. It also estimates the intensity of the sensation. To give an example — we can easily tell which is the heavier of two objects (even though they may be similar in bulk and appearance) by placing one in each hand. The heavier object exerts a greater pressure on the hand and more strongly activates the pressure-receptors, causing a more rapid series of impulses. Or we can "heft" them; that is, make repeated lifting motions. The heavier object requires a greater muscular force for a given rate of lift and our proprioceptive senses will tell us which arm is exerting the greater force. (This is true of other senses, too. We can tell differences in degrees of warmth or of cold, in intensity of pain, in brightness of light, loudness of sound, and sharpness of smell or taste.)

Obviously there is a limit to the fineness of the distinction that can be made. If one object weighs 9 ounces and another 18 ounces, it would be easy to tell, with eyes closed and by merely feeling the pressure of each upon the hand, which is the heavier. If one object weighs 9 ounces and the other 10 ounces, considerable hesitation and repeated "heftings" might be required, but finally the correct answer would be offered. However, if one object weighs 9 ounces and the other 9½ ounces, it is likely that a distinction could no longer be clearly made. A person would be guessing, and his answer would be wrong as often as right. The ability to distinguish between two intensities of a stimulus lies not in the absolute difference but in the percentage difference. In distinguishing 9 ounces from 10, it is the 10-per-cent difference that counts, not the 1-ounce difference. We could not distinguish a 90-ounce weight from a 91-ounce weight, although here the difference is 1 ounce again, and would barely distinguish the difference between a 90-ounce weight and a 100-ounce weight. Yet it would be quite easy to distinguish a 1-ounce weight from a 1¼-ounce weight, even though here the difference is considerably less than an ounce.

Another way of saying this is that the body detects differences in the intensity of any sensory stimulus according to a logarithmic scale. This is called the *Weber-Fechner Law* after the two Germans, Ernst Heinrich Weber and Gustav Theodor Fechner, who worked it out. By functioning in this manner, a sense organ can work over far greater ranges of stimulus intensity than would otherwise be possible. Suppose, for instance, that a particular nerve ending could record twenty times as intensely at maximum as at minimum. (Above the maximum it would be physically damaged and below the minimum it would not respond at all.) If it reacted on a linear scale, the twenty-fold range would mean that the strongest stimulus would only be 20 times as intense as the weakest. On a logarithmic scale — even a gentle one using 2 as a base — the nerve would record at maximum only when there was a stimulus 2^{20} times as strong as that capable of arousing a minimum response. And 2^{20} is equal, roughly, to 1,000,000.

It is because of the manner in which the body obeys the Weber-Fechner Law that we can with the same sense organ hear a crash of thunder and a rustling leaf, or see the sun and a single star.

PAIN

Pain is the sensation we feel when some aspect of the environment becomes actively dangerous to some portion of the body. The event need not be extreme to elicit pain — a scratch or a pinprick will do it — but, of course, as the event becomes more extreme the pain becomes greater. A sensation that ordinarily does not cause pain will become painful if made so intense as to threaten damage. A pressure too great, contact with temperature too high or low, or, for that matter, a sound too loud or a light too bright will cause pain.

Of the cutaneous senses, pain is the least likely to adapt. It is difficult to get used to pain. As anyone who has experienced a toothache knows, pain can continue and continue and continue. This state of affairs makes sense, too, since pain signals a situation in a way that is more than merely informative; it cries for an immediate remedy, if a remedy exists. If pain vanished in time as the sensation of a continuous touch does, the condition giving rise to the pain would inevitably be ignored, with the consequence of serious illness, or even death, rather probable.

And yet when the situation giving rise to pain cannot be remedied, it is surely human to search for methods of alleviating it, if only that a sufferer might die in something less than total anguish. Or, if pain actually accompanies attempts to remedy harm to the body, as it would in a tooth extraction or in a surgical operation, the pain is a positive hindrance and should be removed if possible.

Primitive tribes have in their time discovered that various plant extracts (opium and hashish, to cite two) would deaden pain. These have a *narcotic* ("to benumb" G), or *analgesic* ("no pain" G), effect and are not scorned even in modern medical practice. The most commonly used analgesic still is *morphine*, an opium derivative that manages to hold its own in this respect, despite the possibility of the development of an addiction and despite the development of synthetic analgesics. A mild analgesic in common use is acetylsalicylic acid, better known by what was originally a trade-name, aspirin.

In 1884 an Austro-American ophthalmologist, Carl Koller, introduced the use of *cocaine* as a compound to deaden limited areas, and for operations. (The compound was first investigated by an Austrian neurologist, Sigmund Freud, who went on to gain fame in other directions.) Cocaine is an extract from the leaves of the coca tree, leaves that South American natives chewed to relieve pain, fatigue, and even hunger. (Such relief obviously is illusory, removing only the sensations and not the conditions that give rise to them.) Chemists went on to synthesize compounds not found in nature which showed properties equal or superior to cocaine and yet possessing fewer undesirable side-effects. The best-known of these is procaine, or to use its most common trade-name, Novocain.

In order to make major surgery humane, something was needed

that would induce general insensibility. The first step in this direction came in 1799, when the English chemist Humphry Davy discovered the gas nitrous oxide, and found that upon inhalation it made a person insensible to pain. He suggested that operations might be conducted while a patient was under its influence. Eventually it did come to be used in the dentist's office, where it was better known under its colloquial name of "laughing gas." It was not until the 1840's, however, that operations under conditions of insensibility were first performed, and then not with nitrous oxide but with the vapors of ether and chloroform. Of the two, ether is far the safer and it serves even now as the most common substance in use for this purpose.

A number of men contributed to this development, but chief credit is usually given to an American dentist, William G. T. Morton, who first used ether successfully in September 1846 and arranged a month later for a public demonstration of its use in a surgical operation at the Massachusetts General Hospital in Boston. The American physician Oliver Wendell Holmes (better known as a poet and essayist) suggested the name *anesthesia* ("no feeling" G) for the process.

The method by which anesthetics produce their effects is not certain. The most acceptable theory seems to be that (since they are always fat-soluble compounds) they concentrate in the fatty sections of the body. This would include the myelin sheaths of nerve fibers, and there the anesthetic acts somehow to inhibit the initiation of the nerve impulse. As the concentration of anesthetic is increased, more and more of the nervous system is put out of action. The sensory area of the cortex is most easily affected, whereas the medulla oblongata is most resistant. This is a stroke of fortune, since heart and lung action are controlled from the medulla and these activities must on no account be suspended. Surgery without anesthesia (except under emergency conditions where anesthetics are simply not available) is now practically unheard of.

And yet pain is amenable to modification from within, too. It is subject, though to a lesser extent than the other cutaneous sensations, to thalamic modification. Each sense is channeled into a different portion of the thalamus, which by this means distinguishes among them. A region in the very center of the thalamus called the *medial nuclei* also makes the sort of distinction that is interpreted by us as "pleasant" or "unpleasant." A cool shower may be interpreted as either pleasant or unpleasant on the basis of the temperature and humidity of the surroundings, and not directly on the temperature of the water. A caress may be pleasant under one set of conditions and unpleasant under another, although the same touch sensations may be affected in the same way. Usually, pleasant sensations are soothing and unpleasant ones are upsetting.

Even pain can be modified by the thalamus in this fashion. It may never, under ordinary and normal conditions, be actually pleasant, but the degree of unpleasantness can be sharply reduced. This is most noticeable perhaps in the manner in which, under the pressure of conflict or the stress of strong emotion, injuries are suffered without conscious pain. It is as though there are situations in which the body cannot afford to be distracted by pain; in which it seems to discount possible injury as unimportant in the light of the greater purposes at hand. On the other hand, the fear of pain, and apprehension as to its effects, will heighten the intensity of its sensation. (Folk wisdom marks this phenomenon with the well-known phrase to the effect that the coward dies a thousand deaths and the brave man dies but once.)

There is a social effect on the experience of pain, too. A child brought up in a culture that considers the stoic endurance of pain a sign of manliness will go through barbarous initiation rites with a fortitude incredible to those of us who are brought up to regard pain as an evil to be avoided whenever possible. The modification of pain can on occasion be made a matter of the conscious will through determination and practice; and Hindu fakirs, having nothing better to do, can pierce their cheeks with pins or rest on beds of nails with utter callousness.

Ordinary men and women, who do not make a profession out of the suppression of pain, can nevertheless be induced to suppress it by suggestion from outside, provided their own conscious will has more or less been put out of action. This undoubtedly has been known to individuals throughout history, and many men have earned reputations as miracle workers by their ability to place others in trancelike states and then to substitute their own will, so to speak, for the suspended will of the subject in the trance. The most famous example of such a man was the Austrian physician Friedrich Anton Mesmer, who in the 1770's was the rage of Paris. The phrase "to mesmerize" is still used to mean "to put into a trance."

Mesmer's work was riddled with mysticism and was generally discredited. In the 1840's a Scottish physician, James Braid, reopened the subject, studied it carefully and objectively, renamed it "neurohypnotism," and brought it, minus its mysticism, into the purview of recognized medicine. It is now known by the abbreviated name, *hypnotism* ("sleep" G).

Hypnotism is by no means a device for making men do the impossible through some mystic or supernatural means. Rather, it is a method for inducing a subject to exert a form of conscious control that he can exert under some conditions but ordinarily does not. Thus, a man can be persuaded to suppress pain under hypnotic influence, but he could do that without hypnotism if, for instance, he were fighting for his life or making an agonized effort to save his child from a fire. But hypnotism, no matter how proficient, could never enable him to rise upward one inch in defiance of gravity.

The interoceptive, or visceral, sensations are almost always pain. You may drink hot coffee or iced coffee and be conscious enough of the difference while the liquid is in your mouth. Once it is swallowed, the temperature sensation (except in extreme cases) vanishes. Nor is one ordinarily conscious of touch as food makes its way through the alimentary canal, or of simple pressure. Internal pain is felt, however, under appropriate conditions, but not necessarily as a result of stimuli that would cause pain on the skin. Cutting the internal organs, even the brain itself, causes little or no pain. The walls of the intestinal tract are, nevertheless, strongly affected by stretching, as through the distention produced by trapped gas, which gives rise to the pains of colic or indigestion. In similar fashion, the distention of blood vessels in the cranium give rise to the all-too-familiar headache. The pressure of blocked fluid can likewise give rise to pain, such as that produced by gallstones and kidney stones. Inflamed tissues can be a source of pain, as in appendicitis and arthritis. Pain can also be induced by muscle spasm, which gives rise to the well-known "cramp."

One distinction between visceral pain and cutaneous pain is that the former is much less subject to localization. A pain in the abdomen is usually quite diffuse and it isn't easy to point to an area and say "It hurts here" as is possible if one has barked one's shin.

In fact, it is quite likely that when pain can be localized, it may appear at a spot more or less removed from the actual site of the sensation. This is then called *referred pain*. The pain of an inflamed appendix (the appendix being located in the lower right quadrant of the abdomen) often makes itself felt in the region just below the breastbone. Also, the pain of angina pectoris, which originates through a reduction in the blood flow to the heart muscle, is generally felt in the left shoulder and arm. Headache can be a referred pain, as when it arises from strains of the eye muscles. So characteristic are these wrong locations, actually, that they can be used in diagnosing the actual area of trouble.

At this point, I wish to pause. Before passing on to the special senses, it is only fair to ask whether we have really exhausted the list of the general senses. Probably not; there may well be senses so taken for granted as to be ignored in the main, even today. For example, it seems quite likely that we possess a "time sense" enabling us to judge the passage of time with considerable accuracy. Many of us can rouse ourselves out of a reasonably sound sleep at some desired time morning after morning, and do so often, with surprising precision. In addition, it has often been tempting to suppose that senses exist — perhaps in other living organisms — of which we ourselves are completely ignorant. It may be possible somehow to detect radio waves, radioactive emanations, magnetic fields, and the like. One can only answer, "Well, perhaps."

It is even suggested that human beings (or just a few gifted individuals) have such extraordinary senses, or, better yet, are capable of perceiving the environment through means that are independent of any sense. The last is called *extrasensory perception,* a phrase customarily abbreviated as *ESP.* Examples of extrasensory perception are: *telepathy* ("feeling at a distance" G), where one can detect another's thoughts or emotions directly; *clairvoyance* ("see clearly" French), which involves the ability to perceive events that are taking place at a distance, and out of reach of the senses; and *precognition* ("know in advance" L), the ability to perceive events that have not yet taken place.

All these, plus other abilities of the sort, are very attractive matters. People would like to believe that it is possible to know more than it seems possible to know; and that "magical" powers exist which perhaps they themselves might learn to use. Extrasensory perception of one sort or another has been the stock in trade of mystics, witch doctors, and self-deluded individuals throughout history. It has also been the stock in trade of a large number of deliberate rascals and knaves. The alleged extrasensory powers of so many individuals have been shown to be fraudulent (even where many sober and trustworthy individuals were ready to swear to their legitimacy) that men of science are reluctant to accept the reality of any such cases at all, whatever the circumstances.

In recent years, the work of the American psychologist Joseph Banks Rhine has given the study of ESP a kind of quasi-respect-

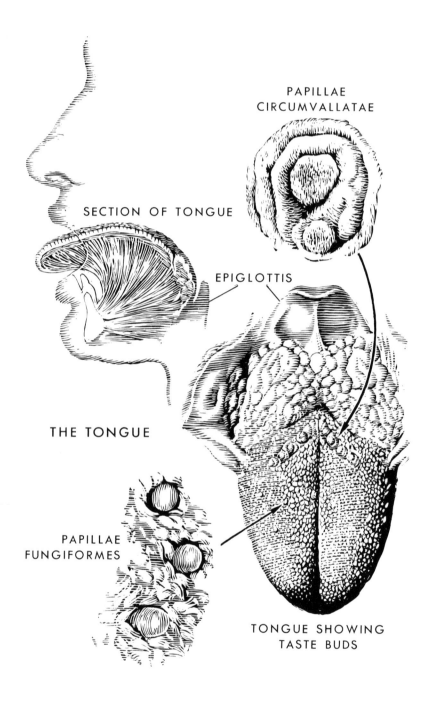

PAPILLAE
CIRCUMVALLATAE

SECTION OF TONGUE

EPIGLOTTIS

THE TONGUE

PAPILLAE
FUNGIFORMES

TONGUE SHOWING
TASTE BUDS

ability. Phenomena not easily explainable except by supposing the existence of some form of ESP have been reported. However, these phenomena depend so heavily on statistical analyses that are at least arguable, on individual subjects whose supposed abilities are strangely erratic, and on controls that many scientists feel to be inadequate that most people will not accept the work as significant. Moreover, the loudest proponents of ESP and like phenomena are not those who seriously study it (and who are generally most moderate in their suggestions), but are precisely those mystics whose antipathy toward the recognized procedures of scientific analysis make them the spiritual descendants of the grand fakers of the past.

TASTE

The general senses, by and large, respond to physical factors in the environment — to mechanical forces and to temperature differences. Of the special senses, two, hearing and sight (which will be discussed in the succeeding chapters), likewise respond to physical factors: sound waves in the first case and light waves in the second.

Differing from all of these are the senses of smell and taste. They respond to the chemical structure of molecules. In other words, of two substances resting on the tongue with equal pressure and at equal temperature, one will stimulate numerous nerve impulses and the other will not. The only difference between the objects seems to be their chemical structure. The same is true of two vapors breathed into the nose. For this reason, smell and taste are grouped together as the *chemical senses*.

The tongue is the organ primarily involved in taste. It is covered with small projections called *papillae* (pa-pil'ee; "nipple" L). The papillae at the edges and tip of the tongue are small and conical in shape, resembling the cap of a mushroom (*fungus* in Latin) when seen under magnification. These are the *papillae fungiformes*, and they give the tongue its velvety feel. Toward the rear of the tongue, the papillae are larger and give the tongue a certain roughness to the touch. These larger papillae are surrounded by a little groove, like a castle surrounded by a moat. They are the *papillae circumvallatae* ("wall around" L).

The actual taste-receptors consist of *taste buds* distributed over the surface of the papillae and, to some extent, in adjacent areas of the mouth. These are tiny bundles of cells that make up an ovoid structure with a pore at the top. Four different types of taste buds have been described. Each is usually considered to respond to a particular variety of substance and its nerve impulse is interpreted in the central nervous system as a particular variety of taste.

It is customary to classify tastes into four categories: sweet, salt, sour, and bitter. Each of these is elicited by an important group of substances. Sweetness is elicited by sugars, saltiness by a number of inorganic ions, sourness by acids, and bitterness by alkaloids. The usefulness of such a categorization seems clear. Sugar is an important component of foods. It is easily absorbed and quickly utilized by the body for energy. Any natural food that is sweet to the taste is usually worth eating, and sweetness is interpreted by the thalamus as a pleasant sensation.

In contrast, the most likely origin of a sensation of sourness in foods as they are found in nature is in unripe fruits, which have not yet developed their full sugar content and are therefore not as edible as they will soon be. Sourness is ordinarily interpreted as unpleasant. The same is even truer of the sensation of bitterness, since the presence of alkaloids in plants is usually a sign of poison and, indeed, it is the alkaloids themselves that are often both intensely bitter and intensely poisonous. Bitterness is therefore intensely unpleasant, and a bitter morsel of food is likely to be discarded at once; even the initial bite is not swallowed.

Saltiness is a rough measure of the mineral content of food. Sodium ion and chloride ion, the components of ordinary table salt, from which the taste takes its name, are by far the most common inorganic ions in food. Whether saltiness is pleasant or unpleasant would depend on the concentration of salt in the bloodstream. Where the salt level is low, either through mineral deficiency in the diet or through excessive loss of salt through perspiration, saltiness becomes a pleasanter sensation than otherwise.

The different kinds of taste buds are not evenly distributed over the tongue. The tip of the tongue is the portion most sensitive to sweetness, and the back of the tongue is most sensitive to bitterness. The sensations of saltiness and sourness are most easily detected along the rim of the tongue. Nor is the tongue equally sensitive to each variety of taste. It is least sensitive to sweetness; table sugar must be present in solution to at least 1 part in 200 before it can be tasted. This is reasonable, since such a comparatively dull sense makes it certain that anything that does taste sweet contains a large amount of sugar and is worth eating.

Saltiness is less uniformly desirable than sweetness; salt can be detected in a solution of 1 part in 400. Sourness, which is distinctly undesirable, can be detected (in the form of hydrochloric acid) in a solution of 1 part in 130,000. Last of all, bitterness, which is the most dangerous, is, usefully enough, the most delicately sensed. One part of quinine in 2,000,000 parts of water will yield a solution that is detectably bitter. Notice that I speak of solutions. In order for anything to be tasted, it must be dissolved in water (or in the watery saliva). A perfectly dry piece of sugar on a dry tongue will not be tasted. Starch, which is related to sugar chemically but differs in being insoluble, is tasteless.

The manner in which a particular substance gives rise to a characteristic taste is not known. The fact that some of the tastes are stimulated by a veritable grab bag of substances does not make the problem of finding out any easier. Sourness is the most orderly of the taste sensations. All acids liberate hydrogen ions in solution, and the taste of sourness is stimulated by these hydrogen ions. The intensity of the taste of sourness varies with the concentration of hydrogen ion, and this seems understandable enough.

Saltiness is stimulated by many inorganic ions other than the hydrogen ion, of course. Yet some inorganic compounds, especially those of the heavy metals, are bitter. To be sure, this is useful, since these compounds of the heavy metals are generally poisonous. Why should it be, though, that salts of lead and beryllium are liable to be sweet? Lead acetate is called "sugar of lead," and an alternate name of beryllium is "glucinum," which comes from the Greek word for "sweet." This would certainly seem to be unfortunate, because salts of both lead and beryllium are quite poisonous. However, both are rare elements that are not likely to be consumed in the ordinary course of nature.

Sweetness also offers puzzles. This sensation is stimulated by the presence of hydroxyl groups (a combination of an oxygen atom with a hydrogen atom) in a water-soluble molecule. Nevertheless, the various sugars, which resemble each other very closely in molecular structure — down to the possession of equal numbers of hydroxyl groups, sometimes — can be quite different in sweetness. A substance such as glycine (this name too comes from the Greek word for "sweet"), which is not related to the sugars and does not possess an ordinary hydroxyl group, is sweet to the taste.

Oddly enough, there are synthetic organic compounds, also not related to the sugars in any way, which are not only sweet but intensely sweet, and can be detected by the tongue in much smaller concentrations than ordinary sugar can. The sweet taste of the best-known of these synthetics, *saccharin* ("sugar" L), can be detected in a concentration 550 times more dilute than that required before sugar itself can be tasted. This means that one teaspoon of saccharin will sweeten 550 cups of coffee to the same extent that one teaspoon of sugar will sweeten one cup of coffee. And there are substances even sweeter than saccharin.

Nor is taste entirely uniform from individual to individual. This is most noticeable in the case of certain synthetic organic compounds that give rise to widely varying subjective opinion. There is a compound called phenylthiocarbamide (usually abbreviated as PTC) which some 70 per cent of those people who are asked to taste it report as having a pronounced bitterness. The remaining 30 per cent find it completely tasteless. Such "taste-blindness" might seem to be a purely academic matter, since it concerns a compound not found in nature. Notwithstanding, there is speculation as to whether other compounds among the many that do occur in nature may not taste differently to different people, and whether this may not account for at least some of the personal idiosyncrasies in diet.

What we popularly consider the taste of food does not, of course, arise solely from the sensations produced by the taste buds. There are general sense-receptors in the tongue and mouth which also play a role. Pepper, mustard, and ginger all stimulate heat-receptors as well, and menthol stimulates the cold-receptors. The feel or texture of food stimulates touch-receptors, so these too play their role in the palatability of the dish. A smooth jelly-like dessert will seem to taste better than a lumpy one of the same sort, and an oily dish may seem repulsive even though the oil itself has no taste.

However, by far the greatest contribution of nontaste to the general taste of food is that of the sense of smell, which it is now time to consider.

SMELL

Smell differs from taste in the matter of range. Whereas taste requires actual physical contact between a substance and the tongue, smell will operate over long distances. A female moth will attract male moths for distances of half a mile or more by virtue of the odor of a chemical she secretes.* Smell is there-fore a "long-distance sense."

---

* Although smell does not require the actual contact of a solid or liquid sub-stance with the body, it does sense the molecules of vapors. These molecules make contact with the body, so the sense does involve physical contact after a fashion. However, since we are not usually aware of vapors as we are of solids and liquids, and since vapors travel long distances as a result of diffusion through the air and actual transport by wind, it is still fair enough to think of smell as operating over a great range.

The other senses too may be differentiated in this way. Touch, pressure, and pain all require direct contact, usually. To a lesser extent so do the temperature senses, although these can also be detected at a distance. You can detect the heat radiated by a hot stove from the other end of a room and you can detect the heat radiated by the sun from a distance of about 93,000,000 miles. However, the detection of heat (or, to a lesser extent, cold) at a distance requires a stimulus of considerable intensity, and in order to detect the mild temperatures we ordinarily encounter, we must make physical contact.*

Hearing and sight, the two remaining senses, are like smell — long-distance senses — but for most forms of mammalian life smell is *the* important long-distance sense. Smell has its advantages: sight is (in a state of nature) dependent on the sun and is to a great extent useless at night, but smell is on day-and-night duty. Also, hearing is dependent on the production of sound, and if animal A is trying to locate animal B, animal B may succeed in refraining from making a sound. Odor, on the contrary, is beyond conscious control A hidden animal may be quiet as the grave but it cannot help being odorous.

Carnivores, then, commonly detect their prey by the sense of smell, and herbivores detect their enemies by means of it. Furthermore, the sense of smell can make the most amazing distinctions. It is the grand recognition signal whereby a bee will know others of its hive, distinguishing its own hive smell from all others, and a seal mother will easily recognize her offspring from among thousands (which to us all seem identical) on the beach. In the same way, a bloodhound will follow the scent of one man (even an old scent) crosscountry with unerring accuracy.

---

* Cold is not a phenomenon independent of heat; it is merely lack of heat. You detect heat by sensing the flow of heat from an outside object into your skin and you detect cold by sensing the flow of heat from your skin into an outside object. The temperature of the skin rises in the first case and falls in the second. Fires are at least 600 Centigrade degrees warmer than our skins but we rarely meet objects at temperatures of more than 100 Centigrade degrees cooler than our skins. That is why we are easily aware of feeling heat at a distance but not so aware of feeling cold.

Among primates generally, and humans especially, the sense of smell has been displaced for long-distance purposes by the sense of sight. This is the result not only of a sharpening of sight but of a deadening of smell. Our sense of smell is far less delicate than that of a dog; this shows up in the physical fact that the area of smell reception in our noses is much less, and so is the area of the brain given over to the reception and analysis of olfactory sensation.

Even so, the sense of smell is not as rudimentary or meaningless among human beings as we might think it to be as a result of too strenuous a comparison of ourselves with dogs. We may not be able to distinguish individual body odors as readily as a bloodhound, but the truth is, we never try. In intimate relationships odors become individual enough. And there is nothing like a chance odor to evoke a memory, even across many years, of people and situations otherwise forgotten.

The smell-receptors are located in a pair of patches of mucous membrane in the upper reaches of the nasal cavity. Each is about 2½ square centimeters in area and colored with a yellow pigment. Ordinarily, vapors make their way into the upper reaches through diffusion, but this process can be hastened by a stronger-than-usual inspiration, so that when we are anxious to detect the suspected presence of an odor, we sniff sharply.

Since the nasal cavity opens into the throat, any vapors or tiny droplets arising from the food we place in our mouths finds its way without trouble to the smell-receptors. Therefore what we consider taste is smell as well, and, in fact, smell is the major portion of what we consider taste and adds all the richness, delicacy, and complexity to the sense. When a cold in the nose swells the mucous membrane of the upper nasal cavities and deadens the smell-receptors under a layer of mucus and fluid, the sense of smell may blank out temporarily through the sheer physical inability of vapors to make contact with the sensory area. This does not affect the ability of the tongue to taste sweet, sour, salt and bitter, but how primitive and unsatisfying is pure taste alone.

So unsatisfying is it that in the absence of smell the cold-sufferer considers himself to have lost his sense of taste as well, ignoring the fact that his tongue is performing its functions faithfully.

The sense of smell, even in the blunted case of man, is far more delicate than is that of taste. The ability to taste quinine in a concentration of 1 part in 2,000,000 shrinks in comparison with the ability to smell mercaptans (the type of substance produced by skunks when those animals are seized with a fit of petulance) in concentrations of 1 part in 30,000,000,000.

Furthermore, the sense of smell is far more complex than the sense of taste. It has proved quite impossible to set up a table of individual smells to serve as a standard for comparison of smell mixtures. There have been attempts to classify smells under headings such as ethereal, aromatic, fragrant, ambrosial, garlic, burning, goaty, and fetid, but these attempts are rather crude and unsatisfying.

The mechanism by which a particular chemical activates a certain receptor — that is, why one chemical smells thus and another smells so — is as yet unknown. Recently, there have been suggestions that chemicals smelled as they did because of the over-all shape of their molecules, or because they punctured the membranes of the smell-receptors, or because parts of the molecules vibrated in some ways. Substances with the same molecular shape, or the same manner of puncturing, or the same fashion of vibrating would all smell the same. However, all such theories are as yet only at the stage of conjecture.

Whatever the mechanism of smell, the sense itself is most remarkable. Although some human senses can be outdone by mechanical devices, smell cannot. The living nose is not likely to be replaced by any nonliving contrivance in the foreseeable future. That is why, in an age of superlative mechanization, the master chef, the tea-taster, and the perfume-compounder are likely to remain immune to the possibility of technological unemployment.

11

OUR EARS

The two senses we are most conscious of are those of sight and hearing. The eye and the ear are our most complicated sense organs and our most vulnerable ones. They are vulnerable enough, at any rate, to give us the only common words for sense-deprivation, blindness and deafness, and neither affliction is uncommon.

Both sight and hearing are long-distance senses, gathering information from afar. To ourselves, as human beings, sight seems perhaps the more important of the two, and blindness a more disabling affliction than deafness. That, however, is a human-centered point of view. For most animals, the reverse would be true, since hearing has certain important advantages over sight. For one thing, sound waves have the property of bending about objects of moderate size, whereas light waves travel in straight lines. This means that we can see something only by looking directly at it, but can hear something no matter what our position may be with reference to it. Any creature on guard against the approach of an enemy can, as a consequence, much more safely rely on its hearing than its sight, especially if it must be engaged in ordinary business of life even while it is on guard. We have all seen animals prick up their ears and come to quivering attention long before they could possibly have seen anything.

To repeat, far and away the most important source of light, as far as any creature other than man is concerned, is the sun. This means that within an area shielded from the sun, as in forest recesses or, better yet, in a cave, the value of sight is reduced or even wiped out. Animals living permanently in the darkness of caves usually possess only rudimentary eyes, as though the vital energies of the organism were not to be wasted on a useless organ.

And, of course, for half the time the sun is below the horizon and sight is almost useless for most creatures. (To be sure, the night is not totally dark, particularly when the moon's reflected sunlight is available. Animals such as the cat or the owl, with eyes designed to detect glimmerings of light with great efficiency, are at an advantage over prey that lack this ability. They go hunting by night for this reason.) And in the ocean below the thin topmost layer, sunlight does not penetrate, so the sense of sight is largely useless. Yet hearing works as well by night as by day. (Better, perhaps, because background noise diminishes as the tempo of life subsides, and there is less distraction from the suspended sense of sight.) Hearing works as well in caves as in the open, and as well in the ocean depths as on its surface.

With comparatively few exceptions, light cannot be produced by living creatures. Even when it can be, as by glowworms or by luminescent fish, so little variation in the nature of the lighting can be deliberately produced that it is used for only the most rudimentary of signals, to attract the opposite sex or to lure prey.

In contrast to this, many creatures, including quite simple ones, can make sounds, and can vary the sounds sufficiently to make use of them for a variety of signaling purposes. (Even the sea is a noisy place, as was found out during World War II, when the growing importance of detecting submarine engines made it necessary to study the background noises produced by booming fish and clacking shrimp.)

The more complex the creature, the more capable it is of varying the nature of the sound to suit the occasion. Obviously not all communication is by sound. A bee's dance can locate a new patch of clover for the benefit of the rest of the hive. A dog's wagging tail communicates one thing and the drawing back of his lips quite another. However, this is not to be compared with the more common communication by sound — with the roaring, whining, chattering, yowling, purring, and all the remainder of the pandemonium of the animal kingdom.

And yet this increasing variability of sound with complexity of creature reaches a sudden discontinuity at the level of man. Here is no smooth advance of variability but a precipitous leap upward. Between man on the one hand and all other species of land animals on the other, there is a vast gulf in connection with sound-making. Even the chimpanzee cannot begin to bridge that gulf. Only man can make at will sounds so complex, so varying, and so precisely and reproducibly modulated as to serve as a vehicle for the communication of abstract ideas.*

Man's unique ability in this respect is twofold. In the first place, only man's brain is complex enough to store all the associations, memories, and deductions that are required to give him something to talk about. An animal can communicate pain, fear, warning, sexual drive, and a number of other uncomplicated emotions and desires. For these, a modest armory of different sounds is ample. An animal cannot, it would seem, experience a wonder about the nature of life, nor can it speculate on the causes and significance of death, or possess a philosophic concept of brotherhood, or even compare the beauties of a present sunset with those of a particular starlit night seen last year. And with none of this, where is the need for speech after the human fashion?**

And even if such attractions could somehow hover dimly in the nonhuman mind, the nonhuman brain would still be insufficiently complex to be able to control muscles in such a way as

---

* I distinguish between man and "land animals" because the dolphins of the sea may represent another species capable of speech (see p. 160).

** This is not to say that all human beings spend much time in pondering abstractions or to ignore the fact that a surprisingly high percentage of our fellows make out with a total vocabulary of 1000 words or so.

to produce the delicate variations in sound that would be required to communicate those abstractions. Nor can one short-circuit matters by supposing communication to consist of something other than sound. Whatever the nature of the signal — sound, gestures, bubbles in water, even thought waves — they must attain a certain level of complexity to make abstract communication possible, and only the human brain (the dolphin's brain possibly added) is complex enough.

In fact, it is possible to make a plausible case for the belief that it was the development of the ability to speak which made the early hominids "human." It was only then, after all, that individual knowledge and experience could be pooled among the members of a tribe and passed on across the generations. No one man, however brilliant, can of himself create a culture out of nothing; but a combined body of men spread through space and time can.

The sense of hearing, complex enough in man to be capable of analyzing the sounds of speech and therefore essential to our humanness, depends upon the conversion of sound waves into nerve impulses. Sound waves are set up by mechanical vibrations and consist of a periodic displacement of atoms or molecules.

Imagine the prong of a tuning fork vibrating rapidly and alternately from left to right. As it bends leftward, it forces the neighboring air molecules together on the left, creating a small area of high pressure. The elasticity of air forces those molecules to move apart again, and as they do so they compress the molecules of the neighboring region of air. Those molecules in turn move apart, compressing still another region. The net result is that a wave of high pressure radiates out from the vibrating prong.

While this is happening, though, the prong of the tuning fork has bent rightward. The result is that in the place where previously an area of high pressure had been formed, the molecules are now pulled apart into the room made for it by the prong bending away. An area of rarefaction, of low pressure, is formed. Molecules from the neighboring region of air rush in to fill the gap, creating a new area of low pressure, which thus radiates outward.

Since the vibrating prong moves first left, then right in regular rhythm, the result is a radiation of successive areas of high pressure and low pressure. The molecules of air scarcely move themselves; they only slide back and forth a short distance. It is the areas of compression and rarefaction that move, and it is the periodic nature of these areas that give them the name "waves." Since they are detected in the form of sound, they are *sound waves*.

The rate at which these waves travel (the "speed of sound") depends on the elasticity of the medium through which they travel; the rate at which a given atom or molecule will restore itself to its position if displaced. In air, the rate at the freezing point is 1090 feet per second, or 745 miles an hour. In other media, such as water or steel, with elasticities greater than air, the speed of sound is correspondingly higher. Through a vacuum, where there are no atoms or molecules to displace, sound cannot be transmitted.

The distance between successive points of maximum pressure (or, which is the same thing, between successive points of minimum pressure) is the *wavelength*. The number of waves emitted in one second is the *frequency*. To illustrate: a tuning fork that sounds a tone corresponding to middle C on the piano is vibrating 264 times a second. Each second, 264 areas of high pressure followed by areas of low pressure are produced. The frequency is therefore 264 cycles per second. During that second, sound has traveled 1090 feet (if the temperature is at the freezing point). If 264 high-pressure areas fit into that distance, then the distance between neighboring high-pressure areas is 1090 divided by 264, or about 4.13 feet. That is the wavelength of the sound wave that gives rise to the sound we recognize as middle C.

THE EXTERNAL AND MIDDLE EAR

We can see that there is nothing mysterious about the conversion of sound waves to nerve impulses. From one point of view, hearing is a development and refinement of the pressure sense. Sound waves exert a periodic pressure on anything they come in contact with. The pressure is extremely gentle under ordinary circumstances, and a single high-pressure area associated with sound would not affect the ear, let alone any other part of the body. It is the periodic nature of the sound wave, the constant tapping, so to speak — not the tiny pressure itself, but the unwearying reiteration of the pressure according to a fixed pattern — that sparks the nerve impulse. A fish hears by means of sensory cells equipped to detect such a pressure pattern. These sound-receptor cells are located in a line running along the mid-region of either side and are referred to as the *lateral lines.*

The emergence of vertebrates onto land created new problems in connection with hearing. Air is a much more rarefied medium than water is, and the rapid periodic changes in pressure that represent the sound waves in air contain far less energy than the corresponding pressure changes of sound waves in water do. For this reason, land vertebrates had to develop sound-receptors more delicate than the fish's lateral line.

The organ that underwent the necessary development is located in a cavity of the skull on either side of the head, this small cavity being the *vestibule.* In the primitive vertebrates, the vestibule contained a pair of liquid-filled sacs connected by a narrow duct. One is the *saccule* (sak'yool; "little sack" L), the other the *utricle* (yoo'trih-kul; "little bottle" L). For all vertebrates, from the fish upward, these little organs in the vestibule represented a sense organ governing orientation in space, something which may be referred to as the *vestibular sense.* The utricle and its outgrowths remain concerned with the vestibular sense in all higher vertebrates, too, including man, and I shall describe this later in the chapter.

From the saccule, however, a specialized outgrowth developed in land vertebrates. This was adapted as a sound-receptor, one that was much more sensitive for the purpose than the lateral-line cells of the fish. It remained, then, to transmit the sound waves from air to the new sensing organ within the vestibule. For this purpose, the parsimony of nature made use of the hard structure of some of the gills, which, after all, were no longer needed as gills in the newly emerging land vertebrates. The first gill bar, for instance, was altered into a thin diaphragm that could be set to vibrating very easily, even by pressure alterations as weak as those of sound waves in air. Another gill bar became a small bone between the diaphragm and the sound-receptor, and acted as a sound transmitter.

With the development of mammals, a further refinement was added. The mammalian jaw is much simpler in structure (and more efficiently designed) than is the ancestral reptilian jaw. The mammalian jaw is constructed of a single bone rather than a number of them. The reptilian jawbones that were no longer needed did not entirely disappear. Some were added to the nearby sound-sensing mechanism (check for yourself and see that your jawbone extends backward to the very neighborhood of the ear). As a result, there are three bones connecting diaphragm and sense-receptors in mammals instead of the one of the other land vertebrates such as the birds and reptiles. The three-bone arrangement allows for a greater concentration and magnification of sound-wave energies than the one-bone does.

Let me emphasize at this point that the hearing organ is not what we commonly think of as the ear. What we call the ear is only the external, clearly visible, and least important part of the complex system of structures enabling us to hear. Anatomically, the visible ear is the *auricle* ("little ear" L), or *pinna** (see illustration, p. 253).

---

* The word "pinna" is from a Latin expression for "feather" and can be used for any projection from the body. "Fin," for example, is derived from the same root as pinna. The application to the ear is fanciful, but reasonable.

The auricle is another uniquely mammalian feature. In many mammals it is trumpet-shaped and acts precisely as an old-fashioned earphone does; an effect carried to an extreme in such animals as donkeys, hares, and bats. The ear trumpet collects the wave-front of a sound wave over a comparatively broad area and conducts it inward toward the sound-receptors, the sound wave intensifying as the passage narrows (much as the tide grows higher when it pours into a narrowing bay like the Bay of Fundy). By use of such a trumpet, which, moreover, is movable so that sounds can be picked up from specific directions, the hearing organ of mammals is made still more sensitive. By all odds, then, the mammals have the keenest sense of hearing in the realm of life.

In man, and in primates generally, there is a recession from the extreme of sensitivity. The trumpet shape is lost, and the auricle is but a wrinkled appendage on either side of the head. The outermost edge of the auricle, curving in a rough semicircle and folding inward, sometimes yet bears the traces of a point that seems to hark back to an ancestry in which the ear was trumpet-shaped. Charles Darwin used this as one of the examples of a vestigial remnant in man that marked lower-animal ancestry. The ability to move the ear is also lost by primates, but in man three muscles still attach each auricle to the skull. Although these are clearly intended for moving the ear, in most human beings they are inactive. A few people can manage to work those muscles slightly, and by doing so can "wiggle their ears," another clear harking back to lower-animal ancestry.

This shriveling of the ear trumpet in man is usually considered an indication of the growing predominance of the sense of sight. Whereas some vertebrates grew to depend upon their ears to detect the slightest sound, perhaps to warn of an enemy, the developing order of primates threw more and more weight on their unusually efficient eyes. With alert eyes flashing this way and that, it became unnecessary to waste effort, one might say, in moving the ear, or in bearing the inconvenience of long auricles for the purpose of unnecessarily magnifying extremely faint sounds. Nevertheless, though we do miss a faint sound that might cause a dog to prick up its ears, our shriveled auricle does not really indicate any essential loss of hearing. Within the skull, our hearing apparatus can be matched with that of any other mammal on an all-round basis.

In the center of the human auricle is the opening of a tube which is about an inch deep, a quarter of inch in diameter, reasonably straight, and more or less circular in cross section. This is the *auditory canal*, or the *auditory meatus* (mee-ay′tus, "passage" L). Together the auricle and the auditory canal make up the *external ear*. Sound collected by the auricle is conducted through the auditory canal toward the vestibule. The canal is lined with some of the hardest portions of the cranium, and the functioning parts of the ear — the actual sound-receptors — are thus kept away from the surface and are well protected indeed. Birds and reptiles, which lack auricles, do have short auditory canals and so do not lack external ears altogether.

The inner end of the auditory canal is blocked off by a fibrous membrane, somewhat oval in shape and 1/10 of a millimeter (about 1/250 inch) thick. This is the *tympanum* (tim′puh-num; "drum" L), or *tympanic membrane*.* The tympanum is fixed only at the rim, and the flexible central portion is pushed inward when the air pressure in the auditory canal rises and outward when it falls. Since sound waves consist of a pattern of alternate rises and falls in pressure, the tympanum moves inward and outward in time to that pattern. The result is that the sound-wave pattern (whether produced by a tuning fork, a violin, human vocal cords, or a truck passing over a loose manhole cover) is exactly reproduced in the tympanum. As the name implies, the tympanum vibrates just as the membrane stretched across a drum would, and its common name is, in fact, the *eardrum*.

Along the edges of the tympanum are glands which secrete a

---

* This is the diaphragm I described on page 249 as having been developed out of the first gill bar of our fishy ancestors.

soft, waxy material called *cerumen* (see-roo′men; "wax" L), though *earwax* is its common name. This serves to preserve the flexibility of the tympanum and may also act as a protective device. Its odor and taste may repel small insects, which might otherwise find their way into the canal. The secretion of cerumen is increased in response to irritation and the wax may accumulate to the point where it will cover the tympanum and bring about considerable loss of hearing until such time as the ear is washed out.

On the other side of the tympanum is a small air-filled space called the *tympanic cavity*. Within that cavity are three small bones to conduct the vibrations of the tympanum still farther inward toward the vestibule. Collectively the three bones are the *ossicles* ("little bones" L). The outermost of the three ossicles is attached to the tympanum and moves with it. Because in doing so it strikes again and again on the second bone, this first ossicle is called the *malleus* (mal′ee-us; "hammer" L). The second ossicle which receives the hammer blows is the *incus* ("anvil" L).

The incus moves with the malleus and passes on the vibrations to the third bone, which is shaped like a tiny stirrup (with an opening not much larger than the eye of a needle) and therefore called the *stapes* (stay′peez; "stirrup" L).* The inner end of the stapes just fits over a small opening, the *oval window*, which leads into the next section of the ear. The whole structure from the tympanum to this small opening, including the tympanic cavity and the ossicles, is called the *middle ear*.

The function of the ossicles is more than that of transmitting the vibration pattern of the tympanum. The ossicles also control intensity of vibration. They magnify gentle sounds, because the oval window is only 1/20 the area of the tympanum and sound waves are once more narrowed down and in that way

---

* The malleus and the incus are the remnants of bones that in our reptilian ancestors were to be found in the jaw, as I explained earlier. They are found in the mammalian ear only. The stapes originated from one of the gill bars of the ancestral fishes, and is found in the ears of birds and reptiles as well as in those of mammals.

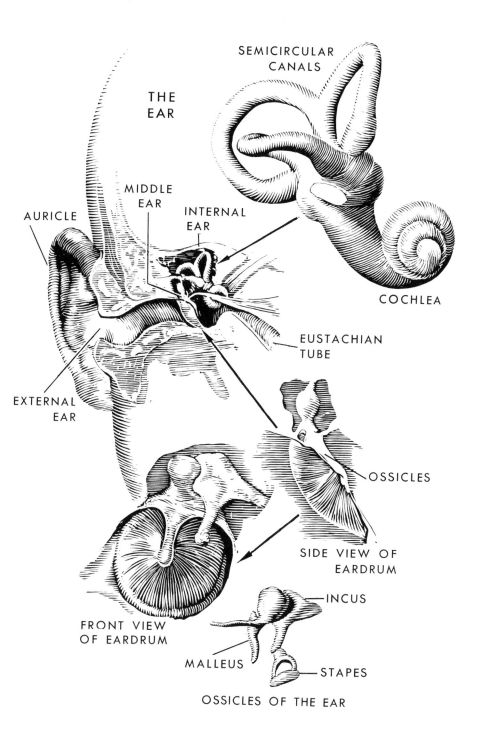

THE EAR

SEMICIRCULAR CANALS

MIDDLE EAR

INTERNAL EAR

AURICLE

COCHLEA

EUSTACHIAN TUBE

EXTERNAL EAR

OSSICLES

SIDE VIEW OF EARDRUM

FRONT VIEW OF EARDRUM

INCUS

MALLEUS

STAPES

OSSICLES OF THE EAR

intensified. In addition, the lever action of the ossicles is such that sound-wave energy is concentrated. The net result is that in passing from the tympanum to the oval window sound is amplified as much as fiftyfold.

The ossicles also damp out loud sounds. Tiny muscles that extend from the malleus to the skull place tension on the tympanum and prevent it from vibrating too strenuously; an even tinier muscle attached to the incus keeps the stapes from pressing too vigorously against the oval window. This action of magnification-and-damping extends the range of loudness we can hear. The loudest sounds we can hear without damage to the ears result from sound waves containing about 100 trillion times the energy of the softest sounds we can just barely make out. These softest sounds, by the way, result from movements of the eardrum of a two-billionth of an inch, and this represents far less energy than that in the faintest glimmer of light we can see. From the standpoint of energy conversion, then, the ear is far more sensitive than the eye.

Sound waves are conducted through the bones of the skull, but the ossicles do not respond to these with nearly the sensitivity with which they respond to tympanic movements, and this is also most helpful. Were they sensitive to bone vibration we would have to live with the constant rushing sound of blood through the blood vessels near the ear. As it is, we can hear the blood-noise as a constant hum if there is a reasonable silence and we listen carefully. This sound can be magnified by a cupped hand, or, traditionally, by a seashell; children are told that it is the distant roaring of the sea.

This filtering out of bone-conducted sound also means that we are not deafened by the sound of our voice, for we do not hear it through bone conduction chiefly, but through the sound waves carried by the air from mouth to ear. Nevertheless, bone conduction is a minor factor and adds a resonance and body to our voice we do not hear in others. When we hear a recording of our own voice, we are almost invariably appalled at its seeming inferior quality. Even the assurance of bystanders that the recording is a precise reproduction of our voice leaves us somehow incredulous.

The ossicles can sometimes be imperfect in their functioning. If the tiny muscles attached to them are damaged, or if the nerves leading to those muscles are, the ossicle movements become somewhat erratic. There may be needless vibration (something like the frame of an automobile plagued with a loose bolt). In that case, there is a continuous sound in the ears (*tinnitis;* "jingle" L), which can be endlessly irritating.

From the middle ear a narrow tube leads to the throat. This tube is called the *Eustachian tube** (yoo-stay'kee-an) after the Italian anatomist Bartolommeo Eustachio, who described the structure in 1563; see illustration, page 253. The middle ear is thus not truly within the body, but is connected to the outer world by way of the throat. This is important, because the tympanum will move most sensitively if the air pressure is the same on both sides. If the air pressure were even slightly higher on one side than on the other, the tympanum would belly inward or outward. In either case it would be under a certain tension and would then move with lesser amplitude in response to the small pressure changes set up by sound waves.

The pressure of our atmosphere changes constantly through a range of 5 per cent or so, and if the middle ear were closed, the pressure within it would rarely match the changing air pressure in the auditory canal. As it is, however, air flows in and out through the Eustachian tube, keeping the pressure within the tympanic cavity continually equal to that in the auditory canal. When external air pressure changes too rapidly, the narrow bore of the Eustachian tube is insufficient to keep the inner pressure in step. The pressure difference then causes a pressure on the tympanum which is uncomfortable and can even be painful. Everyone who has traveled up or down in a rapid elevator knows the sensation. Swallowing or yawning forces air through the

* The Eustachian tube evolved from the first gill slit of the ancestral fish.

Eustachian tube in one direction or the other and relieves the condition.

When the Eustachian tube is closed through inflammation during a cold, the resulting discomfort is less easily relieved, and is one more addition to the annoying symptoms of this most common of infectious diseases. The Eustachian tube offers a route, too, whereby bacteria can penetrate the recesses of the skull and find there a perfect haven. Such middle ear infections are more common in children than in adults. They are painful and hard to treat (though the coming of antibiotics has helped), and can be dangerous.

THE INTERNAL EAR

On the other side of the oval window covered by the stapes is the vestibule referred to on page 248. Both the vestibule and the structures within it are filled with a thin fluid much like the cerebrospinal fluid. Here the sound waves are finally converted from vibrations in air to vibrations in liquid. It is to the latter that the hearing sense was originally adapted in the first vertebrates, and the whole elaborate structure of the outer and middle ear is designed, in a way, to convert air vibrations to liquid vibrations with maximum efficiency.

There are two organs in the vestibule. Lying above and forward are the utricle and the structures developed from it, and lying below and behind are the saccule and the structures developed from it. All the contents of the vestibule are lumped together as the *internal ear*, but only the saccule portion is concerned with hearing. The utricle and attendant structures are concerned with the vestibular sense, and I leave them to one side for now.

The tube that in land vertebrates developed from the saccule is the *cochlea* (kok'lee-uh; "snail-shell" L), which is a spiral structure that does indeed have a close resemblance to a snail shell, except that its width does not narrow as it approaches its central apex, but remains constant (see illustration, p. 253).

The acoustic nerve leads from the cochlea. It is the cochlea that contains the sense-receptors making it possible for us to hear. The cochlea is not a single coiled tube but, rather, is a triple one, all coiling in unison. The upper part of the cochlea, which leads from the stapes and the oval window, consists of two tubes, the *vestibular canal* and the *cochlear canal*, separated by a very thin membrane. This membrane is too thin to block sound waves, and so, for hearing purposes, the two tubes may be considered one. The lower half of the cochlea is the *tympanic canal*. Between this and the double tube above is a thick *basilar membrane* (bas'ih-ler; "at the base" L). The basilar membrane is not easily traversed by sound waves.

Resting on the basilar membrane is a line of cells which contain the sound-receptors. This line of cells was described in 1851 by the Italian histologist Marchese Alfonso Corti, and so it is often called the organ of Corti. Among the cells of the organ of Corti are *hair cells* which are the actual sound-receptors. The hair cells are so named because they possess numerous hairlike processes extending upward. The human organ of Corti is far richer in such hairs than is that of any other species of animal examined. Each cochlea has some 15,000 hairs altogether. This seems reasonable in view of the complexity of the speech sounds human beings must listen to and distinguish. Delicate nerve fibers are located at the base of the hair cells. These respond to the stimulation of the hair cells by the sound waves and carry their impulses to the auditory nerve, which in turn transmits its message, via various portions of the brain stem, to the auditory center in the temporal lobe of the cerebrum.

An interesting question, though, is how the cochlea enables us to distinguish differences in pitch. A sound wave with a relatively long wavelength, and therefore a low frequency, is heard by us as a deep sound. One with a relatively short wavelength and high frequency is heard by us as a shrill sound. As we go up the keyboard of a piano from left to right we are producing sounds of progressively shorter wavelength and higher frequency, and though the progression is in small steps we have no difficulty in distinguishing between the tones. We could even distinguish tones that were more closely spaced — represented on the keyboard by the cracks between the piano keys, one might say.

To solve the problem of pitch perception, the cochlea must be considered in detail. The sound waves entering the cochlea by way of the oval window travel through the fluid above the basilar membrane. At some point they cross the basilar membrane into the fluid below and travel back to a point just beneath the oval window. Here there is an elastic membrane called, from its shape, the *round window*. Its presence is necessary, for liquid cannot be compressed, as air can. If the fluid were in a container without "give," then sound waves would be damped out because the water molecules would have no room to push this way or that. As it is, though, when the sound waves cause the stapes to push into the cochlea, the round window bulges outward, making room for the fluid to be pushed. When the stapes pulls outward, the round window bulges inward.

One theory of pitch perception suggests that the crux lies in the point at which the sound waves are transmitted from the upper portion of the fluid across the basilar membrane into the lower portion. The basilar membrane is made up of some 24,000 parallel fibers stretching across its width. These grow wider as one progresses away from the stapes and the oval window. In the immediate neighborhood of the oval window the fibers are about 0.1 millimeters wide, but by the time the far end of the cochlea is reached they are some 0.4 millimeters wide. A fiber has its own natural frequency of vibration. Any frequency may, of course, be imposed upon it by force, but if it is allowed freedom, it will respond much more vigorously to a period of vibration equal to its natural period than to any other. This selective response to its natural period of vibration is called *resonance*. Of two objects of similar shape, the larger will have a lower natural frequency. Consequently, as one travels along the basilar membrane its resonance will respond, little by little, to lower and lower frequencies.

It was tempting to think that each type of sound wave crossed the basilar membrane at the point where the resonance frequency corresponded to its own. High-pitched sounds with short wavelengths and high frequencies crossed it near the oval window. Deeper sounds crossed it at a greater distance from the oval window; still deeper sounds crossed it at a still greater distance, and so on. The hair cells at the point of crossing would be stimulated and the brain could then interpret pitch in accordance with which fibers carried the message.

This theory would seem almost too beautifully simple to give up, but evidently it has to be abandoned. The Hungarian physicist Georg von Bekesy has conducted careful experiments with an artificial system designed to possess all the essentials of the cochlea and has found that sound waves passing through the fluid in the cochlea set up wavelike displacements in the basilar membrane itself.

The position of maximum displacement of the basilar membrane — the peak of the wave — depends on the frequency of the sound wave. The lower the frequency, the more distant the peak displacement is from the oval window, and it is at the point at which this peak is located that the hair cells are stimulated. The alteration of the form of displacement of the basilar membrane with pitch does not seem to be great. However, the nerve network can, apparently, respond to the peak of the wave without regard to lesser stimulations near by and can record slight changes in the position of that peak with remarkable fidelity. (In a way, this is similar to our ability to "listen," that is, to hear one sound to which we are paying attention, while damping out the surrounding background noise. We can carry on a conversation in a crowd in which many are talking simultaneously, or amid the roar of city traffic.)

Naturally, any given sound is going to be made up of a variety of sound waves of different frequencies, and the form of the displacement pattern taken up by the basilar membrane will be complex indeed. Hair cells at different points among the basilar membrane will be stimulated and each to a different extent. The combination of all the stimulations will be interpreted by the brain as a variety of pitches which, taken all together, will make up the "quality" of a sound. Thus, a piano and a violin sounding the same tone will produce effects that are clearly different. Each will set up a number of sets of vibrations at varying frequencies, even though the dominant frequency will be that of the tone being sounded. Because a violin and piano have radically different shapes, each will resonate in different fashion to these varying frequencies, so one may reinforce frequency A more than frequency B and the other may reverse matters.

In musical sounds, the differing frequencies of the sound waves set up bear simple numerical relationships among themselves. In nonmusical sounds, the various frequencies are more randomly distributed. The basilar membrane of the cochlea can undergo displacements in response to any sound, musical or not. However, we interpret the simple numerical relationships among simultaneous frequencies as "chords" and "harmonies" and find them pleasant, whereas the frequencies not in simple numerical relationships are "discords" or "noise" and are often found unpleasant.

The delicacy with which we can distinguish pitch and the total range of pitch we can hear depend on the number of hair cells the cochlea can hold and therefore on the length of the organ of Corti. It is clearly advantageous, then, to have the cochlea as long as possible; the human cochlea is one and a half inches long. Or at least it would be that length if it were straight; by being coiled into a spiral (forming two and a half turns), it takes up less room without sacrifice of length.

The human ear can detect sound from frequencies as low as 16 cycles per second (with a wavelength of about 70 feet) to frequencies as high as 25,000 cycles per second (wavelength, about half an inch). In music each doubling of frequency is considered an *octave* ("eight" L, because in the diatonic scale each octave is divided into seven different tones, the eighth tone starting a new octave) and, therefore, the ear has a range of a little over ten octaves. The width of this range may be emphasized by the reminder that the full stretch of notes on the piano extends over only 7½ octaves.

The ear is not equally sensitive to all pitches. It is most sensitive to the range from about 1000 to 4000 cycles per second. This range corresponds to the stretch from the note C two octaves above middle C to the note C that is two octaves higher still. With age, the range of pitch shrinks, particularly at the shrill end; children can easily hear high-pitched sounds that to an adult are simply silence. It is estimated that after the age of forty, the upper limit of the range decreases by about 13 cycles per month.

There are sound waves of frequencies outside the range we can hear, of course. Those with frequencies too high to hear are *ultrasonic waves* ("beyond sound" L), and those with frequencies too low are *subsonic waves* ("below sound" L).* In general, larger animals, with larger sound-producing and sound-sensing organs, can produce and hear deeper sounds than can smaller animals. The smaller animals, in turn, can produce and hear shriller sounds. The trumpet of an elephant and the squeak of a mouse represent reasonable extremes.

While few animals are sensitive to the wide range of pitch we are sensitive to, we are comparatively large creatures. It is easy to find among smaller creatures examples of animals that can readily hear sounds in the ultrasonic reaches. The songs of many birds have their ultrasonic components, and we miss much of the beauty for not hearing these. The squeaking of mice and bats is also rich in ultrasonics, and in the latter case, at least, these have an important function which I shall describe below. Cats and dogs can hear shrill sounds we cannot. The cat will

---

* These days the adjective "supersonic" ("above sound" L) is much used. This does not refer to a range of sound frequencies, but to a velocity that is greater than the speed of sound.

detect a mouse's high-pitched squeak which to us may be a faint sound or nothing at all, and dogs can detect easily the ultrasonic vibrations of the silent "dog-whistles" that are silent only to ourselves.

ECHOLOCATION

In hearing we not only detect a sound but to a certain extent we also determine the direction from which it comes. That we can do so is largely thanks to the fact that we have two ears, the existence of which is not a matter of symmetrical esthetics alone. A sound coming from one side reaches the ear on that side a little sooner than it does the ear on the other. Furthermore, the head itself forms a barrier that sound must pass before reaching the more distant ear; the wave may be slightly weakened by the time it gets there. The brain is capable of analyzing such minute differences in timing and intensity (and the experience of living and of years of trying to locate sounds in this manner and observing our own success sharpens its ability to do so) and judging from that the direction of the sound.

Our ability to judge the direction of sound is not equal throughout the range of pitch we can hear. Any wave-form reacts differently toward obstacles according to whether these are larger or smaller than its own wavelength. Objects larger than a wavelength of the wave-form striking them tend to reflect the wave-form. Objects that are smaller do not; instead the wave-form tends to go around it. The smaller the object in comparison to the wavelength, the less of an obstacle it is and the more easily it is "gone around."

The wavelengths of the ordinary sounds about us is in the neighborhood of a yard, which means that sound can travel around corners and about the average household obstacle. (It will, however, be reflected by large walls and, notoriously, by mountainsides, to produce echoes.) The deeper the sound the more easily does it move around the head without trouble and the less is it weakened before reaching the far ear. One method of locating a sound is therefore denied us. The effect is to be seen in the way the majestic swell of the organ in its lower registers seems to "come from all about us," and thereby to be the more impressive. On the other hand, a particularly shrill note with a wavelength of an inch or so finds the head too much of a barrier, and possibly the far ear does not get enough of the sound to make a judgment. Certainly it is difficult to locate a cricket in a room from the sound of its shrill chirp.

The use of both ears, *binaural hearing* (bin-aw'rul; "two ears" L), does not merely help in locating a sound but also aids sensitivity. The two ears seem to add their responses, so that a sound heard by both seems louder than when heard by only one. Differences in pitch are also more easily distinguished with both ears open than with one covered.

Echoes themselves can be used for location of the presence of a barrier. Thus, when driving along a line of irregularly parked cars, we can, if we listen, easily tell the difference in the engine sound of our own car as we pass parked cars and the engine sound as we pass empty parking places. In the former case the engine sound has its echo added, and there would be no difficulty in locating, through the contrast, an unoccupied parking place with our eyes closed. Unfortunately, we could not tell whether that unoccupied parking place contained a fireplug or not. An automobile is large enough to reflect the wavelengths of some of our engine noises but a fireplug is not. To detect objects smaller than a car would require sound waves of shorter wavelength and higher frequency. The shorter the wavelength and the higher the frequency, the smaller the object we can detect by the echoes to which it gives rise. Obviously, ultrasonic sound would be more efficient in this respect than ordinary sound.

Bats, for example, have long puzzled biologists by their ability to avoid obstacles in flight and to catch insects on the wing at night, even after having been blinded. Deafening bats destroys this ability, and this was puzzling indeed at first. (Can a bat see with its ears? The answer is yes, in a way it can.) It is now known that a flying bat emits a continuous series of ultrasonic squeaks, with frequencies of 40,000 to 80,000 cycles per second (and with resulting wavelengths of from 1/3 of an inch down to 1/6 of an inch). A twig or an insect will tend to reflect such short wavelengths, and the bat, whose squeaks are of excessively short duration, will catch the faint echo between squeaks. From the time lapse between squeak and echo, from the direction of the echo and the extent of the echo's weakening, it can apparently tell whether an object is a twig or an insect and exactly where the object is. It can then guide its flight either with an intention of avoiding or intersecting, as the case may be. This is called *echolocation,* and we should not be surprised that bats have such large ears in relation to their overall size.

Dolphins apparently have a highly developed sense of echolocation, too, though they make use of generally lower sounds, since they require reflection from generally larger objects. (Dolphins eat fish and not insects.) It is by echolocation that dolphins can detect the presence of food and move toward it unerringly even in murky water and at night, when the sense of sight is inadequate.

Man has more of this power of echolocation than he usually suspects. I have already mentioned the ability to locate an empty parking spot, which you may try for yourself. That we do not depend on such devices more than we do is simply because our reliance on sight is such that we ordinarily ignore the help of the ear in the precise location of objects, at least consciously.

Nevertheless, a blindfolded man walking along a corridor can learn to stop before he reaches a blocking screen, as a result of hearing the change in the echoes of his footsteps. He can do this even when he is not quite aware of what it is he is sensing. He may then interpret matters as "I just had a feeling —" Blind men, forced into a greater reliance on hearing, develop abilities in this respect which seem amazing but are merely the result of exploiting powers that have been there all the time.

Mechanically, man has learned to use ultrasonic waves for echolocation (in the precise manner of bats) in a device called *sonar,* which is an abbreviation for "sound navigation and ranging." Sonar is used for detecting objects such as submarines, schools of fish, and bottom features in the ocean. In the open air men now make use of microwaves (a form of light waves with wavelengths in the range of those of ultrasonic sound) for the same purpose. Echolocation by microwave is generally referred to as *radar,* an abbreviation for "radio detection and ranging." (Microwaves are sometimes considered very short radio waves, you see.)

THE VESTIBULAR SENSE

The acoustic nerve, which leads from the cochlea, has a branch leading to the other half of the contents of the internal ear, the utricle and its outgrowths, introduced on page 248. It is time to consider in detail their function. In its simplest form, the utricle may be viewed as a hollow sphere filled with fluid and lined along its inner surface with hair cells. (The structure is similar to the saccule and its outgrowths.) Within the sphere is a bit of calcium carbonate which, thanks to gravity, remains at the bottom of the sphere and stimulates the hair cells there.

Imagine a fish swimming at perfect right angles to the pull of gravity — in a perfectly horizontal line, and leaning neither to one side nor the other. The bit of calcium continues to remain at the bottom of the sphere, and it is the stimulation of those particular hair cells which is interpreted by the nervous system as signifying "normal posture." If the fish's direction of swimming tilts upward, the sphere changes position and the bit of calcium carbonate settles to the new bottom under the pull of gravity, stimulating hair cells that are farther back than the normal-posture ones. If the direction of swim tilts downward, hair cells in front of the normal-posture ones are stimulated. Again there is a shift to the right with a rightward tilt and to the left with a leftward tilt. When the fish is upside-down, the calcium carbonate is stimulating hair cells that are removed by 180 degrees from the normal-posture ones.

In all these cases, the fish can automatically right itself by moving in such a way as to bring the bit of calcium carbonate back to the normal-posture hair cells. The function of the utricle, we observe, is to maintain the normal posture. To us that would be an upright standing position, so a utricle used for this purpose may be called a *statocyst* ("standing-pouch" G) and the bit of calcium carbonate is the *statolith* ("standing-stone" G).

This function can be shown dramatically in crustaceans. The statocysts in such creatures open to the outside world through narrow apertures, and the statoliths are not bits of calcium carbonate but are, rather, sand particles the creature actually places within the statocysts. When the crustacean molts, those bits of sand are lost and must be replaced. One experimenter removed all sand from a tank and substituted iron filings. The shrimp with which he was experimenting innocently introduced iron filings into the statocyst. Once this was done, a magnet held above the shrimp lifted the filings against the pull of gravity and caused them to stimulate the uppermost hair cells instead of the lowermost. In response the animal promptly stood on its head, so that the lowermost hair cells might be stimulated by the "upward-falling" filings.

Because the statocyst is located in the internal ear, it is more commonly, though less appropriately, called the *otocyst* (oh'toh-sist; "ear pouch" G). The material within, if present in relatively large particles, is called *otoliths* ("earstone" G), and if present in fine particles is called *otoconia* (oh'toh-koh'nee-uh; "ear-dust" G). Otoconia persist in the utricle of the land vertebrates. The vestibular sense made possible by the utricle is somewhat reminiscent of the proprioceptive senses (see p. 221). However, where the proprioceptive senses tell us the position of one part of the body with relation to another, the vestibular sense tells us the position of the body as a whole with respect to its environment, especially with regard to the direction of the pull of gravity.

A cat can right itself when falling and land on its feet, even though it was dropped feet up. It does this by automatically altering the position of its head into the upright, being guided by the position of its otoconia. This in turn brings about movements in the rest of its body designed to bring it into line with the new position of the head. Down it comes, feetfirst every time. Nor are we ourselves deprived. We have no difficulty in telling whether we are standing upright, upside-down, or tilted in any possible direction, even with our eyes closed and even when floating in water. A swimmer who dives into the water can come up headfirst without trouble and without having to figure out his position consciously.

But the utricle is not all there is to the vestibular sense. Attached to the utricle are three tubes that start and end there, each bending in a semicircle so they are called *semicircular canals*. Each semicircular canal is filled with fluid and is set in an appropriate tunnel within the bone of the skull but is separated from the bone by a thin layer of the fluid. The individual semicircular canals are arranged as follows. Two are located in a vertical plane (if viewed in a standing man) but at right angles to each other, one directed forward and outward, the other backward and outward. The third semicircular canal lies in a horizontal plane. The net result is that each semicircular canal lies in a plane at right angles to those of the other two. You can see the arrangement if you look at a corner of the room where two walls meet the floor. Imagine the curve of one canal following the plane of one wall, that of a second canal following the plane of the other wall, and that of the third canal following the plane of the floor. One end of each canal, where it joins the utricle, swells out to form an *ampulla* (am-pul'uh; "little vase" G, because of its shape). Within each ampulla is a small elevated region called a *crista* ("crest" L), which contains the sensitive hair cells.

The semicircular canals do not react to the body's position with respect to gravity; they react to a change in the body's position. If you should turn your head right or left or tilt it up or down, or in any combination of these movements, the fluid within one or more of the semicircular canals moves because of inertia. There is thus a flow in the direction opposite to the head's motion. (If your car makes a right turn you are pressed against the left, and vice versa.) By receiving impulses from the various stimulated hair cells as a result of this inertial flow of liquid and by noting which were stimulated and by how much, the mind can judge the nature of the motion of the head.*

The semicircular canals judge not motion itself, then, but change of motion. It is acceleration or deceleration that makes fluid move inertially. (In a car at steady speed, you sit comfortably in your seat. But when the car speeds up, you are pressed backward, and when the car slows down, you are pressed forward.) This means that stopping motion is as effective as starting motion in stimulating the semicircular canals. This becomes very noticeable if we spin about as rapidly as we can and continue it long enough to allow the fluid within the semicircular canals to overcome inertia and to turn with us. Now if we stop suddenly, the fluid, thanks to its inertia, keeps on moving and stimulates the hair cells strongly. We interpret this as signifying that there is relative motion between ourselves and our surroundings. Since we know we are standing still, the only conclusion is that the surroundings are moving. The room seems to spin about us, we are dizzy, and in many cases can do nothing but fall to the ground and hold desperately to the floor until the fluid in our semicircular canals settles down and the world steadies itself.

The steady rocking motion of a ship also stimulates the semicircular canals, and to those who are not used to this overstimulation the result often is seasickness, which is an extremely unpleasant, though not really fatal affliction.

---

* The lampreys, among the most primitive living vertebrates, have only two semicircular canals. Their prefish ancestors were bottom-dwellers who had to contend with motions left and right, forward and backward, but not up and down. They lived a two-dimensional life. The fish developed the third canal for the up-down dimension as well, and all vertebrates since — including ourselves, of course — have had a three-dimensional vestibular sense.

12

OUR EYES

LIGHT

The earth is bathed in light from the sun and one could scarcely think of a more important single fact than that. The radiation of the sun (of which light itself is an important but not the only component) keeps the surface of the earth at a temperature that makes life as we know it possible. The energy of sunlight, in the early dawn of the earth, may have brought about the specific chemical reactions in the ocean that led to the formation of life. And, in a sense, sunlight daily creates life even now. It is the energy source used by green plants to convert atmospheric carbon dioxide into carbohydrates and other tissue components. Since all the animal kingdom, including ourselves, feeds directly or indirectly on green plants, sunlight supports us all. Again, the animal kingdom, and man in particular, has grown adapted to the detection of light. That detection has become so essential to us as a means of sensing and interpreting our environment that blindness is a major affliction, and even fuzzy vision is a serious handicap.

Light has also had a profound influence on the development of science. For the last three centuries the question of the nature of light and the significance of its properties has remained a crucial matter of dispute among physicists. The two chief views concerning the nature of light were first propounded in some

detail by 17th-century physicists. The Englishman Isaac New-
ton believed that light consisted of speeding particles; the Dutch-
man Christian Huygens believed that it was a wave-form. Central to the dispute was the fact that light traveled in straight
lines and cast sharp shadows. Speeding particles (if unaffected
by gravity) would naturally move in straight lines, whereas all
man's experience with water waves and sound waves showed that
wave-forms would not, but would bend about obstacles. For a
century and a half, then, the particle theory held fast.

In 1801 the English scientist Thomas Young demonstrated
that light showed the property of interference. That is to say,
two rays of light could be projected in such a way that when they
fell upon a screen together areas of darkness were formed. Particles could not account for this, but waves could — because the
wave of one ray might be moving upward while the wave of the
other was moving downward, and the two effects would cancel.

The wave theory was quickly made consistent with the straight-
line travel of light, since Young also worked out the wavelength
of light. As I have said in the previous chapter, the shorter the
wavelength the less a wave-form is capable of moving about obstacles, and the more it must move in a straight line and cast
shadows. The very shortest wavelengths of audible sound are
in the neighborhood of half an inch, and they already show considerable powers of straight-line travel. Imagine, then, what light
must be able to do in this respect when we consider that a
typical light wave has a wavelength of about a fifty-thousandth
of an inch. Light is much more efficient than even the most
ultrasonic of life-produced sound in echolocation. We may be
able to detect the position of an object by the sound it makes, but
we do so only fairly well. When we see an object, on the contrary,
we are quite certain that we know exactly where it is. "Seeing
is believing," we say, and the height of skepticism is "to doubt
the evidence of one's own eyes."

Light waves contain far more energy than do the sound waves
we ordinarily encounter; enough energy, as a matter of fact, to

bring about chemical changes in many substances. It is quite feasible for living organisms to detect the presence of light by the presence or absence of such chemical changes and to respond accordingly. For the purpose it is not even necessary to develop an elaborate light-detecting organ. Plants, for instance, climb toward the light, or bend toward it, without any trace of such an organ. A response to light is clearly useful. All green plants must grow toward the light if they are to make use of its energy. Water animals can find the surface layers of the sea by moving toward the light. On land, light means warmth and animals may seek it or avoid it depending on the season of the year, the time of day, and other factors.

Detecting light by its chemical effect can, however, be dangerous as well as useful. In living tissue, with its delicate balance of complex and fragile interacting compounds, random changes induced by light can be ruinous. It proved evolutionarily useful to concentrate a chemical particularly sensitive to light in one spot. Because of its individual sensitivity, such a chemical would react to a low intensity of light, one that would not damage tissue generally. Furthermore, its location in a certain spot would enable the remainder of the organism's surface to be shielded from light altogether.

(In order for any substance to be affected by light to the point of chemical change, it must first absorb the light. Generally it will absorb some wavelengths of light to a greater extent than others, and the light it reflects or transmits will then be weighted in favor of the wavelengths it does not absorb. But we sense different wavelengths, as I shall explain later in the chapter, as different colors, so when we see the light-sensitive substance by the light it transmits or reflects we see it as colored. For this reason the light-sensitive compounds in organisms are commonly referred to as pigments, a word reserved for colored substances, and specifically as *visual pigments*.)

Even one-celled animals may have light-sensitive areas, but the true elaboration of course comes in multicellular animals, in

which discrete organs — eyes — are devoted to *photoreception.*
(The prefix "photo" is from the Greek word for "light.")

The simplest photoreceptors can do no more than detect light
or not detect it. Nevertheless, even when an organism is limited
to this detection it has a useful tool. It can move either toward
or away from the light sensed. Furthermore, if the level of stimulation suddenly falls, the obvious interpretation is that something
has passed between the photoreceptor and the light. Flight could
be a logical response, since the "something," after all, might very
well be an enemy.

The more sensitive a photoreceptor can be made the better,
and one method of increasing the sensitivity is to increase the
amount of light falling upon the visual pigment. A way of doing
this depends upon the fact that light does not necessarily travel
in a straight line under all conditions. Whenever light passes
obliquely from one medium to another it is bent or *refracted*
("bent back" L). If the surface between media is flat, all the light
entering it bends as a unit.* If the surface is curved, things are
rather more complicated. Should light pass from air into water
across a surface that is more or less spherical, the rays tend to bend
in the direction of the center of the sphere, no matter where they
strike. All the light rays converge therefore and are eventually
gathered together into a *focus* ("fireplace" L, since that is where
light is gathered together, so to speak, in a household).

To concentrate light, organisms use not water itself but a
transparent object that is largely water. In land animals it is
shaped like a lentil seed, which in Latin is called *lens* and which
lent its name to the shape. A lens is a kind of flattened sphere
that does the work but economizes on room. The lens acts to
concentrate light; all the light that falls on its relatively broad
width is brought into the compass of a narrow spot. A child can
use a lens to set paper on fire, whereas unconcentrated sunlight
would be helpless to do so. In the same way a particular photo-

---

* This is strictly so only if all the light is of the same wavelength. Where it is
not there is another important effect (see p. 295).

receptor could respond to feeble light which, in the absence of lens-concentration, would leave it unaffected.

Since light, left to itself, travels primarily in straight lines, a photoreceptor — whether equipped with a lens or not — will sense light only from the direction it faces. To sense light in other directions a creature must turn, or else it must be supplied with photoreceptors pointed in a number of directions. The latter alternative has much to recommend it since it saves the time required to turn, and even a fraction of a second may be important in the eternal battle to obtain food and avoid enemies.

The development of multiple photoreceptors reaches its climax in insects. The eyes of a fly are not single organs. Each is a *compound eye* made up of thousands of photoreceptors, each of which is set at a slightly different angle. A fly without moving can be conscious of changes in light intensity at almost any angle, which is why it is so difficult to catch one by surprise while bringing it the gift of a flyswatter. Each photoreceptor of the compound eye registers only "light" or "dark" but their numbers enable something more to be done. If an object lies between the compound eye and the light, the insect can obtain a rough estimate of the object's size and shape by the number and distribution of those photoreceptors that register "dark." A kind of rough mosaic picture is built up of the object. Furthermore, if the object moves, individual photoreceptors go dark progressively in the direction of its motion, and others light up progressively as it leaves. In this way, the insect can obtain an idea of the direction and velocity of a movement.

The vertebrates have adopted a different system. Use is made of large individual eyes that concentrate light on an area of photosensitive cells. Each cell is individually capable of registering light or dark. The individual photoreceptors are cell-sized and microscopic; and not, as in insects, large enough to be seen by the naked eye. The vertebrate mosaic of sight is fine indeed.

Suppose that you try to draw a picture of a man's face on a sheet of paper using black dots after the fashion of a newspaper

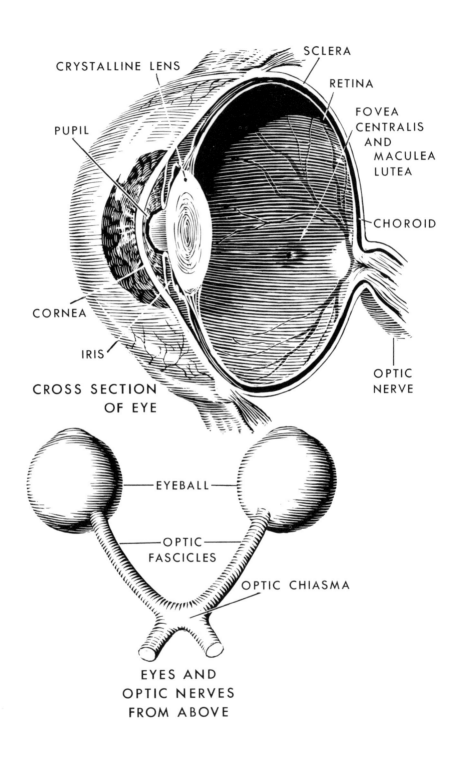

CRYSTALLINE LENS

SCLERA

RETINA

FOVEA CENTRALIS AND MACULEA LUTEA

PUPIL

CHOROID

CORNEA

IRIS

OPTIC NERVE

CROSS SECTION OF EYE

EYEBALL

OPTIC FASCICLES

OPTIC CHIASMA

EYES AND OPTIC NERVES FROM ABOVE

photograph (look at one under a magnifying glass and you will see what I mean). If you use large dots for the purpose, you can't get much detail into the picture. If you use smaller dots (for a picture of the same size) you can make out more detail; still smaller dots, still greater detail.

The "dots" used by insects are the size of the individual facets of their compound eyes; the dots used by ourselves are the size of cells. We can therefore see much more detail than an insect can; our vision is much more acute. In the space which a honeybee might cover with one dot, either light or dark — and that is all the information it would have — we could squeeze in some 10,000 dots in a possibly intricate pattern of light and dark that could yield a great deal of information.

The use of an eye with cell-sized photoreceptors offers such advantages that it has actually been devised by a number of quite unrelated groups of animals. In particular, certain groups of mollusks developed an eye quite independently of the development going on in vertebrates, and ended almost in the same place. The eye of the squid, though possessing a completely different history than ours does, resembles ours closely, part for part.

THE EYEBALL

The human eye, which is just about an inch in diameter, is very nearly a sphere in shape, so the expression *eyeball* for the eye as a physical structure is quite apt. About five sixths of the eyeball is enclosed by a strong, fibrous outermost layer called the *sclera* (sklee′ruh; "hard" G). It is white, and portions of it are visible in that part of the eye to be seen between the eyelids. This is referred to as "the white of the eye."

In the front of the eye, facing the outside world directly, is a section about half an inch in diameter which is transparent. It is the *cornea*. (This word is from the same root as the word "horn," and since thin layers of horn are semitransparent, and since horn and cornea are both modified skin, the name is not as farfetched as it might seem.) The cornea does not really complete the sphere of the eyeball smoothly. Its curvature is sharper than is that of the sclera and it bulges outward from the eye's smooth curve, like a portion of a small sphere set into the side of a larger one. If you close your eyes lightly, place your finger upon the eyelid, and move your eye, you will definitely feel the bulge of the cornea.

A layer of dark tissue, lining the inner surface of the sclera, continues the smooth curve of the eyeball and extends out into the cavity formed by the cornea's bulge, almost closing the transparent gap. This is the *choroid* (koh′roid; "membrane" G) and it is well supplied with blood vessels, some of which occasionally show through the white of the sclera. The portion of the choroid visible under the cornea contains the dark pigment, melanin, which is responsible for the brown or black color of hair, and for the swarthiness of skin. In most human beings, there is enough melanin in this portion of the choroid to give it a brown color. Among fair-skinned individuals with less-than-average capacity for forming melanin, the color is lighter. If the spots of pigment are sparse enough, they do not absorb light so much as scatter it. Light of short wavelength (as, for example, blue) is more easily scattered than light of long wavelength (such as red), so that the visible choroid usually appears blue or blue-green under these conditions, viewed as it is by the light it scatters. At birth, babies' eyes are always blue but as pigment is formed in increasing quantities during the time of infancy, most sets of eyes gradually turn brown. Among albinos, incapable of forming melanin altogether, the choroid contains no pigment and the blood vessels are clearly seen, giving the choroid a distinctly reddish appearance.

The different colors found among individuals in this portion of the eye give it the name *iris* ("rainbow" G). We are particularly conscious of this color, and when we speak of "brown eyes" or "blue eyes" we are referring to the color of the iris and not of the whole eye, of course. The function of the iris is to screen the light entering the interior of the eyeball. Naturally, the more pigmented the iris, the more efficiently it performs this function. The evolutionary development of blue eyes took place in northern countries, where sunlight is characteristically weak and where imperfect shading could even be useful in increasing the eye's sensitivity. An albino's eyes are unusually sensitive to light because of the lack of shading, and he must avoid bright lights.

To allow for changes in the intensity of outside illumination the iris is equipped to extend or contract the area it covers by means of the tiny muscle fibers it contains. In bright light, the fibers relax and the iris covers almost the entire area under the cornea. A tiny round opening is left through which light can enter the eyeball, and this opening is the *pupil* ("doll" L, because of the tiny image of oneself one can see reflected there). In dim light, the fibers tighten and the iris draws back, so that the pupil enlarges and allows more light to enter the eyeball.

The pupil is the opening through which we actually see, and this is evident even to folk-wisdom, which refers to it as "the apple of the eye" and uses it as a synonym for something carefully loved and guarded. It is partly through the variation in its size that we adapt to a specific level of light. Entering a darkened movie theater from the outer sunlight leaves us blind at first. If we wait a few minutes, the pupil expands and our vision improves greatly as more light pours in. Conversely, if we stumble into the bathroom at night and turn on the light we find ourselves momentarily pained by the brilliance. After a few moments of peering through narrowed eyelids, the pupil decreases in size and we are comfortable again. At its smallest the pupil has a diameter of about 1.5 millimeters (about 1/16 inch), at its widest about 8 or 9 millimeters (over 1/3 inch). The diameter increases six-fold, and since the light-gathering power depends on the area — which varies as the square of the diameter — the pupil at maximum opening admits nearly forty times as much light as at minimum opening. (Our pupil retains a circular shape as it grows larger and smaller. This is not true of some other animals. In the cat, to cite the most familiar case, the pupil is round in the dark, but with increasing light it narrows from side to side only, becoming nothing more than a vertical slit in bright light.)

The eye is carefully protected from mechanical irritation as well as from the effects of too much light. It is equipped with eyelids which close rapidly at the slightest hint of danger to the eyes. So rapid is this movement that "quick as a wink" is a common phrase to signify speed, and the German word for "an instant" is *ein Augenblick* ("an eyewink"). Nor is the movement of the eyelid itself a source of irritation. For one thing, there is a delicate membrane covering the exposed portion of the eyeball and the inner surface of the eyelid. This is the *conjunctiva* (kon'-junk-ty'vuh; "connective" L, because it connects the eyeball and the eyelids). The conjunctiva is kept moist by the secretions ("tears") of the *tear glands*, a name that is Latinized to *lacrimal glands* ("tear" L). These are located just under the bone forming the upper and outer part of the eye socket.

When the eyelid closes, conjunctiva slides along conjunctiva with a thin, lubricating layer of fluid between. In order to keep the eye's surface moist and flexible, the eyelid closes periodically, moving fluid over the exposed portion of the eye, despite the fact that danger may not be present. We are so used to this periodic blinking, even when not consciously aware of it, that we are made uneasy by an unwinking stare. The fact that snakes do not have eyelids and therefore have just such an unwinking stare is one factor in their appearance of malevolence.

Some animals have a third eyelid in the form of a transparent membrane that can be quickly drawn across the eye, usually in a horizontal sweep from the inner corner of the eye (the *inner canthus*) near the nose. This is the *nictitating membrane* ("wink" L) and cleans the eye without introducing a dangerous, even if short, period of complete blindness. Man does not possess a functional nictitating membrane, but a remnant of it is to be found in the inner canthus.

Tears also serve the purpose of washing out foreign matter that gets onto the eye's surface. The eye is protected against such foreign matter not only by the eyelid itself but by the eyelashes that rim the lids and permit sight while maintaining a protective (but discontinuous) barrier across the opening. Thus, we automatically squint our eyes when the wind stirs up dust. There also are the eyebrows, which protect the overhang of the forehead, entangling raindrops and insects.

Still, foreign matter will invade the eye occasionally. Sometimes an eyelash will get in so that the protective device itself can be a source of trouble. In response to such invasion (which can be exquisitely uncomfortable), the lacrimal glands secrete their tears at an increased rate and the eyes "water." Eyes will also water in response to the irritation of smoke, chemicals (as in the case of the well-known "tear gas"), strong wind, or even strong light. Ordinarily tears are carried off by the thin *lacrimal ducts* placed at the inner canthus. The fluid is then discharged into the nasal cavity. Usually not enough of it is disposed of in this fashion to be noticed. When the lacrimal ducts grow inflamed during infection, tear outflow is cut down, and we notice the lack of the duct action easily enough since watering eyes make up one of the unpleasant symptoms of a cold.

In response to strong emotions the lacrimal glands are particularly active, and secrete tears past the capacity of the lacrimal ducts, even at their best, to dispose of them. In such cases, the tears will collect and overflow the lower lids so that we weep with rage, with joy, with frustration, or with grief, as the case may be. The escape of tears into the nasal cavity does become noticeable under these conditions, too, and it is common to find one must blow one's nose after weeping.) Tears are salt, as are all body fluids, and also contain a protein called *lysozyme*, which has the ability to kill bacteria and thus lend tears a disinfecting quality.

Despite all the protection offered them, the eyes, of necessity, are unusually open to irritation and infection, and the inflammation of the conjunctiva that results is *conjunctivitis*. The engorged blood vessels, unusually visible through the sclera, give the eye a "bloodshot" appearance. Newborn babies are liable to develop conjunctivitis because of infections gained during their passage through the genital canal. This, however, is controlled and prevented from bringing about serious trouble by the routine treatment of their eyes with antibiotics or with dilute silver nitrate solution.

A serious form of conjunctivitis, caused by a virus, is *trachoma* (tra-koh′muh; "rough" G), so called because the scars formed on the eyeball give it a roughened appearance. The scars on the cornea can be bad enough to blind a sufferer of the disease. Since trachoma is particularly common in the Middle East, this may possibly account for the number of blind beggars featured in the stories of the Arabian Nights.

The fact that we have two eyes is part of our bilateral symmetry, as is the fact that we have two ears, two arms, and two legs. The existence of two eyes is useful in that the loss of vision in one eye does not prevent an individual from leading a reasonably normal-sighted life. However, the second eye is more than a spare.

In most animals, the two eyes have separate fields of vision and nothing, or almost nothing, that one of them sees can be seen by the other. This is useful if a creature must be continually on the outlook for enemies and must seemingly look in all directions at once. Among the primates, though, the two eyes are brought forward to the front of the head, so that the fields of vision overlap almost entirely. What we see with one eye is just about what we see with the other. By so narrowing the field of vision, we look at one thing and see it clearly. Moreover, we gain importantly in depth perception.

We can judge the comparative distances of objects we see in a number of ways, some of which depend upon experience. Knowing the true size of something, say, we can judge its distance from its apparent size. If we don't know its true size we may compare it with nearby objects of known size. We can judge by the quantity of haze that obscures it, by the convergence of parallel lines reaching out toward it, and so on. All this will work for one eye as well as for two, so that depth perception with one eye is possible.* Nevertheless, we have but to close one eye to see that, in comparison with two-eyed vision, one-eyed vision tends to be flat.

With two eyes, you see, the phenomenon of parallax is introduced. We see a tree with the left eye against a certain spot on the far horizon. We see the same tree at the same time with the right eye against a different spot on the far horizon. (Try holding a pencil a foot before your eyes and view it while closing first one eye then the other without moving your head. You will see it shift positions against the background.) The closer an object to the eye, the greater its shift in position with change from one view to the other. The field of vision of the left eye therefore differs from that of the right in the relative positions of the various objects the field contains. The fusion of the two fields enables us to judge comparative distance by noting (quite automatically and without conscious effort) the degrees of difference. This form of depth perception is *stereoscopic vision* ("solid-seeing" G), because it makes possible the perceiving of a solid as a solid, in depth as well as in height and breadth and not merely as a flat projection.**

The fixing of the eyes upon a single field of vision does not obviate the necessity of seeing in all directions. One way of making up for the loss of area of the field of vision is to be able to turn the neck with agility. The owl, whose stereoscopic eyes are fixed in position, can turn its neck in either direction through almost 180 degrees so that it can look almost directly backward.

---

* By cleverly altering backgrounds to take advantage of the assumptions we are continually making, we can be tricked into coming to false conclusions as to shapes, sizes, and distances, and this is the explanation of many of the "optical illusions" with which we all amuse ourselves at one time or another.

** In the days before movies a popular evening pastime was to look at stereoscope slides. These consisted of pairs of pictures of the same scene taken from slightly different angles, representing the view as it would be seen by a left eye alone and also by a right eye. Looking at these through a device that enables the eyes to fuse the pictures into one scene caused the view to spring into a pseudo-three-dimensional reality. In the 3-D craze that hit the movies in the 1950's, two pictures were taken in this same left-eye-right-eye manner and the two were viewed separately by either eye when special spectacles of oppositely polarized film were put on.

Our own less flexible neck will not permit a turn of more than 90 degrees, but, on the other hand, we can turn our eyeballs through a considerable angle. The human eyeball is outfitted with three pairs of muscles for this purpose. One pair turns it right or left; one pair up or down; and one pair rotates it somewhat. As a result, a reasonable extension of the field of vision is made possible by a flicker of movement taking less time and effort than moving the entire head.

EYE MUSCLES

The restriction of field of vision makes it possible for a man to be surprised from behind ("Do I have eyes in the back of my head?" is the plaintive cry), but to the developing primates in the trees, stereoscopic vision, which made it possible to judge the distance of branches with new precision, was well worth the risk of blindness toward the rear. In nonstereoscopic vision there is no reason why the motion of the eyes might not be independent of each other. This is so in the chameleon, to cite one case, and the separate movements of its eyes are amusing to watch. In stereoscopic eyes such as our own, however, the two eyeballs must move in unison if we are to keep a single field in view.

Occasionally a person is to be found who has an eyeball under defective muscular control, so that when one eye is fixed on an object, the other is pointed too far toward the nose ("cross-eyes") or too far away from it ("wall-eyes"). The two conditions are lumped as "squint-eyes," or *strabismus* (stra-biz′mus; "squint" G). This ruins stereoscopic vision and causes the person to favor one eye over the other, ignoring what is seen with the unfavored eye and causing the latter's visual ability to decline.

To be sure, the eyes do not, under normal conditions, point in exactly parallel fashion. If both are to orient their pupils in the direction of the same object, they must converge slightly. Usually this convergence is too small to notice, but it becomes more marked for closer objects. If you bring a pencil toward a person's nose, you will see his eyes begin to "cross." The extent of the effort involved in such convergence offers another means by which a person can judge distance.

WITHIN THE EYE

Immediately behind the pupil is the lens, sometimes called the *crystalline lens*, not because it contains crystals, but because, in the older sense of the word "crystalline," it is transparent (see illustration, p. 274). The lens is lens-shaped (of course) and is about a third of an inch in diameter. All around its rim is a ringlike *suspensory ligament*, which joins it to a portion of the choroid layer immediately behind the iris. That portion of the choroid layer is the *ciliary body*, and this contains the *ciliary muscle*.

The lens and the suspensory ligament divide the eyes into two chambers, of which the forward is only one fifth the size of the portion lying behind the lens. The smaller forward chamber contains a watery fluid called the *aqueous humor* ("watery fluid" L), which is much like cerebrospinal fluid in composition and circulates in the same way that cerebrospinal fluid does. The aqueous humor leaks into the anterior chamber from nets of capillaries in the ciliary body and out again through a small duct near the point where the iris meets the cornea. This duct is called the *canal of Schlemm* after the German anatomist Friedrich Schlemm, who described it in 1830.

The portion behind the lens is filled with a clear, jellylike substance, the *vitreous humor* ("glassy fluid" L), or, since it is not really a fluid, the *vitreous body*. It is permanent and does not circulate. For all its gelatinous nature, the vitreous body is ordinarily as clear as water. However, small objects finding their way into it are trapped in its jellylike network and can then make themselves visible to us as tiny dots or filaments if we stare at some featureless background. They usually cannot be focused upon but drift away if we try to look at them directly, and so are called "floaters." The Latin medical name *muscae volitantes* (mus'see vol-ih-tan'teez) sounds formidable but is rather colorful, really, since it means "flying flies." Almost everyone possesses them, and the brain learns to ignore them if the situation is not too extreme. Recent research would make it seem that the floaters are red blood corpuscles that occasionally escape from the tiny capillaries in the retina.

The eye is under an internal fluid pressure designed to keep its spherical shape fairly rigid. This internal pressure is some 177 millimeters of mercury higher than the external air pressure, and this pressure is maintained by the neat balance of aqueous humor inflow-and-outflow. If the canal of Schlemm is for any reason narrowed or plugged — through fibrous ingrowths or inflammation, infection, or the gathering of debris — the aqueous humor cannot escape rapidly enough and the internal pressure begins to rise. This condition is referred to as *glaucoma* (gloh-koh'muh), for reasons to be described later. If pressure rises high enough, as it only too often does in glaucoma, permanent damage will be done to the optic nerve and blindness will result.

Coating the inner surface of the eyeball is the *retina* ("net" L, for obscure reasons), and it is the retina that contains the photoreceptors (see illustration, p. 274). Light entering the eye passes through the cornea and aqueous humor, through the opening of the pupil, then through the lens and vitreous humor to the retina. In the process, the rays of light originally falling upon the cornea are refracted, gathered together, and focused at a small point on the retina. The sharper the focus, the clearer and more sensitive the vision, naturally.

The lens, despite what one might ordinarily assume, is not the chief agent of refraction. Light rays are bent twice as much by the cornea as by the lens. However, whereas the refractive powers of the cornea are fixed, those of the lens are variable. Thus, the lens is normally rather flat and refracts light comparatively little. The light rays reaching the cornea from a distant object diverge infinitesimally in the process and may be considered to be reaching the cornea as virtually parallel rays. The refractive powers of the cornea and the flat lens are sufficient to focus this light upon the retina. As the distance of the point being viewed lessens, the light rays reaching the cornea become increasingly divergent. For distances under twenty feet, the divergence is sufficient to prevent focusing upon the retina without an adjustment somewhere. When that happens, the ciliary muscles contract, and this lessens the tension on the suspensory ligaments. The elasticity of the lens causes it to approach the spherical as far as the ligaments permit, and when the latter relax the lens at once bulges outward. This thickening of the lens curves its surface more sharply and increases its powers of refraction, so that the image of the point being viewed is still cast upon the retina. The closer a point under view, the more the lens is allowed to bulge in order to keep the focus upon the retina. This change of lens curvature is *accommodation.*

There is a limit, of course, to the degree to which a lens can accommodate. As an object comes nearer and nearer, there comes a point (the *near point*) where the lens simply cannot bulge any further and where refraction cannot be made sufficient. Vision becomes fuzzy and one must withdraw one's head, or the object, in order to see it. The lens loses elasticity with age and becomes increasingly reluctant to accommodate at all. This means that with the years the near point recedes. An individual finds he must retreat from the telephone book bit by bit in order to read a number and, eventually, may have to retreat so far that he can't read it once he finally has it in focus, because it is too small. A young child with normal vision may be able to focus on objects 4 inches from the eye; a young adult on objects 10 inches away; whereas an aging man may not be able to manage anything closer than 16 inches. This recession of the near point with age is called *presbyopia* (prez'bee-oh'pee-uh; "old man's vision" G).

Ideally, the light passing through the cornea and lens should focus right on the retina. It often happens, though, that the eyeball is a bit too deep for this. Light focuses at the proper distance, but the retina is not there. By the time light reaches the retina, it has diverged again somewhat. The eye, in an effort to compensate, allows the lens to remain unaccommodated in order that light may be refracted as little as possible and the focus therefore cast as far back as possible. For distant vision, however, where refraction must be less than for close vision, the lens is helpless. It cannot accommodate less than the "no-accommodation-at-all" that suffices for near vision. An individual with deep eyeballs is therefore *nearsighted;* he sees close objects clearly and distant objects fuzzily. The condition is more formally referred to as *myopia* (my-oh'pee-uh; "shut-vision" G). The name arises out of the fact that in an effort to reduce the fuzziness of distant objects, the myopic individual brings his eyelids together, converting his eyes into a sort of pinhole camera that requires no focusing. However, the amount of light entering the eye is decreased, so it is difficult to see (to say nothing of eyelash interference) and the strain on the eyelid muscles will in the long run bring on headaches.

The opposite condition results when an eyeball is too shallow and consequently the light falls on the retina before it is quite focused. In this case the lens, by accommodating, can introduce an additional bit of light refraction that will force light from a distant source into focus on the retina. Light from a near source, requiring still more refraction, cannot be managed. Such an individual has an unusually far-distant near point. He is *farsighted*, seeing distant objects with normal clarity and near ones fuzzily. This is *hyperopia* (hy'per-oh'pee-uh; "beyond-vision" G).

For light passing through the cornea and lens to focus precisely, the cornea and lens must each be smoothly curved. The degree of curvature along any meridian (vertical, horizontal, diagonal) must be equal. In actual fact this ideal is never quite met; there are always unevennesses, and, as a result, light does not focus in a point but in a short line. If the line is short enough this is not serious; but if it is long, there is considerable fuzziness of vision in both near and far objects. This is *astigmatism* ("no point" G). Fortunately such defects in refraction are easily corrected by introducing refraction from without by means of glass lenses. (The use of spectacles was one of the few medical advances made during the Middle Ages.) For myopia, lenses are used to diverge light minimally and push the focus backward; and for hyperopia, lenses are used to converge light minimally and push the focus forward. In astigmatism, lenses of uneven curvature are used to cancel out the uneven curvature of the eye.

The transparency of the cornea and lens is not due to any unusual factor in the composition, despite the fact that they are the only truly transparent solid tissues of the body. They are composed of protein and water and their transparency depends, evidently, on an unusual regularity of molecular structure. They are living parts of the body. The cornea can heal itself, for instance, if it is scratched. The level of life, however, must remain low, since neither tissue may be directly infiltrated by blood vessels — that would ruin their all-important transparency. Yet it is only with blood immediately available that a tissue can go about the business of life in an intensive fashion.

This has its advantages. A cornea can, if properly preserved, maintain its integrity after the death of an organism more easily than it would if it had been accustomed, as tissues generally are, to an elaborate blood supply. A cornea will also "take" if transplanted to another individual, whereas a more actively living tissue would not. This means that a person whose cornea has clouded over as a result of injury or infection but whose eyes are completely functional otherwise may regain his sight through a corneal transplantation.

Transparency is not easy to maintain. Any loss of regularity of structure will give rise to opaque regions, and the lens, especially, is subject to the development of opacities. This condition can spread so that the entire lens becomes opaque and useless and vision is lost. The possibility of lens opacity increases with age, and it is the greatest single cause of blindness, accounting for about a quarter of the cases of blindness in the United States. Luckily it is possible to remove the lens and make up for the lost refractive powers by properly designed glasses. Since aged lenses have lost accommodative powers anyway, little is sacrificed beyond the inconvenience of the operation and of having to wear glasses, and such inconvenience is certainly preferable to blindness.

The opacity within a lens is called a *cataract*. The ordinary meaning of the word is that of "waterfall," but it is derived from Greek terms meaning "to dash downward" and that need not refer to water only. The lens opacity is like a curtain being drawn downward to obscure the window of the eye. Because the presence of the cataract causes the ordinarily black pupil to become clouded over in a grayish or silvery fashion, the word "glaucoma" ("silvery gray" G) was applied to it in ancient times. When "cataract" came into favor, "glaucoma" was pushed away from the lens condition and came to be applied to another optical disorder (described earlier in the chapter), one to which the word does not truly apply etymologically.

THE RETINA

The retinal coating is about the size and thickness of a postage stamp pasted over the internal surface of the eyeball and covering about four fifths of it. (It sometimes gets detached, bringing about blindness, but techniques now exist for binding it back into position.) The retina consists of a number of layers, and of these the ones farthest toward the light are composed largely of nerve cells and their fibers. Underneath these are the actual photoreceptors, which in the human eye are of two types, the *rods* and the *cones*, obviously named from their shapes. Under the rods and cones and immediately adjacent to the choroid is a film of pigmented cells that send out projections to insinuate themselves between the rods and the cones. These pigmented cells serve to absorb light and cut down reflection that would otherwise blur the retinal reaction to the light falling on it directly.

In animals adapted to vision in dim light, however, the reverse is desired. In them the retina contains a reflecting layer, the *tapetum* (ta-pee′tum; "carpet" L), which sends light back and gives the retina a second chance at it. Clarity of vision is sacrificed to sensitivity of detection. Some light, even so, escapes the retina after reflection has allowed that tissue a second chance, and this escaping light emerges from the widespread pupils. It is why cats' eyes (tapetum-equipped) gleam eerily in the dark. They would not do so if it were truly dark, because they do not manufacture light. The human eye, needless to say, does not have a tapetum. It sacrifices sensitivity to clarity.

The arrangement of layers in the retina is such that approaching light must in general first strike the layers of nerve cells and pass through them in order to reach the rods and cones. This seems inefficient, but things are not quite that bad in the human eye. At the point of the retina lying directly behind the lens and upon which the light focuses, there is a yellow spot (yellow because of the presence of a pigment) called the *macula lutea* (mak′yoo-luh lyoo′tee-uh; "yellow spot" L); see illustration, page 274. In it the photoreceptors are very closely packed, and vision is most acute there.

In order for us to see two separate objects actually as two and not have them blur together into one object (and this is what is meant by visual acuity), the light from the two objects would have to fall upon two separate photoreceptors with at least one unstimulated photoreceptor in between. It follows that the more closely packed the photoreceptors, the closer two objects may be and yet have this happen. In the macula lutea the photoreceptors are crowded together so compactly that at ordinary reading distance a person with normal vision could see two dots as two dots when separated by only a tenth of a millimeter.

Furthermore, in the very center of the macula lutea there is a small depression called the *fovea centralis* (foh'vee-uh sen-tray'lis; "central pit" L) which is right where light focuses. The reason the spot is depressed is that the nerve layers above the photo-receptors are thinned out to almost nothing so that light hits the photoreceptors directly. This situation is most highly developed in the primates. This is one of the reasons why the primate Order, including ourselves, has to such a large extent sacrificed smell and even hearing to the sense of sight. The very excellence of the sense of sight that we have evolved has made it tempting to do so.

Naturally, the retina outside the fovea is not left unused. Light strikes it and the brain responds to that. When we are looking at an object we are also conscious of other objects about it (*peripheral vision*). We cannot make out small details in peripheral vision, but we can make out shapes and colors. In particular, we can detect motion, and it is important even for humans to see "out of the corner of the eye." In this age of auto-mobiles, many a life has been saved by the detection of motion to one side; license examiners routinely test one's ability to do so by waving pencils to one side while having the applicant stare straight ahead. The loss of peripheral vision (popularly called *tunnel vision* because one can then only see directly forward) would make one a dangerous person behind the wheel.

The fibers of the nerve cells of the retina gather into the optic nerve (which, along with the retina itself, is actually a part of the brain, from a structural point of view; see illustration, p. 196). The optic nerve leaves the eyeball just to one side of the fovea and its point of exit is the one place in the retina where photo-receptors are completely absent. It therefore represents the *blind spot*. We are unaware of the existence of a blind spot ordinarily because, for one thing, the light of an object which falls on the blind spot of one eye does not fall on the blind spot of the other. One eye always makes it out. With one eye closed, it is easy however to show the existence of the blind spot. If one looks at a black rectangle containing a white dot and a white cross and focuses, let us say, on the dot, he will be able to locate a certain distance at which the cross disappears. Its light has fallen on the blind spot. At distances closer and farther, it reappears.

The photoreceptors when stimulated by light initiate impulses in the nearby nerve cells, and the message, conducted to the brain by the optic nerve and eventually reaching the optic area in the occipital lobe, is interpreted as light. The photoreceptors can also be stimulated by pressure, and that stimulation too is interpreted as light so that we "see stars" as the result of a blow near the eye. Such pressure-induced flashes of light can appear if we simply close our eyelids tightly and concentrate. What we see are *phosphenes* (fos'feenz; "to show light" G).

The two types of photoreceptors, rods and cones, are each adapted to a special type of vision. The cones are stimulated only by rather high levels of light and are used in daylight or *photopic* (foh-top'ik; "light-vision" G) vision. The rods, on the other hand, can be stimulated by much lower levels of light than the cones can and are therefore involved in *scotopic* (skoh-top'ik; "darkness-vision" G) vision — that is, in vision in dim light.

Nocturnal animals often possess retinas containing only rods. The human eye goes to the other extreme in one respect. To be sure, the rods greatly outnumber the cones in our retinas, since the human retina contains 125 million rods and only 7 million cones. However, the macula lutea, which carries the burden of seeing, contains cones only and virtually no rods. Each cone, moreover, generally has its own optic nerve fiber, which helps maximize acuity. (Yet as many as ten or even a hundred rods may be connected to the same nerve fiber; in dim light only sensitivity is sought and acuity is sacrificed on its altar.)

Man's acuity is thus centered on photopic vision, as seems right since he is a creature of the daylight. This means, though, that at night acuity of vision does not exist for dim light. If one looks directly at a faint star at night, it seems to vanish altogether, because its light strikes only cones, which it is too weak to stimulate. Look to one side, nevertheless, and the star jumps into view as its light strikes rods. (Contrarily, it is because the cones become progressively less numerous away from the macula lutea that we have so little acuity in peripheral vision in daylight.)

The two forms of vision differ in another important respect, in that of color. As I shall explain shortly, specific colors involve only a portion of the range of wavelengths of light to which the eye is sensitive. The cones, reacting to high levels of light, can afford to react to this portion or that and therefore to detect color. The rods, reacting to very low levels, must detect all the light available to achieve maximum sensitivity and therefore do not distinguish colors. Scotopic vision, in other words, is in black and white, with, of course, intermediate shades of gray; a fact well expressed by the common proverb that "at night all cats are gray."

The rods contain a rose-colored visual pigment and it is that which actually undergoes the chemical change with light. It is commonly called *visual purple* (though it is not purple), but its more formal and more accurate name is *rhodopsin* (roh-dop'sin; "rose eye" G). The molecule of rhodopsin is made up of two parts: a protein, *opsin*, and a nonprotein portion, very similar in structure to vitamin A, which is *retinene*. Retinene can exist in two forms, different in molecular shape, called *cis-retinene* and *trans-retinene*. The shape of cis-retinene is such that it can combine with opsin to form rhodopsin, whereas trans-retinene cannot. In the presence of light, cis-retinene is converted to trans-retinene and, if it already makes up part of the rhodopsin molecule, it falls off, leaving the largely colorless opsin behind. (Rhodopsin may therefore be said to be bleached by light.) In the dark, trans-retinene changes into cis-retinene and joins opsin once more to form the rhodopsin.

There is thus a cycle, rhodopsin being bleached in the light and formed again in the dark. It is the bleaching that stimulates the nerve cell. In ordinary daylight the rhodopsin of the eyes is largely in the bleached state and is useless for vision. This does not ordinarily matter, since rhodopsin is involved in scotopic vision only and is not used in bright light. As one passes into a darkened interior, however, vision is at first almost nil because of this. It improves, as noted earlier in the chapter, by the expansion of the pupil to permit more light. It also improves because rhodopsin is gradually re-formed in the darkness and becomes available for use in dim light. This period of improving vision in dim light is called *dark adaptation*. The bleaching of rhodopsin and the narrowing of the pupil on re-emergence into full light is *light adaptation*.

Retinene, under ideal circumstances, is not used up in the breakdown and re-formation of rhodopsin; but the circumstances, unfortunately, are not quite ideal. Retinene is an unstable compound and, when separated from the rhodopsin molecule, has a tendency to undergo chemical change and lose its identity. Vitamin A, which is more stable, is, however, easily converted into retinene, so that the vitamin A stores of the body can be called upon to replace the constant dribbling loss of this visual pigment. The body cannot make its own vitamin A, alas, but must find it in the diet. If the diet is deficient in vitamin A, the body's stores eventually give out and retinene is not replaced as it is lost. Rhodopsin cannot then be formed, and rod vision fails. The result is that although a person may see perfectly normally in daylight, he is virtually without vision in dim light. This is *night blindness,* or *nyctalopia* (nik′tuh-loh′pee-uh; "night-blind-eye" G). Carrots are a good source of vitamin A and can help relieve this condition if added to the diet, and it is in this sense that the popular tradition that "carrots are good for the eyes" is correct.

COLOR VISION

The wavelength of light is usually measured in *Angstrom units,* named for a 19th-century Swedish astronomer, Anders J. Ångstrom. An Angstrom unit (abbreviated A) is a very small unit of length, equal to 1/100,000,000 of a centimeter, or 1/250,000,000 of an inch. The human eye can detect light with wavelengths as short as 3800 A and as long as 7600 A. Since the wavelength just doubles at this interval, we can say that the eye can detect light over a range of one octave.

Just as there are sound waves beyond the limits of human detection, so there are light waves beyond the limits of detection, too. At wavelengths shorter than 3800 A there are, progressing down the scale, ultraviolet rays, X-rays, and gamma rays. At wavelengths above 7600 A there are, progressing up the scale, infrared rays, microwaves, and radio waves. All told, at least 60 octaves can be detected in one way or another, and of these, as aforesaid, only one octave can be detected by the eye.

We are not as deprived as this makes us seem. The type of radiation emitted by any hot body depends on its temperature, and at the temperature of the sun's surface, the major portion of the radiation is put out in the octave to which we are sensitive. In other words, throughout the eons, our eyes and the eyes of other living things have been adapted to the type of light waves actually present, in predominant measure, in our environment.

The entire range of wavelengths is commonly referred to as *electromagnetic radiation* because they originate in accelerating electric charges with which both electric and magnetic fields are associated.* The word "light" is usually applied to the one octave of electromagnetic radiation we can sense optically. If there is a chance of confusion, the phrase *visible light* can be used.

Even the one octave of visible light is not featureless, at least not to normal individuals and not in photopic vision. Just as the

---

* In the case of light, the accelerating electric charge is associated with the electron within the atom.

brain interprets different wavelengths of sound as possessing different pitch, so it interprets different wavelengths of light as possessing different color. Ordinary sunlight is a mixture of all the wavelengths of visible light; this mixture appears to us as white and its total absence appears to us as black. If such white light is passed through a triangular block of glass (a "prism"), refraction is not uniform. The different wavelengths are refracted by characteristic amounts, the shortest wavelengths exhibiting the highest refraction, and longer and longer wavelengths refracting progressively less and less. For this reason, the band of wavelengths are spread out in a *spectrum* which seems to us to be made up of the full range of colors we can see. (The spectrum reminds us irresistibly of a rainbow, because the rainbow is a natural spectrum occurring when sunlight passes through tiny water droplets left in the air after a rain has just concluded.)

The number of shades of color we see as we look along the spectrum is very large, but it is traditional to group them into six distinct colors. At 4000 A we see violet; at 4800 A, blue; at 5200 A, green; at 5700 A, yellow; at 6100 A, orange; and at 7000 A, red. At wavelengths in between, the colors exhibit various grades of intermediateness.*

If the different wavelengths of light thus spread out into a spectrum are recombined by a second prism (placed in a position reversed with respect to the first), white light is formed again. But it is not necessary to combine all the wavelengths to do that. The 19th-century scientists Thomas Young and Hermann von Helmholtz showed that green light, blue light, and red light if combined would produce white light. Indeed, any color of the spectrum could be produced if green, blue, and red were combined in the proper proportions.

* Comparatively few animals possess a capacity for color vision, and those that do are not, apparently, quite as good at it as are the primates, including man, of course. There are interesting cases, though, where other animals may outdo us in some detail. Bees, for instance, do not respond to wavelengths in the uppermost section of the human range. They do, however, respond to wavelengths shorter than those of violet light, wavelengths to which our eyes are insensitive. In other words, bees do not see red but do see ultraviolet.

(Nowadays, color photography and color television make use of this. Three films, each sensitive to one of these three colors, will combine to give a photograph — or a motion picture — with a full color range; and three kinds of receiving spots on the TV screen, each sensitive to one of these three colors, will give a TV picture with a full color range.)

It seems reasonable to suppose that this is a reflection of the manner in which the human retina works. It, like the color film or the color TV screen, must have three types of photoreceptors, one sensitive to light in the red wavelengths, one to light in the blue wavelengths, and one to light in the green wavelengths. If all three are equally stimulated, the sensation is interpreted as "white" by the brain. The myriads of tints and shades the eye can differentiate are each an interpretation of the stimulation of the three photoreceptors in some particular proportion.*

Color vision is, to repeat, confined to the cones, which are not present in the far peripheral areas of the retina. They are present in increasing concentration as one approaches the macula lutea, where only cones are present. The cones themselves evidently are not identical; that is, they do not each possess all three pigments in equal proportion. Instead, there seem to be three different types of cones, each with a preponderance of its own characteristic pigment. The three types are distributed unequally over the retina. Thus, blue can be detected farther out into the retinal periphery than red can; and red, in turn, can be detected farther out than green can. At the macula lutea and in the immediately surrounding region all three are present, of course.

It sometimes happens that a person is deficient in one or more of the photoreceptors. He then suffers from *color-blindness*, a disorder of which there are a number of varieties and a number of gradations of each variety. One out of twelve American males shows some sort of color-vision deficiency, but very few women

---

* This theory does not explain all the facts in color vision, and there are several competing theories, some involving as many as six or seven different photoreceptors. However, the three-photoreceptor theory seems to retain most popularity among physiologists.

are affected.* The lack, most commonly, is in the red-receptor or in the green-receptor. In either case, the person suffering the lack has difficulty in distinguishing between colors ranging from green to red. Very occasionally a person lacks all color-receptors and is completely color-blind, a condition called *achromatism* (ay-kroh'muh-tiz-um; "no color" G). To such a person, the world is visible only in black, white, and shades of gray.

---

* Color-blindness is a "sex-linked characteristic." The gene controlling it is located on the X-chromosome, of which women have two and men only one. Women have a spare, so that if one gene fails the other takes over. Men do not.

13

OUR REFLEXES

Any organism must be able to combine sensation with appropriate action. Some factor in the environment is sensed and some action follows. It is assumed through general experience that the action is brought about by the sensation and would not take place in its absence. If we observe someone make as though to strike us, we duck; we would not have ducked had we not experienced the sensation.

The sensation is a *stimulus* ("goad" L, since it goads us into the action). The action itself, which is an answer to the stimulus, is a *response*. This action of stimulus-and-response is characteristic of life. If we were to come across an object that did not respond to any stimulus we could think of, we would come to the conclusion that it was inanimate; or, if once alive, was now dead. On the other hand, if there was a response, we would tend to conclude instantly that the object was alive. And yet it is not a response alone that is required. If we strike a wooden plank a blow with an ax, it will respond to the stimulus of the blow by splitting; if we set a match to a mixture of hydrogen and oxygen, that will respond to the stimulus of heat by exploding. Yet this does not fool any of us into suspecting the wood or the gas mixture to be alive.

What is required of living objects is a response that maintains the integrity of the object; one that avoids damage or increases well-being. This is an *adaptive response*.

We are best acquainted with our own responses, of course. In ours there exists something we call "purpose"; we know in advance the end we are aiming at. If we are in a fight, we intend to avoid blows because we know, before the blow is received, that we shall suffer pain if we don't. What is more, we intend to strike a blow because we know in advance of the blow being struck that it will help end the fight and enforce our own desires.

Because this alliance of purpose and response is so well known to us, we tend to read purpose into the action of other creatures; even into the actions of creatures that cannot possibly have modes of thought akin to ours. For example, in observing that a green plant will turn toward the light, and knowing that light is essential to the plant's metabolism (so that receiving light contributes to its "well-being"), we are tempted to conclude that the plant turns to the light because it wants to, or because it likes the sensation, or because it is "hungry." Actually this is not at all so. The plant (as nearly as we can tell) has no awareness of its action in any sense that can be considered even remotely human. Its action is developed through the same blind and slow evolutionary forces that molded its structure.

Since light is essential to the plant's metabolism, individual seedlings (all things else being equal) which happen to possess the ability to get more than their share of sunlight will best survive. The ability may rest in a superior rate of growth enabling them to rise above the shade of neighboring plants; or, conversely, in the possession of broad leaves that grow quickly and shade the struggling neighbors, absorbing the light that would otherwise be theirs. It may be a chemical mechanism that more efficiently uses the light received, or one that enables the leaves to turn toward the light so that a "broadside blow" rather than a glancing one may be received.

Whatever the mechanism for snatching at light, the successful snatchers among plants flourish and leave more numerous descendants than their less aggressive competitors. With each generation, those responses that develop, through sheer chance, and happen to be adaptive, increasingly prevail and in the end are all but universal. If, in the course of this slow development, plant individuals arise which, through chance, tend to turn away from the light or manipulate light with lesser efficiency, such strains as they manage to establish will be quickly beaten and will drop out of the game. The same evolutionary development through chance mutation and natural selection holds for all forms of behavior, the complex varieties exhibited by man as well as the simple varieties exhibited by plants.

A nervous system is not necessary for the development of a meaningful stimulus-and-response. As I have just explained, plants, without a nervous system, will nevertheless turn portions of themselves toward the light. Such a turning in response to a stimulus is called a *tropism* (troh'pizm; "turning" G). Where the specific stimulus is light, the phenomenon is *phototropism* ("light-turning" G). The mechanism where this is accomplished is differential growth, which is in turn (see p. 90) sparked by the greater activity of auxin on the shaded side of the growing tip of the stem. When the stem receives equal stimulation from both sides, turning action ceases. (This is analogous to the manner in which we turn toward the origin of the sound, turning in the direction of that ear which gets the greater stimulus and ceasing to turn when both ears receive equal stimuli. The mechanism in ourselves is, of course, completely different from that of plants.)

Once plant life invaded the land it was subject to the action of gravity, and *geotropism* ("earth-turning" G), involving an automatic and adaptive response to gravity, was developed. To take an illustration: if a seed falls into the ground "upside-down," the stem may begin its growth downward, but in the grip of *negative geotropism* bends about and eventually begins to grow upward, in the direction opposite the pull of gravity and, which is ultimately important, toward the light. The root, contrariwise, beginning its growth upward, curves about to head downward in the direction of gravity (*positive geotropism*). Geotropism seems also to be mediated by auxins, but how the distribution of auxins can be affected by gravity is not yet understood. To be sure, a root will veer from its downward path if a rich source of water lies to one side. This is in response to positive *hydrotropism* ("water-turning" G).

Tropisms all involve slow turning through differential growth, but not all plant responses are tropisms. Some are quick responses that are almost animal-like in their resemblance to muscle action (and yet not involving muscles but, rather, such mechanisms as controlled turgor by alteration of the quantity of water present at key spots). And so there are plant species whose leaves fold by night and open by day; there are species with leaves that close at a touch; insect-digesting species with traps that close when certain sensitive trigger-projections are touched, and the like.

There are animal responses that resemble tropisms. An amoeba will move away from the light but a moth will fly toward it.* Nevertheless, the responses of even very simple animals are generally more complicated than those of plants, and to call those responses tropisms would be wrong. For one thing, a tropism involves the movement of only a portion of an organism — such as the root or the stem — whereas an animal is likely to move as a whole. Such movement of a whole organism in response to a stimulus is a *taxis* ("arrangement" G, since the position of an organism is rearranged, so to speak, in response to the stimulus). Thus, the amoeba displays a *negative phototaxis* and a moth possesses a *positive phototaxis*.

Micro-organisms, generally, display a *negative chemotaxis*, which enables them to respond to a deleterious alteration in the

---

* We think with sardonic amusement of the moth who seems so stupidly to fly into a flame that kills it, but movement toward the light is generally adaptive behavior. The hundreds of millions of years that developed this response did so under conditions in which man-made lights did not exist and therefore posed no danger. Unfortunately for the moth, it cannot modify its response to suit the modified situation.

chemical nature of their surroundings by swimming away, and a *positive chemotaxis*, which is an adaptive response to the type of chemical change brought about by the presence of something edible. There is also *thigmotaxis*, a response to touch, *rheotaxis*, a response to water currents, and a number of others.

The nature of the response may not be a simple movement toward or away. A paramecium, on encountering an obstacle, will back off a certain distance, turn through an angle of 30 degrees, and then move forward again. If it encounters the obstacle (or another obstacle) again, it repeats the process. In twelve attempts it will have made a complete turn and, by then, unless completely ringed by obstacles, it will have found its way past. But there is no true "purpose" to this, either, and however clever the little creature may seem to be in the light of our own anthropomorphic judgment, this "avoidance behavior" is a purely blind course of action developed by the forces of natural selection.

THE REFLEX ARC

The tropisms of plants and the taxis of simple animals are generalized responses of an entire organism or of a major portion of one to a very generalized stimulus. Such a generalized response to a generalized stimulus can be mediated through a nervous system, as in the case of the phototaxis of the moth, but with the development of a specialized nervous system both stimulus and response can be refined.

Special nerve-receptors can be stimulated by feebler changes in the environment than ordinary cells can be. In addition, the presence of a forest of nerve endings can make it possible to distinguish between a touch on one part of the body and a touch on another, and the two might elicit different responses. Where a nervous system is involved, in fact, a stimulus need not elicit a generalized response at all. A definite motor neuron might carry the signal required to bring about the response of a restricted portion of the body, of one set of glands, or of one set of muscles.

Where a particular stimulus quickly and automatically produces a particular response through the action of the nervous system, we speak of a *reflex* ("bending back" L). The name is a good one, because the nerve impulse travels from a sense organ along a sensory nerve to the central nervous system (usually to the spinal cord but sometimes to the brain stem), and there the nerve impulse "bends back" and travels away from the central nervous system again, along a motor nerve, to bring about a response. The nerve cell connections along which the nerve impulse travels from initial sensation to final response is the *reflex arc*.

The simplest possible reflex arc is one consisting of two neurons, the sensory and the motor. The dendrites of the sensory nerve (see illustrations, pp. 126 and 304) combine into a fiber that leads toward the cell body located just outside the posterior horn of the spinal cord. The axon of this nerve cell is connected by way of a synapse to the dendrites of a cell body in the anterior horn of the spinal cord. The axon of this second cell leads outward by way of an appropriate peripheral nerve to the muscle, gland, or other organ that is to give the response. Since the first neuron receives the sensation it is the *receptor neuron,* and since the latter effects the response it is the *effector neuron.* The region within the central nervous system where the two make the connection is the *reflex center.*

This two-neuron reflex arc is rare, but examples of it exist even in so complicated a creature as man. More common is the three-neuron reflex arc, in which the receptor neuron is connected to an effector neuron by means of an intermediate neuron called the *connector neuron.* The connector neuron lies wholly within the central nervous system. Even the three-neuron reflex arc is simple as far as such arcs go in highly organized creatures. In mammals the typical reflex arc is likely to have a number of connector neurons, a whole chain of them, that may lead up and down the nerve cord from one segment to others.

A complex reflex arc with numerous neurons taking part allows ample opportunity for branching. A specific receptor neuron may

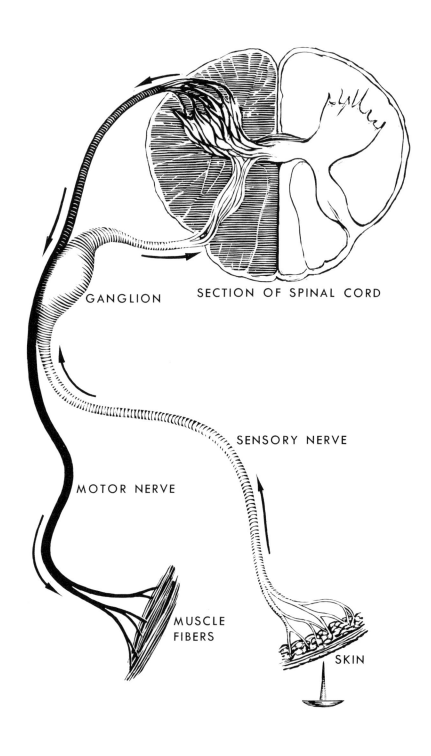

GANGLION

SECTION OF SPINAL CORD

SENSORY NERVE

MOTOR NERVE

MUSCLE
FIBERS

SKIN

end by transmitting its nerve impulse via the various connector neurons to a number of different effectors. For instance, a painful stimulus on the hand may evoke a quick removal of the hand through the contraction of certain muscles. But for this to happen (a *flexion reflex*) there are opposing muscles that must simultaneously be made to relax so as not to hamper the withdrawing motion. In addition, there may be a sudden turning of the head in the direction of the painful stimulus, a sharp uncontrolled outcry, and a contortion of facial muscles. The whole variety of responses may be produced by a simple pinprick that in itself stimulates a very small number of effectors.

At the same time that a flexion reflex takes place in one limb, a *crossed extensor reflex*, sparked by the same stimulus, will take place in the other, stiffening and extending it. So, if we lift a leg in sudden reflex action because we have stepped on a sharp pebble on the beach, we do not usually fall over, as we might expect to since our weight is suddenly unbalanced. Instead, in equally quick reflex, the remaining leg stiffens and our weight shifts.

Another important muscular reflex is the *stretch reflex*. When a muscle is stretched, the proprioceptive nerve endings within it are the receptors of a reflex arc of which the effectors act to bring about a contraction that tends to counteract whatever force is bringing about the stretching. This helps keep us in balanced posture, for one thing. The balance depends upon the equal pulls of opposing muscles. If for any reason a muscle overcontracts, its opposing muscle is stretched, and that opposing muscle promptly contracts in response to the stretch, restoring the balance. If it overreacts, the first muscle is stretched and contracts in its turn.

We are not usually aware of either stimulus or response in this connection. To our conscious selves we seem only to be standing or sitting, and are completely unconcerned with the complex system of reflex arcs that must all cooperate delicately to keep us doing (in appearance) nothing. However, if we suddenly lose our balance seriously, we "catch ourselves" quite without a voluntary decision, and may indulge in violent involuntary contortions in an effort to regain our balance. If the stretch reflex is set off during sleep, the contracting response may again be quite sudden and violent, arousing us and giving us the impression that we "dreamed of falling."

A familiar example of the stretch reflex is the *patellar reflex*, or, as it is commonly called, the "knee jerk." A person being tested for the knee jerk is usually asked to cross his leg and let the crossed leg hang limply. The muscle along the top surface of the thigh has its tendon attached to the bone of the lower leg. If the area just below the kneecap ("patella") is tapped lightly, that tendon is struck and the thigh muscle is momentarily stretched. This initiates a stretch reflex (this one by way of one of the rare two-neuron reflex arcs) and the muscle contracts sharply, bringing the lower leg up in a kicking motion. Because it is only a two-neuron reflex arc, it is a rapid reaction indeed.

The patellar reflex is not important in itself, but its nonappearance can mean some serious disorder involving the portion of the nervous system in which that reflex arc is to be found. It is so simple a reflex and so easily tested that it is a routine portion of many medical checks. Sometimes damage to a portion of the central nervous system results in the appearance of an abnormal reflex. If the sole of the foot is scratched, the normal response is a flexion reflex in which the toes are drawn together and bent downward; but if there is damage to the pyramidal tract the big toe bends upward in response to this stimulus and the little toes spread apart as they bend down. This is the *Babinski reflex*, named for a French neurologist, Joseph F. F. Babinski, who described it in 1896.

Just as a single receptor may in the end elicit the action of a large number of effectors, it is also possible that a particular effector or group of effectors may be brought into play by a large variety of receptors. Small individual painful stimuli over a large area of one side of the body may all cause a reflex motion of the head toward that side, and sudden pain anywhere in the body may elicit an involuntary outcry.

The reflex arc does not involve the cerebrum, so the element of will does not ordinarily enter. The reflex is automatic and involuntary. However, in many cases, the sensation that brings about the response is also shunted into an ascending tract and brought to the cerebrum, where it is then experienced as an ordinary sensation, usually after the reflex response is complete. If, for instance, we inadvertently touch a hot object with our hand, the hand is instantly withdrawn; withdrawn before we are consciously aware of the fact that the object was hot. The awareness follows soon enough, nevertheless, and with physical damage averted (or at least minimized) by automatic reflex action, we can then take the reasoned long-range response of moving the hot object to a safe place, or covering it, or putting a warning sign on it, or cooling it, or doing whatever seems the logical thing to do.

In many cases we are completely unaware of the response we may make to a stimulus. Strong light causes the iris to expand and reduce the size of the pupil. The taste of food will cause the salivary glands to secrete fluid into the mouth, and the cells of the stomach lining to secrete fluid into the stomach. Temperature changes will bring about alterations in the diameter of certain capillaries. We are more a mass of reflexes than we ordinarily realize.

INSTINCTS AND IMPRINTING

The various reflexes I have been talking about are, like the tropisms of plants and the taxis of simple animals, examples of *innate behavior* — behavior that is inborn and does not have to be learned. You do not have to learn to withdraw your hand from a hot object, or to sneeze if your nasal passages are irritated, or to blink if a sudden gesture is made in the direction of your eyes. An infant can do all these things, and more besides.

Such innate behavior can be quite elaborate. One can visualize chains of reflexes in which the response to one stimulus will itself serve as the stimulus for a second response, which will then in turn serve as the stimulus for a third response, and the like. Examples of this are the elaborate courtship procedures among the sexes of some animal species: nest-building, web-building, hive-building, and the intricate patterns of care for the young.

Regrettably, the slow development of such complicated behavior patterns through evolutionary processes is lost to us. Could we trace it, we might easily see how each further link in the chain of reflexes was developed, and how each served to improve the survival chances of the next generation. Behavior patterns do not leave fossil remains, so we can only accept what we find. The necessity of accepting the end-product complications lead the overly romantic to read into the behavior of relatively simple animals the complex motivations of man. The bird in building her nest and the spider in spinning her web completely lack the forethought of the human architect and are not really suitable as subjects for little moral homilies.

Such chains of reflexes give rise to *instinctive behavior* (a term that is falling out of fashion). Instincts are complicated patterns of responses that share the properties of the reflexes out of which they are built. Instinct is usually viewed as a behavior pattern that is fixed from birth, that cannot be modified, that is present in all members of a designated species in an unvarying manner, and so on. Thus, a species of spider builds a certain type of elaborate web without being taught to do so, and may do so, in full elaboration, even if kept in isolation so that it never has an opportunity to see any other example of such a web. Young birds may migrate at the proper time, going to a far-distant place they have never seen and without the guidance of older members of the species.

Nevertheless, this is not absolutely characteristic of all behavior patterns usually termed as instinctive. Some birds may sing characteristic songs without ever having had the opportunity to hear other members of the species do so; but other species of birds may not. In recent years it has come to be realized that there are some patterns of behavior seemingly innate but actually fixed at some time after birth in response to some specific stimulus.

After all, what we call birth is not actually the beginning of life. Preceding it is a period of development within an egg or womb, during which a nervous system develops to what at the time of birth is already a high pitch of complexity. Different reflexes originate at different periods in the course of this development as reflex arc after reflex arc is laid down. In the chick embryo, for example (which is easy to study), the head-bending reflex can be detected 70 hours after fertilization but the head-turning reflex only at 90 hours. Beak-movement reflexes are detectable only after 5 days, and the swallowing reflex does not make itself shown until 8 days after fertilization.

In the human embryo (less easy to study by far) there is also a progressive development. A reflex movement of the head and neck away from a touch around the mouth and nose can be detected in an 8-week human embryo, but such important reflexes as grasping and sucking do not appear until the embryo is at least double that age. To be sure, birth is an important turning point in the developmental process, and by the time it occurs enough reflexes must be developed to make independent life possible, or else the infant will not survive. That is self-evident. Yet there is room for more beyond bare survival.

Such continuity is taken for granted in structural development, where processes sweep past the moment of birth without a pause. The ossification of the skeleton begins before birth and continues after birth for years. The myelinization of nerve fibers begins before birth and continues afterward. Why should this not be true of behavioral development, too? The situation after birth does introduce one radical change. Before birth, the total universe is that of the egg or womb and it is therefore relatively fixed, with limited possibilities of variation. After birth, the environment expands and much more flexibility and variety in the way of stimuli are possible. The "instincts" developed after birth therefore may well depend upon such stimuli in a way that truly innate instincts do not. Chicks and ducklings fresh out of the shell do not follow their mothers out of some innate instinct that causes them to recognize the mothers. Rather, they follow something of a characteristic shape or color or faculty of movement. Whatever object provides this sensation at a certain period of early life is followed by the young creature and is thereafter treated as the mother. This may really be the mother; almost invariably is, in fact; but it need not be!

The establishment of a fixed pattern of behavior in response to a particular stimulus encountered at a particular time of life is called *imprinting*. The specific time at which imprinting takes place is a *critical period*. For chicks the critical period of "mother-imprinting" lies between 13 hours and 16 hours after hatching. For a puppy there is a critical period between three and seven weeks during which the stimulations it is usually likely to encounter imprint various aspects of what we consider normal (and instinctive) doggish behavior.

There is the example of a lamb raised in isolation for the first ten days of its life only. It was restored to the flock thereafter, but certain critical periods had passed and certain imprintings had not taken place. The opportunity was gone. It remained independent in its grazing pattern, and when it had a lamb of its own, it showed very little "instinctive" behavior of a pattern which we usually tab as "mother love." The loss of a chance at imprinting can have a variety of untoward effects. Animals with eyes deprived of a chance for normal stimulation by a variegated pattern of light at a particular time of early development may never develop normal sight, though the same deprivation before or after the critical period may do no harm.

It seems almost inevitable that such imprinting takes place in the human infant as well, but deliberate experimentation on such infants, designed to interfere with any imprinting procedures that may exist, is clearly out of the question. Knowledge concerning human imprinting can only be gained through incidental observations. Children who at the babbling stage are not exposed to the sounds of actual speech may not develop the ability to speak later, or do so to an abnormally limited extent. Children brought up in impersonal institutions where they are efficiently fed and their physical needs are amply taken care of but where they are not fondled, cuddled, and dandled become sad little specimens indeed. Their mental and physical development is greatly retarded and many die for no other reason, apparently, than lack of "mothering" — by which may be meant the lack of adequate stimuli to bring about the imprinting of necessary behavior patterns. Similarly, children who are unduly deprived of the stimuli involved in the company of other children during critical periods in childhood develop personalities that may be seriously distorted in one fashion or another.

But why imprinting? It is as though a nerve network designed to set up a behavior pattern were complete at birth except for one missing link. Given an almost certain stimulus, that final link snaps into place, quickly and irrevocably, with a result that, as far as we know, can neither be reversed nor modified thereafter. Why, then, not have the final link added before birth and avoid the risks of having imprinting fail?

A logical reason for imprinting is that it allows a certain desirable flexibility. Let's suppose that a chick is born with the prescribed behavior of following its true mother, a mother it can "instinctively" distinguish, perhaps through some highly specific odor it inherits and which mother and offspring therefore share. If the true mother is for any reason absent (killed, strayed, or stolen) at the moment of the chick's birth, it is helpless. If, on the contrary, the question of motherhood is left open for just a few hours, the chick may imprint itself to any hen in the vicinity and thus adopt a foster-mother. Clearly, this is an important and useful ability.

We are faced with two types of behavioral patterns, therefore, each with its own advantage. Innate behavior is certain in that it prescribes responses and avoids error, provided the environment is exactly that for which the innate behavior is suited. Non-innate behavior (or "learned behavior") is risky in the sense that if anything goes wrong with the learning process the proper pattern of response is not developed; but it offers the compensation of flexibility in adjusting the pattern to changes in the environment.

Imprinting is only the most primitive form of learned behavior. It is so automatic, takes place in so limited a time, under so general a set of conditions, that it is only a step removed from the innate. There are, notwithstanding, other forms of learning more clearly marked off from innate behavior and designed to adjust responses more delicately and with less drastic finality to smaller and less predictable variations in the environment.

CONDITIONING

A baby is equipped with functioning salivary glands and the taste of food will cause the secretion of saliva by those glands. This is an example of a reflex. It is developed before birth and is thereby innate. It is universal and unvarying in the sense that all babies respond to stimulation of the taste buds by salivating. And it is involuntary. Under ordinary circumstances a baby can't help salivating in response to the taste of food; and, for that matter, neither can you. This is, therefore, an *unconditioned reflex*. There are no conditions set for its occurrence. It will occur under all normal conditions.

The sight or smell of food will not in themselves bring about salivation at first. After an interval of experience in which a particular sight or smell always immediately precedes a certain salivation-inducing taste, that sight or smell comes to elicit salivation even in the absence of the taste. An infant has learned, one might say, that the smell of food or the sight of food means that the taste of food is about to come, and it salivates (involuntarily) in anticipation. Once this association of sight or smell with taste is set up, the response is automatic and resembles a reflex in all ways. However, it is a reflex that is dependent upon one condition; that of association. If feeding always took place in darkness, the sight of food alone would never elicit salivation, since its appearance would never have been associated with its taste. If a certain item of food were never included in the diet its odor would not induce salivation, even though it be a "natural" dietary item for that species. A puppy that has never been fed meat will not salivate in response to the odor of meat.

The reflex that develops in response to an association is therefore a *conditioned reflex*. It is as though the body is capable of hooking neural pathways together to achieve a shortcut. If faced with a situation of "particular smell means particular taste means salivation," a nerve pathway is eventually set up that will give results equivalent to "particular smell means salivation." (This somehow resembles the mathematical axiom that if a = b and b = c, then a = c.)

This has clear value for survival, since a response that is useful for a specific stimulus is very likely to be useful for other stimuli invariably or almost invariably associated with it. An animal seeking food and guided only by its unconditioned reflex is reduced to sampling everything in its environment by mouthing it. The animal will starve or poison itself, in all likelihood. An animal that conditions itself into recognizing its food by sight and smell will get along far better.

A conditioned reflex can be established for any associated stimulus, even one that does not "make sense." Conditioning is not a logical process — it works only by association. The first to experiment with artificial associations that did not make sense was a Russian physiologist, Ivan Petrovich Pavlov. Pavlov began the important phase of his career by working out the nervous mechanism controlling the secretion of some of the digestive glands. In 1889, he carried on rather impressive experiments in which he severed a dog's gullet and led the upper end through an opening in the neck. The dog could then be fed, but the food would drop out through the open gullet and never reach the stomach. Nevertheless, the stimulation of the taste buds by the food caused the stomach's gastric juices to flow. Here was an unconditioned reflex. Pavlov went on to show that, with appropriate nerves cut, the reflex arc was broken. Though the dog ate as heartily as before, there was no flow of gastric juice thereafter. Pavlov obtained a Nobel Prize for this work in 1904.

By that time, however, something new had developed. In 1902 Bayliss and Starling (see p. 4) had shown that the nerve network was not the only means of eliciting a response by the juice-secreting digestive glands. As a matter of fact, they showed that the action of the pancreas was *not* interfered with by cutting the nerves leading to it, but that there was a chemical connection by way of the bloodstream. Pavlov thereupon struck out in a new direction, with even more fruitful results. Suppose a dog were offered food. It would salivate as a result of the taste through an unconditioned reflex; and would salivate in response to the sight and smell alone through early conditioning. But suppose, further, that each time it was offered the food a bell was rung. It would associate the sound of the bell with the sight of the food, and after this had been repeated from 20 to 40 times salivation would take place at the sound of the bell alone.

Pavlov spent the remaining thirty years of his life experimenting with the establishment of conditioned reflexes. Such conditioning can be established for almost any combination of stimuli and response, though flexibility is not infinite. Experimenters have discovered that certain experimental conditions are more efficient in producing conditioning than others. If the stimulus for which conditioning is desired is presented just before the normal stimulus — that is, if the bell is rung just before the food is presented — then conditioning proceeds most rapidly. If the bell is rung after the food is presented, or at too long an interval before food is presented, then conditioning is more difficult.

Some responses are more difficult to force into line with conditioning than others. Salivation is an easy response to adjust and an animal that salivates copiously can be made to salivate in response to almost anything associated with food. On the contrary, the response of the iris to intensity of light is extremely hard to condition to any stimulus but light. (This seems to make sense.

The response to food needs to be highly flexible, because food can appear in a variety of guises and under a variety of conditions; but light is light, and little flexibility in response to it is either needed or desired.)

Different species vary in the ease with which they can be conditioned. In the main, animals with a more highly developed nervous system are easier to condition. They make the association of bell and food more easily. Or, to put it another way, the fact that more neurons are available in the nervous system, and that these are more complexly interrelated, makes it easier to set up new pathways.

Conditioning is distinguished from imprinting by the fact that the former is more flexible. A conditioned reflex can be established at any time and for a wide variety of stimuli and responses, whereas imprinting happens only during a critical period and involves a specific stimulus and response. Conditioning is a much slower process in general than imprinting is, and, unlike imprinting, it can be reversed.

Suppose that a dog had been conditioned to salivate at the sound of a bell and then over a period of time the bell was repeatedly rung without food being presented. The salivary response would grow weaker, and eventually the dog would no longer salivate when the bell rang. The conditioning will have been extinguished.

As is not surprising, the longer and more intensively a particular piece of conditioning has been established, the longer the time required to extinguish it. As is also not surprising, a conditioning that has been established and then extinguished is easier to establish a second time than it was the first. The nervous system, one might say, has made the new connection once, and it remains there ready to hand.

The conditioned reflex has proved to be an invaluable tool in the study of animal behavior; it can be made to yield answers that would otherwise have required direct communication with a lower creature. In the previous chapter, I said that a bee could

not see red, but could see ultraviolet. How can this be established, since the bee cannot bear direct witness to the fact?
The answer lies in conditioning. A creature cannot be conditioned to respond to one stimulus and not to another unless it can
distinguish between the two stimuli. This would seem self-evident. Suppose, then, that bees are offered drops of sugar solution placed on cards. They will fly to those cards and feed.
Eventually, they will be conditioned to those cards, and will fly
to them at once when they are presented, even when food is
not present upon them. Suppose that two cards are used, alike
in shape, size, glossiness, and in every controllable characteristic,
except that one is blue and one is gray. Suppose further that the
sugar solution is placed always on the blue card and never on
the gray. Ultimately the bee will be conditioned to the blue card
only, and will fly to any blue card presented but not to any gray
card. From this it can be deduced that the bee can tell the
difference between a blue card and a gray card when the only
known difference is color. Hence, the bee can see the color blue.

Suppose the experiment is then changed and a red card and
a gray card are used, with the food always present on the red
card. Finally, when enough time has elapsed to make it reasonable to assume that conditioning has taken place (on the basis
of results in the blue-gray experiment), the bees are tested with
red and gray cards that do not carry food. Now it is found that
the bees fly to the red and gray cards indiscriminately. It would
follow that the bee cannot differentiate red and gray. In short,
it cannot see red.

On the other hand, the bee will differentiate between two
cards that to ourselves seem to be identical in color but differ
in that one reflects more ultraviolet than the other. If food is
placed only on one of these cards and never on the other, this
leads to successful conditioning of the bee. It will distinguish
between the two cards even in the absence of food, though we
with our own unaided eye cannot. In short, it can see ultraviolet.

In the same way, we can test the delicacy with which a dog

can distinguish the pitch of a sound or the shape of some object, by conditioning it to that pitch or shape and then noting to what other pitches or shapes it remains indifferent. A dog will distinguish between a circle and an ellipse, for instance. Also, it will distinguish between a circle in which two perpendicular diameters are each ten units in length and an ellipse in which two perpendicular diameters are nine units and ten units in length, respectively. It will further distinguish between sounds varying in frequency by as little as three vibrations per second. Yet it can also be shown that the dog is completely color-blind, because it cannot be conditioned to any differences in color.

14

OUR MIND

LEARNING

Men have in the past sometimes tended to set up a firm and impassable wall separating the behavior of man from that of all creatures other than man and to label the wall "reason." Creatures other than man we might suppose to be governed by instincts or by an inborn nature that dictates their actions at every step; actions which it is beyond their power to modify. In a sense, from such a viewpoint animals are looked upon as machines; very complicated machines, to be sure, but machines nevertheless.

Man, on the other hand, according to this view, has certain attributes that no animal has. He has the capacity to remember the past in great detail, to foresee possible futures in almost equal detail, to imagine alternatives, to weigh and judge in the light of past experience, to deduce consequences from premises — and to base his behavior upon all of this by an act of "free will." In short, he has the power of reason; he has a "rational mind," something, it is often felt, not possessed by any other creature.

That man also has instincts, blind drives, and, at least in part, an "animal nature" is not to be denied; but the rational mind is supposed to be capable of rising above this. It can even rise superior to the reflex. If prepared, and if there is a purpose to be served, a man can grasp a hot object and maintain the grasp although his skin is destroyed. He can steel himself not to blink if a blow is aimed at his eyes. He can even defy the "first law of nature," that of self-preservation, and by a rational act of free will give his life for a friend, for a loved one, or even for an abstract principle.

Yet this division between "rational man" and "irrational brute" cannot really be maintained. It is true that as one progresses along the scale of living species in the direction of simpler and less intricately organized nervous systems innate behavior plays a more and more important role, and the ability to modify behavior in the light of experience (to "learn," that is) becomes less important. The difference in this respect between man and other animals is not that between "yes" and "no" but, rather, that between "more" and "less."

Even some of the more complicated protozoa — one-celled animals — do not invariably make the same response to the same stimulus as would be expected of them if they were literally machines. If presented with an irritant in the water, such a creature might respond in a succession of different ways, 1, 2, 3, 4, each representing a more strenuous counter. If the irritant is repeated at short intervals, the creature may eventually counter with response 3 at once, without bothering to try 1 or 2. It is as though it has given up on halfway measures and, in a sense, has learned something.

And, of course, more complex animals are easily conditioned in such a fashion as to modify their behavior, sometimes in quite complex manner. Nor must we think of conditioning only as something imposed by a human experimenter; natural circumstances will do as well or better. The common rat was alive and flourishing long before man was civilized. It lived then without reference to man and his habitations. It has learned, however, to live in man's cities and is now as much a city creature as we are; better in some ways. It has changed its "nature" and learned as we have; and not with our help, either, but in the face of our most determined opposition.

To be sure, a lion cannot be conditioned, either by man or by circumstance, to eat grass, since it lacks the teeth required to chew grass properly or the digestive system to handle it even if it could be chewed and swallowed. It is, one could say, the lion's inborn nature to eat zebras and not grass, and this cannot be changed. This sort of physical limitation enslaves man too. A man cannot "by taking thought" add one cubit unto his stature, as is stated in the Sermon on the Mount. Nor can he by mere thought decide to become transparent or to flap his arms and fly. For all his rational mind, man is as much bound by his physical limitations as the amoeba is.

If we confine ourselves to behavior within physical limitations, does the fact that behavior can be modified even in simple animals wipe out the distinction between man and other creatures? Of course it doesn't. That the gap (only man can compose a symphony or deduce a mathematical theorem) exists is obvious and incontrovertible. The only question is whether the gap exists by virtue of man's exclusive possession of reason. What, after all, is reason?

In the case of simple organisms, it seems quite clear that learning, in the sense of the development of behavior not innate, takes place through conditioning, and we are not trapped into believing that anything resembling human reason is involved. A bee has no innate tendency to go to blue paper rather than gray paper, but it can be "taught" to do so by conditioning it to associate blue paper, but not gray paper, with food. The new behavior is as mechanical as the old. The machine is modified by a machinelike method and remains a machine.

In mammals, with more complicated nervous systems than are possessed by any creatures outside the class and with, therefore, the possibility of more complex behavior patterns, matters are less clear-cut. We begin to recognize in mammalian behavior a similarity to our own and consequently may begin to be tempted to explain their activity by using the word "reason." A cat trapped in an enclosure from which an exit is possible if a lever is pushed or a latch is pulled will behave in a manner so like our own under similar circumstances as to convince us that it is disturbed at being enclosed and anxious to be free. And when it finds the exit we may say to ourselves, "Ah, she's figured it out."

But has she? Or is this an overestimate of the cat's mental powers? Apparently the latter. A trapped cat makes random moves, pushing, jumping, squeezing, climbing, pacing restlessly. Eventually, it will make some move that will by accident offer a way out. The next time it is enclosed, it will go through the same random movements until it once again pushes the lever or raises the latch; the second time, after a shorter interval of trial and error, the cat will do the same. After enough trials, it will push the lever and escape at once. The simplest explanation is that it has conditioned itself to push the lever by associating this, finally, with escape. However, there would seem to be also a matter of memory involved; a dim process that makes the cat discover the exit more quickly (usually) the second time than the first.

Animal memory has been tested by experiment. Suppose a raccoon is conditioned to enter a lighted door as opposed to an unlighted one. (It will get food in the first and an electric shock in the second.) Suppose it is barred from entering either door while the light is on and is allowed to make its choice only after the light has gone out. It will nevertheless go to the door which *had been* lit, clearly remembering. If the interval between the light's going out and the liberation of the raccoon is too great, the raccoon sometimes does not go to the correct door. It has forgotten. A raccoon can be relied on to remember for up to half a minute; this interval increases as animals with a more complex nervous system are chosen. A monkey may sometimes remember for a full day.

The English biologist Lloyd Morgan took the attitude that in interpreting animal behavior as little "humanity" as possible should be read into the observations. In the case of the cat in the enclosure, it is possible to avoid humanity just about altogether. A combination of trial-and-error with dim memory and conditioning is quite sufficient to explain the cat's behavior. The question is: How far up the scale of developing nervous system can we safely exclude humanity altogether? Memory improves steadily and surely that has an effect. We might conclude that it does not have too great an effect, since even in man, who certainly has the best memory in the realm of life, trial-and-error behavior is common. The average man, having dropped a dime in the bedroom, is very likely to look for it randomly, now here now there. If he then finds it, that is no tribute to his reasoning powers. Nevertheless, let us not downgrade memory. After all, a man does not have to indulge in trial-and-error only, even in searching for a dropped dime. He may look only in the direction in which he heard the dime strike. He may look in his trousers-cuff because he knows that in many cases a falling dime may end up there and defy all attempts to locate it on the floor. Similarly, if he were in a closed place, he might try to escape by beating and kicking on the walls randomly; but he would also know what a door would look like and would concentrate his efforts on that.

A man can, in short, simplify the problem somewhat by a process of reasoning based on memory. In doing so, however (to jump back to the other side of the fence again), it is possible that the trial-and-error method does not truly disappear but is etherealized — is transferred from action to thought. A man doesn't actually look everywhere for a lost dime. He visualizes the position and looks everywhere mentally, eliminating what his experience tells him are unlikely places (the ceiling, a distant room) and shortening the actual search by that much.

In moving up the scale of animal behavior we find that modification of behavior goes through the stages of (1) conditioning by circumstance, (2) conditioning after trial-and-error, and (3) conditioning after an etherealized trial-and-error. If it seems fair to call this third and most elaborate form of modification "reason" it next remains to decide whether only human beings make use of it.

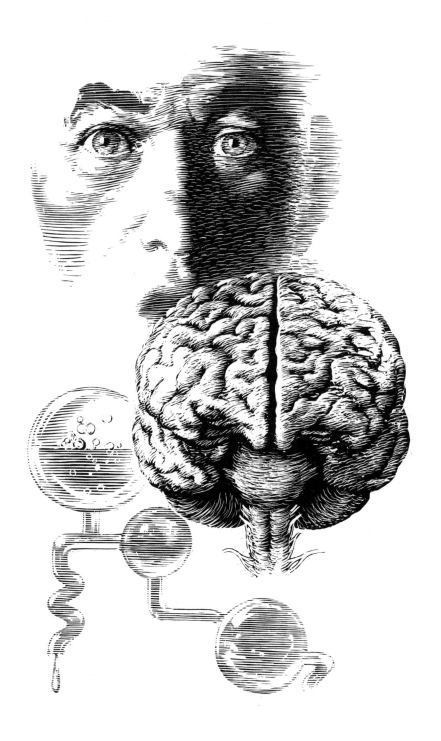

Monkeys and apes remember accurately enough and long enough to make it seem unlikely that they can be thoroughly bereft of such etherealization, and indeed they are not. A German psychologist, Wolfgang Köhler, trapped in German southwestern Africa during World War I, spent his time working with chimpanzees and showed that they could solve problems by flashes of intuition, so to speak. Faced with a banana suspended in air and two sticks, each of which was too short to reach the banana and knock it down, a chimpanzee, after a period of trial-and-error that established the shortness of the sticks, would do nothing for a while, then would hook the sticks together to form a combined tool that would reach the banana. Chimpanzees will pile boxes or use a short stick to get a large stick, and do so in such a fashion as to make it impossible to deny that reason is at work.

At what point in the animal kingdom, trial-and-error is etherealized to a sufficient degree to warrant the accolade of "reason" is uncertain. Not enough animals have been tested thoroughly. If the chimpanzee can reason, what about the other apes? What about the elephant or the dolphin?

One thing is sure. Reason alone does not explain the gulf that lies between man and other animals.

REASON AND BEYOND

But is it fair to compare man and animals on the basis of so relatively simple an act as finding an escape route or a lost object? Can we generalize from finding a dime to reading a book? (The latter no animal other than man can do.) Some psychologists have rather believed that one could. The behaviorists, of whom the American psychologist John Broadus Watson was most prominent, tended to view all learning in the light of conditioned reflexes.

The conditioned reflex differs from the ordinary reflex in that the cerebrum is involved. The cerebrum is not completely essential, to be sure, for a decerebrate animal can still be conditioned. Nevertheless, a decerebrate animal cannot be conditioned as specifically as can one with its cerebrum intact. If an animal is given a mild electric shock on one leg while a bell is sounded, the intact animal will eventually be conditioned to raising its leg when the bell is sounded, even without an electric shock; the decerebrate animal will respond by generalized escape attempts.

If the cerebrum is involved, then it is reasonable to suppose that as the mass and complexity of the cerebrum increases, so will the complexity and intricacy of the conditioned reflexes increase.* More and more neurons can be devoted to "hooking up into circuits" that represent combinations of conditioning. More and more storage units for memory can be set aside, so that trial-and-error can take place among the storage units rather than within the physical world itself.

Given enough storage units for memory and enough room for conditioning, one need look nowhere else to explain human behavior. A child looks at the letter *b* and begins to associate it with a certain sound. He looks at the letter-combination "bed" and begins to associate it with a given word which a few years earlier he had already succeeded in associating with a given object. Speaking and reading become complex conditioned responses, as does typing or whittling or any of a myriad other mechanical skills; and man is capable of all this not because he has something lower animals do not have, but because he has what they all have — only far more of it.

One might insist that the highest attributes of the human mind — logical deduction and even scientific or artistic creativity — can be brought down to hit-and-miss and conditioning. The poem *Kubla Khan*, written by Samuel Taylor Coleridge, was carefully analyzed in a book by John Livingston Lowes called *The Road to Xanadu*. Lowes was able to show that virtually

---

* In fact, in mammals, the conditioned reflex can easily become too complex to be considered a reflex, and many psychologists prefer to refer to the phenomenon as a *conditioned response*. A collection of conditioned responses will form a *habit*.

every word and phrase in the poem stemmed from some item in Coleridge's past reading or experience. We can visualize Coleridge putting together all the word fragments and idea fragments in his mind (quite automatically and unconsciously) after the fashion of a gigantic mental kaleidoscope, picking out the combinations he liked best and constructing the poem out of them. Trial-and-error, still. As a matter of fact, by Coleridge's own testimony, the poem came to him, line after line, in a dream. Presumably, during the period of sleep his mind, unhampered by waking sensations and thought, played the more freely at this game of hit-and-miss.

If we imagine this sort of thing going on in the human brain, we must also expect that there would exist in the human brain large areas that do not directly receive sensation or govern response, but are devoted to associations, associations, and more associations. This is exactly so.*

Thus, the region about the auditory area in the temporal lobe is the *auditory association area*. There particular sounds are associated with physical phenomena in the light of past experience. The sound of a rumble may bring quite clearly to mind a heavy truck, distant thunder, or — if no associations exist — nothing at all. (It is usually the nothing-at-all association that is most frightening.) There is also a *visual association area* in the occipital lobe surrounding the actual visual area, and a *somesthetic association area* behind the somesthetic area.

The different sensory association areas coordinate their functioning in a portion of the brain in the neighborhood of the beginning of the lateral sulcus in the left cerebral hemisphere. In this

---

* It is the existence of such association areas, without obvious immediate function that gives rise to the statement, often met with, that the human being uses only one fifth of his brain. That is not so. We might as well suppose that a construction firm engaged in building a skyscraper is using only one fifth of its employees because only that one fifth was actually engaged in raising steel beams, laying down electric cables, transporting equipment, and such. This would ignore the executives, secretaries, filing clerks, supervisors, and others. Analogously, the major portion of the brain is engaged in what we might call white-collar work, and if this is considered as representing brain use, as it certainly should be, then the human being uses all his brain.

area, the auditory, visual, and somesthetic association areas all come together. This overall association area is sometimes called the *gnostic area* (nos'tik; "knowledge" G). The overall associations are fed into the area lying immediately in front, the *ideomotor area,** which translates them into an appropriate response. This information is shunted into the *premotor area* (lying just before the motor area in the frontal lobe), which co-ordinates the muscular activity necessary to produce the desired response, this activity being finally brought about by the motor area.

When all the association areas, the sensory areas, and the motor areas are taken into account, there still remains one area of the cerebrum that has no specific and easily definable or measurable function. This is the area of the frontal lobe that lies before the motor and premotor areas and is therefore called the *prefrontal lobe* (see illustration, p. 172). Its lack of obvious function is such that it is sometimes called the "silent area." Tumors have made it necessary to remove large areas of the prefrontal lobe without particularly significant effect on the individual, and yet surely it is not a useless mass of nerve tissue.

There might be a tendency, rather, to consider it, of all sections of the brain, the most significant. In general, the evolutionary trend in the development of the human nervous system has been the piling of complication upon complication at the forward end of the nerve cord. In passing from the primitive chordates, such as amphioxus, into the vertebrate subphylum, one passes from an unspecialized nerve cord to one in which the anterior end has developed into the brain. Also, in passing up the classes of vertebrates from fish to mammals, it is the forebrain section of the brain that undergoes major development, and the cerebrum becomes dominant. In going from insectivores to primates and, within the primate Order, from monkey to man, there has been

---

* Both the gnostic area and the ideomotor area are functional only in one cerebral hemisphere (usually the left, but in about 10 per cent of the cases the right). As I said earlier in the book, this existence of a dominant hemisphere is to prevent two separate sets of association-interpretations from arising, as conceivably might happen if each hemisphere were provided with its own "executive."

a successive development of the foremost section of the cerebrum, the frontal lobe.

In the early hominids, even after the brain had achieved full human size, the frontal lobes continued development. Neanderthal man had a brain as large as our own, but the frontal lobe of the brain of true man gained at the expense of the occipital lobe, so if the total weight is the same, the distribution of weight is not. It is easy to assume then that the prefrontal lobes, far from being unused, are a kind of extra storage volume for associations, and the very epitome of the brain.

Back in the 1930's, it seemed to a Portuguese surgeon, António Egas Moniz, that where a mental patient was at the end of his rope, and where ordinary psychiatry and ordinary physical therapy did not help, it might be possible to take the drastic step of severing the prefrontal lobes from the rest of the brain. It seemed to him that in this fashion the patient would be cut off from some of the associations he had built up. In view of the patient's mental illness, these associations would more likely be undesirable than desirable and their loss might be to the good. This operation, *prefrontal lobotomy*, was first carried through in 1935, and in a number of cases did indeed seem to help. Moniz received the Nobel Prize in 1949 for this feat. However, the operation has never been a popular one and is not likely ever to become one. It induces personality changes that are often almost as undesirable as the illness it is intended to cure.

Even granted that the behaviorist stand is correct in principle and that all human behavior, however complex, can be brought down to a mechanical pattern of nerve cells (and hormones)* the further question arises as to whether it is useful to allow matters to rest there.

---

* Actually, it is difficult to deny this since nerves and hormones are the only physical-chemical mediators for behavior that we know of. Unless we postulate the existence of something beyond the physical-chemical (something like abstract "mind" or "soul") we are reduced to finding the answer to even the highest human abilities somewhere among the cells of the nervous system or among the chemicals in the blood — exactly where we find the lowest.

Suppose we are satisfied that Coleridge constructed the poem *Kubla Khan* by trial-and-error. Does that help us much? If it were merely that, why can't the rest of us write the equivalent of *Kubla Khan*? How could Coleridge choose just that pattern out of the virtually infinite numbers offered by his mental kaleidoscope which was to form a surpassingly beautiful poem, and do so in such a short time?

Clearly we have much farther to go than the distance the pat phrase "trial-and-error" can carry us. Briefly, as a change progresses there can come a point (sometimes quite a sharp one) where the outlook must change, where a difference in degree suddenly becomes the equivalent of a difference in kind. To take an analogy in the world of the physical sciences, let us consider ice. Its structure is pretty well understood on the molecular level. If ice is heated, the molecules vibrate more and more until at a certain temperature, the vibrations are energetic enough to overcome the intermolecular attractions. The molecules then lose their order and become randomly distributed; in a fashion, moreover, that changes randomly with time. There has been a "phase change"; the ice has melted and become water. The molecules in liquid water are like the molecules in ice and it is possible to work out a set of rules that will hold for the behavior of those molecules in both ice and water. The phase change is so sharp, however, as to make it more useful to describe ice and water in different terms, to think of water in connection with other liquids and ice in connection with other solids.

Similarly, when the process of etherealized trial-and-error becomes as complicated as it is in the human mind, it may well be no longer useful to attempt to interpret mental activity in behaviorist terms. As to what form of interpretation *is* most useful, ah, that is not yet settled.

The concept of the phase change can also be used to answer the question of what fixes the gulf between man and all other creatures. Since it is not reason alone, it must be something more. A phase change must take place not at the moment when reason is introduced but at some time when reason passes a certain point of intensity. The point is, one might reasonably suppose, that at which reason becomes complex enough to allow abstraction; when it allows the establishment of symbols to stand for concepts, which in turn stand for collections of things or actions or qualities. The sound "table" represents not merely this table and that table, but a concept of "all table-like objects," a concept that does not exist physically. The sound "table" is thus an abstraction of an abstraction.

Once it is possible to conceive an abstraction and represent it by a sound, communication becomes possible at a level of complexity and meaningfulness far beyond that possible otherwise. As the motor areas of the brain develop to the point where a speech center exists, enough different sounds can be made, easily and surely, to supply each of a vast number of concepts with individual sounds. And there is enough room for memory units in a brain of such complexity to keep all the necessary associations of sound and concept firmly in mind.

It is speech, then, rather than reason alone that is the phase change, and that fixes the gulf between man and nonman. As I pointed out on page 246, the existence of speech means that the gathering of experience and the drawing of conclusions is no longer a function of the individual alone. Experience is shared and the tribe becomes wiser and more knowledgeable than any individual in it. Moreover, experience unites the tribe throughout time as well as throughout space. Each generation need no longer start from scratch, as must all other creatures. Human parents can pass on their experience and wisdom to their children, not only by demonstration but by verbalized, conceptual explanation. Not only facts and techniques, but also thought and deductions can be passed on.

Perhaps the gulf between ourselves and the rest of living species might not seem so broad if we knew more about the various prehuman hominids, who might represent stages within that gap. Unfortunately we don't. We do not actually know at what stage of development, or in what species of hominid, the phase change took place.*

PSYCHOBIOCHEMISTRY

The study of the human mind is carried on chiefly by psychologists and in its medical aspects by psychiatrists. Their methods and results are mentioned but fleetingly at best in this book, not because they are unimportant, but because they are too important. They deserve a book to themselves. In this book I am concentrating, as best I can, on anatomy and physiology, plus a bit of biochemistry.

The study of the mind by every means is of increasing importance in modern civilization. There are diseases of the mind as well as of other portions of the body — mental disease, in which the connection between the body and the outside environment is distorted. The message of the senses may be perceived in such a fashion as not to correspond with what the majority are willing to accept as objective reality. Under these conditions a person is said to be subject to hallucinations ("to wander in mind" L). Even where sensory messages are correctly perceived, the interpretation of and responses to those messages may be abnormal in intensity or in kind. Mental disease may be serious enough to destroy the ability of an individual to serve as a functioning member of society; and even if mild enough not to do so may nevertheless put him under an unnecessary burden of emotional gear-grinding.

As scientific advance succeeds in checking the ravages of many physical diseases, the mental diseases become more noticeable

* If it is true that dolphins have a faculty of speech as complex as that of man, then we are not necessarily the only species to have passed the phase change. The environment of the ocean is so different from that of land, however, that the consequences of the phase change would be vastly different. A dolphin might have a man-level mind, but in the viscous and light-absorbing medium of sea water a dolphin is condemned to the flipper and to a dependence on sound rather than vision. Man is not man by mind alone, but by mind plus eye plus hand, and if all three are taken into consideration we remain the only species this side of the phase change.

and prominent among the medical problems that remain. It has been estimated that as many as 17 million Americans, nearly 1 in 10, suffer from some form of mental illness. (In most cases, of course, the illness is not severe enough to warrant hospitalization.) Of those mental illnesses serious enough to require hospitalization, the most common is *schizophrenia* (skiz'oh-free'nee-uh; "split mind" G). This name was coined in 1911 by a Swiss psychiatrist, Paul Eugen Bleuler. He used the name because it was frequently noted that persons suffering from this disease seemed to be dominated by one set of ideas (or "complex") to the exclusion of others, as though the mind's harmonious working had been disrupted and one portion had seized control of the rest.

Schizophrenia may exist in several varieties, depending on which complex predominates. It may be *hebephrenic* (hee'bee-free'nik; "childish mind" G), where one prominent symptom is childish or silly behavior. It may be *catatonic* ("toning down" G), in which behavior is indeed toned down and the patient seems to withdraw from participation in the objective world, becoming mute and rigid. It may also be *paranoid* ("madness" G), and characterized by extreme hostility and suspicion, with feelings of persecution. At least half of all patients in mental hospitals are schizophrenics of these or other types. An older name for the disease was *dementia praecox* (dee-men'shee-uh pree'koks; "early-ripening madness" L). This name was intended to differentiate it from mental illness affecting the old through the deterioration of the brain with age ("senile dementia"), since schizophrenia usually makes itself manifest at a comparatively early age, generally between the years 18 and 28.

One common view of mental diseases is the "environmental theory," which looks upon them as unintelligible if considered in terms of the individual alone. The disorders are considered, instead, to involve the ability of the individual to relate to other individuals and the environment, and the effect of interpersonal stresses on this ability. The disease is hence a function of the individual plus society. In favor of this view is the fact that there is no known physical difference between the brain of a mental patient and that of a normal individual. Favoring it in a more subtle fashion is the ancient view of the fundamental distinction between mind and body — the feeling that the mind is separate and apart from the body, not governed by the same laws and not amenable to the same type of investigation. The physical and chemical laws that have proved so useful in dealing with the rest of the body may be inadequate for the mind, which then requires a more subtle form of analysis.

Opposed to this is the "organic theory," which supports the biochemical causation of mental disease. This holds that what we call the mind is the interplay of the nerve cells of the body, and the mind is therefore, at the very least, indirectly subject to the ordinary physical and chemical laws that govern those cells. Even if a mental disorder arises from an outside stress it is the neurons that respond to the stress either well or poorly, and the varying ability to respond to the stress healthfully must have its basis in a biochemical difference. Favoring the organic theory is the fact that some forms of mental disease have indeed been found to have a biochemical basis. *Pellagra,* a disease once endemic in Mediterranean lands and in our own South, was characterized by dementia as one of the symptoms. It was found to be a dietary-deficiency disease, caused by the lack of nicotinic acid in the diet. As simple a procedure as the addition of milk to the diet prevented pellagra and its attendant dementia, or ameliorated it if already established.

The disease *phenylpyruvic oligophrenia* (ol'ih-goh-free'nee-uh; "deficient mind" G) is characterized by serious mental deficiency. Evidently it is the result of an inborn error in metabolism. In the normal individual, the amino acid phenylalanine, an essential constituent of proteins, is routinely converted in part to the related amino acid tyrosine, also an essential constituent of proteins. This reaction is governed by a particular enzyme, phenylalaninase. In the case of those unfortunates born without the ability to form this enzyme, phenylalanine cannot undergo the proper conversion. It accumulates and is finally converted into substances other than tyrosine, substances not normally present in the body. One of these is phenylpyruvic acid, whence the first half of the name of the disease. The presence of excess phenylalanine, and of its abnormal "metabolites," adversely affects brain function (exactly how is not yet known) and produces the mental deficiency. Here, unfortunately, the situation cannot be corrected as simply as in the case of pellagra. Although it is easy to supply a missing vitamin, it is as yet impossible to supply a missing enzyme. However, some improvement in mental condition has been reported among patients with the disease who have been kept on a diet low in phenylalanine.

This offers a pattern for the possible understanding of the cause of other mental disorders, especially that of schizophrenia. There is always the possibility of an accumulation (or deficiency, perhaps) of some normal constituent of the body, particularly one that manifestly affects brain function and is therefore likely to be found in the brain. In addition there is the possibility of the existence of abnormal metabolites of such substances, metabolites that would themselves interfere with brain function.

The hope that some such solution may exist for schizophrenia is bolstered by genetic data. In the general population the chance of a particular individual developing schizophrenia is about 1 in 100. If, however, a certain person is schizophrenic, the chances that a brother or sister of his will also fall prey to the disease is about 1 in 7. If one of a pair of identical twins is schizophrenic, the chances that the other will become schizophrenic as well is very high, 3 out of 4, or even better. Even allowing for the greater similarities of environment in the case of brothers or sisters than in the case of unrelated persons, there would seem to be a hereditary factor involved. This would mean, according to our present understanding of heredity, an inherited abnormality in one or more enzyme systems and a metabolism that is therefore disordered in some specific manner.

The middle 1950's saw the beginning of a concerted effort to locate a biochemical cause of schizophrenia. For instance, nerve endings of the sympathetic system secrete norepinephrine (noradrenalin), as I pointed out on page 218, and this is very similar to epinephrine (adrenalin), which I discussed on pages 40–43. Adrenalin is an attractive target for suspicion because its function is to rouse the body to react more efficiently to conditions of stress. If mental disease is considered to result, in part at least, from the failure of the body to respond properly to conditions of psychological stress, might it be that the fault lies somewhere in the body's handling of adrenalin?

In the test tube, it is easy to change adrenalin to a compound called "adrenochrome." This is an abnormal metabolite, since it does not seem that adrenalin in the body normally passes through the adrenochrome stage. Interestingly enough, when adrenochrome is injected into normal human subjects, temporary psychotic states resembling those of mental illness are produced.

This is true of other adrenalin-like substances as well. For example, a compound called mescaline, much like adrenalin in molecular structure, is found in a cactus native to the American southwest. The mescaline-containing portions of the cactus are chewed by Indians during their religious rites in a deliberate attempt to achieve hallucinatory episodes. To the Indians, innocent of modern psychiatry, such hallucinations seem to be a window into the supernatural.

Here, then, we have a situation that could be directly analogous to the connection between phenylalanine and phenylpyruvic oligophrenia. Could it be that abnormal metabolites of adrenalin produced by people who happen to be born with a deficient supply of some enzyme or other eventually produce schizophrenia? However, since 1954, when this suggestion was first made, all attempts to locate adrenochrome or other abnormal metabolites of adrenalin in mental patients have failed.

Interest was also aroused in a chemical called *serotonin*. This is closely related to the amino acid tryptophan, which is an essential component of proteins (see p. 10). This relationship is clear in the formulas given here, even for those not familiar with chemical formulas.

TRYPTOPHAN

SEROTONIN

Serotonin is found in numerous organs of the body, including the brain (only about 1 per cent of the body's supply is found in the brain), and it has a number of functions. Some of these, such as its ability to bring about the constriction of small blood vessels and the raising of blood pressure, have no direct connection with brain function, but it seems likely to have some connection with it in other respects.

This was brought home sharply in 1954 when it was discovered (accidentally) that a drug called *lysergic acid diethylamide* could be used to produce hallucinations and other psychotic symptoms. Lysergic acid diethylamide has the same two-ring system that serotonin has (but with a considerably more complicated molecule otherwise) and appears to compete with serotonin for the enzyme *monoamine oxidase*. Ordinarily, monoamine oxidase brings about the oxidation of serotonin into a normal metabolite, one in which the nitrogen atoms have been removed. In the presence of lysergic acid diethylamide, the monoamine oxidase molecules are taken up by the intruder and are unavailable for the oxidation of serotonin. Serotonin accumulates and may finally produce abnormal metabolites. One abnormal metabolite looming as a possibility is bufotenin, a "toad poison" — that is, one of a group of toxic substances found in the parotid glands of toads. This is similar to serotonin in molecular structure and is known to induce psychotic states.

The possibility that serotonin in excess produces schizophrenia is greatly weakened, nevertheless, by the fact that a compound very closely related to lysergic acid diethylamide interferes with serotonin oxidation even more and yet produces no hallucinations. Furthermore, no abnormal metabolites of serotonin have been detected in schizophrenics.

So far, then, the various leads that have arisen in the search for a biochemical basis for schizophrenia (including some I have not mentioned) have led to a series of dead-ends. The search continues, however, and some important byproducts have resulted. There is, for instance, the development of *tranquillizers*. These are drugs that exert a calming effect upon an individual, relieving anxiety and inducing relaxation. They differ from older drugs used for the purpose in that they do not diminish alertness or induce drowsiness. The first tranquillizer to be introduced to the medical world (in 1954) was *reserpine*, a natural alkaloid found in the dried roots of a shrub from India. It seemed significant that part of the complex molecular structure of reserpine consisted of the two-ring combination present in serotonin. This significance was weakened by the introduction that same year of another and even more effective tranquillizer, *chlorpromazine*, which does not possess this particular two-ring combination. The tranquillizers are not cures for any mental illness, but they suppress certain symptoms that stand in the way of adequate treatment. By reducing the hostilities and rages of patients, and by quieting their fears and anxieties, they reduce the necessity for drastic physical restraints, make it easier for psychiatrists to establish contacts with patients, and increase the chances of release from the hospital.

The 1950's also saw the development of *antidepressants*, drugs which, as the name implies, relieve the severe depression that characterizes some mental patients; depression which in extreme cases leads to suicide. It may be that such depression is caused by, or at least is accompanied by, a too-low level of serotonin in the brain. At least the antidepressants all seem to be capable of inhibiting the action of the enzyme monoamine oxidase. With the enzyme less capable of bringing about the oxidation of serotonin, the level of that substance would necessarily rise.

A FINAL WORD

More and more it is becoming fashionable to look upon the brain as though it were, in some ways, an immensely complicated computer made up of extremely small switches, the neurons. And in one respect at least, that involving the question of memory, biochemists are coming to look to structures finer than the neuron, and to penetrate to the molecular level.

Memory is the key that makes possible the phase change I spoke of earlier in the chapter. It is only because human beings (even those not especially gifted) can remember so much and so well that it has been possible to develop the intricate code of symbols we call speech. The memory capacity of even an ordinary human mind is fabulous. We may not consider ourselves particularly adept at remembering technical data, let us say, but consider how many faces we can recognize, how many names call up some past incident, how many words we can spell and define, and how much minutiae we know we have met with before. It is estimated that in a lifetime, a brain can store 1,000,000,000,000,000 (a million billion) "bits" of information.[*]

In computers, a "memory" can be set up by making suitable changes in the magnetic properties of a tape, changes that are retained until called into use. Is there an analogous situation in

---

[*] A "bit" is short for "binary digit" and is either 1 or 0 in computer lingo. It represents the minimum unit of information, the amount gained when a question is answered simply "yes" or "no." All more complicated kinds of information can in theory be compounded of a finite number of bits. A face, for instance, or any other object can be built up of patterns of black and white dots, as in a newspaper photograph, each dot being a "bit," either "yes" for a white dot, or "no" for a black one. Our vision consists of such bits, each cell of the retina, responding "yes" for light and "no" for darkness, representing a bit. Our other senses can be analyzed similarly.

the brain? Suspicion is currently falling upon *ribonucleic acid* (usually abbreviated *RNA*) in which the nerve cell, surprisingly enough, is richer than almost any other type of cell in the body. I say surprisingly because RNA is involved in the synthesis of protein and is therefore usually found in those tissues producing large quantities of protein either because they are actively growing or because they are producing copious quantities of protein-rich secretions. The nerve cell falls into neither classification, so the abundance of RNA within it serves as legitimate ground for speculation.

The RNA molecule is an extremely large one, consisting of a string of hundreds or even thousands of subunits of four different kinds. The possible number of different arrangements of these subunits within an RNA molecule is astronomically immense — much, much larger than the mere "million billion" I mentioned above. Each different arrangement produces a distinct RNA molecule, one capable of bringing about the synthesis of a distinct protein molecule.*

It has been suggested that every "bit" of information entering the nervous system for the first time introduces a change in an RNA molecule contained in certain neurons reserved for the purpose. The changed RNA molecule produces a type of protein not produced hitherto. When further "bits" of information enter the nervous system, they can presumably be matched to the RNA/protein combinations already present. If the match succeeds, we "remember."

This is, as yet, only the most primitive beginning of an attempt to analyze the highest functions of the human mind at the molecular level, and to carry it further represents the greatest possible challenge to the mind.

It seems logical, somehow, to suppose that an entity that un-

---

* The detailed structure of nucleic acids and proteins that makes such immense variability possible, and the manner in which a given nucleic acid can dictate the formation of a particular protein, is a subject of prime importance to biochemists today. There is no room here for even the beginnings of a discussion of these matters, but you can find the details in my book *The Genetic Code* (1963).

derstands must be more complex than the object being under-stood. One can therefore argue that all the abstruse facets of modern mathematics and physical science are but reflections of those facets of the physical universe which are simpler in structure than the human mind. Where the limit of understanding will be, or whether it exists at all, we cannot well predict, for we cannot measure as yet the complexity of either the mind or the universe outside the mind.

However, even without making measurements, we can say as an axiom that a thing is equal to itself, and that therefore the human mind, in attempting to understand the workings of the human mind, faces us with a situation in which the entity that must understand and the object to be understood are of equal complexity.

Does this mean we can never truly grasp the working of the human mind? I cannot tell. But even if we cannot, it may still be possible to grasp just enough of its workings to be able to con-struct computers that approach the human mind in complexity and subtlety, even though we fall short of full understanding. (After all, mankind was able in the 19th century to construct rather complex electrical equipment despite the fact that the nature of the electrical current was not understood, and earlier still, work-ing steam engines were devised well before the laws governing their workings were understood.)

If we could do even so much we might learn enough to prevent those disorders of the mind, those irrationalities and passions, that have hitherto perpetually frustrated the best and noblest efforts of mankind. If we could but reduce the phenomena of imagina-tion, intuition, and creativity to analysis by physical and chemical laws, we might be able to arrange to have the effects of genius on steady tap, so to speak, rather than be forced to wait for nig-gardly chance to supply the human race with geniuses at long intervals only.

Man would then, by his own exertions, become more than man, and what might not be accomplished thereafter? It is quite certain, I am sure, that none of us will live to see the far-distant time when this might come to pass. And yet, the mere thought that such a day might some day come, even though it will not dawn on my own vision, is a profoundly satisfying one.

INDEX

INDEX